The Conquered Brides

Five Novels by

Renee Rose, Ashe Barker,
Sue Lyndon, Dinah McLeod and
Korey Mae Johnson

Copyright © March 2015 by Renee Rose, Ashe Barker, Sue Lyndon, Dinah McLeod and Korey Mae Johnson

All rights reserved. No part of this book may be reproduced or transmitted in any form or by any means, electronic or mechanical, including photocopying, recording, or by any information storage and retrieval system, without permission in writing from the publisher.

Published by Stormy Night Publications and Design, LLC.
www.StormyNightPublications.com

Rose, Renee

Barker, Ashe

Lyndon, Sue

McLeod, Dinah

Johnson, Korey Mae

The Conquered Brides

Cover Design by Korey Mae Johnson

Images by The Killion Group, 123RF/Dl1on, and Korey Mae Johnson

ISBN-13: 978-1508882725
ISBN-10: 150888272X

FOR AUDIENCES 18+ ONLY

This book is intended for adults only. Spanking and other sexual activities represented in this book are fantasies only, intended for adults.

Commanding the Princess

Korey Mae Johnson

PROLOGUE

Some royals got to enjoy dances, great feasts, and lighted halls filled with merriment. Cruelly, in Hohenzollern, all Susanna seemed to get for entertainment was watching her uncle fight her battles for her with emissaries armed only with threats and warnings.

The man before her now was aggressively holding his stance. He was by far the angriest person she'd ever had in her presence. "Princess, many emissaries have come before me, and each has been sent away either with nothing or with empty promises. We can no longer allow your knights to maraud through our lands unchecked. If you are unable to control them, then you must cede the rule of these lands to someone who can!"

Her uncle stepping forward surely announced that she had already ceded control in all but name. He glanced her way as he was speaking, as if he were addressing her. "I hardly think, my lady, that you should allow this man to speak to you in this way!" snapped Lord Eberhard, his seething bark cutting off the emissary before he could continue. Eberhard turned to the man, not even giving his princess the opportunity to reply. "Go and tell your masters that Princess Susanna of Hohenzollern will not be ordered about by the rabble of the Free Cities."

Susanna closed her eyes and took a deep breath as she once again silently cursed the fever which had taken her mother, the plague which had taken her brother, and the bowman whose arrow had taken her father on the battlefield six years past.

When she opened her eyes again, the emissary was still there. He seemed to hesitate before speaking his next words, and she could tell that he was struggling to control his anger. At last, he turned his shoulder to Eberhard and deliberately caught the eyes of Susanna. "Princess, if I have been informed correctly, you are the ruler here and this man," he said, gesturing disgustedly toward Lord Eberhard, "is but an advisor. Those who sent me here bade me return with the answer of Princess Susanna of Hohenzollern, not the words of one of her lackeys."

The words of her uncle, unfortunately, were the only words she could give this man—and everyone else that had come before her throne, for that matter. Susanna knew she could barely decide what to have for breakfast without her uncle overriding her. To be fair, though, her father had always been kept on his toes by his brother as well.

Her problem was simple enough; her own army was more loyal to her uncle than they were to her. Her words were only air, while his words carried weight.

The emissary's threat seemed to carry weight as well, but even as he ranted on, Susanna's attention was drawn not to him, but to the powerfully-built man standing a few feet behind him. His appearance puzzled Susanna. Though he wore the armor of a knight, his bearing was that of a great lord. At last, he stepped forward and covered the emissary's shoulder with his large hand as if to calm him. The emissary was clearly prepared to let him speak the final word.

And speak it he did, even while holding her gaze. "Princess Susanna," the big man began in a voice at once controlled yet still gruff like one who had spent most of his life shouting orders and expecting them obeyed. His measured tone evoked clouds holding a bolt of lightning. "When your father ruled these lands, there was peace between Hohenzollern and the Free Imperial Cities. Do not lightly throw that peace away. I assure you, princess, that if I am forced to return, it will be at the head of an army not even these mighty walls can withstand."

Emissaries had arrived with threats before, but this threat made her stomach clench. She believed this man. There was nothing about him that said that he was a man who bluffed. She turned her head and stared at Eberhard, hoping that he was at least considering this, but the man stubbornly raised his chin.

She had no illusions about Eberhard's loyalty—or lack of it—and if she defied him, he would have her own knights rising against her long before these men were able to journey home, let alone return with an army.

Eberhard, before she could open her lips, grated out a response, but she could barely hear it. Her uncle's blustery words could not pull her attention from the big man's eyes, which were fixed upon her. What she saw in them shocked her, because they held neither anger nor contempt. Instead, they were filled with pity.

Then his eyes left hers and caught those of her uncle. What Eberhard saw in the man's eyes she would never know, but her advisor suddenly saw fit to bring his tirade to an instant end. As the warrior and the emissary turned to leave the audience hall, Susanna slumped in her gilded chair, wishing not for the first time that she had been born the daughter of a peasant.

CHAPTER ONE

Eight Months Later

Silence is meant to be broken. Unfortunately, it had taken far too long for Susanna to realize that, but when she did, she made up for it. At the top of her lungs, she cried, "Where in God's name is Lord Eberhard!" Ladies, her mother once said, speak at volumes not far above a whisper. Today, however, she wasn't a lady. She was a monarch who was completely unable to mask her fury. This was a time she actually needed her uncle's advice, but he was nowhere to be found.

He had left her to her own devices only now when the castle was under siege. She was angry at her own surprise. She should have expected this.

"Princess..." began Ulrich, the captain of the guard, a title whose meaning was somewhat lessened by the fact that Ulrich had held the position for less than an hour. The previous captain of the guard—who himself had served in the role for all of two days—had fallen defending the breach in the south-east wall, and unless Susanna missed her guess, Ulrich was barely more than twenty years of age. Ulrich visibly gathered himself—he wasn't experienced enough to know how to hide his nervousness—then continued, "Lord Eberhard was last seen half an hour ago, heading into the cellars."

He meant to hide, Susanna knew, or perhaps flee through the underground passages that served as the castle's escape route of last resort. He would leave her to face the end alone. "We can spare no men to search for him, but if he is seen," she commanded with cold contempt in her voice, "he is to be executed immediately and his head put on a spike on the walls." She meant it. It wasn't a punishment her uncle had spared his enemies in the past, and she would not spare her own enemy, either.

She paused for a moment to gather herself, then asked the question whose answer she most feared. "Can our defenses hold, Ulrich?" When Ulrich shifted his weight from foot to foot, she realized he was trying to decide on his answer—whether or not to let her in on the reality of the situation. "Do not seek to spare me the truth."

Ulrich's ashen face provided all the answer she needed, but dread filled her nonetheless when he spoke. "In truth, my lady, they cannot hold but a few more hours, even if the men fight to their last breath... and I fear there aren't many who will do so. We must seek to get you out, princess. If we sortie from the west gate with all the men we have left, we might break through their lines long enough to get you to the forest beyond. Or we could take you through the passages in the cellars. Those passages end in the forest, and once you are out, I could send a few men with you while I stay behind with the rest to throw off any pursuit."

His loyalty only deepened the pain which tore at her heart. She could not be blamed for what Eberhard had done as regent before she came of age, perhaps, but she had ruled this castle, at least in name, for two years now. Every life lost defending those walls and gates had been lost because of her failure to stand up to Eberhard in all that time.

If she was to do anything at all as their ruler, now was her last chance. She had family here, and she still had lives to protect. Knowing this, she pulled her shoulders back, took a deep breath for courage, and spoke with soft resignation. "No more men will die in my name, Ulrich. Raise a white flag over the keep and order the archers on the walls to hold their arrows. Leave the gates closed for the moment, and let us hope that whoever leads the enemy will see fit to treat with me."

Ulrich looked stunned, and he did not move for a moment. "But princess, if you surrender, I do not know what their leader will have done with you. He is rumored to be a fearsome man."

"Too long have I lived in fear and let others speak in my name. Today, I will speak for myself, come what may. Now obey this, my final command, and pray that the Lord will grant that mercy be shown to us this day."

After only a moment more of hesitation, Ulrich bowed and left hastily.

• • • • • • •

There was a stillness after the white flag was raised, and everyone was tense and restless, waiting for what would happen next. The surrender had brought hoots of merriment from his army, but he and the men close about him were more experienced, and all knew that a white flag was only the beginning of a surrender.

Gerhard kept glancing expectantly at the battered gate of the great keep, wondering who the princess would send out to treat with them. It had to be a high-ranking official, and Gerhard hoped that she wasn't silly enough to send out Eberhard—that is, if that oaf had the balls needed to come out and face him. He was probably somewhere in the castle, stuffing his pockets with whatever of value he could find.

There was a great stretching in the air and many expectant grunts from the men about him. He whipped his head toward the gate and saw that it was slowly opening. A white-cloaked figure was approaching the gate, a stark contrast against the blood-soaked snow and grime of war all around. Slowly it dawned on him that he was looking at a porcelain-skinned woman who had her head held high as she slowly walked through the mass of men now hemming her in on all sides.

Then Gerhard realized who it was, and he felt like someone had just thrown ice water over his head.

This was no lady-in-waiting or minor noblewoman sent to beg for favorable terms of surrender, although it should have been. He would have never guessed that the princess would come out herself.

The men milled about yet made a clear path between himself and the princess as she approached, and upon reaching him she did not wait for him to speak first. "I am Princess Susanna of Hohenzollern," she told him with a clear, smooth voice. "I've come to beg mercy for the suffering of my people."

He could hear the fear in her voice, but just barely. He had not expected this. He had expected her to bargain, not to beg. Nonetheless, he had to act quickly, before the crowd of soldiers got it in their heads to exact their own justice upon her person. They were a rough bunch, and he didn't want to have to do any more killing today. He could tell by the way some of them growled that he needed to claim a quick hold on this situation.

"Mercy?" he replied loudly so that his men could hear him. "What mercy did your knights show to those whose farms they pillaged and whose daughters they ravished, as you did nothing to stop them?" His orders were to bring her alive to Vienna to face the imperial court, but if he wanted to keep these men—many of them recruited from the very villages her knights had ransacked—from trying to kill her here and now, he needed to let them know he shared their anger.

He expected a defense of her actions, or perhaps even pleas for his mercy, but her response stunned him. "I do not beg mercy for myself, but for my people. I stand before you prepared to accept whatever justice you see fit, if only you will spare the innocent women and children of this castle, and the men who fought bravely to defend it."

Gerhard paused, considering. This rabble of an army the nobles of the Free Cities had cobbled together was going to sack this castle, take everything that they could carry, and probably try to burn the rest, that much was certain, and he would be hard pressed to keep them from having their way with any woman they could lay hands on. Men like these thought women to be little more than the spoils of war.

The princess looked at him through glistening eyes, but no tears spilled down her cheeks. Still, his heart began to clench and a part deep inside him demanded that he acquiesce. When he spoke at last, he spoke loudly again so that everyone could hear him.

"I am Gerhard of Bavaria, and you have my word that the lives of your people will be spared. If women are taken from this castle, they will be taken as wives, and they will be treated well by the men who take them." He paused again, before speaking directly to his army. "You may take whatever plunder you can find, but if any man among you commits rape or murder, I will have him hanged!"

The relief on the face of the princess filled Gerhard with a strange joy, though he knew his next words would bring the fear back to those beautiful eyes. He had to deliver the emperor's message, something he had been dreading since he'd first caught sight of her eight months before. "As for you, princess, you will be brought to the court of the Holy Roman Emperor in Vienna, where you will stand trial for your life."

• • • • • • •

Susanna was accustomed to the feeling of fear. For the past several years she had wondered each morning if Eberhard would choose that day to put an end to her by some nefarious means, thus removing the only remaining obstacle to his absolute rule over Hohenzollern. How she'd lived one-and-twenty years without being poisoned was beyond her, and in a way she had grown used to thinking of herself as living on borrowed time.

It wasn't the decree itself that rattled her. She had expected that much since she looked out her windows over a week ago and saw the army marching toward the castle. What made her bones feel like they were about to crumble was the hard-jawed gaze of the army's commander, the same man who had warned her that this would happen all those months ago. He was impossible not to recognize with his dark brown eyes, the color of wet soil, and the untrimmed chestnut curls which fell over his eyes.

She was going to beg to see her little sister and to say goodbye to her cousins… but now she thought better of it. She had asked enough favors from this enemy, and she was fortunate to have been granted as much as she had, because he did not look like he was in good humor.

A soldier reached to touch her from behind, but even as she turned to jerk herself away, the commander—who was apparently known as Gerhard—stepped forward and cuffed the man across the cheek so hard that she heard a loud, meaty crunch. With a sharp intake of breath, she spun and watched the two face off.

"Touch her, and die," she heard Gerhard state coldly. "Anyone touches her, and they will answer to me," he decreed. "She will be brought to justice in safety. She is property of the Holy Roman Empire now!"

She frowned at this and tried to keep her chin raised. Property of the Holy Roman Empire. What a phrase with which to end her rule. She took a deep breath, trying to gain courage, trying not to think about the days ahead, or about her kin who were still in the castle. She would have given anything just to look up at her home one last time, to see the people who were left watching her from the ramparts... but she knew she couldn't. She had to stay strong. She had to remain proud and royal.

"Rennio!" the commander suddenly boomed, turning behind him, looking past what seemed to be his personal guard. "Where is Bishop Rennio?"

"He's drinking," the man replied, rolling his eyes. "Already."

The commander grunted his disdain and then turned to a young boy and ordered that Rennio be found and brought to him. As the boy hopped off, the commander turned back to Susanna and stepped toward her. He put his hand around her forearm and tugged her close to him. "I will not harm you as long as you do not attempt to escape," he said in a tone which almost seemed gentle.

She blinked at him. "Where would I go?" she asked defensively.

"Just don't try anything. You'll be guarded, and the men outside are not gentlemen. They're not loyal. They're not your subjects. Do I need to frighten you with details of what might happen, or are you going to be a good girl and stay where I put you?"

She pressed her lips together in anger. If she were an empress of ancient Rome, she would have thrown this man to the lions. "I will stay wherever I am led, my lord. You have no need to worry on that account."

A drunken, cloaked man stumbled out of the rabble just as Gerhard's lip actually curled up slightly into a smile. She was lucky for the distraction, because that small grin Gerhard had failed to hold back made her want to slap it off of his face, and she couldn't. He still had the power to take back the mercy she had come out to beg him for.

She turned, and since she'd heard the 'bishop' before his name, she had expected Rennio to look something like a priest or even a monk. Instead, this man had long, not-particularly-clean-looking hair, a messy beard, and a bright nose. He was probably in his early thirties but had the bearing of a much older man. He looked like he was barely holding down his drink.

Gerhard turned from her and put his arm around Rennio, who immediately soured at whatever Gerhard was saying into his ear. Just as Rennio appeared about to complain, Gerhard grasped his shoulder hard and continued speaking to him so quietly that she could barely make out even the smallest word.

"Fine," Rennio huffed, and then stepped forward and grabbed her arm far too hard and without apology. "Come with me, princess."

Gerhard bowed his head when she looked at him in the hopes that he would explain why she was being taken away by the drunkest man in attendance, and merely said, "I will see you later this eve, Your Highness."

She had no time to respond with anything as sarcastic as she'd have liked, or anything at all for that matter. Rennio, once he started moving through the sea of men, was surprisingly steady for a drunkard and very, very fast. He had the feet of a mountain goat as he stepped down the hill over stones and objects, guiding her seamlessly out of the way, nearly so quickly that she couldn't keep up with him. She realized that she hadn't moved as quickly as she was now since she was a child, and she wondered why he'd decided that this sort of speed was necessary.

She had expected, because of the gruff surliness of the men she'd encountered so far and the yells and insults of random soldiers around her, that she was going to be put into a stockade where men could throw rotting food or dung at her. She was very surprised, and happily so, when Rennio slowed down outside of a tall, red-canvas pavilion that was one of the largest in the entire camp. She imagined it might have suited a king just fine, and the fact that it was apparently going to be her jail cell was more than surprising. She imagined this was like her family's liberal tradition of giving the soon-to-be-executed an extra blanket and a nice meal before they were hanged.

He pulled open the flap of an entrance wide enough for her to enter and finally let go of her arm. "After you, Your Highness," he said, although there was a cheeky lift in his voice. She ducked her head under the heavy curtain and walked inside.

The pavilion was covered floor to ceiling in thick tapestries and heavily lighted with several hanging lanterns. It almost seemed cozy, with open trunks filled with books and what seemed to be personal belongings. She eyed a large pallet of goose down as a place to curl up into the fetal position and wish for this to all be a bad dream.

Just as her eyes were adjusting to the light within the pavilion, she heard a rough man's voice say from behind them, "Do you plan on protecting her, bishop?"

Slowly, Rennio turned and stepped back out. She tiptoed toward the door as he answered smoothly, "Why would I have to protect her? You heard the orders—she's not to be harmed until we get her to Vienna."

"She's ours. We fought for the right to the women in that castle!" a new voice hissed on the other side of the curtain.

"You want the women like a whore wants a husband. Just because that was your hope doesn't mean it was what you were paid for," Rennio replied in an unconcerned manner, like a man talking about the weather. "You have full rights to go and claim any of the beautiful ladies within the castle walls for wives, as the commander said."

"That ain't fair!" another man growled.

"Rape isn't fair, either. Plenty of people will get fucked today, and this is just your turn. Stop stomping your feet like surly children. And if you even look at this tent again I will pluck out your eyes, I promise to God!" Rennio's voice suddenly got extremely fierce. "And I will not perform your last rights, either."

She blinked at the cloth in front of her eyes, then stepped toward the entrance with curiosity, wondering if she should try to leave the pavilion and race back up the hill and toward Gerhard, since it seemed impossible that Rennio could stop three men from taking anything they wanted.

The language outside soon became so foul that she wondered if they were really speaking the same language any longer, and she lost track of the argument. Her attention was grabbed again when she heard the clang of steel against steel. Then the tent flap fell aside a little and she saw a black boot step inside only to be pulled back out a moment later.

There was swearing outside now like she had never heard before in her whole life. Every word was absolutely vulgar. "Dip your wick somewhere else, or I'll make sure it doesn't dip into anything else again!" Rennio was now threatening, sounding like he was gritting his teeth. Again, he wasn't sounding very… well, churchy…

She stepped forward and pulled the flap of the tent open to watch as the sword fight went on not eight feet from her. She had never seen real swordplay anywhere near this close up before, and she watched, fascinated. Despite the fact that she was almost certainly going to be sent to her death one day soon anyway, Rennio was braving three men at once on her behalf.

Rennio held the sword with such ease, and with such skill. She knew less than nothing about swordplay, but she could tell that he was vastly more skilled than any of the three men he was fighting. The men tried to hold him back several times to gang up on him, but Rennio's quick feet paced away from them. Then he lunged dangerously and quickly toward them, parrying and slashing as if the sword were an extension of his own arm.

One of his lunges took one of the men off guard, and the man fell back onto the ground, trying desperately to scramble away to safety. But there was no escape from Rennio's sword and the man was soon pinned to the ground by the tip of the blade. "I promised you, didn't I?" Rennio gritted with a cruel smile at the man.

Her heart flying into her chest, she pushed herself out of the tent. "Rennio, no—don't hurt him."

The other men—who had paused in shock to see their friend about to be gored—jumped back in response to her scream. They stood, puzzled. Rennio, however, didn't even flinch. "Princess, it is vital for your health that you turn about and walk back into the tent," he said, not drawing his eyes off of the pinned man.

"Please, Your Excellency… There's been enough blood spilt. They're angry, and they've had too much to drink." This she was merely guessing—their body odor was so strong that she couldn't smell the scent of ale or mead over it, but they looked unsteady on their feet as she glanced at them. "Spare him, I pray you."

Rennio finally glanced at her and then heaved a loud, heavy sigh that she supposed was to signify how much not killing the man had put him out of sorts. "Fine. Be on your way. Lady or no, the commander would not be as forgiving as I," he told the man in low, firm tones, and then pulled the tip of his sword away.

The man and his friends scurried quickly away before Rennio could turn his body toward her. "Do you have a death wish?" he said, the corners of his eyes scrunching with skepticism and his mouth taking an unpleasant twist. He put his sword back in his sheath and then walked toward her. "I ought to take a birch to you!" he chastised, and for a moment she feared he would actually do it. His expression was that of an angry parent whose child had stepped in the way of an excited horse. He gave her arm a violent jerk. "What were you thinking? Never step out of the tent. This is the only time I will tell you. If those men had a brain between them, they would have taken you then as I had the other man pinned. I cannot fight and protect at the same time." He grabbed her upper arm and again forced her toward the pavilion.

She hadn't thought of that, and she couldn't now. Her knees felt shaky, and as he entered the tent with her, the only thing she could think of was how dearly she wanted to sit down and collect herself. That brief episode had moved too quickly, and though she hadn't exerted herself much, she still felt short of breath.

As if he had read her mind, he brought her toward the down pad she had eyed earlier and let her collapse upon it. "You're already showing yourself to be more trouble than you're worth. You'll be the death of us yet, mark my words."

He marched over to where she noticed a whole cask of mead was standing. She frowned as she watched him take a mug and place it under the lever before yanking on the wooden tog, quickly filling up his mug. He stepped toward her and crouched down, passing the mug into her hand. "Drink some of this," he ordered, then added with a grunt, "I made it myself."

She looked into the liquid and then sniffed it. In the end she was unimpressed and put it down. She wasn't thirsty, nor was she hungry. She was cold, and lost, and already lonely despite her company. Out of habit, she looked around for her ladies in waiting to exchange an expression and maybe a whisper or two, but then realized that of course there were none here.

She no longer had a court. She had no ladies, she had no servants, she had no castle, and she had no lands. She was an exile who would journey to Vienna, where she would die. Susanna felt as though her heart had dropped and was now beating in the pit of her stomach.

"You're not going to cry, are you?" Rennio asked, sounding like if she cried then he would surely judge her for it.

If only she could cry. She felt like tears had been either trained or bred out of her; the last time she remembered shedding a tear was when she was ten years old. "No," she replied, keeping her voice steady and her bottom lip stiff.

"You might as well get your crying over with. No doubt you'll start doing it eventually and it will be awkward for everybody involved. There's no handmaidens to clean up your tears for you and whisk you away or whatever it is they do. Now that it's only you and myself, and I plan to ignore you in any case, cry to your heart's content."

Her heart still panged, her stomach still clenched, and even the smell of the mead was making her stomach roil. "I'm not going to cry," she replied firmly. She was far more likely to vomit first, since every time she realized where she was, what had happened over the last week, and that she'd never see any of her friends again, her stomach clenched and rolled.

She lifted her chin, trying desperately to find her voice and strength again. Despite the fact that her uncle had given most of the orders, she had still been the ruler of this whole region. She had honed a regal bearing since birth, and she decided she would keep her dignity. Trying to muster her most authoritative tone, she asked, "I heard that you are a bishop. How is this possible?"

"Are you… ordering me to tell you?" he drawled, looking confused.

She supposed that it might have sounded like that. She was a princess—that's how she was supposed to sound. In control and confident. "No, I am not," she admitted. "But I am curious nonetheless."

"Good. Just as long as you're not ordering me. You're not my princess, you know… You're not a ruler at all anymore. You have about as much power as one of the pigs tied to the meat wagon," he said, gesturing his own freshly-poured mug in what seemed to be a random direction.

It was then that she found herself scrambling toward the entry to the pavilion, where she vomited. The image of being slaughtered like a pig was simply too much.

Her reaction had surprised even herself. She had thought she was doing a fine job of choking down her nerves, but her stomach had apparently decided that it was under far more pressure than it had been in the past.

"Oh, damn it," she heard in her ear somewhere as she was heaving, well aware that there were dozens of soldiers staring at her. She felt a warm hand on her back as she continued to empty her stomach. Finally, she collapsed on the ground, where she remained for a moment before she was picked up with a mighty groan into Rennio's arms and carried back to her pallet of cushions. "Women!" he huffed to himself, as if he had predicted that she'd do this.

She didn't respond, but instead merely curled up with a groan and a shudder, feeling like she was facing misery unlike any she could have imagined.

He left the tent, and in about an hour, she felt him return. He pressed some leaves into her hand. "I had the mess cleaned up. Take this, the mint will help the feeling and the bad taste," he promised. "Mint helps the stomach."

"Thank you," she wheezed, weakly pressing the leaves into her mouth and chewing on them tentatively. The sharp taste of the mint was welcome in her mouth, making her feel slightly refreshed.

"I am a bishop," he admitted out of nowhere after he watched her for a few long minutes.

She had no idea what he was talking about until she realized, with a trickle of annoyance, that he was keen just to pick up the conversation where it had left off more than an hour ago when he had made her ill with his cruel words.

"At least… I was. The pope decided I would be more valuable on the battlefield than behind the pulpit. Now… I'm more of a soldier than I am a man of God." He grumbled then pressed back onto his feet, apparently to rediscover his tankard of mead. "Since then, I've owed my life to Gerhard more times than I care to count. All I know is I'm not doing what I thought I was going to do a decade ago. Believe it or not, my goal was to be pope by the age I am now."

"Thirty?" she guessed, then raised an eyebrow. "Well, that was quite optimistic."

He snorted out a laugh. "I'm an optimistic person!" he said, as if the statement itself was the punchline to a joke.

She felt herself, even if very faintly, truly smile for the first time in days. The man seemed much too dark and surly to feel happiness, let alone optimism. She couldn't imagine anyone who looked less likely to become pope. "Are priests allowed to kill?"

"The response to that is not as simple as you might think," he replied simply, in the same tone she had overheard used in a war room, when one of her father's knights was explaining something to her that her mother didn't seem to consider important to teach a young woman. "I wouldn't worry your pretty little head on these matters," Rennio continued.

This made her pull herself back up into sitting. "Pretty little head, indeed! If you think you have an answer that would sail above my head, then you are sorely mistaken. As my father once said, *respice, adspice, prospice*. I do not fear learning." She regretting quoting Latin as soon as she remembered that he was a bishop and he surely spoke it as well. He would not be impressed.

"Oh, so there is fire in your gullet, eh?" he said with a laugh. "Though examine the past, present, and future," he translated, "are very pretty words for someone who just lost their country, I must admit."

Her stomach roiled again, and she clapped her hand tightly to her gut. He was right, after all—she had just lost her country. She had lost her kin—her wonderful cousins, her little sisters, and all without a suitable goodbye. She might have lived under the control of a tyrant, but at least she had known happiness with her other company. She had been so proud to have the respect so many other women would have died for. Yet, that was all a memory now; it had passed her by...

She cuddled back down on her pallet. "I keep forgetting I'm a prisoner."

"Surely I would as well. Gerhard does have you in his private tent and not outside in the stockade, after all..." He hummed thoughtfully. She couldn't tell any longer if Rennio was being serious or not.

"Why doesn't he?" she huffed, tired of being bullied by a smelly drunk who just happened to be good at swordplay and insulting princesses who had just lost everything. "Why doesn't he just tie me to a block and have done with me?"

"Maybe if you ask him nicely," he retorted, then finished his mug of mead and refilled it.

She sighed, done with talking to him and shaking her head silently as she reflected how her whole life had been tossed into complete madness. The good news about being guarded by a drunk, however, was that he was only horrible when he was awake, which wasn't for very long. Before long, he was snoring loudly from his high-backed chair with his chin tilted up, his mouth open, and a half-full tankard of mead still resting on his lap as he slept.

She pulled herself up into standing, looking around the pavilion and getting attracted by a trunk that was overflowing with books and papers. She knelt in front of it and sat back on her feet as she began to peruse the pages and covers.

Gerhard must be extremely rich, she realized. He had more than fifteen books with him, all with perfect, handwritten pages in delicate script.

She knew she didn't have long on this earth, but she was chomping at the bit for anything, absolutely anything, that could distract her in the few short days she had left. She would even settle for being distracted for a few short hours. Her mind was crowded with thoughts and worries, and she had no power to fix any of the problems that ailed her.

As she was pulling out books, two in French and one in Latin, she dropped a scroll out onto the floor. She carefully picked it up, but before she put it back into the trunk again, she noticed an outline that made her realize that she wasn't holding writing or even a letter, she was holding some sort of charcoal sketch that had been blurred slightly from touch and movement.

It was the portrait of a girl, with long robes and braided hair, looking out with large, doe-like eyes, with freckles stretched across the nose. The character looked all too familiar. It looked like her, but... it couldn't be. Then she noticed that atop the girl's head was a crown.

Her eyes widened with awareness, and then she looked skeptically down at the portrait. There had to be a reason that he had a portrait of her, she thought. Perhaps there had been spies trying to teach him what she looked like so that he could apprehend her when he took the castle…

And then she found a rolled up painting, unrolled it, saw that it was a portrait of her that her father had once sent to the emperor when he was alive and trying to find a husband for her, and rolled it up just as promptly. She opened up another piece of paper. A drawing of just her eyes. Then one of her face, then one of her face from the side. And then one of just her hands.

She closed the trunk as if a fire had caught inside of it. She understood that her life had gone mad, but she couldn't fathom this.

She picked up one of the books at random and brought it along with her to a nearby lantern, determined to ignore everything she saw. Any infatuation Gerhard might have had with her simply didn't matter. He had said himself that she was his prisoner, and that she would be taken to Vienna, and the time between now and then was too short to care about anything, particularly whatever her enemy had seen in her eyes.

CHAPTER TWO

A different Gerhard came into the pavilion than had put her in the company of Rennio. Gerhard that morning had been a grimy man of war. The man who stepped into the pavilion, however, was clean... and without a shirt.

He looked at her and spoke as soon as their eyes met. "Put a fur around yourself, princess. You're going to catch your death sitting on the ground there."

"Not any more than you'll catch yours," she said, unable to keep from looking at all the bare flesh. She found it extremely difficult to keep her bottom lip from dropping straight to the floor.

He stood, giving her a twisted expression filled with confusion, and then looked down. It was as if he had just realized he wasn't wearing a shirt. "Ah, well—movement warms the flesh," he replied, but he walked toward a nearby trunk, opened it, and began rustling out a clean tunic.

She doubted that; she had a feeling he had cleaned himself off before stepping into her presence.

After pulling the shirt down on himself, he turned and seemed surprised to find Rennio sleeping there. "I see you're well looked after," he mentioned to her grimly.

"Believe me, he's better company when he's asleep," she found herself retorting under her breath.

He suddenly gave a laugh that had her looking up, loving the sound. She never thought she'd hear laughter again. "Oh, I believe you. I've known him over twelve years."

Although it was not exactly in good manners, she was unable to restrain her grimace at that.

Again, he laughed and then fished out a fur-lined vest from his trunk and pulled it on. "Oh, I have some stories to tell, my lady."

He stepped toward her and grabbed a blanket that was near her, then slowly dropped it over her shoulders. "There," he said, apparently now satisfied.

She leaned her neck back to look him up and down with new eyes. She had known he was good-looking before, but she hadn't thought of him as handsome until just this moment.

"Princess?" she heard above her, and found that Gerhard was looking at her, his head slightly cocked to the side, as if he had asked her a question.

She blinked at him.

"I asked if you were hungry. Thirsty? Both? I could get you most anything you might desire," he offered, gesturing to the entrance to the tent.

Susanna frowned, unable to see what his design was. If he was trying to get on her good side, than he should know better than anyone that she didn't have any power left behind her crown. In fact, her crown was still behind the castle walls, probably being pillaged right about now, if Eberhard hadn't taken it on his way out.

Then she decided to do what she'd always done. Demand to know. "Why are you bothering to be kind to me?"

He seemed to freeze, even stop breathing for a second, and then he said, "There's no reason not to be kind."

"You have lots of reasons to not be kind to me," she argued firmly, feeling her cheeks flush. "I am the ruler of a castle you have just vanquished. Who are you? How did you come to lead this army? Are you a prince? A duke?" Her tone was a little brazen, but she let it be. She felt out of her skin at the moment, awkward and strange and alone, and she didn't like it.

He hesitated a few moments before speaking. "I'm not a prince or a duke," he admitted finally, straightening his shoulders. "I'm the bastard son of one of the emperor's uncles, born to a maid in the imperial household and a cousin to the emperor by blood though not under the law. We were quite close as boys, the emperor and I, and often practiced our swordplay together." Gerhard paused, then continued, "I have no noble title. I earned my current position by fighting well and winning many battles over the years."

She could understand his place in the world better now, but knowing his connection to the emperor made her heart sink. He was definitely going to hand her over, and there was nothing to be done about it.

His jaw locked as he ground his teeth together. "Does that displease you?" he asked, his lip curling slightly with simmering agitation.

"I don't know if I could be any more displeased than I was this morning, commander," she replied. "My plate's very full. Mostly with my impending demise. I can't say I'm looking forward to it, at the very least."

He pursed his lips together, his eyes looked over her, and he frowned. "I'm getting you something to eat."

"No, thank you."

He left, anyway. She sighed and shook her head. A cold breeze filled the tent when he strode out, and she realized that it was already dark outside. She hadn't noticed because of her nearby lantern. "Stubborn man," she grunted to herself.

When he returned, which was only minutes later, he gave Rennio a good kick with his boot and he woke up with a start, splattering his mead all over the tapestries covering the ground. "Wh-What? Oh. It's you."

Gerhard grunted. "It's me. And if you're not done being useless, please do it elsewhere."

Rennio's eyebrows rose and he said, "You just want me to leave you alone with her?"

"In a manner of speaking," Gerhard verified snappishly.

Rennio took a swig of his mead. "Not proper. You're a hot-blooded man. She's an unmarried woman. Bad precedent to set after you just gave all your men blue ballocks."

"That wasn't a suggestion. Just a warning that a pummeling will soon begin," Gerhard replied dryly, looming over the bishop.

Rennio took that as his cue to pull himself noisily out of his chair and toward the door with an unsavory belch. "You've always been a tyrant," he complained on his way out. He continued to murmur about how he didn't get any respect for all the work he did, especially considering that his worth was twenty times that of most men's.

Gerhard rolled his eyes and then set a plate on a nearby table. "Wine, and some food, my lady. Come have some. You have to be famished."

"I'm not," she assured, but she closed her book and rose to her feet as gracefully as she could. "Tell me the news from the castle. Are my people being treated well?"

He sighed and pulled the chair Rennio had been sitting in toward the table. "Yes, although your people, especially the women folk, have given me and my captains headaches all day. They probably will all tomorrow as well. Not just the castle matrons, either. Just about every bloody female in that bloody fortress needs a good birching." He adjusted his sleeves. "Must be something in the water, making the women stubborn and silly as mules. And now I see they take after you. Eat it. You've already spent your whole day cold, and I don't want to see you ill."

"I wouldn't mind getting ill," she replied, though a surge of pride welled up in her. She was actually quite glad that so many were giving Gerhard's men trouble still, not just sitting down and bending to their enemy's will. "Hopefully I'll catch something and be able to give it to the man who'll lop off my head as my last hoorah."

He rolled his eyes. "You shouldn't think the worst. The Emperor is a good man. He'll give you a fair trial," he assured flatly.

She raised an eyebrow. "Do you really think that?" She saw him take in a couple of deep, defensive breaths as he readied to verbally joust with her, but she didn't wait for him to respond. "If you think the emperor can afford to let enemies get away unscathed, than you are woefully naïve."

He pressed his lips together, but his gaze didn't linger on her for long. "Your journey doesn't start for days, in any case. I want you safe until then, and taken care of."

"I thank you." And then she just stood there.

He looked back at her, now much more intense. "I have a headache from dealing with the promise I didn't have to make to you at all. Can you please do the smallest thing I ask of you?"

"Are you still going on about the food?" she asked, unable to even spare the plate a glance. She was too exhausted to eat, and interestingly enough, she liked making him upset. Somehow, it made her feel like she once again had at least some element of control in her life. "Are scraps of food supposed to make me feel better?"

"They're hardly scraps. I gave you the best I could find," he argued, even seeming stung. "Stop being a brat, princess. It's less than becoming."

She lifted her chin; she hadn't been called a brat by anyone in her whole life. "I'm not a brat. I'm a princess," she gritted.

"Not any more. Now stop acting like a child." She had a feeling it wasn't about the food anymore. He was trying to force her to do something just to show that he could, that he was the master, and that he could rule a princess.

She took a deep breath, but it did nothing to abate her anger. It only made her frustration simmer to a boiling point as he stood there, looking at her like she was being silly. "I am not acting like a child. You are acting like a deranged brute. It's bad enough that you take my whole kingdom from me. My life. My friends. I'm not going to stand here and—" She picked up her cup of wine and threw it at him. Unfortunately, he ducked, but she never stopped her tirade. "—do what you tell me as if you're my master! Bullying me like I'm a dog!" He stepped forward so she picked up a leg of roast chicken and threw that at him as well. That hit him in the forehead, despite his attempt to avoid it.

"Calm down!" he barked furiously, pointing his index finger toward her.

She didn't listen. She couldn't calm down; she was at the edge of her sanity, and slipping off the edge. "Treating me like a—a—!" She picked up the whole wooden plate and threw it, seeing it clip him in the shoulder and spill the extra food everywhere. "—child! I won't have it!"

She continued throwing anything in arms' reach at him, and then when she ran out, she turned to grab more things. She didn't know why, but every time something cracked against him, the better she felt. It didn't strike her that she was in any danger until he marched behind her, grabbed her elbow, and spun her around. He gave her a hard shake. "Stop this. Calm yourself, Susanna."

She slapped him and enjoyed the resounding sound that echoed through the room. It didn't quite seem enough to repay him for taking everything precious in her life away from her, but it was a start.

She didn't regret it until she noticed that his face had become a glowering mask of rage. His lips were pursed, his jaw tight. "I have only one way I deal with tantrums, my lady," he threatened, his voice a low rumble, but then he dropped his hand from her shoulders and began to remove his belt.

She blanched white and stepped back, her anger dissolving like mist and only fear remaining. She took a giant step backwards. "Don't even think about it!" she growled.

"I'm done thinking about it," he assured her, advancing just as quickly as she was retreating. "If you think this will give me joy, then…" he paused. "Actually, it will. Nothing is better than putting a spoiled child in her place, no matter how high she's born."

Her cheeks burned. "I am not a child."

"The food wasted on the floor indicates otherwise," he retorted, and then reached out to grab her arm.

Susanna was very used to be being treated like glass, so this was an awful lot to be taking in so suddenly. Her mother made sure her nursemaid or a servant held her hand whenever she went up and down the stairs in fear of her falling. Her food was sampled by a trusted taster before it ever reached her mouth in fear of sickness or poisoning, and not even her father had ever raised a hand to her. That's what her whipping girl had been for—and she thought it worked because she had been good friends with the whipping girl until she was married outside of the kingdom. She studied and obeyed as well as she could back then to make sure that her friend wouldn't get whipped.

That being the truth of things, Susanna had never felt so physically threatened in her life.

"Let go of me!" she cried, trying to jerk his grip off her arm. She began to fight him with all the strength she had in her. Eventually he had to come behind her and pin her arms up against her chest as he brought her over to the desk and sat down upon it.

"The more you struggle, the more I'll enjoy this," he told her warningly, trying to wrestle her down across his knees.

She used all of the strength she had to wrench her body to the right and stumbled onto the ground. He made a second reach for her and she made a squealing noise she usually reserved for when she was surprised by very large rodents and very hairy spiders, and darted away from him, waving her arms in the air. Even she was surprised when she actually made it to the flap of the pavilion and into the cold winter air around them.

"My lady, not one more step!" she heard Gerhard's voice boom from behind her. She spun in place and realized with surprise that he wasn't as close as he had sounded. He was at the entrance of his pavilion, looking at her like she was a child standing at the edge of a cliff with a mixture of horror and anger on his face.

Chills ran down her arms, and not because of the cold air. His anger was unbearable, mostly because she was very unused to dealing with anger from anyone but her uncle. No one else had ever dared to be angry with her, and the fact that he still had his belt in hand didn't make her want to return to him.

She turned back around and, running as fast as she could through the sea of men, whores, swords, tents, and fires, she made for the tree line. She was already worried that she had no plan for when she got there. She couldn't escape, she had no idea how to keep from getting hunted back down, she knew, but at the same time she couldn't very well just submit to a punishment like she was some disobedient child.

Not used to running, she tired easily, and her toes quickly felt numb in the thin layer of snow under the soles of her slippers. She kept clipping the sides of tents and people, and eventually she tripped over a branch that jutted out from the ground and her body very ungracefully tumbled down next to a fire with two rabbits spitted atop it.

"Well, well! What do we have here?" a voice said above her. She was already beginning to acquire flashbacks from Rennio's fight earlier that day. Two of the largest boots she'd ever seen stood in front of her face.

She put her hands out in front of her and slowly raised her upper body so that she could crane her head up toward the largest and hairiest man she'd ever encountered in her life. How her fortress had been taken had suddenly become oh-so-clear. They hadn't needed to ram the door down. They'd just needed this man to come and smash it in himself. "It looks like you're far from home, little girl."

His dialect was that of eastern Bohemia, and she had the hardest time deciphering his tone, so she had to assume that he planned to eat her next—either that or something equally horrifying. Now, she was too frightened to move. "I thought they had all the maidens up in the keep?"

"Maybe they did, but some have been married off already," another man said with a shrug. With immense relief, she was beginning to realize that they hadn't recognized her as the princess. "Maybe she got away from her husband? Or hell, Arlo, she might be running away from the keep itself!"

"Well, she certainly got quite a ways!" Arlo hummed, but then bent down and grabbed her arm to yank her into standing. As soon as she was on her feet again, however, she felt the desire to crumple herself into the fetal position. Somehow, that position seemed safer.

She looked him in the eye, which was habit since the princess looked down to no one, but she quickly regretted it. Firstly, it strained her neck, and secondly, the eye-contact seemed to confuse the beast.

"Why, hello there, beautiful…" he finally said, grinning widely and exposing the fact that he was missing two of his front teeth. He sat down on a nearby log and pulled her along with him. "Don't you fancy a seat on my knee, love? No need to go out into the dark. You'll get eaten by a bear!"

She felt like she was going to eaten by a bear, anyway. Even when she jerked with all her strength she couldn't seem to move even a single inch away from him. "Let me go!" she demanded sharply through her gritted teeth.

He laughed as if she was playing some sort of cute game, and then said, "Be nice, now. That's no way to treat your future husband, my dear."

"Future husband?" she echoed, narrowing her eyes at the furry brute. "You've got to be out of your mind! Unhand me now!"

"Future husband, aye! I'm not married, and I could see myself plowing some striking lads into this lovely belly of yours!" He reached his hands around her waist and put them up toward her breasts. "Got some tits on you, too!"

She gasped as his meaty hands grasped her breasts through her bodice, squeezing her flesh painfully. She tried to push his hands down and off of her, but he and all the other men around the fire only laughed and hooted merrily. She had a horrible feeling that everyone except her found her horror and disgust amusing.

"Let go of me this instant or I'll scream!" she warned.

"You'll be screaming anyway, lovely—I'm a big man!" the laughter around her was renewed. She scanned the darkness outside of the circle for Gerhard or Rennio, but she could barely make anything out of the shadows moving around. It was far too dark, far too noisy. Gerhard was never going to find her.

She grabbed the man's thick, beefy arm and gripped downward with one hand and up with the other, as if trying to rip his skin in half.

"Oy!" he said, annoyed, gripping his arms around her even tighter. "Keep doing that, love, and I'm going to think you're too impatient to wait for the priest in the morning! Come here and give us a kiss, now!" he leaned forward and she did the only thing she could think of: she spit on him.

Her mother—a woman who surely didn't even know how to spit—was probably rolling around in her grave right this very moment, but in no worlds would Susanna let her first kiss be given by two lips that looked like two pink slugs. Although she hoped he would be stunned enough to let go of her, all that spitting did was stop his kissing advances. A low, worrisome 'oooh!' moaned through the circle as the big man held her by one arm and reached up and wiped the spit out of his eye with the other. He looked at his fingers even as she cried, "Let go of me, you boar!"

"Well, aren't you the feisty one?" he said, his tone now low and holding no laughter. "I think I need to teach you a lesson in manners, don't I?"

Her eyes widened. The men around them once again began to hoot and holler with robust laughter, and she was already tired from trying to get off his lap. When he grabbed her with both hands and shoved her down across his large thighs, she had no chance of fighting him off, and she knew it.

The only thing she could do was pray and scream for help that would never come. There wasn't anyone on her side. Her army had been vanquished and her kin had been conquered and were probably being married off against their will at that very moment.

"Help me! Someone help me!" she cried anyway. It was difficult to tell herself to just accept this immense amount of humiliation and let him spank her, that it couldn't be that bad, and that she would most definitely have worse done to her sooner than she'd like.

"Shut up, woman! You're splitting my ears!" he told her, and she felt one of her hands, which she was trying to pinch his skin with, pinned behind the small of her back. He began to pull up her skirts.

"Dooon't!" she quavered, thrashing her legs, trying to find the ground, or his leg, or anything at all to touch or kick. All she found was air. Air that was very cold on her calves.

No man had ever seen her bare bottom, and she had hoped to keep it that way. She had only two layers on, which wasn't enough to keep her particularly warm even when she was fully dressed, and as he bunched her linens up over her back, she didn't know if she was going to burn with shame or die from the cold on parts that had no business being exposed to the elements.

"Rahh!" she growled, sounding like a wild lioness in her own ears and biting the man right on the knee. He yelped, picked her up, and moved her further to the side across his knee so that her head was now hanging by the ground and her ass was very high in the cold night air. Then he proceeded to do exactly what she had been trying to escape in the first place: he spanked her.

At least she imagined that he would have called it a spanking. She probably looked like a chastened toddler to the eyes of all the men surrounding them. She, however, knew better. Children couldn't bear this sort of pain. She felt like she was getting beaten with a wooden oar, and all she could think about was how completely unfathomable this sort of pain had been just moments ago.

Dots were appearing in her vision, either because her heart was going to beat clear out of her chest, or because she was practically hanging upside down, and all of her screaming—which she couldn't control, she was certain—was making it very hard to breathe.

Certain that she was going to asphyxiate, she began to cry out for Gerhard.

"Gerhard! Please!" she cried out between the loud, rhythmic 'slaps' of the oaf's immeasurably large hand as he heated her backside with one sharp, resounding blow after another. She could barely believe she was crying out for her own jailer, especially one who had also tried to spank her only mere minutes ago. Even if he'd heard her, he would have been unlikely to rescue her, but there was simply no other person to cry for.

"I've never seen a grown woman cry like a little spoiled brat!" one of the oaf's companions said as her voice began to crack and The Oaf adjusted her once more over his knee since all of her otherwise futile wiggling was finally making her fall off of his lap. "Look at her! Like she's never been laid a hand on in all her life! Smack her good!"

The Oaf did, renewing his smacks although she could feel him shudder with laughter under her body. She did something then that she hadn't done for years—something she didn't even think she could do anymore. She cried. Tears began to stream down her face, unbidden and uncontrolled, and she began to hiccup violently as her screams of pain and agony turned to helpless sobs.

Her audience snickered, and it only made her cry harder until the spanking stopped all of the sudden with the shout of a familiar voice.

"Put her down this instant, soldier, or I swear I will run you through!"

She was literally shoved off of the giant's lap in a single instant. She hit the ground and rolled in the dirt until she found herself looking up at a shadow that only looked familiar when the firelight flickered on his visage. It was Gerhard, standing tall with a sword in his hand. He glanced in her direction for only a moment before regaining eye contact with Arlo.

"What were you thinking?"

"Well, you said we could have the women around here if we take them to wife! I'm taking her to wife! Looks like the lass was trying to escape from the castle!" Arlo said, standing up. Although he was over a head taller than Gerhard, his tone was obviously defensive.

Gerhard narrowed his eyes even as he slowly crouched down to her level. He grabbed her hand with surprising gentleness and helped her to her feet. "You're not taking this one to wife. She's not available," he told him, although his words were hard to hear as she continued to hiccup.

She adjusted her dress and then wrapped her arms around herself.

"She looks available to me! Though she's a brat, for sure! Spit right in my face, she did! Like some sort of alley cat!" Arlo waved a hand toward her with anger, but Gerhard put an arm around her waist and pulled her toward his hard body.

"I've become aware of that, Arlo," Gerhard sighed, and she realized that he was on first-name terms with this ruffian. His arm seemed warm around her as he put his sword back into his scabbard and began to turn her away from the crowd around the fire. "Now carry on."

They trudged back in the direction Susanna had run from before, and Gerhard held his body closer to hers than any guard. She still couldn't seem to calm down—it was as if some sort of floodgates had opened and now she was going to have to let the world drown in her dramatic onslaught of tears.

He moved his lips close to her ear. "Are you alright, princess?"

She took a deep breath, but when she opened her mouth to say, 'Yes, of course I am, you fool!' a sob rolled off her tongue instead, which she then swallowed down with a gulp before nodding.

"They didn't recognize you," he assured her, as if that was supposed to make her feel better. "They were just drunk, playing around."

"It—it didn't feel like playing around to me!" she sputtered, suddenly flashing hot with anger. Instead of arguing with her like she expected, he pulled her even closer and gave her upper arm a consoling squeeze.

Suddenly Rennio stumbled in front of them. She could barely make him out in the light, but his silhouette in the moonlight was indistinguishable because of his wild hair and his robes. "Good!" Rennio panted, putting his hands on his sides as he tried to catch his breath and speak at the same time. "You found her safe! Now I hope you can beat her to death! What were you thinking? You are the worst prisoner imaginable! We told you not to leave the pavilion. At least I did. I told you over and over and over. Not because we don't want to chase you down in the forest, either. You could have been assaulted by any one of these men, you nitwit!"

"Rennio, enough," Gerhard immediately chided, walking right past the priest and seeming to continue to ignore him even though he trailed behind.

"She saw earlier what sort of men are out there! They're not as loveable as I am!" Rennio ranted on, beginning to trudge along at her other side, only not nearly as close as Gerhard was. "Idiot females," he grumbled underneath his breath, none too quietly.

She heard Gerhard snort derisively. Then he said very quietly in her ear, so that she wasn't sure she'd heard him correctly, "I'm sorry I didn't get to you sooner. I couldn't see where you'd run off to. I had gone in completely the wrong direction. I am most sorry." His apologies made her insides twist, mostly with confusion. She wasn't sure why he was giving them to her, especially since he was probably going to beat her himself, like he had planned to earlier. Another part of her, however, felt glad that he seemed to feel as though he had let her down in some way, as if he actually had some concern over her safety.

She normally could judge people and their intentions very well, but she couldn't judge Gerhard. She had no idea what his intentions were, and why he would even rescue her at all. His actions couldn't be more puzzling since he was apparently a man who was paid to deliver her to her executioner. She couldn't decide whether to fear him, hate him, or trust him.

All she was sure of was how warm his body felt and how much she enjoyed having his arm around her. Enemy or not, she didn't want him to let her go.

CHAPTER THREE

Gerhard's heart was still pounding in his ears. He had walked through army encampments on plenty of nights before, but he hadn't once realized what a labyrinth they were until tonight as he searched for Susanna.

He had felt guilty about pressing her as soon as she left the pavilion. She was afraid and under an enormous amount of pressure. She had lost her world that day—so what if she skipped a meal or two?

He had just been looking forward all day to being able to come home and care for her, spend time with her, and when she refused to accept even the most basic of his gifts, his disappointment turned to fury... just like it had always done. But this time, he was with his lady.

His lady with the coal-black hair... Who was in his arms, invading his senses with the scent of soap and lavender. He had dreamed of being this close to her all year, and finally it was realized.

All he had wanted to do since he saw her was pick her up in his arms, carry her to bed, and bury himself into her. Instead, it seemed like the whole world was between them.

"Thank God they didn't know you," he told her again, now more to console himself than to console her. A feeling of dread crossed his thoughts as he said it out loud. They would have had their way with her if they'd known it was their enemy, the same woman they had been bawdily disclaiming while they were getting their blood boiling before the battle. His decree would have meant nothing to a crowd of drunken rogues. Fortunately, perhaps because they were drunk, they hadn't realized how well she was dressed or how lovely her hair was, still done up and veiled skillfully. It should have given her away.

Arlo, one of the largest brutes he'd ever seen, wasn't a truly bad man. He was just an idiot. He didn't even know his own strength; he'd probably thought he was just giving her a couple of chiding pats. Gerhard couldn't tell if Susanna was crying from the pain or the humiliation of being spanked like a child. Maybe it was a mixture of both that had upset her.

Of course, he'd been of a mind to give Susanna a spanking earlier himself, so he saw the appeal in it. In fact, if he was being honest, he was jealous that Arlo had seen that beautiful, round ass of hers before he'd been able to glimpse it himself.

"Come on, let's get you indoors," he said, still feeling her tremble in his arms and knowing that the snow beginning to gently fall from the sky wasn't helping.

"I-it was awful," she quavered. She looked like she was trying to stop crying in the same way he'd seen a fish swim against the current; she was trying so hard that it seemed like she was only making it worse.

"I know," he told her, with another squeeze. "I know it was awful. I would rather you not have had that experience, Susanna, and certainly not in front of all those people. Please don't run from me again."

"And now you're going to beat me, too," she sniffled.

He brushed his thumb over the velvet covering her arm. "No. I will not punish you—I think you've been punished enough for the night," he told her, although he had promised himself when he was mad with worry looking for her that he would throttle her when he found her.

Gerhard was glad when they finally reached his pavilion, where one of his guards was already sleeping outside with ale in his hands, worn out by the celebrations around them. He tilted his shoulders back and raised the tent flap before guiding the princess into the tent by the small of her back, not liking the space it left between them. The space where he had held her to him felt cold and incomplete.

Rennio was about to walk right in after them, and Gerhard put his hand out to stop him. "Where do you think you're going?" he asked, raising an eyebrow.

"To get warm and go to sleep," Rennio replied in an exasperated tone normally saved for dealing with snotty children. "Where else?"

Gerhard wasn't particularly zealous about the idea of having another person in the tent. The reason why Rennio was such a good guard for the princess was because he was an excellent soldier, could think for himself, and most importantly, he'd had an injury when he was younger than prevented him from advancing on Susanna himself.

That being said, he certainly didn't want him being any sort of distraction for either the princess or himself this evening. He wanted to be alone with her; he had waited so bloody long to be with her that he didn't want his oldest friend fucking that up for him, especially because he feared that he wouldn't have long with her.

He shook his head. "I don't think so, Rennio."

Rennio shot him a bewildered look. "What do you mean 'you don't think so'? I've been running through the camp looking for her, just because you couldn't keep her in the tent! Now you won't even let me in?" He pulled his head back and then crossed his arms, studying Gerhard with a knowing glance. "Oh. Oh. I hadn't seen it before."

"What?" he demanded, figuring that Rennio knew absolutely nothing. Rennio knew as much about women as a pine tree knew of poetry. Women were completely outside of Rennio's realm of experience or knowledge.

"If you want a night of making love, just go ahead and tell me. Might do her good, since she only has about a week left before she's given over to the emperor," he added, sarcasm rolling off his tongue. "I think she has enough to worry about without your attentions, my friend." Rennio leaned forward, then clapped his hand around Gerhard's arm. His brown eyes glanced toward the castle as he added, "Go pick yourself out a good wife. Have some children. You're close enough to retirement, and you've lived through your youth. You've waited long enough to start breeding."

He hated when Rennio called it 'breeding'. It made him sound as if Rennio viewed himself somehow apart from the human race. As if his horrible manners alone didn't make that impression strongly enough... "Please do not call it breeding. I'm not a Viking," he begged dryly, knowing that the women in that castle held absolutely nothing for him. He wanted Susanna. He wanted her all to himself, every part of her, and he wanted her now and forever.

He had waited all year, then all day knowing she was in his tent, waiting for him. All he wanted to do was go in there and soothe her pain and run his fingers through her hair and torture himself by not having his way with her. "I think she's done with company for today, that is all."

"It's cold out here!" Rennio reminded stubbornly.

Gerhard walked inside the tent, grabbed a fur, and then threw it outside. "Goodnight, Rennio."

"I'll remember this injustice!" Rennio warned, but Gerhard knew that he wouldn't. This was not the first time he had been kept out of the pavilion, and neither Gerhard nor Rennio were strangers to sleeping on the ground without anything to keep them warm. A fur, a warm fire, and a jug of ale would suit all his needs, and he could get that anywhere. "I'm not a dog you can order about!" he cried, but then he wandered off grumbling and scratching himself.

When Gerhard came inside he was treated to a vision, for Susanna was untying her lace veil, which had become askew during her spanking. He watched her, wordlessly, as she fixed her hair, black and beautiful. "Take down your hair," he asked her, his throat feeling dry.

She looked up, her eyes round and her cheeks flushing. "Pardon?"

"I want to see your hair," he repeated. Part of him wanted to cringe at his boldness, and beat around the bush for months or years in a long courtship, but he didn't have that sort of time, and he didn't live that sort of life.

Her brows flickered a little before she dropped her shoulders and asked, "Why?"

"Because you're beautiful," he replied, stepping forward, feeling nearly like he had fallen into a trance. "And because I've been dreaming of you with your hair down."

He froze; he might have gone too far with that one.

She was still, like a deer being hunted in the wood, and he was certain that he had frightened her, put her guard up.

Instead, a smile broke out across her face. It was the warmest smile he had seen in an age, accompanied by white teeth and twinkling eyes. Her tear-stained cheeks was suddenly the only trace left that she had ever been crying at all. "You are too bold, sir," she told him in a chuckle, then tisked. "What about my hair is so important?"

Her smile was contagious, and he continued to step toward her. "It's dark as river stone, and it makes your skin look so pale, like porcelain." He stood close enough to her to feel the heat coming off her body. He reached out, and she flinched her face away, though not much, not enough. She allowed him to touch the pads of his fingers to the side of her cheek. It was so soft, so warm, and after a moment she pressed her face into his hand like a kitten might, closing her eyes and taking a deep breath.

"You are a horrible enemy," she told him in a dreamlike mutter.

"We're not enemies tonight," he said quietly, shaking his head. "Live in this world with me, Susanna. Let me undo your hair and take care of you for one evening, I beg you." And he was begging. He wasn't sure if he could stop if she asked him to, but somehow he knew she wouldn't.

He noticed her shoulders tense, and her eyes fluttered as if just waking. He reached for her crispinette, which hid her braids with enlaced pearls. He unpinned her hair and the crispinette came free. Her braid seemed to explode from its confines and draped through his fingers as long, black curls.

"My mother would have never permitted me to wear my hair down," she said quietly, though with humor in her tone.

"Why not?" he asked, stroking his fingers through her hair, savoring the silky softness of it and the way it smelt like flowers.

"She thought my hair was wild," she told him.

"What a crime," he said, pulling off her other crispinette and tossing it before her on the table. "You have the hair of a goddess, Susanna."

"You shouldn't call me that," she told him, with a sharpness from sudden unease. "You shouldn't use my Christian name like we're familiar."

He combed his fingers through her hair, slowly looping the thickness around his fist. He pulled her head back, firmly but not harshly, and she made a little gasp as her eyes trained themselves upon him. Her expression was proud, but it was also excited.

"I will be familiar with you, Susanna," he told her, his voice a rasp. He wanted her so badly. He wanted those pink, rose petal lips.

"I don't know you," she panted.

"Have you ever been kissed before?" he asked her, easing his grip on her hair.

She pressed her lips together but then shook her head ever so slightly. "No," she replied in just a breath.

"Then you'll remember me as the first man to do this." He let go of her hair and gripped her face with both hands, lacing his fingers behind her neck. He had sacked cities and beheaded dukes, spoken his mind in front of the emperor more times than he could count, but he had never felt bolder than he did in this very moment.

He kissed her, pressing his lips hard and hungrily against hers and tasting her mouth deeply. He had nearly forgotten what fear felt like, but now he felt it brewing in his stomach. He didn't want her to be leery of him. He just wanted her to let go of everything, of her kingdom, of her old life, and just be joined with him. He had fantasized about this moment for ages—the moment where a princess could make love with a man such as him without cringing. He wanted her to just kiss him back.

But she wouldn't. Deep as his kiss was, it was one-sided.

He stopped kissing her and just held her face in his hands. The prettiest, sweetest, and most innocent face he had ever seen. Far too innocent for the lady of a great castle to have. Her uncle had at least done this much—by ruling her kingdom, he had also kept her out of the politics. There was no world-weary hardness to her. Maybe that's what captivated him... or maybe it was those light blue eyes. "Beautiful," he said, petting her cheeks with his thumbs.

"You shouldn't..." she swallowed. "You shouldn't kiss me."

"Why?" he asked her, still gazing at her and stroking her cheeks. She still hadn't pushed him away or cried out, and until she did, he wouldn't move.

"Because... Because you're not my husband, nor my betrothed..." she replied unsurely, quietly, and then her eyes closed sleepily, like a cat's.

"If you were one of those women up in the castle, you would have been mine already," he assured her. He grinned and pulled her body closer. "I would have singled you out, hunted you down, carried you off, married you, and taken you to wife in less than an hour's time."

Her eyes widened and her porcelain cheeks began to flush. She opened her mouth to reply, or maybe even to chide him, but then she closed it. After a couple of tries, she swallowed and asked, "Why me, sir? I am nothing any longer. Spending your time with me will get you nowhere and bring you no privileges. I have no more kingdom, and I will lose my crown after the trial."

He squinted at her, wondering if she just couldn't reason that someone could like her for more than just her crown. "Because I love being in the same country as you. Breathing the same air. I love the way you look at me. I love this small nose," he kissed her nose, "and these pink lips," he kissed her lips, "and this wrinkle that appears between your eyebrows when you're worried," he kissed that too. "I have been dreaming of you since I met with you for barely over an hour eight months ago, and I want to find out how much you'll devastate my world when I spend just one night with you."

"But you nearly beat me," she protested, sounding a little short of breath and beginning to tremble slightly as his hands continued to caress her.

"You make my blood boil," he agreed, and then kissed her again.

This time, she put her hands up and onto his chest, and shoved slightly. Just before he ended the kiss, however, she balled up her hands into his tunic, and kissed him back.

Lightning felt like it had struck through him from each of his toes to the tips of his ears when she kissed him back. His cock, which had already been quite hard, now strained as if determined to break free of his clothing of its own accord.

He dropped his hands from her head down to her waist, slinging one arm around her to bring her body in closer to his own while, with the other, he grabbed her bottom.

"Oh!" she squeaked, suddenly ending the kiss and attempting to jerk her body away.

For a second, he didn't know if it was his brazen grasp that had her thinking twice, or the passion that was beginning to spark between them. And then he remembered, "You're still sore," he said, not as a question.

She didn't reply, just blushed and averted her eyes.

He pulled her close to him and nibbled at her jawbone until she began to calm and melted into his embrace once more. As soon as she did, he began to pluck at the buttons that laced her gown. She froze, holding in her breath, but she didn't stop him.

As the lacing became more intricate and difficult to undo properly, he pulled himself away and slowly turned her around, gathering her thick black hair and carefully putting it over her shoulders so that he could look at the fastenings that held her velvet dress together.

He pulled the cloth down her arms and toward her waist, then untied her two layers of underskirt. When the fabric was pooled around her knees, he kissed her neck and then stepped back to admire her in the lantern light.

His breath stopped.

Susanna was the most beautiful thing he had ever seen before in his life, and he hadn't even seen the front of her yet. He focused on her bottom, which was beautiful as could be, somehow even more so with pink blotches covering it from her spanking. In a way, the scene struck him as extremely domestic. As she stood, she trembled and looked over her shoulder shyly at him.

He pulled off his tunic in a single motion and then, suddenly raging with energy, he stepped forward, swooped down, and picked her up into his arms. She thrashed around after squealing slightly from surprise, but then he found her simultaneously smiling, biting her lip, and covering what he could only assume were the most glorious breasts he'd ever see with her small, fair hand. "I've never seen skin glow so perfectly in candlelight," he told her, and wondered if he was being possessed by a poet. He felt like one tonight; he felt overwhelmed by everything that was happening and everything that he was feeling. The world had never felt so right and wonderful.

He brought her to the pallet of cushions and laid her down on them carefully. "Don't move a muscle," he demanded as she began to reach for the nearest fur. He stood back, trying to pull his boots off and nearly falling on his face doing it. He had never been so eager to bed a woman in his life, not even his first.

She laughed slightly as he stumbled and he grinned at her. As soon as he could, he crawled onto the pallet and over her body, then nipped her playfully on the stomach.

He could already smell her sex, and he slowly moved his hand over her slender thigh, leaving a trail of goose pimples. He found her slit with his fingers. She was wet and hot for him.

"Gerhard!" she gasped, crunching her body upwards.

He put his other hand on her stomach and kissed her belly again. "Shh."

"What are you doing?" she demanded.

"Has a man never touched you here, my beauty?" he asked her, then pressed his thumb down into her wetness until he found her swollen little nub.

"Of course not!" she replied as if he was being scandalous just to mention it. He wasn't surprised. Though most noble women he had ever met, unmarried though many of them were, weren't virginal, Susanna looked at him like she was fascinated by his every move. That look filled him with fire.

He moved his body down and kissed along her knee. He was glad that she hadn't been taken before. He wanted her as his. He didn't want to think about the future, about what lay in store for her. He just wanted her all to himself, right now, as if there was no tomorrow at all.

He rubbed his thumb back and forth over her quim until her body began to writhe and she let out small, quiet little whimpers. She tried pressing her thighs together, and with a chiding tsk, he spread them back apart. "Relax, Susanna. I'm taking care of you this eve," he reminded her.

She chewed at her bottom lip, looking more girlish than regal now.

Unable to keep from grinning like a cat in the proverbial cream, he kissed her inner thigh and began to move his mouth toward her center.

"Gerhard!" she chided.

"Shhh!" he told her, continuing to pet her moist lips with his tongue. "Shh…" He lapped at her, and her body bucked. He moved his hands, gripping them around her waist and then gripping her sore ass. She gasped and growled, continuing to buck against the sensations.

She sat up slightly, even grabbing his hair with her fingers, but without pulling. "Gerhard," she whimpered pleadingly.

He lapped at her honey even harder, closing his eyes in bliss. He listened to her moan and writhe, varying his pace to match her movements until he felt like he was about to explode himself. At last he moved up between her legs, spread them wide apart, and put the head of his cock up against her lovely quim. Despite the cold in the room, her body had a sheen of sweat on it, and she looked like she was in a dreamy state of lust. She looked at him heatedly through slitted eyes as he rubbed his cock through her wetness before moving it toward her entrance and pressing forward.

She growled suddenly, her body bowing. "It won't fit," she said as he halted at her tightness.

"This is my quim," he growled back. "And I will have it." He bucked his hips forward, moving further up her tight channel as she moaned, her nails raking down his back. He gritted his teeth, pulled out slightly, and then pushed again. She gasped and he felt himself slide in deeper until he was fully inside of her, all the way to the hilt. He stayed like this for a long moment, putting his hands on both sides of her face and then kissing her deeply. This felt so right, being inside of her, being joined with her.

He was surprised when she began to writhe under him, spurring him to continue thrusting. He reared back and buried himself in her again and again, even stopping to raise her knees up higher so that he could plunge still deeper into her wonderful heat.

Never had he felt so close to anyone before, and never had he felt like his entire body was going to explode and dissolve like a spark. "Damn it, Susanna," he told her, feeling like he was going to climax at any moment. He could feel her inner muscles begin to contract down on his member, and he thought that she had already had her pleasure until suddenly she sat up, gasping, and wrapped her arms tightly around him as she spasmed powerfully around his cock. He groaned and clenched his teeth, beginning to spill his seed deep inside her as he held her weight in his arms, cradling her on his lap as he knelt on the pallet.

He felt like he had never spent so much seed in his life, and as he finished, they sat still, panting and gripping each other until he turned and dropped against the pallet like a felled tree. She screeched slightly as their weight hit the pillow, and then they laid there, panting, their arms and legs entwined in each other's.

He had his eyes closed as he took in everything that had happened. His dream had finally come true, and all he wanted was to rest so that he could do it again. He wanted to do it forever.

"I didn't know I could do that!" she giggled once she got her voice back.

"Do what? Take all this man into you?" he teased, pumping his hips and pressing his still-buried cock deeper into her.

She laughed and shook her head. "No. I just…" she closed her eyes and took a deep, happy breath. "I never knew I could… feel that way. I…" She bit her lip. "Now I think I know why I was told to wait until marriage before I was allowed to share in that."

He laid his head back onto a cushion as she snuggled against his stretched out arm. "Why?" he asked.

She snorted. "Because I'd never want to leave after that!"

They both chuckled for a long moment, but eventually silence overtook them, and he brushed her hair behind her ear. "You are the most beautiful creature I've ever beheld," he told her with a sigh.

"You keep saying that," she smiled.

"Because it's true," he replied. "You are." He frowned contemplatively and then asked, after a short silence, "Why did you never marry, Susanna?"

She frowned and her eyes darkened slightly. "My uncle chased off most suitors. He said it was because he was picky for me, but really… I know the truth." She sighed. "If I'd married, he wouldn't have had his power."

"All the more reason for you to have tried to find a husband," he replied. "I know even the emperor tried to offer for you."

"Yes, but that obviously came to naught. Though I'm glad the portrait that I exchanged with him came into good hands," she said, raising an eyebrow.

Now it was his turn for his face to heat. "You… saw the paintings, didn't you?"

"Painting—singular," she corrected, "and obsessive sketches," she replied with a sly smirk. "I must have made an impression on you somehow."

He stroked the side of her face again. Yes, she most surely had. Her entire manner had entranced him. He had even liked the way she moved. He'd never thought it possible for a man to be so completely beguiled by a woman until the day he stepped into Hohenzollern. "You were the star in my sky. Although I did my best to ignore that," he admitted bitterly. "I didn't want this spell you have over me to be like this. But… I saw you, and my world went off kilter," he admitted.

She gave him a chiding look, as if there was some part of what he was saying that he was making up. "I should have let you see my hair earlier," she teased. "Perhaps then I could have made you captain of my guard and none of this would have happened."

He smiled but then looked bashfully down and circled her perfect, swollen nipple with a lock of her black hair. "Your mother said your hair was too wild to wear down?" he asked, mostly to hedge away from the melancholy they could so easily fall into. She was his prisoner, after all, and he had just sacked her kingdom. It threatened to come between them like a cold breeze beating on a window shutter.

She smiled mischievously. "My nursemaid said that my mother's heart nearly stopped when I didn't come out blonde like she was. She had the most flaxen hair when she was a girl. When she saw my black hair, she worried that I would never marry." She gave a slight laugh. "If my mother had her druthers, I would have been married by eleven."

"Eleven?" he gasped, shocked.

She nodded. "Yes, and it would have been far better. My brother, Nathaniel, was still alive then and so was my father. I could have escaped all that transpired after." She looked around, but didn't look at her surroundings in particular, but seemed to gesture with her glances at the celebration that still roared outside. "My sister's too young to have the crown. I would have had a husband that would have taken power from Eberhard, or... well, it would have been Eberhard that would be going to Vienna." Her lips tightened slightly at this.

He hated that man so much at the moment, hated how the mere thought of him was ruining their happy moment together. "He will face his judgment. He will not get far," he promised her, then petted her hair. She seemed to sadden, and so he continued, "I know men like your uncle very well. I understand there was surely nothing you could do. Some men are like avalanches—if you stand in their way, they will roll you over and crush you. I wish I had done something then—like killed him with my bare hands," he rumbled tersely.

Now it was her hand reaching out to him. She slid her hand over his chest, along his breast bone. "I remembered you, as well, you know," she admitted quietly, coyly glancing up into his eyes and then back down to follow the patterns her fingers were drawing over his chest.

He was surprised by this, he had to admit. He hadn't thought it was possible for her to remember him. It was nearly a year ago now, and he knew there wasn't anything memorable about him. He'd barely gotten to speak to her, since her uncle was so aggressive toward him. "You did?"

She nodded. "I don't see how I could have forgotten. You have a very recognizable face and voice," she told him.

He grinned impishly, unable to help himself as he pulled her closer by clamping his hand over her bottom and pushing himself deeper into her. "I do?"

He didn't feel so mischievous when he saw her frowning. She looked deep in thought. "Your threat revolved in my mind for this full eight months since," she told him. He watched her long, black lashes flutter on her smooth cheeks. "When do we go to Vienna?"

He closed his eyes, then hugged her closer. He didn't want to talk about Vienna. He didn't want to leave this moment! He sighed and begged, "Let's not talk about Vienna now. That's the future. Let's enjoy what we have right now."

He held her close, stroking his fingers through her hair as he felt her breathing against his neck. He enjoyed her warmth, even the sound of her breathing.

After a moment, she asked, "So why did you have Rennio guard me of all people?"

He gave a laugh so hard that he pulled out of her, then rolled onto his back. As he pulled her into a nook between his chest and his shoulder, he answered, "Let's not talk about the bishop, either."

"He's an odd sort of man, is he not?" she asked, glancing up at him.

"Yes, but he's also a man I trust. That's why I had him guard you. He might be a horrible conversationalist and he's got the manners of a goat, but he would never seek to have his way with you." He grinned. "I'm the only one who can do that."

She giggled slightly under him, then blinked at him with innocent round eyes. "What about you?" she asked. "Do you have a family and a home?"

He shrugged and rubbed his hands together idly. "I own a sizable amount of land in Bavaria which I've purchased over the years."

"Purchased with your spoils from sacking castles like mine?" she asked pointedly.

He smiled, not letting her ruffle him. "Yes, some of it, but most of it with money I've been paid to defend one castle or another so that one lord can prevent some other lord from acquiring spoils at his expense."

"But you don't actually have a home, then, just lands you own?" she pressed him.

"I've had a modest estate constructed on my lands, and I pay a steward to manage it for me, at least until I'm ready to retire and live there myself."

"And your wife?" she asked, cocking her head to the side.

He shook his head and smirked at her. "No wife. Which is too bad because my steward is ten years my junior and already has five children. Every time I stop by the estate, he has a new addition."

She gave a small, though very real laugh. His stomach twisted at the sound, and his eyes followed the way her perfect, pink lips opened and curved with delight at his description. "He's younger but wiser, then?" she asked teasingly, her eyes twinkling at him.

He gave a laugh. "Oh yes. Most surely he is the wiser of us. He chose a peaceful life, while I chose this." He motioned to the pavilion surrounding him. "I nearly freeze to death every winter. I'm paid well, but money only goes so far out here. Sometimes I think that I'd trade my every last coin for a warmer blanket."

She smiled up at him. It was a beautiful smile, though her teeth weren't perfectly straight and her front teeth were larger than others. Her smile seemed almost childlike, he thought, which might have been why she didn't use it often. Her mother had probably trained smiling out of her. She snuggled back into him, saying thoughtfully, "I think I was at my wisest when I was ten years old. I ran away for a full five days before I was found," she told him, and he knew she was smiling against his chest. "Those were the happiest five days of my life. I did nothing but get dirty, run around, and eat berries in the forest." She laughed. "When my father's men found me, I was covered head to toe in mud and the berry stains stayed on my mouth for three weeks!"

"They didn't serve you berries at the castle?" he asked her, chuckling.

She shook her head. "Yes, they did of course... but they're not the same as grabbing them right off of the bush. My wet nurse used to take me on walks on a forest trail and she had me far too spoiled on exercise and fresh air for my parents' tastes." She twisted her mouth slightly as if remembering something distasteful. "After that they gave me a tutor so strict I was lucky to be allowed to look out the windows until my father died."

The thought of her as a little girl who just wanted to go out and play, to be anything other than a princess, was an image that was quickly melting his heart.

"I'm glad I got this time with you," Susanna said to him sleepily.

"Me as well, sweeting," he told her, looking up at the ceiling as the closest lantern flickered its last, and died, leaving them both in darkness. He reached over and pulled a couple of large furs over their bodies, taking care to make sure it covered all of her, including her feet.

"I'm glad it was you who took my castle," she told him dreamily.

He petted her until he heard her breathing heavily against him, sleeping. Every now and then, he felt the tickling of her eyelashes as her eyes moved behind closed lids. He envied that she could sleep so well despite everything that rested on her shoulders.

He feared she was right about Vienna. He was supposed to send her off to the emperor, and he didn't know how he could possibly do that. He would never feel whole again, that he knew. Once she was gone, he would just be left empty, with a memory of what it was like to be full. He'd go through the rest of his days feeling like his heart was dying of hunger.

It was impossible to imagine a worse torture than that. But how could one deny an emperor and live to tell about it?

• • • • • • •

"Rennio, get up," he hissed, tapping what looked like a giant, furry rock with his foot. "Rennio!"

Rennio didn't move even a hair, and Gerhard was just about to give him another shove with his boot when the furry rock replied, "Do I look like a dog to you?"

"Actually..." he muttered in reply.

"If you wanted me to wake up in the middle of the night to sing you a lullaby, then you shouldn't have kicked me out onto your doorstep to surely do several things that would not have pleased the Lord."

Whenever Rennio spoke like he remembered that he was a bishop, Gerhard's eyes would reflexively roll. He was the least orthodox man in the world, of that he was absolutely certain. He had claimed himself that he had only become a bishop because his uncle was very wealthy and Rennio wanted the free books that tended to come with the position.

"Come on, Rennio. I need to speak with you," he begged, nudging him with his toe again.

"Speak."

"In private," Gerhard specified, looking around at the other sleeping, snoring men in blankets around the campfire.

"You're going to have to wait until dawn then," Rennio informed him, rolling onto his other side.

"I have a proposition for you that, if it goes well, will include a casket of wine as large as an ox," he promised.

Rennio grumbled. "A small ox?"

"A very big one. Biggest ox you could find," he promised, whispering with enthusiasm now. He crouched over Rennio and put out his hand. "Come on."

Rennio, apparently more awake now that future wine was on the table, got up and wrapped his cloak around him. They marched out to where no soldiers were around anywhere to be seen in the pale moonlight.

"Alright, now we're alone. What is this about?" Rennio grumped.

Gerhard frowned and then took a deep breath. "You've always been my closest friend, Rennio," he began.

"Out with it. Stop trying to butter me up. It's making me nervous."

"I need you to help me fake a death," Rennio stated clearly. "And make it so the fault could never be traced back to me."

He could make out Rennio raising one bushy eyebrow dubiously. "Is that all?" he asked cynically. "Your death?"

"No. Not mine... hers." Gerhard rubbed at his arm, feeling suddenly very cold and very nervous. "I can't let her die, Rennio."

Rennio snorted. "Of course you can't. Don't you think I've seen all those silly sketches in your trunk? Did you think I wouldn't put together who they were of?" He heaved a groan. "But what about the emperor? Are you just going to lie to him?"

"I think if she dresses below her current station she could walk straight up to the emperor and he'd not notice her. He knows I mean to retire into the country this year, anyway, Rennio. He's been telling me to get married for years."

"Yes," Rennio agreed. "But I assure you he didn't mean for you to marry the Princess of Hohenzollern!"

Paranoid, Gerhard looked around, shushing Rennio, and then he crossed his arms across his chest. "Rennio, she's an innocent. She was born under an unlucky star, that is all. I won't have her die for it."

"You just want to bed her," he doubted with a grumble.

"I have bedded her," he snapped. "I want more than that. I want to marry the girl. Give her a life." He could feel Rennio looking at him skeptically in the darkness. "I want her," he added flatly.

"I have no doubts that you do, but it's very difficult to go from ruler of that," he gestured toward the steep hill that was topped with the great fortress of Hohenzollern, looking intimidating and immense in the moonlight, "to being the wife of a man with no title or birthright."

"I think she'd surprise you," he replied, firm in his resolve. If she could look back fondly to a week of her childhood where she was running around in the forest eating berries, then he couldn't fathom that it would take the girl very long to assimilate to being his wife.

"She'd better, Gerhard!" Rennio snapped. "What you're asking is dangerous. If someone was to find out that you made off with the princess, the emperor would hunt you down. He wouldn't care at all that you were playmates as children or even that you saved his life at least once. He can't let his enemies go unpunished."

"He has Hohenzollern," he replied defensively. "I am not taking anything that he needs. I am not betraying him. If we are able to fake her death, then he wouldn't know any better."

There was a long silence during which the bishop began to pace back and forth. After a few minutes, Rennio finally stopped and turned toward him. "We cannot be conservative about this. We need to make sure that witnesses are convinced she has died, but of course we won't have a body to bring back. Not to mention we have to appear as though we couldn't possibly be involved. It will be risky for us and for her."

Gerhard perked up, recognizing Rennio's tone. Rennio had a plan, he knew it. "What's your idea?" he asked, leaning toward him.

Rennio shook his head. "You're not going to like it."

He put his hands on his hips and stood straight and confident. He already began to feel a little better. "Try me."

CHAPTER FOUR

"Wake up, you whore!"

Susanna woke up with a start, finding herself in the middle of her cushioned pallet with naught covering her but a fur. She had barely spent longer than a moment nude in years, and it took her awhile to remember what she'd done the night before, then she felt the pinch of discomfort between her legs. She was no longer a virgin.

She looked up and saw Rennio hovering over her. He threw her clothes down on her. "Get dressed!" he growled.

"What—"

"Shut up, or I'll drag you out there naked!" he snapped, and Susanna, her heart suddenly feeling like it was controlled by a hummingbird, quickly began to pull her underclothes on. She hadn't dressed herself since she was an unruly child who wanted to be up and about before her nursemaid was ready to dress her. Since then, her clothing had become more complicated.

She moved quickly, her body flushed as she looked up and saw Rennio still leering at her. "Turn yourself away," she demanded.

He suddenly stepped forward, then leaned down and grabbed her hair, snapping so loudly that anyone outside of the pavilion was sure to have heard him, "You don't order me around, you bitch! You're nothing! You have no power over anything! Now get yourself dressed so you can get out of Gerhard's sight! He wants you to stop stinking up his tent!"

The gravity of his words only set in as she was trying to tie her underskirt onto her waist. For a moment she paused and let them slam against her soul.

Nobody had talked as sweetly to her as Gerhard had the night before. Despite the cold winter that was approaching outside, Gerhard's words had been able to warm her down to her toes. He was handsome, sweet smelling, and had large, gorgeous hands and a chiseled jaw. He was the type of man she had never known she always wanted. Last night, after being so caring and sympathetic after her run in with the brute soldier, Gerhard had been able to awaken something deep inside her, and her body had reacted as if he had cast a spell on her.

It had been glorious and fulfilling. She'd felt closer to Gerhard in those few short hours than she had felt with anyone in her whole life.

And now he wanted her out of his sight? How were they at one second two halves of the same whole and by the morning she was something that needed to be disposed of? She had gone from being in the height of bliss into the deepest pit of hell.

"Hurry up!" he growled.

Rennio was an enigma, too. He had been unpleasant yesterday, but he hadn't been wicked or cruel. He hadn't even been aggressive. "Wh-why are you being so terrible?" she begged, finally able to pull on her dress.

"Because of all the goddamned trouble you've caused! We've fought a war over your incompetence! Damn women—you can't even take control of a cake without fucking it up!"

Her eyes widened and she turned away, hoping he wouldn't see that her lip had now begun to quiver. She had known yesterday that her enemies were sure to be less-than-kind with her, but she had at least thought they're be horrible right away, and not all of the sudden after she'd given one of them her maidenhead!

At that mere thought, she felt as though she had swallowed a stone. Her throat tensed and she could barely breathe.

She fumbled with her braids, her fingers feeling numb and not dexterous at all. Her handmaiden was the one who used to fix her hair, and although she had spent time playing around with the hair of her sister and cousins for fun and leisure, she hadn't attempted to fix her own hair in ages. She clumsily tried to arrange her hair into buns and then tried her best to pin on her crispinettes, knowing it would look horrible if she had a looking glass to inspect it all.

She turned and said as clearly as she could beyond the lump in her throat, "If you could be so kind… I need help tying up the back of my dress."

Rennio rolled his eyes dramatically and then marched behind her where he none-too-gently began to lace the back of her velvet gown. "As if I care if your tits are hanging out!" he replied then, loudly. She blushed, wondering why he had to say everything so loud that it even hurt her ears. He wasn't on a stage, for God's sake.

He handed her cloak to her then, although she was surprised that he would bother. She was nearly about to forget about it, feeling rushed and jittery, but was relieved when it was in her hands and she threw it around her shoulders and closed the clasp at the neck. She was sure she looked like the very devil, but at least she would be warm.

"Come on, you move slow as the grave," he claimed, suddenly grabbing her arm and thrusting her out the door.

As soon as she was outside, she was seized on either side by two guards who gripped her upper arms. There were soldiers all around her, crowded in tightly, as she was dragged through the camp. The atmosphere around her seemed even tenser than it had been the day before when she came through the castle gate to surrender.

She felt completely winded; yesterday she had been emotionally prepared for the worst, but sometime during the night she had begun to gain the smallest sliver of hope. She had been made happy by her enemy, after all, at least for a brief time. Perhaps that is why now she felt like there was a ball of ice in her stomach, one which only felt larger after the crowd began to shower her with rotting vegetables.

She had no idea where they were leading her. She looked over her shoulder and saw Rennio, but nowhere she looked could she see Gerhard. Did he know that she was being treated this way? Rennio had said that he did, but Rennio seemed like the type of man who might speak an untruth just to get under her skin.

She cried out when she was suddenly hit on her shoulder by something hard. With fury, she turned and realized that someone had thrown a small rock at her. When she turned, she saw a boy of ten covered in mud who made a face at her. She was just swallowing down her fury when she was hit in the cheek with something else.

Cold horse dung.

Never had she felt so insulted before in her life, and she didn't even have the time to stand still and digest her emotions as they continued to drag her through the field of enemy soldiers. She took a deep breath, trying to ignore what was being thrown at her, keeping her head high and proud like the princess she had been. She wouldn't allow them the satisfaction of seeing her upset.

That was until she finally caught sight of Gerhard, who was holding open the door of a cart that had been turned into a small cage. It looked like it had once carried goats or chickens. Now, it looked like it would carry a princess. Gerhard merely looked at her with a dark, disconnected look that was so unlike the man she had made love to the night before that she wondered if it was the same man at all at first.

"Princess Susanna!" Gerhard greeted with a cruel tilt of his lips. His words were loud enough to be heard throughout the crowd, or at least fifteen men deep. "May I introduce you to your new kingdom?" The guards propelled her toward him, and although she pin wheeled her arms, she fell down into the cold mud. Sputtering from the cold, she was grabbed by the scruff of her robe and lifted from the ground. Gerhard's strong hold freed her of the mud but then he thrust her into the open cage, which she quickly realized wasn't empty after all. There was a baby pig in there with her.

"Hail Susanna! The princess of the pigs!" he cried out to the crowd as he slammed the door of her cage shut behind her. There was a loud roar of

"Hooah!" from the whole army, who laughed and then continued to throw rotting food into the cage at her. The baby pig squealed with delight and immediately began to munch on a cabbage leaf.

She looked through the bars of the cage and up at Gerhard, who now would barely spare her a single glance. How was this even possible? She had thought that they had something between them, she'd thought that she meant something special to him! All those drawings, all that time looking deep into his eyes and seeing only a man who wanted to be something to her.

Now, the only thing he seemed to want to be was a complete prig! Her bottom lip began to tremble again and she struggled not to cry in front of all these people. She would not break down.

"Soldier, take this filth to Vienna. Let the emperor meet out justice to her!" Gerhard demanded in a loud bark, and again the soldiers cheered around her. In moments, there was a violent jerk as the large horse carrying her cart pulled forward.

She watched as the crowd parted around her and more food and dung was tossed on her through the wooden bars. At least there were no more rocks... but at the moment that wasn't much solace. As the cart moved forward, she watched Gerhard, curious if he was going to look at her with even a sliver of regret. But as he watched her being carried off, he showed no expression.

Her heart felt broken, but she wasn't able to cry as she had last night after getting her spanking. For some reason that pain was able to open her up and wring out most of her depression. Now, she was beginning to realize that no tears would come even if she did want them to.

She looked upwards at the hill, at Hohenzollern, and it came to her that she would never see her home ever again. She saw the faint outline of people watching from the ramparts, but she couldn't make out faces. She wondered if her sister could see her, or any of her kin, but then she hoped that they couldn't, that they would never know how she was carried off.

There was a small snort and a nudge on her thigh. She looked down and saw the little face of the piglet looking up at her, and as she watched, it invited itself onto her lap. She placed her hands around its warm, chubby little body and she melted a little bit, feeling the stone in her throat return. At least something in this world seemed to like her...

• • • • • • •

The cart was far away from the army before they were joined by several men on horseback a couple of hours later. Apparently, they were her guard to keep her safe from highwaymen. Rennio, unfortunately, was among them.

"It took you long enough!" the cart driver snapped. "I was nearly thinking of turning around!"

"It's his fault," one of the soldiers, a large, bald man, grunted unhappily as he jerked his head in Rennio's direction. "My wife could pack a whole trunk faster than it took him to pack his satchel!"

"Well, the commander was suddenly in a rush to get her as far away from him as possible," Rennio replied defensively. "Gave me absolutely no time at all to prepare!"

"Prepare what, packing your dresses?" another soldier teased. All the other soldiers laughed.

"They're called robes," Rennio replied with weary exasperation, then took a swig of his horn, which she had a feeling was filled with ale or wine rather than water. She had scorned food the night before, but now her lips were parched and her stomach was growling. She licked her lips.

Rennio seemed to notice and leaned his horse toward the cart, putting out his horn. "Wine, your majesty?" he asked, mockery in his tone.

She pursed her lips together in response to his sarcastic tone, but then she reached for the horn. He pulled it out of reach just as her fingers had nearly grasped it. He laughed, pulled it back, and then took a mouthful of wine, only to spit it on her a moment later.

She heaved a cry like an angry animal, unable to put her emotions into words. He laughed. "We'll feed you at camp if you're a good girl," he mocked.

The pig snorted, sounding angry on her behalf. She knew it was probably just coincidence of course, but it endeared her to the little animal even more. Rennio even glared at the piglet in response and then turned away as if told off. The pig, as if wearied by the effort, turned back around on her lap and lay down, continuing to warm her against the chill of the wind that was beginning to become so violent that it was making the cart sway back and forth.

As the hours paced on, her nose began to feel numb from the bitter cold, which she actually found to be a blessing. It made it nearly impossible to smell the stink of her confines. She sniffled loudly, then rubbed her nose against her sleeve, mostly in an attempt to warm it.

"Stop your noise!" Rennio growled at her as he trotted his horse along by her. Apparently her chattering teeth and her sniffling were beginning to offend him.

"Oy, bishop! Leave her be!" one of the soldiers groaned. "I've seen dogs treated better. I thought you were supposed to treat her kindly."

"I had to read too many men's last rights this week to treat her kindly. Make no mistakes—it's jezebels like her that doomed us out of the garden in the first place," he replied, taking another swig of wine.

She squared her shoulders. "What harm have I done to you?" she asked him defensively, nearly as surprised at his harsh turn around as Gerhard's. He had never been particularly nice, true. But he hadn't been particularly mean or nasty, either. It was as if he hadn't met her before that day and then simply decided to blame her for every sin of humankind. Yesterday she had thought that, even though he obviously didn't take his religious duties very seriously, he wasn't a cruel man.

He then listed far too loudly to be necessary all the things her uncle had done in her name as she stared blankly at the back of her cage, not bothering to listen. She was contemplating what must have happened overnight, what sort of evil seemed to possess these men, because the world was undoubtedly crueler today than it was yesterday.

She sat back in her cage and looked up at the sky above. Her dolling up that morning had obviously not done any good. Somehow this actually bothered her, though she hadn't ever been accused of being particularly vain. She had hoped she would at least be able to be presented to the emperor looking more like a princess during her trial, and not so much like a pig farmer.

"Can't you please at least let me have a blanket?" she begged him, trying to get her chattering teeth to still, gathering the piglet into her robes to be closer to her belly. "I'm going to die of cold."

He snorted. "Enjoy the cold. All you'll have is hellfire soon enough…"

She shriveled at his cold inhumanity. "You are the most hateful person I've ever known!" she spat.

He pointed to the pig. "Complain to someone who gives a damn," he told her coldly.

It hadn't been a bad idea. Not that she complained to the animal, but she found him cuddly and even loveable. She felt at least that the pig wouldn't turn on her by tomorrow morning.

"Stop," Rennio called to the soldiers at the front of the carriage that were leading the way. It was now the tenth time the party had needed to stop so that Rennio could find a bush for privacy.

"Christ! My horse doesn't shit as much as you do!" one of the soldiers, a very sturdy and frightening looking man with a head shaved entirely bald yet a beard down to his chest, groused with a groan. She had a feeling that they had no choice in the matter. Rennio must have outranked them all. "I wanted to get across the river before nightfall!"

"Just camp here," Rennio said, waving his hand as if he thought the soldier was being ridiculously whiney.

"We can't camp here! I keep telling you, this is the worst spot to be. There's nothing for the horses, and there's no way to protect ourselves from the wood! On the other side of the river there's far better shelter. Don't be an idiot, priest!" the man bellowed. "Just hurry this time!"

"Fine, fine," Rennio sighed, but then he wandered off and didn't hurry at all. The soldiers left behind were finally beginning to talk amongst themselves about who would go out looking for him before Rennio finally came back just as the sky was getting even darker.

Susanna began to have a bad feeling. The soldiers were very unsettled and upset, and their nervousness permeated the air around them until she was even more worried about the journey than she had been previously, only this time she didn't even have any idea why. Not until they came upon the river, at least.

As soon as she caught a single glance at the raging, black water, she began to feel just as frightful as the horses who were stomping their feet all around her, making the carriage heave to and fro. She grabbed the wooden bars with her scraped hands, trying to steady herself.

"This looks dangerous," Rennio stated with annoyance.

She wanted, more than anything, for one of the soldiers to slap him across the face. It was certainly not a far jump to assume that that's exactly what they wanted to do, anyway.

"That's why we wanted to go over earlier! So we could see better over the crossing!" the bald soldier all but shouted at Rennio, who seemed unfazed. "Now let's hurry before we can't even see our feet!"

As they slowly guided their horses to the edge, their steeds once again stomped and whinnied at what they were going to be forced to do. The water wasn't very deep—it would probably only go up just past the knee—but it seemed like it was moving far too swiftly to safely cross. Apparently, however, they were going to cross nonetheless. She gripped her piglet tightly against her, ignoring its unhappy snorts.

With a lot of complaining amongst the screaming of unhappy horses, the company slowly entered the fast-moving stream, and the cart jerked violently as the horse reared.

She held her breath, absolutely certain that the cart was going to fall sideways into the water and she was going to drown. The horse slowly settled down and then, suddenly, a huge gust of wind picked up, the water below the carriage wheels surged, and she heard the wheel beneath her body break.

She screamed as the cart, horse and all, heaved onto its side, and the cage immediately filled with ice-cold water that made her scream with pain and fright just before it went up over her head. The cart had gone free somehow, and she was swept below the water in the wreckage.

The piglet screamed and kicked his little feet, trying to climb up on her to get out of the cold water. She held it in her arms and kicked out with her feet as hard as she could. She didn't think it would have worked as well as it did, because the cage fell into splinters with the first kick, several bars falling out and being swept downstream in huge pieces. She rushed through the bars and into the water, which immediately got deeper. She felt her head sink beneath the waves for a terrifying moment but then she bobbed back up. She tried wearily to swim toward the riverbank, though it seemed like she couldn't even move an inch in the right direction.

The stream pulled her even faster, spinning her body out of control, and all she could do was kick and try to keep her head above the water, holding onto the squirming pig as they were swept around a bend. She heard the river roar up ahead and even though she couldn't see, she had an uncanny feeling that they were coming up toward a drop of some sort. The rushing water sounded hollow and expansive, like a waterfall she used to walk under when she was a child… which wasn't good.

Her arms and legs were so numb with the cold that they felt useless, and her soaking wet dress, underskirts, and cloak made her feel as though someone had tied a sack of stones around her waist.

"Drop the pig!" she heard someone shout from somewhere nearby.

She gripped the piglet tighter as she sputtered and choked, looking desperately around in the darkness while trying to keep her head above the water. She couldn't see anyone, and she imagined that she had to be far away from the party that was charged with bringing her to Vienna.

Suddenly she felt hands reach around her. "Susanna!" a voice cried out simultaneously. The arms were strong, and warm. The pig screeched. "Drop that bloody pig and hold onto me!" a man's voice demanded in her ear.

She held her breath, still trying to kick against the current even as the man held her tight. They were both jerked suddenly backwards against the current and she realized that whoever had her was tied to a rope. She gave a choked cry in surprise. "Damn it, I've got you. Hold on!"

She wasn't going to drop the pig. It oinked in her ear unhappily, and she took a deep breath in as her eyes burned from the water. She was able to see now that it was Gerhard that had her held firmly with one strong arm. She was surprised, but her brain refused to wonder at it. It was too concentrated on her survival and the extreme cold all around her.

He slowly pulled them to shore and, as soon as his feet were steady, he picked her up into his arms and carried her up the stream. "Damn that stupid pig," he said, and she could hear that his breath sounded like he was in the midst of shuddering. Apparently he, too, was cold as could be.

She couldn't respond. Her chest felt constricted by the cold, and she stayed perfectly still as he pulled her up into a wagon and placed her onto a dry surface. He bent over her and loosened her arms from the pig, which squealed and shook itself off as Gerhard focused on getting her cloak unfastened. As if her clothes were poisoned, he moved quickly, his teeth chattering every bit as much as hers were. "We have to get you dry," he told her as he peeled off her cold layers. She laid there, feeling numb and paralyzed with confusion and cold. She felt absolutely helpless—she wondered if she could move much more in any contingency. He threw a giant blanket over her, and she curled up into it. She saw his figure shuck his own pants off and then redress. He jumped down from the covered wagon where he had placed her, leaving her nestled among dark shadows of crates or boxes.

There was an unhappy squeal and little hooves hit the boards near her body, and then the piglet nuzzled into her, nosing its way under the blanket. Less than five minutes had passed since she was rescued from the water, yet already she was in another wagon, and the horses were underway, being directed through the dark.

"G-G-Gerhard!" she stuttered, speaking to the ceiling, suddenly wanting to know what had just happened, where she was, and where she was going.

"Shush!" he demanded. "Keep quiet, sweeting," he replied earnestly. "Keep quiet."

She had no trouble doing that. She was mostly invested in making sure her fingers and toes regained blood flow. Every part of her body felt sore down to the bone and being wrapped in the warm, dry blanket was heavenly.

She wasn't sure if they stopped at all during the night. She kept drifting into a deep sleep, despite the wobbling of the wagon and the screeching of the wheels beneath her. It was hard to believe that Gerhard could drive the cart through the night without any rest at all, but she woke up when the wagon finally came to a stop, and when it did, a dull light lit up the canvas overhead.

She heard the sound of a sigh and then Gerhard jumped up on the back of the wagon and, picking up a second blanket, slowly lay down next to her. He ended up lying on the pig's tail, which was apparently a big insult to the little beast, because it squealed, got up, and danced angrily about before settling down between them.

Susanna watched him as he looked down at the pig for a second, surely deciding whether or not to boot the presumptuous animal out of the wagon altogether. He twisted his lips and then looked up, meeting her eyes. She suddenly felt so full of emotion that it seemed just as hard to breathe now as it had in the icy cold water. She didn't even know what to say or how to start asking what had just happened and why he had saved her from the water.

He reached over and put his hand on her cheek. "I am so sorry, sweeting. I know yesterday was hell for you, and I'm completely responsible for putting you through it. I can't even imagine all the humiliation you felt, and I did not want to be the one to have done that all to you... but it was a necessary evil."

Her eyes narrowed and she sat up on her elbow. "Necessary evil? They threw horse dung at me, Gerhard! How could you possibly imagine how that made me feel? You can't possibly have any idea! You took my kingdom and my family and my life, and then you decided to go ahead and take my pride as well," she snapped, her face heating with rage as she recalled her humiliation.

He pulled himself up on his elbow as well, and she noticed that he was dressed in a tunic complete with a hood. He looked like a beer merchant, not like the commander of an army. "Susanna, calm yourself. It's over now, and you have to understand that it was all for show. I think the world of you. I did all that for your happiness!"

She snorted. "Oh, yes. I could tell. I'm ecstatic. And the falling into the river? Was that also the plan?"

He shrugged and did look slightly sheepish. "Yes, but I was there to fish you out before you hit the waterfall."

She flopped back down onto the boards under her with a thump, unable to believe this.

"Susanna, I want you for my own," he assured her, but not in a gentle manner. His tone was deep and exasperated, tired. "This was the only way I could make that happen! You had to be put in a position where you would appear certain to have died but in which your party wouldn't expect to find a body. That river claims several victims every year, and rarely is anyone found!" He took a deep breath, and then reached again for her face. She shrunk away from him in protest. "Come," he cooed, "let's not quarrel."

"Let's not. You nearly murdered me to help me as a friend," she huffed sarcastically, covering her weary eyes with her fingers.

"Susanna—I have done all this to be your husband. This is the price we had to pay!" he argued.

She felt like someone had just dropped her down a very deep hole, and her mind went completely blank for a long moment before she unlaced her fingers from over her eyes, one by one. She slowly turned her head to look at him. "To be my husband?" she repeated, incredulous.

He clenched his jaw, but otherwise did not respond. His eyes looked into hers, stubbornly, as if egging her on to argue with that.

"You can't be my husband. I haven't consented to that!" she reminded.

His bottom lip dropped open. "I don't care if you consent or not! I already took your maidenhead, Susanna! You are mine! You gave yourself to me willingly, which is a lot more than can be said for a lot of your subjects still within the walls of your castle. Men are drawing straws for some of them. You are with a man who at least cares about your happiness—one who's put himself at risk of treason to save your life already!" He rolled over, as if that finished the conversation. "You can't possibly be that picky. No woman could," he finally said, after closing his eyes as if he meant to drop into a deep sleep.

She narrowed her eyes to slits and stared at him. "You cannot force me to marry you. You were horrible to me, and you let everyone you know be even worse! I will never forgive you for that."

He looked up toward the ceiling, "Yes, you will forgive me. I have given you everything you ever wanted. Life, freedom." He turned his head slightly toward her and looked at her. "Don't you understand, Susanna? The Princess of Hohenzollern died in the river, never to be recovered. You're only Susanna, now. Susanna is a bride of Hohenzollern that I have claimed as mine—as is my right—and she will be going home with me."

She had never felt a sensation like this before. On one hand, she had been so frightened for nearly a year that she would end up being executed by the year's end, and in Gerhard's estimation, she no longer had to dread that end. She might be able to live to an old age after all, which is something she had never quite believed before. The possibilities which presented themselves as a result of having that many years at her disposal were almost overwhelming.

Yet to say he was extremely presumptuous was a gigantic understatement after she had spent all of yesterday feeling like he had reached into her chest and pulled her heart out. She would have marched out of the wagon right away if she wasn't completely nude. As it was, she felt trapped.

"You need to rest more, Susanna. You were restless all evening. You will feel better," he promised, reaching out for her.

"Don't touch me," she muttered angrily, pulling her piglet to her chest and scooting away from him the few inches that she could. Their bodies were tightly nestled between towering boxes on each side.

He didn't listen to her. Even as she squirmed away, he moved closer to her until he rolled onto his side, pulled out his arm, wrapped it around her, and pulled her against his chest. "Be still."

"Let me go!" she muttered angrily.

"I'm not letting you go, Susanna. Ever. Now be still, or I will chastise you. I'm exhausted and out of good humor to deal with your stubbornness, as sweet as you look to me with fire in your eyes." His lip curled into an impudent grin, as if he knew full well that she wanted to slap his face and walk right out of the wagon. She squirmed against him and he locked his arm even tighter around her body.

The piglet, apparently feeling too squished for comfort, then took his turn betraying her. He moved from where he was creating space between them and then laid behind Gerhard's head, as if having decided to warm him. Gerhard opened his eyes just to turn his head and glare at the pig as if he didn't approve of the act of favoritism, but then hooked his leg around her. "Stop squirming," he told her sleepily.

She did, but only because she was too weak from the fright last night to fight against him. Soon she would make him sorry. He just didn't know how frightened he should be yet!

CHAPTER FIVE

"Susanna, please come here," Gerhard asked. He had been traveling with the princess for three days, and although they'd been blessed in that they hadn't been approached by anyone of the original party that might have been looking for her, she was still silently protesting him. "I want to keep you in sight."

She appeared, though slowly, back into his line of sight, glancing toward him very briefly before turning her back and continuing to ignore him. If she didn't stop being so cold to him, he was going to lose his mind. She literally talked more to the damn pig than she did to him. "I'll show you how to make a fire, eh?"

He tried to send her a helpful smile, but that was only ignored. Since he had woken up the morning after fishing her from the river, she had never seemed to settle in his arms like she had after they'd made love. Every attempt he'd made to be loving toward her led to her immediately drawing away, and even when he hugged her to his body at night, her body went frigid.

Rennio hadn't joined them yet, but he could almost hear him make a joke about married life beginning already. The night they'd made love, they had fit together like two puzzle pieces. Now they'd obviously spun out of alignment. All he had to do was get her back to looking at him in the right light.

Susanna turned away from where she was washing up in the cold river water, which she had stepped into so that it came up to her bare ankles.

Just as he opened his mouth to try to get her attention again—despite the fact that he was certain that she had heard him quite well the first time—she bent down and patted her pig, who rooted around on the riverbank. "It sounds like the commander wants to start forcing me to do more things today, Grunter. Doesn't that sound charming?" she asked the pig conversationally, her tone dripping with sarcasm.

He ground his teeth together for a moment as he tried to gather his patience. It was true that he didn't like anyone opposing him, but she seemed to take a delight in not doing anything she was told. If he asked her to come, she'd stay. If he told her to eat, she'd refuse. If he told her to wash, she'd go to sleep. If he told her to go to sleep, she'd stay up all night, trouncing around outside the wagon with the pig.

She might have called that pig 'Grunter' but he had been calling it 'Bacon' since the first morning, still upset that she hadn't let go of it in the river. It had frightened him to death, because he'd had to hold her to him and pull them both out onto shore with only one arm. She'd had both of her arms on the pig.

"Susanna, come here and start speaking to me, or else I swear I will start to lose my temper," he warned.

Finally, she stomped toward him. "Why would I care a pittance over your temper?" she demanded, which was the first thing she'd said to him in easily forty-eight hours.

At least the silent treatment had ended. "Because you do not want to feel my hand on your saucy little bottom," he threatened firmly. "That's why. You're acting like a child about all this."

"About all what?" she retorted, putting her hands on her hips, "You wanting me to thank you for freeing me when I'm still your prisoner?"

He rolled his eyes and stuffed pine needles underneath the firewood, then pulled his flint out of his pocket. "If I didn't go out of my way to mistreat you, they might have expected something. It's folly to think that I'll never see anyone in my army again, and when they see you—and they will—I don't want them to even consider that you and the princess are one and the same. Now they'll never suspect I married you after how I let everyone treat you. They would look at you and never suspect that you and the princess are one in the same. They'll just assume you look similar, by some odd chance. That goes with Rennio as well—he had to facilitate your escape, so he made sure that he treated you the worst."

She shook her head firmly, stubbornly remaining angry. "I think he was just looking for an opportunity to treat me like filth," she pouted, crossing her arms in front of her chest. "And I'm not just angry because of how you treated me—although it was horrible and you have to be the worst suitor that's ever been born—I'm angry because you can't just decide my future for me! I don't even know where you live."

He had been clacking his flint against the stone, trying to create a spark that would light the pine needles, but now he stopped. Though he stayed crouched, he straightened slightly. "I'm not exactly a peasant, princess. I may not be a duke or a prince, but I am a man of good means. I've had women chase me down, begging me to take them to wife."

She raised her chin saucily. "Then why didn't you take one of them?"

"I'm not having this argument," he sighed, and then continued sparking the flint, eventually earning himself a small flame that quickly spread to his firewood. "Your opinion on this matter is inconsequential! It's done. You're with me, you're under my protection, and I won't argue about it any further. For God's sake, you might be carrying my child as we speak!" he reminded firmly.

He looked up and saw her face suddenly turn red. He actually thought it was very cute, because it made her freckles far more pronounced than they usually were, but he could never tell if she was angry or embarrassed. Her silence after his statement was disconcerting.

"Did you sleep with me to bind me to you?" she demanded, wincing at him with what looked like pain.

"Susanna," he sighed. "No, I did not. Come and sit—"

She spun her heel and quickly began to tromp away, stomping dramatically back toward the water and then down the bank.

For a long moment, he had decided that he wasn't going to follow her. She would eventually come back, hopefully done with her tantrum.

After five minutes passed and she didn't return, he began to mutter to himself that he was going to have to give her another—and this time, much sterner—talking to about just walking off in the middle of the woods. It unsettled him to see her go out of sight. Although they hadn't had an easy couple of days, after all, she was still precious to him. Her presence made him feel at peace, and when she was away from him, he felt so full of unease he couldn't stand it.

Time ticked by, and he chalked it up to his own paranoia and perhaps the fact that he was, on the whole, too controlling. She might have been his woman, but that didn't mean she didn't have the freedom to walk a few feet out away from him.

After nearly an hour without her return, however, he had worried himself into knots. Something had to have gone wrong. The fish he had caught in the river for their breakfast was already cooked, and he had been certain that she would have been back by now. It was cold, and the bank was icy and covered with snow. What if she slipped and hurt herself?

He picked up his sword, just in case, and buckled the leather sheath around his hips before he took off, following her footprints left behind in the snow, jogging to catch up with her.

When he heard the howl of a wolf, the hairs on his neck stood on end and he put the wind under his feet, nearly slipping across the ice and snow in several points as he jumped over logs and bushes to follow the sound and the remaining footprints.

Another low, resounding howl rung out in the cold air, and he heard a loud squeal.

He drew his sword and launched himself into the clearing ahead of him, shouting, "Susanna!" He saw the princess wielding a stout branch in her defense, with the frightened pig running about around her skirts, trying to hide itself away from the four wolves closing in on them.

His entrance drew the attention of two of the wolves, and he didn't hesitate to charge. He wanted all of the wolves upon him and far away from Susanna, who was swinging her branch back and forth as if it were a sword, crying, "Get back! Get!"

The first wolf wasn't a problem. It charged him head-on, and he was able to rid the earth of it with a single slice of his sword. The second wolf, however, jumped toward his face. It knocked him to the ground and went for his throat, but he got his sword between them just in time to drive it through the beast's chest. The whimpers of the dying wolf, which he quickly shoved off his body, attracted the attention of other two that had remained nipping at Susanna's swinging branch.

Taking advantage of the distraction, Susanna clubbed one hard upon his head with her branch, leaving it motionless on the ground as the last wolf charged at Gerhard. He got his sword back into position and readied his stance. The wolf came at him, snapping his fangs. The beast was quick, but Gerhard was quicker, and a savage stroke from his sword sent the wolf's head tumbling to the ground, followed an instant later by its now lifeless body.

There was silence in the clearing after that, except for the pig who apparently couldn't be quieted even to save his skin. Susanna ran toward him and was soon at his side. "Gerhard!" she panted. "Are you alright?"

He was both panting and shaking with emotion as he looked Susanna over. There wasn't a spot of dirt on the white wool dress he had gifted her just the day before, back when she still wasn't speaking with him. She looked fine, although pale with a pink nose from the cold chill in the air.

He had never been so thankful that he had moved fast. Four wolves could have torn her apart. He pulled her body to him, wrapping his arms around her and cradling the back of her head as he kissed her forehead.

All of his dreams had nearly died on the ground. He would have done anything for her, and she could have died while she was still angry with him. Now, he was livid that she had been in that clearing in the first place. He hugged her tighter, trying not to shake from his surging adrenaline. He felt her arms wrap around him as well, and he slowly allowed himself to calm.

"You are the most foolish woman I ever met," he told her, feeling breathless. "You cannot go this far from me by yourself."

"I am sorry," she replied, her voice also quiet.

He pulled back from her and shook her hard. "Don't you know you might have been killed? You had nothing to protect you. You were alone! I told you to stay in my sight!"

She swallowed and shook her head, still looking dazed. "I know, I know, I am sorry!"

Without another word he grabbed her forearm and pulled her firmly in the direction of their camp. His mind was reeling with images of what might have happened to her. How had he ever thought himself paranoid! He knew what could happen—he'd seen victims of wolf attacks many times before. They were all too common, especially in the winter months when their prey was scarce. And Susanna had gone marching away into danger just to pout!

"Gerhard, speak to me," she begged, and by her tone she had to have known that she'd upset him greatly.

"I'm tired of letting you play the role of spoiled princess with me, Susanna. As I told you, you are no longer a princess. You are mine. You will be my wife, and I will not see you risk your safety. Do you understand me?"

"Y-yes," she said uncertainly, sounding apologetic. "I said I was sorry, Gerhard, I—"

"You will be sorry," he gritted. "You're going to be one sorry girl when I'm done with you. I'm going to give you a whipping you'll not forget anytime soon!"

She tried to stop and then dug in her heels when she stumbled slightly, finding that he wasn't planning on stopping until they were safely back at camp. "Gerhard, stop!" she whined. "Stop, please. Be reasonable—I was upset, I needed air!"

"And now you need a good spanking," he retorted, yanking her back into step with him. Bacon had no objections—he was leading the way, apparently as eager to gain distance from the wolf attack as he was, oinking as only a living pig could.

She was trying to fight him now, slapping at his arm. "Please, I was grateful! Can't you just let me be grateful?" she demanded.

"I am very glad you're pleased with me, sweeting," he gritted, "but I have to show you that, although I'll be a patient husband with you, there is certainly still a line that I expect you not to cross. Anything that risks your safety is over that line."

Again she began to dig in her heels until she had become entirely dead weight to him. With a roll of his eyes, he bent down and, in a fluid motion, hoisted the young woman over his right shoulder and continued to march on. He found this easier, despite the fact that she was pounding on his back with her palms and the side of her fists. She was not the strongest lass, probably since she'd had no reason to develop physical strength in her life. That would surely make disciplining her an extremely easy task for him.

He stepped into the camp and then finally put her down near the campfire. She looked like she meant to bolt, but he held her arm firmly and snapped, "Susanna, desist!"

She calmed slightly, looking up at him with round eyes, filled with fear and anticipation. "Look at me," he said, pointing at his eyes. He didn't want the woman that he was falling so quickly in love with to look at him with fear. However, he did need her to heed him and to trust him. "I know I've done things to you that you are having trouble forgiving me for, but I want you to look at me now and tell me that you still don't trust that I think the world of you."

She looked around, back and forth, but then she straightened. She took a deep breath and then put a hand across his chest. "I do know that. I do trust you. I just… wanted you to feel some of the rejection that I felt."

He picked up her hands and brought her fingers to his lips and kissed them. "I will never forsake you, Susanna. That is my vow to you. I've loved you like the sun since I met you. Do you think I would harm my sun, Susanna?"

She blinked at him, seeming to soften, but didn't answer.

"Trust me to guide you without causing you harm. I will have you cry, and learn, and then we will be done."

She suddenly chewed her lip, which he had only seen her do once, and that was when they had been making love. It made her seem so uncertain. "Please, why can't we forget it?"

"Because I will fear that you have not learned this unless I teach you," he replied, then curled his fingers around her palm.

Ever so slowly, after what seemed like an age of silence, she nodded. Her cheeks were already glowing.

"Please remove your dress, my love, and prepare for your punishment. If you take your punishment well, it will go swiftly, and then we can move on together," he told her as gently as he could, although her eyes averted with shame.

He let her hand go and turned toward the covered wagon which kept the treasures he had collected during the last few years of service, leaving her to undress by herself. He looked through his trunk, looking for the leather strop he used to sharpen his shaving blade. He had no doubt that she would probably disobey him again in the future and perhaps require even sterner chastisement, but for now he wanted to make sure he had an implement that he remembered from boyhood as having a sting to it without the bruising of wood or firmer leather.

He tried it on his thigh a few times and, satisfied by the feeling and even the sound itself, he jumped back down from the wagon.

Susanna was holding her skirts in front of her naked body, looking at him with wide-eyed innocence as she shivered in the cold air. He wasn't sure if she clung to her skirts for warmth or because she was embarrassed.

Lord above, he still thought she looked like a goddess. He walked up to her and held his hand out before carefully grabbing the bundle of cloth in his hands. He put it on a nearby stump, not paying attention to the clothes that were taken off but rather what those clothes had covered.

She was pressing her thighs together now, nervous, unsure, and probably chilled by the cold air, and had her arms wrapped around her bare breasts, keeping them from his gaze. He made sure that he wore a serious expression and that he didn't look as lecherous as he wanted to.

He grabbed her hand and then led her over to the wagon where he sat down on the edge and pulled her body between his parted legs. He reached up, and after he looped a lock of her hair around his finger, he grabbed a fistful of her hair and pulled her head toward his so that he could kiss her mouth.

She kissed him back, and her kiss felt forgiving. He hoped his did as well. After this, a new chapter of their lives would begin.

He ended the kiss and then guided her body over his knees. He smoothed his hand across her thighs and bottom, drinking in his fill of the beautiful sight. He had been in the company of many females before Susanna, but at the moment he couldn't remember what any of them looked like. He was more certain than he'd ever been about anything that she had the finest ass in Christendom.

"What is my beautiful sweeting going to do from now on when I tell her to do something?" he asked her, squeezing one of her still-pale globes.

After a moment of silence during which she hummed and searched for an answer, he prompted, "Are you going to obey me?"

"Yes," she murmured submissively.

"Do you know why?" he asked her.

She shook her head.

"Because I would never order you to do something without it being important to your safety, my love. Never. You are my best treasure; I wouldn't break you. I like you stubborn and wild as you are." He found himself grinning for a moment, but then he remembered that the reason they were in this position was because she had been almost eaten by wolves. Recalling that was beyond sobering.

"But when I tell you to do something," he began to lecture, bringing the leather up above her bottom and then bringing it down with a loud, deafening crack. Her whole body flinched. "Then you—" he struck again, "will," and again and again, "obey me!"

She kicked her legs out, but she hadn't wailed. It sounded from her grunting like she was trying to grit her teeth to keep from crying. Unfortunately, her crying was the entire point. He began to slap the leather down across her tender flanks in earnest, not leaving an inch of flesh untouched from the middle of her milky thighs to the top of the cleft of her ass. She began to try to fight him and the pain, but he easily subdued her, clamping her knees behind one of his own and then hoisting her bottom up even higher.

He didn't have much space to swing the strap in this position, but he wanted to be able to aim without worry of hurting the exposed, puffy lips of her sex, and he wanted the intimacy of having her close to his body through this. In any case, her backside was quickly turning a delicious shade of red.

Finally, she yelped in pain and once she did, she began to cry out loudly and often, trying to kick even more violently than before. As she tried desperately to squirm off of his lap, she sobbed dryly, "Please stop. I'm sorry, I am! Please. Please!" Her shout of 'please' became a refrain.

"I want you to stay safe!" he gritted out, slapping the strop down hard on her bare cheeks over and over, hard and fast.

It wasn't a minute later that he heard her dry sobs turn to full tears. Her struggling began to change from desperate and clawing to more submissive. She was still squirming, and was certainly miserable, but she was also much more subdued that she had been before. He let his hand rest across her naked bottom, which was hot to the touch, and then gave her a few more smacks. "Are you going to behave for me?"

"Yes," she cried miserably.

"Why?" he demanded.

"B-because," she sobbed, "b-because I love you."

He stopped spanking then and immediately pulled her up to him. Although she was still crying, he put his hands on the bottom of her face, tilting her gaze up until her blue eyes met his. "You love me?" he asked, breathily. He had wanted to hear that, had dreamed of saying it to her. They hadn't known each other long, though, and he'd thought that the fervor of his affections for her had to have been one-sided. His heart felt light suddenly and he was filled with relief.

She nodded and blinked, letting a stream of tears release. Whimpering and looking almost ashamed, she explained, "Nobody had ever looked at me the way you did that first night... I thought... my heart broke when I thought you hated me." Her bottom lip quivered, and he pulled her up into his arms until she was straddling him.

"It was the hardest thing I've ever done," he told her, then kissed her wet cheeks one by one before he kissed her mouth.

Her mouth was hot heaven to him. He pulled her up and carried her clumsily over to the pallet he had stretched in the middle of the boxes of cloth and jewels and laid her out like a sacrifice. He kissed her mouth, then chin, then neck, slowly lapping at her warm skin until his lips met with her puffy pink nipple, which he sucked into his mouth.

She gasped and curled upwards, stretching her arms out and threading her fingers through his hair. He teased her nipples with his teeth, groaning as her body writhed under him, feeling strengthened by her pleasure alone. "I need you inside me," she whined, spreading her legs apart for him wantonly and moving her hand down to part his trews.

"I could never deny you anything," he told her, reaching down to help her free his member from its linen confines and then pressing it firmly up against her entrance. "Do you want this deep inside of you?" he murmured hotly.

She nodded and bucked her hips up toward him. He pressed himself slowly into her. "Susanna, you're so wet for me," he hissed with pleasure.

He thrust deep inside of her, hard. She screamed, and he froze, but then she lifted her body and pressed her lips upon his and he realized that she was screaming with pleasure. With a curl of his lips, he pressed her shoulders against the pallet and began to buck his hips in earnest, fucking her body with long, hard thrusts, filling her deeply with his own flesh. "I love you, Susanna," he panted, and he meant it. Nothing could feel more like heaven than this moment. It felt so good he nearly wanted to scream himself!

"My goddess," he said, combing his fingers through her hair as he pounded into her with desperation. She was groaning, loudly.

He wanted to be there forever, but the pressure inside of his cock was building to levels he could barely contain. He was gritting his teeth, trying to hold on to this moment, but as her muscles began to flex with her climax, he emptied himself into her with a roar.

She cried out with him, her sheath gripping him over and over until he felt like he had no more essence left. She had emptied all the energy from him.

Panting, he laid down beside her and pulled her close to him so that he could stroke her hair and look into those captivating eyes of hers. For the longest time they didn't say anything at all and instead just lay together.

"Princess, I want you to marry me. Say you'd choose to, even if I wasn't forcing you?" he asked her, although he couldn't help but grin at her, since the sultry curve of her lips was contagious.

She kissed him. "I'm only Susanna, remember?" she chided against his lips. "I suppose you'll do," she teased. "But only because you're so good in bed."

The pig squealed outside and Gerhard lifted his head, glared in the direction of the back of the wagon, and then dropped his head wearily. "You know he probably just ate our breakfast," he grumbled. He added as she giggled, "I should make him into breakfast..." He nibbled her lip.

"Do we plan on leaving this bed this morning anyway?" she asked him, fluttering her long eyelashes at him seductively.

He grinned. "Absolutely not."

EPILOGUE

Amity "I knew it," Rennio groaned as he sat on a bench outside an inn on the path to Tyrol, holding a half-drunk mug of ale in his beefy hand. It was supposed to be their rendezvous point, and was toward the end of their journey after nearly three weeks on the road. "You kept the damn pig."

"How was the emperor?" replied Gerhard as he carefully placed the piglet on the ground. It ran right up to Rennio and rooted around his boot.

"In an extremely good mood," Rennio replied, looking down at the piglet as if he didn't appreciate its cuteness and then looking up at Gerhard judgmentally before taking a swig of ale.

"...and?" Gerhard couldn't believe that was all, but Rennio did like building up suspense.

"Lord Eberhard was caught. I don't know if you realized that, since you were busy sinfully fornicating off in some distant keep somewhere," Rennio replied, flicking a crumb off his table.

Susanna, standing next to Gerhard, squeaked with surprise. She quickly settled, her lips pulling down at the sides into a frown. "I can't imagine that boding well," she grumbled.

Gerhard, who was also shocked by the news, asked, "Why not? We didn't want him to get away."

"He's a liar and a cheat who can spin a good tale, though. Nobody's better at saving his own skin," she replied, shaking her head back and forth.

"Yes, and he did. I found him along the way to Vienna. He told a very interesting story. Something about the princess being to blame and that he was forced to send the knights pillaging neighboring lands, and so forth. I was quite entertained. By the time we made it to Vienna, however, he told a different tale. He admitted to everything—keeping power over Susanna's army, threatening her with death if she challenged him, ruling the kingdom as a tyrant... Gerhard, my friend, you would have been astounded by how truthful he was. It was a godly sight."

It was hard to be certain who was more surprised by this, Gerhard or

Susanna. They both just stood there for a moment in open-mouthed astonishment.

"How is that possible?" Susanna demanded. "Why would he ever tell the truth? He'd be killed for it!"

"I can be very persuasive, my lady," Rennio replied innocently, and then sent Gerhard a look full of meaning.

He knew Rennio quite well, and though he had a lack of manners and any sort of patience, virtue, or sobriety, he did have a passion for justice. Enough of a passion that he would take it at the edge of a blade, or worse. He didn't want to say anything in front of Susanna, for the idea of torture, even of one of her enemies, would probably make her go pale.

Susanna plopped down in the seat across from Rennio, looking stunned by this news. "He told the truth..." she said under her breath. She was apparently having trouble believing this.

"Yes, and I'm given to believe that you would've been allowed to live as well, which might please you, had you not lost your life during that terrible tragedy in the river. It pains me to think of it, but at least memories of you live on in our hearts..."

Gerhard laughed out loud at this, though Susanna looked somewhat less amused. "In our hearts indeed," he said with a grin.

"So tell me, friend," Rennio began, eyeing Gerhard with amusement, "does your love for this woman extend beyond the grave? Will you still see fit to marry her despite her untimely demise?"

Gerhard walked over and sat next to Susanna so that he could pull her up into his lap. "Yes, I mean to marry this goddess," he answered Rennio even while looking into Susanna's eyes and putting his hand on her cheek.

The piglet squealed with annoyance as Rennio batted him away lightly with his boot, and Susanna looked over at Rennio and took a deep breath. "And I thought all this time that you were horrible," she told Rennio. A crease appeared between Rennio's brows as if he wasn't sure whether he was insulted. "I am very pleased to be wrong."

"See, what did I tell you, love? He's only horrible half the time." Gerhard looked across the table and asked, "Are you going to stay not-horrible enough to marry us?"

Rennio rolled his eyes. "Weddings are a little below my pay-grade," he said loftily. "Wait until you get home to that nice little estate you've had waiting for you in Bavaria all these years, then have a big to-do with your local priest and your neighbors and such." He took another swig of his ale and added casually, "And let me know how it goes."

"I'm afraid it's important that we marry before I bring her home as my bride..."

Rennio rolled his eyes. "Why?" Then he suddenly answered his own question and his eyebrows rose nearly to his hairline. "Don't say you've bred her already?"

On any other day, it might have been Gerhard's turn to roll his eyes. But he'd been feeling quite pleased indeed since Susanna admitted to him that she'd missed her monthly flow and had even been feeling ill the last couple of days. Nothing sounded better to him right now than the idea of settling down and starting a family with her on his quiet little estate.

Susanna blushed. "Don't call it breeding like I'm some filly!" she demanded of Rennio.

"Well, excuse me," Rennio replied sarcastically. He nodded toward her but eyed Gerhard. "And if anyone should ask, how did you come by this new wife of yours? She does look suspiciously like a particular princess who recently met an unfortunate end."

"I doubt that many of my humble neighbors will have had cause to be in the presence of a princess, so I suspect that the resemblance will go unnoticed. If anyone should remark on it, however, I'm sure that my bride would consider it a great compliment to be thought similar in appearance to one so beautiful as the late Princess Susanna of Hohenzollern."

Gerhard paused long enough to kiss Susanna deeply, finally breaking off only when Rennio cleared his throat as loudly and obnoxiously as possible.

"As for how I came by her," he continued, "she's just a pretty girl I carried off from a castle I conquered, of course. She fought me at first, but I think she's finally starting to like me. She might even learn to love me one day," he finished with a smile, before kissing her again, even more passionately.

Rennio and the piglet both grunted in disgust.

THE END

The Knight's Seduction

Renee Rose

CHAPTER ONE

Daisy gripped her sword, staggering under the weight of the chainmail. Her intent had been to join the fight to hold Hohenzollern but now Princess Susanna had run a white flag up after Lord Eberhard abandoned them. The sounds of splintering wood and the screams of the dying had stopped, for the moment.

Daisy struggled under the heavy war gear she'd just taken from the armory and donned over squire's clothing as she climbed to the top of the turret to watch her lady negotiate with the sacking army. Below, in the bailey, Lady Natalia herded children, including the lady's small stepdaughter, into the chapel.

Panic coiled in her belly, slithered up her spine and strangled her. *Not again.*

She knew too well the fate that befell women when a castle is sacked by mercenaries. She'd lost her two sisters and her own innocence because of what had happened the last time. It was the reason she'd disavowed men forever. She wished the fighting had not stopped. She'd rather go out there and die as a soldier than give those monsters one moment of lewd pleasure with her body.

The portcullis opened wide and soldiers streamed into the bailey and then through the castle doors, whooping and calling with the excitement of plunder. She set down the heavy sword and fit an arrow to her bow, but she couldn't make her fingers release it. It was one thing to be willing to die to save Hohenzollern. It was quite another to take someone's life in her name. And shooting a man was far different from hunting a buck in the woods.

Kill or be killed, she schooled herself. *Do it.* She sighted down the length of the arrow at the melee below.

A large burly knight caught sight of her from down below and boomed, "Stand down, squire! Your lady has surrendered."

She bristled. Her lady may have surrendered, but she had not. She aimed the arrow at the knight. His armor would protect him. She let it fly, just for the satisfaction of defying him and his orders. It struck his chest plate, glancing off.

He did not roar or shake his fist. He levelled a stare at her that made her shift on her feet, somehow calmly conveying she had made a grave mistake. Fear tightened in her gut, but she held firm. He continued looking at her as he headed inside, presumably to come after her. Let him. Maybe she'd get lucky and he'd kill her before he realized she was female.

In just a few short minutes, the door behind her opened and the enormous knight stalked through. His helmet dangled from one hand and he made walking in heavy armor look easy. "I told you to stand down," he said. "The princess has surrendered. Hohenzollern is ours."

Daisy didn't speak, because she didn't want to give away the fact that she was female. Her helmet and chainmail should disguise her well enough. She gripped her sword with both hands and charged at the knight.

He didn't even draw a weapon, he simply struck her across the chest plate with his forearm, causing her to fly backward and land on her rear end. "Come now, lad," the knight said, his voice kind, "the fight is over. I admire your bravery, but it's time to lay down your arms."

Curse him for being so decent. Why couldn't he just fight her? She'd rather he ended things quickly. She struggled to her feet, readjusting the helmet on her head. Her sword had flown from her hands, and she stooped to pick it up, hefting it in the knight's direction.

"Enough, boy," he said, not looking even slightly concerned by her attack. He knocked the sword from her hands with a quick chop to her wrists and cuffed the side of her helmet. The metal clanked against her skull, sending her staggering to the side. Retrieving the dagger from her boot, she charged, aiming the blade at his armor, not really wanting to hurt him.

"I don't want to hurt you," he lectured as he jumped out of her path and gave her backside a kick that sent her sprawling in one direction, the dagger flying off in the other.

To her horror, her helmet rolled off. She looked up to see surprise bloom on the knight's face, followed by amusement.

"No," she said quickly, trying to scramble back.

"What do we have here?" he asked, reaching down to offer her a hand.

Instead of taking his hand, she aimed her foot for his privates and let it fly.

The knight moved shockingly fast for a man his size. Before her foot reached its target, he snatched her ankle and yanked up, effectively dangling her upside down by one foot.

"Stop," she yelled. "Let go of me. Let me down!"

He chuckled, a low rumbling that made her armor reverberate. "Not until you stop fighting, lady. The battle ended. Now, lay down your weapon. No one is going to hurt you."

She didn't believe that for a second. She reached for the floor with her fingertips, kicking her free leg.

"What's your name?" he asked.

"Let me go."

"I asked you a question, little one."

She continued to kick and thrash, but when it became evident she could not escape his grasp, she grumbled, "Lady Daisy, sir."

"Lady Daisy, will you promise to behave if I put you down?"

"No." She gave a few more kicks for good measure. He couldn't hold her up there forever; his arm would surely tire soon.

Instead of angering him, her refusal made him laugh.

He caught her other ankle and stalked to the edge of the turret, holding her out, beyond the edge. "Would you care to revise your answer?"

She looked down at the ground far below, her stomach hurtling into her mouth. Her mind may have wanted death, but her body went completely still.

"That's better," he said. He brought her safely back and eased her down, then lifted her to her feet. He stood and gazed at her with amused benevolence, his eyes glittering as if finding a woman in a squire's costume was the best surprise of his day. He had a ruggedly handsome face. If she cared for men at all, she would have found him appealing, both in appearance and personality. But she did not care for men. Not at all.

She took a step backward.

"Fear not, lady. I mean you no harm." His brows drew together. "Did I hurt you?"

She rubbed her forehead where the steel helmet had knocked when she fell. "No, mostly my pride."

He continued to frown and stepped closer, reaching for her head.

She jerked back, but not before he caught her, cupping her skull. He tipped and turned it, examining the lump. She flinched at his touch, his huge hands covering most of her head. He stood close, the masculine smell of leather and sweat reaching her nose, his chest plate bumping against hers. Her knees buckled and she wobbled on her feet.

· · · · · · ·

"Easy, lady," Barrett said, catching the maiden's elbow. "Are you swooning?" He couldn't believe he'd struck a lady down, not once, but three times.

"No, sir," she said breathlessly. She blinked up at him with her large blue-green eyes as if dazed. He hoped he hadn't scared her too much by hanging her over the edge. Of course, he'd had no intention of harming her, but a little fear never hurt for gaining cooperation.

"Are you sure?"

"Please, sir," she murmured, pulling out of his grasp. She looked adorable in the ill-fitting chainmail, like a child playing dress-up. She turned away, as if dismissing him from her presence, and looked down over the bailey. Letting out a gasp, she reached for the bow she'd used earlier. "Put down that harp," she shouted down, fitting an arrow and aiming.

He wondered where and how she had learned to shoot. Sauntering to the wall, he leaned on his forearms to watch the entertainment.

Edgar, one of his mercenary soldiers, carried an enormous harp out to his horse.

"You there!" she cried. "Put down my harp or I'll shoot."

Edgar stopped and looked up at them. Addressing Barrett, he said, "Are you going to let her speak to me like that?"

He shrugged, entertained by the pluck of the maiden. "I might," he said with a grin. Turning to the lady, he asked, "Do you play it, lady?" Ladies did not play harps—minstrels did. He did not know why she would have a harp.

She did not move her gaze from her target. "Aye. It's mine and I play it. I'd rather die than let some oaf who can't tell music from his own vapors carry it off."

He chuckled. "Edgar, can you play a harp?"

Edgar looked exasperated. "No."

"Then it stays with Lady Daisy. Penrod," he called down to his squire. "Take that harp from Edgar and bring it to me." As he offered the determination on the fate of the harp, he realized the future of the lady herself hung in the air.

She turned to him, grateful surprise softening her features into pure loveliness. "Thank you, sir," she exclaimed and started to run toward the door. She didn't make it far, as she tripped over her fallen sword, the armor making her clumsy so that she could not recover and toppled once more to the floor.

He bit back a laugh as he righted her and reached for the buckles under her arms. "Let's get this armor off you, shall we?" he said congenially.

She flushed, allowing him to unfasten the armor, but looking uncomfortable. He shucked the heavy plates and chainmail and stood back, drawing in a breath. She wore boy's clothing, her shapely legs outlined clearly in the leggings. Though she cut a slight figure, her well-proportioned body had soft curves in all the right places.

Penrod threw open the door from the castle, his breath short from running up the stone staircase. "The lady's harp," he said with a bow.

"Thank you, Penrod," she said with a tiny dip. Her manners showed the grace of a true lady, which he'd seen lacking when she'd been hollering over the edge of the turret. The contrast of refinement with bravado fascinated him.

Gerhard of Bavaria, the man who'd led their army to attack Hohenzollern, lifted his voice from the bailey below. "Remember, any woman you touch, you marry! Take your time and choose wisely. We will line them up against the wall for the picking."

The idea of Daisy joining the lineup made him clench his fists at his side.

Her eyes widened in horror at the pronouncement. She started toward the edge at a run, as if to jump off the tower.

He lunged forward and caught her about the waist. "Fear not, Lady Daisy, I'll not allow you in that assembly. I will claim you as my own wife," he said, deciding in that moment he would never trust her to anyone else.

Her face turned pale and she jerked free. "What?" she exclaimed, looking alarmed. "No! I cannot. I am meant for no man," she said in rush.

"Oh, yes, my lady. Every woman will leave here with a man. The princess has bargained for the safekeeping of the women and Gerhard has promised her they shall all go as wives, not slaves."

Her eyes filled with tears. "I cannot marry."

He stiffened. "Do you already have a husband?" Why did that idea irritate him? He should be happy she had a man to look after her so he didn't need to take her on.

"No. The princess and her father before her granted my freedom from marriage. I was never to wed." She tucked her arms around her torso, shivering from the cold.

"You are a nun?"

"Yes!" she exclaimed, grasping onto the idea. "I'm married to our lord."

He narrowed his eyes. "You may be skilled at archery, but lying is not your gift. I'm sorry, but you leave here today as a bride, whether to me or someone else."

"I cannot," she whispered.

The more she argued with him, the more determined he became to keep her. "My name is Sir Barrett. My birth was not legitimate, but I am the son of a prince and I serve as the commanding knight at Rothburg, where my half-brother rules. I also earn a living as a mercenary at times, so I have enough silver to keep you as you are accustomed and I will do my best to ensure your comfort and happiness."

"He is a fair and kind master," Penrod piped in.

He smiled at his squire. "Thank you, Penrod."

The lady flushed. "Sir, I did not mean to question your suitability. I am sure you would make a most chivalrous husband. I just cannot marry a man."

"Do you love another?"

"No, sir," she exclaimed, so quickly that he had no doubt of the veracity of her words.

"Well, look around. If you see another man you prefer, I will release my claim." His teeth clenched as he spoke the last words.

She cast her eyes out to the bailey, but gave her head a small shake.

"Please, I will go as your servant, but I do not wish to be a wife. I will serve in your kitchens, or wherever you have need of me."

He frowned. "No. You are a lady and you will be treated as such. You will come as my wife. Enough arguing, now. You are freezing out here. Let's gather the rest of your things before they are taken like your harp," he said, grasping her elbow and propelling her toward the door.

"Sir Barrett," Penrod said, trailing behind. "Should I look for a wife?"

"I don't know, Penrod," he said, as they stepped down the spiral staircase. "It seems to me like you have just discovered the fun of rolling a serving girl in the hay. Are you sure you're ready to care for a wife? It's a big responsibility, and one I would not allow you to do poorly."

"Why did you decide to take a wife now? You always said you wouldn't."

He felt Daisy's eyes on him, waiting for the answer. "I would not trust her keeping with any of the other men," he answered lightly. He couldn't explain the other reasons because he didn't understand them yet, himself. Daisy was special—he'd known it the moment he laid eyes on her. She was a bundle of contradictions—a refined lady who shot a bow and arrow and played the harp. His attraction went beyond her beauty or her courage. Perhaps it lay in the combination of it all—along with the underlying vulnerability that made him want to protect her to the death.

"Where is your chamber?" he asked when they arrived at the base of the stairs.

She darted a nervous glance at him and swallowed. "Over here," she said, leading him to the main floor, then up the stairs of another tower. She opened the door to what must be the maiden's room, an expanse of six pallets and trunks lining the floor. "This is mine," she said, pointing to one of the trunks.

He shook his head. "We cannot bring the entire trunk. You'll have to pick your favorite things and a dress to change into now." Because he sure as hell wasn't going to let her walk through the castle in those leggings. He'd be beating the men off her.

She opened the trunk and took out a few dresses, hair combs, and ribbons. "Is this too much?" she asked.

He left one of the dresses for her to wear and picked up the rest of the bundle, handing it to Penrod. "Take these and the harp. Wait outside the door."

Penrod obeyed and Daisy stood looking at him uncertainly. She held the dress up to her torso. "Do you have to—would you mind turning around while I change?"

He lifted his eyebrows. She'd have to get used to showing herself to him sooner or later, but he didn't have to push the point now. Folding his arms, he turned his back and began to remove his own armor. He heard a rustling, then a gust of cold air hit his back. Whirling, he saw her head disappearing as she climbed out the window.

He cursed and dashed to the window just as his lady screamed.

Daisy had lost her grip and clung to the windowsill by just the fingertips of one hand, her legs kicking wildly below her. Before he could grab her wrist, her fingers slid and she dropped. She screamed again and caught the water spout, which she clung to with both arms, her legs thrashing.

He snatched her up by the armpits and hauled her inside, his heart thundering. She'd nearly died there. The idea that she risked her life to escape him disturbed him. She had courageously defended the castle, but she seemed particularly afraid of marriage.

She shook in his arms, her breath coming in gasps.

He sat down on a chair and held her on his lap. "That was foolish," he said mildly, stroking her back to quiet her.

"Yes," she agreed in a shaky voice.

• • • • • • •

Sir Barrett's arms enveloped her, his enormous body dwarfing hers. It felt odd and not altogether unpleasant to be held as if she were a small child. She did not look at Sir Barrett but she could feel his breath against her neck.

"I ought to punish you," he murmured.

She stiffened as her imagination took flight. That's right. Despite his courtly manners, he had laid claim to her. Unless she escaped, he would become her husband and master. How would the huge knight choose to punish his wife? What things would he punish for? Would he thrash her? A mixture of fear and something else slithered in her belly. Her entire body grew prickly and warm despite the open window.

She needed to make him understand she could not be a wife. She could not offer her body up night after night for that horrific act. She looked at the door, but remembered his squire stood just outside. Sir Barrett had dropped his armor and sword by her door, but a dagger hung from his belt, just within her reach. Could she use it on him? She doubted it. She shivered and he lifted her to her feet.

"Get dressed now, lady. We must to get on the road or we'll not make it to Rothburg by nightfall."

He moved to close the shutters to the window, which still stood open.

Desperation took hold. Without a plan, she lunged forward and snatched the dagger from his belt.

He whirled, his hand flashing out and snatching the dagger. He grasped her arm and slapped the flat of the blade to her backside. "Now you most certainly earned a punishment," he said, not sounding the least bit angry or even disappointed that she had just attempted to threaten his life. In fact, he seemed almost amused.

Dropping the dagger into his scabbard, he picked her up by the waist and carried her back to the chair. She caught a look of merriment in his eyes just before he tugged her across his thighs and lifted her tunic up her back. His huge paw clapped down on her upturned backside and she jerked, closing her mouth to the squeal that rose to her throat. He applied his hand four more times then created a new panic in her by yanking down her leggings to expose her bare bottom. She struggled against his hold, but he held her fast with an arm around her waist.

He picked up spanking again, slapping one cheek then the other in rapid succession. "We're going to have a hard time together if you insist on trying to kill one or both of us," he remarked, sounding quite calm considering how hard his hand connected with her stinging cheeks.

"I wasn't going to kill you," she said, as sulky as a child. Her initial gratitude at being punished with nothing more than his hand faded as her buttocks grew sore under his continued assault.

"No? What were you going to do, my lady?"

"I know not! I just—"

He chuckled, his hand still slapping a steady rhythm. "I enjoy your pluck, little one. But you've proven yourself dangerous. I will have to bind your hands until I'm sure you won't kill me or run off."

She wiggled and bounced, trying to dodge his hefty palm.

When she kicked her legs, he said, "You earned this spanking, little one. Lie still and take it or I'll use my belt instead."

She froze, crossing her ankles together and squeezing them to keep from moving. The strange, squirming sensation in her belly returned. "Please," she cried. "Please, just let me go."

"Go where, sweet lady? I will gladly free you if you can prove to me you have a place to go where you will be safe and well cared for. Do you have such a place?"

She moaned. Of course she had no such refuge. And her poor bottom burned as if on fire now. More than that, she wanted out of the humiliating position. She imagined the picture she made with her leggings around her thighs and her bare bottom angled up for his view. And could he see... the other?

"Forgive me!" she cried.

He stopped spanking and lifted her to stand between his knees. "I do forgive you, little one. I know you're just frightened about what your future will hold," he said. "But I still cannot allow bad behavior to go unpunished."

She could not bring herself to look at him, her eyes dancing around the floor. Her face burned nearly as much as her bottom. She bit her cheek to keep her lips from trembling. It would be foolish to cry from a simple hand spanking. Still, she did not know how to act after the humiliating punishment.

Fortunately he did not demand she answer to him eye-to-eye. Instead, he bent down and pulled her leggings to her ankles, then wrestled them off over her boots.

She tugged down her chemise, which had been tucked inside her leggings, trying to cover her intimate parts.

He stood and pulled her tunic off over her head, leaving her in just the chemise. "Bring me your dress," he said. He sounded perfectly businesslike, as if stripping and dressing women was an ordinary activity for him.

Her face still burning with embarrassment, she darted to the trunk and picked up her gown. She didn't bring it to him, though. Instead, she pulled it over her head as quickly as possible, anxious to cover her body. She sensed him behind her and whirled.

He picked up her wrists, one of her ribbons dangling in his hands. "Hold them together for me," he said.

She considered resisting, but realized she wouldn't succeed, and her bottom already smarted enough from the spanking. She didn't want another one. She took deep breaths, trying not to panic as she held her hands out.

He wound the ribbon around and around.

She stood on trembling legs, her emotions brewing just beneath the surface. She hardly knew what to think or how to act after that spanking. She certainly wished it had never happened. Part of her wanted to curl up and cry, the way she had as a child, but that was foolish—it hadn't hurt that much. Still, she felt quite chastised—ashamed of her foolish and desperate actions. She also experienced a curious fluttering sensation in her stomach. Not fear so much as... something else.

Her bottom clenched just looking down at the knight's large hands. She stole a glance at his face. He had a rugged appearance with a large head and strong, square jaw. Smile lines around his eyes and mouth softened the look. He wore a bear claw on a cord around his neck and his barrel chest rippled with solid muscle under his tunic. Her skin prickled at being so close to him. Or was that his heat burning right through her dress to warm her skin?

He wrapped the entire length of ribbon before tying a knot.

At first she thought it might be easy to escape a simple ribbon, but he'd fastened her wrists so securely she could not twist or wiggle them at all. Grinning at her, he bent forward at the waist and caught her hips with his shoulder, heaving her up like a sack of potatoes.

"My lord," she exclaimed. "Please... this is entirely undignified."

"Sorry, lady," he said, striding toward the door. "You gave up your right to be dignified when you tried to climb out that window." He opened the door and stepped out in the corridor. "And you gave up your right to the free use of your hands when you reached for my dagger. For now, you must resign yourself to being at my mercy. And if I were you, I would remember there are consequences to your actions."

His squire fell in behind them, looking amused, but Sir Barrett growled, "Not a word, Penrod."

"Of course not, sir," the young man said, his expression turning blank as he hurried to keep pace.

CHAPTER TWO

For a man who had not come looking for a woman or wife, Barrett's sense of victory at claiming Daisy soared as he carried her out. He loved everything about her, from her misguided courage to the way she'd turned docile when he chastised her. And oh, that spanking...

His mind had been seared by the sight of her bare buttocks bouncing under his hand and the humility with which she'd stood before him afterward, unable to meet his eye. She would be easy to correct, as a wife. Her defiance had been sparked by fear, not pride. Once he earned her trust, she'd be tame as a kitten. Not that he minded her misbehavior or additional opportunities to correct her.

The castle priest stood by the portcullis, performing brief marriage ceremonies for each couple departing. He dropped Daisy to her feet and stood behind her, wrapping his arms around her and covering her bound wrists as they faced the priest, simply out of respect for the church.

The priest looked grim, as if he did not approve of the task given him, but knew no better option. He cleared his throat. "What is your name, sir?"

"Sir Barrett."

"Sir Barrett, wilt thou have Lady Daisy to be thy wedded wife, to live together after God's ordinance in the holy estate of matrimony? Wilt thou love her, comfort her, honor, and keep her, in sickness and in health; and forsaking all others, keep thee only unto her, so long as ye both shall live?"

He rubbed Daisy's arms to comfort her trembling. "I will," he answered solemnly. He worried what would happen when Daisy refused her half of the vows, but the priest wisely skipped the lady's part altogether.

"Those whom God hath joined together let no man put asunder. Bless our brother and sister, oh lord. We pray for your guidance that Sir Barrett may honor his vows until death parteth him from his wife." With this pronouncement, the priest fixed him with a beady stare.

He quirked a smile. "My vow is true."

The priest placed a hand on Daisy's head, his brows knit with concern.

"May God watch over you and protect you as you begin your new life."

"Thank you, Father David," she said, her voice sounding choked.

"I will watch over and protect my wife," he said, more gruffly than he intended.

A line of couples had gathered behind them. Lord Gallien of Minrova held a reluctant lady's arm and appeared to be reasoning with her. Daisy cast an anxious look over her shoulder.

"She will fare well," he assured her. "Lord Gallien is a well-bred and chivalrous knight." He lifted her into his arms, cradled baby-style this time, and carried her to where his small troop had gathered.

With a little maneuvering, he managed to arrange her in the saddle before he mounted behind her. Penrod untied his rope and handed him the reins. "I will pack her things in my saddlebag and take the rear, my lord."

"Thank you, Penrod," he said, urging his horse forward to lead, one arm wrapped around Lady Daisy's narrow waist.

She sat ramrod straight, as if to avoid touching him as much as possible. Even so, her warm thighs nested against his. Her soft bottom, spread by the saddle, pushed back against his cock, nearly making him groan as it thickened in response. Her hair smelled fresh, reddish lights glinting in the weave of her blond braid. She wore no hair covering, which seemed strange, but he preferred her this way, her beauty shining without obstruction.

She twisted in the saddle to look back at Hohenzollern, pain showing in her expression. He wondered how many loved ones she had lost that day.

"What will happen to Princess Susanna?"

"She will be taken to the holy Roman emperor for trial."

Daisy gasped. "But she's done nothing. It was all Eberhard, her uncle."

Barrett agreed, but he doubted the princess would receive much sympathy. "We will pray for her safety," he said.

Daisy swallowed. "For everyone leaving Hohenzollern," she said, her words sounding strangled.

"I am sorry, my lady," he said softly. He didn't regret taking her as his wife, but he pitied her loss.

Her focus jerked to his face, surprise registering. Her eyes brightened with tears, but none fell. She nodded. "I believe you," she whispered.

His heart skipped to hear she might not blame him entirely. He leaned forward and kissed her temple. "I will take good care of you," he said. "I promise."

She turned to face forward without answering.

His eyes traced the elegant curve of her neck and it took all his self-control not to lean forward and nibble on the little shell of her ear. He would have plenty of time to woo her later. Now she deserved a little restraint. He picked up the hood of her cloak and covered her head to remove temptation and protect her against the wind.

Penrod caught up and he picked up the pace, riding swiftly to reach Rothburg by nightfall. They arrived just in time for supper.

As they waited for the gates to open, Daisy stared up at the castle.

"It's not nearly so big as Hohenzollern," he said, fearing she found it lacking.

"But far better tended," she said, her gaze sweeping over the outer wall and gate.

He remembered that Hohenzollern had shown some wear, as if repairs had not been kept up in the last few years. "Yes, my brother always has the men working on upkeep," he said. His mount surged forward when the gates opened, eager for his stall and fresh hay. When they arrived, he dismounted and handed the reins to a stable boy, then lifted his new wife down. He loved the feel of her slender waist under his hands. He could hardly wait to strip off her clothing and... he shook his head. Patience. Supper first. Then seduction.

He washed up with the basin of water outside the castle door and dropped his armor and weapons in the arms room. Turning Daisy to face him, he removed her cloak and sent Penrod up to his chamber with her things.

She held out her wrists for him to untie her but he shook his head, smirking. "Sorry, lady, you have not yet earned my trust. For now, you'll have to rely on me to be your hands."

She flushed, frowning.

He led her to the dining hall where the men shouted their greetings. "Aha, there, Bear! You captured a lady!"

"Is she a lady or slave? Look, he has her bound!"

"I see you conquered Hohenzollern. You should have brought Princess Susanna back here hogtied!"

He ignored them and led Daisy to the high table, where his half-brother, Prince Erik, sat.

Erik stood and clasped his forearm. "Welcome back, brother. How fared the battle at Hohenzollern?"

He bowed. "Well. The princess surrendered today on the condition all women would be taken as wives, not slaves." He could not keep the foolish grin off his face.

Erik raised his eyebrows, looking amused. "I never expected you to return with a wife," he said.

"May I present Lady Daisy. I found her bravely defending the castle with her bow and arrow."

Erik chuckled, his gaze traveling to her bound hands. "I take it she comes unwilling?"

"Aye, but she'll get used to me in time," he said and the men at the table laughed.

"If you can't control her, why don't you just give her a taste of the strap?"

one of the knights called out.

"Oh, she'll feel my belt when she displeases me," he said mildly.

Daisy delighted him with a shiver beneath his grasp and he patted her little arse to remind her of his mastery. Oh, how he hoped she would test him again. He would love to have her bent over his knee again. Perhaps the next time he'd insist she be naked for her punishment.

He sat down on the bench near the prince, pulling Daisy to perch on his lap.

She struggled, trying to slide off his knees and onto the bench beside him.

He tugged her back against him. "Where do you think you're going, little one?"

"Please, Sir Barrett," she murmured in an undertone, as if trying to avoid a scene.

"I'm sorry, love. Your hands are tied. You will need me to feed you and that makes my lap the best place for you to sit."

● ● ● ● ● ● ●

A flush of heat burned from Daisy's sex all the way up to her face. Sir Barrett's body connected with too many parts of her own for comfort. His torso melded to her back, his muscular thighs supported her bottom, and both arms surrounded her.

"Please, my lord. This is unseemly."

His hand connected with the part of her bottom available to him in a light, but symbolic spank. Her bottom crawled at the memory of his earlier paddling.

"My lady, you are mine now, given to my care. Do not argue with me." He pulled a piece of bread from the loaf on the table and held it to her lips.

She meant to refuse. After all, she should not eat like a trained dog from his fingers, especially with everyone looking on, as if she was their entertainment for the evening. But her mouth heeded her stomach's desire rather than her head's, opening and accepting the fresh bread.

Barrett brushed a crumb from the corner of her mouth and she ducked her head in embarrassment. She had never felt so self-conscious about eating in her life.

"What?" he asked, his thumb returning to stroke her lower lip.

Her breath shortened. She tried not to look at him, but her eyes disobeyed, sliding to the right and meeting his liquid brown gaze. She did not breathe at all.

"You're lovely," he murmured.

It seemed they were the only two in the room. With all her effort, she managed to look away, pulling her face from his grasp and staring down at the table.

"Sweet Daisy," he murmured, his voice seductive. "Try this."

God help her, she had to look.

He had piled a piece of cheese upon the bread and dipped it in his wine. It was the same food she ate every supper, and yet she had never seen anything so tempting in her life.

She made the mistake of looking his way again, her gaze landing on his mouth. Such sensuous lips. Would he kiss her with them? Her own lip still tingled from his touch. Her mouth watered, though she wasn't sure if it was for the morsel of food he held or something else. She leaned forward, opening for the bite.

"Good girl," he praised, popping the food into her mouth.

It tasted delicious, the mixture of the three flavors exploding in her mouth. She chewed, watching him watching her. Strange tingles shot through her body.

One corner of his mouth turned up. "You're hungry." It was a statement, rather than a question. It embarrassed her, as if being hungry said something about her character. Mayhap he sensed her appetite went beyond the food. He fed her another bite, brushing crumbs from her lips once she'd taken it on her tongue.

She shifted on his lap, in a curious state of unrest. How did this man have such an effect on her? She hated men. She certainly had never thought about kissing one before.

"Lady Daisy, are you a relative of Princess Susanna?" Prince Erik asked.

Her stomach tightened and she swore Barrett scowled before his expression turned blank. She swallowed her food and turned her attention to the prince. "No, my lord. I was born in Balenhof. Prince Frederick took me in as a lady-in-waiting to his daughter when my castle was sacked eight years ago."

She shifted again. Sir Barrett had begun stroking her, his large warm palm sliding down the side of her ribs and over her flank, then reversing. Before she could stop herself, she'd made a low humming sound, like a cat purring.

Sir Barrett's mouth turned up again and she stopped the hum, sitting up straighter. What was wrong with her? Did she actually *like* being manhandled by this burly knight?

Some traitorous part of her screamed *yes*.

She shoved it forcibly away. She could not encourage him. The most important thing tonight was to make him understand she could not consummate the marriage.

Sir Barrett continued to feed her until she shook her head and mumbled, "No, thank you."

"Lovely manners, Daisy," he said, the rumble of his low voice reverberating through his chest against her back. He picked up his goblet of wine and pressed it to her lips.

She drank several sips, certain he would spill it into her lap, but he read her perfectly, somehow knowing when she'd had enough to drink, and righting the goblet. He drank down the rest of the wine and lifted her to stand.

"Did you not eat?" she asked in dismay.

He grinned. "Aye, I ate along with you. Did you not notice?"

She ducked her head. She must have been too wrapped up in herself to realize.

"Come. I'll show you our chamber."

The mention of the word *chamber* brought a renewed sense of dread. She chewed the inside of her cheek, trying to think of something she might tell him to keep him from forcing her into that terrible act. She shuddered.

"Fear not, little one," he said, probably noticing her shiver. "I will be gentle."

She blinked back tears, any hope she'd had that he might not intend to consummate the marriage dashed.

He led her up the spiral stairs to the solarium, a large room with a high, domed ceiling. Instead of a pallet, he slept on a prince's bed, raised from the floor and covered with a beautiful woven blanket. A tapestry hung on the wall, in rich purples, red, and brown. It depicted a large bear standing on its hind legs.

She gazed at it, then glanced at the bear claw around Sir Barrett's neck.

"They call him 'The Great Bear,'" Penrod remarked, seeing her stare. He crouched at the hearth, building a fire.

"Sir Barrett, you mean?"

"Aye. When he leads the mercenary army, instead of Prince Erik's, they ride under the banner of a bear."

"Enough, Penrod," Sir Barrett said mildly. "And add more wood. I don't want my lady wife to be cold."

Penrod smirked and looked as if he might say something, but Sir Barrett raised an eyebrow and the young man seemed to think better of it. He added two more logs and stood, approaching his master.

Sir Barrett waved him off. "I will undress myself," he said.

Penrod bowed and left, closing the door softly behind him.

Sir Barrett unwound the ribbon binding her wrists, then loosened the tie that held her bodice. She caught the edges of it before it fell open and backed away.

He allowed her retreat, stripping off his tunic and then undershirt.

"Sir Barrett... my lord husband?"

He smiled indulgently at her. "Yes, love?"

"I-I cannot lay with you."

His brows drew together. "You can and you must, else the marriage will not be complete."

Her mind searched about for something to say. "I mean, I cannot tonight," she ad-libbed.

"Why not?"

"Uh, well, you see... I have my monthly courses. So you'll have to wait."

"I will punish you for that lie," he said without any trace of anger. He stepped toward her. "I think you must want to be spanked again. Did you enjoy it, little one?"

Again the strange slithering sensation in her belly. She backed up until she hit the wall. "No! Of course I didn't. Why do you think it's a lie?" she asked, desperately continuing the pretense, though it would be easy enough for him to disprove.

"I have already had your bottom bare once today. Have you forgotten? I suppose I did not make enough of an impression." He sauntered closer. "What is it, Daisy?" he asked, his voice gentle. "Are you afraid I'm too big? That I will hurt you?"

She seized on his suggested reason. "Yes, sir," she said, nodding vigorously. "You are far too large." She blushed furiously when she realized he may have meant his manhood, not his entire stature.

He smiled, reaching her and wrapping his warm palms around her waist. "I promise I will make it as pleasant as possible, my sweet wife. There may be a little pain, but only the first time. And I assure you it ends with a great deal of pleasure."

She shook her head, blinking back tears. "Please... I don't want to. Please don't make me."

He frowned, looking genuinely concerned. Cupping her chin, he lifted it. "You are truly terrified, aren't you?"

The tears began to spill. She dropped her eyes and nodded.

"Of me or of the marriage act?"

"Not of you," she said, her voice wavering.

"Look at me," he murmured.

With great effort, she lifted her gaze.

"Did something happen to you to make you so afraid?"

She didn't know how he had guessed such a thing. A sob choked her throat. "Please," she begged, losing all semblance of control.

In a flash he scooped her up into his arms and carried her to a chair, where he sat with her cradled in his arms.

She didn't even think to fight him—her body nested into his as if they were made to fit together. She tucked her face into his neck and wept in ugly, messy sobs. Just admitting her ruin brought back the terror of that day: watching her sisters raped and murdered, her own terrible violation, ended abruptly by another knight pulling him off her. *That one's too young, Wolfhart.*

She'd taken her chance and run, escaping with an old serving woman to Hohenzollern.

"Were you raped, Daisy?" he asked quietly.

She swallowed and nodded into his neck.

"One time, or an ongoing abuse?"

She shuddered. She'd never considered it could've been even worse. "Just once. When I was still a girl."

He rubbed her back and stroked her hair as she hiccupped, burrowing against his muscled chest. "I'm sorry," he murmured. "Do you wish to tell me about it?"

She shook her head.

"Very well. When you're ready to confide, I will be waiting. So is this what you were trying to tell me back at the Hohenzollern? That you could not marry?"

She sniffed and tried to straighten up, but he pulled her head back against his shoulder. "Yes, sir."

"Bear," he said softly. "My friends call me Bear."

• • • • • • •

She fingered the bear claw around his neck. "Is that why you wear this?"

He covered her hand with his own. "No. It's the other way around. I killed this bear when I was young, and the men have called me by it ever since. Of course, it's also short for Barrett, so it suits me, I suppose."

His talk of himself seemed to help, because she calmed down, her breath smoothing out, her head becoming heavier against his shoulder.

"You think all coupling is bad now?" he probed.

She gave a wry bark of laughter, the kind with tears behind it. "I know it's not bad—at least not for others—but I simply cannot—"

"Easy, lady," he said, rubbing her stiffened back. "I will not force you. But I also will not release you from this marriage or your obligation to me as my wife."

She sat up and twisted to look him full in the face, her expression questioning.

"Daisy, I propose we make a bargain."

She looked wary.

"I give you my word, I will not couple with you. Not until you ask—nay, beg me to." And he did intend to make her beg. Bringing a lover to the edge while denying her release would have her on her knees eventually.

She made a scoffing sound. "I'm quite certain I would die first."

"Aye," he said, "You have proven your willingness to die. But wait—I have not finished. You will offer me your body, that I may teach you the pleasure of passion, and that you may learn to pleasure me—all without engaging in the actual act of consummation."

Her brow furrowed in confusion. "I do not understand."

"There is more than one way to find pleasure with a woman or a man. I propose to leave out the one that gives you trouble, if you will allow me to teach you the others."

Her blue-green eyes widened, but the wariness had gone. She studied him, as if measuring the meaning of his words. "Will it hurt?"

He gave a decisive shake of his head. "Never," he promised. He opened his mouth, ready to launch into a long treatise on pleasure, but she nodded her head.

"Yes."

He hid his surprise. "Yes? You will agree?"

"I know not why, but I do trust you, Sir Barr—I mean, Bear."

He kissed the top of her head. "I'm honored. There is one more small thing you must promise me."

"What is it?"

"You will not pleasure yourself. You will only come to me to learn of pleasure."

She gave a short laugh. "You need not worry about that."

He lifted a brow. "You do not pleasure yourself?"

She lifted her chest. "Certainly not. Do you?"

He chuckled. "When I cannot find a suitable partner, yes."

Her smile faded and though it was probably wishful thinking, he hoped she'd been jealous to think of him with other women.

He lifted her to her feet. "One moment, sweet lady," he said as he walked to the door and opened it.

Penrod slept in the antechamber, ready to serve at the first bark of his voice. He scrambled up from his bed. "Do you need another log on the fire, sir?"

"No, Penrod. Please go to the kitchen and fetch me a dish of butterfat."

Penrod gave him a strange look, but knew better than to question the order. "Of course, sir."

He shut the door and turned to his bride, advancing slowly. She did not look nearly so afraid now, which pleased him. He didn't want her unwilling. He wanted her writhing with passion under his hands, begging him to take her. It would take some coaxing, but he didn't mind. Teaching Daisy the pleasures of love would be a privilege. And while he intended to push her boundaries, he would never violate her trust. In fact, the entire seduction must be deeply rooted in her faith in his word, or else he'd never get anywhere with her, as scarred as she was.

He plucked the thread tying her braid and broke it, unraveling her thick flaxen hair until it fell in waves across her shoulders. Her breastbone rose and fell rapidly but she stood docilely allowing his touch. He reached for her loosened bodice. "I like you in green," he purred, slipping his thumbs under the edge of the neckline and pulling it open.

She held her forearms across her breasts, holding up the gown, but her eyes conveyed only curiosity. He tugged the fabric out of her hold and slid it down her body, over the curve of her hips until it fell in a pool at her feet.

Her fingers twisted in her chemise, as if she would hang on to it for dear life if he tried to remove it.

"Take off your boots," he instructed her, moving away to give her space. Winning Lady Daisy's submission required a combination of taking away her autonomy and demanding her compliance.

A light tap on the door signaled Penrod's return. Daisy shrank back, out of the view of the door. He opened it just a crack to receive the butterfat and thanked Penrod. Sitting back down in the chair, he beckoned to Daisy. "Come here, my lady. It is time for that spanking."

She froze. "You are—are you...?" She stopped and shook her head as if to produce the proper words. "Must you?"

"I'm afraid so, love. Marriage is based on trust. You must know I will honor my word to you and I must believe the same of you. When you lie, you erode that trust."

She flushed, looking genuinely chastened. "I shall not do it again."

"Daisy," he said, lowering his voice rather than raising it. "When I bid you come to me for a spanking, you would be wise not to stall or drag your heels. Else it will go far worse for you."

She moved immediately, lurching forward, then slowing her steps as she arrived before him.

"Thank you," he said, reaching for her waist to guide her over his knees. His pulse quickened at the feel of her soft form on his legs, her hip pressing against his thickened cock, the sight of her skin through the sheer chemise. He took his time sliding the hem of the shift up to her waist. The sound of her breath came like tiny gasps. He brought his hand down on one of her cheeks with power.

She yelped, her body jerking.

He rubbed away the sting, losing himself in the delicious sensation of her well-toned arse under his hand. He slapped the other side with equal force, then rubbed. Continuing with the slow pace of slapping and rubbing, he warmed her skin. He had no interest in doling out real punishment—his intention lay in seduction. But he also couldn't allow their marriage to get off on the wrong foot by letting a lie go unpunished. He picked up the pace, omitting the rubbing between spanks.

Daisy began to wriggle and writhe over his thighs, her feet kicking up.

He continued only until the color on her bottom began to hold, then he stopped and stroked her tantalizing cheeks. He took a bit of butterfat on one finger and slid it between her legs.

She jumped, her legs and torso stiffening, her thighs clamping together.

"Easy, girl. This quim is mine now. I will keep my word, you must keep yours." He wriggled his finger between her tightened legs. He had asked for lubricant because he feared it may take him some time to coax out a response, but he found her folds slick and plump. He nearly groaned at the sweetness of it. "There," he said, his voice rough. "It's not so bad, is it?"

She whimpered.

"Spread your legs," he commanded.

She did not move.

He delivered four more slaps to her quivering bottom. "I said, open your legs for me, Daisy." He waited.

After a moment, her thighs parted, but only by a finger width.

"More. Spread them."

"Sir Barrett…" Her voice sounded plaintive.

"Yes?"

"Nothing—I don't know." Her legs opened a little further.

He smiled. He hoped he'd stoked her fire and she was experiencing the discomfort of sexual tension. He rubbed and circled the little nubbin of pleasure at the top of her opening and she began to undulate her hips. He doubted she even understood what she was doing and he certainly didn't want it to stop, so he said nothing.

Everything about her intoxicated him—the scent of her arousal, the lurid sight of her bottom rising and lowering for him. He slid one finger inside her. She froze, stopping the thrusting. He did not encounter any resistance, but he'd known she was not a maid. Her channel still seemed tight so he worked it with one finger before he added a second.

"Good girl," he murmured. "You're doing well. Just this first time I might bring you to completion." She needed to know how sweet the reward could be before he withheld it.

She craned her neck to look over her shoulder at him and he knew she had no idea what he meant.

"Your pleasure," he clarified.

He dipped the thumb of his other hand in the butterfat and slid it between her crack.

Once more, she protested, squeezing her buttocks together and straightening her legs.

He shoved his fingers in and out of her with more force and she thrashed wildly on his lap, looking as if she would swim away if they were in water. Abruptly, he pulled out his fingers and began to spank her rapidly.

She squealed.

"Your bottom belongs to me, too. Every part of you, my dear. You are mine to train." He stopped spanking her. "Spread your legs and push your bottom back for me."

He didn't expect her to comply as readily as she did. She arched her back, opening her thighs.

"Good girl," he praised. This time he started with her back hole, pulling open her cheek with one hand and rubbing a circle of butterfat around her anus.

She made a little gasping sound and started to kick, but seemed to catch herself.

He pushed at her tight hole and waited. Within a few seconds it opened to him and he pressed his thumb inside.

She made an alarmed sound in her throat.

He worked her back hole slowly, massaging all around the entrance, then sinking his thumb in deeply. With his other hand, he began to circle her clit.

She gave another cry, kicking her legs and bucking.

He shoved two fingers inside her sex, pumping them at the same time he thrust his thumb inside her.

"No," she cried, wriggling with desperation. "What? Wait—" and then she came, the muscular contractions of her sex squeezing his fingers in ripples of release.

• • • • • • •

She gasped as her body jerked and bucked of its own accord, spasms emanating from deep in her core. She'd never experienced such a thing, nor had even known it could happen. Was this what Sir Barrett meant about her *completion*? A delicious warmth and relaxation soaked through her limbs, starting in her sex and traveling out.

Sir Barrett slipped his thumb out of her arse, causing her to groan. He stroked his fingers all along her slit, which seemed far plumper than she remembered it ever having been before. Her traitorous body opened to his touch, not seeming to remember her past trauma.

Lifting her to stand, Sir Barrett looked at her with amusement.

She probably looked a mess. Heat warmed her face and her eyes did not easily focus.

"There, that wasn't so horrible, was it?"

It hadn't been horrible. It had been embarrassing and uncomfortable at times but also wonderful and... *wrong*. "Yes, it was," she said weakly.

He gave her bottom a gentle slap. "Another lie," he said. Her eyes darted to his face to see if he intended to punish her again, but he still appeared amused, though his smile had a feral quality that kept her on edge. Lifting the skirt of her chemise, he slipped it up over her hips.

She fought him when it reached her breasts, holding her elbows tight against her sides to prevent him from completely disrobing her.

He chuckled. "You will sleep without covering in my bed, love. I need unfettered access to you at all times."

Her sex contracted at this pronouncement, even as she continued to fight him on removing the underclothing. Why did he need constant access to her body? What else did he intend to do to her? Her eyes traveled down to his crotch, where they widened at the sight of his substantial cock bulging beneath his leggings.

"I will honor my promise, little one," he assured her.

Her eyes skittered around the room, as if the answer to her dilemma would appear, but nothing surfaced. Reluctantly, she relaxed her arms, allowing him to tug the chemise over her head.

"Good girl," he said, scooping her up as if she were a baby and carrying her to his bed. He pulled the covers back and settled her on the mattress.

She gasped at the sensation and looked up at him with wide eyes.

"It's goose-down. Do you like it?" he asked, crawling in beside her.

The feather mattress cocooned her in soft poufy warmth. "It's incredible, my lord. How—" She stopped and flushed, realizing she might offend him by asking how he came by such a luxury. All the finery of his room spoke of the highest breeding, and yet, he had told her he came from an illegitimate birth.

"I have made quite a bit of silver with my mercenary endeavors. I lead my brother's men when he needs me, and when he gives me leave, I have a troop I gather to go to battle for hire."

"And that was how you ended up at Hohenzollern?"

He gave a faint smile. "No, I'm afraid my brother sent me with a small troop to represent Rothburg in the attack on your home."

"Just a small troop?"

"It was symbolic. We had no doubt Hohenzollern would fall, but Erik wished to show our support for the cause."

Her chest had tightened at the thought of Hohenzollern's fall and it must have showed, because he touched her cheek. "You've lost everything twice now, haven't you?"

Abruptly, she burst into tears. She tried to hide her face, but he pulled her against him, tucking her into his chest and stroking her head. She sobbed until all her tears had gone and she collapsed against him, exhausted.

"Daisy?"

She lifted her head.

He pushed her onto her back and leaned on his elbow, brushing the wisps of hair back from her face. "Did any part of what I did with you remind you of your rape?"

She stiffened at the word 'rape,' but something about the matter-of-fact way he discussed it—the thing she had kept locked inside as her dark secret for so long—released some of the darkness around it. She considered, then shook her head. "No," she answered honestly.

"Good," he said. "Because I never want you to experience those feelings with me."

She swallowed, not sure if that was possible. After all, his game was clearly seduction, and hers was to avoid coupling at all costs.

"Sex is like a language. In its highest form, we use words to praise God. In its lowest, we hurl them to insult or harm those around us. So it is with coupling. It can be used in love, in worship, for mutual pleasure. And also for violence."

She eyed him warily. His words made sense, but she didn't want to let go of her armor and believe.

"I only want to teach you pleasure, Daisy," he said. "Can you believe that?"

She sucked her cheek between her teeth and looked away.

When her eyes returned, Barrett was inches from her face. She jerked as his mouth covered hers, pushing her hands against his chest in a moment of panic. He lightened the kiss, releasing her mouth and claiming it again, stroking and caressing her lips until she began to move her lips against his, returning the kiss. He lifted his head and smiled down at her, brushing his thumb across her cheek. "Sweet wife. I know you didn't want to be taken away or to marry an oaf like me, but I promise I will do my best to make you happy here."

She turned her face into his chest and buried it there. "You're not an oaf," she said into his ribs.

He blew out the lamp and kissed her hair. "Good night, angel."

CHAPTER THREE

Waking for the first time with his naked wife beside him made his staff so hard it tented his leggings. Just the smell of her skin would have been enough, but she looked so beautiful lying next to him. The tension in her face had disappeared and her long lashes fanned out on her cheeks, making her look as delicate as a flower. He slid his hand along her side, stroking down to her hip, then returning up to cup her breast.

She tensed.

He rubbed his thumb over her nipple until it stood up, then he pinched.

Daisy gave a surprised squeak.

He slid his hand down the flat plane of her belly until he reached the silky thatch of curls between her legs.

She pressed her thighs together, but he pried open her top knee.

"Leave them open," he commanded, desire roughening his voice.

"Please, Sir Barrett—" she began as he slid his middle finger over her delicate folds. Her natural lubrication began to flow immediately and he spread it up and down her pleats while she gasped and jerked.

He began to circle her stiffened peak at the same time he bent his head and caught her nipple between his lips.

"Ah... ah," she moaned, arching and contracting, shifting around in confusion.

"That restlessness is desire growing within you."

She shook her head. "No, it is not," she said breathlessly.

He began to penetrate her with one finger, pressing the heel of his hand firmly against her pleasure center all the while.

Daisy groaned.

"It is, little wife. You feel that sense of urgency. You think you want me to stop, but in fact, you want me to go on."

"No—" she gasped.

He sucked her nipple hard, then released it, removing his hand from between her legs. "No?"

She let out another gasp and blinked up at him.

"I will not bring you to climax until you beg me to take you, the way a man takes his wife."

She rolled away, her cheeks flushed. "I care not about climax," she said in a shaky voice. She climbed out of the bed and snatched up her chemise, tugging it over her head as if she could not cover herself quickly enough.

"I will make you care," he said. "And do not forget—I forbid you to touch your own quim. It is for me and me alone. I will most certainly punish any attempt on your part to pleasure yourself. Understand?"

She shook her head, then changed the motion to a nod.

"Answer me when I speak to you," he said. "Or are you looking for more punishment?"

"Yes, sir. I mean no, sir," she said, hurriedly stepping into her gown.

He walked over and took the laces from her trembling hands, cinching the bodice for her. He had the perfect view of her two ripe breasts, lifted and framed by the gown. He took his time tying a bow, his fingers brushing the creamy skin of the tops of her breasts.

Her lips twitched, her eyes darted about the room. He still smelled the scent of her nectar on his fingers and from her.

"Give me your hands."

"What?" she asked, looking dismayed. "Why?"

"I still cannot trust you, love, especially outside of my locked chamber. I have to bind your wrists again."

"Surely not. I have not attempted escape since you brought me here, nor have I threatened your life again."

He smiled his most wicked smile. "I'm sorry, lady. You still have not earned my trust."

She huffed, her jaw setting in a stubborn line.

He picked up her wrists and wrapped the same ribbon around them.

"Wait," she said, trying to pull her hands away. "I—"

He raised his eyebrows when she stopped speaking. "Yes?"

Her face flushed crimson. "I need to use the chamber pot."

His lips curled into a slow grin and he resumed the wrapping of ribbon. "Then you shall have to rely on me to help."

Her jaw dropped. "No."

He shrugged. "You have nothing to hide from me. You are my wife. You will bear my children. I will see and know every part of you in the most intimate of ways."

She shuddered, beginning to look genuinely distressed.

"Come," he said, tugging her bound wrists in the direction of the privy screen. Once there, he pulled up her skirts and balled them in a bunch in front of her. "Hold this," he said, placing it in her restricted grasp. Holding her by the armpits, he tilted her backward, over the chamber pot.

She squeezed her eyelids shut, looking miserable. Nothing happened. She opened her eyes and gave him an adorable pleading look. "I cannot. Not with you here. Please leave me—"

"No," he interrupted stubbornly. "This is your one chance to use the chamber pot. If I were you, I would take it, else you'll be the laughing stock of the castle if you have an accident at the breakfast table."

She cringed, then narrowed her eyes. "You are insufferable."

He chuckled. "You're not the first one to say so," he said lightly.

She began to pee, and it took effort not to smirk.

"All finished?" he asked politely.

She made a huffing sound so he left her dangling over the pot. "Yes, I have finished," she snapped.

"Yes, I have finished, sir?" he suggested.

She rolled her eyes. "Yes, I have finished, sir," she said, glaring daggers.

He smirked and lifted her upright, helping her rearrange her skirts. "Come, my lady. Let us break the fast together."

She sniffed, lifting her nose in the air and walking to the door, which, of course, she could not manage to open. He reached from behind her. "Allow me," he said with a bow.

She made a grumbling sound in her throat and he popped her backside with the flat of his hand. "That's enough, little wife."

At the table, they wrestled once again over whether she would sit upon his lap.

"Still haven't tamed her yet, Barrett?" one of the knights called out with a chuckle. Daisy shot him an angry look.

"I rather like her wild," he admitted, pulling her firmly onto his knees and holding her captive with an arm around her waist. "Be good, little girl or I will lift your skirts and spank your naughty little bottom right here in the dining hall," he warned in a low voice in her ear. "Believe me when I say it has been done before, and the men rather love the entertainment."

• • • • • • •

Daisy wanted to spit in Barrett's face. His games were not amusing. His treating her like a prisoner or a child incensed her.

"Good morning, brother," Prince Erik said, looking at them with amused curiosity.

She found it interesting that he addressed him as brother, fully claiming their relationship.

"Good morning," Barrett said with a grin. "Where do you want me today?"

"Well, it appears you have your hands full, but I'd like you to supervise the reconstruction of the south wall."

He nodded. "Of course." Returning his attention to her, he lifted the bowl of warm porridge to her lips.

She turned her face away. She would go hungry before she let him feed her again.

"Do you want that spanking here, Daisy?"

Her bottom automatically clenched at the word *spanking*, and hot tingles crawled across her cheeks as if he had already delivered a few stinging blows. Maddeningly, a drip of moisture caressed her folds, dampening her skirt below. Dearest virgin, what if it soaked through her skirts and he felt it on his thigh? She tried to shift, but he held her too close to move.

Why did he have this effect on her? She'd become all quivery, her body trembling, her breath short. She would never forgive him if he spanked her in public. His ability to stir such responses angered her further. She pressed her lips together to keep from snapping that she hated him.

He lifted the bowl again.

She had no choice but to drink from it.

"Good girl," he said.

Her sex pulsed. She watched the bowl approach, as if in slow motion. Her rational self tried to stop the impulse, but it was too late. She shocked them both by sinking her teeth into the meat of his thumb, cutting through skin and tasting blood. She released it as quickly as her jaws had snapped, and looked at him in horror, knowing she'd just gone too far.

He had jerked in surprise, slopping porridge down the front of her dress, but strangely, he made no sound—no roar of surprise, no angry tirade.

She waited, trembling like a leaf, for him to upend her in front of the entire castle and give her the promised public spanking. Had that been her goal? Impossible—it was too horrible to even contemplate. And yet, if not, why had she baited the bear, so to speak? Perhaps she'd lost her mind.

Her stomach twisted in knots and her palms sweated. Her sex seeped moisture, somehow not understanding she was in real trouble now.

"I'm sorry," she attempted, knowing his punishment would be severe.

Without a word, he lifted her off his lap and stood, propelling her to the stairs and up to his chamber.

She stood, wringing her hands as he shut the door. "Forgive me, Barrett—sir... my lord," she tried again.

She saw a glimmer of a smile on his lips and her heart picked up speed. He pointed to the bed. "Bend over and lift your skirts."

She walked, weak-kneed to the bed and folded her torso over the feather mattress. She could not figure out any way to lift her skirts with her wrists tied, but she made a show of attempting it so he would not think her disobedient.

"I'll get them," he said behind her.

She twisted to look over her shoulder and saw he carried a riding crop.

Leaping back to her feet, she whirled. "Is-is that truly necessary? I mean, could you not bend me over your lap and use your hand as you did before?"

He tapped the crop in his palm. "I would love to, but it takes quite a bit more time to make an impression that way, and my brother needs me outside today."

She shivered. *I would love to.* He probably did love spanking her. And yet he was not a cruel man. What could it mean?

He turned her and pushed her upper back down to lay on the bed, throwing her skirts up over her head. "Eight strokes for biting. You will count each one." Before she had a chance to draw a breath, he delivered the first searing stroke.

She squealed and stood on her tiptoes, squeezing her bottom cheeks together, tucking her tail like a naughty dog.

"I asked you to count them," he reminded her.

"One," she gasped.

He landed another one. "One, *sir*," he corrected.

"One, sir, two, sir," she said quickly, hoping he hadn't meant for her to repeat number one.

He chuckled. "I'll let you get away with that just this once." He brought the crop down again.

She gasped. A terrible burn from the first welt had begun to set in, even as the shock of the third ricocheted through her body. "Three, sir," she managed.

"Good girl," he murmured, though she did not know what merited the praise.

He sliced the crop through the air three times quickly, making her clamp her mouth closed on a scream. Without thinking, she started to scramble away, onto the bed.

"Daisy," he said, keeping his voice low. "Back in position."

"Four, five, and six, sir," she said as soon as she had caught her breath. Reluctantly, she pushed her legs back down to present her bottom for his chastisement. "I'm sorry," she whispered.

"We're almost finished," he said, applying the cruel leather rod on a diagonal across her buttocks.

"Seven! Seven, sir."

"One more." He caught her on the underside of her buttocks, right where cheek met thigh.

She lifted to her toes again, sucking in her breath. It was three long beats before she could speak. "Eight, sir."

"Thank you, Daisy," he said, his voice soft and gentle.

She didn't wish to remain bent over with her naked, striped arse on display, nor did any part of her want to move.

Barrett appeared behind her and she tensed. He began to rub her buttocks firmly, spreading the localized pain of her welts to the whole of her bottom. Her flesh blazed with stinging heat and though she had disliked his touch at first, it began to ease the intensity of the whipping. It also caused those strange spiraling sensations to swirl in her stomach and a pulsing to begin in her sex. She hated to admit it, but some part of her might actually like the overbearing way he handled her. Had she wanted to be spanked? Impossible.

He lifted her to stand, tossing her skirts down and brushing her hair away from her face. "Eight licks and not a tear. I knew you were brave," he said, although he sounded a bit sad, as though it had pained him to whip her. "I can lock you in my chamber for the day or you can come outside with me, but I can't allow you free rein to roam about the castle on your own."

"I'll come outside with you," she said immediately. The idea of being locked alone in his chamber all day frightened her.

He looked surprised, but pleased. Picking up her cloak, he wrapped it around her shoulders, fastening it at the throat. "You will have to behave or you'll get the crop again, and I don't imagine your poor bottom could take that," he said, reaching behind her and giving her throbbing backside a squeeze that pulled her body against his.

She meant to push him away, except her legs did not hold her and she fell against him. He wrapped strong arms around her and held her close. She should not cling to him like a child who needed reassurance, except she did, actually, crave something from him. She lifted her face, not knowing what she would say, and to her dismay, her eyes filled with tears.

One spilled and he brushed it away, peering down at her with kindness. "My intent is not to break you, Lady Daisy. Only to gain your cooperation."

More tears spilled. She had never cried so much in front of another person, at least, not that she could remember. Not even after she'd fled to Hohenzollern. And yet, he did not seem alarmed by her weeping. Rather, he seemed to accept the tears as his tribute and wiped them away with his thumbs.

"Do you need to stay here and have a cry? I can come back for you in a little while."

She shook her head, shamelessly pressing herself closer.

• • • • • • •

He pulled her against his chest and kissed the top of her head. How insensitive of him. Just because she hadn't cried during her thrashing, didn't mean she was ready to be paraded out through the castle moments later. He embraced her, rubbing her bottom to minimize bruising.

She moaned, and he became alert. Desire or pain? Mayhap a bit of both. He cradled her head and lifted her face, brushing his lips softly over hers. She responded and he kissed harder, claiming her mouth with the authority provided him as her husband. When he broke away, she looked dazed.

"Ready?" he asked softly.

Her head wobbled as she nodded.

He smiled to reassure her. Escorting her out in the bailey, he found the back wall that had been wrecked in an attack in late autumn. Repairs had to wait for one thing and another, but Erik was wise to have the men work on it now, even in the cold of winter. Facing spring raids without a proper defense could be the end of a small kingdom like theirs.

The men stood waiting for him, some lounging about, sprawled on their arses. They scrambled up when he arrived, lifting their chins and chests in the fashion of the Roman army.

"Couldn't get started without me?" he groused.

The higher ranking men looked flustered. "Prince Erik said you'd be out to direct us, sir."

He grinned to show he hadn't been serious. "And so I am," he proclaimed. He attempted to push thoughts of ravishing his lovely bride from his mind and took in the scope of the project.

"Hans and Adam, set about collecting what we need to mix a mortar. The rest of you get busy hauling rock. I want it sorted into piles of small, medium, and large. We'll need more than what's here, too. So Fritz, Andreas, and Herbil, bring the wheelbarrow outside of the wall to bring more stone in. That's it, men. Get busy."

"Did you bring your new wife to haul stones as penance for that bite she gave you this morning?" Adam asked with a lewd grin.

He cursed inwardly and snatched the man up, wrapping one fist in the fabric of his shirt and cocking the other to pound his face. "Do not. Speak disrespectfully. About my wife," he growled loud enough for everyone to hear.

"Forgive me, sir," Adam exclaimed, his face pale.

Barrett held him bent backward, his arm ready to strike for a long moment before he released him with a shove. "Anyone else have a wisecrack about my lady wife?"

A chorus of *no, sir* answered.

"Very well. Get to work."

He turned to Daisy. He had hoped few had noticed the bite in the dining hall and he had chosen not to punish her publicly because he wanted her to feel comfortable at Rothburg. Humiliating her more than he had already done would be inconsiderate, at least until she had settled in.

Daisy's eyes were round, but she surprised him by saying, "I will move stone if you untie my wrists."

He gave a short bark of laughter. "Nay, lady. I'd have a dagger in my back the moment I turned around."

She looked disappointed, as if her request had been genuine. She took a step closer to him. "I'm sorry about the bite," she said in a low voice so the others would not hear. "I do not know what came over me."

Mayhap he was a fool, but he believed her. He cupped her face and stroked her soft skin with his thumb. "You're forgiven, wife. But that doesn't mean I can trust you."

"No," she agreed, her shoulders dropping.

"Stay where I can see you, love," he said and joined the task of sorting stones, heaving the largest rocks. When he turned around, he realized Daisy had decided to help anyway, picking up the smallest stones between her bound hands and making a neat pile against the wall.

"Daisy," he called. "Come here."

She looked up in surprise and walked over.

"What are you doing?"

She stuck her chin out at a defiant angle.

God, he'd come to love the spunk in her.

"I'm helping. While it is quite impressive to watch you work, I think I should get quite bored doing nothing." Her eyes had traveled across his chest and over the muscles in her arms, and she blushed, as if she just realized what she'd admitted.

He smiled. "All right, little one. I will set you free if you wish to work. But if you give me any trouble at all, you'll be locked in our room for a fortnight. Understand?"

She shuddered. "Yes, sir."

He unwound the ribbon from her wrists, sorry when he saw how raw they'd become from twisting against the binds while laboring. "You'll stay right beside me. And if you even think of throwing a rock at me..." He raised his eyebrows and gave her his most stern look.

To his surprise, she giggled.

He grinned. He'd rather have her laughing at his authority than angry. He was determined to win her heart, even if he had to keep her chained to his side for a year to do it. So far, he'd found her enigmatic. One moment easy to manage, the next a feisty spitfire. Of course, she might be putting him on—simply pretending to soften until she had her opportunity to escape. She certainly had the intelligence for such a game.

That idea bothered him more than he'd like to admit.

Daisy set to work at a pace that wouldn't last, picking up midsized stones, far too large for her to carry. Her face grew red from exertion, little beads of sweat forming at her hairline, despite the cold. She threw off her cloak and continued.

He watched her as he worked, his cock growing hard. Was it wrong to be aroused by a lady in hard labor? Probably. But it spoke to an animalistic need of finding a mate capable of survival. Daisy would not die in childbirth like his mother, one of the castle's serving wenches, had. But more than her capacity to bear children, seeing her hard at work, without a single complaint reignited an old dream of his: leaving Rothburg and purchasing his own small property.

Without a strong woman at his side, such a dream would never come to fruition. He had enough silver to buy the property, but hadn't had the lady. Certainly he could have picked any wench from the castle and she would've worked her fingers to the bone for him. But he fancied a loftier life.

As a bastard child, born of a serving wench but acknowledged and raised by a prince, he didn't really fit anywhere. His father had promised him if he pledged his sword to his younger half-brother, the rightful heir, he would always have a place at the high table of Rothburg. And so it had been. He did not covet Erik's title or his inheritance. His brother treated him as well as he would a full-blood sibling. But no lady at Rothburg would marry him. They wanted a nobleman. A true knight, rightfully born. Not a bastard. And while he had ventured out to make his own fortune as a mercenary, he had never even thought to take a lady from another castle as his wife.

Would it bother Daisy to have a bastard for a husband? He glanced at her again. She looked exhausted, still lugging heavy stones to and fro.

"Take a break, Lady Daisy. You're looking tired."

She ignored him and kept working.

He moved behind her and wrapped his arms around her waist. "Enough," he murmured in her ear. "You'll ruin your pretty hands."

· · · · · · ·

Daisy spread her palms to examine them. They were raw and swollen. What did Sir Barrett's look like, then? He had been hauling enormous stones all morning with a bite wound. She picked his palm off her belly and opened it. He had hard callouses to protect his skin, but the wound looked swollen and bruised with angry red outlines on the dirt-filled punctures.

"Don't worry, I can still spank with this hand," he murmured in her ear, his words sounding less like a warning than a seduction.

The unnerving fluttering sensation started in her stomach again. Did Sir Barrett *enjoy* spanking her? She thought again about his words that morning when she'd pleaded he spank with his hand instead.

I would love to.

Did he mean he would love to accommodate her request? Or he really loved to spank? The muscles between her legs clenched at the memory of being upended over his lap, her bottom jiggling at the slaps from his bare hand. Those very same muscles had been affected—each stinging blow had spoken directly to her core, stimulating and vibrating. Her bottom, still throbbing from her whipping that morning, tingled as if his hand was still upon it.

"You men need a bit of refreshment?" a female voice called out from behind them. A serving wench stood behind them, one hand on her hip, the other carrying a bucket of fresh water and a dipper.

"Over here, Margrite," Barrett summoned.

The girl sauntered over, looking Sir Barrett's body up and down and licking her lips. "It's so honorable to see the master works as hard as the men," she said, her voice a sultry purr.

Daisy took an instant disliking to the girl. Why did she speak so intimately to Barrett?

He ignored it, and filled the dipper, holding it up to Daisy's lips. She started to refuse, but he ordered, "Drink." Even without her wrists bound, he served her.

She hardly knew what to think about that. She drank from the dipper, daintily at first, then deeply as she realized her thirst.

"That's it," Barrett encouraged.

When she finished, he drank from it himself and handed it back to the wench, who curtsied low enough to show her cleavage.

"They say it's the reason you make such a good commander," Margrite said, continuing her flirtation.

"Go on, Margrite, the other men are thirsty, too," he said, giving her backside a slap.

She giggled and looked at him coquettishly over her shoulder as she scampered away.

Daisy's jaw clenched. "Are you in the habit of slapping the backsides of all the women of the castle?"

To her great satisfaction, Sir Barrett froze and looked like a guilty boy. "Forgive me. I am not accustomed to answering to a wife. I suppose you do not take kindly to such a thing?"

She folded her arms across her chest. "I most certainly do not."

The moment of looking chastened passed. He stepped closer. "I was just trying to get rid of her. But you can punish me later if I gave offense," he said with a wolfish grin.

Her neck and chest grew warm as a ridiculous vision of him offering his bare, muscled bottom up for her small hand rose in her mind. Her eyes dropped below his waist, peeking at the way his strong legs filled out his leggings. When they returned to his face, she found him smirking.

"Do you not have work to do?" she snapped, flustered.

He chuckled. "Aye, my lady. I will return to work."

She watched him, admiring the huge bulging muscles under his shirt. She considered what Margrite had said. He probably did make an excellent commander. She rested a while, but had no inclination to sit, since her bottom still hurt too much, and standing around watching grew tiresome. Eventually she began to work again. Her muscles ached and her hands had been scraped raw, but she enjoyed being outdoors and exercising her body.

She had never been the sort of lady who relished sitting inside and spinning with the ladies. She had certainly done her fair share of weaving, but Prince Frederick, Princess Susanna's father, had given her a fair amount of freedom. They'd pitied her, she supposed. When she'd come to their castle, she'd scarcely eaten or spoken for weeks. It had been a traveling minstrel with a harp who finally coaxed her out of her trauma. Prince Frederick had been kind enough to buy the harp from the minstrel, who gave her lessons over the course of a month before he left, rich enough to buy himself a new instrument.

After that, she'd learned every song she could from the traveling bards and provided music and song for the king's table. It kept her apart from the others. Made her strange enough that no man should seek to wed her. That, and her longbow practice. She taught herself, at the tender age of twelve. Perhaps it had been foresight, because even then, she feared their castle would be sacked. Much more so after Eberhard, Princess Susanna's uncle took over as commander of their troops.

She practiced on a target, day after day, until the squires stopped teasing her. Later, when she grew older, she took up hunting and trapping—always alone, though many a squire offered to accompany her.

A bell rang for dinner, and Sir Barrett appeared beside her, offering his arm like a gentleman. She almost asked if he intended to tie her wrists again, but bit back the impulse in time. She did not want to suggest it if he had decided it was not necessary.

He swung one leg over the bench in the dining hall and tugged her onto his lap.

She winced, squirming at the soreness.

"Do you prefer the hard bench?" he asked in her ear, mistaking her squirming as an attempt to free herself.

"Yes, I do," she said, her stubbornness rising.

He pushed her off his lap and she grunted at the impact of her raw flesh with hard wood. Ridiculously, she found she missed his lap. Not because of her sore backside, but because she suddenly felt quite alone in a totally foreign environment. As much as she'd hated his manhandling, he'd made it easy for her to fit in at Rothburg. Her place had been simple: she belonged to Barrett. Now she sat facing the rest of the high table, seeing the curious faces for the first time.

She remembered the prince, Barrett's half-brother. Beside him sat a pretty woman who must be his wife, the princess. A dozen other men and women sat at the high table with them.

"You've untied her," one of the knights remarked.

"For the moment," Barrett said, cutting a piece of meat and placing it on her plate.

"He's really not a complete ogre," one of the ladies-in-waiting said, looking sympathetic.

"How would you know?" Sir Barrett shot back, breaking a chunk of bread off the loaf and splitting it between their plates.

The poor lady became flustered, as if Sir Barrett had suggested she had carnal knowledge of him. "I wouldn't know anything like that!" she exclaimed and everyone at the table laughed.

"Daisy, you are welcome to join us in the spinning room after the meal," the princess offered.

"Not today, thank you," Sir Barrett answered for her. "I cannot trust her to roam about unsupervised."

The princess looked puzzled. "Why not?"

"She's shown a propensity to try to either kill me, kill herself, or make an escape."

Everyone at the table stared at her, and she flushed. She wanted to deny it, but of course, it was true. Now they probably all believed her to be half-mad. She shot Sir Barrett an angry look, and as usual, he grinned. Catching her nape in his large palm, he tugged her head forward and planted a kiss on the top of it. "I didn't mean to embarrass you," he murmured so only she could hear.

God help her, she wanted only to crawl up into his lap and let him comfort her. She truly must be going mad.

CHAPTER FOUR

Barrett locked Daisy in his room after the midday meal. She looked so tired after eating, he didn't want her to go back outside and work. She protested a little, but he showed her that she would have a view of him from the window and if she wanted to come out after resting, she could call to him.

When he returned to the solarium, he noticed a great many people loitering about in the tower stairwell and on the landings. At his doorway, he discovered the reason: the most beautiful music emanated from his room.

Smiling, he unlocked the door and slipped inside. Daisy sat on the bed, the harp between her legs, her fingers dancing along the strings and the sweet honeyed notes of her voice rising to match the music.

She did not notice him at first, but when she did, she abruptly stopped playing and stood up.

"Please don't stop."

She looked peevish. "Is it time for supper?" she demanded, ignoring his request.

"Yes," he said. "Are you hungry?"

She looked away, toward one of the windows. "Please do not lock me in here again," she said stiffly.

He frowned. "Why did you not call to me, as we arranged, if you wished to come down?"

She stalked past him, toward the door.

He caught her about the waist and hauled her back against his front. "Answer me when I speak to you," he murmured in her ear.

"I felt foolish, all right? Your men already think I am fodder for their jokes—"

"That is not true," he said, then amended. "Or perhaps I should say I will not allow any jokes at your expense." He turned her in his arms, distressed to see tears glinting on her eyelashes. "Little wife," he said, cupping her chin. "I would flatten any man who insulted you."

She blinked rapidly, meeting his gaze and swallowing.

"You are my wife, subject to my rules and punishments like every wife here at the castle. If the men enjoyed our public difficulties, it is only because you are so beautiful and they are unused to seeing me attend to a woman. I'm certain they love seeing your fire as much as I do."

Her lips moved, then closed again. She swallowed. "My fire?"

He showed her the swollen bite mark on his hand. "Aye, your fire. Tell me, which is more exciting to watch—the training of a new colt, born in captivity, or of a wild stallion?"

She raised an eyebrow. "Are you saying I'm a wild stallion and you're taming me?"

"Well, mayhap a mare," he said with a grin.

She rolled her eyes. "I thought you said you weren't trying to break me?"

He chuckled. "So I did. And I meant it. I am trying to woo you, little bride." He grasped her braid and tugged her head back, nipping at her neck. "And I will not stop before your heart is won."

"My heart or my body?" she asked drily.

"Your body already belongs to me," he reminded her, traveling up her neck to take her earlobe into his mouth. "The little matter of our consummation will soon be settled. Nay, it's your heart I aim to capture and keep for my whole life long." He touched his fingers to the fluttering pulse at her throat. "I think that excites you."

She pulled away, stumbling back. "No, sir. It does not. I assure you, men do not excite me."

He gave her a wolfish smile. "I've never seen two women together, but it might interest me to watch."

She gave him an effectual shove. "I'm not interested in women, either, you boar!"

He laughed. "Mind your manners, or I'll have you over my knee before supper. In fact," he said, scooping her up by the waist and carrying her kicking and thrashing to the bed. "Let's see how your little bottom fared after that thrashing I gave you this morning."

"Stop," she squealed. "No more spanking! No, please!"

"Good," he said, wrestling her to his lap on the bed. "I'm glad you've finally learned to fear my punishments."

"Stop it, you oaf."

He delivered a slap to her wriggling arse. "Now I am an oaf? I wasn't planning on spanking you, but if you keep it up, you will soon be sorry."

"What are you doing?" she demanded, craning her neck to look over her shoulder. "Not... the other thing?"

"What other thing?" he asked, hiding his smile as he pushed her skirts up to reveal her pert, round bottom. He ran his roughened palm lightly over her skin. She bore marks from the whipping that morning but it did not look quite so tender as it had hours before.

Daisy had stiffened, her struggles ceasing as she lay over his thighs, panting, seeming to wait to see what he would do.

He took his time, lightly stroking her baby-soft skin, tracing circles around her twin globes, trailing his palm down the backs of her thighs. After a moment, he smelled the scent of her arousal. He pulled one of her thighs open and lightly brushed a finger along her slit.

She jerked and tried to close her legs, but he had anticipated her move, and held her thigh open.

"You're wet for me, Daisy," he murmured.

"I... I don't even know what that means," she said.

"I know, love. You don't know anything about passion yet. But I will teach you. Little by little I'll win your trust until you believe that what I offer you is something altogether different than what you've known."

"Please," she pleaded, sounding distressed.

He gave her bottom another pat and pulled her skirts down. "Let's go down for supper," he said, lifting her to her feet.

She hurried to the door without looking at him, but to his satisfaction, did not open the door. She stood facing the exit, waiting for him.

He smiled. Either she feared going out without him, or she was growing fond of him. Probably the former, but he'd take what he could get.

·······

Sir Barrett had a bath sent up to his room after supper. To Daisy's annoyance, the same serving wench from outside, Margrite, was one of the women who carried up buckets of warm water. She paced a small path near the window where she'd watched her... *husband* all afternoon. It seemed impossible she could be married, and yet Father David had pronounced them man and wife. She now had a husband. She belonged to Sir Barrett.

How odd that the thought did not distress her nearly so much today as it had the day before. The bedding part, yes. She still did not want to have anything to do with coupling, not even the electrifying things he had done to her the night before. But she liked Sir Barrett, despite it all. He had spanked her—three times already. He had tied her wrists and made a spectacle out of feeding her on his lap. He had locked her in his room like a prisoner of war and yet... she could not hate him. She could not even dislike him. In less than two days' time, he'd already become familiar to her. Here at Rothburg, he was the only person she knew. But more than that, she felt close to him. As close as she'd felt to her sisters, God rest their souls. He knew her darkest secret, after all.

Margrite and her cohort clomped into the room again, carrying two more buckets, which they emptied into the wooden tub in the center of the room. "Is that enough for you, my lord?" Margrite asked.

Sir Barrett looked at the water level. "Yes, that should do. Thank you."

Margrite set her pail down and sauntered over to stand far too close to Sir Barrett. "Would you like us to bathe you, my lord?" she asked in a sultry voice.

Sir Barrett smirked. "No, I have a lady wife for that now," he said, tossing Daisy a wink.

"Are you sure?" Margrite asked, her voice dripping with honey. "We could show her how you like it…"

"Out," he said, making a shooing motion with his hand. "Go on, move out. I am married now, and your flirtation offends my wife." He did not seem angry with the wenches, though, only amused.

It irritated her even more to think he offered that same patient amusement with all of her antics. Mayhap she was not special to him at all, but just a female who offered a challenge for his seduction. She folded her arms across her chest and glowered at him when they left.

"You cannot be angry with me for the girls I tumbled before we were married. I will not be unfaithful to you unless you drive me completely from our bed."

A cold, sinking sensation took hold in her abdomen. It was the answer to her dilemma—the way to be rid of his amorous intentions. And yet, the idea of him lying with another made her almost dizzy with nausea.

She looked up to find him studying her. "You are actually considering it, aren't you?" he asked, sounding offended for the first time since she'd met him.

She hesitated. Lying would only earn her another trip over his knee. She shook her head and turned away. "I'm just—confused," she said, which was truth.

"Fair enough. Come here, little wife and learn to serve your husband."

She walked to him and knelt at his feet, unlacing his boots.

His large hand tangled in her hair, mussing her braid. He lifted the plait and cut the thread securing the end with the blade of his dagger. "Unwind your hair," he said, his voice deepened.

She closed her eyes, breathing. Why did such a simple command have an effect on her body? Her breasts had grown heavy, the nipples tight and achy. The now-familiar swirling sensation had taken flight in her belly. Her fingers shook as she unwound the braid until her blond hair fell across her shoulders in thick waves.

Sir Barrett pulled off his tunic and undershirt, revealing his chiseled muscles. She had never found men appealing, but the mere sight of his chest made her heart pick up speed. Something about the power so evident in his naked form made the muscles clench between her legs in a mixture of fear and… what? Desire? Surely not.

She scrambled back and lurched to her feet, away from him when he pulled off his leggings. It may have been better to stay close, because now she had a clear view of his manhood, standing straight out like a jousting rod.

She must have shown her shock, because he grinned and covered it with one fist as he stepped into the tub. "Don't be afraid of it. I'll never take you before you're ready."

"Before I ask, you mean," she said.

"Yes, that, too. But I mean after you've asked, when you've given yourself wholly to me. I still would never let it be difficult for you."

Panic at the topic only added to her confusion. "I-I'm afraid I do not understand you, my lord."

"Come over here," he said.

The last thing she wanted to do was get closer to his naked body. But they had made a bargain, and if she wanted him to uphold his end, she had to keep hers. She came two steps closer.

He patted the floor beside him. "Right here. Kneel by my side and wash me."

Bubbles of fear fizzed inside her but she obeyed, lowering to her knees and picking up the scrap of linen. Her hands refused to touch him with it, though. She just remained there, frozen by his side, staring into the water at his enormous cock.

"Wash me," he commanded, his voice a shade more stern. She pushed up her sleeves but he shook his head. "Take off that gown or it will get soaking wet."

It was a reasonable request, but it made her heart skitter around in her chest like a rabbit on the run from a hawk. She stood up and peeled off the dress, praying he would not also ask her to remove the chemise. Lowering back to her knees, she dipped the cloth in the water and dabbed his knee with it.

Sir Barrett's beefy arm snaked around her waist, the heat from his flesh seeming to scald her. "Higher," he murmured.

It took her a moment to understand what he meant, and when she did, she was sure she blushed. She pushed the washcloth a little higher up his thigh, following the contour of hard muscle.

Sir Barrett's hand stroked up the back of her thigh.

She scooted her knees closer to the tub, as if she might escape his touch.

Of course his hand remained attached, traveling ever higher until he gripped the very top of her thigh, his fingers just brushing the outer lips of her sex.

She froze, the washcloth unmoving on his upper thigh.

Barrett's other hand came down on top of hers in the water, guiding it toward the place she had purposely refused to look.

She resisted, but he did not allow her to withdraw her hand. "I know it must seem grotesque to you," he said, at the same time his finger began to slide lightly over her folds.

"Yes," she agreed. She did find a man's anatomy offensive.

"Go ahead and take him," he coaxed, pressing her fingers around the base of his shaft.

"Please," she said, this time trying to back her knees away from the tub. "I don't—" She stopped when her efforts to retreat caused Sir Barrett's fingers to press into her sex. She bit back the little cry on her lips as he began to circle one finger on a particularly sensitive place. She tightened her fist reflexively, only to feel his cock grow in response. "Oh," she exclaimed, trying to release his manhood, but held fast by his other hand.

"Go on, Daisy," Barrett said, his voice sounding rough.

"I can't," she whispered, her thighs quivering, a mysterious moisture dripping down her leg.

"You're doing so well, little girl." As his fingers continued to delve in and out of her folds, he guided her fist up and down his length.

She squeezed her eyes closed. "Oh," she moaned, her embarrassment and unease equally matched by the powerful and growing need to have his fingers push deeper or faster.

• • • • • • •

"Do you feel the moisture in your quim, Daisy?"

She made a small sound of assent.

"That is how your body readies for me. It makes sex pleasurable. Without it, you might experience pain." The flash of knowing on her face made him sorry he mentioned it. He wanted to avenge her rape, to tear that man or men apart with his bare hands. He kept his tone easy, though, for her sake. "When I said I'd never make it difficult for you, that is what I meant. You see, right now, your little quim wants me."

The feel of Daisy's slick sex under his fingers felt even sweeter than her hand around his manhood. He wanted to bring her over the edge again, to show her pleasure in every way he knew how. And yet he had resolved not to allow her to climax until she asked him to take her properly.

That didn't mean he couldn't reach completion, though. He tightened his hand over hers, closing his eyes. His feet began to press against the wall of the tub, his legs tightening and straining. His cock had been aching for release since the moment he first saw his Daisy. He pushed her fingers right up to the sensitive rim and back down again, as he began to thrust one finger inside her tight channel.

The sound of her labored breath and little squeaks excited him further. As his seed surged down his shaft he slid a second finger inside her, pumping them rapidly.

"Oh, please," she squealed plaintively.

"No, Daisy," he managed to say, removing his fingers at the same moment he found his desperate release. He lifted his hips and came into the cloth, to keep the water clean.

She gasped, staring, then scrambled back and stood up. After a moment, she asked in an unsteady voice, "Why did you say no?"

He finished washing quickly and stood up. "I meant you were not allowed to finish. Your turn in the tub; it's still warm."

She looked at the bath dubiously, her brow furrowed. "Finish?" she asked.

He smiled at her sweet innocence. "Climax. You may not climax unless I give you permission, or until you have begged me to consummate our marriage."

She appeared uneasy, as if just beginning to understand the implications of his plan. She hadn't moved from her place, so he strode over and pulled her chemise over her head in one swift movement.

"In the tub," he said, slapping her arse.

She yelped and lurched forward, climbing into the tub and drawing her knees to her chest as if to hide her body from his view.

He stood over her, peering down. "There's no hiding yourself from me," he said. "I will soon begin punishing any attempts to hide or keep yourself from me. I am your lord husband and your body belongs to me. You'd best get used to it."

She looked up at him, her eyes wide and frightened, but her perfect pink nipples stood in stiff peaks. He knew her mind battled her body at times like this and he rather enjoyed watching the war.

"Show me," he commanded, because she had not moved from her position.

She moved her knees an inch away from her breasts.

"Spread your feet wide," he said. "Show me your charms."

She looked aghast. "My lord... surely this is not... proper?"

He grinned. "It is proper for a man to have carnal knowledge of his wife, is it not? I have made a significant concession in light of your fears. But you must hold up your end of the arrangement. Now open your thighs."

She cringed, but slowly inched her feet apart.

The water did not obscure his view of her silken curls and the treasures that lay beneath. He made a show of looking her body up and down. "Beautiful," he remarked.

An enchanting blush colored her cheeks, her lush lips opening as she stared up at him.

"You didn't know that, did you?" he asked, surprised at the sudden realization.

She flushed a deeper shade of rose. "I never wanted to be," she answered.

"You've been hiding from men."

The tiny pink tip of her tongue darted out and moistened her lips. "Yes.

I refused to cover my hair. I learned to trap and hunt like a boy, to play harp like a minstrel, to make myself seem eccentric."

He crouched down to her level. "If the men of Hohenzollern passed you by, they were fools."

She nibbled her lip. "You don't find me... odd?"

He held her gaze. "I find you fascinating, intoxicating, beyond compare. Last night when I lay down beside you, I thanked God for my good fortune."

She dropped her eyes to her hands. "You flatter," she mumbled.

He walked around to her side of the tub and lifted her out, handing her a dry linen. "I speak truth."

She dried off and reached for the discarded chemise.

"Ah, ah," he scolded. "No clothing in bed. Don't you remember?"

She looked pained, but dropped the chemise.

He scooped her into his arms and carried her to the bed, where he laid her gently down. She thrashed a little when he lowered his own body over hers, but he didn't put any weight on her, staying on his knees and forearms as he kissed down her neck. He dragged the tip of his tongue across the slope of her collarbone, cupping one breast in each hand and kneading. He began to torture her right nipple between his fingers as he suckled the left, teasing her with nips and bites, pinches and caresses.

She made the most erotic little grunts of protest, her belly tensing and releasing.

Keeping one hand focused on her breast, he crawled lower, kissing down her fluttering abdomen until he reached her little triangle of dark curls. He planted a kiss at the apex of her folds.

"No," she said, sounding panicked. "What are you doing?"

"I'm teaching you pleasure," he said.

"No... please," she said, trying to push him away with her legs.

"That's a spanking," he chortled, rolling her to her belly.

"Ack," she exclaimed. "No!"

"All I hear is no, no, no," he said, slapping her squirming bottom with each word. He didn't hold back, hoping a little pain might help release her nerves. He pressed one hand down on her low back to pin her in place and spanked her over and over again, until her bottom took on a beautiful shade of pink.

He rolled her back over. "Naughty girl," he scolded. "If you can't open for me, I shall have to help you. Do not move," he said sternly.

She delighted him by letting out a little whimper and writhing about on the bed.

His cock forgot about his earlier release, standing eagerly at attention at the sight of Daisy's naked form. He grabbed some jute rope from his supplies and returned, picking up a new linen washcloth on the way. He tore the washcloth into strips and wound one around her ankle to protect her soft skin from the rough rope.

She watched him with wide, frightened eyes as he wrapped and knotted the rope over the swath of linen.

Tossing it underneath his wooden bedframe, he picked it up on the other side, tugging until her leg opened to the side.

For all their jesting about taming horses earlier, she did have the look of a nervous filly now, peering at him from the corners of her eyes, her chest rising and falling with quickened breath.

He caught her other ankle, pulling it wide, so she lay with her legs spread open, her sex mercilessly on display. He wrapped and tied the ankle, then gave her wrists the same treatment.

She tugged at the ropes, twisting and fretting.

"Shh," he said, crawling over her and brushing her cheek with the backs of his fingers. "Easy, little girl. I'm not going to hurt you. I promise."

She said nothing, but her eyes remained fixed on his, her breasts lifting and falling open with each short breath. He kissed down her centerline again, using a little tongue, sucking in places. Settling between her splayed legs, he slid a hand underneath her bottom and squeezed the warm flesh of one cheek as he brought his mouth to her glistening sex.

• • • • • • •

She jerked at the velvety caress of his tongue, but the ropes would not allow her to get away. She strained anyway, somehow needed to resist, to prove she did not want this, not any part of it, even though it felt… so… A wanton sound escaped her lips.

"You like that, don't you, little girl?" He nibbled at her outer lips.

"No," she wailed, though it sounded more like another lusty moan. "Sir Barrett," she pleaded breathlessly. "Bear? Husband?"

"My lord and master?" he suggested, grinning wickedly before diving back down and teasing her with the incredible undulations of his tongue. Flick, suck, nibble… he tortured her endlessly as she squirmed and rolled her hips to and fro.

"Please," she panted.

"Please, what, my love?" he asked, slipping one finger inside her and curling it to hit her inner wall.

She panicked, the sensations overwhelming, an urgency—some unknown bodily need taking over. "Don't… oh, please, oh, please." She tugged at her bonds, fluid trickling shamefully from her sex.

"Take me, Bear," he prompted. "Just say it, and I'll give you sweet release."

Sweet release sounded like what she needed. But no, she couldn't give in. Sounds came out of her throat—strange and desperate. Keening, mewling notes like an animal in heat. "Please, Bear," she pleaded.

"Say it," he urged.

"I... can't," she said.

Abruptly, he pulled his finger from inside her and shook his head. "No?" he asked.

She stared up at him, bereft without his touch. "Please," she pleaded once again, though she did not even know what she wanted.

He appeared disappointed as he freed her of the ropes. For a moment, she thought he would punish her by depriving her of all touch, but blew out the lamp and climbed up beside her, wrapping an arm around her waist and pulling her snugly against him.

She closed her eyes, melting into his warmth, drinking in his strength. After a while, his arm grew heavy and his breath deepened. She lay in the darkness, unable to sleep. Her entire body still rioted with need—her sex pulsed, her breasts had grown heavy and her nipples tight. The feather mattress seemed too hot tonight. She kicked the covers off her legs. The cool air did nothing to soothe her fire. She rubbed her feet together to release a little pent-up energy.

She reviewed every single thing Sir Barrett had done or said to her that day, examining his actions, looking for fault. She felt irritable; she'd gladly bite his hand again if he put it in her way, even if it did mean a whipping. She slid her hand over her hip to her naked buttocks, squeezing one cheek to remember the sting of his hand, the agonizing welts of his crop. Why did that make her stomach somersault?

The pulsing between her legs had only become more insistent. What had he done to her? The memory of his tongue circling and penetrating brought a fresh wave of heat crashing over her. She slid her hand between her thighs and touched the wetness there. What had he said? Her body was readying for him? The sensation of her fingers against her sensitive pleats sent ripples of pleasure down her inner thighs. She began to stroke herself the way he had done, exploring her own anatomy with interest for the first time.

As she probed and teased, the same sort of urgency came over her. She began to pull against her mons, stretching her legs in the opposite direction, tightening her buttocks and thighs. Her bottom clenched and relaxed, undulating in rhythm with her hand, satisfying her and yet creating more need at the same time—like the scratching of an itch that only grows and grows.

Suddenly, a huge hand clamped down over hers, stilling it. "Naughty, naughty girl," Barrett murmured in her ear. "Are you allowed to touch yourself?"

She groaned and pulled her fingers against her mons.

"Ah, ah," he tsked, pulling her hand out from between her thighs and pushing her to her belly. "That's a spanking, and I'm not inclined to go easy on you, either," he said.

She hardly minded. A spanking might help scratch her itch.

He slid his fingers between her cheeks and found the shameful moisture. "Very naughty, Daisy. You're soaking wet," he said, taking his time to investigate, renewing her burning need with each circle of his fingertip.

"Ahh," she moaned, pressing her hips into the bed and lifting them over and over again.

But he withdrew his fingers, bringing his hand crashing down on the middle of her buttocks, just above her sex.

She moaned again, her fingers burrowing into the soft woolen mattress. She lifted her bottom for more. If he wanted to punish her, she would take it—every swat. Hopefully it would quench the burning desire, put out the flames of lust she never wanted to feel.

He repeated the action, spanking her in the same delicious place where the reverberation went straight to her sex. He moved from where he'd been sitting beside her to the head of the bed, sitting with his back against the wall. "Lay yourself over my legs for a proper spanking," he said, his voice gravelly.

She obeyed, crawling up to him and draping herself willingly over his thighs. To her satisfaction, he picked up exactly where he'd left off, spanking the sweet spot that went straight to her core. She arched for him, offering her bottom up, seeking each slap. It seemed like he could spank her all night and she'd never complain. She wanted it as much as she'd wanted his fingers to continue their tease. She tensed when a finger from his other hand slid between her buttocks, finding her most private hole. He circled the rim of her anus, all the while he continued to spank and she shattered, her body shivering, her hands diving between her legs as she bucked her hips.

Barrett kept spanking until it had passed and she collapsed in a limp heap. Even then, she would not have minded if he continued spanking her all night. The pain felt good, somehow. "I didn't say you could climax, Daisy," Barrett murmured.

She could not even bring herself to beg forgiveness.

"I ought to whip you with my sword belt for that."

A second climax sent her bucking at his words.

He rubbed her bottom with hard, punishing strokes. "I think you'd like that, wouldn't you, my naughty little wife?" He bent over and kissed one of her blazing cheeks, confirming her suspicion that he was not in the least bit angry with her over the broken rule. All the irritation she'd directed toward him when she'd first laid down morphed into affection and even optimism. Mayhap this marriage might work for her, after all.

If only she could hold him off from ever consummating the thing.

CHAPTER FIVE

"Good morning, love." Barrett stroked his palm up the baby-soft skin of Daisy's back, noticing how rough his hands seemed in comparison.

She rolled over and blinked at him. She looked so innocent, so unspoiled. He had planned to continue his sexual torments with her that morning, but he couldn't even bring himself to kiss her lips. Her beauty made his chest ache. He wanted more than just her body, he realized. As he had explained to her, he wanted her heart, mind, and soul. Every piece of her.

"Good morning," she said, a tinge of color coming to her cheeks, as if she just remembered how they'd ended the previous night.

He kissed her forehead and rolled out of bed to get dressed.

"My lord?" she asked, sitting up and pulling the covers to her armpits to hide her bare breasts.

"Yes, Daisy?"

"Are you going to…" she dropped her eyes to the bedcovers, "lock me up again today?" she asked, plucking at a stray thread.

His heart twisted. "No, sweet girl," he said before he'd even had a chance to consider his options. "Did you say you liked to hunt?"

Her face lifted, shining with expectation. "Aye, my lord. Will you take me?"

Resisting her child-like joy would be an impossibility. "If you promise to be respectful at breakfast this morning."

She beamed, slipping out of bed and running, hunched over as if to hide her body, to slip on her chemise. "I promise," she said, jumping when she discovered him right behind her.

He wrapped his arms around her from behind. "All spoils go to your master," he murmured in her ear.

She melted back against him, in what he considered his best-won victory yet, and laughed a deep, throaty laugh. "Of course, my lord."

At breakfast, he sat down on the bench and watched her eye the bench and him with uncertainty. To his shock, she chose his lap.

"Ah, the little bird has been tamed," Erik remarked. "Does that mean you'll let her stay in with the ladies today?"

He smiled. "Mayhap after dinner. This morning, I am taking her hunting with me."

The knights and ladies of the high table looked perplexed. "Hunting?"

"Aye. The lady likes to hunt."

Several people exchanged glances, but he didn't care. Daisy's eccentricities made him all the more proud of her.

"That's what became of the ladies of Hohenzollern without a man to rule there," one of the knights remarked.

"All the more fortune for me," he remarked lightly, leaving them to decipher his meaning.

Daisy sat perfectly still, politely waiting for him to give her permission to begin.

"You may eat," he said.

He enjoyed the feel of her on his lap where he could inhale her sweet scent and feel her soft warmth. He looped an arm around her waist and stroked her side and legs, feeling her stiffness ease with each passing moment.

When they finished, they went to his chamber where he helped her into her cloak and picked up his riding crop. "Do you know what will happen if you try to escape me today?" he asked, reaching out and patting her bottom with the crop.

"I won't," she said, turning away dismissively.

He swung the crop and caught the underside of her bottom, making her leap forward and grab her bottom.

"I said, I wouldn't," she exclaimed, turning around and glaring.

He caught her up in his arms, joining her hands in rubbing away the sting. "Do not glare at me. If I think you need a taste of my whip to remind you to behave, I will use it."

"You," she said furiously, attempting to push him away.

"This little bottom is mine," he said, squeezing it possessively. "Mine to punish or pleasure as I see fit. Do you need another reminder before we go?"

Pride warred with practicality in her expression and he hoped she would test him again, but she shook her head. "No, sir."

He smiled and touched her nose. "Smart girl." He offered his arm. "Shall we?"

She took his arm and they walked out to the stables where Penrod had already saddled his destrier and a pretty roan for Daisy. She stroked the mare, introducing herself and speaking softly in the manner of someone well-accustomed to horses. He helped her into the saddle, then mounted his own stallion and led the way out of the castle gates and into the forest.

The day was quiet. A light dusting of snow had fallen during the night, making everything look clean and white, the snow catching the sunlight and sparkling. They rode side by side, following a path through the trees.

"It's beautiful," Daisy breathed.

He smiled, enjoying her happiness.

She turned to him. "Thank you so much for taking me out today," she said. "I can't stand being cooped up inside."

"Nor can I," he said.

"You don't mind having a wife who prefers to act like a man?"

He bit back a laugh. "Little Daisy, you are nothing like a man. And no, I meant it when I said it was my fortune to have a wife who likes to hunt, for now we have something we can do together." He gave her a wink.

She looked at him doubtfully. "I think everyone at Rothburg will pity you for your poor choice in wives."

"Enough," he said. "Rothburg will accept you, just as you shall accept her. Do not fret over it."

She didn't answer, but within a few moments looked content again, taking in the scenery. They saw a buck and she had her arrow fit to her bow before he did, but his horse stepped on a stick and the buck startled and ran.

They rode for over an hour before they stopped to rest. He helped her from the horse, catching her waist and guiding her along his body as he lowered her, until she landed at his feet, her slender form pressed against his.

He expected her to protest, but she looked up at him expectantly. He bent and caught her lips, tasting her sweetness. When she returned the kiss, he went rock hard. Grasping the back of her head, he took her mouth more insistently, licking into her lips.

• • • • • • •

She gasped, pulling away from Barrett, a bit frightened by his invasion. He abandoned her mouth, kissing down her neck, nipping at the place it met her shoulder. He slipped his hand inside her cloak, cupping her breast and squeezing it.

Her legs grew weak. He pulled open the laces of her gown, baring her nipple to the cold air, where it stood up in a hardened point. He flicked his tongue over it and she groaned, the contrast of warm to cold making it burn. "What are you doing?" she croaked.

"What do you think I'm doing?" he murmured, grasping her bottom with one hand and pulling her even closer.

He had her completely off-balance. If he released her, she would fall backward onto the ground. She clung to his arms, giving up maintaining herself apart from him. Barrett would never let her fall—she knew it instinctively, even though it cost her to give up her own independence. She let go, stopped trying to keep her toes balanced on the slippery ground and relaxed into him, letting his strength bear her weight.

He picked her up, pulling her legs to straddle his waist, and carried her to a fallen log, which he brushed off and sat upon. "You know what I think?" he asked, his voice low and seductive.

"What, sir?"

"I think if you tried sex in some new and fresh position, you wouldn't even know we were coupling. Like this one for instance." He yanked her hips closer to his body and she realized her sex lay just above his manhood.

She attempted to push back, but he held her close, gripping her bottom with both hands and grinding her quim against the bulge in his leggings. "Barrett," she cried, bringing her fist down on his shoulder.

"Don't be naughty or I will have to warm your bottom for you," he warned.

A shivering had begun in her sex and spread down her legs, making her toes scrunch up in her boots. Moisture had begun to pool again. She wondered: what would the harm be in trying it this way? He was right; nothing about the position or the feeling in her body reminded her of her first time. She rocked her hips, joining him in the grinding motion, testing the sensations it produced.

Both breasts tightened, heavy and full. She ground against him harder, a sigh escaping her lips.

Barrett pulled out the skirts trapped between them until her hot core rested right on top of his bulging hose. His cock moved beneath her, twitching and straining.

She panicked, rearing to scramble off his lap.

"Easy, easy, easy," he soothed, catching her before she fell face first onto the ground and lifting her to her feet. "You're all right, little one. Nothing is going to happen until you say yes. I promised you that, did I not?"

She stamped her feet, smoothing her skirts and trying to calm her racing heart.

"Did I not?" he repeated.

"Yes, sir," she said, her eyes filling with tears.

"Oh, Daisy," he said, catching her up in his arms. "Please don't cry. You can trust me, my sweet. I'm not going to force you."

She nodded, sniffing. "I know. I know that, I do. I just…" What had happened? She hardly knew herself. "I guess I got scared. Something reminded me." She shuddered. It had been the thought of his manhood that frightened her. It had been manageable the night before, when she had a bit more control in how she touched it, but today had been too fast. "I'm sorry," she said. She started to cry again. "I truly am sorry. I cannot be your wife. I'll never be able to give what you want me to."

"Hush," he said. "You will, love. It's only been two days. We have our whole lives together. I am not worried—you should not be either. You can trust me, Daisy."

She nodded, brushing the tears away. "I do," she said. "I really do."

He looked cheered by that. "Let's start back. We don't want to miss the midday meal." He helped her back onto her horse.

Her bare quim hit the saddle and the slickness of her juices made it slide. It felt so different from before; what did Barrett do to her body that made it react this way? She sucked in her breath at the sensation it produced. It was not quite as intense as Sir Barrett's lap had been, but she still found a wonderful wave of heat each time she rocked back. They began to ride and she rocked into a delicious rhythm, rubbing her sex over the smooth leather. She stole a glance over her shoulder to see if Sir Barrett noticed her undulations, but he wore a blank face.

She continued, growing slightly dizzy, her breath staying high in her chest, coming in quick little gasps. She rubbed harder and faster until her muscles seized. She squeezed the saddle tight with her inner thighs as her bottom tightened and the muscles in her core contracted over and over again. When it passed, she slumped in the saddle, her muscles relaxed and warm.

When they arrived back at the stable, Sir Barrett helped her down. "You are in big, big trouble," he growled.

She drew in her breath in dismay, her bottom clenching convulsively.

He didn't say a word as he led her up to his room, swishing the crop ominously through the air. He shut the door and tapped the bed with the crop. "Bend over."

She stole a glance at his face, but could not read whether he was truly angry or not. She bent over, leaving her skirts down, since he hadn't instructed her to lift them.

He tossed them up her back. "Four strokes for being a very naughty wife," he said, tapping her bottom with the crop. "Did you think I would not notice what you were doing in that saddle?"

"I'm sorry, sir," she said meekly.

"You broke the rules. You may not refuse me and then pleasure yourself. Only I will decide if and when you receive pleasure. That is twice you have defied me."

"Yes, sir."

He brought the crop down across her low buttocks.

The tenderness from the whipping the previous morning came back tenfold. She groaned. Another line of fire landed across her bottom. She broke into a sweat. He whipped her again and she yelped, lifting her torso as if to escape. He pushed her back down and applied the last stroke. She squealed and reached back, covering her bottom with her hands and hiding her face in the covers.

• • • • • • •

Daisy looked adorable when she'd been spanked. Truly, she took correction so sweetly it made him want to claim her, devour her, show her she was his entire world. She lay bent over the bed, clutching her welted buttocks like a sorry little girl, her sex glistening between her legs. He leaned over her, covering her torso, lacing his fingers over the tops of hers.

"This is another position we might try," he murmured, praying she hadn't been forced from behind. She didn't struggle, so he went on. "I could take you right now, little girl." He pressed his thickened cock against her plump folds. "I see you're ready for me."

She tightened her fingers around his, breathing hard.

"I think you want it, Daisy. I know you want it, but you're scared. After I've possessed you in every way and every position, I will banish all other memories you have of men."

She turned her head and he saw unshed tears glistening in her eyes.

He froze. "What are those tears for?" he asked.

"I want to believe you, Bear."

Hope skipped across his chest.

"Believe it, little one. I will make you forget. You will only know me, my body, my love, my touch. I promise you that."

She closed her eyes, looking troubled. "That would be so sweet."

Saddened by her pain, he lifted her off the bed and stood, holding her against his body. After a while, he said, "I need to check on the progress of the wall. Do you wish to come with me?"

She still looked small and withdrawn. "What is my alternative?"

He smiled, toying with her braid. "I won't lock you in my chamber. You are free to sit with the other ladies, if you like. In fact, you probably should, I think they are anxious to know you."

She nodded. "I agree. Thank you, Bear."

He kissed her forehead. "Be good, little one."

"I will."

He left her, his heart heavy for the burden his little wife carried, the trauma he hadn't yet found a way to take from her.

· · · · · · ·

Daisy laid on the bed for a while, rubbing her sore backside, her mind swirling over all the new thoughts Sir Barrett had given her about making love. She had never pleasured herself before. Maybe she had touched herself a little as a child, before her mother told her it was wrong. But she didn't remember the incredible sensations—the heat and need, the relaxation afterward.

She was tempted to touch herself again, not to purposely disobey Sir Barrett, but because she just needed to understand it all better. And while he punished her, she didn't actually believe he minded all that much. This was part of his game, and she was breaking rules, but at least she was playing it with him.

But the thought of meeting the ladies drew her off the bed and out the door. She found them in the spinning room, laughing and talking.

"Come in," the princess called, seeing her hesitate at the door.

She curtsied and came forward.

The princess stood from her wheel and came forward, taking her hands. "Forgive me; I feel I have not given you a proper greeting. I am Annika. This is Greta, Ute, Grite, and Elsa. Greta and Grite are my cousins, and Elsa is my sister. Ute is Prince Erik's sister."

She curtsied again. "I am Daisy. I have been serving as lady-in-waiting to Princess Susanna of Hohenzollern."

"Welcome to Rothburg. Sir Barrett has had you so… occupied. Are you all right?" she asked, peering into her face.

She felt the stares of all the women, and blushed. "Yes, my lady."

"Sir Barrett has not treated you with the chivalry he is usually known for," Annika said, speaking slowly as if choosing her words carefully. She glanced at the other ladies.

"But it's plain he is quite taken with you," Greta added quickly. She was the same lady who had told her Sir Barrett was not a complete ogre the day before.

"Yes, yes, I agree. It is wonderful to see him so engaged with a lady—unusual for him," Elsa said.

"Does he not… has he courted any ladies before?" She didn't know what compelled her to ask, because she definitely did not want to hear the answer. Her body tensed, her fingernails pressing into the flesh of her palms.

"No, not since I've been here," Annika said, looking to Ute.

"Never," Ute said definitively. "He probably didn't think any would have him, since he's a basta—" She stopped when the rest of the ladies gave her warning looks.

Daisy drew herself up, heat suffusing her face. "I don't care one whit about the legitimacy of his birth," she declared. "I am proud to be his wife." She lifted her chin, daring one of them to say he was unworthy.

Annika darted forward and grasped her hand, tugging her to a chair beside her. "Sir Barrett is a brave and noble knight, well-deserving of a well-bred wife like you. Please take no offense. Rothburg has its hierarchies like all castles. Sometimes it is easier to find a mate elsewhere, as he has."

Her cheeks still burned, but when she searched the princess' words, she could not find any offense, so she let it go.

CHAPTER SIX

The blizzard came out of nowhere. It had been cloudy, yes, but she hadn't felt this storm coming. She needed to get back to the castle immediately or she could be lost out in the woods. This was the kind of storm where men became disoriented, freezing to death only to be discovered a mere twenty yards from a building.

She grasped the four white rabbits she'd trapped and ran through the snow, the cold air burning her lungs and making her chest ache. The path would be lost soon, but she wasn't far. She had only walked a half mile or so, if she remembered correctly. She picked up her speed even more, the toes of her boots sliding out behind her with each step. Almost there, almost there.

Thank God—she thought she saw the castle up ahead. Which meant she must be out of the woods. The snow blew too hard to even see the trees. She'd come out to trap, with the idea of sewing rabbit fur into the collar of Sir Barrett and Penrod's cloaks. She made a poor wife in terms of weaving, but the fur would set them apart, give them something special.

Why hadn't she told anyone where she was going? If she got lost out here, no one would even know where to look. Not that she would want them to risk their lives over her stupidity. She tripped and fell into the snow, the icy flakes searing her face. Cursing, she struggled to her feet and ran on. Yes, that must be the castle up ahead.

She reached the gates just as a rider tore out of them at a breakneck speed. He must have seen her because he turned the stallion sharply in her direction, causing him to rear and whinny.

Barrett.

He had come for her. Relief, gratitude, and fear poured from her in equal measures. His destrier galloped toward her, not slowing in the least. Was it him? As he passed her, he bent down and caught her about the waist, wrenching a choked scream from her throat. She clung to the rabbits and he set her on one knee, guiding his horse in a circle and back through the gates.

He didn't say a word.

She had no breath to speak, but if she did, she would not have known what to say to him. She teetered precariously on his knee, supported only by the strength of his arm. She did not dare steal a glance at his face, but she could feel anger pouring off him in waves. He rode the horse straight up to the castle doors and dropped her to her feet.

"Wait for me in our chamber," he said tersely.

She rushed forward, not looking back, her heart thundering in her chest. She thought to give the rabbits to Penrod to take to the kitchen, but she did not think she could manage a conversation. Instead, she removed her wet cloak and boots and carried everything up the stairs with her. She did not have to wait long.

Barrett burst in the room, his dark eyes flashing. He looked every part his namesake: a great, growling bear—vicious and terrifying in his huge stature. She stepped quickly back, but he closed the distance between them and swept her off her feet, carrying her to the edge of the bed, where he sat and plopped her over his lap.

He began to spank her immediately, one hand tugging up her skirts, while the other already lit into her.

She tried to lie still, not wanting to further anger him, but her body had a mind of its own, jerking and wriggling under the punishing blows. By the time he had bared her bottom, the cold numbness in her buttocks had worn off, replaced by terrible, hot pins and needles.

"Ahh… ah," she grunted. "Oh."

"What were you thinking?" he demanded, speaking at last, but not pausing in his spanking, even for an instant.

"I didn't know it would storm," she protested, squeezing her eyes shut. The pins and needles were easing and now her entire bottom blazed.

"Did you ask my permission to leave the castle?"

"No, sir," she said. Tears choked her throat, threatening to spill.

"Why not?" he demanded.

Though he'd surely seen the rabbits, she still did not want to spoil the surprise. She did not answer.

He spanked even harder, his huge hand like a wooden paddle, punishing her poor bottom with each heavy blow. "I asked, why not?" When she still did not answer, he picked her up from his lap and set her on her feet, giving her a shove toward the wall. "Stand in the corner," he barked.

She tripped, scurrying away from him. She'd never been made to stand in a corner before, and she didn't think it would be worse than the spanking she had just received, but it was.

"Keep your skirts lifted to show me your naughty bottom. I am not nearly through with you," he growled.

She picked up her skirts and bowed her head, unable to stop the tears that had been threatening. Out of the corner of her eye, she saw Barrett bury his head in his hands, looking defeated. She felt even worse. She sniffed and his head jerked up, as if in surprise.

"Daisy," he said, his voice much softer. "Come here, love."

Fresh tears streaked her face at the endearment. He couldn't be so angry anymore, if he called her 'love.' She walked to stand before him, still holding her skirts up, as he'd ordered.

"Forgive me for my temper," he said heavily. "I was afraid for you, that's all." He reached out and grasped her hips, pulling her closer. "Come here. I'm sorry I scared you."

"You didn't scare me," she lied.

A flick of his eyebrows showed he knew the truth. "Well, *you* scared *me*. I forbid you to leave the castle walls without permission. Ever. Do you understand me?"

She nodded, swallowing back a fresh wave of tears. "I'm sorry, my lord."

"I'm going to give you the worst strapping of your life."

"Yes, sir," she murmured. She hardly cared about the punishment, although she knew it would be awful. Her only concern was to make things right between them again. What could she offer him, except four dead rabbits?

• • • • • • •

Daisy slowly lowered herself to her knees at his feet, surprising him with her humility. When she reached for his manhood, his surprise turned to shock.

He ought to stop her. It was wrong of her to try to distract him from her punishment this way, but curiosity and desire got the better of him.

She palmed his cock through his leggings, then wrestled it free. She stroked it the way he'd shown her in the bath, sliding her fist up and down his length. Her expression looked half-frightened, half-determined. Of course he would have preferred aroused or excited, but he found her actions touching, considering how difficult it was for her.

She leaned her face forward and gingerly stuck out her tongue.

His cock surged with excitement just to see her intent. He resisted the urge to grab the back of her head and thrust in like she was a serving wench. Instead, he waited, holding his breath and watching as she flicked her tongue on the rim of his penis. After a just a few such flicks, his breath grew ragged. She lifted her eyes to him, her tear-stained cheeks flushed with color.

"Take him in your mouth," he muttered, his voice rough.

She opened her lips wider and accepted his length, looking uncertain.

"That's it," he said. "Keep going, Daisy, it feels so good."

She seemed encouraged by his words and picked up speed, sliding her mouth up and down his length. She didn't take him very deep, but he didn't mind. He wanted it to last forever, but he also wanted her first time to be easy. When she came off and looked at him uncertainly, he covered his fist around hers, pumping.

"Stick out your tongue," he grunted. She obeyed, and he pressed the head of his cock against it while he slid her hand up and down his length. "Open your bodice," he ordered.

She fumbled with the laces as he continued rubbing the head of his cock against her tongue. When she pulled open the front of her dress, he came, decorating her breasts with his seed.

She looked down at his artistry, confused, and he pulled her up to his lap and wiped it off with his sleeve. He cupped the back of her head and kissed her.

"I didn't know what had happened to you," he said, regretting his temper. "No one knew where you'd gone. I feared you'd run away, and I knew you wouldn't live through that storm." A muscle twitched under his eye.

She lifted her hand to touch his cheek.

"Were you running away?" he asked, his voice cracking. He had to know.

"No," she said immediately. "I went trapping, that's all. I didn't feel the storm coming—I'm sorry."

"You should have asked me first," he said.

She dropped her eyes, and didn't answer. The third time she hadn't answered him.

He cupped her chin and lifted it. "Were you afraid I would say no?"

"I wanted to go alone," she said, looking away.

His heart thumped in his chest, though he hardly knew what he feared. She kept something from him, though, and it bothered him. "Why?" he demanded.

She fidgeted with her skirt, then her shoulders sagged and she looked up. "I wanted the rabbit fur to line your cloak. I'm a terrible weaver—"

He cut her off by smashing his lips against hers, claiming her mouth with a bruising ferocity. He yanked her dress off her, then the chemise. Now he had forgotten her punishment, his love pouring out in a passion that would not wait. Standing, he picked her up and placed her in the center of the bed. He ripped off his own clothes and nudged her legs apart, settling between them. His cock nestled between her legs, and he caressed her with it, gliding his hardening shaft along her moistened slit. She stared up at him, her eyes wide but trusting.

"I'm sorry I scared you," he murmured as he lowered his lips to her neck. "I would never harm you, I hope you know that." The head of his cock found her opening and rubbed over it, requesting entrance.

Her fingers twined in his hair. "I believe you," she whispered.

He nipped her shoulder, pushing his manhood against her tight entrance, entering by a tiny measure. "Say yes, Daisy."

She said nothing, her breasts lifting and lowering with quickened breath.

"Daisy," he said more urgently.

"Do what you want with me," she whispered.

He nearly plunged deep into her, but at the last moment, he withdrew. He didn't want it this way. Not as a punishment, or something she gave as penance. He wanted her to want it as much as he did, to beg him for it. With effort he pulled back from her and rolled to his side. He thought he saw disappointment on her face before he got up, but that was probably just his own reflected back at him.

"Where are you going?" she asked, sitting up and clutching the open bodice of her dress to her chest.

He gave her a sad smile. "Away from the temptation of you," he said.

She looked lost, as if he'd abandoned her. "Why didn't you take me?"

He shook his head. "It's just that I want you to truly desire it. Not to offer because you're trying to get out of your strapping."

She flushed a deep pink, scrambling out of the bed. "I did not offer to distract you from my punishment," she cried defensively. "I only wanted—" She stopped and blinked. Then swallowed and looked away.

"You only wanted what?"

"I didn't like you angry with me. I wanted to show you I was sorry."

He swept her up in his arms. "Sweet little wife. I'm not angry anymore. And I accept your apology." He kissed the top of her head, then summoned some resolve. "I am still going to teach you a lesson with my belt, though."

Daisy said nothing, just remained pressed against his body, as if drawing strength from him.

"Take off your clothes."

• • • • • • •

Daisy drew a breath as she allowed her dress to fall open and spill to her feet. She clutched the skirt of the chemise in her fingers, but hesitated, embarrassed.

"One…" Sir Barrett began to count.

She sprang into action, tearing the chemise off and dropping it on top of the gown before he got to 'three.' She stood blushing before him as he took a long, leisurely survey of her body. Warmth pooled between her legs.

"Turn around," he commanded.

She bit her lip and rotated, showing him her backside. Her bottom still tingled and burned from the hand spanking he'd given her. She heard the sound of his footsteps moving away, but she did not dare turn to see what he was doing, since he had not given her permission.

"Daisy, come here," he said after a few moments.

She turned to see he had folded several blankets and stacked them on top of one another. Realizing his intent, genuine fear rooted her to the floor.

"Daisy," he repeated, not raising his voice.

She forced her feet to move forward, her heart pounding painfully against her ribs. She'd never felt more vulnerable in her life.

He reached out his large hand as if to comfort her and she placed hers in it. He led her to the side of the bed and tapped the stack of blankets.

Her body felt leaden as she crawled on top of the stack designed to lift and present her bottom for his chastisement. The skin on her back, bottom, and legs crawled in anticipation of the leather belt. "Please, sir," she found herself begging before he'd even started. "Forgive me."

"I have already forgiven you, little Daisy, but I need to be sure you understand this lesson."

"I do understand it," she assured him, her palms both cold and sweaty at the same time. She could almost hear the frantic thump of her heart pulsing in her ears.

"I'm not going to go easy on you; this rule is a serious one for me. I do believe your intentions came from your sweet and loving heart, and I will take that into consideration. Do you need me to tie your hands to keep you from reaching back?"

The question only drove more fear into her. "No, sir," she squeaked.

He picked up his belt from where he'd discarded it on the floor and wound one end around his fist until the remaining length was a bit longer than his forearm. He pressed a hand into her low back and slapped the belt across her raised buttocks.

She squeezed her eyes closed and held her breath to keep from crying out. He brought it down a second time and then a third. It was not as horrid as the riding crop had been. She thought she could handle it until she began to doubt he would ever stop. She abandoned her attempt to lie still and quiet after twenty-five strokes. Her bottom blazed and she was sure she could not take any more. Each new slap of the thick leather caused her to jump and kick as she wriggled all over the pile of blankets. Without thinking, she reached back to try to cover her poor welted flesh.

"Naughty wife," Barrett murmured, grasping her two wrists in one of his large hands and holding them against her low back. He returned to whipping her and she began to cry.

"Please, Barrett. Please. I'm so sorry," she begged.

On and on he whipped, until she gave up all fight and lay sobbing into the covers. She did not even notice the whipping had ended until Barrett scooped her up into his arms and settled on the bed, holding her cradled against his chest.

She clung to him like a child, soaking his shirt with her tears as he stroked her back and kissed her hair. "I'm sorry," she sobbed.

"You're forgiven, angel," he murmured. "It's all over now."

She drifted to sleep nestled against Barrett, exhausted.

When she woke, he had gone. Her bottom still throbbed from her spanking and she imagined her eyes must be red and swollen from crying. She wondered if he had locked her in the room. She dressed and tested the door and found it open. She shut it again, not willing to show her face in the castle until she felt more like herself.

The rabbits were gone and a fresh fire burned in the hearth, so Barrett could not have been gone for long. She lay on her stomach and thought about her husband.

She loved him. He had been so worried for her safety and so careful with her—only spanking with his hand while he was angry, and apologizing for scaring her. And even though the whipping had been sound, she didn't mind. She took it as proof of his love—he would not allow her to endanger herself without consequences.

And yet, she still couldn't give him what he desired. She understood why he had not taken her, even when she'd offered, but she didn't think she could do it the way he wanted. She would never beg for it, would never actually *want* to have sex. The only thing she wanted was to please him. Maybe that would be enough…

• • • • • • •

Barrett returned to his chamber before suppertime. Daisy had not appeared that afternoon and they had both missed the noontime dinner, so she must be hungry. He found her lying on her stomach on the bed.

His heart lurched. Had he spanked her too hard? He knew he had not, and yet it had been difficult to mete out a real, serious punishment. He felt even more protective than usual for her now. "The door was not locked, Daisy. Did you think I had confined you as punishment?" he asked.

She pushed to sit up. "No, sir. I suppose I am hiding," she said.

His heart stopped. "From me?" he asked in a choked voice.

"No," she said, climbing off the bed and walking to him. "Not from you," she said softly, placing her hands on his chest.

He covered them with his own. "Nobody overheard your whipping, if that's what you fear."

She pressed her face against his chest. "You whipped me hard," she said. It sounded more like an observation than a complaint.

He lifted her chin and smiled down at her. "I had to be sure my naughty wife learned her lesson." He grew sober again, remembering how frightened he'd been. "Did you?"

She nodded and rubbed her backside. "Yes, sir."

He reached behind her and squeezed her sore little bottom. "On nights when I've had to punish you soundly, you will give me your bottom hole to show me you're sorry." He had not planned any such punishment, but his cock hardened when he invented it in the moment.

She looked up at him searchingly. Of course she did not know what he meant.

Earlier he had not wanted her to offer sex as penance, and now here he was demanding she give him her most private entrance for his plunder. He shifted his aching cock in his leggings. "It's suppertime now. At bedtime I will show you what happens to naughty wives."

She bowed her head submissively, which only made his cock surge more insistently against his leggings. That he'd won her trust and respect meant the world to him.

He held out his arm. "Come, let us eat. You may sit on my lap if the bench is too hard for you."

She took his arm and they went downstairs where she sat meekly on his lap, teasing his cock with the feel of her soft, round arse.

He made her fetch the butterfat after supper and asked her to bring it to him in their chamber.

She arrived, blushing, but not appearing overly frightened.

"Take off your clothes," he instructed.

For the second time that day, she undressed under his watchful eye. He would never grow tired of seeing her in her full beauty. Her peach-tipped breasts bounced when she released them from the confines of her bodice, her hips swayed as she shifted to step out of her dress. She clasped her hands in front of her sex, as if to hide it from his view.

He sat in a chair near the dressing table, where the butterfat lay. "Come lie over my lap," he said.

She obeyed, taking his hand and allowing him to guide her into place.

"Reach back and hold your cheeks apart for me, Daisy."

She shot him a worried look over her shoulder, but complied.

He scooped a dollop of the butterfat with his fingers and rubbed it over her darkened hole, watching the way it puckered and released each time he touched it. "You see, when you're naughty, Daisy, I will make your bottom sore all over. Not just your pretty cheeks," he said, pinching her swollen flesh between his fingers and thumb and giving it a gentle shake. "Your bottom hole may be punished also. Or it may be pleasured. But this is for me to decide."

She made a small mewling sound as he rested his thumb against her anus and tapped it.

"Which would you prefer tonight? Shall I punish your bottom hole?"

He'd pressed until the reflexive contraction of her opening released and he slid in.

She stiffened, her legs straightening out behind her, her back arching.

He slapped the back of her thigh. "Don't fight me or I'll have to give you another spanking. And I'm quite certain you don't want that, do you?"

"No, sir," she answered quickly.

"I didn't think so." He massaged the inside of her tight channel, working the oil into every tiny crevice, inside and out.

She moaned, holding perfectly still for him, her head held up, alert.

"Who does this little bottom belong to?" he asked sliding his thumb into the second knuckle.

"You, sir," she yelped. "Ahhh..."

"Pleasure or pain, Daisy? Which do you prefer?" he asked as he pumped his thumb in and out of her hot orifice.

"Pleasure, sir," she said. "Oh, please..."

He made circles with his thumb inside her arse, widening and stretching her tight hole to accommodate him.

"Oh, please," she repeated, her voice rising in pitch.

He could wait no longer. Keeping his thumb embedded in her arse, he lifted her to her feet. "Back over the stack of blankets," he directed.

She did not move, probably confused about how to do so with his thumb still intruding. He shoved his thumb deeper, using it to propel her forward.

She gasped, taking tiny, tight steps to the bed and stopping when she reached the side of it.

"Up," he commanded, swinging his other hand to catch the back of her thigh.

She yelped and climbed up on the bed, crawling slowly forward to drape herself over the blankets.

"Good girl," he praised, sliding his thumb out.

He washed his hands and scooped more butterfat from the dish, applying it liberally to his straining cock.

He crawled over her. "Naughty wives take it in their bottom holes," he said, pressing the head of his cock against her tiny entrance. "Be a good girl and let me in or I'll have to give you another spanking."

"No," she whimpered.

The lubrication and stretching worked their magic and her tight hole opened, allowing him to slowly push forward. He entered little by little, stopping and giving her time to adjust and watching closely for any panic or trauma on her part. "Reach down between your legs and touch your quim, Daisy."

She obeyed, lifting her hips just enough to slip her hand down.

"I want you to tell me what it feels like." When she didn't answer, he prompted, "Tell me, Daisy."

"It's wet," she whispered.

"Mmm, that's just how it should be. What else do you feel?"

"It's slippery."

"I want you to stroke it, Daisy," he said. "Find the places where it feels the best."

He gave her a few moments to begin, then started to move in and out, gliding easily with the help of the butterfat.

Daisy moaned.

"Did you find a good place?"

"No... yes... I don't know," she said, her voice stretched thin by a wail.

"Give me your bottom, Daisy," he growled. "You've been a bad girl. Show me how sorry you are."

"Yes," she cried. "I've been a bad girl. Take my bottom. I'm sorry!"

It took all his effort to hold back and not plunge into her with his full force. Her acceptance of his dominance fed his passion until he could no longer take it.

"Bad, bad girl," he scolded, pumping his cock into her arse as his seed surged down his shaft. He spent inside her, then eased out and pulled her to her side, nested against him. He kissed her hair and snuggled her. "Good girl, Daisy. You did so well. I'm so proud of you."

She held the hand he'd wrapped around her and kissed it.

CHAPTER SEVEN

With her husband's permission, Daisy went out to check her traps the following week. She hadn't thought he would allow her to go alone, but it seemed he trusted her not to leave and to be able to take care of herself, so long as the weather was not threatening.

Barrett had been touchingly sweet with her ever since the whipping. He had not pressed the issue of their consummation, seeming to accept what she had given him as enough for the moment. She still didn't know what to think of it all. The way he'd taken her had been intense—both discomfort and pleasure all tied up together. She'd been caught up in giving herself to Barrett—pleasing him, and she'd never once been afraid or reminded of her first, terrible loss of innocence. Mayhap he was right; it could be different with him.

She'd been willing to try, but he hadn't pressed the issue, and she had no intention of initiating it herself.

She found one rabbit in her traps and she carried it back. As she approached the gates, she saw three riders entering. They did not wear the Rothburg tabard and she did not recognize them. When she arrived, the three newcomers were walking from the stables. She stopped cold, her heart leaping to her throat and choking her.

Wolfhart. She would recognize that evil rat anywhere. As if she were still that ten-year-old child screaming beneath him, terror flooded every part of her being, leaving her frozen to the ground, staring.

He sauntered up. "Greetings, lady," he said, looking amused at her gaping interest in them.

He didn't remember her. Of course he didn't. He'd probably raped hundreds of women and children.

She forced herself to curtsy, bowing her head as they passed. She stared at their backs, her eyes narrowed, fear morphing to pure hatred. She would make him pay for her sisters' deaths. She would make him pay dearly.

She picked up her skirts and raced up to the solarium to think and make a plan. She considered telling Barrett. He might love her enough to avenge her sisters. But to ask someone else to murder in cold blood, to damn his soul along with hers, wouldn't be right. No, if she wanted Wolfhart dead, she'd have to do it herself.

She searched Barrett's things for a dagger or other suitable weapon, but found nothing. She'd have to take one from the armory, or else steal a kitchen knife. And she would need to get Wolfhart alone—she might be able to kill him, but she certainly couldn't kill all three of the men. How would she lure him away?

The only thought that occurred to her made her sick.

But she had no other choice. Squaring her shoulders and steeling her nerves, she went back downstairs to search the armory for a dagger. She found a small one that would require quite a bit of sharpening, but it would do. She stuck it in her boot, then went to the chapel and knelt before the altar.

Dear God, forgive me for what I am going to do.

God would not forgive. She imagined her soul literally tearing away from her body as she contemplated her actions. The blackness inside her was as horrible as it had been the day her sisters died, as if the eight years in between had never happened.

She sniffed, realizing tears were streaming down her face.

"Bless you, my child. Do you wish to confess?"

She jumped, tweaking her neck as she whipped her head around to see Father Albert, the elderly priest, standing behind her.

She tried to say "No, thank you," but instead she just began to sob.

The priest pulled up a chair beside her, handing her a handkerchief and looking kindly, but unruffled by her tears, as if he was accustomed to administering to such hysterics. He made the sign of the cross over her. "God hears your prayers, Lady Daisy."

She tried to speak, but only hiccupping came out.

"Tell me your troubles, child," the priest said gently.

"My two sisters were raped and killed by a man here at this castle," she said, her words barely intelligible between sniffles and chokes. "He took my innocence. And I mean to exact revenge."

The priest said nothing for a long time. Then, at last, he asked, "If your mind is made up, why do you cry?"

She drew in fluttering breaths, trying to regain control of her emotions. "Because my soul will be forever lost," she said.

He nodded. "Yes, my child. Our lord has decreed, *thou shalt not kill,* and yet you intend to take justice into your own hands. Do you not trust God will mete out the justice this man deserves? Or could you not bring your case to Prince Erik, or to your husband and ask for justice to be served here on Earth?"

"Why is their justice different than mine?"

The priest considered. "It would be fair and impartial."

She shook her head. "I will not ask anyone else to kill for me. I would not wish their souls to be damned along with mine, which still would bear the stains of blood."

The priest bowed his head. "I beg you to reconsider, child. Do not act in hatred or haste. Love thy enemy, find forgiveness, and pray to God for the justice that is richly deserved."

She knew he was right, but her mind was made up. She stood up on wobbly legs and curtsied. "I thank you for your counsel, father," she said, her chest as hard as stone. "But I must do this. Please pray for my soul."

She returned to her chamber with a whetstone to sharpen the dagger.

• • • • • • •

Barrett walked back to the castle after checking on the rebuilding of the wall. Daisy had acted strange at the midday meal. Her eyes had been red, as if she'd been crying, but she denied it, redirecting the conversation every time he pressed her. He'd get to the bottom of it later. He didn't intend to let her keep secrets from him, especially if something was bothering her.

As he entered the castle, he caught sight of his wife in the armory and he froze. Something immediately struck him as odd. She was speaking with Wolfhart, the mercenary knight who had shown up earlier that day, and her tone seemed secretive, almost... seductive.

"I might be able to sneak away after supper," she said, her voice pitched low. "I will meet you here, if I can."

Ice cold washed through him. His feet froze to their spot as he gaped in disbelief. Daisy, unfaithful? Impossible. She did not like men. Or sex. Nausea nearly made him retch. Mayhap she did, just not with him.

He turned, just as she looked over and caught his gaze. He closed his eyes to block her out, stumbling forward, finding his way up the steps to the solarium. The soft patter of her feet running behind him barely registered above the rushing sound in his ears.

He drew in deep breaths to calm himself. What a fool he had been. He thought she just needed taming. Here he had been forcing himself on a woman who found him repulsive. A damn fool.

"Barrett." She caught his arm when he reached the door.

He pushed forward, resisting the urge to fling her off. He tried to shut the door in her face, but she flung herself forward. He closed his eyes and turned away.

"Barrett—"

"I don't want to hear it," he said dully, keeping his back to her. He picked up her harp and her few items of clothing and strode to the door, placing them outside it. "I will not keep an unwilling woman. Our marriage is not consummated; you are free to go."

"No," she cried. "You've misunderstood. I am not unwilling."

"I thought you did not like men. But now I see it is only me you do not care for."

"That is not true!" Tears streamed down her lovely face. "I cannot explain now, but I hope that by tomorrow you will understand that I only ever cared for you."

He looked away, disgusted. "Get out," he said. "You are no wife of mine."

Weeping, Daisy left the room, closing the door softly behind her.

He picked up the ewer and smashed it against the wall, shattering the crockery into dozens of pieces.

• • • • • • •

Daisy left her harp and things and ran down the steps, her vision blurred with tears. What had she done? If she lived past this night, her life would mean nothing. She had just ended her marriage, the only good thing that had happened in her life, in favor of revenge.

Would it be worth it? Would her sisters thank her for their justice?

She ran out of the castle and through the bailey, straight through the gates. She wore no cloak, and the wind whipped at her face with a satisfying bite. She ran into the forest, not stopping until her side contracted and she doubled over to catch her breath.

She should just keep walking. Walk until she froze to death. At least that way, she would die with a clean soul and spare Barrett the pain of ever seeing her again. But no, better to die avenging her sisters. Otherwise Barrett would never know why she'd betrayed him. The priest would tell him when it was all over.

She didn't even dare think of the possibility of exacting revenge and living. How could she go on with a blackened soul? Nor did she dare think about what would become of her if Barrett never believed she loved him. She walked until her hands and feet were numb and her teeth chattered.

No. The priest had been right. Justice was best served by God, not her. And she refused to die without making sure Sir Barrett knew what he meant to her. She turned back. She needed to find the old priest again, to confess it all. He'd spoken wisely; he would know what she should do.

Darkness had fallen by the time she returned. She walked through the bailey, straight to the chapel, skipping supper. The old priest was not there, but the hearth was still warm and she sat beside it until the feeling returned to her hands and feet like shards of glass piercing her skin. Her stomach growled but she ignored it.

An odd sense of peace came over her after the emotional tumult of the day. She would not commit murder. Somehow she would get Sir Barrett to forgive her. It was not too late to put her world to rights again.

She heard the sound of the door open and her spirits lifted. The old priest would advise her.

"There you are, woman," a deep voice said. The terrible deep voice that had haunted her nightmares.

She jumped to her feet in dismay. "Sir Wolfhart. Forgive me. I've had a change of heart," she said, her blood racing through her veins. "I cannot keep my tryst with you."

He walked forward, a terrifying leer on his face. "Of course you can. You are here, I am here." He reached out and grabbed her head, bringing his mouth down on hers and forcing his tongue in her mouth as she screamed.

She fought him, but he knocked her down to the floor with the back of his hand across her face. Pain exploded in her cheek and her vision went black. When it cleared, Wolfhart had straddled her thrashing hips and was ripping her bodice open to expose her breasts.

"No," she screamed, shoving uselessly at his chest. Remembering the knife, she bent her leg up to grasp the dagger from her boot, but her fingers did not quite reach.

He pulled his manhood out from his leggings and she screamed as loud as her voice would screech. Wolfhart struck her across the mouth, splitting her lip.

"What's going on here?" The voice of the old priest reached her ears. "Get off her."

"Get out of here, old man," Wolfhart snarled. "Adam! Siman!"

Her relief at Father Albert's arrival turned to dread when she realized Wolfhart had just called in his two henchmen, who would surely kill the old man if he interfered. She fought even harder as she heard the two men enter.

The clang of the church bell split the air. The resourceful priest must be pulling the cord to alert the castle. She prayed they would not kill him for it.

She contorted, twisted her hips to the side and stretching her fingers toward her boot. If only she could reach the dagger...

Wolfhart yanked her skirts up, tearing the fabric in his haste.

No. She would not allow him to rape her a second time. She would die first. She screamed again, the furious cry going on and on until his fingers closed around her throat, cutting off her air. The sound of men's shouts and the clash of steel came from the doorway. Still strangled for breath, she caught the handle of her dagger as her vision began to grow dim.

She lifted the dagger, but before she could bring her hand down, Wolfhart flew off her as someone attacked him.

Sir Barrett.

Stars danced before her eyes as she struggled for breath. Blood filled her mouth and her head swam. She curled up on her side and saw Sir Barrett fighting with both Wolfhart and one of his men. The other lay dead in the doorway. She tried to stand up, but could not catch her breath or strength.

Prince Erik and other knights had arrived, but Sir Barrett did not seem to need any help. His sword flashed out, first to the right and then the left as he went after both men at once. He moved his huge frame with great speed, shifting and swinging, somehow herding his two foes together, backing them against the wall. He ducked as Wolfhart's sword swung for his neck and lunged forward. His sword stabbed through Wolfhart's chest, withdrew it and beheaded the other man in less than a breath's time.

She opened her mouth to scream again, but only a croak came out. The bodies of Wolfhart and his man had hardly fallen when Barrett appeared at her side, scooping her into his arms and cradling her against his chest.

Tears stung her eyes at the evidence that he still cared.

"You see, Lady Daisy," the priest proclaimed, loud enough for all to hear. "God delivered justice for your sisters' deaths, without any blood upon your hands, or the hands of your husband, who acted in self-defense."

Barrett turned his eyes on her in surprise, but said nothing, stepping over the bodies to carry her past the prince, Penrod, and all the others, straight upstairs to his chamber. Her things still sat outside the door, a reminder of their horrible quarrel. He pushed through the door and laid her gently on the bed as if she were made of glass and might break.

"Barrett—"

"Shh," he hushed, soaking a piece of linen in the washbasin and coming to her side. He dabbed at her split and swollen lip, cleaning the blood from her face. She searched his expression, but he showed no indication of his feelings. Did he understand now that she had been seeking vengeance, not sex? Had he forgiven her?

She caught his hand and pulled it to her lips. "Make me yours," she croaked. "Please. I need you. Please take me."

Still, his face showed nothing. He blinked down at her for a long time, unmoving. Then he slowly began to remove his clothing.

She pushed up on her elbows, tugging her torn dress down. Sir Barrett helped her when she reached her waist, pulling as she lifted her hips, his dark eyes locked on hers. She shivered and he froze.

"You don't have to do this," he said, the first time he'd spoken to her since their terrible ending that afternoon.

"I need you. Inside me. Please, Bear."

He studied her, then nodded and returned to removing his clothing. He shucked his tunic and undershirt, the bulging muscles of his chest rippling with his movements.

She swallowed, remembering the swiftness and power in those muscles—the way he had just defeated three men at once to rescue her. She started to flinch reflexively when he removed his leggings, but made herself look upon his manhood. Barrett would never force her, never harm her with it.

He crawled over her and she lay back, trembling. He nudged her thighs open and settled between them, his stiffened shaft prodding her sex. He cradled her head in his hands and gazed down. For the first time, she saw emotion on his face—pain. He stroked the hair back from her face and lightly brushed her throbbing cheek, his expression darkening.

"Please, Barrett," she begged, trying to distract him from her bruises.

He lowered his head to one of her breasts, sucking the nipple into his mouth until she felt an answering tug between her legs. He flicked the other nipple, making her gasp. He kissed down her stomach and bent her knees up toward her shoulders, spreading and lifting her sex. Lowering his head, he licked into it, running the tip of his tongue along her folds, then swirling it over the most sensitive place. She grasped his head, trying not to kick him as he sent shocking sensations rippling down her legs. He licked until she moaned and whined and then he withdrew and lifted both ankles in the air.

·······

The position raised Daisy's bottom and pushed her delicate quim forward and open. Barrett raised his hand and brought it down, right across the middle, catching both cheeks and her sweet little sex.

"Oh!" she cried, squeezing her cheeks together and lifting her bottom higher.

He began to spank in earnest, striking every area of her exposed bottom, thighs, and sex with each well-aimed slap.

"I'm sorry, Barrett," Daisy gasped, her little bottom bobbing and dancing under his hand, trying to escape the punishing slaps.

He paused and rubbed her reddened cheeks. "So am I, Daisy," he said gruffly. "I knew you were mine, I should have trusted that."

"So you're not angry?" she asked.

"Oh, I am angry," he said honestly, resuming spanking whilst she gasped and twisted. "I'm angry that you didn't confide in me and let me help you. I'm angry you told Father Albert and not me." He knew that was stupid, but he resented that the old priest had been privy to her dilemma while he had been in the dark. He stopped spanking. "And I'd like to kill that monster all over again now that I understand what he did to you and your sisters."

"Barrett..." she whispered, her eyes pleading.

He parted her legs, wrapped them around his waist, and lifted her torso up so he held her like a child, cupping her heated bottom in his hands.

She did not seem to require the comforting he thought she needed. She bit his ear, kissing along his jaw. "Please, Barrett, I need you to make me wholly yours. Punish me as you wish, but please take me tonight."

Dear God. His urge to protect her after what she'd been through warred with answering her needs. If it had been up to him, he would have tucked her in bed and held her all night, leaving discipline and sex for later, when she had recovered. But she seemed to crave this. Maybe they both did.

He lowered her to the floor, turned her to face the bed, and pushed her torso over. "I'm going to spank you, little one." He tucked a pillow under her chest to keep her bruised cheekbone from touching the bed and stroked her back. He drew a breath, remembering the pain of believing she had betrayed him. He picked up his riding crop and tapped her bottom with it. "Never, ever offer yourself to another man, not for any reason," he said gruffly. He did not wait for her to answer before he whipped the crop through the air, catching her smartly across both cheeks.

"Oh," she gasped and stood on her tiptoes, hugging the pillow to her chest. "I won't, Barrett, I promise," she cried when she'd recovered her breath.

"Do not keep secrets from me," he said, swinging the crop again, landing another stripe just below the first one.

"Ah... I won't keep secrets," she said in a strangled voice.

He struck her again, changing up the pattern of speaking before swinging. "You will not endanger yourself or try to protect me." He whipped her two more times. "*I* protect *you*," he said emphatically.

She reached her hand behind her, not to cover, but opening and closing her fingers as if she wanted him to grasp it. The gesture completely broke him. He clasped her little palm, dropping the crop and rubbing her hot arse with his other hand. His fingers strayed between her legs and he found her quim dewy with moisture.

Should he take her from behind? He didn't want to evoke any part of the position she'd just been in with Wolfhart. He nested his hips against hers, his erection sliding between her legs. He shivered at the feel of her nectar when he brushed along her beckoning sex. He squeezed her hand and bent it behind her back, pressing it there as he rubbed the head of his cock at her slick entrance.

She shifted on her feet, but did not move away.

He applied a little more pressure, paying attention for any fear or panic from Daisy. She held perfectly still, seeming to wait. "I'm going to make you mine, Daisy," he said, speaking to distract her from any discomfort. "You've always been mine, but tonight I will be sure you know it with every fiber of your being."

"Yes," she breathed.

He pushed more insistently, advancing an inch, then another. "I will take you in every way possible. I will teach you to find pleasure in every act, every form of lovemaking." He eased all the way into her tight channel and remained there, giving her time to accommodate to his size.

"Barrett," she gasped.

He rubbed her back. "Daisy?"

"I'm all right. Go on. Please."

He chuckled and withdrew an inch, pushing back into her firmly.

"Oh…" she moaned.

"Do you like that, little one? It feels good, doesn't it?"

"Yes, sir," she whimpered. "More."

"More," he repeated, satisfied. He stroked in and out of her, slowly, caressing her quim with his cock, relishing the feel of her hot, wet tissue enveloping him. "You feel so good," he rumbled, beginning to lose his careful control.

"Yes, Barrett, more," she cried.

He picked up speed, pumping in and out of her as her channel grew more and more slick. He released her hand and gripped her elbows to plow in with more power, thrusting up on each in-stroke.

"Yes…" she whispered. "Please.…"

He forgot gentle, thrusting with his full desire, showing her all the passion he'd held back since the day he first took her to his bed. "Daisy, yes," he ground out through clenched teeth, his climax roaring down his cock and exploding into her.

She cried out, her muscles tightening around his manhood as she shuddered and squeezed with her own beautiful release.

He remained inside her, closing his eyes and enjoying every last pulse and twitch. Easing out, he scooped her up into his arms and carried her to the bed, settling with her cradled like a baby in his lap.

"Sweet Daisy," he murmured.

• • • • • • •

Daisy snuggled against her husband's strong body, enveloped in his affection and love. Consummating their marriage had been so much easier than she imagined. She had found only pleasure, no pain; only Barrett, not her demons from the past. She had thought she could never give herself to a man. She had thought she would hate a man who tried to take from her, yet her husband demanded all and she gave it gladly.

She wanted him to take and use every part of her. She wanted to learn to please him. Barrett gave her a sense of security she hadn't had since before her family's death. Like she belonged somewhere, was safe and most important, loved.

"Little wife?" Barrett said, putting a finger under her chin to lift it from his shoulder.

"Yes, sir?"

He smiled, as if he liked the submissiveness of her answer. He studied her face without speaking for a moment. "Would you ever…" he broke off, looking uncertain.

She sat up, giving him her full attention.

"Would you—" He stopped and shook his head. "Daisy, how do you like living here, in this castle?"

She furrowed her brow. "Everyone has been kind to me. Is that what you mean?"

He looked frustrated with himself. "No, what I mean is… do you require a fine castle? Would you ever consider a smaller abode? One that belonged to us?" He looked at her with apprehension, as if he cared very much about her answer.

"I do not require anything but you, Bear," she said softly. "Why? What are you thinking?"

He drew a breath. "I know not if Erik would allow it, but I have enough silver to buy us a plot to build a house and work the land. It wouldn't be Hohenzollern or Rothburg, but it would be our own. I think some of my mercenary soldiers would come with us to work it and we could—"

"Yes," she interrupted. "You were meant to be king of your own castle. I would love to make a home with you."

"It wouldn't be fancy. You might have to…"

"Work?" she asked, smiling. "I don't mind. Would I have any help with the women's work?"

"Yes," he said quickly. "At least, I hope so. I think we could support six or eight servants if we're quite careful."

"And what of Erik? You require his permission?"

He looked troubled. "Aye. I owe him my loyalty. He has given me a place of honor in his life and his castle and I pledged my sword to him as a knight."

"What do you think he'll say?"

He shook his head. "I know not, honestly."

A light knock sounded at the door. "Bear?"

She yanked the covers over her naked body. "Who is it?" she whispered.

Barrett looked taken off-guard. "My brother," he murmured.

"Ask him now," she urged in a low voice.

Barrett gave her an uncertain look, then leaped out of the bed and pulled on his hose and undershirt. "One moment, brother," he called out, tossing her a chemise. "Stay there, under the covers," he murmured, helping her into the shift and tucking the blankets around where she lay propped up in bed. He opened the door and stepped back to allow the prince to enter. Penrod scurried in behind him and built up the fire.

"How is she?" Erik asked in a concerned tone.

"Bruised, but safe, thank God," Barrett said, pulling a chair to the side of the bed and offering it to the prince. He sat on the bed, stroking her leg over the blankets.

"Daisy, I do not mean to bother you if you are unwell," the prince said kindly. "But I want to be sure I understand what happened this night."

She nodded, drawing a breath. "Of course, my lord."

"Can you tell me now, or do you wish to wait until the morrow?"

She plucked at her fingers, her heart beginning to pick up speed. Would the prince judge her responsible for the men's deaths? She had intended their murder, after all.

Barrett must have seen her trepidation because he leaned forward and stroked her arm. "Do not be afraid of my brother. He is a fair and just ruler."

She nodded, her gut twisting in knots. Slowly, she recounted her tale, which Barrett had not yet heard from beginning to end. She told them of her sisters' deaths and her rape and escape to Hohenzollern. She admitted her plan to kill Wolfhart. Tears began to spill down her face. "I had changed my mind, I swear it. Please believe me. Father Albert had counseled me not to take matters into my own hands and I meant to heed his advice. I had gone to the chapel to speak with him again."

"I believe you," Erik said simply.

Barrett squeezed her fingers.

"And then, you must know the rest. Wolfhart found me in the chapel and tried to force himself upon me. When Father Albert tried to stop him, his men drew their weapons on him. And then Barrett came and ended it all."

Erik nodded. "Yes, that is exactly how Father Albert told it as well, Daisy. Thank you for telling me in your own words. It seems a simple story: Wolfhart and his men tried to avail themselves of our women and were killed for it." He started to stand, but Barrett stopped him with a hand on his arm.

"Brother," Barrett said, clearing his throat. He glanced at her, as if for support, and she gave him a little nod of encouragement.

Erik searched his half-brother's face when Barrett hesitated.

"I wish to buy a plot of my own," Bear said in a rush.

Erik said nothing for a long moment and she held her breath, waiting. "I will be sorry to lose you," he said at last.

Barrett exhaled. "You will allow it?"

Erik gave a half-smile. "You are a free man. I doubt I or anyone else could stop you from doing something you wished to do." He sighed. "I guess I always knew this day would come." He looked at Daisy and smiled. "I didn't guess you would leave me for a woman, though. I thought someone would make you a better offer, or you would stay in one of the castles you sacked with your mercenaries."

Barrett squeezed her hand. "Daisy was my missing half," he said, making her heart trill.

"Have you a plot in mind to purchase?"

Barrett shook his head. "Not yet. Mayhap they'll sell off part of Hohenzollern's holdings and I could build a structure."

"If you're going to build a house, would you consider the north fields of

Rothburg? There's eighty acres—that should be enough. Then you'd be close enough so we could call on each other to defend any attacks."

Barrett looked elated. "Are you sure you can part with that much, brother? If so, I would gladly buy it from you. How much do you ask?"

Erik rubbed his stubbled face. "Consider it my wedding gift." He smiled. "It's my way of keeping you close."

Barrett's face reddened with emotion and he stood from the bed, clasping forearms with Erik, who also stood. "Thank you, brother. You honor me," he said, bowing his head.

EPILOGUE

Daisy giggled and dashed ahead of her husband who thundered down the hall of their new home behind her.

Barrett caught her, as she knew he would, coming up underneath her and scooping her high into the air.

She shrieked like a child with fearful delight as he carried her, running, to their chamber.

"I told you to rest after dinner, did I not?" he demanded when they arrived inside.

"Aye, and I told you the garden should be weeded while the soil was still wet—ack!" She squealed as his huge palm landed on her backside.

"Little wife, when I give you a direction, I expect you to obey. And when you do not, you know perfectly well there are consequences."

"I should think if you are so worried about my condition, you would not think of spanking me," she said, placing her hands on her hips and attempting to look offended.

He swatted her again. "I'm not thinking of spanking you, I am spanking you," he said, wrapping a strong arm around her waist and bending her forward while he landed several hard slaps to her backside. "Lift your skirts, little girl, and stand in the corner."

She giggled, far more excited by his dominance than afraid. She loved to bait her bear, and gain some precious time alone with him, where she had his undivided attention. She stood in the corner, lifting her skirts above her waist.

"Hmm, which implement should I choose for a naughty wife?" Barrett said.

She peeked over her shoulder to see him standing in front of the box where he kept the little wooden paddle he'd made her, the strop—an old belt he'd shorted and split down the middle—the riding crop, and a wooden spoon from the kitchen. He picked up the strop. She ducked her head before he turned and caught her peeking.

"Come here, my naughty little wife," Barrett said.

She turned to find him sitting on the bed, the strop in his hand. Despite the fact that she goaded him into this spanking, her stomach still did a somersault at the sight of him. In the two years since they'd married, she'd had every form of punishment out of him. Most were like this—he meant them, but his mood was light and they always included lovemaking.

A few times he'd been genuinely annoyed or angry with her. Those spankings were terrible. It wasn't about how long or hard he spanked, but about her state of mind during the punishment. She would inevitably end up crying, sometimes even before he'd started. Barrett would make sure she did not sit comfortably for the next two days, then hold her and speak gentle reassurances until she knew he had forgiven her.

She stood in front of her husband now, her legs beginning to shake.

"Ah, now she takes me seriously," Barrett said with a smirk. He tugged on her dress, which she still held up to her waist. "Take this off. I want you naked before me."

She pulled off her dress and chemise and covered her belly with her palms. Her waist had only just begun to expand—it hardly showed in her clothes, but naked, the new shape stood out.

Barrett's face went soft when he gazed at her. He pulled her between his knees and stroked her hips, bottom, and thighs. "How do you feel, really?" he asked, peering up at her face with concern. He'd been monitoring her like a hawk since the first day her courses were late. That day he'd forbidden her to return to her work in the garden, insisting she rest, instead. She had waited until he'd left and returned to her work, anyway.

"I am a little tired," she admitted.

"You need more sleep. And more rest. I appreciate your willingness to work so hard, but when I give an order to rest, I expect it to be obeyed."

She wrapped her hands around his face and leaned down to kiss his head. "I love you," she said softly.

He caught her hanging breast and squeezed it. "Over my knee, you naughty girl. I'm going to whip you and then I'm going to punish your bottom hole."

She shivered with the combination of fear and excitement. She bent over his leg, resting her torso on the bed beside him.

He brought his hand crashing down on her upturned bottom in swift, firm strokes, warming her flesh and sending sparks of desire off in her core. "Naughty, naughty girl," he said, continuing his steady beat.

As if preparing for her its own punishment, she felt each spank in her bottom hole, the jiggling and jolts going straight to her most vulnerable orifice. By the time he paused and rubbed her heated flesh, she was panting.

"Who is the master of this house?" Barrett demanded.

"You are," she said, her words sounding muffled in the bedcovers.

"That's right. So who gives the orders?"

"You do," she said, then gasped as the first stripe of the strop licked across her buttocks.

"What happens if my naughty wife doesn't follow my orders?" He brought the strop down a second time.

"She—I—get spanked," she choked out.

"That's right," he said. He struck her again. "And I do enjoy spanking you." He laid a fourth stripe below the first three. "But in this case," he said, slapping the flexible leather across her burning bottom again. "I would have preferred you obey."

"Sorry," she wailed. And she already was. Pregnancy made her more sensitive and the strop hurt much worse than usual.

Barrett never stopped just because she apologized, or when she cried. He had his own criteria for deciding when she'd learned her lesson, and it was always long after she believed she'd reached that point. Indeed, he continued to strop her, tanning her backside with neat rows that ran from the middle of her buttocks to the backs of her thighs.

"Ow, Barrett, please!" she wailed, starting to scramble in panic.

He held her clamped tightly, still administering the leathering. "Who is your master?" he demanded again.

"You are!" she gasped in a rush. "You are my master."

He continued spanking. "When I give you an order, what should you do?"

"Obey it! Obey it. Forgive me, my lord!"

She felt real tears threaten, her emotions always close to the surface since she'd been with child. What had begun as a fun spanking now had her genuinely remorseful.

As if Barrett knew, he stopped spanking and rubbed her tender flesh. "It seems you don't take my discipline seriously," he said.

"I do," she sniffed.

He rubbed her back. "You're a good, sweet wife and I know you'll work hard to please me the next time I give you instructions, won't you, Daisy?"

"Yes, sir."

"Do I need to tell you what will happen to you if you don't rest the next time I tell you to?"

"No," she said. But then curiosity overcame her. "What will happen?"

"I will whip you at that moment. And then I will paddle you before bedtime. How do you think that will feel on an already sore bottom?"

She knew she must be blushing at his suggested punishment.

He rubbed her bottom. "Crawl up and lie on your stomach," he said, his voice sounding rough.

She obeyed, a slow pulse beginning in her sex as she contemplated the next part of her punishment. Her husband arrived above her, naked, and covered her body like a blanket, his warmth cocooning her as he carefully held his weight off her. He kissed her neck and she pressed her bottom back, seeking more than the light touch of his cock between her legs.

He slid into her without requiring his hand to guide him and she groaned at the delicious pleasure. She'd been expecting her bottom hole punishment, so this reward came all the sweeter. He moved in and out, pressing his hips against her tender buttocks, shoving deeper, filling her completely.

She moaned at the exquisite pleasure of it. Her body had seemed ever-ready for sex since she'd been pregnant, and it seemed to be all she thought about. Their kitchen maid had told her if she craved lying with her husband during the pregnancy, it meant she carried a boy. She hoped so—the thought of a miniature Barrett running underfoot brought joy to her heart.

Barrett began to push more insistently, slamming into her on each upstroke.

She spread her legs farther and pushed back at him, her cries growing more excited.

Before either one climaxed, Barrett pulled out.

She groaned.

"Reach back and pull your naughty bottom cheeks open for your back hole punishment," Barrett said.

Moisture seeped from her sex. She obeyed, reaching back to spread her cheeks for his plunder of her most intimate hole.

He rubbed the head of his cock, still slick with her juices, over her tight opening. "Take a deep breath," he commanded.

She inhaled.

"Let it go and open for your master."

She exhaled, willing all the muscles in her bottom to relax and allow his entry.

He pushed in, the head of his cock entering her.

She gasped at the intensity of the stretching, the feeling of fullness. The urgency to climax came immediately, from the very first in-stroke. "Please?" she begged.

"Not yet, naughty girl. I have to punish you thoroughly," he said, though his own need was evident in his voice.

"Oh, please, Barrett," she cried, fisting the covers, clenching her teeth in a silent scream of need.

He pushed in and out, torturing her with terrible desire, until she heard his breath grow ragged.

"Barrett, yes!"

"Good girl," he said, burying his cock deep in her ass two more times before he let loose and came.

The muscles of her sex did not contract as they usually did during climax, but she experienced the after-effects just as if they had, her body turning to jelly, an overwhelming sense of bliss and relaxation pouring through every limb.

"Good girl," Barrett crooned again, nibbling at her ear.

She sighed contentedly as he eased out and wrapped her up in his strong arms. "I love you, husband."

"You are my everything, little Daisy. My entire world. I hope you always know that."

She nuzzled against him, enveloped in his love. "I do, my lord," she murmured, her eyes drifting closed for the nap Barrett had asked her to take that afternoon.

THE END

The Widow Is Mine

ASHE BARKER

CHAPTER ONE

My feet pound the cold flagstones as I dash the length of the deserted great hall. The servants have already fled the palace, at least those who were able to discover a way out, past the besieging forces. Those less fortunate, or less quick off the mark, are milling in the bailey, confused, fearful, desperately seeking solace with loved ones. Such soldiery as remains in the castle linger on the battlements, or are preparing to surrender the besieged keep to the army now surrounding us. I have little time left.

Unseen in the shadows, secreted in the corner of the hall, I listened as my cousin Susanna conferred with Ulrich, the commander of our garrison. All is lost, this great castle is about to fall to the enemy. For all his youthful inexperience Ulrich knew it, Susanna too. And I see no cause to doubt that outcome either.

For the women of a conquered foe, surrender is a disaster. We will be seen as the spoils of war, our bodies, our lives at the mercy of a rampant, hungry, victorious army. Rape is a foregone conclusion, bloodshed and murder likely enough. The fate of children might be less precarious, but only marginally so. The little ones will be unprotected, afraid, and will likely witness atrocities that will scar them for the rest of their lives. I want to spare Sophia that. My dear, adored Sophia.

So I run. I run for my own life and for that of my stepdaughter. With the death of my husband just half a year ago, care of his orphaned daughter was wrested from my hands. Guardianship of the child transferred to the court of Hohenzollern, nominally to my second cousin, Princess Susanna. In truth, Lord Eberhard would have controlled Sophia's fate, but mercifully one small three-year-old female who slipped into the palace nursery never attracted his notice.

Now, if I understood correctly what I overheard, Lord Eberhard is gone. He has disappeared. He fled to save his own hide. Susanna has ordered his execution and I doubt any will weep at his passing, though they have yet to run him to earth.

The Widow Is Mine

I would have loved to continue as Sophia's mama, but as the penniless widow of the count of Chapelle, a childless third wife at that, I lacked any power or influence. I consider myself fortunate to have been invited to join the Hohenzollern court as one of Susanna's ladies as this has meant I could remain close to Sophia. I see my stepdaughter daily, play with her, watch her grow. I had hoped our situation might remain thus throughout her childhood years, and later perhaps, when Sophia has no need of me, I could take the veil. I harbour no desire to marry again. Twice is enough.

But none of that will come to pass. Our world is upturned, our lives forfeit for the self-serving stupidity of Lord Eberhard.

Well, my life is lost, as will be that of Princess Susanna and the rest of the nobility here. But our conquerors will spare the children. Surely, they will not butcher innocent babies. If we are able to get the little ones to sanctuary, to the palace chapel perhaps, they might well be spared.

So I run for the stairs, charging up two flights to reach the nursery where seven frightened little faces await me. Their nurse is huddled in the corner with the two smallest ones; she at least has not deserted her post. Sophia rushes into my arms as I burst through the door.

"Mama, mama. Too much noise. Too loud." She buries her face against my skirts and clings to the woollen fabric.

I crouch to comfort her, my heart twisting in anguish for the terror these little mites are experiencing. The screams from within the castle walls, the shouts of the army outside, the crash of rocks hurled from the enemy trebuchets breaching our outer defences. The din must be truly terrifying. And likely to get worse.

"Hush, sweetheart. You will be safe, I promise." *Please let it be so.* "But we must leave here. We must hurry. Come with me now." I stand and take her small hand in mine. "All of you, follow me. Quickly."

"Where are we taking them, my lady?" The nurse stands, a baby in each arm.

"The chapel. We can seek sanctuary for the children there. Here, give me one of the babies. I'll lead the way, you follow at the rear."

The nurse—her name is Annis perhaps, though I am not certain—wastes no time in further discussion. In moments we have lined up our charges and the frightened children are filing between us as we scuttle along the empty hallways. The sounds of battle from outside are more muted as we pass through the bowels of the fortress, or maybe the fighting has ceased. If so, we only have minutes before the gates are splintered and the opposing forces overrun us. We emerge into the corner of the bailey and run the final few yards to the chapel entrance. I chance a glance sideways at the utter chaos surrounding us. The entire population of Hohenzollern must be gathered here, the scene one of panic and pandemonium. No one pays us any regard as Annis and I herd our small charges into the dark interior of the chapel. I slam the door shut and draw the bar across, then offer up a prayer that the commanders of the imperial army will show mercy to innocent children when the door is eventually breached.

"Where is Edmund?" One of the slightly older boys steps forward, his expression fearful.

Edmund? I gape at him.

"Edmund de Richy, son of the duke of Styria. He is fostered with us." Annis explains, her tone matter of fact.

I applaud this servant's calm in the face of such catastrophe. If we survive this ordeal I shall tell her so and do what I am able to seek her advancement.

"He was unwell and went to use the privy. My lady, if you would wait with the little ones, I will go and seek him." She holds the baby in her arms out to me, clearly intending to return to the nursery.

"No. Annis—is it Annis?" At her quick nod I continue. "You remain with the children. I will go."

Annis is young, no more than seventeen summers. She is pretty, and will offer a tempting sight to the imperial foot soldiers who are probably even now flooding our courtyard. I am but a couple of years older and I have no illusions about my own likely fate. I am a member of the royal household, however lowly my station within it, and I can see no cause for optimism regarding the outcome of this day. I will not survive it. There is no need though for Annis to take further risks with her life. She has proven herself to be a loyal and diligent servant and the children will be as safe with her as it is possible to be. If one of us must return to the castle, it should be me.

I bend to hug Sophia.

"I will return soon, sweetling. Be brave and do as Annis says while I am away. She will take care of you." I kiss my adopted daughter's beloved, tear-stained face, praying it will not be for the last time. But I whisper my sweet lies in the grim knowledge we will probably not see each other again in this life.

• • • • • • •

Back out in the bailey the scene remains one of sheer madness. Servants, guardsmen, peasants from the village who sought safety within the castle walls all now milling together, their desperation etched on their faces. I see many more children. These too could be, should be sheltered within the chapel. Alas, the task is beyond what I can accomplish alone. I grab the elbow of a woman, a capable-looking soul who is at least not beset by weeping. I urge her to collect as many youngsters as she is able and see them safe to the chapel. She seems to understand what I want her to do, and starts shepherding the children together.

I am but halfway across the bailey when the huge oak door to the keep opens. Princess Susanna emerges, flanked by Ulrich on her right and Father David, the castle chaplain on her left. Their faces are grave as they descend the short flight of steps and start to make their way through the milling hordes thronging the yard. They pass close to me, and I reach out to touch my cousin's white gown.

"Your highness, is there anything I can do to help? Anything at all?"

The princess turns to me, her smile sad. She looks defeated.

"Tally, thank you, but no. There is nothing can help us now but the mercy of the imperial commander. I go to plead for it."

My name is Natalia, but my cousin's use of my less formal name, known only to my family, almost breaks my heart. Even now, in the face of certain death, she is kind to me. She was always sweet, gentle, and generous. She has been as much a victim of her incompetent, greedy uncle as the rest of us who are trapped here, and she will pay the greatest price.

"Would you like me to come with you? I could…"

She places her hand on mine and squeezes. "No, cousin. I must do this alone. Enough lives have been lost here, and now I will salvage what I can. Perhaps in the future, if you enter a convent as you have said is your intention, you will pray for me."

I fight back my tears as I reply. "I will pray for you now, princess. For all of us."

Susanna's lips tremble as she gives me one last, sweet smile. I stand, motionless, my vision blurring as my cousin continues on to the outer gate, her escort beside her. The two men help her with the heavy bar, then stand back as she opens the portal and slips outside.

Ulrich and Father David close the gate behind her, and Susanna is gone. I hesitate for a few moments, then my sense of urgency returns. I scramble through the crowded space, rushing to regain the main keep. I retrace my path back to the nursery rooms, but find no sign of the missing heir to the duchy of Styria. Perhaps he has ventured out onto the battlements. It would not surprise me. I do not know this lad, but I am well aware that the misguided and gory enthusiasm of young boys can lead them into dangerous places. My own brothers were always getting into scrapes as we grew up, and their youthful fascination for warfare earned them both early graves.

I exit the castle from one of the upper doors leading directly onto the lofty walkway. Most of the bowmen have abandoned these positions and are occupied at Ulrich's direction attempting to restore some semblance of order in the lower courtyard. From my vantage point up here I see no real evidence of success yet. Neither do I see young Edmund.

Cautious, I make my way along the ramparts, peering through the archers' holes set at regular intervals. From here I can see the massed hordes of the enemy army, my first actual glimpse of them. The troops look rough and cruel, above all bloodthirsty. They may be battle-weary but these troops sense victory, and crave the spoils that go with it. My stomach clenches, my fear almost crippling me. But I have to go on. I have to do what I can, even now, in these final moments.

I reach a slightly more elevated position and stop to survey the scene below me, beyond the castle walls. Princess Susanna is clearly visible in her white gown, her slight form dwarfed by the imposing man towering over her. I recognise him. The mercenary who spoke so directly to the princess when the delegation came here all those months ago. They had been sent by the emperor to deliver his ultimatum. I was newly widowed then, only just arrived at court. I listened, as did we all, as this commander issued his threat. His promise. He has fulfilled it.

I cannot hear what is said between them now, but I watch as the commander steps aside and gestures the princess to pass him. Two of his knights flank her as she does so. She disappears from my sight as the ranks of soldiers close behind her.

The commander makes another gesture, and more knights appear at his side. They confer briefly, then their commander turns and marches after the princess, away from the castle. The knights approach the drawbridge. They are followed by scores of men, all massing at their rear. The procession passes almost beneath me as they advance on the gates.

I know by the sound of chains clanking and metal grating that the gate has been lowered, allowing them to enter unimpeded. I turn to view the scene within the castle walls now. I am mesmerised, frozen in place as I watch our people flee in terror from the advancing army.

A movement catches my eye, in the turret on the opposite corner of the bailey. As I watch, an arrow is loosed from the narrow window to score a direct hit in the breastplate of a burly knight in the melee below. Too little, too late I fear. The knight appears unharmed, but even so by his scowl and angry shout I judge him to be less than best pleased by this assault. He heads for the entrance to the turret and I fear that last, lone archer may not survive this day either.

It's all over. I can do no more. I am sorely tempted to curl up and hide where I am, in the hope that I can remain unnoticed. Even as that forlorn thought flutters through my head, one of the imperial guardsmen looks up and catches sight of me. He grins, a toothless leer, and nudges the ruffian beside him. I back away from the edge as they laugh and point at me. One of them makes an obscene gesture with his hand, confirmation if it were needed of what they plan for me. My courage deserts me; I turn and flee along the battlements.

I reach the first flight of stairs and hesitate. Whether to run down into the mayhem that is unfolding and hope to lose myself there, or seek to scramble back inside the keep and perhaps find a place to hide. That second option evaporates as the door from the castle bursts open and men start to pour through. Cornered, I choose the stairs. Perhaps even now I can elude the worst of this.

The two guardsmen are waiting for me at the bottom. One of them grabs me by the arm and slams me face-first against the hard stone wall.

"I saw 'er first. You can 'ave what's left when I'm done." His companion seems intent upon staking his claim.

"Bollocks. I caught 'er. She's mine an' ye can wait yer turn." A meaty hand seizes the back of my neck, the grip vicious. The soldier squeezes and I go still, rigid with fear.

"Maybe we could fuck 'er together, ye can have the front an' I'll take the back. I like a nice bit of arse."

The two soldiers discuss their vile intentions as though I was unable to hear them, as though I was just a piece of insensible meat. I do not doubt that is all I am to them. My face is flattened against the cold stone but I scream, my throat burning with the effort. My cries for help are drowned in the din all around me. Who would come to my aid in any case? I struggle as best I can but, despite desperation lending me a strength I did not know I possess, I am unable to break free of the vise-like grip on my arm or neck. Fighting by pure instinct alone I use all weapons at my disposal, though they do not amount to much. My feet, my head, my elbows. With an angry growl the ruffian spins me around and I succeed only in earning myself a vicious backhand across my face. I slam into the wall behind me before crumpling to the earth at my feet. I curl into a foetal position, waiting for the inevitable.

"What the fuck is this? Did you not hear your orders regarding the treatment of women in the castle? Mayhap I should have you nailed by your dicks to yonder door. Would that improve your hearing, I wonder?"

The harsh, stern voice rings across the bailey. Maybe rescue is at hand after all, though I don't dare raise my eyes to look. Heavy footfalls draw near, several men by the sound of it. There is shuffling as my assailants seek to back off, to slink away.

"Find some stocks for these vermin. I'll deal with them later." There are sounds of a scuffle, plaintive wailing as the men who would have raped me are dragged away. A few seconds pass, then, "Get up, my lady." The same voice, perhaps a little gentler now but still a tone that resonates with authority.

Even so, I prefer not to obey. I remain where I am.

"Can you hear me? I said, get to your feet. Now."

I shake my head and tighten the grip of my arms around my knees. My protector has done his Christian duty, now surely he'll have other matters to attend to. Surely he'll move on and leave me alone. I open my eyes a crack to behold two solid feet encased in iron-plated boots, topped by muscular legs clad in fine quality leather breeches. I do not raise my eyes any further than his knees.

"My lady, look at me." It seems he is not in any undue hurry to be off. A hand in my hair draws my head back, tipping up my chin. He's not rough exactly, but his touch is firm. I do not resist.

"Open your eyes."

The tone has gentled still further. I begin to think this man may not mean me harm. If he simply intended to claim me for himself by right of rank he would have no need to talk to me, much less to reassure. I hold my breath as I lift my eyelids and look at him.

He is beautiful. Beautiful and terrible at the same time as he looms above me. He is bending at the waist, leaning over me, but his full height must be approaching six feet. Vivid blue eyes meet mine, hold mine. He wears armour, a tunic of chainmail glistening over a stout leather jerkin. His head is bare. His hair is blond, just a shade or two darker than mine, and falls to his shoulders. It is flattened as though he has only recently removed his helmet. His hands are ungloved, I note, and he retains his grip on my hair, whilst his other hand cups my chin. I wince, the bruise from the punch I received still throbbing. His eyes narrow, but I do not think his anger is directed at me. He turns to issue a command to a soldier at his right hand.

"Twenty lashes. Each. Then they will be discharged without pay. See to it."

"At once, your grace." The man scurries away.

Your grace. A duke then. I peer at him but do not recognise the handsome visage before me. I am sure I would have never forgotten if I had encountered him in the past. My first husband was the youngest son of a duke, and my second husband a count. I have moved in reasonably exalted circles but not met this man before.

"Are you able to stand?" That smooth timbre. My stomach clenches, and so does something else, something lower.

I nod, my eyes never leaving his, but when I attempt to get up my legs will not hold me. The duke's arm is suddenly around my waist, lending me the support I need.

"My thanks, sir. I appreciate your assistance. All of it."

"What is your name, madam?"

"I am Lady Natalia de Chapelle, my lord."

He frowns, as though attempting to place me. "That name is familiar to me. You are a member of the royal household?"

"I am, my lord. My husband is—was—the count de Chapelle."

"Yes. And a witless, cowardly buffoon if I recollect correctly. He *was* your husband, did you say?"

"I am a widow, my lord. These last six months."

"My condolences, madam, both on your marriage and on your widowhood. Then you are one of Princess Susanna's ladies, I assume."

"Yes, sir." I regard him, and hope to keep my gaze level. There will be no mercy for the royal household, but perhaps my end will be less cruel that I had feared a few moments ago. This duke is not to be trifled with as my assailants have discovered to their cost, but he has offered me no violence yet, nor even the threat of it, despite bearing little regard for my late husband. A swift and painless death might yet be mine.

"The royal ladies, at least those who are still here, are to assemble by the castle entrance." He turns to another of his guards. "Erik, see to it that Lady de Chapelle reaches there safely if you will, please."

The man nods and steps forward. Acting on instinct, I shrink back against the duke. His arm tightens around me. "You will be safe now, my lady. Go with him."

I turn in my rescuer's arms, and I'm oddly bereft when he releases me. "Sir, may I know your name?"

He executes a stiff, formal bow. "You may. I am Stefan, duke of Richtenholst."

"I am indebted to you, your grace. Please, one last question if I you would permit it?"

He lifts one eyebrow, and waits. I interpret that as his consent to continue.

"Why are the women of the castle to be assembled as you describe?"

Is that a hint of pity I detect in his austere visage? My stomach clenches in apprehension.

"Any of our forces who wish to select a bride from among the unmarried women of Hohenzollern will be permitted to do so. You are there to be inspected. And chosen. I suspect you will not be a widow for much longer, my lady."

I gasp, horror-struck. A humiliating, cruel death is to be avoided, it seems, but the alternative will be little better in my view.

"No! I will not marry again. I refuse to do this. I am to enter the church."

He tilts his head to one side, regards me with something akin to wry amusement. "I suspect not, my lady."

"I have been married twice already. It is enough."

"Twice? You are an experienced woman of the world then, and will be much in demand. Tell me, Lady de Chapelle, how old are you?"

"I am almost a score years, your grace."

"And two weddings to your credit already. Your previous marriages must have been short-lived, my lady. What happened?"

I stiffen, defensive though I know not why I should be. "I was first married at fourteen. My husband was but fifteen. He died of a fever after just half a year. I was next wed at seventeen, but the count was much older than I. He was kind to me even so. He died of a heart seizure and I was very sorry to lose him."

Again that wry smile. "Kind to you? I am glad to hear it, and more than a little surprised. The count must have mellowed in his old age, for he was without doubt a vicious bastard in his youth. And you were the death of him it would appear. An old man with a young and pretty wife—always a fatal combination. Let us hope your next husband is made of sterner stuff." He makes a half turn, as though he does at last consider his business with me to be concluded and he has other weighty matters claiming his attention.

I am baffled by his remarks regarding my husband, but now is not the time to enquire into what past hurts this duke is still harbouring. In desperation I grab his leather-clad arm. "There will be no 'next husband.' I have told you, I will not marry again."

His features harden at my outburst and he glares pointedly at my hand, still clutching his sleeve. "Matters are not yours to control. You will have no choice. Erik…?"

I realise my error immediately. The conqueror will not permit such resistance from the vanquished. But I will beg if I must. "Please, your grace. Please, you do not have to do this. You could let me go. Please."

He regards me for a few moments, his lip quirking in a half-smile, his expression regretful. "I am sorry, Lady Natalia. Your fate is sealed." I have no doubt now. That *is* pity I discern in his features, but it will be of no aid to me.

I watch the duke's retreating back as he strides away across the bailey, stopping once or twice to issue instructions. The imperial soldiers rush to carry out his bidding; clearly he is a man who demands respect, and he gets it. The guard, Erik, takes my elbow and directs me toward the centre of the courtyard where a cluster of our women are already gathered.

I avert my eyes as we pass the stocks where my assailants are shackled, their rough shirts ripped to expose their naked backs. They would have done far worse to me, but still I pity them now.

• • • • • • •

"My lady, you have been injured." Berthe, the young servant who normally takes care of the ladies of the household hustles over to me, ready to dab at my bruised face with her apron. "They are animals. Nothing but pigs, all of them."

"I am fine, Berthe, really. I was attacked, but one of the imperial commanders intervened, and I am here, am I not?" *But for how long?*

A crowd is gathering around us now, all men, all of the opposing army. The menfolk of Hohenzollern are nowhere to be seen, probably imprisoned to keep them out of the way until the castle is sacked and perhaps burned. We are bombarded by a continuous chorus of 'turn around,' 'let's see the goods then,' and, from the more direct, 'show us yer tits, wench.' Some of the women are even complying, posing for the entertainment of our audience. Maybe they hope to secure a more lenient spouse by their cooperation now.

I pull my dark cloak around my shoulders and fix my gaze on the ground before me. I am not unattractive, but no beauty either. Maybe my plain but even features will not be to the taste of these men.

"That one. That one there, in the cloak. She is the high and mighty little bitch who got our Kurt flayed." The voice is whiny and the dialect low German, the speech of the north.

His meaning is clear enough. I shudder and take a step backwards.

"I am in need of a wife. I will have her." The nasal tone is similar to that of my assailant. My heart is thumping as I edge back still further, until I come up against the exterior wall of the keep. It is to no avail. My arm is once more seized in a rough grip and I am dragged forward, out of the dwindling group of unclaimed females. I look up into the features of my latest captor, and can at once see the family resemblance. I last saw the face of his brother, if that is the kinship, as he backhanded me at the foot of the battlements staircase.

"Our Kurt'll get 'is turn on you after all. Ye'll serve all of us, whore."

I shake my head, desperate now. I am beyond pleading, in utter despair. Why did I so fear death if this nightmare is to be the alternative?

"Choose again. This one is not for you." The sweet and blessedly welcome voice of the duke of Richtenholst interrupts my frantic struggles. Will he be able to save me a second time?

"I am not wed, my lord. We was told we could choose any, no matter the rank, as long as we marry 'em." My prospective husband is as eager as was his brother to stake his claim, it seems. I am unable to contain the sob that escapes me.

"Choose another." The duke's tone is low and even, and dripping with authority.

"Nay, my lord. I want this one, no other will do."

"Then you will take no bride this day. Walk away, man. Now, else you will answer to me as your liege lord."

"But, I..."

The duke steps right up to my would-be husband and prises the man's fingers from my arm, one by one. In truth, he meets with little resistance now. When I am free he shoves me behind him, a position I do not mind in the least at this moment. He crosses his arms in front of his chest and regards the waiting soldiers, as though daring any of them to defy him in this. I cannot see his face, but the duke seems calm, confident, though none of his personal guard are within easy reach of us. It seems that his grace's personal authority will carry the day. Oh, God, I do so hope.

"Do I have to make it even plainer for you? You cannot have this lady. The widow is mine."

CHAPTER TWO

I have no notion, not the faintest idea, what possessed me to claim the widowed Lady de Chapelle as my bride. I suspect my household will be equally perplexed since I have made it my business to avoid any contact with the house de Chapelle since the count's disastrous and incompetent warmongering cost the life of my elder brother some twenty years ago now. Frederick was a young knight in the count's service, there to learn the art of warfare though not from one with any serious aptitude for it as far as I am able to discern. I was but a boy when my brother was killed, ambushed by brigands whilst patrolling his lord's estates. Frederick and his two comrades were hopelessly outnumbered that day despite their being men at arms a-plenty drinking ale and enjoying the comforts of their barracks at Chapelle's keep. The count was warned repeatedly that the marauding villains hiding out in the forests surrounding his castle were well-armed and dangerous, but he knew better. He judged them to be nothing more than a rabble of disorganised peasants and refused to dignify the threat they posed by increasing the number of guards patrolling his lands.

They were not the unruly, ineffective mob the count mistook them for. The outlaws were armed, trained, and deadly, as any commander with a grain of sense would have known. Chapelle was an arrogant fool, oblivious to the safety of those who served him, or relied upon him for their protection. He was altogether too fond of ale and wenching too if his reputation was at all deserved, and I have no reason to doubt it. Until now. His widow claims he was kind to her. I suspect the kindest thing he did was to die on her.

Which brings me back to my current situation. I have no need for a wife, nor any desire for one. My needs are met well enough without such recourse. But it seems I am committed now.

Maybe it was the lady's beautiful grey eyes. Or perhaps her hair the exact shade of finest ermine, which has been shaken loose from her coif and now falls in shining waves, framing that heart-shaped face and begging for the twist of a man's fist in those flaxen tresses. Not a classical beauty but without doubt there is something extremely arresting about Lady Natalia. Alluring even.

And there I have it. I want to fuck her. I want to fuck her very much indeed, and it seems marriage will be the price. So be it.

I turn to regard the slight figure, now silent behind me. Her sobs have subsided, but I doubt I have seen the last of her tears. "Remain close, madam. I have other matters to attend to here before I can see you to safety in my tent." I do not wait for the lady's agreement before striding off in the direction of the castle stables. Her obedience is a foregone conclusion.

She has no choice.

The soft tread at my heels confirms that Lady Natalia is obeying my commands. A good start, though I know it will not always be so. Part of me looks forward to her first defiance of my dictates, her first chastisement at my hands. For that is what drew me to her. That flicker of submission in her lovely, frightened eyes as she cowered at my feet, the healthy trepidation even as she began to trust my intentions. A lady should fear her husband, just a little. Just enough.

I am aware of it the moment she breaks into a trot to keep pace with me. I do not slow down. In the stable block I confer briefly with my master of horse who is organising the removal of the bloodstock here. Fine animals all, and they are to be mine in recompense for my support to the imperial cause these recent weeks. In truth, I would have acted without reward. The menace posed by the marauding knights of Hohenzollern needed to be stopped; the people of the Free Cities are entitled to expect protection and they will have it. They do have it now.

The lovely creature hovering at my elbow does not, unless I decide to offer it to her. Which of course I will. She is to be my duchess.

"Sir? My lord?" Lady Natalia's voice trembles, but only slightly. Even so, I realise I must do what I may to reassure her.

"Yes?" My response was curt, more so than I intended. Natalia flinches, and I curse myself. I must do better if I am to gain her willing response.

The lady continues; I cannot fault her courage, nor her tenacity. "Earlier, in the bailey, you mentioned that you recalled my husband. My late husband…"

"Yes." I curse my less than guarded reaction on first hearing the name of Chapelle. I would not have this matter come between us now, though it is inevitable that Lady Natalia should become acquainted with my family history. It is widely enough known that I am a second son, and that I inherited following the death of my brother. The older members of my household staff will recall the circumstances, and make the connection. Better that I deal with it now, probably.

Lady Natalia continues. "You met my husband then? I do not recall that he mentioned you to me."

"I never met the count de Chapelle. I knew of him though."

"You did not like him."

"No, I did not." An understatement if ever I was guilty of making one.

"May I ask why, my lord?"

I draw in a long breath. "You may." I pause, briefly consider gilding the truth somehow to make it less stark. I opt in the end for a more direct approach. "Your husband was responsible for the death of my brother."

Lady Natalia gasps and steps back, her lovely eyes widening. Shock perhaps, and maybe fear too. I find I care for neither very much.

"I... how? I mean, I had no idea..."

"It was a long time ago, my lady. Twenty years. I doubt you were even born then."

"But, what happened?"

I provide a brief account of Chapelle's less than stellar performance as a military commander, doing the best I can not to betray my bitterness by my tone or words. I suspect I do not entirely succeed as Lady Natalia's features have turned from pale to ashen by the time I complete the story.

"You are still angry."

"Of course I am angry. My brother died a senseless death, and your late husband was the cause of it."

"Perhaps he did not know. I am sure he would never..."

"He knew. He was advised of the dangers posed by allowing outlaws to establish a presence on his lands. He just didn't care as long as his own skin was safe. He sent others out to face the perils while he remained secure at home."

The small figure before me stiffens and draws herself up to her full height. Her forehead still barely reaches my shoulder. "You are seeking vengeance then?"

"I am what?"

"You will have your vengeance on my husband then, all these years later, through me. Is that why you have decided to marry me?"

God's precious bones! Where is this coming from? "No, my lady. You can be assured that were I of a mind to seek vengeance upon your incompetent, self-serving fool of a husband I would have directed my attention at him, or at those more directly connected to him. Not at a child bride he merely took to lighten his declining years."

"Then why...?"

"Drop it, my lady. Be assured that I bear you no ill will for your late husband's crimes against my family. He is gone now, and good riddance. Let us not speak of him, nor be reminded of him further. Now, if you will allow me a few minutes, I am almost done here."

I turn from her to complete my inventory of the Hohenzollern horseflesh, relieved to have got this awkward business out of the way.

A few minutes pass in silence, then Lady Natalia speaks again.

"I was wondering, if I may request, sir...?" She pauses, hesitant. I turn from my perusal of a particularly fine filly to bestow on her my undivided attention. I even manage a smile since I feel I owe her that much. It is enough, and she continues.

"Sir, what will become of the children?"

I frown in confusion. This I did not anticipate. "You have children, madam?" It was to be expected, I suppose. Two marriages, after all.

She is quick to dismiss that notion. "No, sir, no I do not. I am referring to the children of the castle. They have sought sanctuary in the chapel."

"Ah, I see. They will be taken to Vienna I expect, with the other prisoners."

"Prisoners! But, my lord, they are only babies..."

"I phrased that badly, my lady. The imperial forces do not make war on infants. Sanctuary will be respected, but the children will in all likelihood be conveyed to Vienna. There they will be cared for in the court of the holy Roman emperor, until other arrangements can be made."

"Arrangements?"

"They will be fostered, or guardians appointed. I am certain you are aware of this process, my lady."

"Yes, but I wanted to know that they will be safe."

"They will. As will you, if you obey me and cause me no trouble." In truth, Lady Natalia does not really strike me as the troublesome kind, but women have surprised me in the past. My late wife offers a prime example. She certainly departed this life with an alacrity I found most startling.

"Why are you so concerned about the welfare of babes when you have no children of your own at risk here? What is your particular interest?"

"None, sir. None at all. I was just—wondering. That is all."

Is it? I suspect that is not all, nowhere near. But I have pressing work to complete if this castle is to be secured, further unnecessary bloodshed averted, and the wealth of Hohenzollern collected and redistributed with some degree of equity.

"Follow me. I will see you safe into our encampment outside the walls."

Again, I do not wait for my bride's acquiescence before striding from the stable.

She follows hard on my heels, clearly anxious not to be left to her own devices once more. This time I moderate my pace. I have made my point.

I am waylaid several times on my way across the courtyard, settling questions, issuing further commands, clarifying matters. On each occasion Lady Natalia halts beside me and remains silent. I find this encouraging.

At last we reach the outer gate and she trails through it in my wake. We attract several enquiring glances from the troops who have not yet entered the castle but chose to remain in camp. None of them sees fit to comment on the lady's presence. Just as well, I am in no mood to issue further reprimands. Though I may make an exception for Lady de Chapelle herself.

I turn to regard her slender form, now several feet to my rear. "Do not drop behind, my lady. I wish to see you safely installed, then I must attend to my other duties. I do not have all day to dally."

"My apologies, sir." She pulls her cloak more tightly across her chest and breaks into a trot to catch up and remain at my side.

At the castle gate we are delayed by a throng of our men, all accompanied by females from among the Hohenzollern household, most of whom are in various states of distress. There is much weeping, and a number of our soldiers are experiencing not inconsiderable difficulty in preventing the women's imminent departure. The ladies are far from happy.

"You, man, what is this? Why are you congregating here?" I tap the soldier closest to me on his shoulder, a gesture that causes him to temporarily divert his concentration from the struggling servant girl in his clutches. She succeeds in landing a well-aimed or perhaps merely lucky foot in his private parts, and he crumples with an anguished groan. Moments later the girl is haring across the bailey.

I'm not sure my response is entirely one of remorse as I bend to aid the man to his feet. He appears less than grateful for my assistance.

"What did you do that for? I 'ad 'er. Fine wench too. Shit! Where did she go?"

"Over there, I think." I indicate a direction opposite to that taken by the fleeing girl. "Now, answer me, man. What's this crowd doing here? Don't you have better things to attend to?"

"It's the priest, my lord. He's doing the marrying at the gates."

"I beg your pardon."

"Gerhard of Bavaria said all the women who were taken from 'ere 'ad to go as wives, so the priest is doing the weddings at the castle gate. There's a queue, my lord. An' I was in it. If you'll excuse me, my lord, I think I'll be needing to round up my bride again."

He's not wrong, so I nod and step back to allow the eager bridegroom passage. He mumbles his thanks as he makes his unsteady way across the courtyard. I silently wish his reluctant bride luck as I ponder the dilemma now facing me. I have no wish to create my new duchess in a botched ceremony on a battlefield, but at the same time it would undermine Gerhard's command if I were to ignore his dictate.

I reach for Lady Natalia's hand and edge the pair of us around the milling crowd in the direction of the drawbridge. As we draw close I can see the priest standing on a mounting block, speaking the necessary words over couple after couple as they pass before him. The ceremonies are brief to the point of almost non-existent, reinforcing my concern that such unions may not be universally recognised. Still, it's the best that can be achieved in the circumstances, and my responsibility is to uphold the practice.

I tug Natalia along until we are standing before the priest. He barely looks at us as he mumbles the words, and makes no attempt at all to elicit my lady's consent. This is probably a wise precaution, given her present aversion to the matrimonial state, but in the longer term will not suffice. I resolve to secure the services of a priest at the earliest opportunity, and one not acting under duress. Mercifully my bride makes offers no argument as the words are recited, and I hustle her away as soon as the ceremony is concluded.

My tent is at the far end of our encampment, close to that of Gerhard and the other commanders. It offers few luxuries, but will afford a degree of privacy. And safety.

As we draw near I spot the hulking figure of Karl, who serves me in an undefined capacity. A member of my personal guard, his duties span those of companion, bodyguard, manservant, and squire. Born of peasant stock, he would not ordinarily hold such a position in my household, but as Karl's services, and his friendship, have become invaluable to me, I allow his status to remain ambiguous. He seems similarly content with his situation.

Karl is crouching before the entrance to my battle tent polishing my helmet. I chose not to wear it to enter the castle, a deliberate display of confidence to reaffirm to the conquered people of Hohenzollern that further resistance will be futile. He straightens, regarding my diminutive companion with a mixture of suspicion and sympathy.

Karl is a hardened warrior. He carried me from a battlefield in Lombardy some ten years ago now. He was just a common foot soldier then, but I rewarded his aid with a position in my personal guard. Since that day he has been at my side during more battles than I care to recall, and is no stranger to the brutality of warfare. He is a ruthless killer when such is required, a fact I have had cause to appreciate on a number of occasions. But he is not cruel, not a vindictive man, and always merciful in victory. He looks from me to my lady's battered face, one eyebrow arched in disapproval.

"Not my doing." I have no notion why I feel inclined to account for myself to Karl, but it is a habit I find difficult to shed. I growl my denial as I gesture Lady Natalia to precede me into the tent.

"Right then." Karl follows us inside, hovering by the drawn back entrance flap. "So, are we taking prisoners now, my lord?"

There are occasions when I reconsider the wisdom of permitting Karl such free rein with his opinions, though on balance our arrangement works. I opt for making introductions.

"Karl, may I introduce Lady Natalia de Chapelle, widow of the late count de Chapelle, and the next duchess of Richtenholst."

That expressive eyebrow lifts again, but Karl refrains from making any comment. He will no doubt be stunned at the mention of a new duchess, and he cannot but be aware of the circumstances of my brother's death. Instead he turns to Natalia and bows from the waist. "My lady, it is a great pleasure to make your acquaintance. Would you like to sit down, perhaps? Could we offer you a drink, or some sustenance maybe?"

My bride-to-be opens her mouth to respond but I forestall her. "Natalia, this is Karl, my—servant. He will take care of you while I am away."

She makes no response, merely chews on her lower lip. I accept that most people find Karl an intimidating individual at the first encounter, further reassurance will not go amiss. "You will be perfectly safe with him, my lady."

I hope she is convinced, though her countenance suggests otherwise. Still, I have pressing business to see to back in the Hohenzollern keep. Karl's actions will doubtless speak louder than any words of mine right now, and I have every confidence in him. I turn my attention to my manservant. "Thank you, Karl. I know I can rely on you to see to my lady's comfort. I have matters still requiring my urgent attention within the castle, and I must consult with Gerhard too regarding the transport of prisoners."

I regard the small, cloaked woman standing in the middle of my tent and I cannot help but observe her nervous hand-wringing. "I must leave you for a while, my lady, but Karl will see to your needs."

"Yes, of course, I… Wait, my lord. You said you would be meeting with Gerhard. Is he the commander of the imperial forces? The man who came to Hohenzollern all those months ago?"

"He is. Do you know him, my lady?"

She shakes her head. "No, but I was at court he came to Hohenzollern and, and—threatened to return. Then I saw him talking to my cousin earlier today. I was watching from the battlements when Susanna surrendered the castle."

"I see." In truth, I do not entirely understand this interest in the fortunes of the princess whose dereliction of her duty brought the castle to ruin. I have the impression Lady Natalia has more to say however. I wait.

"What will happen? To Princess Susanna?"

"She will be taken to Vienna, to the court of the holy Roman emperor. There she will stand trial."

"Trial? But why? She has committed no crime."

Lady Natalia appears distressed at the treatment meted out to her kinswoman. I have some sympathy with that as I surmise they may have been close, but I see no merit in encouraging my bride to consider matters to be less serious than they are. I am as certain as I may be of Princess Susanna's eventual fate.

"She had ample opportunity to comply with the commands of the emperor. And she was under no illusions regarding the actions necessary to stave off military enforcement. She chose to defy the emperor, and will now pay the price for that."

"What price? What will happen to her?"

"That will be the emperor's decision, but I think it likely she will pay for her misdeeds with her life."

"No! No, my lord. That cannot happen. It would be unfair, a gross injustice."

Lady Natalia's distress is palpable. If nothing else, Princess Susanna of Hohenzollern inspired great loyalty among her ladies. I fear that loyalty is misplaced for the princess has been sorely derelict in her duties as a monarch.

"I cannot agree, my lady. The injustice has been served on the landholders surrounding Hohenzollern who have suffered the ruination of their property, theft of their crops. The princess brought her fate upon herself."

"No, she did not. It was all Lord Eberhard's doing. He was the one who controlled the knights, whose instructions were obeyed. Susanna had no influence."

"She was the ruler of Hohenzollern. It was her responsibility, hers alone, to curtail the excesses of her knights. She failed to do that."

"Susanna was bullied by Eberhard, intimidated, as we all were. She could not prevent what happened. If anyone should stand trial in Vienna, it is he."

"As indeed he will, when we capture him. But that will not absolve the princess of culpability in this matter."

"No, this cannot be. She…"

I have heard enough. I raise my hand to halt the flow of words. "Princess Susanna's fate is in the hands of the emperor. Her trial will be a fair one, and her fate dignified, as befits her rank."

"But…"

"Enough, my lady. I must leave you now. Please remain here until I return. I bid you a good day, until later."

I make a small bow, nod to Karl, and leave them to become better acquainted.

• • • • • • •

"A bride? I had no notion you were considering remarrying, Stefan." Gerhard makes no attempt to conceal his amusement as he hands me a glass of rich red wine. Gerhard has chosen to receive me not in his own personal tent, but instead in the headquarters tent where battle plans were drawn up in the preceding days. I find this odd, but I say nothing of it to him. "I hear you have selected a lady of some considerable experience. Twice widowed already, I gather. Do you not find this ominous at all?"

News of my hasty marriage has preceded me. My commander was already aware of the broad facts of the matter but now seems intent on gaining the finer details from me. I know that Gerhard is just teasing, but I am in no mood to encourage my commander's banter. I have to hope he will not take it amiss. Gerhard is my friend as well as my commander on this excursion and I would not normally be so taciturn. We have enjoyed many a frank exchange over several mugs of fine ale, but on this occasion I do not feel inclined to explain my sudden decision to claim Lady Natalia as mine—not that I would be able to summon much in the way of convincing explanation.

I settle for something innocuous, hoping to be able to leave it at that. "She seems harmless, and compliant enough. Do you have further instructions for me or is our business here all but concluded?"

My attempt to change the subject fails. Gerhard is not to be distracted.

"You are keen to regain your hearth at Richtenholst? I cannot say I blame you, blessed as you are with a new bride and all. What did you say her name was?"

"I did not. So—are we done here?"

He chooses to ignore my unforthcoming response.

"The widow of the count de Chapelle, I understand—I cannot say I am able to place the lady."

Gerhard is nothing if not persistent. And well-informed. I wonder who has brought him this detailed report of the recent changes to my domestic arrangements. They were certainly quick off the mark.

He continues, his amusement at my discomfiture splitting his face in a wide grin. "Compliant, you say?"

I sigh, resigned to the need to supply at least some details to satisfy my commander's curiosity. I take a deep draught of my wine. "She seems agreeable enough, though I have only just met her. I am confident we will get along well enough together."

"Why marry her though? You know that you did not have to go so far."

"Your edict to the men was clear enough, Gerhard. I well know your preference for leadership by example. And we all bore witness to your promise to the princess. How fares she, anyway?" I seize on this opportunity to change the subject, or at least deflect Gerhard's interest from my own domestic concerns.

His brow furrows. He appears uncomfortable, ill at ease despite our resounding success in seizing this castle. "She does well enough, in the circumstances."

I recall the impassioned pleas of my bride-to-be. However wrong-headed, Natalia is convinced of the princess's innocence. I reflect that there will be few others likely to raise a voice in her defence, and perhaps there may be some room for mitigation.

"Natalia—Lady de Chapelle—is adamant that the princess bears little responsibility for the events here over recent years. She insists that Lord Eberhard is solely to blame, and that Princess Susanna is as much a victim of his tyranny as anyone else."

Gerhard pours himself another glass of wine and stares into its ruby depths before responding. "I find that hard to accept. Don't you?"

I shrug. "Mayhap. The trial should establish the truth of this matter though."

We exchange a glance. I suspect that neither of us can envisage any circumstance in which the princess will escape blame, however sympathetic her accusers. And they will not be sympathetic. Someone will be required to answer for the crimes of Hohenzollern, and as its ruler it will be she. And rightly so. Meanwhile, we have further work to do here.

"I learned, also from Lady Natalia, that the children of the royal household had sought sanctuary in the castle chapel."

"I see. They are still there?"

"No, not any longer. I have taken the liberty of removing them from the chapel and making arrangements for their safe transport to Vienna. I am intending that they join the convoy taking the prisoners to the imperial court."

"Good. The convoy will be well guarded so their safety should be assured." Gerhard smiles, the matter settled. "Now, compliant you say, this Natalia of yours. I hope it is so. She should suit you very well then."

I groan. Despite my best efforts Gerhard was not to be deflected from the object of his interest for long. I need to make myself scarce, or be prepared to satisfy his curiosity. I down the remainder of my wine. "I have every expectation of her complete suitability. Now, if you will excuse me, sir, I will complete my duties. I am hoping to leave for Richtenholst in the morning."

My commander barely has a moment to nod his assent before a commotion in the entrance to the tent arrests our attention. There is a murmur of voices outside, growing louder. Karl enters. He looks uncommonly flustered. My heart sinks.

"Your grace. It is Lady Natalia, she is gone."

CHAPTER THREE

The tent flap drops behind the duke of Richtenholst, leaving me alone with his hulking manservant. Despite his ferocious appearance the man—Karl—does indeed seem gentle enough. And polite. He offers me a bow, then follows his liege from the tent, to return a few minutes later with a tray of food. Simple fare, just bread and cheese, some slices of cooked meat that I identify as rabbit, and a mug of ale. I had not realised I was hungry, would have refused the food had it been offered. But as soon as Karl sets down the tray and retires again to attend to whatever duties are calling him, I help myself to a slice of the cold meat.

It is surprisingly good, and I have soon cleared the contents of the tray. Thus fortified, I begin to take in the details of my surroundings. The tent is rectangular in shape, quite large, and better furnished than I might have expected. Not that I can claim vast experience of the finer details of such accommodations. The first thing that I notice is that it is warm in here, courtesy of a pile of hot stones deposited in a small pit in the centre of the tent. These were replenished by Karl whilst I ate, encouraging me to remove my cloak. There is a bed, ample size for one but perhaps a little small for two. I prefer not to dwell on that detail. There is also the table that bears what is left of my repast, and two chairs, one of which I am presently occupying. A large bowl of clean water has been set on a stool in one corner, and beside it a jug. I assume these to be intended for the duke's ablutions. There is no provision for what I might consider more private functions, but I daresay in the masculine environment of a military camp, such necessities are dealt with as and when they arise. There is a large chest against one of the walls, where I imagine the duke's possessions are held secure.

My own possessions, and those of the rest of my family I do not doubt, are by now in the hands of the soldiers who will have looted the defeated castle.

Exhausted, I lie down on the bed to contemplate my new circumstances, and those of the people close to me.

I fear for Princess Susanna but I know she is beyond my help. I can but hope that the duke will convey the information I supplied to those who are holding her, but I have little optimism on that matter. He did not believe me. He remained convinced of Susanna's culpability, so why would he argue in her defence?

That leaves Sophia, as far as I am aware still safely ensconced in the sanctuary offered by the chapel. Dear lord, I hope it is so. And I thank God that I was able to see her safe there before encountering the duke of Richtenholst. If he had seen her, identified her as the child of his old enemy… There is little in the way of family resemblance that I have ever discerned, but even so. The duke might be inclined to disregard my connection to the count de Chapelle, but he would not ignore Sophia, a direct descendent. He as good as said so. He told me that were he minded to seek revenge, he would direct his vengeance toward those more directly related to the dead count. I cannot but be convinced that his old enemy's only surviving child would be the prime target.

The duke seems to be a man of honour and as such should not harm an innocent child. But these are desperate, violent times, and husband or not I hardly know him. I will not take that risk.

Thank the good lord that Sophia is safe. I have every confidence that Annis will take care of her to the best of her ability, and of the other little ones. Surely the imperial armies will respect their claim to the protection of the church.

But what if they don't? Will Annis be sufficiently assertive to establish their claim? Will she possess the required fortitude? Might she even desert her charges? I doubt that, but once the notion has occurred to me it takes root. My head is soon awhirl with any number of dire possibilities, a host of catastrophic outcomes. The upshot is, Sophia needs me. The children need me, and it is my duty to see to their safety if I am able.

The duke instructed me to stay within his tent. If I knew he planned to return soon I would do so, and rely upon being able to convince him to use his authority to ensure the wellbeing of the children. I can protect Sophia's identity, she could leave with the rest. He was not specific as to his movements, but I had the impression he would be gone for some time. I cannot risk waiting for him, especially as there is no guarantee he will aid me.

That leaves but one course of action for me. I must return to the chapel to help press the claim for safe passage for the little ones. I have no doubt that the duke will find me there and he will be angry at my disobedience, but I might even be able to claim sanctuary myself. So much for his insistence upon becoming my third husband, and for that sham of a marriage ceremony.

I roll from the bed, entertaining the very real hope that I may not be called upon to occupy it again. My aspiration to take the veil and live out my life in quiet seclusion might not after all be a forlorn one. If I can just elude Karl and the other troops surrounding the tent…

I step to the entrance and peep out. Karl is just outside, no more than a few feet from me. He is supervising the labours of a young lad aged perhaps fourteen who is intent upon his task of polishing a pair of stout leather boots. Neither of them looks up. I duck back inside. There will be no escape by that route.

I cross to the opposite side of the tent and drop to my knees. The canvas walls are firmly secured to the hard earth, pegged there by sharp iron stakes that have been driven into the earth, no doubt by the formidable Karl. There is sufficient gap beneath the edge of the canvas to slip my hand under and grasp the nearest stake. I take a firm grip, but cannot shift it so much as an inch.

I sit back on my haunches, disappointed and frustrated, but my determination is undiminished. I *will* be free. I *will* return to see Sophia to safety.

I recollect the remains of my meal, and in particular the small dagger which Karl supplied to enable me to cut up my bread and cheese. I scramble back across the tent and find the implement still on the table, discarded with the now empty trencher. I turn it over in my hand. The knife is far too tiny to be of much use as a weapon, but as a tool it will pass muster. I can carve out a slit in the canvas wall and slip out of the rear of the tent.

Then what? I can't just march through the enemy camp and back across the castle drawbridge. But there may be another way, a way that could work and gain me re-entry to the keep. Several escape tunnels lead from the castle in various directions, and I have a good idea where at least some of these emerge. More or less. It was common knowledge among the ladies of Hohenzollern that one of the tunnels exits into the thickly wooded area about half a mile to the north west of the castle walls and just a few hundred yards from where I now find myself. If I can escape from this tent without drawing any notice, and make my way out of the camp unseen, I will have ample opportunity to seek out the tunnel under cover of the trees. Then it will be a simple matter of making my way back through the underground passageway into the castle. By now all those fleeing will have made their way through. I should have the route to myself.

It will be dark in there, but as far as I am aware there is just one straight tunnel leading to a storeroom under the stables. There is no maze of underground caverns in which to become lost. I *can* do this.

My course decided, I waste no time. The dagger slices through the canvas with ease and I peer out of the hole to survey my escape route. For once this day luck seems to be on my side. The rear of the duke's tent gives on to open countryside. There are no soldiers between me and the stand of trees where the tunnel entrance is concealed. If I remain low, crawling along the ground if necessary, the meadow grass will provide ample cover. I should not be spotted.

But I must move quickly. Karl might return at any moment. My lord the duke could even decide to check up on me, though I doubt he will. He has other priorities. I pull my cloak around me, though in truth it is made of thin weave and offers little additional warmth. I tuck the dagger in a pocket in my cloak, draw in a deep breath, and wriggle through the opening I have fashioned.

Outside, I lie still for a few moments, hardly daring to breathe. I await a shout, the flare of a torch, the pounding of running feet to indicate that I have been spotted. Nothing. Just silence. I lift my head to look around me. One or two soldiers can be seen scurrying about their business within the confines of the camp, but out here, beyond the perimeter, there is no one. Still, I am cautious as I make my way across the meadow behind the tent. I remain on my hands and knees, opting for secrecy at the expense of speed. Even if my escape is discovered—*when* it is discovered—it will be assumed I have fled away from the castle, seeking to put distance between myself and the tender mercies of the imperial forces. That illusion will not last long. I will be discovered with the children in the chapel, but by then my mission will be completed. I will have done all I am able to secure the safety of my adopted daughter.

After that my own fate is less certain, though despite my optimism as I formulated my plans I imagine the most likely outcome will be that the duke will reclaim me as his bride. My freedom will be curtailed thereafter. There will be no subsequent escape for me. Mercifully though the duke has given me no reason to suppose he will harm me. He will be angry, but I think not violent. At least I hope not.

I reach the trees and at last I dare to stand up. I look back across the meadow, regretting the trail of flattened grass I have left, though that could not be helped. A few minutes of helpful rippling by the fresh early December winds will do much to eradicate my tracks. The longer it is before my escape is discovered, the more chance I have of eluding capture for long enough to achieve my aim.

So far so good. I lift up the front of my heavy woollen skirts and head on into the cover of the trees.

The trail I left provides me with the clue I need to help discover the tunnel quickly. The undergrowth in the wood is trampled, the vegetation battered by the pounding of feet as our people made their escape not many hours ago. I find it simple enough to follow the track back to its source, a dark cavern between two upright rocks. There is hardly enough space for one person to push through, and I am astonished that so many have succeeded in making their escape this way. The evidence is clear though in the path worn through the woodland.

I peer into the entrance, and regret the lack of a torch. From just a few feet in I will have to find my way by touch alone. I estimate the length of the tunnel to be maybe half a mile, though of course that assumes a direct route. It will be slow going, in pitch dark, but the task will not improve for waiting. I grit my teeth and squeeze my body between the stones.

Within seconds the darkness is total. It envelops me, oppressive, bleak, and very, very cold. I stretch out my hands beside me and find I can touch the walls on either side, just with the tips of my finger. The tunnel is narrow, and was clearly not designed for the mass exodus it has achieved this day. I shudder as I imagine the claustrophobic effect of this tiny space filled with bodies, people panicking, running for their lives. It would require but one among their number to trip and that unfortunate soul would be crushed by the feet of those behind. At least now there is only me.

I inch forward, my eyes trained on the blackness ahead. Although becoming accustomed to the lack of light I can pick out nothing, not even the vaguest of outlines. I listen too, my ears cocked for any sign of pursuit, or of life ahead of me. I could even now meet with some straggler seeking refuge beyond the castle.

There is nothing. I shuffle onward, cocooned in my own tiny world, a world of silence and absolute darkness. I'm startled when my right hand is suddenly clawing on thin air. I have lost my contact with the tunnel wall and I am grasping at empty space. A side tunnel? Please, God, no. I could so easily become lost in here, never to be found.

I stand still, fighting back panic as I stretch my arms out in all directions. The fingertips of my left hand are still touching the cold, damp earth of the tunnel wall, but there is nothing to my right. I shuffle forward. My right hand straight out in front of me, and soon meet with the clammy wall dead ahead. A bend in the tunnel, then. This implies a greater distance to travel, but is less worrisome than the prospect of negotiating my way, blind, through a network of passages. I will my heart to stop its frantic thumping and turn to face the onward path.

A few yards farther on I encounter another deviation to my route, this time a sharp bend to the left. I make the turn and inch forward. I am horribly conscious of the mass of earth surrounding me, I feel entombed, buried alive. My heart is pounding again, my breath laboured. The air in here is fetid, yet bitterly cold. The surface beneath my feet feels to be on a slight incline and I imagine I could be descending right into the bowels of the earth. I pause, concentrate on drawing in deep, even breaths. I must not lose my composure now, though panic is only just below the surface.

My right foot slips on a wet patch of clay and I almost stumble. There is no way to know where I am putting my feet, so I press on with even more caution. At this rate it will take me hours to reach the castle, but it cannot be helped. To turn back is even more unthinkable.

By now my absence may well have been discovered. Has the duke been informed? Is he even now commanding his men to give chase across the countryside? I have lost track of time, cocooned in this dark and silent catacomb, my only sensation that of intense cold. I cannot even tuck my frozen fingers into the folds of my cloak as I need to extend them to feel my way along the dank walls.

I shiver, gritting my teeth to keep them from chattering, and continue on.

I hear something. A faint scratching, somewhere in the murk ahead of me. Rats? I shudder but press on.

The sound reaches me again, closer, and louder. Heavier. Something a good bit larger than a rat is sharing this tunnel with me. Perhaps some tardy soul is even now making his escape.

"Hello? Is someone there?" I call out into the velvet darkness and wait for the answering voice.

Silence.

I try again. "Is anyone there? Show yourself."

I remain still and quiet, listening intently. I pick up a soft sound, a footfall perhaps, but of one who has no wish to encounter anyone else in this dark domain. My companion is close, very close. I sense him. Moments later, I hear his breathing.

"It is safe, I am not with the imperial forces. Please, show yourself."

I advance another cautious step, and another, my hands searching the gloom in front for something, someone. Anything.

A whisper, the merest breath of air. He is here, beside me, inches away yet still choosing to remain concealed. I turn to my right, still searching. I am seized and hurled bodily against the opposite wall. The breath leaves my lungs in a rush and I gasp, in shock, in terror.

The next moment he is upon me, hauling me to my feet only to plant a vicious blow to my ribs. I am sure my assailant is a male, though his larger, heavier bulk the only evidence I have to go on. I sag against the damp rock at my back, at the same time bringing my knees up in some sort of defence.

The only saving grace is that if I am unable to see him, he cannot see me either and he has now expended his advantage of surprise. I succeed in connecting my kneecap to his groin. He lets out a growl of pain, crumpling to the ground.

"Bitch! Fucking whore."

He is writhing, wriggling at my feet. I can hear him, his fingers are clawing at my ankle, trying to drag me to the ground also.

I cannot see him. But I know that voice.

Eberhard!

"You!" I am beset by an overwhelming fury at this man who has brought such catastrophe on us all and even now skulks in the earth, seeking to escape whilst the rest of us suffer for his actions. I drag my foot free and aim a kick at him, not entirely in self-defence.

"I'll fucking kill you, bitch…" Eberhard continues to grope around my feet, trying to secure a decent hold on me. I have the advantage, at least for now, of being the one standing and I manage to extricate myself from his clutches again. This time I take a precautionary step back, out of his reach.

"Bastard. You ran to save your own miserable hide. The princess has surrendered the castle, and herself, to the emperor's forces while you, you slither in the earth like the worm you are."

I astonish myself at the difference even a day has made to my attitude. I was as intimidated by Lord Eberhard as everyone else, but no more. Now my overriding reaction to him is contempt. Bitter, scathing contempt.

The impact of my lucky blow is fast dissipating. Eberhard is starting to breathe more easily, and it is only a matter of a few moments now before he gets to his feet and is upon me again. I may not be so fortunate in my retaliation next time. I turn and run, hoping I can keep ahead of him. And that I have chosen the correct direction to make my escape, for in truth I have no idea which way I am facing and whether I am now heading for the exit, or deeper into the tunnel. I can but hope Eberhard is equally confused.

After but a few feet I crash headlong into the tunnel wall. I crunch my forehead into the stone, but I am driven by pure terror and ignore my injury. I scramble along the damp rock face, grabbing at any handhold to retain my balance. I offer up prayers that I might elude Eberhard, and so far the lord appears to be on my side.

I pause, listening. I hear his footsteps, but they are faint. And becoming fainter. He is moving in the opposite direction. I must assume that the snivelling coward has opted to save his own skin rather than chase me. I heave a long sigh of relief, convinced that he will not get far. If Eberhard is able to find his way out into the forest he will be surrounded by the imperial armies. I cannot imagine he will elude them for long, and when he is captured, surely then the truth will emerge and Susanna will be released.

I hope so. Oh, I do hope so. Meanwhile, I have my own pressing concerns to attend to. I re-gather my wits, wait a few moments to allow my heartbeat to slow and my breathing to settle, and then I push forward again.

My progress is slower than before because my head is throbbing and my ribs ache where I took the punch from Eberhard. Heavy bruising I expect, if not a cracked rib or two. I lift my fingers to explore the lump on my forehead and they come away sticky with blood. Far from reassuring the children with my presence among them, I am likely to terrify the poor creatures.

Perhaps I should go back, seek out the duke, and beg his mercy. I should tell him of Eberhard's flight. Would that be my most constructive course now?

Contemplating my best options I step forward, onto nothing. I stumble, my knees buckling as I desperately try to keep my footing on the slithery clay. It is to no avail, and I fall headlong to the floor of the tunnel, my right ankle twisting under me. I scream as the wrenching pain shoots up my leg. Shocked and stunned I lie still, willing my heart to steady again, and the agony in my ankle to abate even a little. My heart does eventually oblige me, but my ankle has its own ideas and continues to throb, the pain relentless.

I shuffle around onto my bottom and draw up my knees. I pull my cloak around me in a vain attempt to ward off the piercing chill now working its way through to my very bones. I cannot remain here long, I must keep moving, however slowly. I brace my left leg under me and try to push myself up, leaning against the wall. I succeed, after a fashion, and manage to prop myself against the side of the tunnel. From there my progress is a series of awkward hops, and the outcome is inevitable. It is not many yards farther before I am again rolling on the ground, this time with scraped hands to show for my efforts.

Sobbing now, I manage to get to my feet once more, or should that be foot? My progress is almost imperceptible. I am numb with cold, dizzy now from the blow to my head, near paralysed by fear, virtually immobilised by my injured ankle, and my hands are so cold I cannot feel them, let alone the route forward. I am not going to make it to the castle, and with gnawing dread I face the fact that I am too far into the tunnel to be able to make my own way out again. And even if I could, what then? No one is likely to find me in the woods.

I sink to my knees, defeated. With enormous effort I drag myself against the tunnel wall and there I curl up into a tiny ball. This miserable place will be my grave.

CHAPTER FOUR

"What the fuck do you mean? Gone? How can she be gone? I told you to take care of her." I glare at Karl, unable to comprehend that he has let this happen.

"Aye, my lord. You did. You never told me to guard her though. I didn't think she was a prisoner. In fact, I did ask you…"

"Well, of course she was a fucking prisoner. We just ransacked the bloody castle."

"You introduced her to me as the next duchess of Richtenholst, my lord. I had assumed this to be a station to which she might aspire with a degree of enthusiasm, not one she would flee from at the first opportunity."

I stride past him, enraged yet more by Gerhard's relaxed chuckle at my rear.

"Do not let me detain you, Stefan. I can see you have pressing matters clamouring for your attention. Please offer my compliments to your bride. If you can find her."

I manage—just—to refrain from suggesting my commander commit a most unsavoury act upon his unsuspecting hunting hound. His compliments indeed. I'll offer the lovely Lady Natalia my riding crop against her delicate buttocks when I get my hands on the ungrateful wench.

Karl falls into step beside me. He has no trouble keeping up despite my punishing pace as I stalk back in the direction of my now abandoned tent.

"Are you sure she's gone? Might she just be seeking a private spot to…"

"She is gone, sir. Sliced a hole in the back of the tent and slithered away across the open countryside. I have men following her trail."

I turn to gape at him. "She had a knife?"

"Aye, my lord. I gave it to her. For her food."

"God's bones, give me strength. You armed her? You actually gave her the weapon?"

"As I think I have already mentioned, my lord, you did not make her position in your tent entirely clear to me. I had no reason to mistrust her. And to the best of my knowledge she has not attacked anyone with the implement."

I reply with an inarticulate grunt and head off again to check my tent for myself, though I have no real cause to believe Karl has somehow overlooked the lady. His sanguine reaction to my displeasure does nothing to lighten my mood, not least as the man is right, as he so often is. I have no inclination to acknowledge that truth right now however. Gaining my destination I fling back the tent flap and march in. I glance around, taking in the remains of my lady's meal still strewn across my table top, and the slight indentation on my bed to suggest she may have taken her rest there before embarking on this latest madness.

What was the little fool thinking? That she could trot unhindered around a battlefield? Make her pretty, mincing way among our rough and ready troops and attract no unwelcome attention? Surely today's events would have disabused her of any such notion. I instructed her to remain in my tent because I knew she would be safe there. Surely she understood that, if nothing else.

The fluttering of the loose canvas on the far wall tells its own story, the flap of material showing exactly where my reluctant duchess made her exit.

"I looked in on her. She was lying on the bed, and she appeared to be sleeping. She had eaten the food I brought for her. I had no wish to disturb the lady further so I left her to her rest. I was right outside though and I did not leave. She must have seen me and known she would not be getting past this way." Karl has pursued me inside and is now stationed by the door, his arms folded across his chest. "You should have told me how things stood between you. Had I known, I would have taken better care of our duchess."

Our duchess indeed. I stalk back past my unrepentant servant and pace around the outside of my tent to survey the damage from there. The path taken by Lady Natalia is clearly defined, heading across the meadow toward a small wood. Several of our men can be seen entering the stand of trees in pursuit. I will join them in a moment. First I wish to make a closer inspection of her escape route. The grass is flattened in a solid trail rather than sporting the separate indentations that would be made by a person's feet. I ponder that for a few moments before arriving at the most likely conclusion.

"She crawled through the grass to make sure she was not seen." Crafty little minx. Determined, too. I have much to address with Lady Natalia, when I finally have her back under my protection once more.

Karl nods. "I arrived at the same conclusion. She is on foot so she cannot have got too far. She was fast asleep on your bed less than an hour ago."

"Or pretending to be." I growl my retort.

Karl shrugs. He does not wait for my instruction before starting off in the direction of the trees. He takes a few paces then turns to me, his expression puzzled. "But why would she come in this direction? Why would she not head away from the castle if she was so bent on escape? Surely she did not intend to attempt to hide out in yonder copse."

I believe I can explain that, at least in part. "She's trying to get back into Hohenzollern."

"What? Why would she do that? And how...?"

"I don't know why, but as for the how… There are several underground passages, escape routes leading from the castle in several directions. We've been finding them and blocking them up for most of the day but still a great many of the castle's occupants got away through those catacombs below ground. It's my guess Lady Natalia has some notion of traversing the route in reverse."

"But, how will she find the entrance to one of these tunnels out here?"

"Perhaps she knows where it is. We observed dozens of people streaming from these woods when the castle first fell to us. Our mission was to capture the princess, and as we had her we allowed the rest to flee if they chose to. There must have been an exit somewhere in the trees."

"But, if the tunnels are all blocked now…"

"Exactly. She'll become trapped in there, unless she can find her own way out again." I know my expression is grim as I contemplate the likely outcome if we do not find her soon.

From the expression on his face I can see Karl shares my concern. "I do not imagine she will. It must be pitch black in there. And cold enough to freeze the balls off Lucifer himself."

Quite. I turn to face our camp again and spot a couple of men loitering by a cask of ale. I cup my mouth in my hands intending to shout them over, but settle instead for a piercing whistle. It lacks gravitas, but is more effective. Both leap to startled attention.

"You two. I need torches. Gather as many as you can find and follow me. Be quick about it." I holler my instructions across the intervening distance.

The men rush off to obey my command. At a run now, Karl and I head into the trees.

We find the entrance to the tunnel easily enough, the path to it etched into the earth by the many pairs of feet that have tramped through the wood this day. It is impossible to discern Natalia's specific tracks in the battered, muddy earth, but I'm near enough certain she will have gone that way. Nothing else makes any sense at all.

The entrance is narrow, marked by two upright pillars of roughly hewn stone. Inside it is every bit as dark as Karl suggested, and deathly quiet. No sound of female footsteps, nor even cries for help.

I lean between the stones and call her name. There is no response. Nothing. I try again, louder this time but can still evoke no answering cry. I fall back on my whistle, sure that sound will penetrate through the underground passages. She must have heard that, if she's in there. And she has to be in there. Why does she not answer?

The sound of running feet in the woodland surrounding us announces the arrival of our torches. Karl and I take one apiece, light them, and without further ado squeeze through the portal stones.

The tunnel is only just wide enough for us to walk two abreast. I can manage to stand upright, but Karl is several inches taller than I am so has to stoop. The smoke from our torches creates a choking atmosphere. We will not be able to remain in here for long.

I lead the way, Karl behind me. We make good speed, but we have light. I have to assume Natalia did not. The chill in here is already penetrating my thick leather tunic, and despite the warmth from our torches this place is deathly cold.

Did Natalia possess warm clothing? I have to confess I do not recall, though I doubt it. Had she thought to do so she could have taken a heavy cloak from my chest in the tent, but when I glanced around my quarters nothing seemed to have been disturbed.

Foolish woman. I grit my teeth. There is no point contemplating the many and various means I could employ to teach her the error of her ways until I get my hands on her. And even then…

The passageway bends to the right, narrowing a little now. Then to the left, and drops away in a slight incline. We don't slow down. I'm calling to Natalia, but still no reply. We round a slight curve, and I see her.

A small, still form, huddled in a grey cloak, lies a few feet in front of us. I rush to her, crouch beside the motionless bundle. Karl is close on my heels.

"Is she…?" His normally confident tone has deserted him. He is every bit as worried as I am.

"Alive? Yes, I think so. I bend over, place my cheek close to her mouth and feel the slight riffle of air. "Yes, she's breathing." I reach for her hand, and my heart sinks. "Christ, she's freezing. We need to get her out of here."

Even as I speak I am assessing her ravaged face, the dried blood from a deep scrape on her forehead marring her already bruised complexion. A head injury as well as exposure. *Dear Christ.*

"Give me your torch. I'll lead the way, you carry milady." Karl does tend to forget the chain of command in moments of dire urgency. I see no merit in reminding him at this juncture. I hand him my torch and lift Lady Natalia in my arms.

Karl sets a cracking pace but I have no trouble keeping up. In moments it seems we are at the entrance again. Karl squeezes through the stones first, tosses the torches to the ground, and turns to take Natalia from me. I scramble after them.

Karl sets Natalia down on the rough ground, and I get my first look at her in daylight. She's pale, her skin almost translucent, with an ominous blue tone to her complexion. Her eyelids flutter, she appears to regain consciousness for a few seconds, then drifts off again.

The first order of business is obvious. "We need to get her warmed up." I clutch her to me, wrapping her in my own warm cloak, but I know this won't be nearly enough. "Get back to our camp as quick as you can and get everyone set to boiling water. Find a bathtub—Gerhard has one I believe. I'll bring Lady Natalia. Hurry."

Karl nods, and is gone, sprinting through the trees. I pick up my bride and follow his path at a slightly more sedate pace. By the time I arrive back at my tent Gerhard's personal servant is just leaving.

"The bath, my lord." He gestures behind him.

I spare him a grateful nod as I carry Natalia inside. The tub is set in the middle of my floor and is already steaming. As I stand there, my bride still cradled in my arms, three soldiers enter, each carrying two buckets of hot water. They empty them into the bath and bow to me as they leave.

"We'll need more," I yell at their retreating backs.

"We know that, my lord. More is on the way." Karl has entered the tent, also carrying pails of steaming water. "There's enough here to get started though. Shall I help you to undress her?"

The impropriety of my servant's suggestion is ignored given the dire circumstances in which we find ourselves. Every second may count now. I place Natalia on the bed. "Yes. Could you get her shoes?" Even as I speak I am hauling the useless cloak from her body.

Karl unties her deerskin boots and tugs. Natalia gives a low whimper, as if in pain.

"My lord, look at this." Karl is cradling Natalia's right foot, now bared.

I glance at it, wincing at the purples and blues marring her delicate skin.

"Now we know how she became trapped then. She must not have been able to continue on foot."

Karl murmurs his agreement as between us we turn her over, unlace the back of her woollen gown and drag that off too. Only when we are down to her shift does Karl step back. He bends over the bath and dips his hand in.

"Hot, but not scalding. This should be fine. I will bank up the hot stones, my lord. We need this place to be warm. There will be more hot water when we need it."

I could insist that he leaves, but I will need his further assistance. If Natalia feels I have compromised her modesty she can take that matter up with me later. If she lives. I untie the loose ribbons that fasten her undergarment at the front, then I lift her from the bed to slide it from her shoulders.

Karl's eyes meet mine as we both spot the dark bruise extending from just below her right breast around her ribcage. The lump on her head and sprained ankle I might just believe could have been caused by stumbling through the pitch black tunnels. But this? I no longer believe all Natalia's injuries to be accidental.

There will be questions, lots of them. But first, we need to revive her. I pick up the nude form and with no further ado I place her in the steaming water.

I reach around her to bend her knees in order to ensure that her head is submerged, only her face remaining above the surface of the water. I am aware that heat is lost through the head, so perhaps it can be absorbed that way just as easily. Christ, I hope so.

I position myself at the end of the tub, one hand behind Natalia's neck to support her. With my other hand I start to rub her chilled limbs, attempting to stimulate her circulation. It is not enough.

"Karl, help me. You massage her legs."

He utters not a word as he takes his place at the foot of the tub and lends his efforts to mine.

The water is clear and clean, and does nothing to conceal the slender form of Lady Natalia. I observe that she is quite beautiful. Her body is exquisite, perfect, and achingly delicate. I struggle to detach myself from that fact in the face of more pressing concerns. Naturally, Karl does not comment though his expression indicates he too appreciates my future bride's obvious attractions.

Should I resent this? I cannot find it in me at present. I simply want her to survive and I am glad of my servant's aid.

Long minutes pass, and neither of us speaks. There is nothing to say any more. We continue our ministrations in silence. A couple of times Karl collects additional buckets of water from just outside the tent and pours them into the cooling bath. At last, Natalia's skin begins to pinken, losing that ghastly blue tinge. Her limbs seem less relaxed under my fingers, as though her frozen muscles are once again regaining their function.

She draws in a long, ragged breath. Her eyelids flutter.

"She's coming round." Karl releases his hold on her leg and stands. He grabs her cloak, which we had discarded on my bed, and folds it into a rough wad. "Here. Prop this behind her head."

We arrange the makeshift pillow, and at last I dare to let go of her.

"I will leave a blanket warming by the stove. If you need me I will be just outside." He has reached the door before I find my voice.

"Thank you, Karl."

He nods, and is gone. I am alone with Lady Natalia. And her eyes are open.

I smile at her, cup her face in the palm of my hand. Her expression is confused, though this gives way to fear.

"My lord...?" Her voice is thin, a soft whisper.

"You are safe now. Just relax, and come back to me slowly."

"I... I... Where am I?"

"In my tent. Where I told you to stay, you might recall. I believe my instructions were sufficiently clear."

"I was... It was dark. So cold."

Time enough for remonstrations later. At this moment she needs comfort. "I know, love. But you are safe now. And warm again, yes?"

She nods, her eyelids drooping again. She looks exhausted, but just for a moment. Her eyes are suddenly open again, and this time her expression is one of alarm. And urgency.

"Eberhard. He was there, in the tunnel. I saw him. He, he... attacked me."

This I had not expected. I pause. "Eberhard? Are you certain? It was dark in there, as you say..."

"I knew his voice. It was him. I know it. You must hurry, you might yet apprehend him."

"He is still in there?"

She shakes her head. "No. He ran away. I believe he was making for the forest. He is on foot, you might be able to catch him."

I have no intention of hurrying anywhere this night and will trust others to run the desperate Eberhard to earth. Right now it is time to get my wife out of the bath and tucked up in bed.

I stand and strip off my tunic, glad of Karl's efforts to heat the tent. I pick up the blanket he has spread out close to the stove and lay that on my bed. Then I crouch beside the tub and slide my arms under Natalia's body. I lift her from the water.

She gives a soft mew of protest as the cooler air caresses her body, but is soon content again as I lie her on the warm blanket and wrap her in it.

"What about Lord Eberhard? You should be…"

"I will send Karl to report the sighting to Gerhard. We will have him, fear not, Natalia. For now though, it is enough that I have you still."

Propping myself up in my bed, I lift her swaddled form and position her on my lap, her cheek resting against my chest. Her hair is dripping wet so I reach for another blanket to wrap around her head and thus prevent our good work being undone.

"I am naked." Her voice is still weak, but improving.

I grin down at the top of her head. "Not any more, strictly speaking."

"You undressed me."

"Yes. We needed to get you warmed up, and a hot bath was the best way."

"We?"

"Karl, and me."

"Ah, Karl." She hesitates, then, "I must remember to thank him."

"I already did, but you may talk to him yourself tomorrow."

She says nothing for a few moments, then, "I thought I was going to die."

Me too. I don't share that thought with her. "You did not die though. We followed your tracks and found you in time."

"You came for me." Her statement is delivered in a tone of near wonder.

"Of course. You are mine. I thought I had made that perfectly clear back there in the courtyard at Hohenzollern. I take good care of what is mine." My tone has hardened, deliberately so.

"Sir…?"

Ah, she has picked up on it. Good. We'll be getting to that aspect of things soon enough. But first… "You hurt your ankle? And your head."

"I, yes. Crashed into the rock as I fled from Eberhard. Then I tripped and twisted my ankle. I could not walk."

"I see. Is the ankle still painful?"

She attempts to flex it. Her sharp hiss of pain is my answer.

"You will need to keep your weight off that for a while. You have bruised ribs too."

"Eberhard hit me. He said he would kill me, but I managed to escape."

More than will be said for that bastard when I get my hands on his miserable carcass. "Are you injured in any other way?" *God, please, no more.*

"No, I do not think so. I scraped my hands, but they are not so sore now."

"That is good. Did you lose consciousness when you hit your head?"

"No, I do not think so."

"You were unconscious when we discovered you, so I wondered. Do you feel dizzy, or confused?"

"I am not dizzy, and only confused about why you would go to so much trouble to help me."

"You are my wife. My responsibility."

"But, why would you wish to marry me? I have no dowry, no lands nor fortune. No influence anywhere. I bring you no advantage. I bring nothing at all to this match."

"I have my reasons, and I will share them with you. Soon."

My reasons for claiming her are simple enough. I want to fuck the lady. Now is not the time to say this though. I do however have another related matter to convey to my bride to be.

"I told you to remain here, in my tent. Was anything at all unclear in my instructions to you?"

"I… no, my lord. But…"

"But?"

"But I needed to return to the castle. I had to make sure everyone was safe."

"Everyone? You know where Princess Susanna is. You are aware of the fate of the other women of the castle. You shared that fate. Who else were you concerned about? So concerned you would almost lose your own life for them?"

She is silent, appears to be considering my words. I wait, but nothing further is forthcoming.

"Natalia? You are already in enough trouble. Do not compound your punishment by lying to me now."

This has her attention. "Punishment? What punishment?"

"You disobeyed me. I have yet to hear any reasonable excuse for that. Unless you can come up with some persuasive reason why you found it impossible to remain in the safety of my tent, as instructed, I intend to punish you for your behaviour."

She is gazing up at me, her beautiful eyes widening, darkening to a deep, stormy grey. "What do you intend to do?"

"I will spank you. Hard. This will hurt, Natalia, but I hope it will prove to be the deterrent you so badly need. You are my wife, and I expect your obedience, and your honesty. Do you understand?"

"Yes, my lord. But you have no need to beat me. I am sorry. Truly I am. I will never do anything like that again."

"I hope not, for your sake. And I said I would spank you, not beat you."

"What is the difference?"

"Ah, my lady, there is a difference. In time you will come to appreciate that. For now though, we have business to settle, you and I."

"You intend to spank me now?"

Her voice is breaking. She is afraid. A little fear is healthy, but this is too much. I stroke her back, my palm circling between her shoulder blades as I seek to soothe her.

"No, not now. Now you need to rest. You need to regain your strength, and stay warm. I want you to go to bed, sleep, and perhaps think about what has happened today. Try to reconcile yourself to your new situation if you can. In the morning you will accept your punishment, then we will move on and not speak of this again."

"How will I sleep, knowing... knowing this? If you are going to punish me, please do it now. I want this to be over with."

Ah, my sweet, too easy.

"No. I will decide when you are to receive your punishment. The events of this day have taken their toll, and I will not lay a hand on you tonight."

"But you cannot expect me to..."

I place my finger across her lips. "Hush. I expect you to obey me, and not to argue. So now, if you are quite dry, I would like you to get into bed and wait for me there."

Her expression is shocked. I manage to conceal my grin.

"You intend to sleep with me? In this bed? Tonight?"

"I do. Having gone to all this trouble to combat the effects of your foolhardiness, I intend to make sure you remain warm."

"But, you cannot. It would not be decent."

"It is decent enough. You are my wife, after a fashion. I grant you the ceremony at the castle gates was not entirely satisfactory, not the way I would have chosen to make you my duchess, but it will certainly suffice until I can make a more robust arrangement. We will seek the benefit of a more orthodox ceremony as soon as the opportunity presents itself. For now though, we will both get some sleep. In the morning I will spank you, then we leave for Richtenholst."

I do not wait for her further response. The time has come for acquiescence, not debate. I stand, lifting her to her feet. I deposit her with care, mindful of her injuries. I peel the damp blanket from her, and I am pleased to note that she offers no resistance. Despite the angry bruising to her body and face she is still a lovely woman. I take a moment to admire her nude beauty as she stands before me. Then I draw back the blankets. I pick her up and lay her in the warm cocoon, pulling the covers up to her chin.

I offer her a smile, I hope one offering sufficient reassurance to enable her to at least contemplate slumber. I walk across the tent and lift the flap. Karl is stationed outside.

"Karl, I need you to take a report to Gerhard. Natalia encountered

Eberhard in the tunnels. He attacked her. She believes him to be making his escape through the forest."

"Can we trust her account, my lord?"

A fair question. Until this day Natalia and I were on opposite sides of this conflict.

"You saw her injuries. I am inclined to believe her. And she has already made it plain she harbours no loyalty to Eberhard."

Karl nods. He seems to share my logic in this. "I will seek out Gerhard immediately, your grace."

"Thank you. And please ensure we are not disturbed. Lady Natalia is fatigued and we are retiring for the night."

"Of course, my lord. Please convey my good wishes to milady. I trust she is not too uncomfortable."

"I will. She has been hurt but she will heal. She wants to thank you for your assistance today."

"It was my pleasure, sir. Good night." He saunters off into the gathering dusk, in search of ale and other female company, I daresay. He has earned it.

I return to my bed and gaze down at my bride. She watches me, apprehensive but quiet. I will settle for that. I remove my leather belt and woollen chausses, choosing to ignore Natalia's maidenly gasp as her eyes are drawn to my cock. I have been hard since she regained consciousness, and this state seems set to persist. In time my lady will become better acquainted with just what that means for her. For now, she may look her fill.

I slide under the blanket and lie next to her. The bed is small, she is pressed against me.

"Let me hold you, Natalia."

Again, she hesitates. But then comes obedience as she curls her slim body against mine. I wrap my arms around her, my cock hardening yet more at the feel of her soft breasts pressing against my torso. Tomorrow will prove an interesting day.

"I have you, my lady. Sleep now."

CHAPTER FIVE

I open my eyes, my brow furrowing at the sudden onslaught of bright wintry sunlight. I am momentarily perplexed. Where am I? This is not my chamber at Hohenzollern. This place is too—warm.

The source of heat shifts, and I become aware of the living, breathing *male* presence beside me. The events of yesterday come clamouring back into my mind.

The castle is taken, conquered. The royal family are captured, imprisoned, or have fled. Or, as in my case, been claimed as brides. My husband-to-be is sleeping at my side, his huge, naked form both warm and vibrant, and utterly terrifying.

I am also nude, and as the events of yesterday rush back at me I recall why this is. I attempted to escape, believing I might make my way back into the castle by way of one of the underground passages. I had planned to return to Sophia, to be assured of her safety. Instead, I almost lost my life. I owe my very survival to the duke of Richtenholst, the powerful presence slumbering beside me.

I really should not be snuggled up to him in this manner. Even were we properly wed, it would not be quite seemly. Certainly I never shared a bed nor any other such intimacy in either of my previous marriages.

I shift, intending to ease myself away from his solid body. At my first movement he tightens his arm around me, holding me secure against him.

"Where are you thinking of making off to now, my lady?"

His voice is rich and deep. I sense the vibrations in his chest as he chuckles.

"I was, I mean, I thought… I am sorry, my lord. I did not intend to wake you." I do not usually stammer, but he seems to bring out such nervousness in me I find it hard to string two sensible words together.

"I don't doubt that. But since we are both now awake, shall we get on? We have much to accomplish this day. Starting with your spanking."

I stiffen, press my lips together. I knew, of course I knew this was coming.

I remember full well his words of last night. But I had wondered in some optimistic corner of my brain if he might forget. Or relent. It would seem not.

I am not above begging if that might help my plight. "My lord, please. This is not necessary. I am truly sorry for what I did yesterday and for all the trouble I caused you. Such will never occur again, I swear that."

"It pleases me to hear this. I accept your apology, and your promise."

Thank heaven.

"So now we have only to deal with the matter of your suitable chastisement, then it will be done with."

Oh. Oh, no.

He continues. "Unless of course you remain too fragile following your exertions of yesterday. You took quite a battering. How are your ribs this morning?"

My lord the duke eases himself up into a sitting position, his back propped against the headboard. I peer up at him from my safe haven among the blankets and furs. Despite my dire circumstances, I have to confess he makes a magnificent sight.

I had little opportunity to study his features yesterday, but as I view him now in the clear morning light, I confess the duke is an uncommonly handsome man, though his features possess a certain severity. I suppose that comes with his station, and his profession as a soldier. His dark blond hair reaches his shoulders, and is both thick and wavy. It looks soft too, and I suppress an unaccountable urge to run my fingers through those tawny locks. His eyes are blue, a piercing, deep shade that puts me in mind of the kingfishers that inhabit the banks of the river flowing along the borders of Hohenzollern. His azure gaze is now locked on mine. His lips are full, and they curl in a friendly enough smile. Despite his intent, his demeanour toward me seems pleasant.

His chest is broad, the muscles there clearly defined. They ripple under his tanned skin, reminding me that his power over me is physical as well as legal. If he intends to spank me, he will. His arms are solid, the strength there plain to see. He said he would hurt me. I have no doubt of it.

"My lady, your ribs?"

I draw a deep breath to expand my lungs, and find the effort neither too taxing, nor painful. I test the area of bruising with my fingertips and find it to be tender but not sore. I consider laying claim to a greater fragility than would be accurate, but decide against that. The best I might achieve is a delay, and throughout the period of waiting I would be tense, afraid of what was to come. Better to get this done with now.

Probably.

"I, I am fine, my lord."

"I see. And your head? Any remaining dizziness or headache?"

I shake the head in question. He nods his.

"Your ankle will not be affected by what I intend for you, but I shall ask anyway. Can you stand? Can you walk?"

"I believe I shall be able to do so, my lord. After a fashion."

"That is good. But you are shaking, my lady." He lifts one eyebrow, whilst also reaching to caress my cheek. "You are afraid of your first punishment at my hands, I understand that. Be assured that you will come to no harm from me."

I work to regain some semblance of control, though in truth he is right. Despite my determination to see this matter concluded, I am terrified. I contemplate even now attempting to make a run for it, but the dull throbbing in my ankle convinces me this would be futile. Counter-productive even. I have no wish to provoke him further.

Except that he does not have the appearance of an angry man. He seems calm, amused almost. And in no particular hurry to lay into me.

"If you need a private moment to relieve yourself first, that will be fine with me. Or perhaps you are hungry. Your spanking can wait until you have broken your fast, though I will insist that you remain naked."

At his mention of a private moment my bladder makes its presence felt. I would appreciate that comfort, though I can find no appetite for food.

"Is there a privy I could use?" My voice sounds so small, pitiful even. Can he discern the threat of tears? My pride hopes not.

"Madam, this is a battlefield populated almost entirely by rude foot soldiers. There is no privy. There are however several buckets scattered around the tent from your bath yesterday, and you are free to make use of one of those. I will allow you a few minutes alone."

He throws back the blankets that have been covering his lower body and stands up, his back to me. I am treated to a fine view of his taut buttocks and powerful thighs as he reaches to retrieve his chausses from the floor. He pulls those on and turns to me.

"You have your five minutes. Use them well. And my lady, you are shortly to endure a hard spanking, my hand on your bare bottom. If you so much as think about repeating your escapade of yesterday I will take a switch to your arse. You really do not want that. Not on the first day of your married life." He tips me a polite nod from the doorway, then ducks through the opening to leave me to my toilet.

I stare after him for a few moments, resenting the implied further threats. I have given my word, he had no need to reiterate the details of my predicament. Sulking will avail me nothing however. I shove back the blankets and leap into action. Or rather, I hobble. I extricate myself from the snug furs and perch on the side of the bed shivering. The December morning is chilly, despite the still warm stones making up the stove in the centre of this tent. I wonder, did the duke replenish them during the night? Or perhaps it was his servant, Karl. The servant I know I must face this morning too.

I get to my feet and try an experimental step forward. My ankle throbs, but it is bearable. My ribs trouble me hardly at all. I manage to make my way to the bucket closest to me and use it to do what is necessary. I would take it to empty outside but the duke ordered me to remain unclothed.

I comb my fingers through my hair, but with no looking glass available to me I cannot properly braid it. I draw it back into a loose, rough plait, but by now I feel sure my allotted time must be almost up. Modesty propels me to scramble back into bed and I curl up under the covers to wait.

The duke does not keep me waiting long. He re-enters the tent, halting just inside the doorway to regard me. His features bear an odd expression, somewhere between amusement and regret. But I detect no sign of a reprieve.

"Are you all right, my lady?"

I nod.

"Ready then?"

Again I nod, but not so fast this time. I know this is going to happen. There is no merit in drawing it out. But even so...

The duke strides over to the table and pulls out one of the chairs. He turns it to face the bed and seats himself upon it. His bare torso is glistening, droplets of water clearly visible on his skin, and his hair is darkened by the remaining damp. He must have completed his ablutions whilst outside.

"Stop cowering among the furs, Natalia, and get yourself over to me. Now." His tone has hardened, and the temperature in the tent seems to me to drop. I know better than to delay any longer. This is inevitable, and it is happening now.

I slip from the bed and stand beside it, my weight balanced on my left leg. I cannot resist the urge to cross my arms in front of my chest.

The duke frowns. "You said you were able to walk."

"Yes, my lord. A little."

Despite my reply he stands and comes toward me. At his advance my courage fails me and I step back with a small, frightened squeak. I turn to face the wall, cowering, ready to plead for whatever mercy he might see fit to grant me.

He does not speak to me. Instead he places his hands on my shoulders and turns me to face him, then gathers my shivering form against his chest. He enfolds me in his arms, murmuring into my hair.

"Be still, little one, calm down. I mean you no harm." His hand works large, soothing circles across my back, between my shoulder blades, then reaching lower, to my waist, my soon-to-be spanked bottom.

"My lord, please, I am sorry. Truly." I am sobbing now, my tears moistening his chest.

He tightens his arms around me, pressing me against him. "Trust me, Natalia. I will take care of you. I would never injure you. This will soon be over."

"But, I am so scared."

"I know that, and I know you regret what you did." He pauses, but continues the calming massage. After a few moments he continues. "I promise you I will be a firm husband to you, but a fair and loving one also. If you cannot bring yourself to accept your punishment now then we will leave it. I will not drag you, weeping and screaming across my knee. But I do want you to accept the discipline you have earned, and to learn from it. If not now, then soon. Can you do that, my lady?"

He does not press for my answer. He just holds me, and he waits.

At last, gulping, I succeed in mustering some semblance of control. And courage. And, incredibly, trust. His words have affected me, in particular his promise not to force his discipline upon me. He is asking me to willingly accept my fault and the consequences of it. I think, now, that I can.

"Very well, my lord. I am ready."

He uses one hand to tip my chin up, meeting my gaze. He smiles at me, then dips his head to lay a soft kiss across my lips. He releases me from his solid embrace, then turns. He wraps his arm around me, taking my weight.

"I can see that your ankle pains you. Let me help."

With his aid I make my way to the chair, where he retakes his seat.

"You will lay yourself across my lap, with your hands and feet on the floor."

I gulp, brush the remaining tears from my face, and chew on my lip for a moment. Then I shuffle to his side. I adopt the position he has instructed, determined to quash my sense of humiliation that he has placed me in such an undignified posture. *Sweet Jesu', let this soon be done.*

"That's good, but could you lift your bottom up a little higher for me please?"

So polite. I have no option but to shift around until I am poised just as he wishes, my bottom raised for him to spank.

"That is fine. I will spank you until I feel you have had enough and I will decide when your punishment is complete. You can make as much noise as you like. I fully expect you to be somewhat vocal. But you are not to move until I tell you to. You will not lift your hands to try to protect your bottom, nor will you kick. You will remain in this position, quite still, until I am finished. Is that clear?"

"Yes, my lord." I clench my buttocks, anticipating the first spank.

"Do you have any questions about why I am punishing you?"

He seems to be in no hurry to start. I whisper my response, desperate for this to be over. "No, my lord. I know it is because I disobeyed you."

"Yes, that. And also because of the danger you put yourself in. I left you here to ensure you were safe. By leaving the security of my tent you placed yourself in peril. As your husband it is my responsibility to protect you, to ensure your safety. I will not permit you to compromise that, now or in the future. Do you understand?"

"Yes, sir. I think so."

"We will see. But for now…"

I scream as the first spank lands on my right cheek, but manage not to move. The second swat sears my left cheek, and I cry out again. The spanks continue to rain down on my upturned bottom, and I swear that despite his promise to take care of me he is hitting me as hard as he can. The punishing blows all blend into each other as he delivers the spanking, hard and fast, until my bottom feels to be on fire. Yet still he continues, setting a truly blistering pace. I lose count at twelve strokes as he shifts slightly to better reach my upper thighs. I am sobbing, and can no longer hold the position. I lift my right leg, and he pauses.

"Do you want me to start all over again, Natalia?"

"No, my lord. But my ankle hurts."

"I see. Then I will overlook your disobedience on this occasion. But be assured, Natalia, that while in the course of a punishment I expect absolute compliance from you. I will make allowances on this occasion only."

"Thank you, my lord."

"Your bottom is clenched. I want it soft, relaxed. Accept what is happening, do not try to resist. This will continue until you submit to your punishment."

I groan, mortified, and allow my body to go limp across his knees. I can do nothing to help myself. I have to bear this and hope it soon ends.

"Good girl. Stay soft now and this will soon be over."

I do not entirely take his meaning, but my brief surge of pleasure at his apparent approval is soon dispelled as he resumes the spanking, dropping the hard slaps all over my unprotected buttocks and thighs. I am still sobbing, though no longer screaming. The pain is harsh, severe, my body feels to be aflame. But it is bearable, as he said it would be. I hate this, I am in agony, but I have ceased any resistance and I will survive it.

"Natalia? Are you still with me?"

"I… what did you say, my lord?" My head is swimming, I am confused, uncertain. My backside is stinging, but the onslaught seems to have stopped, at least for now. Is he finished?

"We're done. You may get up if you like, but I would prefer you to remain where you are."

"What? Why?"

"Part your thighs for me, my lady." His tone has softened now, his voice almost velvety.

"Your grace, I do not think…"

"I prefer not to ask you again, Natalia." He has laid his palm on my smarting rear and is caressing my buttock. I wince, but the hurt soon recedes, to be replaced by—what? He is generating an unaccustomed sensation of warmth, but not the painful smarting heat of the spanking just moments ago. This is more a soft, seductive assault on my heightened senses, insistent yet tender too.

I part my legs, and hold my breath.

"Good girl. Let me make this feel good for you." His fingers slip into the crease between my buttocks, questing, exploring. I gasp as his fingertip finds the private pucker of my anus, circling the tight opening before delving lower, between my delicate folds.

My late husband used to touch me in a similar way, but it never felt like this. There is no similarity. The duke's touch is assured, skilled, he seems to know exactly how to arouse me, and despite my recent degradation at his hands, my response now is swift. And powerful. Irresistible.

"Your grace, you should not…"

"No? Should I stop then?" He punctuates his words with another gentle caress across the lips of my quim, then sinks two fingers deep inside me.

"Oh, my lord! Sweet Jesu'…" I let out a low moan and fail to resist the impulse to squeeze my inner muscles around his thrusting fingers.

"I am not to stop then?" His tone is light, but I detect the serious edge to it. He requires me to answer.

"No, your grace. Please do not stop. Not quite yet."

He chuckles, and delivers a couple of deep, driving thrusts into my soaking quim. "Not quite yet, then. On one condition."

His fingers inside me go still, though his palm continues to massage my tender buttocks. The pain radiating across my rear now feels sensuous, heightening my enjoyment of what else he is doing to me. The contrast between almost-pain and pure pleasure is delicious, exquisite. I need him to continue.

"Condition, my lord? What condition?" I think I would have agreed to sell my soul to Lucifer if such were required to convince him to resume his delightful stroking.

"It does seem to me, as a general rule, that if a man should find occasion to place any part of his anatomy inside the body of a woman, she should be able to bring herself to use his given name. I would have you call me by mine. It is Stefan."

"Stefan. Yes, please…"

He chuckles again. "Better. Now, let us see what happens when I…" He shifts his position, twisting his hand just a little.

I let out a startled shriek as my body starts to convulse around his fingers. He rubs, and something seems to ignite within me, a clenching heat radiating through my shuddering body. The duke—Stefan—continues his ministrations, and the pleasure builds, threatening to overwhelm me.

On occasions, rare occasions, I experienced something similar during my second marriage, but nothing so intense. My late husband's touch was pleasurable, but never so—compelling. If Stefan stops whatever it is he is doing to me, I suspect I might attempt to do him some injury. I writhe on Stefan's lap, panting, squeezing, gasping as his fingers continue to pleasure me. I want more, but I could not possibly articulate what I desire more of.

Stefan seems to know, and his skilled touch works me to near frenzy before he suddenly stops. I let out a groan of frustration when he withdraws his fingers, then clutch his neck when he turns me in his arms and lifts me. He carries me to the bed with two long strides and lays me upon it on my back. He settles alongside me and slides his hand between my thighs again. This time I do not wait to be instructed, I spread my legs as wide as I am able. Modesty is for now forgotten. I simply need.

Stefan plunges two, or perhaps three fingers into me again, but at this different angle he manages to rub the heel of his hand against that most sensitive piece of flesh at the opening. I squirm, and my body is clenching again. I bend my knees, thrusting upwards in an attempt to increase the friction.

"Be still, Natalia, Allow me to do this for you." His fingers continue their relentless, driving motion as he leans over to brush his lips across mine. His kiss is gentle, undemanding, though I know he could, would take command entirely if he chose.

"Tally. I am Tally."

"I beg your pardon?"

"While any part of your anatomy is inside me, I am Tally. It is not my given name, but my family call me that."

His low chuckle is warm, sensuous. "Ah, Tally then. Come for me, Tally. Now."

"I do not understand. What is it that you want?" My voice is breathy, I am finding it difficult to concentrate in the face of the near overwhelming pleasure burgeoning within me. No part of my body is unaffected, I am trembling, tingling, on the verge of ...

"Now, Tally. Let it go now."

In the next instant I am flying. I have on occasions watched the birds gliding above me and dreamed of what of would be like to join them, to swoop and soar in the air, weightless. This is it, this is that sensation. I am spinning, swirling, my body and mind no longer my own, seized by an irresistible spasming that seems to start in my core and pulse outwards to the very ends of my fingers and toes. I am scared, and exhilarated at the same time. This is incredible, wondrously terrifying. But regardless of my discomfiture, my confusion, I am powerless to stop what is happening.

Nor would I wish to. It is glorious, though the sudden release leaves me limp. The intensity of the sensation recedes, my body relaxes. I feel boneless, and utterly content.

I lie still, Stefan's arms around me. I no longer care that I am naked, nor that he has spanked me, hurt me, frightened me. He has delivered the most exquisite experience of my life, I have encountered nothing of this sort in the past. Somehow he knew just how to touch me, how to caress and arouse me. He controlled my response, and made it seem so effortless. I turn to him and blurt out the first thing that comes to mind.

"Thank you."

"My pleasure, Tally."

The use of my family pet name from his lips sends another sweet tingle through me. It carries with it an intimacy, offering a promise of something comforting and safe. But as I lie in his arms, savouring his hard warmth, his solid strength, the crushing reality of my situation descends. I know this is a promise of something I cannot, must not, have.

I have made promises also, to myself, to Sophia, and to God. In truth, the prospect of becoming the duchess of Richtenholst is one I could readily enough warm to, I suspect, but there is more at stake here than just my happiness. This was a stolen moment, a rare gift of pleasure snatched from the crumbling wreckage of my life, an aberration no doubt brought on by the stresses and terrors of the last days.

"Tally? Are you ready to get dressed now? We have much to accomplish this day." His grace hauls himself up to a sitting position, and I go with him. He pats me on the backside, the tap playful and I'm realise that my bottom is no longer especially sore. "Shall I play lady's maid for you or would you prefer me to summon Karl?"

"I can dress myself, my lord." I try to move away from him, intending to seek out my clothes from yesterday. I dread to contemplate the state they will no doubt be in after my adventures in the tunnel.

"Ah, back to the formalities are we? Mayhap you require my fingers to be inside your sweet cunt once more, to remind you of our new status."

I turn to him, my face no doubt betraying my genuine shock at his crude remark. Unrepentant, the duke grins at me and stands up. He picks up a blanket from the floor and tosses it in my direction.

"Cover yourself, Tally. I expect Karl has breakfast for us, and some clothes for you. Naked, you are a truly beautiful sight, and one I would not be averse to sharing with my loyal servant and companion. But from the expression on your face I surmise that you may have other ideas about that."

He strides to the entrance of the tent and leans out. "Karl, our stomachs are under the impression our throats have been cut. What do you have for us?"

With a startled squeak I am galvanised into action. I drag the blanket around my shoulders and grip it tight, every inch of me covered except for my head. I am only just in time as Karl saunters in bearing a tray. He sets it down on the table, offers a nod in my direction, and leaves again. Moments later he is back, this time carrying a bundle of clothes. He drops those on the bed in front of me.

"Yours, I understand, my lady. I hope they are among your favourites. I am not normally called upon to select a lady's garments." The look Karl directs at the duke could best be described as baleful. The man seems to consider himself put upon.

For my part, I am grateful. And confused.

"Thank you, Karl. They are mine, but how did you…?"

"I encountered a woman in the castle when I went there to seek out your possessions. Berthe? She was intent upon guarding the royal chambers from defilement by our troops but I managed to prevail upon her good nature. She took some convincing but I can be insistent when such is needed. The woman finally agreed to show me which chamber you used, and where your belongings were kept."

I am stunned again, horrified at the fate that has seemingly befallen poor, loyal Berthe. What form did Karl's 'persuasion' take?

"Did you hurt her? Please, tell me that she lives still." My gaze swivels from one man to the other as Karl turns to me, clearly astonished.

"Hurt her? Lady, I value my hide too much to have risked such folly. Mistress Berthe remains safe and well. You will be able to ascertain this for yourself soon enough as she has insisted upon joining our party. She travels with us to Richtenholst." He turns to address the duke. "Such was her price for aiding me yesterday. I judge the woman to be a faithful and skilled servant, my lord, and I expect her to prove an asset to your household. Perhaps your new duchess will be requiring a lady's maid…?"

The duke frowns and appears to be considering the matter. He shrugs and helps himself to a slice of cold meat from the tray. "Mayhap. Do you want the woman, Tally?"

Again I am nonplussed. He is inviting my opinion. I gape at him, nodding. Berthe? Sweet Berthe is to come with me. I am to know a familiar face among strangers. "Thank you, my lord. Yes, Berthe is a good servant. She will work hard and…"

His grace dismisses my gratitude with a wave of his hand. "You have Karl to thank, not me. It seems neither of us will be called upon to dress you after all. Karl, how go our preparations?"

The manservant levels his attention once more upon the duke. "I took the liberty of reclaiming a number of other items which my lady may find useful on the journey, my lord. I have those stowed with our own supplies ready to leave. I trust that too meets with your approval?"

The duke shrugs, seemingly unconcerned one way or the other. "I'm sure Natalia will appreciate your efforts. I don't suppose you could see your way clear to reclaiming my tunic and boots? And make sure the horses are readied. I want to leave within the hour."

"Leave, my lord? You are leaving?" I quash the surge of disappointment this news elicits. I should be relieved. I am not.

"*We* are leaving, my lady. And at some point on our journey we will need to press a priest into service. You are not yet my duchess, at least not to my full satisfaction. I intend to remedy that at the earliest opportunity."

"No! No, sir, I cannot marry you."

"No? It is probably a little late for such sentiments, and after this morning's sport I really believe you should." His grace has managed to locate his own boots and is dragging them onto his feet. His leer at me is pure lust.

I squirm lest Karl should spot it and surmise at least some of what has already passed between myself and the duke, but the man seems intent on collecting the discarded buckets from last night and clearing them from our sleeping quarters. I have cause for further embarrassment when Karl discovers the vessel I used to relieve myself earlier. He makes no comment though, just picks it up and strides from the tent.

"Lady Natalia, please get dressed. Then you will eat. We will be a long time on the road and weddings cans be taxing work. You will require a full belly."

"No, my lord. I cannot come. I will not. I will not be your wife. I am to be a nun."

Again that chuckle. "My lady, you would make a singularly poor nun. I do, however, detect the makings of a decent duchess. Get dressed now, please."

I gather my makeshift cloak around myself. I am scared, my stomach is churning, but I feel compelled to make a stand. "I will not. I have told you, I am to take holy orders."

"You will take orders, Natalia, but they will not be holy. Your clothes, then break your fast. Do not make me repeat myself again."

The memory of my spanking at his hands is too recent for me not to shiver in alarm. His tone has hardened, his expression no longer teasing. But I must make him listen. He must see that this is impossible.

"I am promised to God. It has always been my intention to enter a convent."

"Your plans have changed. Christ has ample brides already. Our convents overflow with them. I am sure the good lord can spare me just one. If you insist upon spending half your life on your knees I have no objection to that, but it will not be in a cold chapel."

"This is blasphemy, your grace. And I do not understand you, where else would I kneel?"

His sensual leer forewarns me that somehow I have drifted into a trap, an ambush of which I had been blissfully unaware. "You may kneel at my feet, Natalia. Naked, of course. You will take my cock in your mouth and worship that."

The flush reaches to my very bones. Heat engulfs my features. I cannot, simply cannot believe he has uttered such a thing to me. How can he be so crude, so, so… explicit? And what earthly reason might my quim have for the sudden wet gush that sends moisture dribbling down my thighs?

"My lord, you are, you are… despicable. I allowed you to spank me, and to touch me. I should not have, I should have fought you. I should have protested, even though you would have easily overpowered me. But even so, there is no reason for you to say such things to me. I am a lady, not a, a…" My words trail off. I cannot bring myself to mouth the denial.

"A whore?" The vocabulary of the duke of Richtenholst is hampered by no such scruples. He stands and approaches the bed, then takes my chin in his hand. He tilts my face up, forcing me to meet his steady gaze. "No, you are not a whore, not in the usual course of things. You are a lady, a respectable lady of the royal court. But in my bed, you are *my* whore. And this is not to be deplored. This is what I want from you. It is what I will demand. Your willing surrender. And you will love it, Tally. All of it."

"I will not. I cannot."

"You can and you will. And you will start now, by obeying me. You know the consequences if you do not."

"Your threats do you no credit, sir."

"We are talking of promises, not threats, Natalia. I made my promise to you earlier, before I spanked you. You know how it is to be between us." He pauses for a moment or two, just long enough for me to recollect his words. He told me he would be a firm husband, but fair too, and loving. I have had a glimpse of all these qualities, and privately I own that were it not for Sophia I would gladly accept what he offers. It seems though I am to have no choice in the matter.

His palm slides from my chin and down my neck, dragging the blanket with it. He reaches further, pulling the fabric from around my shoulders to pool at my waist. It never occurs to me to resist. His hand cups my breast, lifting it, feeling the weight. His thumb brushes my nipple, and I gasp. Still he does not allow me to drop my gaze.

"Do not test me further on this. I will be back in a few minutes. I expect to find you dressed, fed, and ready to accompany me as we embark on our journey to Richtenholst. Until then, my lady…" He leans down to kiss my lips.

Then he is gone, the tent flap swinging behind him.

CHAPTER SIX

What is it about the wench that has me in such knots? She's pretty enough, granted, with her hair the colour of pale honey, and her little heart-shaped face. Her grey eyes alternate between dove-like acceptance and stormy defiance. I crave both. I knew her body would be perfect, and it is. She is slender, supple, on the surface she appears fragile but I detect an inner strength. Her peachy bottom, upturned, inviting her punishment is a sight that will remain with me for many a day. Rarely have I gazed on such perfection. And her response to my touch was divine, her climax given to me on command.

Nun indeed. She would shrivel and die in some chilly cloister. She may resist now, but she will bless the day I laid an alternative future before her. A future she was born for, a life her body was made for. I can, will, mould her, for her own pleasure as much as mine. And we will find joy in each other.

But first, there will be pain. There will be resistance. I will overcome that. I will spank it out of her, and I will pleasure her to distraction. She will not regret becoming my duchess.

I make a circuit of our encampment checking on Karl's preparations for our departure. It is a needless task; I am merely marking time until I must return to my quarters and learn whether or not the lady has obeyed me. I hope so. While further punishment does hold a certain attraction, I was not exaggerating when I told her that I would take a switch to her backside. If I must discipline her again this day, her treatment would be harsher. I doubt I would find her sweet quim wet and welcoming after a few strokes of wet willow. At least, not this first time.

No, it is better that she obeys me now, and we proceed on our way.

I cannot delay any longer. I turn on my heel and stalk back to my tent.

Natalia is fully dressed, seated on the end of the bed. She looks like a frightened sparrow, and utterly miserable. Her gaze lifts to mine as I enter. Her lovely eyes are glistening. I glance from her to the table. The tray of food is untouched.

Disobedience? Or have fear and misery robbed her of her appetite? I opt for the latter.

I approach her, but rather than towering above her this time I squat at her feet. Her face registers her surprise.

"My lady, you must eat. Please. Just a little now, and more later perhaps?" I school my features into a gentle smile, determined to calm my bride rather than add to her alarm.

She makes no move, so I stand and select several morsels for her. I assemble these on a slice of brown loaf and present the food to her. To my relief, she takes it and starts to nibble on a hunk of cheese. I force myself to remain patient while Natalia picks her way through ham, cheese, a small mug of mead, and some honey dribbled onto the bread. Despite her protestations she actually consumes a hearty meal, and I am content we can safely set out.

Karl has selected her clothes well. She is wearing some sort of warm woollen gown and stout boots, and the cloak he has draped on the bed looks weatherproof enough to ward off the December chill. We will be travelling south and the climate will become milder as we approach Richtenholst, but here in Hohenzollern the winter's grip is starting to settle over the landscape. I would not wish to save my lady from frostbite yesterday, only to have her freeze to death on a mountain pass in Bavaria.

I pick up the cloak and drop it across her shoulders, stepping in front of her to tie the ribbons at her throat. She is motionless under my ministrations. I offer her another smile, one intended to reassure though I fear it falls short.

"We leave now, Tally. Come, you will ride with me." I usher her from the tent, leaving Karl to disassemble it when we have gone. He will follow us and catch up in a few hours.

My horse is tethered a few yards from the camp, chewing the sparse grass and snorting white plumes into the chilled morning air. A veritable monster of a stallion and as black as the night, Hades stands at over seventeen hands high, towering over me and most other men. My bride is dwarfed by him. An experienced warhorse he knows his craft and has served me well for several years. He looks the part, though when not in armour he is a gentle giant, content to graze and grow fat if I would let him. He has work to do today carrying the two of us, but I have no doubt of his strength. He will need it to service the several fine mares I have selected from the Hohenzollern stables.

I loosen the tether and grasp the reins, then swing into the saddle and reach down for Natalia's hand. She offers it with a degree of nervous reluctance, but I haul her up before me easily enough.

"On, boy." At my murmured command the warhorse starts forward. Our journey has begun.

With the exception of Karl and a handful of men who will remain to assist him in the heavy lifting as our camp is dismantled, the rest of my knights and guards travel with us, as do the maidservant recruited by Karl and whose name escapes me at this moment, and the troop of Hohenzollern horses. Our force is formidable, certainly sufficient to convince any brigands roaming the countryside to seek easier pickings elsewhere. I do not fear for myself, but Lady Natalia's safety is also my concern.

The next two hours pass in near silence. I check that Natalia is comfortable, and warm enough. She answers my queries in the affirmative, her back rigid, her eyes fixed straight ahead. After a couple of leagues her posture is slipping, she is clearly tired, her muscles tensing under the strain. I invite her to lean back against me.

"Thank you, my lord, but I am perfectly comfortable."

I lean in to lay my lips close to her ear. My words are for her alone.

"I spanked you earlier for disobedience and for endangering yourself. Lying to me will invite even harsher retribution. You will feel the sting of the switch against your delectable bottom soon enough, my lady. For now though, I invite you again to lean on me. You can relax. Sleep if you will. I will not let you fall."

My words are met by a sharp hiss of breath, then, slowly but surely, my bride leans back into my arms. I shift her a little to ensure she is both comfortable and secure, then draw my cloak around her small form, enveloping her in warmth. I hope it will be enough.

Several hours pass. The silences between us are lengthy, but companionable enough. The beat of hooves at our rear signals Karl's arrival. The convoy carrying most of our belongings is some way behind him, destined to arrive at Richtenholst a day or two after we do.

Karl's destrier canters alongside mine. He answers the enquiring tilt of my chin with a curt nod to signal all went well with our departure from Hohenzollern, before wheeling his steed around to take his place in the convoy a few yards behind us. I note that he has brought his mount up alongside the cart carrying the new servant.

It is nearing nightfall when we crest a small hill to see a village laid out on the other side. A scattering of dwellings can be discerned in the gathering gloom, rough constructions made of mud, stones, branches, and whatever else the villagers could find to cobble together. The roofs are mainly thatched. Most important of all though, I see a church.

The chapel is modest, but I do not doubt it will serve our needs well enough, provided the priest is in residence. I haul on the reins to pull Hades to a halt and turn to scan the column at our rear. Karl spurs his horse forward to regain my side.

"What village is that, do you know?" I point down the hillside.

"I know not, sir. Would you like me to ride down ahead of the rest and enquire?"

"No, but you can accompany me. Bring half a dozen men. And the maid. We'll be having a wedding."

Natalia stiffens in my arms, but has the good sense to remain silent. I am relieved. I will permit her to speak freely when her words are for my ears only, but I will not accept insurrection in front of my men at arms. This marriage is to happen, and it is to happen now.

The chapel is mercifully more impressive upon internal inspection than it appeared from outside. The walls are plastered in smoothed mud and painted with colourful frescoes that cast a suitably reverent mood for the undertaking I have in mind. The altar is adorned with a red damask covering, and gold candlesticks perch at either end though the candles are unlit. The font is small, embedded into the wall. Rows of rough wooden benches serve as seating, and from the numbers supplied it would appear the chapel is well used, though we are the only occupants now.

"Approach the dwellings close by, find out the whereabouts of the priest, and have him attend us here." I send one of my guards to do my bidding whilst Karl moves about the small church lighting candles. The flickering glow creates an illusion of warmth in the place, though barely.

I cast a glance at Natalia. She is white-faced, and looks nervous, though not inordinately so. I suppose it is her right; this is her wedding day after all.

"Would you like to sit for a while, Tally? We must wait for the priest to arrive."

She obeys me in silence, her shoulders drooping beneath her voluminous cloak. I find her apparent dejection to be a sight I do not care for. Apart from the potential impact on my prospects for domestic contentment, her mood puzzles me. I spanked her, true enough, but the pleasure I gave her afterwards amply made up for the discomfort and indignity.

In truth, I was gentle with her. I know she enjoyed my touch, responded to it with a passion and fervour I could not have dreamed of. To the best of my knowledge she had no prospects at Hohenzollern apart from those afforded by her connection to the royal house. Any such expectations are gone now, the princess is taken prisoner, Hohenzollern destroyed. She should be jumping with joy at the opportunities and security offered her by this marriage. Certainly, it is an improvement on the life of poverty, prayer, and perpetual toil that would likely have been hers had she entered a convent.

I seat myself alongside her and stretch my arm across her shoulders. She begins to stiffen, would have turned from me but I firm my grip and pull her around to face me. Her eyes are downcast, but I catch the glitter of moisture on her lashes.

"Why the tears, my lady? I have sworn to be a good husband to you, and asked nothing from you in return save honesty and obedience. This is not such a bad bargain, is it?"

She does not answer me, though I see her lips working. I have the unhappy suspicion she is fighting back sobs. I cup her chin with my hand and lift her face.

God's blood, even so woebegone she is lovely.
"Is it, Tally?"
"What, sir? Is what?"
"This, marrying me. Is it such a bad bargain?"
"No, my lord. It is not, but…"
"But?"
"What will happen to me, my lord? If I refuse to marry you?"
"You cannot refuse. You already tried that as I recall, but look, here we are, in a church, awaiting the arrival of the padre."
"If I did not say the words though, what will happen?"

I draw in a long breath, considering my response with care. If she was a virgin maybe, in love with another perhaps, I might relent. A forced marriage would ultimately benefit no one. She is no innocent, I know that, and her arousal by the spanking I delivered suggests that while she may not fully appreciate it yet, her natural desires are not incompatible with mine. It also makes a mockery of her assertions regarding taking the veil. She would simply wither away in a convent.

"Is there someone else, another man perhaps?" Unlikely, but I have to ask.

She shakes her head, her denial vehement. "No, no, of course not. I told you my reasons. I am… I was to be a nun."

"You were, perhaps, but no more. You are to be a duchess. And in answer to your question, if you do not give the proper responses you will accompany me into yonder vestry where you will bend over and lift your skirts. I will remove my belt and apply it to your delightful bottom until such time as you inform me that you have reconsidered and are ready to attempt the ceremony again."

"You would beat me? Here, in a house of God?"

"Beat you? No, I would never beat you as you put it. But I will spank you if need be, and I will use whatever implement I deem most effective and appropriate. I *will* spank you here, and I trust in the lord to sympathise with my dilemma. You owe me your obedience, and I will have it."

"Not yet. I owe you nothing until I do become your wife in a true ceremony. Your property."

"A moot point, my lady. I beg of you, do not push me on this as you will not win."

A rattle of the outer door at the end of the knave heralds the arrival of the guard I dispatched to find the priest. He is accompanied by the padre himself, rushing toward us in a flurry of brown robes.

"Your grace, my apologies that I was not here to greet you. I was busy about the lord's work, attending to the needy among my flock. I have many responsibilities, you understand…" The priest comes to a halt before me, his visage lit by a willing, and I suspect optimistic, smile. Without doubt he views my unexpected visit as an opportunity to enrich his ecclesiastical coffers. He is probably correct in that assumption, I am prepared to pay handsomely for a speedy resolution to my current state of uncertainty. The sooner Lady Natalia's station is elevated to that of duchess of Richtenholst, the sooner we can all move on.

"Indeed, and I apologise for the disturbance. I have need of your services, father…?"

"Father Paul, my lord. And I have the honour of addressing the duke of Richtenholst, I understand?"

"You do. And this is Lady Natalia de Chapelle, widow of the late count de Chapelle." I reach out my hand. To her credit and my relief Natalia takes it and rises to her feet. She makes a graceful curtsy to Father Paul before positioning herself at my side.

"Of course, of course, I am delighted to make you your acquaintance, my lord. My lady. And how may I help you this evening?"

"We wish you to perform a wedding. Between myself and Lady Natalia."

"Now? Tonight?" The priest's demeanour is less enthusiastic now, though only marginally. "This is most—sudden."

"Yes, now, tonight. And I can appreciate that our plans might seem somewhat precipitous from your point of view. My betrothed and I have however been aware of our intentions for a while." A short while, in fairness, but I see no need to trouble this busy padre with the details. "We have witnesses," I gesture to my men at arms. "We have a bride and a groom, and a generous purse with which to bless the parish funds, so perhaps we could proceed?"

Mention of the purse does the trick. The priest beams at us both.

"Of course, at once. If you would just step forward my lord, my lady, and kneel before the altar. And your witnesses…?"

"Karl, Berthe, you will serve, will you not?" I am relieved that I took the trouble to learn the girl's name as I gesture to the two of them to follow us down the aisle to face the altar, where his reverence is already fiddling with his incense and such other trappings. He turns to face us, prayer book in hand. His countenance is beatific, no doubt at the prospect of my likely generosity.

"A widow you say? May I enquire who gives this lady in marriage?"

"Gerhard of Bavaria, though he is regrettably not able to be present in person. You are of course free to make enquiries, though perhaps you could do that afterwards. I would not wish to delay, nor to be forced to seek a different church to bless our union."

"That will not be necessary, my lord. Not necessary at all. Perhaps if one of your attendants could act as proxy for his lordship…?" My implied threat of the lost revenue has dispelled any remaining doubts on the part of the priest. I summon the nearest of my men at arms to join the wedding party at the front of the chapel. Now all I need is for Natalia to do her part.

She does. Tally speaks her responses in a low but even tone, exchanging vows with me. Ten minutes later we emerge from the church as man and wife, and the priest is several silver pennies the richer.

I chance a brief glance at my new bride. She looks positively wretched. I had intended to press on for Richtenholst immediately, but the sight of Tally's depressed features generates a more urgent need. This marriage needs to be consummated, and quickly. My own desires aside, though I confess they are substantial, my bride needs to rediscover the joy to be found in intimacy. She needs to be fucked, and she needs that to be done both thoroughly and well. And it needs to be now.

"Karl, do you think you might secure us lodgings for the night?"

Before Karl has any chance to respond, Father Paul is chirruping again at my elbow, this time drawing my attention to the dwelling of one Mistress Lars who has a clean and weather-tight barn we might like to make use of.

"She had a man, and two grown sons, but they are all gone now. She would be glad of the coin, my lord, I am sure. And she will provide you with adequate sustenance too, I can vouch for that. She's my sister, you see…"

Ah, right, a family concern. Still, it looks like this will be the best we can manage at short notice.

"Thank you, father. Could you direct us to Mistress Lars' home, please?"

"I will take you there myself, my lord, with pleasure. Please, follow me."

I am not sure whether the good father's diligence is borne of a desire to see us comfortable in our lodgings or a reluctance to allow potential further income to slip through his fingers. After all, we might still remount and carry on our way. We do not do that though, and the next half hour sees us cosily ensconced in Mistress Lars' own cottage.

The priest's sister would not hear of us sleeping in her barn. She insisted that Lady Natalia's wedding night must be conducted in more salubrious surroundings. Whilst I might have struggled to apply that description to the humble widow's cottage, the place is at least clean and warm and I am happy enough to hand over two more silver pennies for the privilege of using it for the night. Mistress Lars draws our attention to the pot of lamb stew simmering on the fire, then bustles off to oust her brother from his bed. I suspect the padre could end up in the barn.

Meanwhile, Natalia and I are quite alone.

CHAPTER SEVEN

I am numb, though not from cold. His grace made sure of that on our journey here, insisting that I snuggle up close to his body, absorbing his warmth while he enveloped me in his thick cloak.

I was warm, comfortable, I even slept. I was in his arms, and I felt safe there. Even his brute of a horse seemed less terrifying after a while, the steady gait beneath us, the rhythmic clip-clop of the steel-tipped hooves pacing the distance, laying mile after mile behind us, taking me farther and farther from Sophia.

His grace told me she would be taken to Vienna, which lies somewhere to the east of us, I think. I have lost my bearings somewhat, though I know our destination lies south of Bavaria. Richtenholst is a long way from Vienna, from Sophia.

Richtenholst. My new home, whether I wish it or no.

It is done now, I am wed. I obeyed, as I always do when intimidated. I gave my responses, and I did what was expected of me. I am married, for the third time. This time though it is to a man I hardly know and already fear.

He hurt me. He spanked me, and he will do so again when the mood takes him. He as good as said that. He has talked of using a switch on me, and his belt. I will be black and blue, if I survive at all.

"It is our wedding night, Tally. I intend to make it memorable for you."

The duke's voice is soft from across the small room that serves as living area and sleeping quarters for Mistress Lars. I lift my gaze to meet his, conscious that I am wringing my hands together. It is a nervous habit. I suspect I will be doing it a lot from now on.

My husband is lying on the narrow bed. He looks at ease, comfortable. Everything that I am not. He smiles at me, and despite my inner tension my stomach flips over. My quim is damp too, disgustingly so. There must be something in the human condition that creates this reaction to wedding nights, I can think of no other explanation for my embarrassing condition. Though neither do I recall any such effect with either of my previous nuptials.

To the best of my recollection both those occasions were somewhat stilted, painful, and not especially pleasant.

Based on this morning's demonstration of the duke's prowess, and my incredible response to it, I do not expect tonight to follow the same pattern. What I do expect lies somewhat beyond my powers of description.

"I would like you to undress, please. When you are naked, come and lie here beside me." He delivers his instructions in a calm, matter-of-fact voice, his expression inscrutable.

I do not move.

"Tally, I think you know by now that I prefer not to have to repeat myself." His tone has hardened, gone is the lover-like lilt. Now his words are tinged with an edge of command, a timbre that demands obedience, expects it. I have no doubt that he will punish anything other.

I should be afraid. I *am* afraid, but it is more. Without doubt I am aroused too, my inner muscles clenching at the harsh, uncompromising thread of steel that laces his curt commands. I do not want to be here, I have not chosen to be here, did not wish to be his wife. But regardless, here is where I find myself, Stefan's duchess, and I have enough experience of the married state to know what is coming next.

I untie the ribbons at my throat and slip the cloak from my shoulders. Mistress Lars has banked up the fire so the room is warm. Still holding my husband's gaze, I reach behind me for the ties fastening my kirtle. I loosen them and slip that from my shoulders too to pool around my feet. Clad now in just my shift, I break eye contact as I bend to pick up my clothing and drape the garment over the back of a small wooden chair. I do not look back at him as I perch on the chair to unfasten my sturdy leather shoes and remove those too.

I am left in just my heavy cotton shift. It is serviceable, fashioned for warmth not seduction, though I doubt I would need to apply much in the way of effort. His grace seems to know what he is about, he is in control here. My role is to obey.

Despite the unexpected intimacy that occurred between us this morning, nudity does not come easily to me. The duke's instruction was quite specific though; he told me he wanted me to be naked. I see no viable alternative but to obey him. I am embarrassed, mortified with humiliation as I stand to slip the remaining garment from my body. My every instinct screams at me to cover myself, at the very least to wrap my arms across my chest, but I fight that urge. He would simply instruct me otherwise if I tried such a tactic and I would be compelled to submit yet again to his wishes.

The duke rakes his eyes along my body, from the top of my head to my toes. His expression does not alter. Seemingly satisfied with his perusal, he pats the mattress at his side, a reminder that I have not yet fully complied with his requirements. My heart is in my mouth as I move toward him, concentrating on putting one foot in front of the other until I reach the narrow cot. Taking care not to touch him, I lie down at his side.

At first I lie on my back, staring up at the ceiling. Then it occurs to me that he may expect something less passive from me. Anxious not to attract further censure I roll onto my side to face him.

"My lord, I am not sure what…"

"No matter, Tally. I am sure, sufficient for us both. Lie on your back, please, and put your hands above your head."

His tone is less harsh now, though could hardly be described as soft. When he spanked me this morning he instructed me to remain still. Perhaps he intends such again. I position myself as I have been told, only to squeal in alarm when he takes my wrists in one of his hands and produces a strip of fabric from somewhere beside him. In moments he has tied my hands together, and secured them both to the bed frame behind my head.

"My lord, release me. Please, there is no need for this. I will not fight you…" Thrown into a sudden panic I am struggling, tugging at my bonds but to no avail.

The duke says nothing to calm or further alarm me. Nor does he make any attempt to prevent my hopeless thrashing around. Instead he lies beside me, waiting until I exhaust my efforts, until I finally accept that there is to be no escape until he unties me. At last I lie still, regarding him with a heady mix of dread, and what I am starting to realise is anticipation. He has shocked me, scared me, but still I am eager to know what he intends to do to me now.

"Are you comfortable, Tally?"

I shake my head slowly. Comfortable would not be the correct description.

"Too tight?" He gestures at my bound wrists.

Again I shake my head.

"Ah, the problem lies here then." He extends his hand to tap my temple with the tips of two fingers. "You think you should not like this, so you tell yourself that it is awful. You struggle, you fight to be free, when all the while you just want me to touch you. You want to be at my mercy, though perhaps right now you do not know why that should be. Am I right, Tally?"

"I am not certain what I want, my lord…" This much at least is true.

"No? I have some idea, and I intend to show you, my lovely little Natalia. I intend to teach you. Do you intend to be my willing pupil?"

"I cannot. I do not know what you mean."

"You will. I have tied you to the bed this time. You fought, but you have accepted the restraints, and I consider that to be enough. For now. Soon I will introduce you to a blindfold, or a gag, and you will accept those too. I intend to explore your beautiful body at my leisure. I will touch you, lick you, kiss you. Like this perhaps…" He takes my nipple between his thumb and forefinger and squeezes it.

I gasp at the contact, then squeal as the pressure builds to become painful. At once he releases me. He leans over to plant a kiss on my stomach, then drifts a little lower to circle my navel with the tip of his tongue.

It tickles. I have never liked that feeling, and delivered by his grace with such consummate skill the sensation is unbearable. I arch my back under the featherlike caress in a hopeless attempt to throw him off.

He stops after a few moments and props himself up on one elbow, to peruse my body. He seems especially interested in my breasts. I glance down to see that my nipples are swollen and hard, like deep pink cherries tipping my not especially ample curves.

"Tell me, Tally, which did you like best? I am about to touch you again. Should I torture your nipples, or tickle your tummy? Your choice."

In truth, I hated being tickled, but I fear what further pain he might inflict on my nipples. "I prefer the tickling, my lord."

He turns his head to meet my gaze, his expression playful but somehow serious too. My belly clenches, though this time with unease.

"Your first lesson, my sweet—here, in our bed, I make the choices."

He leans in to take my nipple in his mouth. I groan, the sound evolving into a low moan as he sucks hard. It feels heavenly, absolutely divine. Is this what he means by torture? My vocabulary is developing fast.

He scrapes his teeth over the tender, distended nub, and I shiver. This is more ominous. He is not hurting me, but he could, he so easily could. I am vulnerable, helpless, but it is that very edge of danger that makes the sensation so intense, so heady. My quim is soaked, the moisture surely dribbling onto the bedding beneath me. I arch again, this time to thrust my breast upwards, offering him more.

Begging for more.

He lifts his head, now taking the pebbled bud between his fingers again. He rolls it, his touch gentle though firm, the tender peak slick from his mouth.

"You like this? You like me to touch you this way?"

I close my eyes, allowing my head to drop back against the pillow.

"Answer me, Tally. I want to know what you like, and how you like it."

"I like that, my lord."

"Stefan. You will call me Stefan. We have a new rule. Whenever you are naked in my presence you will use my given name. If you do not, if you forget, I will spank you. Do you understand?"

"Yes, my lo... Ah!"

I let out a scream as he squeezes hard and twists my nipple between his fingers. "Stefan! Stefan!"

"There, you are learning already. So you agree to this new rule of ours?" His caress has softened once more, but I am wary now, my body primed for some new assault on my senses. He has not hurt me, or if he has the pain has been fleeting. But in just a few minutes, using nothing more than his fingertips and his lips, he has brought me to this state, stretched taut as a bow string, my every sense attuned to whatever he might do to me next.

"So, for the avoidance of doubt, you understand and accept my new rule? Yes?"

"Yes, Stefan." My voice is breathy, the words forced out between gasps of pure pleasure as he continues to roll the pad of his thumb over my nipple.

"And you like to be touched in this way? You like me to stroke your nipples, to squeeze them, to suck them and lick them?"

"I… yes, Stefan. I like this. But it hurts when you squeeze."

"A little pain is good. It hurts, but not much. Not *too* much. Shall I squeeze again?"

No. "Yes."

He chuckles, the sound low and sensuous, melodic almost. "Ah, my sweet little whore. I shall enjoy you." He tightens his grip, increasing the pressure again.

This time when he twists the hard nub in his hand I hiss and arch my back, but I do not cry out. He holds me there for several long moments, suspended between pain and pleasure, before he releases me.

"Such rapid progress, sweet Tally. Now tell me, do you like being bound?"

"I do not know, my lord."

He squeezes my nipple hard, and I scream out loud. That was definitely pain, not pleasure.

"My name?"

"Stefan! Please, please…."

He releases me. "Try to remember the rules. I do not want to be unnecessarily harsh with you, but you have agreed to these conditions, so I will be enforcing them. On the next infringement I will turn you over and spank your bottom. And you really would not like that as it would mean I could no longer do this for you…"

His fingers are again at my nipples, the caress firm, sensual, and utterly delightful. My emotions are scattered, my wits in turmoil as he flips me between intense pain and erotic bliss. My responses are beyond my understanding, but despite the occasional flirtation with something akin to brutality I know I want it to continue.

"So, you do not know if you like being bound, Tally? You seemed certain enough at first, when you fought to be free. You did not like it then."

I moan again as he shifts his attention to my other nipple, subjecting that to the same tender attention.

"I was not expecting it, so I was surprised. And very scared. But now, now I believe I might get to like it." *Heaven preserve me, where did that come from?*

"That is good. Now, I have another idea for something you might get to like. Spread your legs wide for me."

"I, Stefan, I…"

"Love, honour, and obey, Tally. Do I need to remind you of the consequences? And I think by now you might believe me when I tell you, you will love the honour I am about to do you, when you obey."

I do believe him, why would I not? I spread my legs, my knees straight and my ankles now perhaps a yard apart.

Stefan grins at me, shaking his head. "Tally, let me explain. I intend to lick your quim, then I'll fuck you with my fingers while I suck on your plump little clitty. For this I need better access than you are allowing. When I tell you to spread your legs wide and promise you joy, I do not expect you to play the modest virgin for me. Show me your cunt, my whore. Present it to me. Offer it to me. Beg me to take it."

I turn my head to meet his gaze. His eyes are intent, pinning me to the bed as surely as his bonds have fastened me there. In some curious display of mental gymnastics it is almost as though I am outside my body, watching from a distance, as if some stranger has slipped into my consciousness and is doing these outrageous things. My movements are slow, but I obey him. I bend my knees and bring them up toward my chest before opening them as far as I am able. I am exposed, waiting. Hoping.

One corner of Stefan's mouth lifts in a satisfied half-smile, and I offer him a tremulous grin in return. I am drawn back into this moment knowing I have pleased him, and this makes me proud. I will do anything he asks of me, just to win that smile from him again.

"Well done, love. Now you may lie still, and enjoy what is to happen."

I close my eyes, conscious of the shift in the bed as he moves. I know he will be positioning himself between my thighs, looking at me, at my most secret self, but I find I do not mind. Well, not overmuch. The cool draught of his breath flutters across the exposed lips of my womanhood, and I wonder if he has blown on me on purpose. It happens again, and I know.

My entire body jerks as he draws his tongue slowly around the entrance to my quim, but I recover and hold myself still for him. This position is difficult, not comfortable, but he has demanded it and I will comply.

He circles the lips of my sex again, then opens them with his fingers to plunge his tongue inside. I am astonished, it had never occurred to me that he might do such a thing, but he has. And it is wonderful, so intimate, so intense.

"Oh, Stefan…"

"Is this good?" He has replaced his tongue with a finger as he talks to me. He is stroking it in and out of me, each movement slow, deliberate.

I can only nod, so wholly focused am I on the sensations he is generating at my very core.

"I will always keep my promises to you, Tally. You may rely on that."

My inner walls are stretched as another finger joins the first, and his head dips toward me again. This time though it is that sensitive nub just at the front of my slit that attracts his attention. It is swollen, just as my nipples have grown and hardened under his caresses. He takes the jutting bud in his mouth and sucks on it.

It is too much, the thrill too intense. I shatter, my senses scrambling in every which direction. I thrust my pelvis up, desperate, demanding as I squeeze hard around his fingers. My quim is clenching, though not through any effort of mine. I am spinning again, loving the sensation of weightlessness, a rhythmic pulsing that wracks my entire body, gripping, twisting, and eventually relaxing to allow me to drift back into myself.

The waves of pleasure recede and my writhing dies away. Eventually I lie still, my eyes closed as my world rights itself. I feel dizzy, a little lightheaded perhaps, confused certainly. Twice now he has touched me, created such intensity of sensation that I lost control of my body, my responses. I had heard of such a thing, in those naughty whispered conversations girls sometimes indulge in, discussing the mysteries of married bliss. I had thought such stories to be a myth, a wishful fantasy woven to soften the harsh reality of a life filled with duty and pain and culminating usually in the perils of childbirth.

Not so, it was real. Is real, here, now, with this man as my husband.

I prise my eyelids open. He is close to me, propped up again on his elbow as he gazes down at me. His face bears an amused smile, perhaps laced with a trace of indulgence. His grin widens and he leans in to kiss my mouth.

I part my lips under his, then widen them further as his tongue slides into my mouth. I suck on it, loving the taste of my body on him, my wetness. He angles his head to deepen the kiss, tilting my face back to gain better access. I tug at my bonds, wanting to wrap my arms around his shoulders, hold him to me.

He breaks the kiss with a low chuckle. "Not yet, my beautiful little bride. I am not nearly done with you yet."

My gut twists in helpless excitement even as I prepare myself for the possibility of pain. Who knows what this wonderful, dangerous, beautiful man will do next?

He stands, waits for a few moments to look down on me, spread out on the narrow bed waiting for him. I shiver despite the warmth of the fire.

"My apologies, madam. I should not keep you waiting, at least, not tonight."

He makes a mock bow and steps back a pace to remove his leather belt, then his linen tunic. He drops those on the floor as I gaze at his magnificent torso. I am gnawing on my lower lip, my mouth dry in this moment. Somehow Stefan knows. He crosses the room in two paces to pick up the cup of mead left on the table with the remains of our repast of lamb stew. He returns to the bed and crouches beside it.

"Drink." The command is soft spoken, and he slips his hand beneath my shoulders to help elevate my upper body, just enough that I can take a few sips without choking.

"Thank you, my lord."

"Ah, such a short memory. Roll over, please, and bring your knees up."

Again I have forgotten to use his given name. He said he would punish me, and it seems he will. This time, though, I find I face my chastisement with far more equanimity. A spanking might hurt, but he will not harm me. I know this, I am sure of it. And with the pain comes such exquisite pleasure—afterwards.

I twist my body, finding he left sufficient slack in my bonds to enable me to turn to lie face down. I bend my knees under my body in a kneeling position but with my face on the mattress.

"Lift your bottom up, Tally. And feel free to scream."

I barely have time to draw in a breath before a blaze of fire explodes across both my buttocks. I let out an anguished yell and jerk away from him. Turning my head I see his belt, so recently discarded, dangling from his right hand.

"Oh, sweet Jesus. No more, no more…" My voice is a strangled croak.

"We are not done yet. One more, on each side. You will not forget my name again, I suspect. Get back into position and present your bottom for further punishment. You will learn this lesson here."

I have rolled to my side, my body curled in a near-foetal position. Stefan stands beside the bed, the belt swinging. He waits for me to compose myself and do as he has instructed me.

And I do it. From some secret, hidden place I did not know I had, from somewhere deep within myself, I discover the courage, the fortitude, the determination to submit.

The remaining two strokes are delivered with ruthless efficiency, searing my buttocks with liquid fire. I cry out with each stripe, but I do not move again. Even after he has finished and the belt lies once more on the bare earth floor, I remain still.

Stefan is moving around the room. The rustle and swish of fabric against skin tells me he is undressing. I am curious, but still too stunned to shift so much as a muscle.

"I am happy to take you in that position, but you might prefer to lie on your back."

"I am scared to move. It hurts."

"That will soon pass." I wince as his palm flattens over my tender, smarting bottom. His touch is gentle now, a slow, light caress that seems to absorb the pain and soothe my throbbing skin.

"Your arse feels hot, and you will have bruises from this night. Your flesh is soft, tender. Were you never been spanked before this morning?"

"No, my… No, Stefan. Never."

Conscious of my error I hold my breath, but this time he chuckles. "I want you to obey me, but I will not punish you again tonight. Best you do not store up further retribution for tomorrow though, would you agree?"

"Yes, Stefan. Thank you."

"So, do you want to move?"

I manage a small nod and wriggle cautiously back onto my side, then complete the turn. The press of the mattress against my still smarting bottom is uncomfortable but not unbearable.

Stefan stands, and for the first time I catch sight of him in all his naked glory. In all his naked and truly enormous glory.

I have only the dimmest recollection of seeing my second husband so displayed, and my first husband not at all. For sure neither one of them was endowed with even a fraction of my current lord's size. I would have remembered. Without doubt.

And it will not do. I am a small woman, in every respect. There is no way that he will be able to… That I can…

"No, my lord. You will not fit. You are too big."

"So quickly you forget, Tally. Have a care. Tomorrow is going to be a difficult day for you as it is. As for your other concerns, you are tight, I know that. It has been a while for you, I realise. We will take this slow, but please be assured, I know what I'm about and we will be extremely compatible."

He shifts to kneel on the bed, reaching for my knees to draw them apart. I am dreading the next few minutes, but I appreciate the futility of further argument. And surely, despite appearances to the contrary, one man is much like another. I am no virgin, I will survive this.

Stefan has promised.

CHAPTER EIGHT

The expression on Tally's face puts me in mind of a cornered hind I once observed during its final moments as it faced a pack of hungry wolves. The inevitability of the outcome was assured, no serious hope of escape remained, but still the tenuous possibility of some sort of reprieve hovered, tantalising, just beyond the desperate creature's reach.

I am not entirely sure I care for the comparison, and if I believed further delay might alleviate my bride's fears I would be happy to give her the time she needed. Well, perhaps not happy, but I am convinced it would make no difference in any case. Tally needs to conquer her trepidation, and she can only accomplish that with experience. Delightful, exquisite experience.

I will do what I can to deliver. For reasons I am only starting to understand, this matters to me. To her.

I shift to position myself between her knees, drawing her legs up. She offers no resistance, allowing me to arrange her as I like for my penetration. Her eyes are tightly closed, her beautiful mouth working as she chews on her lip. On impulse I reach for her, rub the pad of my thumb over her mouth. She parts her lips and I slip the tip of my thumb inside. Her mouth fastens on it and she suckles, the soft tug so intensely erotic I have to fight down the urge to ram my cock into her body, deep and hard, right to the hilt.

Instead, I use my other hand to stroke the velvety lips of her quim, drawing comfort from the welcoming moisture I find there. Not for the first time, Lady Natalia's mouth is saying no, but the rest of her body is screaming yes.

I slide the head of my cock into her hot, wet entrance, taking the time to look down at that spot where our bodies are soon to be joined. The pink velvet of her sweet cunt, the lips stretching around the glistening, swollen rod soon to be buried inside her. So sweet. So adorable.

I press forward, keeping a harsh rein on my lust. It would be easy, much too easy, to rush this and to hurt her. She's so tight, I know she'll struggle to accept what is happening, at least at first. But soon, provided I take plenty of time over her, and can manage not to terrify the poor woman half to death…

Not that I've enjoyed too much success on that front so far. I fear that last spanking may have been one too many, especially for her wedding night. I will be more patient with her, more tolerant. I will.

Or maybe not. Her peachy little bottom is altogether too much of a temptation. Better that I strive to awaken the appetites I now know with certainty lurk beneath that innocent demeanour. My own beautiful whore, delighting in the same desires that drive me.

I ease further inside her, taking care to stop each time she gasps in pain. This is tight, so deliciously snug, the walls of her cunt gripping my cock like a glove. She's hot and wet, very ready, but so tiny. She is not fragile though, I am certain of that. I will not break her, nor will I harm her.

I would not do that, not for the world.

Another half inch, then an inch. I sink the head of my cock deeper, bury it between her soft folds. I let out a sigh of pure contentment, pressing forward, easing my way inside. I want to thrust, the urge near overwhelming, but I maintain a savage grip on my own desires.

Another half inch, and…

God's sweet bones, what is this?

I press again, a tentative, experimental nudge. This time there is no mistaking it, that thin, quivering barrier guarding her quim and blocking my way.

Twice married, twice widowed. She has said herself she is not a virgin. But the proof of it is here.

My first wife was pure when we wed. I took her maidenhead, and I recall the sensation most vividly. I am not wrong. I am confused, astonished, but not wrong.

Tally's eyes remain tightly shut, her face screwed up in a grimace of pure concentration, of steely determination to face and conquer the inevitable. She has courage, this little bride of mine. She will need it.

I contemplate stopping at this point, pulling out. I might attempt to talk to her, seek to understand this conundrum. But to what end. She is my wife, this is to happen between us. She will not leave my bed a virgin.

There is but one way, really, and I see no merit in drawing out the agony. I lean forward, plant my hands on the mattress on either side of her head. I tilt my hips back, position myself with care for a smooth, strong thrust, and I do it.

Tally lets out a high-pitched scream, a shriek of pain, fear, shock. I expect all of that, even if she does not. My rod drives home, I am fully embedded, balls deep inside her. The first part of my mission accomplished, I hold still, my weight supported on my hands and my knees as she arches under me, writhing on the bed.

"Please, please stop. What have you done? Hurts…" Her moans and cries are pitiful, her desperation near palpable. She believes I have injured her, and not without reason. I lower my upper body to hers to trail my lips across her chin, her face, finally settling on her neck.

Incredibly, she goes still beneath me, though her chest is heaving and I can feel her rapid pulse under my lips.

"Easy, sweetheart. You are safe, No more pain, I swear that to you."

"What have you done? It has never felt like this, never hurt like this…"

"I know, little one, I know that. Trust me, I will make it good from here."

"I cannot. You cannot, this is wrong. You have injured me."

"Not injured. I hurt you, 'tis all. Just for a moment, but no more. Am I hurting you still?"

She hesitates, her eyes opening a fraction. She frowns, as though contemplating my question. Then, she shakes her head.

Thank God. Thank you, God.

"You were a virgin, sweetheart. I have no notion how or why, but that is the truth."

"That is not possible."

I shift a little to brush my lips across hers. There will be no further merit in debating this now. We—I—have weightier matters to attend to. Like fucking my wife and doing a good job of it.

"Hush, love. We will talk later. After."

I withdraw my cock, almost pulling out of her. Tally's face is a gorgeous mix of arousal—despite everything, her body is already responding—and pure shock. Disbelief. I share her bewilderment, though I can also discern some comic irony in our situation. Twice widowed and still a maid. She might have made a nun after all.

Not now though. Now, she is mine. All mine.

I slide my cock back into her in one long, smooth stroke, filling her to the hilt. Her body stretches around me, her grip fierce and clinging. She lets out a low moan, and this time I do not think it to be one of discomfort. I wait for a moment, then repeat the action.

More moans, and the walls of her quim quiver around me. Women may feign much, but not that, never that. My little Tally is loving this, and she is not alone in her bliss.

It is a snug fit. She is hot, and so slick my cock glides in and out with ease as I set up a steady rhythm. Slow at first, each stroke full length, allowing her a moment between each thrust to adjust, to accept. I contemplate releasing her hands, but decide against that when her inner walls start to convulse around me. She is here, in this moment with me and I see no cause to distract her.

"Stefan? I, I… oh!" Her long moan is one of utter contentment now as she lifts her hips to thrust back against me.

"Is this good?"

"Yes, I think... Oh, yes, yes, yes!"

She is writhing around now, her cunt squeezing me hard as she seems to seek more friction. I quicken the pace, thrusting harder in response to her unspoken demand. Still it is not enough. She locks her ankles in the small of my back as though she would never let me go.

Could she find her release just from my penetration alone? Perhaps, I am aware many women can and do, and I trust my little Tally may be one of those. But now, this first time, she needs more from me. And in truth, if I am to outlast her, I need to conclude this with some alacrity. I slide my hand between our bodies to find her sweet, throbbing clitoris and lay the pad of my thumb over it. I circle, the pressure even, just enough to focus all her senses in that one spot.

"Stefan, please... harder. I need more..."

"You shall have it. You shall have all of it. Come for me again, sweetheart." I increase the pressure, rubbing the sensitive button at the same time as I fuck her hard.

Her response is all I could have hoped for and more besides. Her head rolls back, her eyes closing on a breathy, guttural moan as her entire body spasms. For long, luscious seconds she is locked in the throes of her climax, shuddering with the effort, her muscles clamping hard around me as I bury my cock in one last, driving thrust. I never let up the firm caress on her clit as I hold that position and savour the moments until her passion spends itself. Tally's cries of delight are still echoing around the tiny room as I withdraw and plunge deep one last time, this one for me as I empty my aching balls into her.

Later, I hold her small, trembling body in my arms. She is draped over my chest, her breasts pressing against me and one slender leg slung across my hips. I am sure she has no idea of the alluring picture she makes in our newfound intimacy. I am not certain how much time has elapsed, a few minutes perhaps though it may be longer. My own breathing and heartbeat have returned to normal, but Tally is still shivering. I suspect she is still experiencing the residual effects of her first coupling rather than reacting to any chill in the room, but even so I reach to draw the blanket over us as she snuggles closer. Only when her breathing is steady and the shivering has subsided do I attempt to talk to her.

"That was unexpected, my little one." I nuzzle the hair on the top of her head, inhaling the delicate fragrance that is unique to her.

She does not reply at once. I smooth my palm across her naked back in large circles, waiting, reassuring I hope.

"I am sorry. Truly I am, my lord. I had no idea... You must think me a fool. A ninny."

"My lord? I had thought we were past that now..." I lower my palm to her bottom and pat the soft flesh by way of a gentle reminder. "And just to avoid any doubt, let me make it clear what I think of you. I find you to be a beautiful woman, a sensual and responsive bride, and a unique, precious gift."

"But, I, I mean, you expected. When we first met, you said that my experience would be valued by my next husband. Yet when it comes to it, I am, I am…"

"A virgin?" I do try to be helpful, when I can.

She nods, her face buried against my chest.

"Not any more. How do you feel? Any soreness?"

"No, my lor… Stefan. You were very kind, considering."

"Considering?"

"Your disappointment. You must feel cheated."

"Must I?"

"Of course. This is not the wedding night you planned or expected. I have ruined it."

I've heard enough. I'm tempted to spank her again, but that really would be too much for her. Instead I haul her up my body in order to plant a quick kiss on her mouth, then I toss her onto the bed at my side, on her back. I pin her hands in place with mine as I lean over her, my face just inches from hers.

"Let me make my position clear, my lady. You are my wife, my bride. You are beautiful, obedient, courageous, and you are blessed with the tightest, hottest, wettest cunt it has been my good fortune to sink my cock into in many a long year. Fucking you was my absolute pleasure, and will be again. And again. I did not care whether you were a virgin or not, and in any case that is all behind us now. You are mine, all mine, and I expect we will do very well together."

"You do not mind?"

"I do not. But I would like to understand how this state of affairs came about."

Her face flushes, her embarrassment obvious.

"I thought, I mean, my first husband was just a boy and not well enough to, to… I knew my first marriage was not consummated. Everyone knew that."

"Okay. And the second one?"

"I thought he did, I mean…"

"He never hurt you? As I did, at first?" I know he did not, he could not have. But Tally needs to understand the difference in order to make sense of this.

"No, never."

"What did you feel?"

"Rubbing. A lot of rubbing, and his fingers—inside me."

"It felt good?"

"It… did not feel bad exactly."

I suppress the urge to chuckle, though I sense Tally would not see the funny side right now. Even so, some comment is called for.

"Madam, I would have a promise from you if you please. If, on any occasion after my lovemaking, you feel moved to describe the experience in those terms—it did not feel bad exactly—you are to make that sorry state of affairs known to Karl at the earliest opportunity. He will have instructions upon hearing this to take me down to the moat surrounding my keep at Richtenholst and drown me."

"Drown you? Why? I do not understand."

"You will, in time. So, when I fucked you just now, did that feel bad? Exactly?"

Her eyes widen, her expression incredulous. "No, not bad, not at all. It was glorious. Oh, not at first, but very soon." She pauses, appears to be considering something. Then, "I should thank you for your kindness. For being gentle when I did not deserve it."

"What is this about deserving? You are precious to me. I will always be gentle with you."

"Except when you spank me?"

Is that a hint of mischief I discern in her pretty eyes? Is my little bride teasing me? Now this is promising.

I lean down to rub the tip of my nose against hers. "Especially then, if you did but know."

She is silent for a few moments, and squirming against the bed as though testing the remaining soreness in her derriere. Her face brightens into a soft smile.

"I do know, Stefan."

"I am forgiven then?"

"You might be. First, I will require that you make love to me again. And maybe another time after that."

"This sounds fair. I will not tie your hands this time, nor will I spank you, probably. Though I do expect you to scream."

Her lips curl in a sensual grin, her eyes alight in a way I have not observed before. "Make me, my lord."

CHAPTER NINE

The journey to Richtenholst passes quickly. The duke and I have established a comfortable rapport. We chat, we ride in companionable silence, we eat together beside the campfires that Karl produces with little effort. He seems to just click his fingers and the flames burst forth to lick beneath a rabbit or duck or some other such fare collected on our route.

Often Karl and Berthe share our meal, the four of us at ease together while the rest of our entourage arrange themselves around us in protective circle to ward off predators of the four- or two-legged varieties. That said, Stefan does not appear unduly cautious, and his confidence has increased as we have neared his own lands.

We have made good time and Stefan tells me he expects to see the turrets of his mighty keep before sunset this evening. We will arrive after dark, but that is preferred to remaining on the road for a further night.

I have shared my husband's bed, rolled up with him in his blankets to ward off the cold, covered only by a rough canvas. I have been warm enough, but Stefan is irritated by the lack of privacy. His caresses within the confines of our bedding are intimate, his kiss sweet and sensual, but he has not made love to me since we emerged from Mistress Lars' cottage into the thin light of a wintry dawn, the morning after our wedding. My body was sore in places I had only just begun to discover, and even now, after two days on the road, the memories of that night are no less vivid.

Stefan has made no mention of my ridiculous naivety in believing myself to be anything other than an innocent virgin. In truth, I can hardly credit it myself. How could I have possibly imagined that my previous husband's furtive, peremptory fumblings were anything more than that? I lacked experience, I never questioned, even though the gossip among ladies which I was privy to as a married woman bore no comparison to my own reality. I simply accepted my passionless, unfulfilled existence as my lot in life.

There is nothing of the passionless or unfulfilled about my new husband. He is, quite simply, magnificent. He is demanding, dominant, a man to be obeyed. But the reward for obedience is his dazzling company, his witty conversation, his ready smile. His touch is exquisite, promising infinite pleasure. But above all that, he is kind to me. He seems ready to like me. Perhaps to even love me.

I have been so incredibly lucky I should be offering up prayers to sweet

Mother Mary and all the saints to thank the heavens for my good fortune. Why, instead, am I burdened by such despair, such bleak, confused misery? Why can I not give myself over to my new life, to my new husband, and look forward to a rosy future as duchess of Richtenholst? Why, I might even be blessed with my own babies soon, to make my life complete.

I had assumed myself to be barren, but now I know the reason I never conceived. All that has changed, there is now every chance.

But my life is not complete. Will never be complete. I miss Sophia. I long for her, I worry and fret over her. I imagine her alone now, a small, bewildered, abandoned child among strangers. I hope the imperial court will be kind to her, for she needs a lot of love. She is now beyond my influence and my help, and perhaps has been since her father's death. But whilst we remained at Hohenzollern I was close to her, I was a familiar presence. And if I am honest with myself, she gave me a sense of purpose. I felt needed.

Stefan enjoys me, but I doubt he needs anyone.

My plans to join a convent were driven by a pressing desire to remain close to Sophia, as well as a need for stability, for security. My life has always been aligned to that of a man, first my father, then each of my husbands, and my fortunes were dictated by theirs. I have been a daughter, a wife, then a widow, cast into the uncertain purgatory of relying on the charity and goodwill of others. No more of that. I want, need, the security of knowing that my future is my own, and not subject to the vagaries of fate. The cloister offered me that, and within the church I could envision some way of maintaining my precious connection to the little girl I have come to adore.

But no longer. Stefan offers me the security I crave and much besides, though the price is high. I have lost Sophia. There is nothing I can do to cling to her, our future was always out of my hands. I can only pray that she is safe and happy. She is not mine, she never was. My head knows that, the laws of this land tell me that. But my heart is not listening.

I no longer fear that Stefan would exact retribution against Sophia for her father's actions. She is in Vienna, miles from us, but not beyond his reach were he so inclined. My husband is stern, but he is also a fair man. He would never hurt an innocent child. But neither could I expect him to sympathise, nor to help me to maintain contact with the daughter of his old enemy. In accepting me without the burden of my previous marriage as a spectre between us, we agreed to set the past aside. He has done that, and somehow I must do likewise. But it is so hard. I miss Sophia. I long for her. I always will.

"When we crest yonder hill, if the light holds, we should be able to see the castle. From there it is perhaps a two-hour ride." Stefan's low tone interrupts my private grieving, his warm breath feathering across my cheek as he leans down from his position in the saddle behind me.

I turn to him and manage to drum up a smile. In truth, he deserves more, but it is all I have for him.

He frowns at me, his expression one of concern. "You *will* be happy there."

"I know. I am looking forward to seeing it, my new home."

"Indeed? You have a look of one about to ascend the gallows. Why so forlorn?"

He misses nothing. "I am not forlorn. I am—nervous." This is not entirely untrue, I do harbour reservations about the warmth of my welcome. Stefan married me having had no prior discussion with his family. He has not shared the details of his household with me, but I assume he has kin awaiting his return to their hearth, and some of those will perhaps remember the events of twenty years ago. Even if they bear no malice they will at the very least be surprised to have a new bride thrust into their midst, and I know of no reason to assume my welcome is assured.

"Why nervous? Richtenholst needs a duchess. You will do admirably."

"I will try my best to fit in, my lord."

"You will fit in, and it will be effortless. My people will adore you. I should mention though, I make that six times you have omitted to use my given name. You know the rules, you have continually disobeyed them, and therefore we have a problem. I intend to avail myself of the first opportunity to rectify it."

A sensual smile accompanies his 'threat,' but even so, I am indignant. "But, I am not naked. I thought the rule just applied to the times we are alone and…"

"A fair point, and one I will take into account. But you are to receive a thorough spanking as soon as we are alone. And if you insist, I will deliver it whilst you are naked."

My bottom tightens, my quim already starting to moisten. I lean back against him as he wraps his arms around me and buries his face in my neck. Under the heavy fabric of his cloak that is draped around the pair of us, he cups my right breast with his left hand. He continues to control his mount one-handed as he palms my curves, first one side, then the other, his gloved fingers scraping across my nipples. The caress is even more erotic for its roughness, and both tips swell to rub against my clothing.

"You will love your spanking, little one. When we arrive, and we are settled, you will come to me and ask me for it."

"My lord?"

"Ah, how you love to live dangerously. Your bottom will be so sore and I vow you will sleep on your stomach for the rest of this sennight. But still, you will ask me for it. You will say please, and when we are alone you will lie across our bed and raise your skirts for me. You will lift your bottom up for me to punish. Won't you?"

I do not answer. Indeed, I cannot answer. My head is whirling with sensuous images and my quim is wet. He can do this just with words, and with a casual caress. How much more can he accomplish when he sets his mind to it?

"Won't you, Tally?" Stefan's tone has firmed, the shift so subtle as to be almost imperceptible. But I know.

"Yes, sir. Stefan. You will spank me, and I believe I may love it."

"Good enough, my lady."

My first glimpse of Richtenholst comes perhaps an hour later as we round the grassy summit to the range of hills that lies between us and our destination. The countryside is spread out below us, a deep, fertile valley, the bountiful nature of this land obvious even in this inhospitable season. The keep itself dominates the landscape, perching halfway up the mountainside on the opposite side of the valley. The castle is constructed of pale sandstone, which takes on an almost golden hue in the fading winter light. A red pennant flies above it, flapping in the distant breeze. The light is still good enough to make out the moat that surrounds the keep, a sparkling ribbon of silvers and greys. Tiny ant-like buildings are scattered across the surrounding lands, close enough to draw on the protection of the castle whilst still proclaiming their proud independence.

"Do the villagers live outside the castle walls the whole year round?" At Hohenzollern only the most intrepid or the most foolhardy would venture far from the solid walls of the outer bailey.

"Many do, though they would be quick to seek protection inside were we to be attacked."

"I see. They feel safe in their homes then?"

"Of course. This is a peaceful region and I intend for it to remain so. That is why I was persuaded to join Gerhard's force when it became necessary to ride against Hohenzollern. The excesses of Princess Susanna had to cease."

I do see that there was problem, and I can even appreciate the need for the solution which transpired, but I cannot let his mention of Susanna's culpability remain unchallenged.

"You should direct your justice at Lord Eberhard. I have told you, the attacks on neighbouring provinces were none of Susanna's doing."

"The emperor and his court will determine the facts and take whatever action is required." Already Stefan is spurring his horse on, quickening the pace now that his home is in sight. The rest of the column at our rear do likewise. All are keen to seek their beds this night. Stefan's rough caress of my body ceases. He takes the reins in both hands as Hades breaks into an easy canter.

It is full dark by the time we approach the outer dwellings but the populace are at their doors to greet us. Their lord has been recognised in the distance, and they are glad to see him safe home. Occasional cheers ring out, spontaneous clapping. Stefan is liked and respected here, and again the image of Lord Eberhard comes to mind. He was despised and hated, but above all feared. Never would the peasants of Hohenzollern have interrupted their evening meal to see him safe home.

The great gates of the castle are opened to us as we grow near, the drawbridge lowered to offer access. We clatter across the wooden bridge and into the bailey where a flurry of grooms hurtles from the stables to grab the reins of our mounts.

Stefan flings his ribbons to one lad, who catches the flying strands with an alacrity that speaks of long practice.

"See Hades settled, Con, if you please." Already my husband is swinging his leg from the saddle. His descent is agile, and moments later he is reaching up for me to slide into his arms. Once my feet are in contact with the flattened earth of the courtyard, he steadies me and turns me to face the castle entrance where it would seem his entire household is pouring forth to bid him welcome. The charge is led by two boys, aged perhaps nine or ten years, who bound whooping across the bailey.

Stefan steps forward and bends to encircle each one with an arm as they reach him, their own smaller limbs wrapping round his neck. He says something to each in turn, though his voice is muffled and I cannot pick out his words. The boys can though, and after the first flush of exuberance has passed they turn to face me, their features solemn.

Stefan straightens. "Alexander, Fabian, I have the honour of presenting to you Lady Natalia, the duchess of Richtenholst. My wife, and your new mama."

The boys' faces are agog. They look to each other, then at Stefan, their father it would seem, for confirmation of this incredible state of affairs. I share the sentiment. I have heard no mention up to now of sons, though I have never asked about Stefan's family. Uncertain how to greet them, I settle for simply stretching out my hand.

"I am delighted to make your acquaintance, Alexander, Fabian."

Each boy takes my hand and shakes it, their manners impeccable. The taller one, Alexander, even overcomes his surprise sufficiently to execute a small though somewhat formal bow. He turns to his father, his expression one of discontent. My heart sinks; a resentful stepson is not a complication I had anticipated.

"Father, now that you have a wife, does this mean I am no longer required to aid you in removing your boots at night?" From the boy's expression I do not believe he harbours any desire for a lightening of his responsibilities.

Stefan ruffles his hair, the gesture one of easy affection.

"Less of your insolence, lad. I'll have need of your services for a good while yet so you will continue in your current duties and studies until Karl or I tell you different. Unless of course Lady Natalia also finds herself in need of your assistance, in which case I trust I can rely on you to treat her with every courtesy."

"Yes, sir. Of course." Reassured, I hope, that a new stepmama will not disrupt his relationship with his father, Alexander turns his attention to me once more. "What is your opinion of carrots, my lady?"

This conversation is not proceeding quite as I expected. I consider for a moment before answering. "I like them. Very much."

The boy frowns and I wonder if I uttered the wrong answer. It would be a pity, but I had few clues to go on.

"I see. That is a relief as we have had an uncommonly good harvest this year and our storerooms are overflowing with them. We eat nothing else and I am heartily sick of carrot soup. Do you know any other ways to cook carrots?"

The culinary arts are not among my greatest strengths, but I fear this is not the time for needless humility. "I have some expertise in this matter. I believe I may be able to come up with something."

My response appears satisfactory. Alexander nods and shifts his attention back to his father.

"I have practised my swordplay, as you instructed. I can best Fabian every time." Alexander is seemingly no more inclined toward a humble disposition than I am. We should do very well together. I intend to work at it.

"You cannot!" The smaller boy tips up his chin, ready to take issue with such an outrageous claim. "I win at least half the time. And you only get the best of it at all because you are bigger than I am. I am faster, and more cunning." The brave words are punctuated by a bout of frenzied arm waving, a mime of Fabian's alleged expertise at swordplay if I am not mistaken.

His brother is less than impressed. "You are a baby. You should remain in the nursery with Clare, not totter around the lists, tripping everyone up."

"Father, he lies! I…"

"Hush, is this any way to greet our new duchess?" Stefan crouches before the two lads, his expression stern. They go silent at once. "I will watch your practice in the morn and assess your progress for myself. Both of you."

"Carrot soup indeed… That boy never thinks of anything but his stomach. Welcome home, my lord. And welcome to you too, my lady." This last is delivered by a stout woman of middling years who has been hovering on the fringes of our small group.

Stefan rises to his full height again. "Thank you. May I present Lady Natalia, duchess of Richtenholst?"

The woman bobs a quick curtsy. Stefan continues. "Helena is our cook. Her husband, Otto, is my bailiff and between them they ensure our comfort here."

As mistress of this household, however newly risen to that position, I expect I will have much to do with Helena and Otto, though my experience of running a large home and estate is limited indeed. I will be reliant upon their assistance. And their goodwill. I step forward to offer my hand.

"I am delighted to meet you, Mistress Helena. Perhaps you will have time to talk with me soon, to advise me on how matters are run here. I have much to learn about Richtenholst." I have much to learn about everything, in truth, but I see no point in expanding on that.

Helena's beaming smile seems genuine enough. "Of course, my lady, as soon as you are settled and rested. And fed." She turns to my husband again. "Sir, we have prepared a feast in readiness for your return. If you would like to take your ease inside, food will be served in the great hall."

"Thank you, Helena. We are more than ready for that." He takes a couple of paces in the direction of the front steps, then stops. He turns to me, his hand outstretched.

"Come, Tally. I would show you your new home."

I take his hand, but he just uses the contact to tug me to his side. There he loops his arm across my shoulders and drops a kiss on the top of my head. The careless gesture seems artless, but I know better. He has embraced me, kissed me in full view of his entire household, making clear the affection he has for me. My position here is assured.

Together we ascend the short flight of stone steps leading into the castle. I gasp at my first sight of the great hall, the vaulted ceiling soaring above us and the walls hung with thick tapestries. The stone has been rendered and lime washed to reflect light and increase the impression of space. The wall hangings lend colour and vibrancy, but the exposed walls are brightly painted in the reds, browns, and yellows of ochre. A huge fire roars in the grate on the far wall, the warmest spots around it already claimed by several large hunting hounds. The room is moderately warm despite its size and the inclement weather outside.

A table is set on a small raised dais at the end of the hall, and eight seats are arranged along it. The rest of the hall is furnished simply, a long table running the entire length, flanked by low benches on both sides. Servants are scurrying to and fro laden with dishes, plates, steaming bowls of food. They deposit these on the tables and rush off for more.

Much of the floor is covered in rushes, clean I note, apart from the end where the top table is situated, where clay tiles have been used. The room is amply lit by torches set into recesses in the walls. The overall effect is one of cosiness, a bustling, friendly home where all are busy, all are welcome, all are cared for.

Stefan leads me in the direction of the dais, nodding and smiling at the servants we pass, greeting each by name and accepting their smiles of welcome. Fabian and Alexander are hopping alongside us, each bursting with excitement at the return of their father, vying for his attention. He answers their eager questions, confirming that yes, Gerhard is at least seven feet tall, the moat at Hohenzollern was filled with ferocious beasts with huge teeth, and the imperial army was beset on all sides by fearsome foes. Even so, Gerhard, Stefan, and their brave armies prevailed, and have returned safe to their loved ones to feast on carrot soup.

At the mention of loved ones, Stefan halts. He steps onto the dais and scans the room as his sons seat themselves in the chairs which I assume they normally occupy. At a brief word from Stefan they move along one seat, to make space for me beside their father I assume. Stefan is still peering about, looking for something. Or someone.

His eyes light on the bottom steps of a spiral staircase opening into the hall at the far end. I follow his gaze to see a movement in the shadows there, a small figure almost hidden from view. Stefan smiles and turns to me.

"Please be seated, my lady." He gestures to one of the chairs positioned at the centre of the table. I seat myself next to Alexander, who does not seem concerned at the new arrangements. "If you would excuse me for one moment please, my lady." Stefan offers me a bow and strides from the dais.

He marches across the hall to the shadowy staircase, and crouches when he reaches it. A few seconds pass before the small figure steps forward into the light.

It is a tiny girl, no more than three or four years old. She stands before Stefan, shifting from one foot to the other, her nervousness very much apparent. At this distance I have no idea what words are exchanged, but eventually she steps forward to hug him around his neck. His arms fold around her and he stands, picking her up. He returns to the top table, the child clinging to him.

He takes the seat beside me and arranges the little girl on his lap. Her face is buried in the soft leather of his tunic, her tiny fingers curled into fists, which she has tucked under her chin. She turns her head just enough to stare at me, her dark eyes wide. She is impossibly pretty, but so timid it is painful. I attempt a smile, but this simply causes her to bury her nose against Stefan's chest again.

"Clare, I would like you to say hello to my new wife. This is Natalia. I call her Tally and I think perhaps you can too." He glances at me, his eyebrow lifted in inquiry.

This is a far less formal introduction and I sense some delicacy here. Stefan was sure of his sons, handled them with easy, gentle authority. With this little girl, he is on eggshells.

"Yes, of course. And I may call you Clare, I hope."

I am talking to the back of her head, but even so I observe what will have to pass for a nod. I press on.

"We will be friends, you and I. We will have to be, for we are girls in family of men and we must look out for each other. May I rely on you to help me if I get lost in this huge castle?"

Another brief nod, unmistakable this time.

"I am relieved for I had been worried. I will require your assistance, I am sure. And now, I wonder if you could tell me what is good to eat among all these delicious dishes. What is your favourite, Clare?"

The small head turns and Clare surveys the feast laid out before us. I have yet to discern a surfeit of carrots, but perhaps those are to come. The child considers the rich and varied fare, taking her time, then points to a plate of what I suspect may be apple dumplings.

"Thank you. I will start with those then. May I serve you a helping too, my lord?"

"Yes, if you would, Tally. Clare, would you like to take your seat next to Fabian?"

The little head shakes, and Clare buries her fingers in Stefan's tunic.

"She has been naughty. Again. She broke your mirror. I told her you would be angry, and that she would be punished when you returned." This from Fabian, speaking around a mouthful of pigeon pie.

Stefan's warning frown suggests he has not appreciated Fabian's intervention in the matter of the mirror. However this does perhaps explain the child's reluctance to greet Stefan on his return.

"My mirror. I see. How did that happen, Clare?"

His tone is gentle, but even so Clare is weeping quietly. She clambers further up onto his lap, clinging to Stefan as though she expects to be hurled from his embrace at any second. In fact, his arms tighten around her. He strokes the back of her head and her shoulders, murmuring nonsense into her hair. It is clear he adores this little girl, mirror or no.

Eventually, with a last gulping sob, she stops crying. She turns in Stefan's arms to lift her tear-stained face. Her mouth is still quivering.

"I am sorry, papa. It was dark, and it fell."

"Tell me about it, love."

"I woke up in the night. I heard a noise, and I thought it was you. I thought that you had come home. I wanted to see you so I got out of bed and went to your solar. B-but you were not there. I was looking for you, and I banged into the mirror. The big one that stands beside the window. It fell and it broke. Otto came. He had a lamp. He called for Mathilde and told her to see me back in bed. In the morning the pieces of the mirror were gone, I do not know where it is now."

"The shards of glass might have injured someone, so I buried them."

I turn my head at the new voice. A tall man in his middle years has taken a seat on my other side.

"Ah, Otto. I was wondering where you might be. You will by now have heard that we are honoured by the presence of a new duchess."

"Indeed, my lord. And may I say what pleasure it is to meet you, my lady. This keep will benefit from a mistress." His gaze is fixed pointedly upon the tiny figure huddled in my husband's lap. I wonder if disciplining small girls is to form part of my housekeeping duties. I do hope not, for I shall have no aptitude for it.

"Clare, you should not wander around the castle at night. Not on your own, and not without a light." Stefan's tone is serious now, and when Clare would have pressed her face into his chest again he cups her chin and holds her gaze. "If Otto had not come when he did, you might have been injured. You could have cut yourself and I would not have wanted that. You are my very precious little girl and I do not want anything bad to happen to you. I will punish you, but it is not because I am angry about the mirror. It is because I want to keep you safe. Do you understand that?"

She nods, her eyes filling with tears again.

"Tomorrow you will help Otto to clean the mirrors that remain to us. You are to spend all morning at it. That is to be your punishment. You will work hard and you will not complain. Is that clear?"

Clare nods, the faintest of smiles playing at the corners of her mouth. She looks as though a huge burden has been lifted, the weight of the guilt she has carried, and perhaps fear of her punishment too.

I know that feeling.

CHAPTER TEN

I should insist that Clare take her usual seat in order that I can devote my full attention to my new bride on her first evening in my home, but I do not have the heart for that. Instead, I allow her to remain in my lap while we eat.

Her eyes are fixed on Tally. Clare observes every move my wife makes, listens to every word. She is fascinated, and I sense terrified too. She has already lost one mama, perhaps she fears accepting this new one lest disaster might strike a second time. I have not the words to reassure her, so I fall back on kindness and as much patience as I can muster. This has ever been my strategy with Clare, and hope that these will be sufficient to bring my timid little goddaughter out of her shell. Now though, I have Tally too to aid my efforts and I hope the pair of them will become close. I do my best, but Clare needs a woman's love.

By the time the repast is over Clare has fallen asleep. I shift her in my arms to find better ease for both of us.

"She is a pretty child. Did you say that she is cousin to your sons? Your niece then?"

I turn to Tally, who has been quiet by my side throughout the meal. I suppose Clare is not the only female here somewhat awed by the circumstances in which she finds herself. I shake my head.

"Strictly speaking, she is not. Clare's father, Edmund de Ranelagh was one of my knights, a man of courage and honour. I liked him very much."

"He is dead then?"

"Yes. He died at my side in battle, in Lombardy." I pause to recollect. It was a skirmish in which I might well have lost my own life but for Karl's intervention. But fate was on my side that day. It was not on Edmund's. "He fell as the battle drew to a close. We carried him from the field, barely alive. He died after perhaps an hour. In that time though he charged me to see to the welfare of his widow and unborn child. Eleanor, Lady de Ranelagh, did not choose to reside here at Richtenholst though I invited her to join our household. She and my own late wife were cousins, but they did not like each other overmuch. I think we were all a little relieved that Eleanor chose to maintain her home separately in a manor house about five miles from here."

Tally frowns, and I realise this is the first time I have mentioned my first wife to her. Until meeting my sons a couple of hours ago I doubt she even contemplated the possibility that, like her, I had been married previously. But Juliana is dead now, has been gone for over a year. I loved her well enough and mourned her passing, but my concern is with the living. I return to my story.

"Clare was born a few weeks after her father died. I am her godfather. Juliana, my wife, was her godmother. We would see Clare occasionally, when Eleanor would come here for feast days and the like. I was away at the emperor's court when a messenger arrived here with the news that Eleanor was ill. I was to learn later that she had been caught in a downpour and took a chill, which turned to a fever. Despite the tension that had always existed between them, Juliana insisted it was her Christian duty to care for her cousin, so she left for the manor house. Perhaps if I had been here I might have dissuaded her. Still, her mission was to no avail, and Eleanor was dead within a couple of days. Tragically, Juliana was not far behind her. My wife contracted the same fever, and did not recover either.

"I returned to Richtenholst to find my household in confusion, my boys motherless, and an orphaned Clare awaiting me. The messenger who brought the news of their deaths had brought Clare to Richtenholst with him, a tiny girl aged just two. Up to that point I had left the parenting to Juliana. She was good at it and ran my household with an efficiency that left me in awe. Otto and Helena were doing all they could, but their new responsibilities in the wake of Juliana's sudden demise were overwhelming. No one knew what Clare's future might be, whether she would remain here or not, and I suppose she became lost in the chaos. Had I been here her security would have been confirmed at once and she would have been adopted into my family. By the time I arrived home, she was already withdrawn, a silent, timid little presence. As her godfather, it is my responsibility to care for her. I do my best but she is only now starting to regain her confidence and she is easily upset."

"You are a good father."

"I try to be, though I confess it is not always easy. I am improving with practice."

"I will help, my lord."

I scan Tally's features, and I am somewhat surprised to see tears in her eyes. She is clearly moved by Clare's story, and I hope this bodes well for their future relationship. I cannot demand genuine affection between my wife and my adopted child, but that will not deter me from hoping.

"I know, and I appreciate it. I will welcome your aid with Clare. She is not an easy child, but I have sworn to care for her, and I will."

"That is very kind of you, especially as she is not a blood relative."

"You are not the first to offer such an observation, and it never fails to baffle me. I am not Clare's sire, but she is my responsibility as I was the liege lord of her parents. Her father died in my service, her mother was related by marriage. I swore to Sir Edmund that I would care for his family and I intend to keep my word." I meet her gaze, and hold it. "You need to understand, Tally, I will protect those who rely on me. This includes you now. All my children are very dear to me, my sons and this little girl who ended up in my care. Mine is a close family and as my wife you will be at the heart of it. I will not insist you love my children as I do, I realise that would be futile. But in time, perhaps you might grow close."

"I apologise. I meant no offence. It is just that…" Her words trail off, though I wonder if perhaps she has more to say on the matter. I wait, but nothing is forthcoming. I trust I have made my position clear as far as my children are concerned. Now, it is time for a shift in the mood.

"I will send for Helena soon, to take Clare to her chamber. Then you and I may retire, Tally."

My bride's startled expression suggests she has not forgotten my promise to redden her bottom at the first opportunity. I know what she is anticipating, a hard spanking followed by an equally hard fucking. A pleasant enough prospect to be sure, but not exactly what I have in mind.

As my cock starts to stir in readiness, my need for Helena becomes more urgent. It is one of the qualities of a fine servant that she would anticipate her lord's needs and Helena does not disappoint. I get to my feet, Clare still cradled in my arms, at the very moment the cook appears from the kitchens. She hurries over to my side.

"Ah, the poor little poppet. She must be exhausted. Shall I take her, my lord?"

"Thank you." I relinquish my burden. "See her safe to bed. And Helena, would you assign a maid to watch over her for the next few weeks. If she awakens in the night and has a wish to go wandering around, I prefer that she does not do so unescorted. And she is to have a light."

"Of course, my lord. Mathilde will be well suited to the task. I will see to it."

I wait until the pair have disappeared up the narrow staircase before turning my attention back to my two sons, bickering as ever.

"You two should seeks your beds also. I expect to see both of you out in the courtyard soon after first light tomorrow. I will be ready to inspect your progress with the sword and the longbow so I hope your performance lives up to your boasts earlier."

I have had this conversation with my sons on many occasions and I know what is to come. I halt the answering rush of enthusiastic assurances with a raised hand. "Enough. Let your actions speak for you. Now, 'tis late so away to your chamber."

They know when not to press me further. Both get to their feet and start to make their way across the hall, after Helena. Halfway to the staircase Fabian stops. He turns, then rushes back to fling his arms around my neck.

"I missed you so much. I am pleased you are home."

I fear my attempt at a stern demeanour slips a little as I hug him in return. "It is good to be back, my son. Though you and I still need to have a conversation about what you said to your cousin. You know how timid Clare is, how easily frightened. I rely on you and Alex to take care of her when I cannot be here."

"I never meant to upset her. But it *was* your favourite mirror. It belonged to our mother."

"I appreciate that. But as your mother would have been the first to point out, things can be replaced. People cannot. Clare is a part of our family now and we must all take care of her. Will you help me with that?"

Fabian nods, earning himself a final pat between the shoulder blades.

"Off with you. I will see you in the morning. Do not be late." He scampers after this brother. I watch him trot across the hall and cannot conceal my smile. He is a good lad and I am proud of my children, all of them.

But now, I am at last alone at the table with Tally.

"I meant what I said. I will help, with Clare I mean. I thought perhaps I might clean the mirrors with her in the morning. Otto must have other matters to occupy him." She is smiling at me, her expression uncertain, as though she still doubts her place here. I aim to dispel those fears. But first...

"I expected nothing less but still I am pleased to hear you say it. I am sure Otto will appreciate the help and I want you to get to know Clare. Now though, I think I should make you acquainted with our bedchamber." I lean in, my next words are intended for her ears alone. "How is your bottom, sweetheart? Not still sore I trust?"

Her face flushes, the redness creeping from her neck upwards. I love it when she does that. My cock swells in my chausses at the mere anticipation of seeing that gorgeous bottom displayed for my punishment once more. Soon. Very soon.

"Follow me." I stand and march across the hall.

The soft footfalls behind me are sufficient evidence to convince me that Tally is not entirely dismayed at the prospect of another spanking. I smile to myself as she trails in my wake. I take the stairs two at a time and lead the way to the master chamber. I open the door then stand back to gesture her inside.

I am familiar with the room, but of course Tally is not. Once inside I allow her a few moments to gaze around her and assess her new environment. The room is comfortable enough, I would accept no less. The fire casts a soft warmth that fills the chamber. I hate the cold and my servants have instructions to keep the fires in my quarters well-tended. The floor is made of wood, but strewn with a variety of rugs so bare feet are an option. A garderobe is discreetly enclosed behind a screen, and sweetened by bunches of pungent herbs refreshed on a daily basis.

The stone walls have been rendered with lime and mortar that excludes all but the most determined draughts, then painted in a design to imitate stonework, decorated with five petaled roses. The usual ochre shades of reds and browns have been supplemented by greens and blues that I purchased on my travels around the surrounding kingdoms. I could flaunt my wealth in the great hall downstairs, and I do so to some extent, but I have always preferred to reserve the greatest comforts for my own private enjoyment. And now Tally's. I dislike austerity and have the means to indulge my tastes, so the comforts of my private chamber are further enhanced by thick hangings and tapestries collected over several generations, which adorn my walls and also serve to retain the heat.

Tally no doubt takes in much of these details, but her attention is mainly riveted on the solid bed in the centre of the room. It is old, belonged to my father, and I believe my grandfather before him. It has stood in this chamber for at least three generations and is likely to see off several more. The bed curtains, embroidered by my grandmother with the vivid reds and golds of the Richtenholst crest, hang from the ceiling. They provide both warmth and seclusion, and are pulled back now to reveal the mattress stuffed with down, and the straw-filled bolster at the head.

The room is lit by two torches, their glow mingling with the firelight to create an atmosphere that is intimate yet quite sufficient for me to enjoy the glorious sight of my bride's naked bottom.

"Tally, I recall you mentioned a preference for being naked when I spank you." That is not exactly what she said, but I am an optimist.

She casts me a nervous glance. "Yes, of course, Stefan. But it has been a long journey, and although our welcome has been warm enough I am fatigued. I wonder, could we not just go to bed?"

It would seem my bride is an optimist also.

"Tally, I do not appreciate being kept waiting. Undress, please." I harden my tone on purpose, just a little, sufficient to end this procrastination. I want her compliant, but not cowed.

I must have managed to strike the right balance because Tally makes no further ado, divesting herself of her kirtle and undergarments. I detect a slight hesitation before she unlaces her chemise and slides it from her shoulders to reveal her exquisite breasts. It would seem there has been some rekindling of her modesty after our enforced abstinence this last two days and nights. I intend to dispel that.

Despite the warmth of the fire she is shivering, her eyes downcast. She is nervous, no doubt feeling vulnerable. Knowing this I offer no praise, no compliments on the exquisite perfection of her body now bared to me.

Instead I feign indifference, requiring her to quell those doubts herself. I leave Tally to stand in the centre of my chamber, nude, whilst I perch on the edge of the bed to unfasten my boots and kick those off. Then I pull my tunic over my head and rid myself of my shirt. This will do for now. I settle on the bed, my back against the headboard.

I summon her to me with a hand gesture. She approaches, her expression apprehensive. She is gnawing on that bottom lip again. I doubt that habit will persist for much longer, but I intend to enjoy it while it lasts.

"Lie across my lap and fold your hands in the small of your back." I am careful to maintain a low, even tone. She needs to know that I mean what I say, and that I am calm even though she is not.

She obeys me in silence. This is progress. The last time I put her over my knee I recall her protests were most vigorous.

"Make yourself comfortable, and tell me when you are ready."

She wriggles on my lap, causing my already solid cock to twitch and strain against my chausses. Perhaps I should have stripped completely after all. Still, we are here now. She reaches behind her and clasps her hands together at the base of her spine.

"I am ready, Stefan."

I am gratified to note that she is becoming quite good at getting my name right. Such an avid pupil. This night I have another lesson for her.

I lay my palm on her pert, round buttock and caress the delicate globe. There is no hint of redness or of bruising from my earlier attentions, which is both relief and disappointment to me. I like to see a woman carrying my marks, but I have no wish to cause either too much discomfort or unnecessary harm to her. I will view Tally's pale, delicate curves as a blank canvas this evening.

I draw my hand over her bottom, making large circles, first on one side, then the other. I press on hard, my fingers sinking into the firm yet soft flesh. Tally lets out a sigh, and appears to be enjoying this despite her obvious trepidation that my caress may be a prelude to a more challenging episode.

I continue to stroke as she arches her back to offer me more of her bottom. I suspect she is doing this with no conscious thought, just relaxing into the moment.

The first tap, when I deliver it, is so soft, so light as to pass unnoticed. I massage her curves a little more, then drop another light smack on her pinkening cheek. Still no reaction. I continue, increasing the intensity by increments until the sensation starts to register.

"Oh. Oh, Stefan." She breathes the words on a low moan.

I increase the pressure again, just a little, nothing to jar, nothing to disturb the intimacy of this moment. The pleasure is shared. I admire the deepening hue of her bottom as the spanking builds, and Tally writhes under my hand, her soft moans all the response I need to hear.

I maintain the intensity of my slaps for several minutes before ramping the pressure up again, just enough to elicit a gasp. Tally clenches her buttocks, the relaxed softness replaced by tight, wincing flesh. Her bottom has darkened to a bright crimson, the heat radiating from her tender skin. She whimpers, and I know this is enough. I have brought her to the point of pain and edged her slightly beyond. She is uncomfortable and expects to become more so in the coming few minutes. She is anticipating a punishment, after all. Instead I begin our descent, reducing the severity of the blows, interspersing sharp slaps with gentle caresses to soothe the burn away. At once her bottom softens again and she relaxes under my ministrations, allowing her body to sag in relief, boneless across mine.

As my palm finally comes to rest on her heated skin she is still. Her fingers are loose, no longer clasping her wrists. She is not quite asleep, but very nearly so.

I slip my fingers into the crease between her buttocks and seek out first her quim, then her clitoris. She parts her legs as I trace my fingers through her folds, her wetness coating them. I stroke the tip of her clitoris. She thrusts her hips up, her back arches in wanton invitation. I sink two fingers inside her, delivering three or four quick thrusts before withdrawing my hand and concentrating on her sensitive clit again.

I knew she is close to her climax, I can see it in the clenching of her buttocks and the eager thrusting of her hips. I can hear it in her breathy moans, and I can feel it in the quiver of her soft, swollen bud under my fingertip.

I use my free hand to thrust inside her again, the strokes long and slow, and never letting up on her plump clitoris until her body convulses in gasping, moaning delight. Her quim is spasming around my fingers, her clit throbbing. Her legs are spread wide and I lean over to see the delicate beauty of her sex, open and welcoming, begging to be fucked.

I intend to oblige her. But first…

As the shudders of her release die away I withdraw my fingers from her cunt to again explore that secret hollow between her clenching buttocks. This time I find her tight arse, the muscle there pursed in determined innocence. I circle it with my finger, spreading her own juices there. I press, not hard, but enough that she knows what I am about.

"Stefan, no, you cannot."

I shift to rest my elbow on her back, a signal to her to remain still.

"Lift your bottom up for me. Let me see this."

"You cannot mean to, I mean, not… there."

"Yes, there. Show me."

"I, I…"

"Tally, show me." I continue to press my finger against the sphincter, and she relinquishes her inner struggle, relaxing enough to allow the tip to penetrate.

"Lift your bottom. I wish to see what I am doing."

She is hesitant. I will insist, we both know that, but in the end it is not necessary. She does as I have instructed. I use my other hand to part her buttocks as I dip just the top of my middle finger in to her arse, as far as my first knuckle. Tally groans, her mortification no doubt complete. But she does not stop me. Nor does she protest again.

I withdraw my finger, then sink it into her again. My movements are slow and I know I am not hurting her. This is all about submission, my will over hers, her body accepting my demands. I continue to stroke in and out, each thrust shallow, gentle. She lies still, her arse slackening as her resistance ebbs away. Time for one last push of her limits.

"Tally, I want to continue with this, but if you ask me to stop, I will. Do you want me to stop, Tally?"

I wait, my finger maintaining the intimate intrusion as I allow her to mull over my request. I know she is not comfortable with what I am doing to her, I fully appreciate that she would prefer me to roll her onto her back and fuck her. But will she say that, or knowing what I want will she seek to please me?

"No, do not stop. I… it is alright."

I smile to myself. It is indeed alright, and I intend to reward her beautiful submission. I apply my free hand to her clitoris, still swollen from her climax of moments earlier, and I rub.

"Ah, oh, Stefan, I… Oh."

Tally's release is swift, less intense than before, but all the sweeter for that. God's blood, she is exquisite.

Her gaze is still hazy, unfocused as I lift her from my lap and roll her onto her back. I spread her on my bed, her limbs outstretched in glorious abandon now, a far cry from her fearful trembling earlier. I watch her stretch languorously as I rid myself of my remaining clothing, then crawl alongside her.

"I want to be inside you."

"Yes." Her reply is a throaty whisper as she lifts her knees and spreads her thighs wide.

I position myself at her entrance and thrust hard. Her virgin arse benefited from my gentle side. That time is now spent. I drive my cock balls deep inside her, relishing her cry of almost-pain as I fill her tight cunt. I withdraw, then plunge into her once more. And again. Each stroke is long and fast, intended to give no quarter. She asks for none, lifting her legs further to hook her ankles over my shoulders.

So wanton. So absolutely perfect.

I pound into her, the walls of her channel squeezing around my rod as her arousal builds. So responsive, so demanding, her groans of pure pleasure echo around my chamber. Our chamber now. My own release will not be long. I slow my thrusts for a brief moment, just sufficient time to slip my hand between our bodies and attend to her clit with the pad of my thumb. It has the desired effect. Her back arches as she returns my thrusts, seeking the friction I am denying her. I pick up the pace again, fucking her mercilessly until she convulses around my cock.

    I am but seconds behind her. My balls tighten and my cock gives one final leap as I drive it home. I hold still, her delectable body trapped, unresisting beneath mine as I pump my seed into her.

CHAPTER ELEVEN

It is full daylight, several hours since dawn I would say judging by the bright glow spearing through the window. I turn to my side, but I already know I am alone. Stefan's side of the bed is empty, cool. He is long gone.

He did stress to his sons the strict requirement that they be ready to demonstrate their newly honed fighting skills soon after first light, so I assume he has gone down into the courtyard to drill them. It would not do for their mentor to be late, and I know Stefan well enough by now to be sure he will never be derelict in his duty.

I roll onto my back, gazing up at the curtains gathered into a rosette above me. I contemplate my new situation.

Stefan is a fine man, a loving father. He is handsome too, wickedly so. His skills in the bedchamber seem limitless. His people respect him, his keep is well protected, runs with an efficiency that does credit to all who dwell here, but owes most to its master. He sets the tone, the standards, and he enforces them.

I have been welcomed here, accepted. And this despite the astonishment this household must have experienced on learning the duke had wed again. At a word from their lord they just adapted, set another place at the top table, and continued on.

My husband is full of surprises, but perhaps the greatest of these has been the revelation of the tender father who lurks beneath that stern exterior. His sons respect and adore him, though with not a hint of fear that I could detect. He is firm with them yet patient and affectionate too, giving of his time.

More astonishing still was his kindness to his little ward. He was gentle and loving even when discipline was required, caring of her needs. If he can be so accepting of an adopted daughter, surely he would understand my own attachment to Sophia. Perhaps he would allow me to remain in contact with my stepdaughter, or even visit her on occasion. I appreciate he would not welcome the daughter of his enemy here, but he might permit me to go to Vienna.

I could ask him. Perhaps. Soon.

Stefan promised to be a stern but attentive husband to me, and thus far has fulfilled that undertaking. I find myself uncertain which facet of my husband I prefer, his sternness or his gentler brand of lust. Perhaps they are two sides of the same coin. It may be that the harsh, demanding demeanour he adopts so often is a mask behind which lurks an inventive sensuality that takes my breath away.

The spanking he delivered last night was—incredible. It was glorious, like nothing I could have imagined. Even as he hurt me, I wanted more. Maybe not too much more, but my husband knew the exact moment to pull back. The effect brought back an almost forgotten memory from my childhood, of the cunning herbal concoction my nurse once used to counter the pain of a broken wrist when I tumbled down a stone stairway. I drifted into some inner mist, aware of everything, but it all seemed to be a long way away and I was detached from the pain. My muscles went to liquid, my bones to porridge. I lay there and, and I let him do anything he wanted to me.

He shocked me when he insisted on exploring my most intimate places, but somehow it was alright even so. Because it was Stefan, and I know he will not harm me. I know, with absolute certainty, that whatever he asks of me I will do. I trust him. I want to please him.

I would not wish to disrupt the delicate balance that is between us now. I will wait for the right moment, then I will broach the matter of Sophia with him.

A soft knock at the door interrupts my musings. It opens and Berthe steps inside. She closes it behind her, then peers at me from across the room. She looks concerned.

"My lady, is there anything you need?"

I wriggle to a sitting position and shake my head. "I am fine for now, thank you. I was intending to rise quite soon though."

"The duke left instructions you are not to be disturbed, madam. He informed me that you will be fatigued from your journey and should rest in bed awhile."

"I see. That is kind of him, but…"

"He is most considerate, my lady. And handsome too."

"Indeed. I…" I hesitate, wondering how to phrase my next question. I do not know her well, but I like Berthe and I know her to be a diligent lady's maid, though at Hohenzollern her duties usually revolved around Princess Susanna and the more senior members of the household. "Berthe, it is pleasant to see you. But if I am not to be disturbed…?"

"I just wanted to see for myself that you are faring well, my lady. I have travelled with you, and with my lord and I am aware that he…" She draws a deep breath before ploughing on. "I know that he is stern, and I have heard the sounds of, of…"

Oh, dear lord, do all the servants know? What impression must they have of us? Of me?

"Berthe, I can assure you I am well. Very well. 'Tis true my lord has an unorthodox approach, and as you say, he is somewhat demanding. But I am perfectly at ease with it." Not entirely true perhaps, but I suspect I am on that journey. "I would ask that you not discuss this matter with the other servants."

Berthe stiffens, her indignation apparent. "I would not, my lady. Never. I like the duke, he is a fine lord and I know how to keep my silence. I will respect your privacy. Karl is also aware of how matters stand, though he did not learn it from me."

Yes, I suppose he would be. It is apparent that he and Stefan are close, though it surprises me that the manservant has discussed such a private matter with Berthe.

"You and Karl are friends then?"

Berthe's healthy blush is sufficient to confirm the impression I had been forming. I am not the only female to emerge from Hohenzollern to find herself attracted to one of our conquerors.

"It is nothing, he is a foolish, rough sort, and altogether too ready to put his hands where they have no business to be."

Ah, yes, Karl has much in common with the duke.

I hope Berthe is not unduly troubled by his attentions, though I will always harbour a certain fondness for Karl. His aid on the night of my capture and subsequent escape helped to save my life. I doubt Berthe will find a better man here. Apart from Stefan himself, of course, and he is mine.

I relax in his bed, now my bed also I hope, for he has said nothing of any separate chamber that I might occupy. But even as I stretch out here marvelling at my good fortune in attracting the notice of this wonderful man, I know I do not deserve it. My pleasure is marred by my guilt at having abandoned Sophia, however reluctant I was to do so. My happiness has come at a price, and I miss my darling girl so much. How long might I have to wait before I see her again? And when I do, will she still remember me? It would take but a few short months, and perhaps another kind mama to care for her, and I would be forgotten.

"My lady, what troubles you?"

I had momentarily forgotten Berthe's presence as she moves quietly around the chamber picking up my discarded clothing from last night. She is my one remaining link with the past, the only other person here who knew Sophia and who might understand my sense of loss. I decide to confide in her.

"I am worried about Sophia. His grace tells me that she and the other children were sent to Vienna, to the emperor's court. I just hope she is safe, and happy, but there is no way to discover her fate."

"If the duke says she went to Vienna with the others, do you have cause to doubt that?"

"No, no, of course not. It is just that she is so little, so young to be alone among strangers."

Berthe places the clothes she was folding on a chest and comes to sit on the edge of the bed. Her actions speak of a familiarity that may not be appropriate, but I need her quiet strength now. She takes my hand in hers.

"My lady, may I speak to you plainly?"

"Of course. Always."

Her smile is rueful. "Perhaps not always, but today, yes. I know how much you loved Sophia. We all knew that, the lady's maids and the ladies of the household. You spent all your spare time with her, you cared for her, you taught her to sew, and she was starting to learn her letters, was she not?"

I nod, viewing Berthe through the soft sheen of tears. Who will teach Sophia her letters now?

"You were her stepmama, and you did your duty to her for as long as you were able. You might even have escaped the castle when Hohenzollern fell, but you saw to her safety before your own. You owe her nothing more. Responsibility for Lady Sophia's future lies in the hand of others now and you are not in a position to aid her. You have other concerns, a new family who require your love. In time you will have babes of your own, I am sure. I know you will not forget Sophia, but times have changed, for all of us. You must move on and seize the opportunities you now have."

The tears fall unchecked. I know Berthe is right, her words are those of sound reason, good sense. She is practical to her core and she has my best interests at heart.

"If I cannot take care of her myself, I would wish for a kind and loving mama for her. I love her, so I can desire nothing less. But is it so wrong to wish it could have been me?"

"No, my lady. I do not believe it is wrong. But it is not to be, not now."

"She is to be my secret then, just someone in my past not to be spoken of?"

"You could speak of her. You should. The duke would not take that amiss, I am sure. He is fond of children, he will understand."

Will he? I hope so, I am just starting to dare to think he might, but I am not sure. He is fond of his own children, and of those he assumes responsibility for, where he feels an obligation. Sophia would be the orphaned child of a lord he despised. I did not tell Stefan about her before we left Hohenzollern because at that time I was so afraid of what would happen to her, to all of us, at the hands of the conquering army. That, coupled with Stefan's animosity toward my late husband guaranteed my silence as I sought to protect her. Now, it may be too late.

Stefan has made it clear he expects me to devote my attention to the family here at Richtenholst, and of course I will do that. I will do it to please him, and because I am already drawn into my new home and all that entails. I need to show him that I have fully embraced my role as mama to his children before seeking his indulgence regarding a child who is no longer my responsibility and was never his.

I stiffen my resolve, manage a watery smile for Berthe and make up my mind. I will live in the present, and I will endeavour to let the past go. She is right about this. I must move on, I have no alternative.

"I will leave you for a little while, my lady. I believe one of the other maidservants is on her way to build the fire up, though I swear this room is already quite warm enough." She glares at the flames roaring in the grate and shakes her head in disbelief. We were never so profligate with firewood at Hohenzollern, 'tis true. "If you need anything just summon me. Or tell the servant when she arrives."

She pats my hand one final time before she stands, straightens her heavy woollen skirts, and leaves me to consider her words.

My thoughts drift, inevitably, to Clare. Poor frightened, insecure Clare, the tiny girl who Stefan adopted. Her story is a sad one, and has taken its toll. I promised my husband I would spend time with her this morning and I intend to honour my word.

I push my legs from under the furs. Instead of the usual chill of a winter's morning, this chamber is pleasantly warm. Perhaps too warm, as Berthe observed. The fire must have been lit for a couple of hours at least and the chamber is cosy.

The door opens at that moment and a young maidservant enters carrying an armful of logs. Seeing me awake she tries to execute a curtsy, but the attempt is ill-fated. Several logs tumble to the floor and she juggles the rest. The outcome is precarious to say the least, and I scoot from the bed to relieve her of the remaining firewood.

"My lady, I am so sorry. No, please, there is no need for you to…"

I deposit the rescued logs beside the hearth and return to collect some of the stray pieces of wood scattered around the floor. The maid dumps her cargo beside the grate also and joins me. Together we retrieve the remaining logs and pile them by the fire ready for use.

"My apologies, your grace. I should not have been so clumsy. It was just, I did not expect you to be awake. And I tried to carry too many. I wanted to save a second trip down to the woodpile…"

"I understand, and it is of no matter. We have sufficient logs now, and I suspect it will be some while before we require more. Did you light the fire…?" I pause, trying to recall if I was introduced to this servant last night but if so I cannot remember her name. "I am sorry. Did we meet yesterday?"

"No, my lady. I was in the kitchens, then I sat with Lady Clare while she slept. I am Mathilde."

Ah, right. The servant who was to be assigned to watch over Clare at night. And it would seem the same maid who has responsibility for lighting fires in the early morning. Mathilde's duties are heavy.

"You must be tired then. Were you awake the whole night?"

"No, your grace. I laid my pallet across her door so Lady Clare would wake me if she tried to leave. She slept soundly the night through though. Indeed, she was still sleeping when I checked a few minutes ago, but I should really be getting back to her. His grace was most insistent that she be attended. Is there anything else I can do for you before I go? The fire is good for now, as you say, but I could bring you food, something to drink perhaps. Water for your toilet?"

"I should like all those, please, when you are able. As for Lady Clare, when she awakens would you bring her to me here please as well?"

"Here, my lady?"

"Yes. Please."

"Very well, but it may take little while to get her suitably dressed. She can be quite stubborn regarding her clothes."

"I see. In that case bring Lady Clare, in her sleeping attire, and such clothes as you deem suitable for the day. She can get dressed here, with me. It is probably warmer than her chamber."

"No, my lady, it is not. But I will bring her to you."

She bobs me a curtsy, rather more accomplished than her previous attempt, and leaves the room. I hop back into bed to wait for my little project to arrive.

I do not have long in which to contemplate my next move. Mathilde returns after a few minutes, a rather bedraggled little girl beside her, clasping her hand as though it were her last link to anything resembling security. Mathilde has bundle of clothes under her arm, and she places those on a chair close to the door.

Clare is carrying a floppy doll fashioned from rags, which she clutches in her free hand. Her hair is tangled, her loose plaits unravelling before my eyes. She peers at me from the relative safety of the maidservant's skirts, her expression wary.

"Good morning, Clare. Did you sleep well?"

No answer. Clare tightens her grip on the doll and on Mathilde's hand.

I press on with my campaign. "I am hungry. Mathilde was just about to bring food for me, to break my fast. Would you like to join me?"

Still no response. I slip from the bed and pad barefoot across to the doorway where the pair still stand. I crouch in front of Clare.

"Your dolly looks hungry. Mathilde, what does dolly like to eat?"

The maidservant picks up the cue without further prompting. "She likes milk, my lady. And sometimes a little oatmeal too. Eggs if we have any."

"Excellent. Please, could you bring those then? And for myself some bread and cheese if you would be so kind."

The maid extricates her hand from Clare's with some difficulty and bobs her brisk little curtsy again. "At once, your grace."

She is gone, leaving Clare and me to regard each other with I daresay some doubts and considerable trepidation on either side.

"Dolly looks cold. Let us tuck her back in bed to wait for her breakfast. Then we can shut this door and keep out the draughts." I stand and push the door closed behind the tiny figure, then I offer my hand to Clare. She eyes it with undisguised suspicion. Seizing the initiative, I reach down and take the child's hand, then allow her no opportunity to protest as I march her back to the bed I so recently shared with Stefan. I lift her up and deposit her in the middle of the bolster, then slip in beside her. I arrange the blankets around her feet and legs, tucking her in.

I lean against the headboard and wrap my arm around her thin shoulders. She stiffens, but makes no move to pull away. I treat that as encouragement.

"So, Clare, you are to clean mirrors this morning. I will help you."

She hugs the doll to her chest, then turns to peer up at me. "Otto is to do it. Papa said."

Her first words to me are defiant, though her tone is not. She fears displeasing Stefan again.

"I asked your papa if I could help you instead, and he agreed. Otto has many other duties to see to, and I like to clean mirrors. So you and I will do it. I do not know where all the looking glasses in the castle are though, so your papa said that you would show me." I trust that invoking Stefan's authority will win the day for me.

"And Mimi."

"Mimi?"

She lifts the doll, who close up I can see is badly in need of some repairs. Not to mention a good wash. I surmise this must be Mimi.

"Mimi too, of course. We will wait here for Mathilde to bring our tray, and we will eat. Then we will ask Mathilde to help both of us to dress. After that you can show me where the mirrors are and we will clean each one. If Mathilde does not have other tasks she must attend to perhaps she could help us too. That way it would not take as long, and we might have time to play later. Do you play hopscotch, Clare?"

Two dark eyes, wide with curiosity, regard me from beneath a tangled thatch of blond hair. She shakes her head.

"Then you must learn. Today. We shall play in the great hall. After the mirrors."

She smiles, and I know I have her.

· · · · · · ·

"Why so sad?"

Stefan's voice interrupts my reverie. Startled, I turn to watch his approach. I am seated at the high table in our great hall, alone for once as Clare is off playing somewhere. She has hardly left my side these last days as I have settled into my new home, my new life as Stefan's duchess. I set aside the clothes I have been sorting and offer a smile to my handsome husband as he crosses the hall.

My heart twists at the sight of him, so tall, so dark, and so forbidding, but under that exterior lies a sensuality which continues to stun me. Each night, and several mornings too, he delights me with his touch. Sometimes gentle, sometimes less so, but always he fulfils me.

He has spanked me again, twice. Once it was a punishment for getting his name wrong yet again. We were in the solar, and he ordered me to our chamber. I squealed and wriggled, begging him to stop as he turned me across his knee and flogged me with his belt. By the time he stopped I was still and quiet, accepting of his discipline. I was unable to sit in comfort to two days. That night though, he tied me face down to our bed, my wrists and ankles bound to the posts, and proceeded to spend the next hours exploring every inch of my body with his tongue. I lost count of how many times he brought me to a shattering climax. Eventually I begged him to stop and allow me to sleep. He did, but not before making love to me with an aching tenderness that left me weak.

The second spanking, just yesterday, was pure eroticism. I lay on our bed, face down of course, the rolled-up bolster under my stomach and my bottom lifted for him. I spread my legs on command, and I suspect I may have purred when he caressed my buttocks. I longed for him to slip his hand between my thighs to test my wetness. I no longer experience any embarrassment at my response to Stefan's touch. I relish it. At last I could bear the waiting no longer and I begged him to touch me, to spank me, to fuck me. He just chuckled, that wonderful, sexy laugh he has, and plunged three fingers into me. He promised me the spanking if I allowed him to explore my most private place with his finger.

So, I did. And it was—not bad, exactly. I did not voice that opinion though, having no desire to see my husband drowned in the Richtenholst moat. I swear my clitoris swelled as he slid his finger into me, that sweet spot throbbing until he took it between his finger and thumb and squeezed. My climax was so intense, the joy of it so overwhelming, that I may have passed out. The next thing I recall he was slapping my buttocks, raining light, rapid taps all over my bottom and thighs, and occasionally right there on the lips of my quim too. It was so good, so sensual, I could have wept. Perhaps I did. I might again.

My release seemed to persist for long, long minutes, one small climax after another, each one punctuated by a heady, greedy arousal, always begging, always demanding more.

At last Stefan heeded my pleas and drove his cock into me. He continued to slap my buttocks whilst he fucked me, pushing me to one last, shattering orgasm. This time he found his release too. The heated wash of his semen inside me is a sensation I have come to relish, not least as it will surely result in one of the most precious gifts he could offer me.

A child of my own.

"You look unhappy, and not for the first time. Why is that?" Stefan takes a seat opposite me, his glance puzzled as he takes in the pile of small items of clothing piled in front of me.

"I am fine. Really. I was just looking through these things of Clare's. Some will need to be mended, others are past that."

"You are very good with her. I am grateful for your time, and your efforts."

"She is a sweet child. I like her."

"She likes you. And from Clare that is an accolade indeed. She is sparing in her favours."

I grin. He is right there. It took me two days of almost unbroken monologue before she would respond in more than couple of grudging syllables. Now, she is a chatterbox and sometimes I might long for a little peace. But not much. I love that she is happy, relaxed around me, and enjoying my company.

"I should go find her, check that she is alright."

"She is. I just saw her playing hopscotch with Otto. I gather I must relieve him later. I confess it is not a game I am familiar with."

"I can teach you, my lord."

"Thank you. And after, I will repeat my lesson regarding the use of my given name, for I fear you are proving particularly stubborn in learning it."

Ah, a spanking. I clench my bottom in anticipation even though I fully appreciate this will hurt. "Your belt, my lo… Stefan?"

"No. On this occasion I will require you to go down to the coppice beside the village and select a suitable switch. In fact, you may bring several as I have no doubt you will be presenting your delightful bottom for punishment on regular basis."

I nod. "Of course. Several."

"But you have distracted me. You have not answered my question."

"Your question?"

"You seem so sad, so downhearted much of the time. Do I make you unhappy?"

"No! No, Stefan, Definitely you do not."

"I thought not for your response in our chamber, whether to punishment or to pleasure, is always, shall we say, enthusiastic? So, what then? Do you dislike Richtenholst?"

"No, the castle and surrounding lands are beautiful. I love it here."

"But?"

"There is no but."

"Do not lie to me, Tally. Never that. I see the unhappiness in your eyes, I hear it in your voice when you talk to Clare, and even to my boys. What can I do to relieve it? What is it you need?"

Stefan misses nothing. Even when I hope to conceal my longing for Sophia, even though I never mention her name, he somehow knows there is something, someone ever in my thoughts. I need to at least try to explain.

"I love my life now, here, with you, your sons, and little Clare. But still, I miss my old life. I had dreams, plans, people I loved, and they are gone."

"You wish to return to Hohenzollern? It will be a very different place in the future."

I shake my head. Hohenzollern was the place I wanted to be as long as Sophia was there. Now, I can think of no better place to be than Richtenholst.

"The church then? You still harbour a wish to take the veil?"

I shrug. At peril of damning my immortal soul I admit to myself that my interest in taking holy orders was rooted in a desire to remain close to Sophia, nothing more than that. My vocation was selfish in origin.

"I consider your infatuation with entering a convent to be misguided, but if you truly yearn for the peace of the cloister I would prefer to know it."

"Why? What difference would it make? I have no choice. I never did. And even if that were my ambition, my heartfelt aspiration, what could come of it now? I am your wife, with all that entails. I could never become a nun."

He cups my chin in his hand and tilts my face up to hold my gaze. "I suspect you would find it a life lacking in some comforts you have grown to appreciate of late." He cocks his head to one side, his expression intense, and also sad. "I would miss those comforts too, but if that was what it would take to make you happy, I would bow to your wishes. You *do* have a choice, Tally. I want you to choose me, us. I want you to be my duchess but it will only work if you desire it too."

"I do not understand. What are you saying? I *am* your duchess."

"A duchess who desires to be a nun. That is not what I desire from you."

My heart lurches. What does he mean? What is he saying?

"Stefan? I…"

"If you want to join a convent, Tally, I will not prevent it. Indeed, I will aid you in gaining entry to a suitable house, of your choosing."

"You are sending me away?"

He shakes his head. "No. I want you to stay here, with me. Every fibre of my being yearns for you to stay. But I will not hold you here against your will. These last few days I have seen the passion in you, and I have loved it. But I also see the sorrow in your eyes when you think yourself alone, and I will not be the cause of that. Would the cloister make you happy? Is that what you truly desire?"

I stare at him, incredulous, and I blurt out my reply. "No, of course not. Before, yes. But not now."

He holds my gaze, his eyes boring into mine for several moments. At last he nods. "I believe I have the truth from you, at least on that matter. So I return to my original question. Why so sad? And please, no more evasion or half-truths. You will tell me what is troubling you, and you will tell me now."

His features have hardened, his expression quite glacial now. I shiver, despite the fire roaring in the grate. I have experienced my husband's commanding presence before, but never have I encountered this implacable demeanour from him. Something is different here, today. Something brittle and delicate shimmers between us, something that could so easily be shattered.

It is trust, mine in my husband, but also his trust in me to deal honestly with him. He has earned it. It is time.

I bow my head, breaking his gaze at last. My hands twist in my lap, the clothes on the table long forgotten. "Very well, my lord. I will tell you, and I hope you will not think less of me, and of our marriage, when you know everything about the woman you chose to wed in such haste."

"I believe I can accept responsibility for my decisions. And deal with any implications that might ensue. Please continue, Tally."

I drag in a breath, and attempt to gather my scattered thoughts. Where to start? How to even begin to explain? And how will my husband react when he knows? I am about to discover the answer to that.

"You will recall the day we met, at Hohenzollern?"

"Of course. I recall those events in vivid detail. So, what happened that day that I missed?"

"You learned the identity of my former husband, and… and you told me of your previous acquaintance with him. The reasons why you hated him."

"I did. Do you dispute the facts I shared with you? Or take issue with my attitude toward your late husband?"

"No. No, my lord, I do not. I have no cause to doubt your account."

"Thank you. And you asked me then if I was marrying you from some misplaced sense of vengeance. I believe I assured you that was not the case."

"You did, my lord. I have never thought that."

Apparently satisfied on these points at least, Stefan makes no further comment. He waits in silence as I gather my thoughts once more.

"You may also recall I was keen to know what had been the fate of the children in the chapel."

He nods, remaining silent.

"You asked if any of the children were mine, and I said they were not."

"And I now know with absolute certainty that they could not have been. You were a virgin on our wedding night."

"You know better than most that a family can be more complex than that. You too love a child who is not yours by birth."

He frowns, and I discern understanding start to dawn. Still he does not help me out here. The silence lengthens between us as I make an earnest study of my hands.

Stefan reaches for my chin and cups it in his palm. He lifts my face, forcing me to meet his gaze once more.

"Tell me. Say the words. Make me understand this."

His tone is low, demanding, but not unkind. I take courage from that.

"I have a stepdaughter. Sophia. She, she is three years old…"

"Chapelle's child?"

I nod, blinking back tears, silently pleading with him for—what? For his permission to grieve I suppose, to set aside his hostility and allow me to express my loss and mourn it.

"Why did you not tell me of this before? Why keep this matter to yourself when I can see the distress it has caused you? It has not been for the want of opportunity, I have asked repeatedly what was causing your unhappiness and you continued to deny aught was amiss."

"I was afraid. Afraid of what you might do. You hated my husband, Sophia's father. You still do, and I accept you have sound reason for that. I know now that you are a just and fair man, but on that terrible day I had no notion of what was to happen, how the day would unfold or what fate awaited any of us. I did not know what you might do, to me or to the daughter of your enemy if you knew she was within your grasp. I feared the worst so I kept silent."

I halt, tears streaming unchecked down my cheeks as I try to voice the unthinkable. It is so clear to me now that Stefan would not have injured Sophia, he would never do that. But then, on that awful day, I did not know. I really did not. And by the time I better understood the nature of the man who was my husband, my stepdaughter was gone, already on her way to Vienna.

"So, let me be sure I have the right of this. You believed I would exact my revenge for the death of my brother on a small child, a blameless child, even after the true culprit was long dead. Out of what? Spite? Did you perhaps consider me cruel? Given to acts of mindless savagery?" He narrows his eyes in disbelief. "I know I was hard on you that day, and the day that followed perhaps, but did I truly create such an impression?"

I shake my head, sobbing in earnest now. "No, my lord. Well, yes, at first, perhaps, in the confusion, the horror and despair, amid all that was happening. But not as I came to know you. I quickly realised that you would not harm me, and that you would not have harmed a child. But by then Sophia was already gone, sent to the emperor's court. I was married to you, against my wishes, terrified of what the future might hold. Please, please try to imagine how it was for those of us trapped in the castle when it fell. I expected to die that day, I truly did. I was near enough paralysed by fear, beyond reason. My instinct was to hide, to protect. To survive. I made bad choices, I see that now, but desperation will do that."

I am weeping now, transported back into the nightmare that was that day, but this time with the liberty to succumb to my feelings in a manner that I could not have afforded then. When we were first conquered, I suppressed my feelings, my almost blind panic, and I did what I had to do, for myself, for Sophia, for such others I might be able to help. Now, the danger is passed, the floodgates are opened, and I let it all out.

Stefan's arms are around me. I am amazed, I did not expect his tenderness, not now, not over this. Yet I have it. His voice is in my ear, murmuring, comforting, assuring.

"Cry, little one. Let it go. It is over. I have you, you are safe now."

I cling to his tunic, and somehow crawl into his lap. He is rocking me, childlike, in his arms. I continue to sob, for the little girl I have lost, and for the life here I may yet lose if Stefan cannot find it in him to forgive me.

"I am sorry. I should have trusted you. From the very beginning, I should have known…"

"Shhhh, love. How could you have known? Later, yes. But not at first. I know that. I understand that."

"I was wrong. I am so sorry. Can you forgive me?"

"I always do, always will. Eventually. This will be fine. We will make it fine between us, my little Tally."

At last, gulping, I manage to raise my ravaged face to his beautiful one again. From somewhere my husband has produced a kerchief, which he uses to wipe the tears from my cheeks. His touch is gentle, loving. I do not deserve it.

"Are you angry?" He has not said so, and his actions do not suggest it.

"Nay, sweetheart, at least not for the reasons you are thinking. I am not best pleased with you, but we will get to that. First, I wish to know more of this child. Sophia, did you say?"

I nod.

"And she is what? Three years old?

"She will be four in the spring."

"She must have been very young when you married her sire."

"But a few months old. I became her mama. The only one she knew."

"It is clear that you care deeply for her. You remained close then, after her father's death?"

"Yes. Sophia became a ward of the Hohenzollern court, but Susanna allowed me to remain there too. The princess is but a distant cousin of mine, though she was kind to me."

"And all was well, until the imperial army arrived to storm the castle?"

"Yes. I suppose that is so. I always knew a time would come when we would be separated, but I had hoped…" I hesitate as tears threaten once more.

"You lost more than just your home that day, my sweet, I see that now. I wish I had known earlier. I could have offered you reassurance."

"I should have trusted you, I see that now. Berthe trusted you, she told me I could talk to you."

"You should have listened to her. You see, my love, I can appreciate your reasons for concealing the full facts from me whilst we were still at Hohenzollern. I am not entirely without wit or imagination, I can appreciate the trauma of conquest, particularly for women and children. Your assessment of me was wrong, but I can understand how you arrived at it and I do not blame you for your secrecy that day. I was not especially gentle in my handling of you. I required you to comprehend the true nature of your new situation and to submit to it so my treatment of you may have been heavy-handed. I made you fear me, and this was a consequence.

"But you did not fear me for long, not really. Certainly by the time we arrived here I believe we were on a more, shall we say affectionate footing? You saw that I had children too, you know how I feel about them. You could not still have been harbouring doubts as to Sophia's safety at my hands."

"No, my lord."

"So, why did you not tell me? I asked you, and you lied to me. On several occasions."

"I am sorry. Please, forgive me."

"Why, Tally?"

"Because it was already too late. Sophia was gone, I would not see her again. And, you and I were starting to become close. Closer. I did not want to spoil that."

"Honesty and trust enrich a relationship. They do not spoil it."

"I know, but I did not want to displease you. You told me that I was to be a mama to your children, to Clare especially. I did not think you would appreciate my affections being split."

"But they were split, whether I knew it and appreciated it or not. Is that not the case?"

"I suppose so, but I swear I have never neglected my responsibilities here. I would not do that."

"I know you would not. I have no complaints on that score. What I do take issue with, Tally, is your continued attempts to evade telling me the truth. I need you to understand your fault in that regard, and to accept the consequences of it."

I know what that means. He intends to punish me. It will hurt, but I will learn from it. And after, it will be done with. God willing. I meet his gaze.

"I understand, my lord. Do you wish me to accompany you to our chamber?"

"No. You will meet me there shortly. First, you will go to the coppice I mentioned earlier and cut several switches. I leave the selection up to you, but be assured I intend to teach you a memorable lesson and I expect your full cooperation in that. If I am less than satisfied with your choices and forced to make my own trip down to the woods, I will exact retribution for my trouble, on top of that which you have already earned. Do I make my wishes entirely clear?"

"Yes, my lord. Perfectly clear."

"Then go now. Make all reasonable haste and I will see you in our chamber when you return. Do not keep me waiting."

CHAPTER TWELVE

She has not been tardy, I will grant her that much. I turn from the window having watched Tally traverse the bailey below, a bundle of what might be mistaken for firewood in her arms. I doubt any in our household would be fooled though as to the true purpose of the sticks she carries, though no one will be so indelicate as to ask.

I do not care. I will be master of my house, and that includes my wife. I sense that this is a pivotal moment between us. I expect her to scream and squirm and beg me to have mercy, all of that is a foregone conclusion. I will ignore her pleas and deliver the discipline she needs, the discipline she has come to expect from me. Then we will move on from this.

I do not enjoy punishing my beautiful little bride, not like this. Not when the matter is so serious. But I will do what I have to in order to ensure our future together. This is as much about Tally forgiving herself as it is my requirement for justice.

I am not without sympathy for the circumstances that brought her to this situation. The brutality of the fall of Hohenzollern must have been beyond terrifying for those helpless females and children on the receiving end and it is little wonder that Tally behaved as she did that day. Had I not been so preoccupied with the responsibilities of my command, and had she not scared me almost witless with her flight and subsequent near-death I might have given voice to the questions that nattered me even then. The clues were there, in her obsession with the fate of the children in the chapel, her irrational attempt to regain entry to the castle. I could have pressed her for answers.

But I did not, and here we now are. I will deliver the thrashing she deserves for her deception, Tally is unlikely to feel able leave this chamber before tomorrow at the earliest, and then she will still be in considerable discomfort. But she will heal, she will forgive me. I have already forgiven her.

Light footsteps approach the chamber from the hallway outside, then the door opens. Tally slips inside and halts by the door. I stride past her to close it, and I drop the latch.

"Show me the switches."

Head bowed, she offers her bundle to me for my perusal.

"Select one, please."

"Me, my lord?"

"Is there another here who I might be addressing?"

"No, my lord. I am sorry." She glances at the tangle of twigs and draws out one of them. "This one, Stefan."

I take it and swing it through the air. It makes a whistling sound, very satisfying. Tally flinches.

"Excellent. And now another, please."

"Another, my lord?"

"If you please." I hold out my left hand, the first switch dangling from my right.

Tally selects a second one and hands it to me. It joins the first, and this time I swing both together. The accompanying sound is louder, more menacing.

"I believe we are getting there. One more though, I think."

I am aware from her stunned expression that Tally realises where we are headed. She is pale, her fingers trembling as she hands me the third switch. I repeat my test swing, the loud whooshing sound sufficient to strike fear into the most stoic of constitutions. My Tally is right to be nervous, but despite my earlier expectations I note she makes no attempt to plead, nor to beg for clemency. I am proud of her.

"I would have you naked. Put the remaining switches on the floor. Remove your clothes, then bend over the chest." I gesture to the large clothing chest that usually stands under the window, but which I dragged into the centre of the chamber while Tally was at the coppice. I have made the concession of laying a bolster across the top of it, for her comfort, but also to ensure her bottom is raised sufficiently for my liking.

White-faced, Tally struggles to remove her woollen dress and kirtle. Her fingers are shaking, she fumbles with her fastenings but eventually manages to divest herself of her clothing. I could offer to help, but I do not. Instead I hitch my hip on the window ledge, the three switches clasped in my hand and dangling at my side as I regard her efforts. Whatever the circumstances, I always enjoy watching Tally undress.

She pulls her shift over her head and stands naked before me for a few moments. Then without further instruction on my part, she walks to the chest and leans over it. I watch as she positions herself, her feet on the floor on one side, her hands just reaching the floor on the other.

She never looked more beautiful to me, or more perfect.

"On your toes, please. Lift your bottom higher for me."

She wriggles, raising her lush derriere as requested. I move to stand behind her, the better to admire the pink globes. It is all I can do not to drool. I consider fucking her first, but dismiss that. She would not protest, but I know how scared she is of the switching she has coming, and I have no wish to draw this out for her.

"Are you ready?"

"Yes, my lord."

She could ask me how many strokes I intend to give her, but she does not.

"You will remain still until I tell you that you may stand up. You can make as much noise as you please, as I have taken the precaution of asking Mathilde to ensure Clare is out of earshot. Do you have any questions?"

"No, sir."

"Then for the sake of clarity, tell me why I am punishing you."

"Because I did not tell you why I was unhappy. I should have told you all about Sophia. I should have trusted you."

"And in the future?"

"I will always answer honestly any questions you put to me. I swear that I will, but I need you to punish me anyway."

"Why is that, Tally?" I step closer, and trail the switches across her quivering buttocks, from right to left.

"Because I wronged you. This will make it right."

"If ever you so much as consider lying to me again, you will remember this moment, and those that are about to come, and you will think better of it. Yes?"

"Yes, my lord."

"Breathe in, Tally."

I wait a moment as her body shifts, then I deliver the first strike, hard and sharp across her right buttock.

She lets out a short scream, and I pause for a few moments to allow the three perfect stripes to ripen across her pale skin. She is gasping, shifting from one foot to the other but managing to remain in place.

"Breathe in again, Tally."

She does, and my next stroke is directed at her left buttock. It leaves three deep red lines, in beautiful symmetry with those adorning the right side. She is whimpering now, and I know I will not be able to maintain this for long. She is receiving the equivalent of three strokes for every one I deliver, and has thus far not offered any complaint.

I shift my stance, and strike her on the right side again, below the marks left by my first stroke. This time she does scream, loud. Now, we are getting somewhere. I repeat the blow on her left buttock, drawing another shriek of agony from her. If she were to beg me to stop I would not blame her. Neither would I stop. We are not yet done here.

The next two strokes are laid across the backs of her thighs, in that spot that will ensure she does not sit in comfort for the next several days. She is whimpering between the strokes now, but managing to remain in position.

I land two strokes across the centre of her bottom, in quick succession, catching both buttocks. Her whimpers are now groans. She is hurting, really hurting. The crimson marks of my discipline now crisscross her bottom, glowing, livid, etched into her tender skin. I lay the palm of my left hand on her buttock and feel the heat radiating. We are almost there.

"Two more strokes, Tally, then we are done."

She does not answer me, but I discern her slight nod and I know she is still with me in this. I see no merit in delay so I drop the remaining two strokes across her thighs, hard and fast. I am determined to deliver a memorable lesson and I am satisfied with my work.

I drop the switches to the floor and move round to crouch on the other side of the chest, beside Tally's head. I lift her hair, which has been trailing on the floor in a thick, flaxen wave. Her face is ashen, still contorted in pain. Her tears are flowing, her sobs soundless now.

"We are done. You may stand."

She uses her hands to attempt to push herself up, but to no avail. I will not watch her struggle now. I shove my arms under her shoulders and ease her up. Sliding my other arm around her waist, I help her to her feet. She wobbles, and I know her knees are about to give way under her. I scoop her up in my arms and head for the bed.

I lie on it, and arrange Tally on top of me, face down. Her breathing is rapid, jerky, and I lay my fingertips on the side of her neck to feel her pulse there racing too. But it is slowing, steadying as I hold her. I murmur words of comfort into her ear, soft whispers intended to soothe, to reassure. She says nothing to me, but I know she hears me. She kisses me, her lips soft in the crook of my neck.

I wonder, not for the first time, what I did to deserve this most exquisite of women.

• • • • • • •

The first shoots of spring are poking through the hard earth, little green buds sprouting optimism and hope for the future. Karl and I turn our steeds back in the direction of Richtenholst, leaving the men who came out to hunt in the forest with us to strap our kill to the back of a spare mount. Two roe deer and a wild boar, sufficient food to ensure full bellies for a while. Helena and Otto will butcher the carcasses and salt up any meat we will not consume at once.

Tally too has developed some skill in the art of household management. She informs me that she was taught the craft as a child, but never had any opportunity to practice it in her previous marriages. The first time she was but a child and her mother-in-law held the reins of their domestic arrangements. The second time she married a man whose housekeeping had run like clockwork for thirty years in the capable hands of a formidable bailiff. Tally lacked the confidence to challenge for her position, and in any case, the count de Chapelle wanted a pretty young thing to warm his bed, not a chatelaine to warm his hearth. It seems to me he achieved neither, though his loss is my gain.

Tally has been my duchess for three months, and for the most part I would say she was born to it. Clare adores her, and is rarely far from her side. Under Tally's gentle encouragement my little ward has flourished into the happy, outgoing child she should have always been. Alex and Fabian are fond of their stepmama too, though they insist on pretending otherwise. Aloof and preoccupied with their studies and training by day, they gravitate to Tally in the evening as she entertains them with stories or music. She is an accomplished player of the lute, and often strums a song or two for us after our evening meal. Her singing voice is perhaps less impressive, but none of us sees any reason to take issue with that.

It is in my bedchamber though that her finest skills and qualities come to the fore. She is submissive to the core. She will drop naked to her knees, a radiant smile upon her face, at the merest lift of my finger. Her occasional lapses regarding the use of my given name are, I suspect, deliberate as she craves the rough edge of a punishment spanking as much as she loves the sting of a more erotic one. She spends a great deal of her time tied to my bed, a circumstance we both find most satisfying.

She seems content at Richtenholst. More than content. I believe her to be happy and I am relieved for that. I have encouraged her to speak to me of Sophia, and I believe that has helped her to come to terms with her new situation.

There have been difficult times of course, not least the day news reached us of the death of Princess Susanna. She never reached Vienna, having met with a fatal accident on the way there. For my part I regard this as a merciful end, for I doubt the princess would have found a sympathetic audience at court. The outcome of her trial was inevitable, and the penalty would have been death. She met that fate earlier than she might have, though without the indignity of being required to plead in vain for her life.

Tally wept at the news, and continues to maintain that Princess Susanna was the wronged party. From the little I saw of Lord Eberhard I can accept there may have been some truth to that, but we will probably never know. I held Tally, encouraged her to vent her grief and her sense of injustice. It was all I could do, and I hope it was sufficient. She is calm again now and immersed in her role as my duchess.

"Is there further news from Vienna? Princess Susanna eluded justice but the trials of her other nobles should be concluded by now, should they not?"

The Widow Is Mine

I glance at Karl, puzzled by his sudden interest in politics. He never showed such concern previously for matters of state.

"I have heard no word of it."

"I see. It is just that Berthe is perturbed. She insists that the princess was unfairly used, and that the others who were accused with her had only acted under the instructions of that uncle of hers."

"Her grace expressed a similar sentiment. They are both biased of course."

"Could you enquire as to the outcome? It would please Berthe…"

"And that would please you, I do not doubt."

He shrugs, but his sheepish grin is not lost on me. I have known from the moment he added her to our party and brought her with us from Hohenzollern that Karl entertained more than passing fondness for the maidservant. He is smitten. I grant she is comely enough and her disposition seems fair. She has become a valuable part of my household, though the duties of lady's maid to my wife have largely been assumed by Mathilde.

"I will send a courier to Vienna if this will pour oil on the troubled waters of your courtship. Though why you do not simply bed the girl I cannot quite grasp."

"I suspect she would crush my balls in the cider press were I to suggest such a thing without the benefit of holy wedlock."

"Ah. Unless I miss my guess your balls are in a sorry state in either case then. Though I daresay you could consider the wench's alternative. I do recommend it."

Karl's jaw assumes a familiar stubborn angle. "I have no intention of marrying."

I grin at him, and note the uncomfortable shift as he adjusts himself in the saddle. A sorry state indeed.

"I see."

· · · · · · ·

"My lord. I have a request I would like to make of you, if you please."

We are in our solar, Tally engaged on embroidering yet another tapestry whilst I am penning my missive to the emperor seeking details of the Hohenzollern trials. I lay down the quill and turn my attention to my wife.

"Indeed. Let me hazard a guess. You would like me to bind your wrists to the bedposts and lick that beautiful quim of yours perchance? Or perhaps you are in dire need of a spanking?"

Tally stifles a smile. "Those do sound quite delightful suggestions, Stefan. But my request is of a different nature."

Her tone has become serious.

"Then ask me."

Tally has also deposited her needlework. She wrings her hands, a gesture I have not witnessed for some time. And sure enough, she is chewing on that bottom lip again. These are not good indications. I wait.

"My lord…" Another bad sign, but I let her lapse go. After a slight hesitation, she continues. "I understand from Berthe that you intend writing to the emperor regarding the fate of the Hohenzollern prisoners."

Karl must have told his ladylove of my plans. "That is correct, sweetheart."

"Is that what you are writing now, my lord?"

"Yes, it is. Was there something specific you would like me to raise with the emperor?"

"Yes. No, I mean…"

I cock my head to one side and regard her. "Tally, what is it?"

"Would you object if I were to include a personal message with your package?"

"You wish to write to the emperor?"

"No, not the emperor. I thought I might write a short note to Sophia. Would you permit that?"

I regard her across the table. I had not expected this, though in truth the idea has merit. But for one little detail.

"Is she able to read?"

Tally reddens. "No, not really. I had started to teach her, but … I was hoping that there might be someone at the court who could help. Surely someone would read my letter to her. Perhaps even aid her in penning a reply."

"Perhaps. We can but hope. Or we could ensure that outcome by sending your missive in the care of my cousin. Lady Alberta de Lombard is a lady-in-waiting to the empress, a kindly enough soul. And most crucial to our cause, she is mother to five children herself so will have some empathy I daresay. If you write your letter I will ensure it is delivered to Lady Alberta, with the request that she read the contents to Sophia and help her to formulate a reply. How will that be, my love?"

Tally beams at me for several moments before launching herself across the table. Her squeals of delight are ample reward for my flash of brilliance. Indeed, I wonder that I did not think of such a remedy for her malaise before now. I should have sent word to my cousin as soon as I became aware of the situation, seeking news of the child, and urging Alberta to take an interest in Sophia's welfare. Still, I bask in my wife's gratitude now.

"Thank you, thank you, thank you. When is the courier to leave?"

"Tomorrow, at first light. I expect a reply from court within a fortnight."

"I must write my note quickly then so as not to delay his departure. Would you excuse me, please?"

I could kick myself for not delaying the messenger's departure, but it is too late now. Tally scurries from the room, and I content myself by looking forward to reaping the full fruits of her gratitude in our chamber later.

CHAPTER THIRTEEN

It has been almost three weeks since the courier left for Vienna, and still no word. I am not sure exactly what it is I am expecting, though I have every confidence that Stefan's cousin will help if he says she will do so. But Lady Alberta may be busy. She will have other duties, other calls on her time.

I lean against the windowsill in our chamber, scanning the distant hillsides for any sign of a rider heading our way. Already the spring grows late, the lush grasses and early summer blooms are splashing their glorious hues over the landscape.

It is beautiful sight and I know I am lucky to be here. I am fortunate indeed to be able to enjoy a fresh spring morning, in the knowledge that my husband is close at hand, my family too. And as I place my palms on my still flat stomach, I give secret thanks to my maker for the new life just blossoming inside me.

I will tell Stefan soon. Today. For now though I hug my joyous news close, knowing that my own burgeoning happiness makes the wait for a reply to my letter yet more poignant.

A knock at the door disturbs me. I bid my visitor to enter. It is Mathilde.

"My lady, his grace has requested that you join him in his solar. At your earliest convenience."

"I see. Thank you, Mathilde. I will be there presently."

She bobs her curtsy and scurries off about her business. I collect some embroidery and make my way to the solar on the floor below. I enter, to find Stefan gazing from the window. On this side of the keep, the windows overlook the bailey and practice courtyard where the men at arms are put through their drill each day by Stefan and his knights. From my husband's intent expression I surmise he must be observing today's training exercises. He is probably casting an especially critical eye over the performance of two young boys as each vies to outdo the other and gain the praise of their commander. He turns to me as I approach his side, his smile dazzling.

He never fails to take my breath away, this handsome man of mine.

"My lord, you wished to speak with me?"

"Speak? Yes, I suppose so. Though I would much rather fuck you."

Ah, one of those conversations. And so early in the day too. How nice.

I glance about me. "We are quite alone, my lord, and I doubt it would take long."

"You are casting aspersions on my prowess, my lady?"

"As if I would consider such foolhardiness, my lord. I simply thought…"

"I believe I am quite capable of discerning what you simply thought. If you require a spanking may I suggest you come right out and ask for it? I know you too well now to be fooled by all this 'my lord' nonsense."

I lift my chin in a gesture of mock haughtiness. "I was merely being respectful, my lord."

"Is the door locked?"

I step back to it and slide the bolt home. "It is now, Stefan."

My husband seats himself on a low, straight-backed chair in the centre of the room. It has no arms, and in normal use I daresay would be somewhat uncomfortable. It is perfect for spanking though.

"I note you refreshed our supply of switches the other day. You will find them in the chest below the window. Select one and bring it to me. Then you may arrange yourself across my lap and raise your skirts."

I kneel beside the chest and open the lid. There, lying on top of a pile of folded linens, are the half dozen or so switches I cut and brought back from the coppice the day before yesterday. I had wondered where my husband had stored them. This is not a punishment switching so I have no reason to fear his treatment of me this morning. And of course there is also the matter of my delicate condition. I select the switch that seems to me to be most supple, most likely to deliver a sweet, sharp bite, then I close the lid and stand up to pass the instrument to Stefan.

He gestures to me to get into position, so I waste no time in doing so. The cool draught of air across my naked buttocks is an exhilarating precursor to a spanking, and over recent months I have come to love that sensation. I sigh my contentment as Stefan palms my soft flesh, sensitising my skin in readiness. I wrap my fingers around the front leg of his chair and lift up my bottom, adopting just the pose I know he likes without his even needing to instruct me nowadays.

"Are you ready, Tally?"

"Yes, my lord. Perfectly ready. But there is something you should perhaps know before we start."

"And what is that, my love?"

"I believe I am pregnant."

"Believe?"

"My courses are late."

"How late?"

"Almost three weeks, my lord."

"And you only now think to mention this, when you are poised across my lap, your gorgeous bottom raised for my punishment?"

"I intended to tell you today, Stefan. Does it make a difference? To my spanking, I mean?"

"It makes a difference to me. Until I have considered this matter and concluded how I might best spank you without fear of harming you or our child, I prefer to settle for fucking you instead."

"I believe that might be an acceptable alternative, my lord. And since my skirts are already raised perhaps you might like to remain seated as you are and I will straddle you."

"A delightful notion, but that would be you fucking me I fear."

"Does it really matter, Stefan?" I twist on his lap until I am upright, facing him, my legs spread wide on either side of his. I lift his linen tunic to reach the fastenings on his chausses and undo those in one practised move.

"I daresay it does not. Not in the grand scheme of things. Tell me, when did you become so shameless?"

"The day you married me, my lord."

I shift, lifting my body to position his cock at my entrance, then sink down onto him. My quim is already drenched from the near spanking, but the friction is still intense. Still quite, quite sublime.

"God's bones, woman. That feels so damn good." Stefan's sexy voice has dropped an octave or two, his face now buried in the hollow of my neck.

"It does, my lord. It truly does. Now be still and allow me to conclude our business."

I am amazed that he does, after a fashion. It does not take long, and ten minutes later I am snuggled on his knee, my cheek against his chest as I listen to the wondrous sound of his heartbeat.

"May I return to my embroidery now, my lord?"

"All in good time. You distracted me. You may be surprised to learn that I did not summon you here just because I wanted to fuck my wife. Sorry, be fucked by my wife, delightful as that was."

"No, my lord? Did you have some other matter you wanted to raise with me then?"

"I did. The courier has returned from Vienna."

I sit bolt upright, almost crashing the top of my head into Stefan's chin. "What? I did not know that. I have been watching for him."

"Have a care, my sweet, lest you do me some injury. Neither of us would wish that, I am sure. He arrived while the household was still abed. You are eager for news then? Perhaps a reply from Sophia?"

"Was there any news, my lord? A letter for me?"

He shakes his head. "No letter, just documents from the emperor, all addressed to me. Matters he has agreed I am well placed to take care of. One of those matters will be of particular interest to you though, I suspect."

"What matter is that, Stefan?"

He stands and settles me back on my feet. "Come, I will show you."

I take his hand and he leads me from the room. I follow him down the narrow stairs into the great hall where servants hurry back and forth laden with laundry, fresh rushes for the floors, pails of water. The scene is a familiar one to me nowadays, the daily hustle of a large, busy household. We stop at the foot of the stairs and survey the room.

"Over there. Look." Stefan points to the far corner where two small figures huddle over something. Mathilde is hovering in attendance. As we approach the group I hear the high-pitched mew of a kitten, followed by girlish giggles. Clare must be playing with one of the children from the village.

"Be gentle, Lady Clare. She is just a baby. And you must share her." Mathilde's tone is patient, as ever.

Clare picks up the tiny bundle of fluff and hugs it to her chest, just as she did her doll Mimi on that first morning we spent together. She hands the kitten to her companion, another small girl.

My heart lurches, for in this dim light the second child looks just like... I halt, forget to breathe as I stare at the incredible sight, taking in every familiar feature.

"Sophia! Oh, Sophia, can it be? Is it really...?"

I turn to Stefan, perplexed. Clare's playmate looks so much like Sophia but it cannot be. Not here. Sophia, my Sophia is in Vienna, in the custody of the court.

"Mama!" The shriek of joy dispels my doubts. However this miraculous state of affairs may have come about, it has happened. The impossible, the wonderful, the truly unimaginable has actually come to pass. Sophia is here in Richtenholst. I drop to my knees in time to catch her as she concludes her headlong flight down the length of the hall. I hug her to me, my tears dampening her soft hair.

"My baby. My beautiful, beautiful baby girl. You are here. I never thought to see you again, yet here you are."

"Mama, mama, mama," Sophia's words are muffled as she buries her face in my chest, her little arms locked tight around my neck. We hang onto each other, and I make myself the silent promise that come what may I will never allow us to be parted again.

When at last I raise my head, it is to see Stefan seated at the high table, Clare standing on the bench at his side. She has his face between her palms and is gazing into his eyes. It's a staring contest, a game they like to play together. Perhaps distracted by my movement, Stefan turns to me.

"I won. Papa, I won."

"I know, sweetheart. You did well. Could you teach the game to Sophia now, do you think?"

Clare hops down from the bench and comes over to Sophia and me. She takes Sophia's hand and I let her go with reluctance. The pair of them head off to toward the staircase. They seat themselves on the bottom step and are soon locked in earnest conversation.

"Tally, come here." Stefan is still lounging at the high table, but his expression is anything but casual. I walk toward him, my head buzzing with questions.

Why is Sophia at Richtenholst?
How did she get here?
How can I ensure that she never leaves?

Stefan calls out to Mathilde, still hovering in the corner. The servant is as confused as I am. Almost.

"Would you get her grace a drink, please? Some mead, perhaps. Or a little wine. We will watch the children."

That habitual bob, and she is gone, scurrying in the direction of the kitchen, no doubt to consult with Helena on my bizarre behaviour. Still dazed, I take a seat beside Stefan.

He reaches for my hand, and for the first time I realise it is shaking.

"From that display I assume you are pleased to see the newest addition to our family. Not counting this little one, naturally." He pats my stomach, then leans in to kiss my forehead.

"Our family?" Not eloquent, but I am doing my best.

"Yes. I petitioned the emperor for custody of Lady Sophia, which he has graciously granted to me."

"But, why…?"

"Why not? I am head of a noble house; she will be well cared for here at Richtenholst."

"You are being uncharacteristically obtuse, my lord. I mean, why did you petition the emperor?"

"It took me a while to come to terms with the notion, I confess. My hostility toward her father runs deep, but I believe I have arrived at the correct solution for us all. I did not wish to mention my intentions to you, I wanted to be sure I could gain custody of the child before raising your hopes. I was confident, my influence at court is not inconsiderable, but the history between my house and that of the late count de Chapelle is known so I had to convince the emperor that my intentions were altruistic. My reputation is honourable enough, but until the courier arrived just before dawn with the documents, and of course Sophia, I could not be certain of the outcome."

I frown, still trying to make sense of this, to fully comprehend the implications of what Stefan has achieved. "So, Sophia is… what? She is now your ward?"

"Yes."

"What does that mean? For her?"

"It means she is in my care. She will live here, with us, until such time as she marries whereupon I will no doubt be called upon to provide her with a generous dowry. I gather the count de Chapelle died in somewhat strained circumstances so she can expect little in the way of inheritance. Still, I daresay we will manage."

His smile is indulgent, but I do not underestimate the extent of my husband's generosity. And his forbearance. "You did that for me. You took in another penniless orphan, the daughter of your enemy at that, just because you knew I loved her and that I was missing her?"

"Of course. Why would I not? I love you. I want you to be happy. I once, mistakenly, believed that becoming a nun would achieve that for you. I much prefer this solution though."

"Me too. I cannot believe you would do this. For me. For Sophia. Will her presence her not be… painful for you?"

Stefan smiles at me. "I am no scholar, 'tis true, but I hope my intellect is sufficiently well developed that I can discern the difference between an incompetent warmonger, one who has been dead or the best part of a year at that, and a small child playing in the corner of my hall. If there is some physical resemblance between them, it is lost on me since I never met her father. I am confident I will not confuse the two."

"You will grow to love her?"

"Yes, I daresay."

"I don't know how to thank you."

"I suspect you will come up with something, my love." His smile fades and for a few moments his expression is serious. "You know how precious my children are to me. Why would I consider yours any less so? And please be under no illusion, my love, if it is within my power there is little I would not do for you. I love you, so 'tis simple. Even on that first day at Hohenzollern, had I known of Sophia's existence and her importance to you, we would not have left without her. You could have trusted me even then, though I do understand why you did not."

I lower my gaze, ashamed now of my doubts. I was quite certain there was no chance, I knew with cold certainty there was no means by which I might affect Sophia's fate. I have no influence, no power, no friends at court. I never considered for one moment that Stefan might intervene, that he would do this for me. I should have, I see that now.

I make a belated attempt to explain myself. I owe him that much. "I apologise, my lord. It never occurred to me that you would allow Sophia to come here, to be with me. The child of your old enemy, not even my own daughter."

"Allow? What is this talk of allowing? Have I ever denied you anything you needed or desired, if it was in my power to provide it?"

"No, but…"

"And you should realise by now that family is not always about blood. Certainly ours is not. I thought you understood that, your attachment to Sophia is proof of it. Clearly I have some further work to do in convincing you." His expression takes on a more stern aspect as he narrows his eyes at me. "As the switch is out of the question for the next few months I must come up with something else sufficiently compelling."

"I am sure you will not fail me."

"Your confidence is heartening, but I am open to suggestions nevertheless."

"Stefan?"

"Mmm?"

"I love you."

His expression softens and he kisses me. "Thank the dear lord for that. It is about time you got around to telling me."

"If I tell you every day from now on, will it earn me more spankings?"

"Lady Natalia, you are quite wanton. Thank God I married you when I did for you would have made a deplorable holy sister. I fear you will prove a questionable influence on our impressionable girls."

"In that case, perhaps we should retire to our chamber for a short while, my lord. Just to make sure I do not create the wrong impression."

"What an excellent suggestion, my sweet. Even if Clare and Sophia were not traumatised I doubt Helena would approve of my fucking you on this table. I believe it to be freshly polished." He glances around the hall. "Where is Mathilde?"

Just at that moment the maidservant reappears from the kitchen, a mug of ale in one hand and a glass of wine in the other. Stefan meets her halfway across the floor.

"Thank you." He takes the drinks from her. "Lady Natalia and I have some matters of considerable urgency that we must attend to in our chamber. Perhaps you could watch the girls for us now? And ensure that we are not disturbed."

Mathilde grins and nods, though she does have the grace to blush. Would that I still retained such finer feelings.

"She will know. She is sure to know what we are about." I whisper my admonition to Stefan as he drags me up the stairs in his wake.

"They will all know soon enough. You do tend to be most vocal, my dear. I suppose I could gag you, if that helps."

I sigh. "I am sure we will manage perfectly well, my lord, gag or no gag."

He chuckles as he bundles me through the door into our chamber. "No doubt we will. Now, strip, and kneel, your grace."

The End

Conquering Lady Claire

Sue Lyndon

PROLOGUE

Galien sat at the duke of Leuthold's right, his unease rising as the midday meal progressed. He had intended to depart Leuthold two days past, but the duke had invited him and his men to stay longer. Galien thought it unwise to refuse his overlord's invitation and had agreed to prolong his visit, even though the duke's constant questioning grated his nerves.

"Tell me about your intended. She used to live here in this castle, did she not?" the duke asked.

"Aye, the Lady Rhianna. She died when an illness swept through and claimed her father, her mother, her brothers, and many others in the castle." Galien brought his goblet to his lips and swallowed the last of his wine in an attempt to drown his growing irritation.

The emperor had granted Leuthold the dukedom last spring, after the young man's army helped overthrow an attack upon an important trading port, and this was Galien's first visit to Leuthold in many years, a visit made tense by Leuthold's increasingly peculiar behavior. If Galien didn't know better, he'd think the young duke suspected him of some crime or treason. The less-than-casual interrogation had gone on for almost a fortnight.

"Did you know her well? The Lady Rhianna?"

"No, I only met her once as a child."

"Sir Galien, I know you are anxious to return home, but I assure you I have good reason for inviting you to Leuthold." The duke sat back. "I also have good reason for badgering you with question after question."

Galien stiffened and placed his goblet on the table. "What reason is that?"

"To determine your character, Sir Galien."

"My character?"

"Yes." The duke crossed his arms and a brief smile flitted across his youthful face. "I have found you suitable enough for my purposes."

A sense of foreboding struck Galien, for he recognized the look in the duke's eyes. His father had given him that look many a time, always before he issued a command Galien didn't care for. "Suitable enough for what?"

"To marry my sister, Lady Claire."

God's head. Marriage! Galien swallowed hard and felt the blood drain from his face. He'd endured many a lecture from his father in recent months about his responsibility to marry and produce an heir, but he preferred to postpone matrimony until absolutely necessary. He cleared his throat and tried to compose himself. He glanced in his empty cup. Why hadn't a servant refilled his wine yet? "Your grace, I'm afraid I do not understand."

"You will travel to Diterich Castle and fetch my sister. I believe she is still there, though I cannot be entirely certain. I've sent her many letters since her husband's death two winters ago, but she has offered no response. I do not trust her husband's family, and I am taking it upon myself to see her wed again, this time to a man who isn't old enough to be her sire's sire. Are you familiar with Diterich?"

Galien had heard of the castle, and of the elderly Lord Diterich who had outlived his first five wives. "I did not know Diterich had taken a sixth wife, though I did hear of his passing."

Leuthold leaned closer to Galien. "Aye, my sister became his sixth wife, but she did not bear him any children. However, she is still young and I am confident she will give you many sons." He shrugged. "My mother gave my father six sons. I sense your reluctance, Sir Galien, but I am not giving you a choice. You will find Lady Claire and you will make her your wife." The young duke smirked. "And to compensate you for having to spend the rest of your life with my spirited sister, I will extend your holdings into the valley. That means the trading village of North Wenzton is now yours."

Servants passed by and collected their empty trenchers as the minstrels played a merry song that contrasted with Galien's dark mood. From across the hall, the servant girl he'd tumbled on his first night here winked at him. He lowered his gaze, wishing the duke hadn't found him *suitable enough*.

"You will leave on the morrow." The duke of Leuthold patted his back as if they were longtime friends. "See that you find my sister and treat her with kindness. Do not disappoint me. I needn't remind you that I have the emperor's ear."

CHAPTER ONE

Lady Claire blinked up at the white flag raised above the battered keep. All the hairs on the back of her neck stood up, and a knot formed low in her stomach. A tense silence blanketed the bailey, while outside the walls of Hohenzollern triumphant cries rang out.

It was over, or at least the fighting part of it. Claire wasn't so naïve as to think the mercenaries and soldiers who fought on behalf of the emperor planned to march away empty-handed. She covered her mouth with an icy hand to stifle a gasp wrought from the sudden realization. The castle would be looted, or worse. Perhaps the knights would show some restraint, but over half of the army consisted of ruthless mercenaries, the type of men who knew no restraint.

She cast one last glance at the white flag flapping about in the frigid winter wind and made her decision. She had to escape Hohenzollern before the terms of surrender were finalized, before the conquering army streamed into the keep. Gathering up her skirts, she raced into the castle, almost knocking a young knight over in her haste to escape. Before she succeeded in moving by him, he gripped her shoulders and peered at her through the slit in his helmet.

"Sir Roland," she said, recognizing the knight by his eyes, one blue and one green.

"You must depart the castle, Lady Claire. The princess is walking out to meet with the enemy as we speak, but I fear the mercenaries will storm the keep at any moment to claim their portion of the spoils of war, including the women within these walls."

"Tell me how to leave this place and I will." She clutched onto his armor-covered forearms to steady herself, praying he knew of a secret passage that led away from the castle and the carnage of the battle.

"Gather as many women and children as you can and make haste to the cellars. Lady Glenda is waiting there and she will guide you to safety. Go now and good luck!"

Claire nodded her thanks and gave him a sad smile. "God be with you, Sir Roland."

"And with you, my lady."

With a feeling of purpose that superseded her fear, she ran through the halls of the keep, gathered as many women and children as she could find, and bade them to follow her to the cellars. Glenda stood waiting as promised, and after lighting a few torches and handing them to the women who looked most able and alert, the dark-haired lady ushered them down a series of narrow passages, the light of their torches barely piercing the deep gloom of the underground escape route. Glenda paused when at last a faint light could be seen further on down a narrow tunnel. She bid the trembling lady at the front of the line to lead the group out of the tunnel and on to safety in the forest.

"There's an old hunting cottage only a half-day's journey, just keep moving north," Glenda said. "We will find each other there."

Claire's conscience grew heavier and heavier with the knowledge that she hadn't been able to find all her cousins, many of the servant girls, and other ladies who had been visiting the castle. She met Glenda's stare through the dim light and reached for her hands.

"This isn't half the ladies I meant to find, Glenda. They must be hiding in their chambers, or perhaps waiting to see what happens next."

"I've sent two smaller groups out into the forest before yours, Claire."

"Did you see Lady Hazel?"

Glenda shook her head. "No, I haven't seen her since early this morning."

"I must go back and find her."

"Please hurry. I'll wait for you here as long as I can." Glenda squeezed her hands to encourage her, but Claire did not move right away. Something about the surrender troubled her. "What is it, child?" Glenda asked impatiently.

"I am surprised Lord Eberhard agreed to surrender so soon. I imagined that stubborn man would hold out for a few more days at least."

Glenda scoffed. "Lord Eberhard is more a coward than he is stubborn. He joined the second group of women and children I took into the cellars. Pushed ahead of the group and ran off into the dark even as I hollered after him."

Claire's spirits plummeted to her feet. Poor Princess Susanna. No wonder a white flag had been raised. The princess had taken the most sensible course of action under the circumstances to save the lives of her people, and Claire respected her for it. "That bastard," Claire hissed, thinking it especially cruel of Lord Eberhard to incur the anger of neighboring kingdoms only to run when they came seeking vengeance.

"Aye, he's a bastard of the worst kind. We are running out of time. You must go now."

Claire nodded and grabbed up her skirts, grateful that she'd worn her brother's old boots today rather than a pair of dainty slippers. She'd taken to wearing them the moment the fighting began and had slipped a knife into a fold of leather against her ankle. She had no intention of letting some foul-breathed mercenary rut on her. It took her several minutes to find her way back down the passageway with only the light of her torch to guide her, but at last she emerged into the cellars once more, then quickly made her way upstairs.

Servants rushed to and fro through the halls, and Claire stepped in front of a footman. "Are the mercenaries inside yet?" She clutched his arm to prevent him from taking off again.

"Please, milady, I must go and find my daughters." He tugged free of her grasp but paused long enough to divulge the reason for the new chaos that had broken out. "Gerhard of Bavaria announced that there would be no rapes or murders today, but women may be taken as wives."

Her mind spun and for a moment she felt dizzy. "What do you mean?"

"I mean you'd best go and hide yerself, milady, lest you become the bride of some mercenary or a knight from the Free Cities. They've just summoned Father David to stand at the portcullis and perform quick marriage ceremonies. Hide now, milady! Before it's too late!"

The footman dashed off and left Claire alone in the middle of the disorder.

She wasted no time in retrieving the knife from her boot. She clutched the bejeweled handle and set off in search of any remaining women and children. As she made her way to the stairs, she looked upon the great hall and her eyes went wide at the sight of rough-looking, brutish men spilling into the castle. The mercenaries she'd heard the servants whispering worriedly about. Knights too, some bearing crests she recognized from nearby houses, and some wearing crests she didn't recognize at all.

Her heart sank at the sight of ladies and servant girls being forced to stand in a line against the far wall as the men looked them up and down, while others were forced outside. Many of ladies were crying, and Claire's heart went out to them. She wished to save every last one of them, and she held her breath as she scanned the crowd for her young cousin, the very lady who'd kindly asked Princess Susanna to send her an invitation to the castle many weeks ago.

"Claire! My God, it's you!"

Claire spun around and breathed a sigh of relief. "Cousin! Where have you been?" She grasped Hazel's hand and pulled her toward the cellars. "Oh, never mind. Come on."

"Where are we going?"

"Away from here." Claire ran through the halls, desperate to reach the cellars before the soldiers made their way further into the castle. At last she came upon the stairs which lead to the cellars, and she pushed Hazel ahead of her. "Glenda is waiting for us. She's already evacuated three groups of ladies through an underground passage. She will guide us out into the forest."

Hazel rushed down the steps, holding her skirts high, the veil on her headdress flouncing through the air. Claire followed quickly. At the bottom of the stairs, Claire grabbed the torch she had left behind after coming back through the passage minutes ago. Moving quickly through the cellars, she guided Hazel through the door which lead to the underground passage, then handed her the torch. "Follow this passage until you find Glenda or reach the forest! I'm going to see if I can bar this door behind us."

Hazel paused for a moment, then nodded and started down the passage. Claire turned back to the door which concealed the passage entrance from the rest of the cellars, forcing it shut and then searching for a locking mechanism. Unable to find anything after a few minutes, she cursed under her breath, then simply left it closed and hoped for the best.

Glancing down the passage, she didn't see Hazel. Her cousin must be well on her way to safety. After taking just a moment to catch her breath, she would start down the passage herself. It would be hard going without light—she should have thought of that before sending Hazel on ahead with the only remaining torch—but she would have to find her way somehow.

Before she could take a step, however, the door at her back was suddenly thrown open. An arm snaked through the opening and grabbed her roughly, and a large man dragged her into the cellars again. It happened in a blur of movement, and no matter how hard she fought her captor, he didn't falter as he carried her away from the promise of freedom. Almost before she knew it, she had been dragged through the cellars and back upstairs into the great hall. Throughout the ordeal, she managed to conceal the blade of her small knife against her wrist, and she grasped it beside her skirts, determined to hold onto the dagger until the opportunity to wound her captor arose.

"Ah, now let's get a better look at you, milady." The man, whom she suspected was a mercenary, pushed her to sit atop a table and held her upper arms in a bruising grip. She kicked and kicked, but her booted feet only connected with his armor. He wore no helmet, but he still wore full armor and chainmail. She assessed the situation and planned her method of attack, knowing she must aim for his face when the time came.

"I am Lady Claire of Diterich, widow of Lord Diterich. My brother is the duke of Leuthold. If you don't unhand me, I assure you that you will regret it. My late husband's family is powerful and would seek swift justice if you damage a single hair on my head, and my brother the duke would have *your* head for even looking at me." Though she spoke a half-truth, she infused her tone with confidence and lifted her chin. If she spoke it like she believed it, mayhap this man would unhand her.

He tightened his grip on her arms and displayed a yellow-toothed grin that made her cringe. The heavy stench of ale on his breath turned her stomach. An unshaven savage with greasy dark hair plastered to his head, his eyes glistened with more cruelty than she'd ever witnessed from her late husband. At least Lord Diterich had been old and weak, and she'd had no trouble dodging his fists. Most of the time. This man, however, was young and strong, and sickness rose in her throat at the thought of becoming his wife. She turned the dagger around so the point faced him and clutched the handle with renewed determination.

"Ah, such a pretty girl," the man said, his grin widening. His gaze lowered to her bosom. "I've always wanted a taste of a noblewoman, and now I shall have one as my wife. God has surely smiled upon me!"

He backed up to ogle her further and Claire wrenched from his grasp. She swung the knife at his face and slashed deep. His scream pierced the air and he covered his left cheek, staring at her with a look of surprise that quickly shifted to cold anger. She pointed the knife at him, holding it between both her hands. Though tremors besieged her body and her hands shook around the dagger, she put on a brave face and rose up from the table, but when she made to slip around the man, he blocked her path.

"You will let me pass," she said, lifting the knife higher.

"No, I will not let you pass, you fucking bitch. I will make you my wife, and then, little lady, I will spend the rest of the day pounding into your noble cunt." He struck out at her hands and knocked the knife from her grasp. The bloodied weapon clattered to the table, and she backed against the wall.

His fist flew through the air, but Claire ducked and his knuckles crunched into stone. A snarl erupted from his throat and he loomed over her with murderous intent reflecting in his dark eyes. Her blood ran cold.

He raised his fist again, but a large figure knocked him off his feet before he had the chance to swing.

· · · · · · ·

Galien pushed the mercenary to the floor and stood over him with a hand hovering on the hilt of his sword.

"I saw her first," the man spat. "She's mine."

"Aye, but it doesn't look like you're able to handle her," Galien replied with a smirk. "Shall we fight over her?" He inched his sword halfway out of its scabbard, and the drunken mercenary's eyes went wide with alarm. The man turned and scrambled away, leaving behind a bloody handprint on the floor.

"Thank you, sir," the lady said, straightening her skirts. "That was chivalrous of you; however, I am quite certain I could have handled the miscreant myself."

Galien released his hold on his sword and gave a slight bow to the lady.

"You can put your knife away now, Lady Claire."

She clutched it low at her side, eyeing him with suspicion. "I think I'll keep it handy for now." Her thin dark brows narrowed together. "How do you know my name?"

"I overheard you threatening the mercenary." Galien studied the lady before him, taking in her full bosom, narrow waist, and ample hips her dress displayed in an inviting fashion. He still couldn't believe his luck at finding Lady Claire at Hohenzollern of all places. He cleared his throat and stepped closer to her. "I am Lord Galien of Minrova."

"Minrova? I thought Lord Galien was an old man. I did not know he had a son. Of course, there are so many lords and castles of late that it makes my head spin."

"The *late* Lord Galien was an old man. I will inherit my father's title upon my return to the family household. After my departure to find you, I received a missive that he passed away. You may call me Lord Galien if it pleases you." He gave her a wicked smile. "However, I would much prefer you call me husband."

"Husband?" A crazed laugh escaped her, but when he didn't crack a smile she fell silent and stared at him with wide eyes. "You're serious, aren't you?" She pointed her knife at his face and gave him a hard look. The tip of her blade shone dark with the mercenary's blood.

"Aye, my lady, I am serious. Your brother wishes for us to be married. He deployed me to Diterich to retrieve you from your late husband's castle. My men and I joined with the army to defeat Hohenzollern on our way south to Diterich. Imagine my surprise to find you here in this castle, so far from home."

"My brother?" she gasped. "*Which* brother? I have six of them."

"The duke of Leuthold, and my overlord."

Still, the lady did not lower her weapon. He watched as her expression transformed from suspicious to astounded, and then from fearful to suspicious again. "Even if you're telling the truth, you are wasting your time with me. I have no need of a husband, and Leuthold is a fool for thinking I do."

He crossed his arms and regarded her, amused by her stubbornness. Her beauty also mesmerized him. When the duke had none too gently commanded him to marry his sister, he had not been pleased. Being ordered about by an overlord a decade younger than him was riling at the very least, and he had no desire to marry a woman he'd never once laid eyes on. Refusing the duke's orders was not an option, however, so he'd assembled his men and set off for Diterich, his mood dark until the opportunity to battle Hohenzollern arose. Two and a half days of fighting had proven a fair distraction from his father's recent passing and his impending nuptials.

Ah, but the lady's sparkling blue eyes drew him in, especially when anger flickered forth. She had lifted her chin and clenched her jaw, emphasizing high but delicate cheekbones he longed to reach out and stroke. Her full, pink lips called to him, and images of what she might do with that pretty mouth of hers left his cock straining against his armor.

She made a sudden jabbing motion with the knife in his direction, jarring him from his salacious thoughts. He glared at her, annoyed that she viewed him as no better than the mercenary who'd been pawing at her.

"My lady, I am losing my patience with you. I would like to leave Hohenzollern soon. Daylight is fading and I prefer to travel as far as possible before dusk. If we don't dally, we will arrive at my keep before nightfall tomorrow." He arched an eyebrow at her and looked pointedly at the knife, silently urging her to place the weapon down. It wouldn't take him more than an instant to disarm her, but he wanted the lady surrender on her own free will. Trying to gain her trust after forcibly taking her dagger and hauling her out of the castle would be no small feat.

Lady Claire edged along the table, attempting to slip past him. He blocked her path at every turn and held out a hand, beseeching her to surrender.

"Give me the knife, my lady."

"No. Perhaps you should take out your sword so it's a fair fight, my lord," she said tauntingly. The firm set of her jaw and her brave words were betrayed by her trembling hands.

His heart softened to her and he ached to gather her against his chest. He did not know much about the lady he had been commanded to wed, but he knew her late husband had been no saint. Lord Diterich's first five wives had died in their sleep under mysterious circumstances. The elderly lord had been known for his violent temper, as well as his obsession with wealth and power. Galien hoped Lady Claire had not suffered too terribly at his hands. She was far too young to have been married to such an old man, and he wondered at the circumstances that had led to the marriage. Surely she had not been a willing bride.

Around them soldiers issued commands and ladies cried and gasped as they were escorted toward the great hall. Claire's eyes filled with tears as she surveyed the scene, and her lower lip quivered. She met his gaze and anger flared in her brilliant blue depths.

"While you might have heard of my brother, I doubt you are the lord you claim to be. For all I know, you have concocted the story for some sinister purpose."

"I am exactly who I claim to be. Even if I'm not, I am within my rights to claim you as mine. Enough of the knife play, my lady. Hand me the weapon now."

She slashed the dagger through the air and he caught her wrist in a firm grasp. Stepping closer, he towered over her petite form and stared into her frightened eyes, cursing the circumstances of their first meeting. If the rumors about her late husband and his son who now ruled in his place were true, she would have welcomed his arrival at Diterich with open arms. But now instead of her savior, he was her enemy.

He squeezed her wrist just hard enough to force the knife out of her hands. It clattered to the floor and for a moment he simply stared down at her, wordlessly beckoning her to trust him. She struggled against his hold, kicking at his legs and flailing around like a woman possessed.

"Release me!" She landed a hard kick and then winced, her foot hitting his armor.

"If you don't calm yourself, my lady, you will get hurt." He pulled her arms down to her sides and backed her against the table. "Now listen to me and listen well. I am indeed Lord Galien of Minrova, and your brother the duke of Leuthold has commanded me to take you as a wife, even to use force against Diterich to remove you from their castle if necessary. We are leaving Hohenzollern now, and if you continue giving me trouble I will not hesitate to exercise my husbandly right to discipline you, Claire. You will behave, my lady, or you will feel the sting of my sword belt on your bare arse."

CHAPTER TWO

Claire relaxed within Lord Galien's hold and swallowed hard. Heat flooded her face at his threat of chastisement. She bowed her head and felt tears of frustration burning in her eyes. This wasn't supposed to happen. She was supposed to enjoy a nice, long visit at Hohenzollern away from Diterich and her late husband's relatives, especially her conniving stepson. She had eventually hoped to ask Princess Susanna for assistance in traveling to one of her brothers' estates, but now it was too late.

Even if the story Lord Galien told her about Leuthold held true, she did not understand why her brother wished for her to marry the man. Leuthold, along with the rest of her brothers, had stood by without uttering a single protest when their father announced she was to wed Lord Diterich, all for the sake of an alliance that had proven troublesome in the end.

"I would rather not fight with you, Lady Claire." Lord Galien's deep, rumbling voice sent a flutter through her insides.

She inhaled a long, drawn-out breath and closed her eyes, willing herself to wake up in her bed, but when she opened her eyes Lord Galien was still staring down at her and still holding her captive. She tore her gaze away from him and listened as the chaos in the castle started to settle. She heard murmuring voices, punctuated by the occasional shout or bawdy laugh, coming from the great hall around them. The soldiers who apparently weren't bride hunting today rushed by with armfuls of stolen goods, some of them lugging trunks through the halls.

"Do you have any belongings you wish to bring with you?"

Lord Galien's question caught her by surprise, as did the kindness she glimpsed in his dark brown eyes. She cleared her throat. "Aye, my lord. I didn't travel here with much, but if you would permit me to go to my chamber I will gather my things." The longer she stalled, the longer she remained in the castle, the better her chances of escape. If she somehow managed to evade Lord Galien and slip down to the underground passage again, she might find her way into the north woods and catch up with Glenda,

Hazel, and the others.

"Very well. Show me to your chamber and I will have my squires collect your belongings. If you attempt to cause any mischief though, my sweet Claire, I will make you sorely regret it." He snapped his fingers and two squires emerged from the horde of looting men.

The four of them traveled through the halls and up a busy set of stairs. Lord Galien kept a firm hand on her upper arm, guiding her through the crowd. She noticed that he commanded great respect, or perhaps he incited fear, because all the soldiers stepped out of his path and gave him a wide berth.

The armored men swept past them carrying their treasures, everything from golden candelabras, to jewelry, to ladies' dresses. Claire wondered if her chamber had already been ransacked. Once she reached the room she had been sharing in the east wing with Hazel and four other ladies, she frowned at the open door.

"That's it," she said, nodding. "If you would permit me some time to collect my things, I will be quick about it." She glanced into the empty chamber and groaned inwardly to see it in such disarray, but at least some of her belongings remained untouched. The lid of Claire's trunk rested open, but many of her dresses remained hanging over the side. She made to move into the chamber alone, but Lord Galien followed her inside with a possessive grip on her arm.

His assessing gaze swept around the room and he gestured for the squires to enter. "Please collect all of Lady Claire's belongings in her trunk, and be quick about it. I would like to depart Hohenzollern within the hour."

Claire's mouth fell open and she wrenched from Lord Galien's grasp. "I will pack my own things!" she snapped. "All of you, get out! Bloody get out!"

"My lady, I insist you calm yourself."

"I said to get out! All of you!" She required time to think, damn him. She had never intended to marry again. She had already done her duty to her family by wedding the awful Lord Diterich, and she saw no benefit to a match with Lord Galien, for her family or for his. Her brother's command puzzled her, and she hoped to talk her way out of the marriage. Yes, she would speak with the duke before the nuptials took place. Surely Lord Galien would not deny her a visit to her brother's castle on the way to his keep. She took a deep breath and peered into her intended's soulful eyes, fighting off the desire to sink further in his arms. His hold on her had turned gentle, though his censoring gaze burned into her.

"It appears you do not listen very well, do you, my lady?"

"I am sorry for my outburst. Your squires may pack my things. Th-thank you, Lord Galien, for your kindness." It grated her nerves to speak so civilly to the man, but she forced the words out in hopes of garnering his favor long enough to see her to her brother's castle. Her cheeks ached behind the smile she forced.

Lord Galien waved a hand at his squires, but instead of packing up her trunk, the young men slipped from the chamber and shut the door behind them. She inhaled a shaky breath, the sudden darkness in Lord Galien's eyes stirring fear in her heart. The last thing she wanted was to be alone with the man!

"My lady, I will not have you speaking disrespectfully to me or any of my men, squires included. As my wife, your behavior reflects on me, and it is my duty to ensure you are well-mannered and ladylike. Furthermore, I will not be mollified by a fake smile and placating words. No wife of mine will make a fool of me." His harsh tone and his sudden grip on her shoulders made her wince. Still, she hated to cower in fear.

"One marriage was enough for me, Lord Galien. Whatever my brother's intentions are, I wish to discover them before we are wed. I demand that we travel to Leuthold at once so I may have an audience with him."

He lowered his head and a vein on his temple pulsed. "I need to hurry back to my keep, my lady. We will be wed soon and I'm afraid a visit to the duke is out of the question. Already the first snowfall is upon us, and I have business to take care of at Minrova. We will visit your brother in the spring, Lady Claire."

The last vestige of her control slipped and she pushed out of his grasp, then shoved at him with all her strength. She stood, utterly stunned, as he wobbled and almost fell backward on the bed. Panic swirled within her when he righted himself and pinned her with a livid glare. Her mind screamed for her to turn and run away, to try to rush out the door, but her legs became rooted to the floor. When he finally spoke, the quiet anger in his voice washed through her like a rush of cold water.

"Lady Claire, I have just lost my patience with you. Now, I want you to go stand in the corner over there. Put your nose to the wall and do not turn around until I beckon you."

She gulped and stared at the corner he'd nodded at. "Th-the corner? Why?"

"Because I intend to spank your naughty bottom, that's why. I have given you plenty of opportunity to conduct yourself properly, my lady, but you have crossed the line. I have no doubt a sore bottom will help ensure your good behavior for the duration of our trip to Minrova, or for the rest of the day at least."

Disbelief coursed through her, and a warm sensation pulsed between her thighs. She pressed her legs together and wrapped her arms around herself as if to fight off a chill, but she no longer felt cold at all. Heated all over, her shame at the prospect of being disciplined by the stern Lord Galien awakened baser desires she had not experienced since the time she indulged in a long kiss behind the stables with one of her brothers' friends. Her husband had never called up such a yearning within her. She hugged herself tighter and gave Lord Galien her most apologetic look.

"I-I am sorry I spoke to you in such a disgraceful manner, Lord Galien, and I beg your forgiveness for my pushing you. I promise it will not happen again. It is not necessary that you discipline me."

"Ah, but it is very necessary, my sweet lady." His countenance softened a few measures. "If I allow you to get away with such behavior now, it will set a bad precedent. Do not be frightened, Lady Claire, I will only be giving you a light spanking. *This time.* As long as you cooperate with your punishment, I will not use my sword belt. I suggest you turn around and take up position in the corner, little lady, *now,* lest I change my mind about being gentle."

Claire opened her mouth to argue further, but his stern demeanor had her clamping her lips together and turning around. Her gut clenched with apprehension. Taking a deep breath, she moved to the corner and waited for his instruction. Perhaps if she stood here without fussing, he'd reconsider her punishment. A phantom tingle prickled across her bottom cheeks, and she lowered her head as her face flamed. Why did she feel so warm and achy, even as nerves twisted and whirled in her stomach?

The door creaked open and then slammed shut, and she resisted the temptation to turn around. Her shame deepened as she realized the squires had returned. Standing in the corner was embarrassing enough in front of Lord Galien, but the presence of spectators deepened her humiliation. She prayed the stone floor would swallow her up, anything to help her escape her shameful position.

From the clinking of metal on metal going on behind her, she guessed the squires were removing the remainder of Lord Galien's armor, and she next heard what she supposed was her heavy trunk scraping across the floor. The door opened once again, permitting a rush of noise from the soldiers in the hallway, before it slammed shut. She jumped at the sound, feeling a sense of finality at being alone with Lord Galien. She wondered if the hard push still angered him. Now that she had time to reflect, she supposed physical aggression was an appalling way to conduct herself against a lord.

Her mother had tried to raise her to be a gentle, kind woman with a heart full of grace, but Claire had faltered much growing up, constantly disappointing her parents as she got into scrapes with her brothers and their friends. She missed her mother and felt ashamed once again for behaving in a way that would've disappointed her. *A lady always remains calm and gentle, Claire. A lady who resorts to violence will never command respect, and the ability to command respect for oneself is of utmost importance,* her mother told her once after scolding her for punching a boy in the face. At the time Claire had ignored her mother's wisdom.

She sighed and wondered if her mother had been right. Would Lord Galien treat her differently if he respected her? And why did it matter to her so much what he thought of her? They'd just met, and she didn't like him. No, not a bit.

Lost in her thoughts, she didn't hear his approach.

She started when a hand touched her shoulder, and gooseflesh rose up on her arms. The deep voice at her ear wrapped around her like a warm blanket, but the words that came forth struck fear deep in her heart.

"It is time for your punishment, Lady Claire."

• • • • • • •

"Lord Galien, please, I beg you to reconsider." She grimaced when she said *beg*, as if the mere idea of pleading with him lay beneath her.

Well, he intended to show her who was in charge. Besides that, he needed her subdued when they departed Hohenzollern. While he wished to give her a proper wedding in Minrova, he doubted they would make it through the portcullis without speaking their vows. Before he'd ventured into the castle, he'd seen the castle priest brought up to perform the hasty ceremonies after Gerhard's decree.

Galien rested his hands on Claire's shoulders and peered into her startled gaze. She was so opposed to the idea of accepting his discipline that he wondered if she had ever been spanked in her life. "Claire, I want you to close your eyes and take a few deep breaths. Try to calm yourself," he said in the gentlest of tones. For a moment he reconsidered his decision to spank her, especially when a tear trickled down her cheek as she opened her eyes.

"I-I don't want a spanking," she said, her bearing imploring and childlike.

He brushed the tear away with his thumb and fought the impulse to gather her in his arms. The longer he stared at her, the more he wondered if this match had the potential to become more than just another political marriage. "Claire, you have nothing to fear from me. However, when you do wrong, little lady, I will not look the other way. Now come and lay yourself across my lap."

She resisted, but only in a slight pull against him as he guided her to the bed. He sat on the edge and brought her down over his thighs, angling her so her upper body rested over the blankets. His first touch to her posterior was met with a quick intake of breath, and she shifted over his lap, inadvertently rubbing her center atop his growing hardness. Several strands of her dark brown hair had escaped her coif, and he bent to brush the errant locks from her face. A shudder rippled through her and her face bloomed under a pretty blush. He wondered if she felt his cock swelling beneath her, straining against his leggings and seeking out her sweetness. She met his gaze briefly before turning her head to the side, away from his view, but not before he saw her blush deepen.

Where she had gotten the ridiculous notion that she'd spend the rest of her days an unmarried widow, he knew not. She was still young and hadn't conceived a child with her first husband, likely due to the lord's advanced age, and she had many good, fertile years ahead of her. Galien needed an heir, and now that he had located Claire he supposed wedding his overlord's comely sister to be as good, if not better, than any other match he might have made. After Lady Rhianna died, he had decided to put marriage off as long as possible, preferring to satiate his lusts with the tavern wenches from his village, much to the frustration of his father. But now, as he held the nervous Lady Claire over his lap and prepared to chastise her, he rather liked the idea of keeping a wife, filling her with his seed, and watching her grow heavy with his child.

He blew out a breath. By God, what was he thinking? He had met Claire not yet an hour ago and already his mind brimmed with notions more romantic than any he'd ever entertained. Sitting straighter, he gathered her closer and reached for the hem of her dress, deciding it best to get her discipline over with. The poor girl was shaking profusely, and while he knew he must punish her, he wished to end her misery.

"Please, Lord Galien," she said, her voice urgent. "It is not proper for you to see me unclothed." She reached a hand around to prevent him from baring her bottom, but he circled her wrist and pinned it to her lower back.

"I'm afraid I cannot allow you the protection of your skirts," he said, lifting her chemise up with her dress, revealing her pale bare bottom to his gaze. His cock throbbed and longing pummeled through him, clouding his ability to think clearly. She was so lovely, and she was all his to do with as he pleased. Right now it pleased him to look at her, and it pleased him to stroke her naked cheeks while she squirmed and whimpered.

He raised his hand high and brought it down with a resounding smack, leaving a dark pink mark on her delectable bottom cheek. Again, he spanked her, this time slapping the other side. She cried out as if he'd just abused her grievously, and he paused and tightened his grip on her, now holding both her wrists at the small of her back overtop the layers of her dress and chemise.

"Claire, I hardly struck you. Those were light slaps. Why are you screaming so?"

"Because it hurts!"

"It's going to hurt a lot worse by the time I've spanked you properly. I will not have you screaming like a wild cat every time I punish you. I do not expect you to be completely silent, but screaming as if you are being murdered is not acceptable. Now," he said, adjusting her bottom higher in the air and forcing her legs apart, "we are going to continue and I expect you to control yourself for the remainder of your spanking."

With the next slap, she uttered a small gasp and only kicked her feet once, and the improvement pleased him. He continued on, switching from her left cheek to her right one as he spanked, covering the entirety of her bottom. It didn't take long for her pale cheeks to blush as prettily as her face had moments ago. Feeling devilish, he smarted the insides of her thighs and held her in such a way that she couldn't close her legs, then he moved up to bestow attention to the tender curve of flesh where her bottom and thighs met. All the pale flesh on her bottom reddened under his hand.

The soft sound of her crying wrenched at his heart, and he gave her two more hard slaps before stopping to caress her inflamed cheeks. "It's over, my sweet Claire."

She sniffled. "Don't call me that."

"Why not?"

"Because I don't like you, and I'm not sweet. There's nothing sweet about me."

He stroked her punished flesh once more, running his hand over her heated skin, before he pushed her chemise and skirts down. His cock still throbbed and strained to escape his leggings. By God, he couldn't wait to have her writhing naked underneath him in the marriage bed. He was glad she wasn't a virgin and he hoped she might enjoy such pleasures with him later in the warmth of their tent. "You're wrong." He released her wrists. "Everything about you is sweet. I think it is sweet that you were trying to save your friend."

"How do you know about that?" She peered over her shoulder at him, her blue eyes sparkling with question. Despite her widowhood, she possessed a childlike innocence that made him want to spend the rest of his life watching over her, protecting her, and making her smile. He imagined the glimmer in her eyes while she smiled or laughed rivaled that of the sun and stars.

"I watched you for a spell after I followed my men into the castle. Some of them wished to take wives, you see. I regret that I was not able to stop that mercenary from frightening you. I looked away for a moment to speak with my squires, and when I sought you out again you were in trouble. I am glad you were not harmed, Lady Claire." He turned her over, sat her upright on his lap, and wrapped his arms around her.

At first, she resisted meeting his gaze, opting to glare at his chest. Her eyes were red-rimmed, and the impulse to wipe a lingering tear away proved too tempting to resist. Still keeping one arm around her, he reached for her face with his free hand and brushed her tear away with his thumb. As he did so, she glanced into his eyes, her expression fearful and confused.

"Come here," he said, drawing her against him. He nestled her head on his chest and stroked her hair, half of it now fallen from her coif. "Well, my lady, do you think you learned your lesson? Will you behave yourself for the remainder of the day at the very least?"

She remained silent for the longest while, and he almost wondered if she'd fallen asleep in his arms. But finally she spoke, her tone as soft as her body felt within his embrace. "I-I promise to try my best, my lord."

CHAPTER THREE

"No! I will not marry you today. Lord Galien, I implore you to reconsider." Heart pounding a wild rhythm in her chest, Claire stopped in the center of the bailey and balked at the sight ahead.

A pale-faced Father David stood in front of the portcullis, watching as a huge knight approached with a woman flung over his shoulders. She flailed a bit and kicked up her skirts, and her long golden braid swayed with her struggles. The knight dropped her to her feet, and Claire recognized her as Lady Daisy, one of Princess Susanna's ladies-in-waiting. Their marriage ceremony happened in a flash, with Father David only speaking to the knight.

The insufferable Lord Galien clasped Claire's arm and urged her forward now that their turn had come. She tried to dig her heels into the ground, but his strength surpassed hers. By the time they reached Father David, he was practically carrying her. Her outraged cry drew a glance from Lady Daisy, who stared over her shoulder and gave Claire a compassionate look before her knight led her through the portcullis and outside the walls of Hohenzollern.

Lord Galien drew her up to his side and put his mouth to her ear. "Yes, my sweet Lady Claire. You will marry me today, and you will be sensible about it. We haven't a choice. The only way I'm permitted to take you through the gates is if I take you as my bride, which I am fully prepared to do. Your brother commanded I marry you anyway, my dear. Today or a fortnight from now, the timing of our nuptials matters not."

"It matters to me!" Panic filled her, and she looked ahead at Father David, meeting the elderly man's sympathetic gaze. She tilted her head to Lord Galien. "If you make me do this now, on this very day, I will hate you forever."

His dark eyes flashed with humor and he struggled to restrain a smile, his lips curving before he pressed them into a straight line. He obviously didn't believe her, or mayhap he didn't care whether or not she despised him. Flames of anger rose up, burning hot in the face of his indifference to her plight.

"As you just witnessed in the ceremony before ours, the lady's consent matters not on this day. But I wish you would be so sweet as to give it. In fact," he said with a teasing, wistful air. "I dream of looking upon our wedding day with much fondness years from now and remembering my wife having kindly spoken her vows to me, perhaps as an endearing blush stained her cheeks."

She released a sharp breath. "I suggest you shove your dreams up your arse, my lord, because that will never happen."

He reared his head back and laughed. Then he once again put his mouth to her ear, and she sensed his demeanor growing more serious. "All the women lining up behind us are frightened, Claire. If you are calm and cooperate, you might ease some of their fears."

She glanced behind her and spotted four couples lined up, and none of the ladies appeared the least bit happy. They were maidens, all of them younger than her. Damn him, Lord Galien was right.

Very well. She would play along and be sweet, but not for Lord Galien's sake or his bloody dreams. She turned to Father David and nodded with a smile that didn't hurt as much as it should have.

"We are ready, father." She pried her arm from her husband-to-be's grasp and he took the hint and wrapped an arm around her instead. They moved two steps forward and turned to face each other, holding hands and looking into one another's eyes. Her heart beat faster and her blood thumped in her ears.

Father David launched into an abbreviated sort of ceremony, and when it came time for Lord Galien to repeat his vows to her, the world suddenly narrowed. She couldn't look away from the exceedingly tall and broad-shouldered Lord Galien, and a little piece of her broke off and latched onto him when he squeezed her hands in a reassuring gesture, and the strangest thing of all—she swore she detected sincerity in his voice. A lump lodged in her throat and she blinked back tears. Though forced, this ceremony felt so much different than her first wedding, certainly not as frightening. Her annoyance with Lord Galien faded as he continued gazing into her eyes with a gentleness that contrasted with his often firm manner. She suspected he was a man of many layers, and a small part of her delighted at the prospect of getting to know him better.

When it would've been her turn to recite her portion of the vows, Father David tried to press on and skip this part entirely, but she glanced at the priest and said, "I would like to say my part too, father. You needn't skip it." The other ladies were watching, she knew, and she heard at least two of them gasp.

Father David hesitated, but after a nod from Lord Galien the priest complied, and Claire obediently repeated the marriage vows, keeping her eyes locked with Lord Galien's. She told herself she was only doing so for the sake of the maidens waiting their turn, but she didn't know what to tell herself to explain away the increasing flutters in her stomach, especially when Lord Galien leaned down to kiss her after Father David pronounced them husband and wife. His lips pressed warmly to hers, gentle and quick, and she mourned the loss of his closeness when he pulled away.

Husband and wife. A pang of longing quickened in her core, catching her completely by surprise. Being bedded by Lord Galien would surely be different from being bedded by the weak and elderly Lord Diterich, and she wondered how soon he planned to consummate the marriage.

"You honor me today, Lady Claire," he said, guiding her through the portcullis.

A glance behind her showed the next ceremony had begun, and the young lady standing with the knight and Father David did not appear as scared as she had earlier. The ladies waiting their turn also looked more at ease, to her great relief. She caught the gaze of a servant girl she recognized as having newly arrived at the castle and gave the poor thing an encouraging smile before returning her attention to Lord Galien.

They traveled on horseback for the rest of the day, until the sun set over the distant mountains, a range of mountains she had never glimpsed so close before. Lord Galien sat her on his horse in front of him, not permitting her to ride by herself, and each time she squirmed or winced due to her sore bottom, he chuckled and held her tighter.

Though she had argued with him at first over not getting her own horse, she was now grateful for his insistence due to the snowy and rocky terrain. Even when they traveled through the woods the path proved treacherous.

The warmth from Galien's huge body enveloped her, and when an icy wind picked up he tucked a thick wool blanket around her. She both appreciated and detested the care he kept showing her. She was glad he hadn't been cruel to her in any way, but these constant kindnesses made it difficult for her to hate him.

After the group of about twenty knights and squires, as well as three maidens taken as wives, stopped for the night, they erected a series of tents in the time it took her to walk off the soreness from sitting on a horse all day. She held the blanket tight around her shoulders to keep out the chill, since her warm winter cloak had been stolen during the looting. She approached the largest tent once Lord Galien stepped out from it.

"I'm surprised you left me alone," she said, trying to sound bitter. "Aren't you worried I'll try to run away?"

Amusement lifted his expression, his dark eyes glittering in what scarce light lingered as the sun slipped away. "There's just enough snow left on the ground from the last storm that tracking you would be easy. Besides that, I told my squires to keep an eye on you."

At his response, she looked around the camp and spotted the two squires standing near a fire, and the moment she spotted them they ducked their heads as if trying to be inconspicuous. She sighed and gazed up at Lord Galien. "I might wish to escape you, my lord, but I am not stupid. I've no idea where we are, and I am not foolish enough to wander through the forest at night."

"I'm glad to hear it." He pulled her closer and wrapped his arms around her, his features once again turning stern. "Do you know what will happen if you attempt to leave this camp?"

She glared at him hard even as her face grew hot, the shame of her trip over his knee in the castle still fresh in her mind. "I've an idea."

"I want to hear you say it, my sweet Lady Claire. Tell me what happens the next time you misbehave."

She tried to lower her head, but he grasped her chin and forced her to hold his gaze. "You, my lord, are the most infuriating man I have ever had the misfortune to meet."

A grin brightened his features briefly before the gleam in his eyes once again reflected his serious side. "I need to hear you say it aloud, my lady, or I will think you require a refresher." He leaned down, his nose almost touching hers, and the white ribbons of his breath mingled with hers in the frigid evening air. "Now, what happens when you misbehave?"

She clenched her teeth and made an indignant noise. "If I misbehave, you will spank me, my lord." The instant he looked pleased over her response, she added, "That is because, of course, you are a beastly savage."

"Into the tent with you, my sweet Claire, and I will show you just how beastly I can be."

A firm hand guided her inside, and the warmth coming off the braziers welcomed her. He lifted the cloak from her shoulders and set it aside, then turned her in his arms. She stared at his chest, unnerved by the telltale bulge in his leggings. She longed to retreat but he held onto her with purpose. The single bedroll that rested in her periphery seemed to taunt her.

"Look at me, Claire."

The calm command in his voice prompted her eyes to his.

"You have nothing to fear from me." He brushed the back of his hand along her cheek, stroking in a gentle circle. "I have some business to attend to with my men, but I will return soon. Eat something and rest for a while, and most important, be a good girl."

She nodded and watched as he left the tent, thankful he wasn't going to maul her just yet. Her stomach growled and she moved to a small table with a spread of salted meat, cheese, and crusty bread. She poured herself some wine and took a long gulp, then nibbled on a piece of cheese. The constant fluttering in her belly at the thought of what would happen between her and Lord Galien tonight soon chased her appetite away though. She forced a few bites of bread though, knowing she needed her strength in order to keep her wits about her. A second helping of wine dulled her senses and warmed her insides.

Since there was nowhere else to sit, she eased her sore body down onto the thick wool blankets atop the bedroll, wishing she was a thousand leagues away, in a faraway kingdom where ladies could marry for love, or not at all if they so desired, and men like Lord Eberhard and Lord Diterich weren't allowed dominion over a single soul.

• • • • • • •

Galien marched through the camp at a brisk pace, anxious to return to Claire. He hadn't intended to leave her for so long, but the scouts who'd gone ahead had taken longer than expected to report back. The howling of wolves much too close for comfort had driven them on a longer return route, and they had ridden into camp just as he'd been assembling a search party. All was well though, the wolves had moved on and the scouts hadn't glimpsed any other trouble. Tomorrow's journey would be a lengthy one, but as long as the weather didn't turn bad they would arrive at his keep by nightfall.

He entered the warm tent, pleased the braziers were still giving off ample waves of heat. He sought out Claire, finding her tucked under several blankets on the bedroll. A glance at the spread of refreshments proved she had eaten, and consumed her fair share of wine too. After removing his sword belt, he helped himself to the salted meat and downed the remainder of the wine, his thoughts on the small figure in his bed. He doubted she was sleeping, and he cleared his throat and approached the bedroll and the lovely lady nestled under the thick pile of blankets.

It was their wedding night, and he intended to claim what was his.

She blinked at him and sat up. She had removed her coif, and her hair cascaded over her shoulders in a lovely fashion. He couldn't have torn his eyes away if his life depended on it, and his fingers tingled with the impulse to stroke her silky dark locks. But before he reached out, her face melted with sympathy and she sat straighter.

"I am sorry that your father died recently, my lord. I was too preoccupied with other things to give you my condolences today."

"Thank you, Claire. I am touched by your concern for my family."

"Was he ill when you left?"

"No, but he was old. Died in his sleep. My mother passed last winter. It comforts me to know they are together once again. They loved each other very much." He knelt and started working his boots off, then sat beside Claire on the bedroll. "They were strangers on their wedding day too, but they eventually came to hold one another in high regard." He watched as she twisted a jeweled ring around her finger and he felt an unexpected pang of jealousy, even though she lawfully belonged to him now. "Did Diterich give you that?"

She shook her head. "No. It belonged to my mother."

"Is she still alive?"

"She died when I was yet a child, and my father died not long after I wed Lord Diterich." She chewed the inside of her lip. "He perished leading a battle against one of my husband's numerous enemies while Lord Diterich sat in his castle deep in his cups."

Galien wasn't surprised. Lord Diterich had been a snake of the worst kind, and he suspected the days of his family's reign were numbered. One day their enemies would band together against them, just as Princess Susanna's and her uncle's enemies had banded against Hohenzollern. "We have both suffered losses, my lady, but we have each other now. I swear on my mother's soul I will never mistreat you."

She shot him a suspicious glance. "Am I your first wife?"

"Yes. I was betrothed to a lady in my youth, but she perished during an illness that swept through the very castle your brother now resides in." He placed a hand atop hers, stilling her fidgeting. "I met her but once as a child, and back then I was too careless to give a single thought to the future. Now that my father is gone and I have inherited his title, I cannot think of anything but. I hope we have many children, Claire, sons and daughters alike."

She withdrew from his touch and balked at him, her eyes growing wide and her lips parted. "I-I am very tired, my lord, and I wish to rest now. I bid you goodnight."

Galien sighed. The mention of children had likely startled her into worrying about the consummation of their marriage. Her reluctance resembled that of a maiden, or so he imagined. He'd never lain with a maiden before, but enough of his men had plundered an innocent and boasted later to give him an idea.

She burrowed under the blankets, turning on her side and facing the opposite direction. After spending the day with her bottom pressed against his groin, Galien wanted nothing more than to strip her dress off and pound into her. He stared at her small form, watching as the covers rose and fell under her rapid breaths. He ran a hand through his hair, his frustration mounting. He'd never bedded a reluctant lady before. Well, he'd never bedded a *lady* at all. His prior conquests only included willing servant girls and skilled tavern wenches.

He tugged the blankets off Claire and picked her up, situating her on his lap. She kept her head bowed, and he rubbed his hands up and down her arms in hopes of easing her fears. "We are husband and wife now," he said, tipping her chin up.

Her eyes fluttered to the left and then to right before finally settling on him. "Do you intend to claim your marital rights now, my lord?" Her voice trembled along with her body, and he wondered if perhaps it best to get the deed over with.

"Aye, my sweet Claire. I do."

"I cannot persuade you to delay until we reach Minrova?"

His hard cock pressed up against her as she squirmed on his lap. "Does it feel like you can persuade me to delay?"

The reddening of her face proved she had indeed detected his excitement. "Very well." She scooted off his lap.

Galien watched as she lay down on her back and lifted her skirts partially up to expose a hint of flesh above her hosen. His heart thudded and his cock hardened further in his leggings, because he thought for a moment she intended play the role of a seductress. He watched for an inviting smile and a wink, but instead she placed her arms straight at her sides and shut her eyes. She turned away from him and remained still.

He cursed inwardly. The poor girl had braced herself as if for an attack. He hoped Lord Diterich had found no peace in death for all the hurt he had caused Claire. Galien doubted she realized what they were about to do could be pleasurable for them both, and he vowed to see that she enjoyed his touch even if it took until morning.

He stood and shrugged off his surcoat and tunic, tossing them atop the blanket she'd kept wrapped around her during their travels. Keeping his leggings on, he crawled onto the bedroll atop Claire and turned her face, bringing her out of her hiding.

"My wife," he murmured, placing a gentle kiss on her lips. "My sweet Claire." He coaxed her mouth open and ever so slowly delved his tongue in to meet hers.

Rigid to the point of holding her breath, she allowed his kiss but offered no response. That is, until he traced her hip and moved upward over the flat of her stomach to cup one breast. A shudder rippled through her and she gasped, her middle rising up against his for one small instance, and she at last began to breathe through her nose and released a faint moan as he kissed her. She tasted of wine and something else much sweeter, and he drank her in and thrilled when her tongue brushed along his lips. He felt her soften underneath him, and once again her hips rose up to meet his, her center grinding into the hardness still encased in his leggings. Aye, she was sweet, and he rejoiced that the tremors racing through her body were no longer born out of fear. He sensed her calming in his arms, and when he withdrew from what had become a most thorough kiss, she graced him with a coy smile.

"You make me feel different than any other man has," she said with a hint of confusion.

He grinned down at her, taking in the sight of her kiss-swollen lips and the flush that had spread down to her chest. "I shall take that as a compliment, my lady." He toyed with a lock of her hair, choosing his next words carefully. "I don't wish for you to close your eyes and hide from me. I enjoy your responses to me, Claire, and it pleases me that you want me."

He almost checked to see if he'd sprouted a second head, because the look she gave him was one of pure shock. "How do you know what I want?" She wriggled underneath him and pulled at the edge of the bedroll, trying to slip from his hold.

Galien captured her wrists and pinned them above her head in one hand, and with his free hand he explored the swell of her breasts before tugging the ribbon tie of her bodice loose, exposing her further. "I know you are afraid, because that bastard husband of yours never showed you the proper affection you were due in the bedchamber, and you don't understand why your breaths are coming fast and your face is growing hot. Nor do you understand the aching in your loins, my lady, the reason you have thrust so wantonly against my hard cock twice already."

An outraged cry left her lips and she struggled to escape his hold, but her center only pressed against his manhood harder while she fought him, and her eyes soon grew wide and she stilled beneath him, once again holding her breath.

"Stop that," he scolded. "No more holding your breath. I don't want you fainting on me, Claire."

Challenge sparked in her eyes and she didn't release the breath she was so stubbornly keeping in, and her face reddened with each passing moment, eventually taking on a bluish tint.

"*Claire.* Enough. Breathe in and out, my lady, this instant. Stop this childish nonsense at once or I will give you a good thrashing." The obstinate girl held her ground until he had no choice but to jerk her upright. The quick movement prompted her resumed breaths, though not before she dug her nails into his arms in retaliation.

He waited until her face paled to its normal ivory shade as he battled with himself over whether or not to follow through with his threat to chastise her. When her eyes flashed with insolence, he came to a decision. "Turn over on your hands and knees, Claire, and present your bottom for punishment. If you cooperate, I will only give you ten strokes with my sword belt."

CHAPTER FOUR

The resolute glare Galien pinned her with brought Claire out of her bad disposition. His description of her wants and needs had embarrassed her deeply, but regardless of that she felt even more ashamed for having held her breath like a child protesting a nap. Angry red marks lifted on his forearms where she'd dug her nails into him too. How had she let this happen? Now he intended to punish her for the second time today. She watched as he removed the scabbards from his sword belt and doubled the thick leather length in half. Panic and regret welled up in her, and she wished she had not overreacted.

"I'm waiting, Claire. Please assume the position. Hands and knees, bare bottom lifted up to receive ten lashes."

"I will do no such thing! You embarrassed me!" Her voice cracked over words she had intended to speak with confidence.

He stepped closer and blocked out the lantern light, appearing as a shadow until he knelt to look into her eyes. "We are husband and wife. I did nothing untoward to you, and you put yourself in harm with your childish antics."

"I did not put myself in harm, Lord Galien. As you can see, I am fine, and I would have been fine without your interference."

"You also disobeyed me, Claire, and for that you will be punished." He clasped the sword belt tighter in his grip and nudged her. "Hands and knees now, or these ten lashes will turn into fifteen."

Tears burned in her eyes, and she blinked rapidly to keep her emotions hidden. The last thing she wanted to do was break down weeping. She bit her lower lip, needing the distraction of the pain to focus on restraining her tears, and turned onto her hands and knees.

"Very nice." Galien moved behind her, still kneeling atop the blankets. "Now be a good girl and bare your arse to me, Claire."

A wave of submission rolled through and her face grew hotter than the braziers. Time slowed as she reached around and flipped her skirts up, and when she rested on her hands again she found herself leaning down, found herself truly presenting her backside to her new husband. The sudden desire to please him filled her and cooled her fury. He wasn't going to pound her with his fists or drag her through the camp by her hair, the sort of thing Lord Diterich had done before she learned how to read his moods to avoid his outbursts. Instead, Galien meant to punish her for a specific infraction, just as he had in the castle. Somehow this comforted her, even though he was about to cause her pain.

Galien placed a steadying hand on her lower back and dangled the belt against her bottom cheeks as if preparing his aim. "If you remain in position and keep cooperating, Claire, I will make these lashes light. I know you are still sore from earlier, and I hate to cause you pain, but this is for your own good. Please be a good girl for me."

The tears that had been threatening to fall trickled down her face now as she reacted to Galien's soothing words and gentle tone, for they calmed her and lent her the strength to yield to his discipline.

He shifted on the bedroll behind her and the belt cracked across her cheeks, the first lash falling with a mild sting. She exhaled in relief and held position, waiting for the next blow. He didn't make her wait long, and he landed the next two strikes in lines below the first one, but again the pain proved bearable. The fourth lash stung her upper thighs though, and she winced and cried out, her flesh especially tender in this area.

"You're doing very well, Claire. Only six more to go. But before I continue, I want you to promise you will be sweet and submit to my whims tonight, even if it embarrasses you. In return, I promise to give you pleasure and show you the utmost care, but you need to trust me first. Will you promise this for me, sweet girl?"

It was so surreal, resting on her hands and knees with her bottom bared in the middle of a belt whipping, while Galien spoke to her so very calmly, as if he were commenting on the weather. The act of surrendering to him felt more intimate than the kiss they had shared, and the warm sensation of her desire returned to pulse between her thighs. She tried to ignore the longing that coursed through her and focus on answering Galien's question. "Yes, my lord. I promise."

"You please me, Claire, very much."

The final six blows fell in quick succession, the last one packing the harshest sting of all. She cried out and lurched forward, almost breaking position, but she reared back and kept on her hands and knees, waiting for Galien's instruction. A warm hand brushed across her punished flesh, and he stroked her sore cheeks.

"Mm," she said with a sigh. "Thank you, Galien." She supposed it was acceptable to call him Galien now instead of Lord Galien when they were in private. She waited and listened for his objection, but it never came, and she smiled, rather liking the feel of his name on her lips without any formality. She liked hearing her name on his lips as well, especially when he called her sweet Claire. No man had ever used an endearment with her before, not even her father.

He rubbed the sting from her bottom using both hands now, and he tapped the insides of her legs to force her to spread wider. She obliged him, still overcome with the unceasing urge to please him, even though his actions made her face flame. Of course the embarrassment of knowing he had a perfect view of the folds between her thighs made her heart race faster, and she throbbed in her womanly parts and ached for him. She arched her backside higher and trembled as his rubbing hands moved closer to her center, and when his fingertips danced along the outer lips of her quim she jerked into his touch with a whimper.

"Just as I suspected. You're soaking wet, Claire." His voice was strained, but he sounded pleased by her body's reaction to him, and this shocked her and filled her with curiosity.

Why was she getting so wet? His quick intake of breath as he parted her folds put her more at ease with her body's reactions, and she gasped as an intense burst of ecstasy rocked through her. He swirled and applied pressure overtop a place where she'd never been touched, and she moved against his hand, unable to keep still during the onslaught of pleasure. She felt herself building up to something, but before she reached what promised to be a climatic ending, he turned her over and resumed untying the front of her dress. Panting, she peered up at him from under her eyelashes, admiring the sculpted expanse of his chest and the dark spattering of hair covering it.

"Let's get this off of you," he said, his eyes darkening. "I want to see my wife." He lifted her dress over her head and cupped her breasts over her chemise, kneading and stroking the exposed flesh of her cleavage.

Her hardened nipples ached and tented the fabric, and she resisted the impulse to shield herself from Galien's intense gaze. His eyes gleamed black in the lantern light, and she glanced down at the hem of her chemise, knowing he'd insist she lose this item of clothing too. She bit her lip as he studied her, and to her surprise he divested himself of his leggings before requiring anything else of her.

The appearance of his thick, long manhood jutting out set off a fluttering in her stomach, and her breaths came shallow and fast. She swallowed hard and lifted her eyes from his swollen shaft to meet her husband's gaze. He edged forward on his knees with a predatory stare trained on her, and he next slipped her chemise off her shoulders, working it off her with slow movements as he paused time and again to caress her skin in all the right places.

The moment her chemise fell to the ground beside the bedroll, he latched onto one of her nipples and pressed her down atop the blankets. His tongue danced around her stiffened peak, and each hard tug sent a spiral of wicked sensation straight to her nether region. She felt moisture gathering between her thighs, more of the wetness Galien had been so pleased to discover, and she wrapped her arms around him, drawing her hands up and down his back, then through his hair. He traveled on to her other breast, pinching her peak first before taking it into his mouth. His ministrations spawned an even deeper longing within her, and she found herself pressing against his leg, seeking relief from the sweet torment he so mercilessly inflicted upon her.

He pulled back and situated his body over hers with his manhood grazing the opening of her slit, and he dragged it through her wetness, coating the tip of his hardness as he gazed down at her, looking every bit the fierce warrior. He was a powerful man, a knighted lord with vast holdings, and she knew he intended to always command the same respect and obedience from her as he commanded with his men. Although she hadn't wanted to marry him, in this tent, in this moment, she wanted nothing more than for him to command her, to show her the pleasure he'd promised. She parted her thighs and arched up, inviting his entrance.

A growl rumbled out from him, and he clasped her head and claimed her lips, kissing her harder than he had before. She moaned into his mouth and tried to meet the thrusts of his tongue, and she felt his stiffness pressing into her, teasing her entrance with slow and shallow thrusts. An urgent fire lighted within her, and she whimpered and would've begged him to take her if only she could speak. But he kept kissing her, kept holding her steady in his arms and taking all that he wanted.

She gasped for breath when he pulled back, and she searched his eyes, wondering why he hadn't taken her yet. Why was he teasing her so? She felt frantic and needy and ready to combust, and she trembled as her aching transformed to an almost unbearable throb.

"Please, Galien," she said in a harsh whisper. "Why are you doing this to me?"

"What am I doing to you?" He continued the slow and shallow movements, still not filling her up as she so desperately wished he would.

• • • • • • •

"You're killing me, Galien. Please, please, please," Claire said, her head thrashing around as she begged. He relished each frantic plea that fell from her lips, and he enjoyed watching her writhe underneath him while she ached for his cock.

"Ask me for what you want, Claire," he said, now drawing his length through her moist folds.

"I want you, of course!"

He grinned down at her. "That's not specific enough. I want to hear you say, 'Please, my lord husband, will you please pound into my wet quim with your cock?'"

"I've changed my mind. I don't wish to consummate this marriage after all, my lord. I want an annulment." Through her sensual haze, her eyes shone with mischief.

"Is that so, my lady?"

"Yes, sir, I am quite decided about it."

He tapped the tip of his cock against her womanhood, aiming for the swollen nubbin he'd rubbed her moisture over earlier. "You're quite decided, are you?"

She screwed up her face and closed her eyes. Little gasps emanated from her with each tap of his cock on her pleasure spot, and finally she relented. "I-I cannot remember the exact wording you asked for."

"Use your own words then, sweet Claire."

"Please, my lord, will you please…" Her words trailed off and a profuse blush stained her cheeks. She stared at him pleadingly, and released a frustrated sigh when he held fast to his demands. "Very well," she said, arching her hips up. "Please, my lord husband, will you please pound into my, er, into *me* with your co-cock?" She said *cock* in a whisper so faint he almost missed it.

"Such bawdy talk for a lady. I might have to punish you again tonight." He grasped her hips and surged forward, entering her slick channel in one rapid, harsh thrust. The tight warmth of her wet core gripped his cock, and he groaned and leaned further over her, kissing her cheeks and nibbling at her soft earlobe. She shuddered and ground against him, and he withdrew partially and slammed back into her.

Galien set a fast pace of driving in and out of her sweetness, claiming her with all the height of his primal lust. His need for her overpowered his ability to be gentle, but by the wild manner in which she met his thrusts, it was obvious his bride didn't wish for him to take it slow. More than happy to give her what she wanted, he drew her legs atop his shoulders in order to plunge deeper into her tight, moist quim. Ah, she was so lovely and responsive, his sweet Claire. Her hair billowed out on the bedroll around her delicate face, and her bare breasts bounced with the movements of his pounding.

"You belong to me now, Claire."

She met his eyes with a shocked look, and at first he thought she intended to protest his claim on her. But her lips parted and she let out a deep, long moan as she gyrated her mound against his hardness. "Oh, Galien. Galien… my lord…" Her nails dug into his arms, and she closed her eyes as she rode the wave of her release, a release he suspected was her first.

As her moaning and writhing subsided, he slowed and waited for her eyes to open. When they did and her stare fluttered to his, her expression was one of pure contentment. "That… that, my lord, has never happened before."

He cupped the side of her face, and she leaned into his touch with a purr. "I believe this means I have conquered you then, Claire," he said, unable to stop the pride welling up within him over his prowess.

"If this is what being conquered feels like, I invite you to do so again and again."

"Gladly, my lady. Every day for the rest of our lives." Galien's cock throbbed within her and ached for relief, but when he resumed driving in and out of her, he drove excruciatingly slow and after the first few thrusts, he pressed his thumb to her sensitive nub. She jerked underneath him and undulated her hips, matching her moves with his.

Too soon a tingle of pleasure raced up the insides of his thighs and his balls clenched up, his peak imminent. He spread more moisture overtop her sensitive spot and increased the swirls with his thumb. Her legs quaked and her eyes closed, and her insides once again clamped down on his cock. Unable to hold back any longer, he pumped into her faster and groaned as he filled her up with his seed, holding her hips tight and not releasing her until he had spent himself completely.

He withdrew from her and cupped her face, stroking her cheeks as he peered into her enchanting blue eyes that reminded him of the mountain lakes near Minrova.

The intensity of his feelings for her unnerved him, and he had to resist the compulsion to whisper sweet words of affection into her ear. That he even had the urge in the first place startled him. He reminded himself that he'd known her for less than a day, and if he spoke of the warmth spreading through his heart, she'd likely balk at him. Yet in the short time he'd known her, he'd glimpsed many sides of her nature. Her beauty and grace, her sweetness and her stubbornness, and her bravery and kindness. She was a lady who had put the safety of others ahead of herself, a lady who had possessed enough bravery to take on a mercenary nearly twice her size with nothing but a dagger, and a lady who had overcome her fear of intimacy and discovered the passion blazing within her.

He pulled the blankets atop them and tucked her into his side. She rested her head over his heart, and he stroked her hair as his thoughts turned to the future. The death of his father would overshadow the arrival of his new wife at Minrova, but he was certain she would understand. The late Lord Galien's burial would take place in two days, and Galien knew his cousins who'd stayed behind were likely making the arrangements for the late lord to be put to rest next to the wife he had loved so dearly. Galien smiled at the memories of his childhood, of always catching his parents kissing and hugging and making eyes at one another.

The sound of Claire's soft snoring brought his attention back to her. He was thankful for the braziers and extra blankets that allowed her to curl up naked next to him, despite the fact that the cold wind howled outside the tent.

"Sleep well, my sweet Claire," he said, even though she was already fast asleep. In response to his voice, she sighed and snuggled closer to him, draping one leg atop his and burying her face deeper into his chest.

Though his responsibilities as the new lord of his estate weighed upon him, as well as the impending funeral and the sadness at losing his father, the world didn't seem so bleak with Claire nestled in his arms. He leaned down to brush a kiss atop her forehead, and when she sighed again so sweetly in her sleep and her breath tickled his chest, his heart swelled with tender emotion for the spirited lady encased in his arms.

CHAPTER FIVE

Minrova was a large keep that greatly resembled Hohenzollern, and Claire's head spun as she walked the halls in the late afternoon, determined to make the acquaintance of anyone she'd missed meeting last night. She was also determined to immediately take up her position of lady of the house; she'd already visited the kitchens to discuss the evening meal, and she made certain chambers were being prepared for the arrival of several of Galien's relatives, two more cousins, and an uncle and his wife.

A somber mood prevailed over Minrova due to the passing of Galien's father, and Claire hadn't seen her husband since last night when they rode into the bailey under a bright full moon. He'd passed her off to one of the servants, a bashful young woman named Erwyn who was to be her lady's maid. Erwyn had taken her to Galien's chambers and helped her get settled, and she'd fallen fast asleep after a relaxing bath in lavender-scented water. At some point in the night, Galien must have returned, because his side of the bed was crumpled, and she did recall the feel of a warm body pressing into hers in the middle of the night.

She missed him but understood he shouldered many responsibilities, including overseeing the arrangements for his father's funeral tomorrow. She hoped to see Galien this evening though, and she smiled at the memory of their travels back to Minrova. He'd kept her warm and had spoken at length about his family and his holdings and told her much about his home. In the tent, he had commanded her body, and her heart to some extent as well, and the mere thought of their carnal deeds now caused her face to flush. Even thoughts of the spankings heated her cheeks and prompted a tingle to race across her backside, and lower still where it coalesced between her thighs.

She looked around, embarrassed that perhaps someone might witness her flushed state and deduce her thoughts. To her relief, she saw no one aside from a footman at the end of the hall. Satisfied that she was alone, she moved to a window to look down upon the bailey. Her spirits rose at the sight of Galien riding up on his horse. He dismounted and one of his squires led the stallion away.

Claire brightened and prepared to rush downstairs to meet him as he marched to the entrance of the keep, but the sight of a woman blocking his path froze her in place at the window.

For the first time in her life, Claire suffered a stab of jealousy over another woman showing affection to a man. It festered deep and burned, unlike any other form of jealousy she'd experienced, and she felt physically ill with her stomach twisting into tight knots. She watched as the woman touched Galien's arm, and he smiled and laughed at something she said. Her hair gleamed golden in the sunlight, and it wasn't done up properly in a coif or veil. This woman was no lady, and Claire's blood boiled hotter and hotter the longer she lingered at the window, spying on her new husband and a woman who most likely spent her days pandering her virtues.

All the happiness that had flowed through her since their time in the tent faded, and she backed away from the window and sought sanctuary in Galien's chambers. Her chambers now too. Galien said she wasn't to have her own chamber because he wanted her close, and this pronouncement had filled her with warmth—at the time. Now a sense of doom filled her. She sat on the bed and tried to put herself in Galien's place, tried to explain away his actions in an effort to comfort herself.

He hadn't wanted to marry her. Leuthold had commanded it, for reasons she still knew not. She'd discovered Galien hadn't been married before, but beyond that she knew nothing of his amorous ways. Perhaps he frequented the taverns for wenches, or perhaps he'd harbored a fondness for a particular woman before riding off to do his overlord's bidding.

Tears prickled in her eyes and she blinked them back, determined not to allow Galien to affect her so. She reminded herself that her marriage to Lord Diterich had been far worse, for her late husband had flaunted his use of whores in her face, sometimes inviting a servant girl to sit on his lap in the great hall during the evening meal. Claire had never been jealous of Diterich's use of other women—if anything it had come as a relief—but she hadn't enjoyed being shamed so publicly, and a tear finally trickled down her cheek as she recalled the looks of pity other ladies had constantly leveled in her direction. She sniffled and wiped away the moisture coating her face, damning every man she had ever known.

She cursed men for being so weak-willed, and she questioned why God deemed them fit to rule over women, a thought she'd had quite frequently throughout her life.

If she examined why she was so upset with Lord Galien's supposed dalliances though, she supposed it was because she had expected better of him. He had seemed a man of morals, the sort of man who expected those under his authority to be at their very best. The sure and confident way he commanded his men, and the strict manner in which he'd disciplined her and then the tender embrace that had followed after as he comforted her, had painted a picture of a man of high principles. A man she had begun to respect.

A knock on the door startled her from her miserable musings. Claire rose up and crossed the room. "Who is it?"

"Lady Desmona, but please, call me Desmona. I know we shall be good friends," a cheerful voice called from the other side.

Claire opened the door and smiled at a short plump lady with rosy cheeks and a thick mass of curly hair that peeked out from a sheer blue veil. "You must be Lord Galien's youngest cousin. He told me about you on the journey here."

"Aye, I have the misfortune of being related to a scoundrel like Galien," she said merrily, winking at Claire. Then her countenance grew more somber. "I came to visit with my brothers, Trent and Gaston. We were here when Lord Minrova passed, God rest his soul. It was a sad day when the bell tolled over the keep."

"Have you been here long?"

"For a fortnight. Our parents live in the foothills where Hohenzollern's soldiers were frequently attacking. They wished to see me to safety and insisted I visit Minrova for a while, sending me off under the care of my two most annoying brothers."

Claire grinned and edged out of her chamber, shutting the door behind her. She looped her arm though Desmona's and nodded at the hall looming ahead. "Shall we take a walk?"

"As long as we don't go outside," Desmona said. "It's frightfully cold."

They walked to the western wing, where the halls were the widest and decorated with lavish paintings that rivaled those she'd seen in Hohenzollern. Desmona carried the conversation, talking about everything from the weather to her latest embroidery to the most recent news from the Free Cities. Claire listened, enjoying the younger woman's company and the distraction she provided from her fretting over her marriage.

"Has Galien treated you well? If he's given you the least bit of trouble, I will push him out of a window, my dear," Desmona said with a laugh, her high-pitched voice carrying through the halls.

"Yes, he has treated me well," Claire said, not keen to divulge anything more, though she longed to ask if Desmona knew of Galien's relationship with the golden-haired woman.

"I heard your brother is the duke and he arranged this marriage, and by a bit of luck Galien found you but a day's travels away at Hohenzollern. Was it dreadful? The battle, I mean?"

The sound of arrows zipping through the air, glimpsing fallen men in the bailey, and the cold terror of the moment enemy soldiers rushed into the castle resurfaced in Claire's mind. She looked down at the stone floor, unsure of how to answer Desmona's question. The truth was the battle had been the most terrifying event of her life, holed up in the castle with crying ladies and frightened children. The screams of the wounded had haunted her dreams last night. She had tried to be brave, but all through her escape attempt she had been trembling and her heart had been racing.

"It's all right," Desmona said, covering Claire's hand and squeezing. "You don't have to tell me. That was a silly question. I am probably talking too much. Trent and Gaston are always scolding me for saying the wrong things, and for not knowing when it's best to be silent."

"It was terrifying," Claire said, meeting the girl's gaze. "I tried to escape after Princess Susanna surrendered."

"Ah, but Galien found you."

"He saved me from an awful mercenary who wished to take me as a wife." Had Galien not intervened, the mercenary would've likely succeeded.

"That's so romantic," Desmona said. "Your rescuer and your husband. Did you love him at first sight then?"

Claire bit her lip and restrained a laugh. Desmona, bless her and her naivety, viewed love and marriage, and the world for that matter, through a pretty haze of colors. "No, I did not love him at first sight, but I have found him to be a kind and noble man, much more chivalrous than my first husband." Claire pondered telling Desmona about how she'd threatened Galien with a knife in an effort to escape, but she worried the truth might cause the girl to swoon, so she wisely bit her tongue.

"Well, I think it's the most romantic thing I've ever heard. I know you will fall in love with him soon, and he will fall deeply in love with you—if he hasn't already, that is."

Before Claire had glimpsed the golden-haired woman touching Galien's arm and laughing with him, she might have believed Desmona's wistful proclamation. But how could she harbor tender emotions for a man who entertained other women?

• • • • • • •

Galien eyed Claire and decided her demeanor had been overly polite during the evening meal, and he had also noticed she had only taken a few bites of food from the trencher they shared. She was performing again, and it troubled him that she was gracing him with faux smiles and trying to make him believe in her happiness. He leaned close to her and she stiffened.

"Claire," he said in a low voice, "What is troubling you?"

Her gaze flickered to his with obvious hesitance, and she feigned surprise with a shake of her head. "Why nothing, lord husband. I am perfectly fine." Another smile spread across her face, but it didn't reach her eyes.

"I am going to ask you one more time what is bothering you, Claire, and I suggest you tell me. I will not tolerate lies. Now, sweet wife, what has you behaving so strange this evening?"

"Very well," she said, folding her hands on her lap. "I saw you conversing with a lady of questionable repute, a woman with golden hair, and I am concerned about your relationship with her. Furthermore, I would like to know how often you plan to entertain other women. My lord." This time, Claire didn't try to make her voice sweet or offer him a smile. She glared daggers at him, and when she reached for her wine goblet, he feared she intended to fling the contents of the cup into his face.

"Careful, my lady. You wouldn't want to do something you might come to regret." He reached for her hands and held them in both of his, drawing his thumb over the soft undersides of her wrists. By God, Claire was jealous of Agnete, the woman who had spoken with him in the bailey earlier. "Claire, I have spent much of my time entertaining women of questionable repute, particularly in my younger days, and I will not deny it. But you needn't worry. Those days have ended."

"You mean because you were ordered to marry me? I very much doubt you would change your lascivious ways just because you've been forced to take a wife." Anger threaded her words, and she lowered her gaze, her body trembling.

"Claire, look at me."

Hard blue eyes met his. "Do not fret, my lord, for I will not keep you from your dalliances. I simply wish to know why I am not permitted my own chambers, if this sort of thing is your habit. Is it your plan to come to bed stinking of a whore every night and then expect me to spread my legs for you?"

Galien's cousin, Lady Desmona, launched into a coughing fit beside Claire and turned away, reaching for her wine. Others at the head table, including Galien's recently arrived uncle, sported uncomfortable expressions. Claire's voice had carried, whether she had intended it to or not. He gave her the benefit of the doubt and nodded at the bread pudding a servant had placed in front of her.

"Eat that, all of it, and then we will retire to our chambers to finish this discussion in private. You will sit here and be sweet and smile, and not utter another word, Claire. I will not have you making a spectacle."

A smile lit her face and she turned to face him. "I recommend you shove the bread pudding up the same orifice I once suggested you shove your dreams," she said in a hushed tone. She pushed back from the table, stood up, and dipped into a curtsey. "My lord."

Desmona shot him a censuring glance and leaned across Claire's vacant seat. "I promised Lady Claire I would push you out a window if you treated her poorly, cousin. I was teasing, of course, but now I'm afraid I must kindly ask you to stand yourself in front of a window."

"Enough," Trent said, putting a firm hand on his sister's shoulder. "You have no business nosing about in our cousin's affairs."

Desmona glared at her oldest brother, her normally rosy cheeks turning bright red under her rising anger. "Lady Claire and I have become the best of friends, and I will not see her treated so unfairly."

"You will quiet down this instant, sister, or I will call for a birch rod and send you off to bed with a well-punished bottom." Trent directed a reprimanding glare at her until she lowered her gaze, mumbling an apology and a promise to behave.

Galien remained in the hall for only a short time after this, staying only as long as it took his uncle to question him about his new holdings in the valley. The conversation served as a sharp reminder that his marriage to the unwilling Lady Claire was anything but a love match, and the responsibility to make her heel rested on his shoulders alone. He made his excuses and departed the hall, marching straight to his chambers.

He flung the door open and his gaze swept around the room, finding it empty. Cursing under his breath, he searched the halls for his headstrong wife, his anger rising with each moment that he failed to locate her. Finally, one of the footmen claimed to have seen her entering Desmona's chamber, and Galien headed to his cousin's room and burst inside without bothering to knock.

A panicked look flittered over Desmona's face, and he found her stance next to her bed quite odd. She twisted her fingers in front of her in a nervous manner.

"I am searching for my wife, cousin. Have you seen her, or do you know where she is?" Galien approached Desmona and towered over her, hoping a quick intimidation would make her confess, because he very much suspected his cousin was helping Claire hide.

"I haven't seen the poor Lady Claire since you broke her heart during the evening meal, my lord." She swallowed hard and glanced at her bed, just a brief passing of her eyes, but Galien took note of it.

"What's going on?" Trent's voice boomed from the doorway. He entered the room and crossed his arms as he regarded his sister. "I heard Lady Claire is missing, Desmona. Do you know anything about that?"

"As I just told Galien, I haven't an idea where his wife has gone. Perhaps if he treated her with kindness and didn't quench his sinful appetites with the village whores, Claire would not be missing." Her voice trembled and tears glistened in her eyes.

Galien couldn't believe the course of events that had taken place just because he'd had a quick conversation with Agnete this afternoon, the golden-haired woman Claire had become so jealous of. Yes, he had lain with Agnete a few times before, but he hadn't made arrangements to do so again. He'd told Agnete he planned to stay true to his lady wife, and the woman had joked that all the tavern wenches would become destitute having lost their best customer. Had he known Claire was watching, he would've snubbed Agnete and kept walking.

"I think you know where she is." Galien looked at Desmona, and he felt a pang of pity for his young cousin. Her heart rested in the right place, but he doubted Trent would be lenient with her once her complicity in Claire's disappearance was revealed.

"I swear I know not where Claire is hiding," she said, backing against the wall as her brother walked toward her.

"Shall I spank you now or later, Desmona? Because I know you are lying, and I will not tolerate such naughty behavior from my only sister." Trent tipped her chin up and she burst into tears.

"Enough!" a voice from behind the bed shouted. Claire jumped up and moved to Trent, placing a hand on his arm. "She was only trying to help me. I asked her to hide me, because I knew Galien would look for me in our chambers. Please do not punish her."

Galien strode to Claire and grasped her arm, spinning her to face him. "This matter is entirely between Trent and his sister. Now come, we are going to our chambers, to discuss a matter that is entirely between *us*." He guided her out of Desmona's chamber while Trent continued scolding his tearful sister.

The servants rushed out of their path as he marched Claire to their chambers. She had caused a scene in the great hall, and she had also taken advantage of Desmona's sweet, giving nature, and now the poor girl would be sitting as uncomfortably as Claire the next day. All because of a little jealousy. Galien intended to give Claire a most thorough spanking, and then he intended to spend the rest of the night proving he desired no other woman but her.

"Please, Galien, can we slow down?" Tears wavered on Claire's eyelashes, and her lip trembled. She shook in his arms.

He slowed his pace but maintained his hold on her, not giving her the opportunity to escape. "You have erred much this evening, Claire, and I am very disappointed in your behavior."

"Please, my lord, I am so sorry. Please don't be angry." She tried to twist from his grasp as the door to their chambers came into sight. "Galien, no! I don't wish to go in there with you!"

Galien had no choice but to lift Claire up and half carry, half drag her to the door. A footman at the end of the hall ducked his head, tactfully ignoring their quarrel.

"You are making this worse for yourself, Claire. The more you fight me, the harder I shall thrash your bare little arse." After a great deal of effort, he managed to get his protesting lady into their chambers with the door bolted behind them. "Cease, now!" His booming shout echoed off the stone walls.

Claire covered her ears and stilled within his arms, or at least made the attempt. She was shaking so hard her teeth chattered intermittently. "Please don't yell at me," she whispered through an especially hard shudder. "I know I was foolish, and I am so very sorry, my lord."

Holding her out by her shoulders, he studied her frightful reaction to his yell. She'd been scared and shaking before he raised his voice, but not as violently as now. He pondered this for but a moment before realization dawned, and his throat burned as guilt filled him. "Did Diterich yell at you?" he asked in a gentle tone.

She gave a short nod and the tears welling in her eyes overflowed, trickling down her face as she sniffled. "All the time." Her hands still cupped her ears, and he gently pried them away.

"I promise I will not yell at you again, sweet Claire, even when I am especially angry with you. I am sorry I frightened you so. Come here," he said, drawing her against his chest. He rested his chin atop her head and stroked the back of her neck, tangling his fingers in the short soft hairs that had resisted her coif.

Her arms remained at her sides at first, but she gradually brought them up around his waist, accepting the comfort he wished to give her. He cursed himself for raising his voice so. He had never yelled at a lady before, and the guilt of losing his temper nagged at his heart. Regret flowed through him, because in a few moments he had to punish her. After all the trouble she'd caused, he couldn't go easy on her either. His sweet Claire saved him the guilt though when she surprised him with a sudden pronouncement.

"I am ready now, my lord," she said, pulling back but keeping her gaze on his chest. "F-for my spanking, that is."

CHAPTER SIX

"Let us talk first," Galien said, guiding her to the bed. He sank down atop the covers and drew her into his lap, cradling her in his arms with a tenderness that made her want to cry all over again.

She wiped the last of her tears away and wished he'd just spank her. Married men weren't required to be chaste as wives were, and if he wished to tumble a whore now and then what right did she have to stop him? Making a scene in the great hall had been unwise, and she felt doubly guilty for getting Desmona into trouble. Even worse, his father was to be buried tomorrow, and she belittled herself for not keeping her grievances to herself during this time of mourning. Oh, how she had made a mess of things.

"I realize most men stray from their wives," she said, peering into his dark eyes. "It is quite common, and I confess I did not become so upset when Lord Diterich invited a whore into his chambers. I do not know what came over me, my lord, and I beg your forgiveness. You, of course, are free to do as you wish. I hold no dominion over you." How foolish she'd been to think her second marriage would be different than her first.

"Claire, you do hold dominion over me, because I desire no other woman but you."

"Have you been with that woman before? The one with the golden hair?" Pain squeezed her heart, because she already knew the truth.

"Aye, Claire, I have lain with Agnete many times, and other women as well. But not since we've been wed, and I have no plans to seek fulfillment outside of our marriage bed. I give you my word."

"How do I know you speak the truth?"

"Because I gave you my word, sweet Claire." He spoke with conviction, but doubt still waged a battled against hope in her heart.

Many a man had broken promises to Claire over the course of her lifetime, starting with her father. He'd promised she would not wed Diterich once, after the elderly lord first expressed interested in her, and she still felt a jab of betrayal each time she remembered the day her father reneged on his promise. "If you break your promise, I wish for permission to go live with my brother, Duke Leuthold."

Galien sighed and toyed with the blue veil that cascaded down her back from her elaborate headdress. Hesitation overtook his features, and she suspected he intended to refuse her request. It was unheard of for a lady to leave her husband, though to the world it could simply appear as if she were spending a lengthy visit with her brother. At first, anyway. She imagined Galien breaking his promise and bedding Agnete and all the other village whores, and she imagined journeying to Leuthold to spend the rest of her days with a broken heart. Hot tears gathered in her eyes as she envisioned a future without Galien, even if was because he betrayed her with another woman. The moment dragged on, and she wondered if he meant to ignore her ultimatum.

"Very well, Claire. If I break my promise, I will send you to live with your brother."

"Thank you, my lord."

"Know that it will never come to pass, my sweet Claire. When I give my word, I always keep it, and I mean to keep you. You are *my wife*." A possessive edge hardened his words, and his gaze grew intense as he stared down at her, still stroking her veil and her hair.

She sent up a silent prayer that he spoke the truth, for if he broke his promise her pride wouldn't allow her to remain at Minrova, even if she forgave him his transgressions and wished to remain at his side.

"Henceforth when something upsets you, Claire, I expect you to speak with me about it in a civil manner. You imagined that I meant to betray you just because you saw me speaking with Agnete for all of a moment, and you made a scene in the great hall in front of my cousins, my uncle, my aunt, and many of my men."

She shrank under his admonishment, her shame over her behavior making her cheeks flush and her heart ache. The strangest part of all was her desire to be over his lap already. She longed to put the punishment behind them, and in the very core of her being she ached for his forgiveness. But she also feared the impending pain and embarrassment, and she sat still as he continued scolding her.

"I am your husband, Claire, and I expect you to obey me even when we are not in agreement. If you had come straight back to our chambers as I had instructed you to do, your punishment would not have been so severe. But you intentionally hid from me and enlisted the help of Desmona, bringing another into our marriage. That kind of behavior is unacceptable, and I intend to make sure this sort of thing doesn't happen again. Do you understand?"

"Yes, my lord, I understand." She sniffled and felt small in his arms. "I am so sorry, and I am ashamed of my actions."

He pulled her slippers off and reached up her dress to tug her hosen down, and she shifted on his lap to assist with her undressing. Next he removed her headdress and freed her hair from the coif beneath it, and her hair billowed down her back. "Stand up, Claire."

She rose up with his assistance and her stomach went aflutter as he guided her to the center of the room. Without a word, he began unfastening the laces of her bodice, and soon she stood in nothing but her thin chemise. He removed his sword belt and placed it atop a trunk by the wall. He approached her with his arms crossed while he tapped at his chin, as if he was pondering the nature of her punishment. She shivered as though a sudden chill descended upon her, though the servants had already been in to light the braziers for the night, and the room was actually quite warm.

"You will be completely naked for your punishment, Claire." He moved behind her and placed his hands on her shoulders.

Anticipation twisted her insides and merged with her regret, leaving her a bundle of nerves. He had never punished her while she was completely unclothed before. Yes, he had bared her bottom, but her dress had remained on and given her a sense of decorum. Galien meant to strip away all her modesty, and as her chemise drifted to the floor, she felt truly humbled and repentant. She couldn't meet his eyes as he led her back to the bed.

He sat down and forced her to stand between his spread legs, and her lower lip quivered as she stood there naked before her clothed lord husband. Her hands flew up to cover her breasts, but he grasped her wrists and pulled her arms straight at her sides, forcing her to remain exposed and vulnerable.

"From now on, Claire, when you require chastisement, I shall strip off your clothes before I thrash you. I think it makes you more amenable to my authority, and I confess I also like to look upon my wife. Keep your hands in place," he admonished as he stroked her inner thigh.

She trembled and quaked, wishing he'd take her over his knee so she might hide her face in the covers.

"Spread your legs, wife. Good. Now hold this position."

She summoned all her inner strength to stay still as he probed her quim, tracing his fingers along her entrance and tapping against the nubbin where all her pleasure seemed to originate. He wrapped one arm around her body and held his flattened hand upon her womanly core. Heat gathered and pulsed between her thighs, and she looked down, wondering about his intentions. The sound of a stinging slap filled the room, and she gasped and shut her legs tight and shielded her quim from further punishment.

"Please, my lord," she begged. "Please don't spank me there. It isn't proper." She tried to escape his hold, but he pinned her hands behind her back and forced her to remain in place, smacking the insides of her thighs until she opened to his liking. "It hurts, my lord."

"I am your husband and it is my right to punish you as I see fit," he said, shooting her a stern look. "Keep your legs open, Claire, or you will earn extras."

She didn't want to earn extras, especially if those extras consisted of more slaps laid upon her tender nether lips. Squeezing her eyes shut, she endured a quick round of smacks to her quim. She winced and cried out with each blow. Tears coated her face, though they hadn't been wrought from pain. It hurt, but the humiliation of this particular punishment stung far worse than the slaps raining down upon her lips. Despite herself, pleasure also bloomed beside her discomfort, pulsating with each crack of his fingers across her most sensitive spot, that tender bud he'd swirled his thumb over whilst pounding into her.

He paused and parted her lower lips, delving inside with ease, and to her mortification she realized she had grown wet. A sob burst from her and she longed to slip into a crack in the stone walls and disappear. Never had she known shame so great.

"Over my knee, wife," he said, withdrawing his hand from her center. He arranged her over one strong thigh and wrapped his other leg atop hers, and she took it as a sign that this punishment was going to be quite severe. Next, he gathered her wrists at her lower back again. Naked and completely restrained over her displeased husband's lap, she sniffled and waited for the first smack to fall. At least his sword belt still rested atop the trunk, out of reach for the moment.

"I understand why you became upset this evening, Claire," he said, cupping her right cheek and giving it an ominous squeeze. "However, I expect you to conduct yourself like a lady. If you raise your voice at me again in my own hall, I will take a birch rod to your bare bottom. Have you ever been birched before?"

"No, my lord." She'd heard the screams of her brothers taking a birching though, and she had always strived not to land in such trouble as to warrant the use of the birch, and thus as a child she had only received a handful of quick, rather light spankings from her father. Coldness spread through her at the thought of receiving a birching from Galien, and she hoped to never give him cause to mete out a punishment so severe.

"It is a nasty implement, the birch rod. I sincerely hope to never use one on you, Claire." He moved to rub her left bottom cheek now, and she shuddered over his lap, trembling with a mixture of fear and relief that her spanking was about to begin.

"I intend to spank you fast and hard, Claire, and then this will be over. I want you to be a good girl and take your punishment. You were naughty. And this, sweet Claire, is what happens to naughty wives."

The first blow landed, and she clenched her arse and reared over his lap, the sharp sting of it taking her breath away. Before she recovered, he rained a second and third smack down. She wiggled and cried out with each hard spank, and still he maintained a rapid pace as he switched from cheek to cheek with each strike.

"Oh, please, my lord!" After a dozen slaps she was ready for her punishment to be over. The pain of his hand cracking steadily down on her smarting flesh continued to take her breath away, and she gasped and tried to turn over on his lap. When that didn't work, she attempted to slide to the floor, but he tightened his grip on her and kept spanking. Her struggles didn't slow him a bit. And to think she had asked for this spanking—had told him she was ready to be punished.

Once her escape attempts failed, she pressed her face into the blankets and sobbed. When she remembered her promise to Galien to be good and accept her punishment, she sobbed even harder. How quickly she'd forgotten that promise to submit when faced with the unendurable sting upon her bottom cheeks.

He thrashed the tops of her thighs, as well as the tender area of her lower backside. Her wet face stuck to the blankets, and the intensity of the fire blazing across her skin chased away all other thoughts. There was only the pain and the knowledge of what she'd done to deserve this punishment from her husband. *Thwack! Thwack!* His hand didn't seem to tire, and as exhaustion from her struggles and crying fell upon her, she went limp over his lap.

He paused and caressed her throbbing bottom. "The next time you are upset with me, wife, how will you behave differently?"

She sniffled and turned her face to the side, taking in a deep breath before she replied. "I-I will speak with you about it, my lord, in a calm manner." Hot tears poured from her eyes.

"What else?"

"I will not disrespect you again, not the way I did tonight, my lord, for which I am very sorry."

"Good girl. We're almost finished."

• • • • • • •

Galien ceased rubbing Claire's reddened backside and brought his hand down ten more times, rapid blows that tore a howl from her in between her sobs. He then turned her over and enfolded his arms around her, aching to comfort her and needing to feel her close.

"Shh, sweet Claire. It's over now. You are forgiven." He tangled his fingers in her hair and stroked the back of her head.

She sat within the circle of his embrace, her face pressed to his chest and her arms wrapped about his waist. Her shoulders heaved under her cries, and he murmured soothing words into her ear in hopes of helping her calm down. Gradually, her sobs turned to sniffles, and soon after that her sniffles faded altogether. Her breathing stabilized and she simply held onto him as the moments passed, and likewise he held onto her. There was nowhere else he wished to be in this instant in time, nowhere but in his chambers with his sweet lady wife.

"I cannot believe I behaved so outrageously in the great hall, Galien." She peered up at him with red rings around her eyes.

"The matter has been dealt with, Claire. You did wrong and I punished you for it, and then I forgave you, my sweet wife." He kissed her forehead and let his lips linger upon her soft flesh, inhaling her floral scent and never wishing to release her. Oh, she felt perfect in his arms.

She lowered her head and leaned into his chest again, and he strengthened his hold on her as warmth spread outward from his heart. Claire's reaction to her punishment pleased him greatly. She had accepted responsibility for her behavior and felt repentant, and after her spanking she wasn't sulking or trying to escape him. That she sought comfort in his arms after he'd punished her testified to her growing trust in him. His throat tightened with this realization, because her willingness to accept his guidance boded well for their marriage, and above all he wished for their union to be a happy one.

"Do you think Desmona will forgive me for getting her into trouble?"

"Aye, I'm certain she will. I've known her since she was a babe, and she has a kind heart. You needn't worry."

She drew back and met his eyes, and a blush crept over her face. "Are we going to sleep now, my lord?"

His cock shifted beneath her bottom as if protesting the very idea of sleep. He shook his head as he admired her innocent expression. "No, Claire, we are most certainly not going to sleep."

Her blush deepened and she tried to lower her gaze, but he caught her chin and held it between two fingers, and a sharp tremor rocked her and caused her to wiggle atop his lap and the hardness encased within his leggings. Longing flared and he leaned down to claim her lips, clutching her face as he kissed her hard and deep, pressing his tongue into her mouth with all the urgency he felt rising within him. The little whimpers and moans she made as he kissed her drove him wild, and his desire spiked hot and dangerous the moment her tongue at last pressed against his.

When he finally broke away, she gasped for air and moved her bottom over his growing cock, and he caught her occasional wince as her sore flesh brushed too hard over his leggings. The state of her arse gave him an idea, and he pushed her off his lap and arranged her on her hands and knees on the bed.

She peeked over her shoulder at him, her long dark locks in complete disarray and her lips swollen and red from his kisses. "My lord?"

He looked from her questioning gaze to her bright red bottom and punished thighs. "Remain in this position, Claire." Standing up, he worked off his boots, leggings, and tunic while she watched with wide eyes.

"My lord, please. I thought my punishment was over." She trembled and bit her lip.

He crawled up on the bed behind her. "I'm not going to spank you, Claire," he said, understanding her misconception with a pang of pity. The last time he'd forced her into this position had been when he'd taken his sword belt to her bottom, on their wedding night no less.

"Then what do you plan to do?" Her eyes remained impossibly wide, making her appear all the more tempting to Galien.

He rested on his knees behind her and grabbed her hips, bringing her center back against his aching cock. "I plan to take you this way, my curious wife."

"But... but you can't!"

He chuckled. "I assure you I can." He dragged his hard cock through the wet folds of her quim, noting that her level of arousal rivaled that of two nights ago in the tent after her whipping. She shuddered and lifted her hips to meet his entrance, even as she uttered another outraged protest.

"My lord, you can't! Not *this* way."

"Claire, I believe you've forgotten your place in this marriage," he said, driving forward into her sweet tight cunt. "Sometimes your place is on your hands and knees, with your red punished arse up in the air, while your husband pounds his cock into your soaking wet quim."

She cried out with the force of his thrust, and whimpered as he slowly withdrew his length from her tightness, only to trail the tip of his cock through her folds once more, teasing her with shallow plunges and the occasional touch to her nubbin.

"Galien, this is highly improper."

"Is it?"

Though she still argued, her body surrendered to his ministrations. He pushed into her again and started pounding her hard, and her only response was a pleasurable moan as she lifted her hips to meet his thrusts. For all her hesitance and fighting, she enjoyed this position and the deep drives into her slick quim that it allowed. He pulled her bottom cheeks apart, exposing the pucker of her back entrance as he continued on, fucking her with rapid strokes.

He reached underneath her to circle her swollen nub, sliding her moisture over the delicate and engorged bit of flesh while she writhed beneath him in the throes of passion. She'd given up her protests and all resistance, instead giving herself over to her desires, be they proper or not. A cry leapt from her and her head tilted to the side, and she increased the movements of her hips. Her insides clamped down around his cock, and he couldn't hold back any longer. He followed her into the warm pulsing sensation of a release, and when it ended they collapsed on the bed together, seeking one another out in the aftermath of their bliss.

"I believe I have conquered you yet again, Claire."

He felt her smile against his chest. "I think I like this… this conquering."

CHAPTER SEVEN

Time passed in a whirl of activity at Minrova, and though Claire had more responsibilities at Galien's keep than she'd had at Diterich, she enjoyed the constant flow of visitors and goings-on. Desmona, who had indeed forgiven Claire, departed with her brothers not long after Galien's father was buried, and not long after his aunt and uncle left as well. Only a handful of his cousins remained, many of them knights who helped safeguard the keep and all of Galien's holdings. With Hohenzollern's fearful shadow gone, people traveled and traded more freely, and various lords visited from time to time seeking respite from whatever postponed journey they'd decided to finally take.

Galien acted as a fair lord, settling disputes between his subjects with a deftness that she admired. Her respect for him grew each day, and when she accompanied him into the village she noticed children flocked to him. On one notable day, they'd come upon a young girl crying by the well. After discovering the girl's kitten had gone missing, he enlisted Claire's help, as well as two knights, to search for the child's pet. The look in the girl's eyes as he'd returned the tiny black kitten to her waiting arms had melted Claire's heart. Though stern and commanding at times, Galien had his gentle moments too, and she smiled and felt warm all over whenever she remembered this day.

The people of Minrova took a liking to Claire and made her feel at home, particularly those in the keep. She shared her mother's sweet cake recipe with the cook, and after he received many compliments on the cakes, he began consulting her about the meals and smiled when she entered the kitchen. Claire also delighted in helping the younger ladies with their stitching, an art her mother had taught her at an early age. She learned to make precise stitches and create a perfect pattern in her pieces far ahead of her peers, because she learned the sooner she finished her stitch work, the sooner she could escape and run after her brothers. Now she found the work soothing because it reminded her of her mother, and it passed the hours when she was waiting on Galien to return from his duties.

Her evenings were full of passion with her lord husband. Flutters rose in her stomach when she reminisced about their nighttime activities. Each evening he brought her to their chambers and undressed her, often holding her in his lap while they discussed their day. His hands would play about in her hair, and a dark lustful look would flame in his eyes. She grew to love his roughness as much as his gentleness, craving each side of him and willingly giving herself over to his amorous moods, whether he wished to make tender love to her or smack her arse and then pound into her hard.

She tried her best to please him, and she couldn't wait to thank Leuthold for arranging their marriage, for she found life with Galien a far better circumstance than being a lonely, fearful widow. The dark cloud that had surrounded her the day she married Diterich had lifted thanks to Galien. She saw the world and all its vivid colors, felt happiness rising and bursting in her heart on a daily basis, and the longer she was married to Galien, the more certain she was of her growing love for him.

Aye, she couldn't deny it. She loved her husband and suspected he felt the same. After all, he hadn't wandered into the village to seek company with the tavern whores, nor had he invited any to the keep. She'd kept a watchful eye on him after their fight that stemmed from his conversation with Agnete, and she hadn't so much as seen him glance in another woman's direction. After the miserable failure of her first marriage in this regard, she thanked God for blessing her with a loyal husband.

Her peaceful lull was broken one day, however, when she awoke early one morning with a sense of unease. She reached for Galien to discover him missing from their bed, and she slipped on a cloak and ventured to the window. Bright orange flames lit up the darkness in the distance. She gasped and surveyed the horizon, wishing the sun showed more than a thin pink line through the trees. Another fire flared to existence, far enough away from the first one for her to know it hadn't spread from building to building.

These fires were intentional, and her pulse thudded with the suspicious that Minrova was under attack. *Oh, Galien…*

She dressed in haste and slipped into her thickest hosen and dug out her brother's boots from her trunk, wishing she still had her knife. Putting her ear to the door, she listened for sounds of distress, and hearing none she cracked the door and peeked out. A dark feminine figure moved through the dim halls and headed for Claire. It was her lady's maid, and her relaxed expression left Claire perplexed. Hadn't she seen the fires?

"Erwyn. Have you glanced outside this morning?"

"Milady," the young girl said, performing a quick curtsey. "Milord Galien has sent word to the castle that a band of miscreants set two buildings ablaze in the village. Two of the men have been captured, and the rest have been killed."

"Lord Galien is unharmed?"

"No harm came to Lord Galien or any of his brave men. Milord has asked that you remain in your chambers until he returns from questioning the captured villains."

Sharp relief coursed through Claire. "Thank you, Erwyn."

After another quick curtsey the girl turned and disappeared down the hall, and Claire retreated into her chambers to await Galien's arrival. She stood at the window, gazing across the village beyond the castle walls. As the sunlight broke through the trees and over the mountains, the fires diminished into two trails of smoke rising from the blackened buildings. From this distance, she couldn't ascertain what structures had suffered damage, whether they had been houses or storehouses, or perhaps one of the taverns. She hoped all those inside the buildings had escaped without injury.

The hours passed slowly and her impatience swelled as midday drew closer, and still Galien hadn't returned. Erwyn came to help her dress properly with her bodice laced tight, and later the girl arrived with porridge and sweet bread, but Claire picked at her food and spent the rest of the time pacing from the door to the window, her restlessness and worry turning to anger. Why had Galien ordered her to remain in their chambers if the danger was over?

She glanced out at the village and saw no hint of the rising smoke from the fires, and people moved about in the streets, women chatted at the well, and children ran merrily about. The sky darkened though, and each time she returned to look out at the landscape, it grew more ominous still. A light snowfall began but soon turned to a complete whiteout, and she saw nothing from her view except a swirl of white against darkness.

Enough bloody waiting, she thought, and she bounded toward the door with purpose. She intended to find her husband, and after she hugged and kissed him and looked him over to ensure he wasn't hurt, she planned to tell him exactly what she thought of being ordered to remain in her chambers for no good reason that she could discern.

Feeling especially cross, she flung the door open and prepared to exit her chambers, but a large man blocked her path. She gasped and looked into his dark brown eyes. Galien's eyes.

"Going somewhere?" he asked, arching an eyebrow.

She gulped and backed into the chamber. He followed her and shut the door behind him, his gaze censuring and focused solely on her.

"Didn't your lady's maid relay my instructions to you?"

She nodded, too angry to speak.

"Then you were about to disobey. Is that the truth of it?" Something odd and distant flickered in his eyes, a coldness she had never glimpsed from him before. His body vibrated with rage, and his tone reflected a harsh fury she hadn't known he possessed.

"I became impatient and I wished to find you, my lord. I am sorry." She stared at her blue slippers, fear chasing away every bit of anger she'd been harboring.

"Sorry? You're always sorry, Claire, especially after I give you thrashing you richly deserve, yet you continue to disavow my authority again and again. Perhaps I have punished you too lightly."

A flash of terror swept over her. Who was this man standing before her and where had her husband gone? She peeked up and trembled to see Galien methodically taking his sword belt off, removing the scabbards, and folding the leather in half. Her insides clenched with dread, and she started shaking her head as she backed up into the wall, her livid husband following her with his sword belt dangling from his hand.

"I didn't even make it out of my chambers, my lord, and you intend to whip me with that?" Her lip trembled and she wanted to scream out that it wasn't fair, that even though she'd been about to disobey him, it wasn't cause for such a harsh punishment. A spanking perhaps, just a quick reminder to teach her to heed his word, but nothing like this. Not the sword belt, please, not the sword belt...

She suspected he meant to wield it with more force than the last time he'd used it on her, the time he'd given her ten light strokes in the tent. Tears spilled from her eyes because she didn't understand the rage taking over her husband.

"Remove your clothing, Claire, and bend over the bed."

"My lord, please. Don't do this."

"Now, Claire, or this will go much worse for you."

• • • • • • • •

Galien gripped his sword belt and waited as Claire undressed. She fumbled a bit with the laces on her bodice, but she managed to strip off all her clothing and bend over the bed. Her hands shook and she grasped onto the blankets, shuddering breaths revealing the height of her fear. An urge to gather her up in his arms and soothe her worries built up, but he pushed the desire down. When danger visited the village or his keep, he expected all those under his command to obey his orders, including his wife.

Galien and his men had killed five of the marauders and captured two for questioning. The prisoners had been executed of course, but not until after they'd spilled all their secrets while begging for their lives at Galien's feet. The cowards. After hours of interrogating the two captured men, one of whom bore the Hohenzollern crest, it had been revealed that several bands of Hohenzollern knights still roamed the countryside, men who hadn't been at the castle during the siege. The lot of them had ridden over the hill during the siege at Hohenzollern and turned to flee before the conquering army spotted them.

Galien ground his teeth together, all the rage he'd felt during the fight returning. The prisoners claimed a camp of Hohenzollern knights was in the forest not far from Minrova, and a search of the woods had found an abandoned camp, but no sign of the remaining men. Tomorrow, after the storm calmed, they would set out again in search of the cowards and put an end to them once and for all. No one attacked Minrova or any of Galien's holdings and got away with it. He took the safety and well-being of his subjects very seriously, and though he had disregarded much of what his father taught him growing up, this was the one lesson he had taken to heart, the one lesson he held dear, and he intended to honor the memory of his father by hunting the villains down.

Claire might have grown impatient waiting for him, but he had serious business to take care of, and he had wanted her to remain in their chambers, safe and protected within the walls of his keep, so when he'd finished dealing with the attack he knew exactly where to find his lady wife. He'd told her to wait. A simple command, and yet he'd caught her in the act of disregarding his orders.

His anger flared as he considered how frantically he'd be searching his keep at this very moment if Claire had succeeded in leaving their chambers, how worried he would have been that a sly Hohenzollern knight had infiltrated his home and harmed his sweet wife. Mayhap his imagination was running wild with worry, but the fact remained that she had disobeyed him, and for that he needed to punish her. To make her understand that she wasn't allowed to pick and choose which orders to follow and which orders to ignore.

"Spread your legs, Claire." He moved to her side and placed the sword belt on the bed directly in her line of vision. "Wider, wider. Good."

She sniffled and her shoulders shook, but she kept her thighs open as he'd asked. The pinkness of her quim glistened up at him, and he placed one steadying hand on her back and with his other hand reached between her legs to stroke her center, wanting to know exactly how wet she'd become. She always reacted to his discipline in this way, and he found this time was no exception. Though she appeared frightened, her womanly core dripped with copious amounts of her desire. As he prodded her slick entrance, her hips shifted and he caught sight of her secret puckering hole nestled so innocently between her bottom cheeks.

A dark thought crept into his mind, a new way to punish his naughty wife, to help her feel true submission and perhaps think twice before misbehaving again. He pumped two fingers in and out of her wet quim and moved his other hand down to part her arse cheeks. She tensed and tried to rear up, but he pushed her down and continued spreading her bottom to reveal her shy, untouched hole.

"Be still, wife. This is part of your punishment."

"Wh-what are you going to do?" She looked over her shoulder, her wide eyes displaying her utter shock over this new treatment.

"I intend to punish your arsehole, Claire. Naughty wives deserve to be punished in naughty ways." His reply came out stern, his displeasure over her planned disobedience burning hot. At least while he punished her bottom hole, he'd have some time to calm down and the lashes she received with the sword belt wouldn't be fueled by his anger.

She turned her head and hid from him, burying her face in the blankets as her body tensed. "My lord," she said, her voice muffled in the covers. "Please, I beg you, this is a most cruel punishment."

"No," he said with a firmness that made her start. "It's not cruel, Claire. It is just. Cruel would be causing your husband undue worry when he didn't find you where you were supposed to be, not long after an attack by a renegade band of Hohenzollern deserters. I ordered you to remain in our chambers for your safety, in case the threat against Minrova grew, and I also wished to easily find you afterward to hold you in my arms and breathe in your flowery scent and satisfy myself that all was well with my wife."

"I-I am deeply sorry, my lord. I was worried about you and wished to find you first. I know I was supposed to wait, but—oh!" She gasped as he pressed two fingers into her arsehole, using moisture stolen from her quim to guide the way. "Oh, my lord. It hurts!"

He wasn't even knuckle deep, yet she thrashed about on the bed and closed her legs, trying to rise up. He angled one leg in front of hers, preventing her escape and holding her down as he pushed in and out of her arse, delving knuckle deep before withdrawing and pushing inside again. Her hole was hot and tight, and his desire swelled at the thought of taking her snug entrance and giving her a good pounding with his cock.

She cried and kicked her feet to no avail, he didn't ease up on her once, and he eventually pushed deeper, until both his prodding fingers were fully submerged in her tightness. Keeping them still for a few moments, he urged her legs apart again and smacked her thighs until she complied. Fresh sobs erupted from her throat, and she cried pitifully into the blankets.

As expected, his anger began to melt as he punished her, and by the time she stopped fighting him and lay limp over the bed while he plunged in and out of her backside, only a whisper of his irritation remained. He gave her three more deep thrusts before withdrawing from her tight hole. Giving her time to recover, he washed his hands in the water basin and returned to sit beside her while stroking her back, trailing a hand up and down her soft warm skin, thinking she was the most beautiful woman he'd ever known. The sweetest too, and he longed for her punishment to be over so he could hold her and stroke her hair while whispering words of comfort in her ear.

He removed her coif and combed her locks out with his fingers, wishing it were appropriate for ladies to wear their hair down at all times, because he liked the look of her with her hair spilling about her shoulders. She sighed and caught his gaze while wiping at her lingering tears.

"Are you still terribly angry with me, my lord?"

"No, sweet Claire. I have calmed down considerably, and I regret that I frightened you so. I do, however, mean to finish your punishment."

"Must you use your sword belt? Couldn't you just spank me with your hand?"

He gave a shake of his head and stroked her face, brushing away another tear as it trickled down her cheek. "You cannot talk your way out of a whipping, Claire. It's going to hurt, but it will teach you to mind me, teach you to obey your lord husband. You took a vow before God to obey me, and I intend to help you honor that vow, because I want you to be your best, and because I want to ensure you're always safe, and happy."

"Will you hold me when it's over?"

His heart contracted at her request. Of course he would. He always did. "Aye, Claire. I will hold you forever if you wish it." He stood and picked up his sword belt, and it felt unusually heavy in his hand. Moving behind her, he pinned her wrists together, securing her hands at her lower back. "Twenty strokes," he announced, raising the leather high and bringing it down with an echoing thwack.

Claire tensed and whimpered with each lash he rained down, and on the fifth stroke she lurched upward, desperate in her attempt to escape. He pushed her back into position and stuck her upper thighs, three blows in quick succession that made her cry out and beg for mercy. She shook under her sobs and uttered heartfelt apology after apology, and promises to obey him in the future. Despite her discomfort, he continued on and meted out the full punishment, even when the sound of her sobbing pained him, until the belt impacted across her bottom cheeks for the twentieth time. Then he dropped the belt and gathered her in his arms, just as he'd promised.

CHAPTER EIGHT

His loving embrace surrounded her, comforting her and reassuring her of his regard for her. If he despised her, surely he wouldn't offer her such tender care after a punishment. In his arms, she felt the completeness of her love for him, a stark feeling of rightness. There was no doubt in her mind that she loved him, and she was certain he held similar affections for her. Perhaps he loved her as deeply as she loved him. Oh, how she hoped.

She shifted on his lap, her welted bottom sore, outside and *inside*. Shame heated her face as she recalled the reason for the tenderness in her private hole, and how exposed she'd felt when he spread her arse cheeks to punish her *there*, using the wetness from her quim to ease the passage of his fingers. The intrusion had burned and filled her up, and after he'd thrust in and out for a spell, her center had started to ache and throb. Moisture coated the insides of her thighs, evidence of her excitement even during a harsh chastisement.

Galien's heart thumped a steady rhythm and lulled her into a peaceful state. His forgiveness washed over her, and she tightened her arms around his waist, wanting to be as close to him as possible. Her heart swelled with affection for this man who had stormed into her life, rescued her from certain misery with a foreign mercenary, and took his vows to her seriously even before he'd gotten to know her well.

"Are you all right, wife?"

"Aye, my lord. I am well." She nuzzled his chest, inhaling his masculine scent and sighing into his tunic. The aching in her core pulsed harder, and she squirmed and detected the hardness of his manhood beneath her punished bottom. She tilted her face up and Galien captured her lips, pressing his mouth to hers and thrusting his tongue inside.

His rough manner stoked the flames of her desire to burn hotter and she moaned as he kissed her. He lifted her and arranged her legs to straddle him while she continued sitting on his lap, and this position allowed her to feel the brunt of his arousal through his leggings, the hard part of him that he used to conquer her and bring her to the heights of the clouds. No, the stars and the moon.

"Does my wife want a cock inside her?" He pulled back and cupped her face, and her cheeks burned with the coarseness of his speech.

"My lord," she said in a hushed, scandalized voice.

He grinned and flipped her around, placing her atop the blankets on her back. She winced at the feel of her sore arse brushing against the covers, but she spread her legs in invitation, her pulse thudding as he stripped off his clothing. His cock jutted out, so long and so thick.

"My lady," he said, mimicking her tone.

She giggled and sat up on her elbows, eager for him to advance on her.

He gripped his cock and a dark look crept over him as he situated himself atop her, aiming his length for her quim's wet, aching opening. Rubbing the tip up and down, he teased her entrance with the softest touches, driving her into a fever of longing.

"Cup your breasts, my lady. Touch yourself."

Her hesitation lasted but an instant, and his ardent look prompted her hands to her breasts. She cupped the mounds and squeezed, kneaded, and ran her fingertips over her hardened rosy peaks. He rewarded her obedience with a press of his thumb to her pulsating nub, and she lifted her hips to meet his firm caresses as he swirled moisture atop that sensitive spot.

Leaning over her, he trailed kisses up and down her neck and licked the soft hollow at the base of her ear. He moved lower, nibbling her flesh and grazing his teeth over her breasts. A hot spike of desire pierced her when he flicked her taut peak with his tongue, and she arched into him as he moved lower still, and lower, until…

She saw the stars approaching, felt the majestic night descend upon her in a haze as Galien lapped at her wet center, licking her folds over once before focusing his attentions on her throbbing nubbin, circling that swollen bit of flesh until the stars transpired and sparkled bright in the blackness that consumed her. She ground herself against his mouth and rode out the crashing waves, hearing the roar of the water in her ears, or perhaps it was the beating of her heart. She wasn't sure. But she fell apart in his arms over and over again that night, spreading her legs as he pumped into her and spilled his seed, and even as she straddled him and rode his thick cock while he guided her movements.

Before she drifted into a restful sleep, he kissed her forehead and caught her eyes in a lingering stare so intense she feared his earlier anger had returned, but his words dispelled her worries. "I love you, Claire. With all that I am, I love you."

She smiled and kept her eyes open as long as her fatigue allowed it, never wanting this day to end. "I love you, Galien."

• • • • • • •

The next day she watched him ride off into the snow-covered forest with his men, her heart heavy and light at the same time. His dire sense of duty dictated he hunt down the Hohenzollern men and she wished he didn't have to endure such danger, but he had confessed his love to her oh so tenderly the night before. She wavered between heartbreak and absolute elation during the next three days as she awaited his return. She wished to stay in her chambers and keep vigil at the window, but she was the lady of this household, and she had duties to attend to just as Galien did, so she made herself busy with her normal routine and maintained a presence in the halls. She also comforted the women whose husbands had accompanied Galien on his search, hugging them to her side and promising the men would return soon.

She hoped she spoke the truth, and it took all of her strength to hold her head high around the keep and project confidence. In the privacy of her chambers at night though, she curled into a ball beneath the blankets and cried silent tears, wrapping her arms around her body to fight off the pervasive loneliness. Apprehension ravaged her senses, leaving her sick to her stomach and barely able to eat. Was this how her mother had felt each time her father rode off to battle?

The clouds blocked out the sun most days, but at least it didn't snow again. The cold wind blew across the village and whistled against the walls of the keep. She prayed for Galien's safe return at least ten times during every hour of every day, keeping a constant vigil in her heart. The men who stayed behind kept watch over the keep and reported back to her often, though there wasn't much to report. A lack of news was preferable to somber news, she knew, but when a full six days passed, the bleakest scenarios played out in her mind.

She stared across the darkness of Minrova at the end of the sixth day, watching as the sun set beyond the snow-covered mountains. She felt as cold inside as the top of the farthest peak. Standing at the window with a blanket draped around her shoulders and her hair cascading down her back, she willed Galien and his men to ride into the keep. *Come back to me, husband, please.*

A sickeningly familiar sight lit up the sky, and Claire rushed to get dressed and put on her boots, once again wishing for her knife. If she lived through this, she would get another weapon, even if she had to sneak it behind Galien's back.

She glanced outside and spotted three distinct fires. Panic crashed over her, and she rushed out of her chambers, determined to ensure the survival of Galien's people. Her people. They were her people too.

A white-faced Erwyn rounded a corner and bumped into her. "Milady! We're under attack!"

Claire reached for the girl's hands. "I know, and I have a very important job for you, Erwyn. You must gather all the women and children and head for the storage rooms off of the kitchen. It's warm there and close enough to the back entrance and the great hall that you have two options of escape if the walls of the keep are breached."

The fear marring Erwyn's face soon gave way to a purposeful, confident expression. "Aye, milady. I will do so at once." The girl turned and hurried away, knocking on doors as she moved down the hall to summon the women and children into hiding.

Claire ran past her and stomped down the stone steps into the great hall, and exited the keep and found Galien's men mounting their horses in the bailey. She sought out Sir Ceryn, one of her husband's cousins, and the knight in charge of his remaining men.

"Sir Ceryn! Sir Ceryn!" She bounded to him just as he prepared to mount his horse. He paused and peered at her through the slit in his helmet, and the sight of his full armor filled her with dread. Their keep was under a true attack, and judging by the shouts spilling in from beyond the walls of the outer bailey, she feared the enemy outnumbered them.

"My lady, you must remain in the keep. We will protect you, but you must stay inside."

"Any sign of Galien or his men?"

"I'm sorry, my lady, but no." Sir Ceryn mounted his stallion and looked down at her, then nodded at the keep. "Please return inside, my lady. I will not leave the bailey until I see that you're safe inside."

Claire surveyed the two dozen men assembled and ready to rush out to meet the enemy, and she realized she was holding them up. Frustration welled up at her inability to help them, and she gathered up her skirts and inclined her head to Sir Ceryn and all the men in a manner of respect. "God be with you, sirs." She rushed into the warmth of the keep and turned in time to witness two dozen armored men storming out of the bailey with their swords drawn.

• • • • • • •

An eerie orange glow flickered on the horizon, and Galien urged his horse to full speed and shouted for his men to follow him into the heart of Minrova. Screams and the familiar sound of clashing swords reached him, and his thoughts at once shifted to Claire. Was she safe within the fortified walls of the keep?

He struck down a man wearing Hohenzollern colors, and his men did the same as they worked their way toward the keep, felling the enemy as they took the assailants by surprise. Judging by the way many of the Hohenzollern deserters staggered to hold their swords, they must have imbibed too many spirits before committing the folly of attacking Minrova. The cowards had evaded Galien and his men for days, until they found a fresh trail leading in the direction of the village in the late afternoon. They'd ridden hard for hours hoping to reach Minrova in time to assist the men Sir Ceryn commanded in Galien's absence.

Galien surveyed the village during a lull in action and counted five blazes, but the villagers were bravely working to extinguish the flames, and two of the fires were nearly put out. The recent snow kept the deliberately set fires from spreading between buildings, and he moved on through the horde with his men following his lead, striking down every Hohenzollern man who dared cross their path, and riding down those who attempted to flee into the forest. Galien had no mercy for these assailants. "Kill them all!" he shouted over the clashing of weapons. "Take no prisoners!"

Halfway through the village Sir Ceryn rode up with his sword drawn and turned his horse to trot beside Galien. "The keep? Has it been breached?"

"No, my lord. All in the keep are well, including your lady wife. We rode out of the bailey while the Hohenzollern men were still setting the fires, and none of them managed to climb the walls or breach the portcullis. They were ill prepared to fight."

Galien thanked Sir Ceryn, and the men swept through the village carefully in search of any remaining attackers. The few they found offered little resistance were easily felled, and once the village was secured and Galien assessed the danger had passed, he helped to douse the flames of the last two fires, heaping snow atop the diminishing flames until only ribbons of smoke remained to whirl into the dark sky.

His heart slowed from its erratic pounding and he rode for the keep with his men, anxious to hold his sweet Claire in his arms. The Hohenzollern men had obviously lured Galien out of Minrova with the first fires they set, and the cowards had misjudged the capacity of Minrova to defend itself even in his absence. Galien was confident Sir Ceryn would have prevailed over the assailants, but he was still glad to have ridden into the village at the height of the attack. His people were safe, his men were safe, and most important of all, his lady wife hadn't been harmed. He hoped the ordeal hadn't frightened her too much.

After passing his horse off to a squire, Galien strode into the keep, his heavy armor clinking against his chainmail. "Claire!" He searched the great hall and found no one, and he rushed upstairs to their chambers, only to find it just as empty. The blankets were pulled up tight on the bed, and the room appeared tidy except for Claire's open trunk and a pair of slippers in the middle of the floor. He frowned as his concern deepened. "Claire!" Had Sir Ceryn erred in his report? Had some of the Hohenzollern men managed to breach the keep after all?

Galien searched every wing and bellowed his wife's name, and he rushed to the great hall after it became apparent that no one, not even a servant, was to be found in any corner of the keep. His men searched about the keep as well, shouting for someone, *anyone,* to make their presence known. Beyond the kitchen and near the storage rooms, he paused at a door in the dimly lit hallway. The shrill sound of a crying infant had him flinging the door open.

"Claire?"

He blinked and stared into the blade of a knife, and his gaze traveled beyond the weapon to the blue-eyed beauty grasping it between shaking hands. "Claire." He reached for her hands and lowered the knife, then drew her into his embrace. She threw her arms around him and shuddered, and behind her many of the servants waited in the shadows, anxiously peering out the open door. A servant girl rocked and cooed her wailing child.

"I've been calling your name, wife. Why didn't you answer?"

"I'm sorry. We couldn't hear much on account of the baby. Are you all right?" She pulled back and her gaze swept up from his feet to his head, and back down again.

"I am fine. All my men are safe as well. We tracked the bloody Hohenzellorn men in a long circle through the forest that led back to Minrova. They are all dead. They won't hurt anyone else again." He stared at the ladies, servants, and children in the storage room. "All is well. You may come out now," he shouted over the baby's cries.

He escorted Claire to their chambers and called for the servants to bring up a bath. His squires removed his armor and made a hasty retreat, and Galien bolted the door before turning to his wife, a fervent longing for her mixing with his relief at finding her safe, and amusement at discovering her armed and protecting the women and children of the keep, just as she'd done at Hohenzollern.

"Where did you get the knife?" he asked, nodding at the weapon she'd placed on a table next to his sword belt.

"I swiped it from the kitchen," she said, a smile tugging at her lips. "I used to have a larger one with a bejeweled handle, but a beast of a man made me drop it."

He grinned and backed her against the bed and worked her dress open and pushed it down over her shoulders. "A beast of a man? Is that so?" he asked, biting the soft lobe of her ear.

"Oh!" she said, reaching for him as a shiver rippled through her. "Aye, my lord, the beast made me drop my knife, and then he stole me out of a castle and forced me to marry him."

"Forced you to marry him?" he asked with a mock gasp.

"Aye, and he spanked me for resisting him on our wedding night."

"I'm sure he had a very good reason to redden your little arse, Claire."

She trembled as she stood before him in her thin chemise, the taut peaks of her breasts tenting the sheer fabric. He cupped her mounds and squeezed, thinking her size had increased as he trailed kisses down her neck when her head fell to the side. She moaned and her hips lurched toward his, her center pressing hard against his straining cock.

"Tell me," he said. "Does your story have a happy ending?"

She smiled against his lips after he kissed her. "Aye, my lord. The ending is most romantic. You see, the beast conquered my heart, and likewise I conquered his. We love each other very much." She placed his hand on her stomach, her eyes lighting up the room. "And soon we will have a child together, our first of many, I hope."

Excitement abounded in his heart, and he clutched her face and kissed her again. "Are you certain?" He returned his hand to her stomach, rubbing in a circle.

"Aye, my lord, I am quite certain. I just realized it myself not long after you rode off in search of the Hohenzollern men. I haven't bled in two months, and I feel different."

He slipped her chemise off and stared at her breasts before caressing and weighing them in his hands. The slightest swell of her stomach protruded from her narrow waist, and he pinched her nipples until she gasped.

"Oh! Gentle, please. I find I am especially sensitive there."

Of course he responded with another squeeze to her stiff peaks and grinned at her gasp. "My wife," he said with reverence. "My sweet Claire. You have made a fine wife, and I know you will make a fine mother."

She glanced down and blushed under his compliment, her cheeks turning a pretty shade of pink as her hair tumbled in front of her face. He brushed the locks aside and tipped her chin up and stroked her cheek with the back of his hand. "I have a surprise for you too, my lady."

"What is it?"

"The duke of Leuthold is coming to visit in a fortnight. I have been in correspondence with him and as long as the weather holds out, you will see your brother soon."

She stood on her toes to rain kisses all over his face. "Thank you, my lord!" She paused and tucked her hair behind her ears, a thoughtful look coming upon her. "Oh, I have so much to do to prepare for his arrival. I have to speak with the cook, and the servants, and we must see about…"

He pressed a finger to her lips, stilling her speech. "You have plenty of time to prepare, and I am certain your brother will be impressed with the proficient manner in which you manage the keep. Now," he said, stepping back to remove his leggings and his tunic, "into the bath with you, and be careful not to slosh the water over the sides. Last time you took a bath I nearly slipped on the wet stones."

She slipped into the water with a pleasurable sigh and gave him a mischievous smile, then flicked a drop of water onto the floor. "Oh, dear," she said. "Look what I've done."

He stalked to her and arranged her on her hands and knees in the water. "Naughty Claire," he said. "Now I must punish your wet arse." He rubbed more water atop her backside, as well as a dollop of lavender oil, and he slipped one finger into her bottom hole.

"My lord!" She shot him a pleading glance over her shoulder. "Are you really cross with me?"

"I know the last time I touched you here, it was meant to punish, but this is for your pleasure, Claire. And for mine. Try to relax." Keeping his finger submerged in her tightness, he crawled into the water behind her and continued rubbing the oil over her arse cheeks, admiring her glistening backside. He pumped in and out of her bottom hole and paused to smack her cheeks, his hand lightly cracking over her wet mounds.

She moaned and lifted her rump, and he added a second and third finger, increasing the pace of his thrusting while the water sloshed around them. His cock throbbed against her thigh, and his balls drew up tight. Watching her responses for any signs of distress, he withdrew all the way from her shy hole and his desire heated at the sight of her puckering entrance pulsing in the wake of his touch. He applied more oil and nudged her again, this time with four fingers, taking them deep without more than a whimper. Once he felt she was adequately prepared to accept a much larger, harder intrusion, he pulled his fingers from her tightness and situated his cock at her tempting arsehole.

"You forgot about this part in your story," he said, jerking her head back with a hand fisted in her hair.

"What part?"

"The part where the beast fucks your tight virgin arsehole." He surged into her before she had the chance to protest, and her tight entrance clamped down around his cock. "Be a good girl and let me inside, Claire."

"You're too large, my lord. I can't…"

"Yes, you can." He stroked her back and withdrew from her hole in a slow movement before pushing forward again, surging deeper and deeper still. Almost to the hilt, he paused inside her and felt her gradually relax around his manhood. "That's it, Claire. Good girl."

"My Lord Galien." She uttered his name like a plea for him to continue, and he was happy to oblige her. His cock throbbed within the tight confines of her arse, and he had to concentrate to keep from spilling inside her just then.

He pulled out and nudged her dark pink pucker with the tip of his hardness. "Ask me to fuck you hard, my lady."

Her hair flipped about as she shook her head. "My lord, please, I cannot."

"Ask me, or I shall drag you out of the water, turn you over my knee, and smack your bottom until it turns bright red. Do you want a spanking, Clare?"

"No, my lord. I don't want a spanking, I want you to, to take me, please."

"I'll give you one more chance to ask me properly, Claire. Use your manners, say 'please, my lord' and ask me to fuck you hard. Tell me you've misbehaved and need your lord husband to teach you a most memorable lesson."

Her shoulders rose under a deep breath, and she lowered her head until it almost touched the water. "Pl-please, my lord, I have been a naughty girl and I require a memorable lesson from my lord husband."

"What kind of lesson?" he prompted.

"A hard fucking in my arse, my lord, if it pleases you."

Oh, it pleased him just fine. He rubbed her back and moved his hands to grip her hips, and he worked his way into her tightness again, surging deep and withdrawing fast only to thrust into her again, going deeper and deeper with each plunge of his cock into her arsehole.

"This is what naughty wives get, isn't it?" He reached around to stroke her most sensitive spot, locating her nubbin and swirling her moisture around the stiff peak. "Naughty wives get fucked in their bottom hole by their husbands."

"Mm. Yes, my lord," she gasped out, writhing as she met his movements and gyrated against his hand.

A tingle raced up his thighs and his balls felt heavy and tight, and he upped his pace and pounded her faster, delving deep with each thrust as he held her in place. She cried out and shuddered, her body tensing as she found her release. Her soft whimpering as she came down from her peak drove him over the edge, and he pumped into her with a groan, spilling his seed in her most private, naughty hole.

After they caught their breath, he arranged her on his lap in the water, holding her and unable to resist keeping a possessive hand on her stomach. A child. She was carrying his child and he smiled against her hair, imagining how she would look months from now, her belly heavy and swollen. Ah, he couldn't wait, and he decided to tell her as much.

She laughed. "I don't think you'll want me then, Galien. I will be quite fat."

"You will be quite beautiful, Claire, and if you ever call yourself fat, I will give you a sound thrashing and make you stand in the corner with your punished bottom on display."

"Will you be upset if it's a girl?"

"Why ever would I be upset? I'd love to have ten girls, spirited girls with long dark locks like their mother." He tugged on her hair for emphasis.

"The same reason all men want sons, silly. Don't you wish to produce an heir the first time?"

He patted her stomach. "I wish for a healthy child, a boy or a girl, it matters not. We have plenty of time to create a large family, my wife."

"You want a large family?"

"Aye," he said, nodding. "I had my cousins growing up, and a few foster brothers too, but I was an only child and found it lonely at times. I always wished for a real brother or a sister. Did you like having six brothers growing up?"

She trailed her fingers through the dark curls covering his chest. "I suppose so. I did like having a large family. We took care of one another, and no matter where I went, I always felt safe knowing one of my brothers was close by, watching me." She chuckled. "Always ready to scold me and run off to tattle to our parents."

"Perhaps you shouldn't have given them reason to tattle, Claire."

She peered up at him, batting her eyelashes. "But, my lord, however would I have had any fun?"

Restraining a smile, he tapped the tip of her nose. "I cannot wait to interrogate the duke of Leuthold and get him to tell me all about your naughty antics as a child."

EPILOGUE

The keep bustled with activity, all the servants putting forth their best efforts for the duke of Leuthold's visit. Claire sat in the great hall on the first evening of her reunion with her brother, feeling as if she had come to the end of a long and difficult journey. She shared a trencher with her husband, and Leuthold sat to his right at the long table. Their heads were bowed together as they discussed some trivial matter about the training of knights, a subject that bored her to tears. She smiled at the two men though, certain she had never been so happy in her life.

After they finished their talk of knights, Leuthold began telling tales about her childhood, per Galien's request of course. He started with the time she decided to live in a tree, and how it had taken hours to locate her in the forest during a fierce rainstorm. Claire pretended to ignore them as they laughed over her antics.

Her brother sat back and regarded her with amusement after a while, giving Galien that same look she recognized as one of pure brotherly evil. She'd seen that look growing up, and it meant he was plotting something—something more sinister than regaling her husband with ridiculous stories, many of which contained extreme exaggerations.

"It's time you both know the truth about your marriage," Leuthold said, a twinkle in his eye. "Judging by your happiness, I don't see the harm in telling you about your father's plot."

"My father?" Galien asked, his brows drawing together.

"Aye. Your father sent me a letter listing his concerns about Minrova, his chief concern being your refusal to marry and produce an heir. He felt his time was growing short and he asked for my assistance."

Claire grasped Galien's hand, anxious to hear the rest of Leuthold's story.

"I had been writing letters to you, Claire, only to receive no response. I worried for your well-being after Diterich's death. Well, I worried for you before his death, but there was naught I could do to help you then. I decided to order Galien to marry you, sweet sister, after he visited Leuthold and I decided he was…"

"Suitable enough," Galien cut him off, as if they'd had this conversation before.

"Aye," the duke said with a smile. "Suitable enough."

Galien laughed and glanced at Claire. "You should also know this brother of yours extended my holdings into the valley to North Wenzton to compensate me for having to spend the rest of my life with his spirited sister. I believe those were his exact words."

The two men laughed while Claire glared from one to the other, trying to be angry over the bribe but failing. She found herself smiling as relief filled her, because at last the truth had been revealed, and it lifted her spirits that Leuthold did care enough about her to see her married to a decent man, a man whose tender love and firm guidance cleansed her heart of all the hurt she endured during her first marriage. Now Diterich and his cruel family remained but a distant, fading memory.

She covered a yawn, exhaustion sweeping over her. The babe growing inside her left her tired at the end of the day, and sometimes she napped after the midday meal, unable to keep her eyes open even when the sun streamed through the keep's windows.

Galien put an arm around her and gathered her against his side as he rose up. "Please enjoy the minstrels while I put my wife to bed. She must be growing a fierce warrior inside her with all the extra sleep she's requiring of late."

"Nay, not a warrior," she said. "A little beast."

He smiled down at her as he led her from the hall and upstairs to their chambers. Her lady's maid was waiting, but Galien dismissed Erwyn because he enjoyed helping his wife prepare for bed. He stripped her of all her clothing and helped her don a thin white shift.

"Rest now, sweet Claire." He kissed her forehead and placed a hand on the swell of her stomach.

She peered up at him and felt her eyes growing heavier as another yawn stole over her. "Will you wake me up later when you return, my lord beast?" She giggled at the faux stern look he fixed on her.

"Aye, I will wake you later. I think you require a lesson in how to properly address your lord husband. A very firm lesson, indeed."

She drifted to sleep, murmuring, "Firm lesson, yes. I believe that's exactly what I require, my lord."

THE END

Kidnapped and Claimed

Dinah McLeod

PROLOGUE

I almost didn't make it to the dining hall for the evening meal. My stomach was tied up in knots that I felt keenly with every step I took, and I wanted nothing more than to lie down and rest. But I took my duty as the Duchess of Württemberg very seriously and felt that I must be seen with my husband as often as possible.

It was a decision that I regretted almost instantly upon entering the dining hall. As soon as the smells of cooked meat and fish reached my nose, I nearly lost my balance, and would have, if not for the steading arm of my lady-in-waiting at my elbow. I gave her a small smile of thanks, the best that I could summon, and collected myself before walking down the length of the room. Since I was a child, I had become accustomed to being looked upon, which made it easy to disregard the stares that followed me. Only when I approached the head table did I realize that these were not the usual cursory glances.

There sat my husband, the duke, at the head of the table, as was his right. My chair on the other end was empty, of course, though I could not say the same for my husband's lap. I stood stock-still, taking it in and refusing to let even an ounce of emotion show on my face, even though I longed to drop into a faint or turn and flee. I could do neither. I was not common-born, and I had a responsibility in every moment—even horrid ones such as this—to maintain a certain level of dignity.

"Good evening, my lord husband," I called out to him when I was confidant I could keep my voice from shaking. I could let neither anger nor shame show, though I felt them both.

He took his time acknowledging me. It shouldn't have surprised me; Wallace was always content to cause a scene. The woman perched upon his lap, however, had frozen the moment I'd spoken. It was Anne Clover, the maid who handled the chamber pots every morning. She was looking at me, as was every other person in the dining hall, courtier and servant alike. She did not have my gift for hiding her emotions and her shame-stained cheeks were visible to all who cared to look.

Good, I thought, rather meanly. *Let her be ashamed. She should be.* Yet, Anne Clover mattered little. I knew that. It was my husband who should truly be repentant.

Lazily, he sipped his small ale before turning those piercing gray eyes of his onto me. When he smiled, I dipped my head and curtseyed, though I was acting out of habit as much as out of a need to avert my eyes. His smile had been full of menace, as though he knew he was hurting me and had not the energy to care.

When I'd collected myself once more, I rose and returned his smile with one of my own. "I hope you fare well this evening," I said, speaking loud enough for the entire hall to hear. I didn't know what I hoped—perhaps that he would remember himself and shake the servant girl from his lap.

But if anything, his hold on her seemed to tighten, and right in front of me, right before the eyes of the court, he leaned over and kissed her. Anne made a strangled sound, as though her throat was closing up, and perhaps I could have felt sorry for her, if it were any other man's lap she was perched upon.

I surveyed Wallace with cool eyes that belied the heavy pounding beneath my breast. He was a handsome man, of that there was no doubt. He was tall and muscular from the hours he spent fencing and jousting. His hair, which he kept neatly tied back, was long and the color of straw. His most notable feature was not his long, aristocratic nose, but his dark gray eyes which could pierce you with no more than a glance. I longed to be able to copy his cutting manner, but I knew myself to be hopeless at such imitation, else I would have cut him to the quick right where he sat.

"Will you join us, my lady?" he asked smoothly, as though naught a thing were amiss.

I found myself stuck—I couldn't let the court know how seriously this slight vexed me, and yet, my feet felt like lead, so heavy that I could not move them even if I wanted to do so. "Is there a shortage of seating?" I asked at last. "Shall I find a chair more suitable for Miss Clover?"

The girl in question flushed scarlet, much to the delight of onlookers who laughed to see her embarrassed so. I myself felt my lips twitch, but I did not give into the smile.

"She is fine right where she is, aren't you, sweeting?"

The knots in my stomach tightened to hear him coo to her so. When was the last time he'd ever spoken so kindly to me?

"Then I shall take my meal in my rooms," I replied. "Good night, sir." I bobbed a quick curtsey and turned to leave when Wallace's laughter rang out.

"Don't play the fool, Cecily. Come and take supper with us."

My spine froze upon hearing how casually he would speak to me, his own wife. Did he have no regard for my station?

"Thank you, no."

I had taken but one step further when I heard a commotion behind me. I turned my head to see that Wallace had indeed shaken the girl from his lap and was now stepping toward me.

"You *will* eat where and when I say you shall!" he commanded, his booming voice giving the stunned courtiers plenty to gossip about.

"Perhaps, if your dinner companions were chosen in better taste…" I spoke so that only he could hear, trying not to tremble as his eyes narrowed into slits.

"You'd do better to obey your husband," he growled, stalking closer still.

Even though he was still a few feet from me, I could smell his breathe, pungent with drink. "You are not yourself, my lord. You do not realize the scene you are—"

"Why in all hells do you concern yourself with what they think?" he bellowed, sweeping an arm out to indicate the courtiers who dined. "I never do."

"Then perhaps, my lord, you might concern yourself with what *I* think." I was doing my very best to keep the emotion out of my voice, but it trembled despite my efforts. It was a hard mask I was trying to wear, and the mounting shame of this moment was making it harder to maintain.

"Why should I?" he sneered, reaching me at last. "If I want a whore upon my lap, then I shall have one. Who are you to tell me I can't, when you are no better?"

I gasped at the accusation, feeling the beginnings of tears prick my eyes. I did my best to fight them, but I knew it would be a losing battle, just as this one was with Wallace. He was drunk and nothing I said or did would make him recall himself. "I bid you good night," I whispered thickly before turning on my heel.

I would have run, but for the hand that seized my arm, grasping tightly at my flesh. "You shall take your leave when I say and not a moment before," he shouted, his face reddening.

Despite all the countless lessons I'd had on courtly bearing, I was losing myself to his drunken rage. "Please, Wallace—"

"Please!" he snapped, shaking me. "Please?! You are not worthy of my attention," he decreed, snarling. "Get out of my sight before I whip the flesh off your body, inch by inch." He tossed me to the floor then, in front of everyone, as though I was nothing more than a dog to be discarded at will.

A sob lodged in my throat, but I fought it back. He gave me a vicious, mean smile and then turned his back on me, walking back to the table where every courtier—and Anne Clover, of course—sat with gaping mouths and stunned expressions. Never once did he look back.

My ladies swarmed around me at once each one offering assistance, but I batted them away impatiently, standing to my feet and fleeing the room with as much dignity as I could muster. I did not let the tears come until I was safe inside my chambers and my ladies had been instructed to see that no one disturbed me.

I never could have imagined enduring such abuse as my own husband had just put me through. I hadn't thought it possible, and yet, it had happened. When the first tears streaked my cheeks they were laced with sorrow and regret, but the ones that followed were hot and full of righteous anger. By the time my tears cleared, I knew just what I had to do. I would ride for home, for Hohenzollern. Upon learning what had happened, my cousin Susanna, the princess, would surely find room for me.

Wallace would be lucky if I ever returned to him, which I would only do if he got down on his hands and knees and crawled like a beggar. The thought filled me with no joy—I did not wish to return to him at all, under any circumstances, though I knew that if he asked, I must. Never again would I let him command me. *Never.*

I had bid my ladies to return to the hall and take their meal. A few had protested, but I knew it was for nothing but show. I was certain each was eager to be away from me. They must decide what way the duke's favor was turning, and if they could benefit from it in some way. And if nothing more, they would hear the gossip and be plagued with questions after my health. They would relish it, to be sure. There wasn't one in my train who cared more for me than she did her own future.

Once upon a time, I would have thought myself lucky to know who I was, to know that I was royal born and would never have to act so, but now I wasn't so sure. I never would have thought that a husband could treat his wife so cruelly, either. And yet...

I shook the thoughts from my head as I saddled my horse. She'd been a wedding present from the duke, and he'd told me with pride in his voice that he'd named her Fortune, for that was what he'd found when I'd agreed to be his wife. From the moment I set eyes on her, so beautiful with her snow-white coat and so strong, I'd fallen in love. I would have left her for the memories she carried, but I feared that she would fall at the wrath of his hands once he discovered I was gone.

"We're going home," I whispered as I took a moment to stroke her neck. "Get us there quickly, Fortune."

She was an obedient mare, and well trained. She took to the road and even though there was hardly any moonlight to see by, I trusted her to get me where I wanted to be. My mother would know how this should be handled, and I was certain that Susanna would give her leave for me to stay at the castle for a time while I worked this out.

That I would have to go back to Wallace was a certainty, one that made me feel faint. I could hardly get his face out of my mind. It had been nearly purple in his rage as he'd spat those horrible, hateful words: *Get out of my sight before I whip the flesh from your body*. I had no trouble believing that he meant every word and that he would take pleasure in carrying out his threat. Though I knew I had been nothing but the most devoted, dutiful wife I could be, it mattered not. Wallace ruled our household, and my wellbeing would depend upon his mood.

Yes, I knew that I would have to return. My mother would insist that I forgive him, which as a lady, a royal duchess, I would—but only after he dismissed Anne Clover from court and promised me his unfailing fidelity.

I was so lost in my thoughts that I was surprised when Fortune stopped and I realized that we'd made it safely to Hohenzollern. "Good girl," I praised her, patting her flank before I gently guided the reins toward the stable. I would see her safely in the stable before I went to Susanna. She would be surprised to see me, to be sure. I had only made it back home once since my marriage to the duke, and she'd known I was coming. But there was nothing to do for it now; I was here already and everything would soon be explained.

At first, the stable seemed empty. I shouldn't have been surprised—it was time for the evening meal, after all—yet, I was annoyed. Now that I'd dismounted, I realized how hungry and tired I was. I wanted nothing more than to see my horse cared for so that I could seek solace with my mother, and perhaps partake in a bit of supper myself. A movement out of the corner of my eye had me turning my head and when I saw a figure crouching down low, watching me, my irritation grew.

"Are you the stable boy?" I demanded, my voice harsher than I normally would have used, but justified given the circumstances.

"Ah…"

"Whatever are you doing on the floor?" I snapped. "Get up, then. There's work to be done." I held out the reins, arching a brow when he stood, dusted off his trousers, yet made no move to take them. "Well? What are you waiting for?"

"Forgive me, princess, I don't mean to—"

"Oh, for Heaven's sake," I exclaimed, with an unladylike snort of laughter. "You must be new."

"What gave me away, my lady?"

"I am not the princess. Any servant worth his salt would know that." Not that he could be blamed entirely for the slipup. We both had the same thick, dark raven hair. Though mine often spilled in curls down my back, it was held up in pins at the moment. We were of a similar height and build—both with small waists and narrow hips, though Susanna's chest was more endowed than my own. We also shared smooth skin as white as milk and full, rosebud mouths. Still, for all those shared qualities, no one could deny that Susanna had the bearing of a princess, which added to her beauty in a way that I would never know.

"Forgive me, my lady. And whom do I have the honor of addressing?"

I tilted my head to the side, examining him. My first thought was that he did not speak very much like a servant. Nonetheless, I opened my mouth to answer him when it occurred to me that perhaps it would be better if I did not. If he didn't know who I was, then perhaps he would not remember seeing me at all when my lord husband began asking questions. Smiling to myself, pleased with my own cleverness, I dismissed his question with a wave of my hand. "Never you mind. Go about your business and leave me to mine." I'd barely spoken when I felt him move behind me. A sudden chill ran down my spine, and heeding my instincts, I spun around to find him right behind me.

"I would very much like to," he said in a quiet, steady way that would have been comforting but for his unnatural closeness. "But I'm afraid you're my business now."

"I beg your pardon?" I huffed the question, even as my heart began to pick up speed. "Do you forget yourself, sir? Do you forget that you address a *lady*, one far above your station?"

He did not smile, but a twitching around his lips told me that he would have liked to. "You high-breds are all the same, aren't you? Always concerned with your own importance. There is more to the world than you know, princess."

"I already told you—"

"Hush."

The word was spoken softly, but with enough authority to shock me. I took a step back, until I was leaning into my horse. "You do not command here! Why, you are nothing more than a… than a…" I trailed off helplessly, thrown by his calm, by his quiet authority in the face of my anger.

I took a closer look, certain that if I could recognize him, I would recall his master, who would undoubtedly be hearing from me. The man was tall, standing a good head or more above me. He had a full head of copper curls and stubble of the same color marring his cheeks. His lips were lush, the color of ripe berries, and I decided on sight that they were lips unaccustomed to smiling. No, I did not recognize him, not even on a closer look. Though he wore servant's clothing—trousers and sturdy boots, and a long-sleeve white tunic that opened at the chest—somehow he carried himself in a manner that belied his station.

"I do not know why you are here, but it is not the place for you. It would go better for you if you returned at once."

I blinked my large, blue eyes in surprise. "Why? Is there danger afoot?" Something in his expression changed when I said her name and I smiled, finally feeling as though I had the upper hand. "Yes, perhaps I shall go fetch her right now, I think she would like to know there are impertinent stable boys in her household." I turned to go, but I had not gone two steps when I felt his hand close over my arm in a surprisingly strong grip.

"I cannot allow you to do that."

I whirled on him, irritated with his matter-of-fact tone as well as the fact that he would dare lay hands on me. "Who do you think you are?" I demanded. "How dare you touch me!"

If anything, his grip on me tightened. "I'm afraid I can't risk you're leaving. You're going to have to come with me. Just remember, I did try to warn you."

"Warn me about what?" I practically spat the words at him, my fury incensed when he did not so much as blink. "Unhand me, you brute!"

"Come along quietly now, or I'm afraid I'll have to gag you."

The way he spoke without wavering, the dead-set look in his eyes, told me that he would not hesitate to carry out his threat. Yet, I dug my heels in and yanked with all my might. When I did not find myself released, I took a deep breath, preparing to scream at the top of my lungs and alert anyone nearby to my plight. Before I could, however, I felt his hand come down sharply on my backside. It was only once, but it was swift and hard. I opened my mouth to shout my indignation, but his hand came clamping down over my lips, smothering my outraged cries.

"Do as I say, or it'll be worse for you," he promised.

Just then, looking at his stony, unrelenting face, I longed to weep. I knew I was lost—there was nothing I could say or do to stop this stranger from having his way with me. Though I did not trouble to reply, he must have sensed my defeat, because before I knew it I felt his hands around my waist, lifting me back in Fortune's saddle. Before I could utter a word more, he himself was sitting behind me and urging the mare on with a clap of the reins. It was all I could do to hold back the tears as I turned my head for one last look at the castle. The lights shone, seeming like beacons of hope that I'd been riding toward only moments ago. Now, one by one, they faded away. I could imagine the laughter and dancing that was taking place in the dining hall just now. All of the court would go on with their flirting and feasting, none of them having any idea that I'd been there at all.

• • • • • • • •

Though the sun was out, its rays did nothing to diminish the chill in the air. I shivered, my teeth chattering despite myself. My thighs ached nearly as much as my backside from long hours in the saddle and my eyes grew weary of rows of trees stretching as far as the eye could see for my only view. Yet, I would not—indeed, *could* not—cry. It would only delight my tormentor and I had no intention of giving him that pleasure.

He was letting me ride alone as he walked along, but that did not make him a man of honor. Indeed, he was a coward who had stolen me away from the only true home I'd ever known. Tears of anger and frustration, of fear and hopelessness, prickled at my eyes, but I shut my eyes tightly against them. *I will not*, I told myself. *I will not cry*. It was my mother's voice I heard; she'd been strict with me and quick to rap my knuckles if I ever forgot my teachings. Practically from the time I left the breast I'd been reared to be the epitome of a lady, as my parents lived at court and expected that I would do the same.

I liked the life of a duchess—pretty dresses, fine rooms, with servants to wait on me and fulfill my every whim. I was ill-suited to hard rides and I longed to make my complaint known, though I doubted it would mean much to the man who held me prisoner. I looked down at him, walking astride the horse while he held the reins. Idly, I wondered if it was to ensure that the horse did not buck or that I did not attempt to escape.

He'd hardly spoken to me since he'd captured me and carried me off like some wild savage, but that suited me fine. If he had the audacity to address me, I might forget my courtly manners altogether. After all, he didn't deserve courtesy.

"We'll be stopping to rest soon." His gruff voice startled me as it broke into my thoughts. "Then we'll trade places for a while."

I didn't demean myself to answer, but I was horrified by what he suggested. He couldn't mean that *I* would be forced to walk in the snow… surely not! Yet, I knew without asking that it was exactly what he meant, and that however abhorrent the idea was, it was a fate that I must bear. Oh, how horrified my lady mother would be to see me treated thus! Thinking of her, and the fact that I might never see her again, made the tears that had been threatening ever since my abduction spring forth and a sob worked its way from my throat despite myself.

"Are you unwell?"

I ignored the rough man who dared to address me so, trying to get the horrible thought out of my head. Of course I would see her again. I would escape this horror somehow. I would return to Hohenzollern, to those that loved me. I had to believe it—it was the only hope I had to cling to now.

"I said, are you unwell?" he queried again as he tugged on the reins and halted the horse.

A grim little smile curved my lips. "Frankly, no, not that it's any concern to you."

At first, I'd thought he might reply. Indeed, he opened his lips to do so, but in the end he closed them again and continued walking. After a moment, Fortune followed suit. I wished I could feel even the slightest joy at this small victory, but I was too tired, too cold and hungry to feel anything but miserable and frightened.

I'd never given much thought to the fire that was kept burning in my rooms. They were always there, as they should be, and it had never occurred to me to give a moment's notice to who had performed the task. Right now,

I longed for nothing so much as a nice, bright fire to warm myself beside. That, and perhaps my comfortable bed with down blankets piled high as the eye could see.

Instead, I had to content myself with the meager burning of a few twigs that we had managed to uncover from the blanket of snow that surrounded us. I supposed I should have been grateful that my captor had provided that much, but I wasn't in the mood to feel appreciative. Which was why when he offered me a freshly killed, cleaned dove, I only stared at him.

"Your dinner, my lady," he said with only the faintest hint of mockery hiding in his deep voice.

I had watched him roast the bird over the fire, yet I was surprised to find it offered to me. "Thank you, no. I don't eat pheasant."

"This isn't pheasant, your ladyship. It is a dove, and you will eat it. Unless, of course, you wish to starve."

I raised my head to meet his stare, my blue eyes glaring fiercely into his dancing light gray ones. I took the bird out of his hand, steeling myself against the feel of it, and hurled it onto the ground.

I don't know what I'd been expecting, but it was all I could do to keep from flinching. If I'd ever done such a thing in Wallace's presence, I would have paid for it, and swiftly. But when I chanced to look at my captor, his face was inscrutable, his eyes dancing and merry as always.

"Now you must pick it up and eat it cold," he said, as though it mattered not one bit to him. Before I could offer a reply, he had walked around to the other trunk in front of the fire and made himself at home. As much as I wished I could pretend otherwise, I *was* hungry. I couldn't help but keep darting looks at him, and watching him eat his bird made my stomach growl.

But I couldn't be made to play fetch like a common dog! I would rather freeze to death than to let him see me obeying his casually issued command. Instead, I glared at him, daring him to meet my eyes, but he kept right on eating as though it meant little whether or not I did as he'd instructed.

I tried to distract myself by thinking of other things. Perhaps I could work on my escape plan. Perhaps I could distract myself with thoughts of my family, who surely must be looking for me by now. My kidnapper had the upper hand now—I was, after all, a lady and one of small stature and build at that. I could not fend off an attack, nor could I outrun him. But one day, when I'd returned to the castle I'd grown up in, he'd pay for the time he'd stolen from me.

Yet, even thoughts of vengeance fled in the wake of my growling stomach. The longer I waited, the colder I knew the meat would be. Casting another hot, hateful glance at my companion, I eased off the log and walked to where I'd thrown the bird. I snatched it from the snow, wincing to see the dirt and grass that had dirtied it. As I marched back to my seat, I caught sight of him looking at me. When I reached the fire, he held out his hand.

"Give it to me," he said, not unkindly. His voice wasn't even slightly mocking this time. "I'll warm it for you."

Who did he think I was, to need favors from one such as him? I was a royal duchess of Hohenzollern, and I needed help from no one. Glaring at him, I brought the dove to my face and sank my teeth into the cold meat. As I chewed, I lowered the food and glared at him defiantly.

"Very well." He shrugged and went back to eating. Only then did I notice how much smaller his bird was than mine. For a moment, the briefest of instances, I almost felt remorseful of my treatment of him. It fled with his very next words. "The next time you choose to discard the food I offer you, you will not eat. I am trying to be considerate of your... unusual circumstance and of your hardship, but I am not going to be played for a fool, my lady. You will take what you are given or have nothing, and I shan't tell you again."

My cheeks burned with indignation. What right did he have to speak to me so freely? Why, if we were back at the castle... but we weren't. And no matter how hard I tried to tell myself otherwise, I might never make it back. But I would *not* be made a peasant, not by this man, or any other!

"You may address me by my proper title, which is Duchess," I told him, my voice clear and cold. Neither of us spoke again as we went back to eating.

CHAPTER ONE

Hohenzollern Castle

The music swirled around me like a beautiful tapestry of melody and my feet moved obediently in step with my partner.

"Are you enjoying yourself, Lady Cecily?"

I acknowledged the wizened Lord of Archester with the best smile I could manage, stifling a yawn. "Very much so, thank you, my lord."

"And are you eager to be a wife?" he asked as he twirled me around. "Eager to be a duchess?"

I went through the steps fluidly—I'd been taught to dance nearly before I'd learned to walk—easily disguising my annoyance at the personal question. It wasn't as though he'd been the only one to hint around the matter, though he was the only one who dared to ask outright. As the cousin to the princess, I already enjoyed a certain amount of special treatment at court. Now that I was to wed a duke, my star would rise and there was bound to be a certain amount of envy and speculation among the other courtiers. Having never met the Duke of Württemberg before—not that such a thing was uncommon—I was a bundle of nerves, not that I intended for anyone to know it.

Yet, the smile the lord gave me suggested that he knew things I was not saying. "You need not fear, my lady. I hear that the duke is quite an honorable man."

"Indeed, I have been well informed."

"I met him once, I believe."

I was so caught off-guard, I nearly missed a step in the dance, but fortunately I caught myself just in time. I'd never spoken to anyone who had met my future husband and I could not deny my curiosity. I looked at my partner, my cheeks flushed from making such a silly gaffe, and hotter still to see the patronizing smile he'd fixed on me.

I won't ask then, I thought to myself. *Better he think me unfeeling than nothing more than a simple maid.*

"A very intelligent man." He offered up the information like half-hearted alms for a starving woman. Though I didn't meet his gaze again, I devoured the information as though I truly were famished. "He will surely consider himself quite fortunate to gain such a *beautiful bride."*

This time, I did slip in my step. When I looked, horrified, at my partner, he was indeed laughing at me. Mercifully, the music stopped just then and I was able to hide my flushed cheeks as I dipped my head and curtseyed.

"Another dance, my lady?"

I was tempted. I wanted to hear any tidbits he might be willing to share, but I was beginning to suspect that he was only amusing himself at my expense. "No, thank you, my lord. I must confess myself to be a bit tired."

"Very well," he said agreeably, taking the hand I extended to him and bending over it. "I shall look forward to dancing with you again. Mayhap on your wedding day." His teeth gleamed as he teased me once more.

"Mayhap," I agreed half-heartedly, forcing myself to smile as he kissed the back of my hand. I pulled it away a moment before it was courteous to do so, but the Lord of Archester did not seem in the least offended.

After we'd parted I did indeed retire to my room. For now, I was a lady in waiting to my cousin, Susanna, but soon, after I was wed, I would have chambers and ladies of my own. It was a small solace, marrying someone I only knew through others' stories so that I would inherit a small part of his influence and power. Yet, it was what my parents had always planned for me. I'd known all my life that I would marry—indeed, each dance lesson, my tutelage in the fine arts, was to prepare me for it. There had never been a question of choosing another path. As the only daughter to the Lord and Lady of Sheridan and cousin to the Princess of Hohenzollern, there could be no doubt that I would marry to strengthen the family and secure loyalties for the princess. I was no more than a chess piece in this game—that I'd known from the start—but even so, I had hoped that I might make a suitable match.

I hoped and prayed nearly each waking hour that the duke might be such a match for me. There was no doubt that my mother thought him so—for although it was my duty to marry well, I could not believe she would place me with a man who would do me harm—but I would not be able to get a good night's rest until I laid eyes on the man in question and saw for myself what type of man he was. Would he be loving and kind, as I so hoped? Would he find me beautiful, as the Lord of Archester had suggested? Or would he think me plain and set his eyes on a more desirable lady? The thought made my stomach turn. I shut my eyes against the pain and wished that Susanna were back from the evening meal so that we might play a game of cards to take my mind off things. Unfortunately, she and the rest of her ladies were out, leaving me to the lonely chambers and my anxious heart.

There's nothing to be done for it, I told myself as I sat up in the bed, determined to put my fear aside. No good would come from dwelling on something I could not change.

At that moment, the door opened and a pair of the princess's ladies poured in, all whispers and giggles. They halted when they saw me, but couldn't quite hide their smirks behind their hands.

"Jane, Mary," I greeted each of them in turn with as much warmth as I could manage. I had nothing against the girls, aside from the fact that they were vain and silly.

"Your Grace," the one called Jane giggled, giving an exaggerated curtsey.

"Not quite yet, I'm afraid," I remarked with a tight smile.

"What are you doing up here all alone?" Mary asked. *"Thinking of the Duke of Württemberg?"*

I knew she was teasing. I knew that neither of them meant any harm, and yet, even though I smiled, I felt that I would be sick any moment with the looming uncertainty.

A sudden lurching in my stomach brought me out of my thoughts. Doubled-over at the waist, I retched for what had to have been the fourth time in the last hour. Not that I could keep track of time—who could in this mess of swirling snow that blinded one past the point of seeing? I was cold, weak, and miserable, though I refused to say so.

"Are you unwell?"

The gruff voice startled me, though I carefully kept my expression blank. Nor did I give him the scathing reply that readily supplied itself—surely he could hear for himself that I was anything but well.

"You did not eat much," he commented when I did not reply. "Perhaps you have an empty stomach."

"It was probably the damned bird you fed me," I snapped.

He arched his dark brows, clearly unimpressed with my slip in decorum. With the acrid taste in my mouth, I couldn't trouble myself to care about his opinion.

"As soon as we are able, we will stop and you can rest."

I wiped my mouth and regarded him with narrowed eyes. "Oh, please, you needn't trouble yourself on my account."

He made no reply, only yanked the reins to keep the horse moving. My stomach settled long enough for me to doze in the saddle, rocked to sleep by the steady motion combined with my bone-weariness. When we halted suddenly, my eyes snapped open and my body tensed, preparing to face danger. Much to my surprise, I saw that we were in front of a small tavern. True to his word, the man who'd made me his prisoner had stopped, seemingly at the first opportunity.

"I cannot sleep here," I announced, since I could not bring myself to thank him.

"Then do not sleep," he said, as if it mattered to him not at all. "But you need to rest, as do I. We shall take shelter for the night. A hot meal will do you good, I think."

"I will not share a room with you, and certainly not your bed," I continued peevishly. I was not a bit happy about the situation and I was determined that he should never forget it, not even for a moment.

"As you wish, princess."

I rankled at his words. "I am *not* the princess."

"I see. Then what right do you have to think so highly of yourself?"

My lips parted to make a reply, but I found that I could not speak. No one had *ever* dared speak to me so openly before! Why, who did he think *he* was? The one in control, of course, which meant that no matter how gently he spoke, nor what considerations he offered, I would never be able to do more than loath the very sight of him.

"Come," he said before swinging me from the saddle as though I were no more than a common servant. "Let's get inside before you worsen."

As though he had a care for my health! If he had, he wouldn't have secreted me away from the castle, stolen right out from under my family's noses! They would be in such a dither when they discovered me missing!

I walked reluctantly beside him until we'd reached the inn. The woman at the front looked at us without interest when my jailer asked for a room.

"Two, please," I interrupted, my voice sweet as morning wine. "It would be improper otherwise, you see. He is not my husband."

Suddenly, the woman's interest was piqued and she gave my captor a suspicious, eagle-eyed look that would have made a number of men squirm. Anyone, save the one that had abducted me. He only stared back at me with his infuriating calm.

"What's that you say, miss?" the innkeeper queried. "The lad isn't your husband?"

"No! My husband is the Duke of Württemberg, and this man," I jabbed an accusing finger in the direction of my captor, "has been holding me against my will!"

The innkeeper's brow furrowed as she looked with notable concern from my face to his. "Well, what have you to say for yourself?"

"Please, my lady, this woman is—"

"Don't be trying to sweet-talk *me* now, lad! I know your kind! Yes, indeed! You best be out with the truth!" She came around to stand beside me, crossing her arms across her considerable chest. Her nearness gave me a boost of security that I hadn't felt since this entire ordeal had begun.

"Please, madam, I assure you—"

"What's this, now?"

I turned my head at the sound of a new voice and saw a tall, robust man making his way toward us. His dark hair was lined with silver and his eyes were dark as obsidian.

"What's the fuss about, wife?" he demanded of the innkeeper.

"George, to hear this young lady tell it, she's been kidnapped by this man here who's keeping her from her husband!"

I felt nearly weak with relief at her coming to my rescue. Finally, *finally*, I could get back to Hohenzollern. I could nearly feel it within my grasp.

Her husband turned to my abductor, his face as angry as a storm cloud. "What kind of man does such a thing?" he demanded.

"I would never harm a lady," my captor told him smoothly. "And certainly not a single hair on this one's fair head. Truly, sir, this is my wife. She took a spill from her horse not a fortnight ago and has been speaking nonsense ever since. In fact, we're riding to see the doctor now."

I'd begun shaking my head long before he was finished speaking, but I could see that the innkeeper's husband seemed inclined to believe the tale. "No, I've known how to ride since I was a babe, I've never fallen—"

"A lass who's *never* fallen?" he chucked to himself. "Well, now. There's something you don't see every day."

"My father had me tutored in riding right along with the squires!" I protested, missing the glances the man and his wife exchanged. "Why, it is not uncommon for a well-bred woman to know how to ride! The princess herself has never fallen!"

"You can see for yourself what I mean," my captor interjected softly, ignoring the daggers I glared at him. "She's a sweet woman, I swear it, but a bit… daft at the moment."

"I am not!" I spat at him, stomping my foot. "It's true!" I turned to the innkeeper, reaching for her with pleading hands and feeling my hope begin to fade as she backed away, as though my touch would burn her. "Please, you have to listen to me! My name is Cecily, the Duchess of Württemberg! Write to my husband, and he'll come for me. Please, all you have to do is write to him!"

"She is overtired," he said, while turning to me with a pitying smile. "Of course, Duchess, we'll do as you ask at once."

I flew at him then, my hands reaching for his face. I'd never struck another person in all my life, but if he hadn't captured my hands just then, I would have dug my fingernails into the flesh of his cheeks with pleasure and made him bleed.

"I've seen enough," the innkeeper's husband announced, his voice gruff. "Take your wife to bed and be sure to keep her in line while you lodge with us."

"Thank you for your kind understanding, sir."

"He's lying!" I cried, feeling tears well in my eyes. "He's lying, I swear it! If you'll only write to the duke, tell him that I am here…. please."

"Come along now, sweeting," my abductor said, pulling me along. No matter how hard I dug my heels in, it did nothing to slow him down.

"Let me go!" I spat at him. "I won't tolerate this for another second! I—"

"Stop it," he hissed in my ear as he continued to lead me to a room. It was the first time that he'd spoken to me in such a hard voice, and for a moment it did send me into silence. "I will not force myself on you, if that's what you fear. If I'd wanted to take you, I would have done so without paying for the pleasure." He gestured to the inn.

For some reason, the way that he'd said it, the way he insinuated that he didn't find me desirable rankled me even more. "If you want me to stop, take me home! I'm not going to stay here and let you have your way with me!"

"You're causing people to stare," he told me in a clipped voice that was laced with warning.

Proper ladies did not raise their voices and they certainly did not cause a scandal, but I was beyond the rules of gentility now. Let them stare—let him be embarrassed. Perhaps it would be enough to get me my freedom. "I will *not* be forced to—"

He was much taller than me, a head at least, and he had a large, muscled form. He had no problem picking me up and hoisting me over his shoulder, carrying me as though I weighed no more than a barrel of hay. People were indeed staring then, not that he seemed to notice.

"Put me down!" I demanded, battering him with my balled fists and kicking feet. That, too, he ignored, walking toward what I presumed was the room he'd paid for. Still, I was determined not to give up. "At once, you brute!" I shrieked.

He did not heed my words until we were safely inside the room and he'd closed the door behind him. When he set me down, it was not very gently, and I glared up at him from the floor. "I understand that you are not happy to be here," he said, returning my angry stare. "Nor am I pleased to be saddled with such a spoilt little girl. I suggest we both do our best with the situation at hand."

"If you're so unhappy with me, then take me home!"

"I also suggest that you start behaving like the royalty you claim to be," he continued in the same measured tone, as though I'd never spoken. "Or I shall see you soundly thrashed."

I glowered, making my hatred for him plain. If my eyes could have pierced him, he would have bled to death then and there. How *dare* he threaten *me*?

My abductor met my stare, as calm as ever in the face of my wrath. At that moment, he bent his hulking frame over me, and I couldn't help but take notice of how big and broad his shoulders were. They looked accustomed to hard labor, and if his easy handling of me earlier was any indication, all of him was probably hard and muscled beneath his tunic. A single copper curl fell over his eye, which he brushed away impatiently.

"Do you understand?"

A little gasp escaped my lips. First, he had the gall to threaten me, but now I must show acquiescence of my situation, like a chastened child? I wouldn't do it. I *wouldn't!*

Yet, the stern warning in his eyes was enough to temper my anger. I had no true choice here, royalty or not. I had to go along with whatever he wished, regardless of how terrible I might find it. When I was returned home, when he was captured, he would be punished for his crimes, but until then I was subject to his will. And his large, heavy hands told me that he would have no problem carrying out what he'd promised.

His features were hard with determination—his chiseled jaw clenched as he waited for my answer. I knew that if I pushed him, he would deliver on that threat and more, so as much as it pained me, I bowed my head. Though I refused to speak, he must have decided that he'd humiliated me enough for the moment. He straightened and gave me a nod.

"Very well then." After he'd spoken, he offered me a hand to help me from the floor, and I forced myself to accept it without flinching.

CHAPTER TWO

The moment sunlight hit my face, I awakened, wondering how long I'd been asleep. My jailer had warned me the night before that we would be leaving at first light, which gave me cause to wonder why he'd changed his mind. I began to sit up, but as soon as I moved the room spun in a way that made me certain that I would be sick. With a groan, I sank back against the pillows and closed my eyes once more. Even that simple act was exerting.

"You're awake."

"Unfortunately," I whimpered.

"I can see that I was right not to wake you."

My eyelids fluttered open and I peered at my captor. "Why didn't you?"

"I'm afraid you've taken ill. You cried out during your sleep and when I checked on you I realized you were burning with fever."

My hand felt limp and lifeless as I raised it to check my forehead. When I pulled it away, it was damp with sweat. "Oh!"

"No need to worry, princess. I'll see to it that you're well taken care of."

"I'm not..." My words trailed off, for I was too weak to complete even that sentence.

"Yes, I remember. Perhaps one of these days you'll find it appropriate to tell me your name."

I did not bother to reply, choosing instead to turn away from the sound of his voice and try to get comfortable once more. If I'd had the strength for it, I would have told him that there was no cause for it. One way or another, we would be going our separate ways, even if he didn't yet know it.

• • • • • • •

Yet, for all my brave thoughts I could hardly summon the energy to use the chamber pot, much less plot and carry through with an escape plan. *Soon*, I promised myself, even as I allowed myself to be fed broth like a baby. The fever raged on, and there were hours where I lost track of time and where I was. In some moments, I thought myself back at Hohenzollern, safe in my rooms and waiting for my husband to come to me. At others, I thought I was inside Württemberg Manor, hiding from the duke, though I couldn't seem to remember why.

Only in the first hours of the morning did I realize where I was, which was both disappointing and a relief all at once.

"You were crying out," he told me as he brought a wet cloth to my brow.

"I called you… Wallace," I said as I remembered.

"Yes. Who is Wallace, my lady?"

"My… my husband," I whispered through cracked lips. "The duke."

"Do I remind you of him?" His smile was gently mocking, though who he was making fun of, I wasn't certain.

"No," I said, vehemently, though only once the word was out of my mouth did I realize that I didn't mean it to be an insult, as he probably assumed.

"Well." He dabbed the cloth over my cheeks before setting it aside. "We can only be who we are, I suppose. Do you think you can sit up? You really should drink some water."

Without waiting for me to respond, he put an arm underneath me and lifted me until I was sitting upright. Only when he held out a hand and I saw the cup of water put into it did I realize that we were not alone. I furrowed my brow as I peered past him and made out the innkeeper who I'd thought might help me earlier. She looked at me with a face wrought with concern.

"She's losing weight," he commented to her, as though I were not in the room.

"Do you think she's taken ill because of her fall?" she asked, wringing her hands anxiously.

"It's possible. Don't worry, madam." He gave her a brief smile. "I'm certain that she will not infect anyone else with her illness."

"Let us hope it is as you say."

I wanted to tell them that I had not taken any fall, that I was ill from riding such long, hard hours in the cold. I wanted to remind my captor that I would be fleeing at my earliest opportunity, but when he put the cup to my lips, I drank deeply, forgetting every concern except for the need to cure my thirst.

• • • • • • •

Time passed by in a blur. I could not say how long it had been—I had no true recollection of time, only brief flashes of dreams that seemed real, such as being spoon fed like a babe. My captor changed the sheets on my bed once, I recalled, and never left my side. Even when I was not awake, when my mind lied to me about my whereabouts, I could feel him there.

When next I awoke, I found him sleeping, snoring slightly in the chair he'd moved to my bedside. I sat up, and though I felt weak, my head did not spin with the movement. A glance at the window showed me that the sun had not yet risen, yet I was powerfully hungry. I couldn't recall eating more than a spoonful or two of broth for... how long had it been? Hours? Days? Everything ran together in my mind. All I could recall with any clarity was the fact that the man who pretended to be my husband had never left my side.

It was an odd thing for a kidnapper to do, was it not? Yet, he had done it. Not only when the innkeeper was present, but throughout my illness. It made me look at him with appraising eyes, wondering why he should bother. Surely, I was naught more than property to him. A valuable commodity, perhaps, but property nonetheless. I'd been nothing more to Wallace, and I'd come to expect no better from married life.

Suddenly, his words came back to me: *Do I remind you of him?*

I'd responded quickly to the negative, but not for the reason he might have thought. Wallace never would have looked after my health if I'd taken ill, and if he had, it only would have been for show. No, while I was sure he would send a woman or two to tend me, it probably wouldn't have even occurred to him to seek after my health. How strange, that a man that had abducted me and had secreted me away in the middle of the night should care for me thusly.

It gave me a lot to ponder, and ponder I did. Once or twice, as the sun slowly began to rise above the clouds I looked toward the closed door and pondered escaping. Each time, I dismissed the thought, for one reason or another. I told myself that I was too weak, or that I would be caught, that I would only be returned to this room anyway. Perhaps the truth was, as I watched him sleep, I began to wonder what kind of man my captor truly was.

When he awoke, he seemed as startled to see me awake as I was by him. "Good morning. It is still morning, isn't it?"

"Yes. The sun has not been out long."

"You're looking well."

"Ah... thank you."

I watched as he pushed the chair back and stood, wincing slightly as he did so. "You've no need to thank me. I was only stating the truth."

I dropped my eyes and stared at the quilt that had been draped over me. "I do. I... I know it was you that took care of me while I was ill."

"Yes, well, you were probably the most cooperative these last days than I've ever known you to be."

I eyed him sharply, only to see that he was teasing me. "Yes, well, please don't become accustomed."

"I wouldn't dream of it."

"Do we leave today?" I asked, turning away so that he would not see me smile.

"I'm afraid so. As much as I would like to stay one more evening to allow you to rest, I think we've lost enough time already."

I nodded my acquiescence.

"We'll leave as soon as we break our fast. While I'm seeing to our food, you should dress and ready yourself for riding."

I said nothing, which he must have taken for agreement because he left the room without looking back. As soon as I found myself alone, I was on my feet. I wobbled unsteadily for a moment—it was to be expected after all the time I'd spent in bed—before I regained my footing and began to move with purpose. Though I'd only had seconds to think it over, I knew as soon as I saw his retreating back that this was my chance to flee. It might have been the only chance I would ever get, so I needed to seize it. Briefly, I doubted myself—after all, he had taken such good care of me; this was no way to repay him. But I pushed the thought aside and began to dress in haste.

I'd been left in my shift during my illness and I was able to find my dress in a pile of discarded clothing and quickly pull it over my head. Under normal circumstances, I wouldn't have allowed myself to be so careless with my appearance, but things were far from normal. In fact, I had begun to wonder if I'd ever know any sense of normalcy again.

As I paced the room and pondered what to do next, something at the back of the room caught my eye. Momentarily distracted, I peered closer until I realized that it was a door. A door, at the back of the room! Why, whatever could it be for? As soon as the question crossed my mind, the answer supplied itself. It had to lead to a public bathhouse. And mayhap there was a way for me to bypass the bathhouse altogether and find the road that would take me home.

As soon as I'd thought of home, my feet began moving as though of their own accord toward the door. Once I'd opened it, I saw that my theory had been correct. Only a few short feet away was a stand-alone building where the common folk went. Turning my head, I saw that there was a path between the two buildings that surely must lead to the road.

Excited for the first time since my ordeal had begun, I closed the door behind me and walked around the inn to follow the road that had brought us here. I hadn't the faintest idea where I was, but surely if I followed the road we'd traveled, I could find my way home. And if not, God might put someone in my path that could show me the way.

With hope in my heart, I walked as quickly as I dared, though I forced myself to try to act naturally so that I did not call attention to myself. Then again, how did one who had been kidnapped against her will act as though she wasn't afraid, as though every step she took didn't make her fear being caught again? I didn't know, but I did my best.

I had to hurry, as there was no telling when my captor would return to check on me. Mayhap he was there, even now, finding the room empty. What would he do when he found me gone? Would he be relieved to be rid of me? Or would he charge the stables, saddle my horse, and come galloping after me? The thought made me quicken my pace, despite my fear of being seen as out of place.

I should have taken the horse, I thought, glancing back over my shoulder and wishing that I'd had the foresight to head in the direction of the stable. I hated to lose her, yet if I were to go back for her now, my chance would slip through my fingers, and well I knew it.

With each step I took, I began to feel more uncertain in my unexpected freedom. Surely, I should have been elated, and though I wanted to be home more than anything, the barrage of doubts that began to plague me overrode any joy I might have felt otherwise. I'd been too hasty, I realized with a sinking heart. What if I couldn't find my way home? I'd slept a bit along the way, and though it had been a fitful sleep, still it had kept me from noticing if we'd made any twists and turns along the way to finding this inn. What if I got lost? Already, hunger was gnawing at me. If I should find myself in the woods, what hope did I have of finding nourishment? Had I foolishly stranded myself, trading one predicament for another? What about shelter? What about vandals on the road? I had been most unwise to think I could ever look like one of the common folk. Despite the dust on my gown, it clearly was fine cloth and like nothing these people had ever come across. My hair hung free and was not plaited as the women who worked in the fields wore it.

Never mind, I told myself, my lips coming together in a thin, determined line as I marched on. I couldn't afford to worry about that now, not if I was going to have a chance at making it home. Somehow, I would find a family loyal to Hohenzollern and the princess, and they would see me safely returned to the castle.

With my resolution renewed, I clenched my hands into fists at my sides and picked up my pace. The sooner I saw my family the better. And what a tale this would make! I could imagine the entire dining hall listening with rapt attention as I told how I'd been abducted and forced to walk while my captor rode! Who'd ever thought such a thing could happen to a duchess?

A smile quirked at the corners of my mouth when I imagined my cousin's reaction. I knew she'd be horrified and full of sympathy, yet the thought of me forced to live as a commoner would make her laugh and the thought of hearing her familiar peals of laughter made me smile, too.

"What's a fair lil' thing like yourself doin' out here on her own?"

Oh, no! Fear rose like bile in my throat as my head jerked up at the sound of the unfamiliar voice. I'd thought that being caught and dragged back to the inn, kicking and screaming, would be the worst thing that could happen to me. As I took in the leering, gap-toothed man who'd pulled his horse over to speak to me, I revisited that assessment. He was thin, in clothes that bore more resemblance to rags, with stringy black hair and a long, crooked nose. I did my best to school my features so that I didn't visibly wince. It was hard, since the sight of him—and the smell that soon followed—turned my stomach.

"Would you be needin' a ride, miss?"

The way he looked me up and down with those narrowed, beady eyes sent a chill of revulsion along my spine. I swallowed hard to stifle the cry that rose to my throat the moment I realized I was being followed. *Please, not again*, I thought, trying to calm my racing pulse. "I am a woman wed, sir," I said at last, hoping he didn't hear the quaver in my voice. "I am the Duchess of Württemberg, if you please."

His eyes lit with amusement at my tone and his smile widened, revealing a mouth full of dark gaps where teeth had once been. "Beggin' your forgiveness, *my lady*."

I didn't care for the sing-song tone he used, and as he looked down at me with greed in every line of his expression, I realized I'd made yet another mistake. *I never have known when to hold my tongue*, I thought ruefully. *Mother had always said so.*

"It's quite all right." I changed my tune, speaking gracefully with my head held high. "You didn't know. Now, you can see for yourself that I am fine, just out for a stroll. My husband should be along any moment."

"Husband, eh?" His grin stretched even further and I began to feel my heart pounding hard in my breast, certain that he must know that I was lying.

A frisson of fear ran the length of my body at the thought, but I did my best to hide it. "Yes. The Duke of Württemberg."

"I'd be pleased to help you find your, er, husband."

My smile froze, prickling like tiny shards of ice on my face. Somehow, I knew that he intended to do nothing of the kind. "Thank you, but—" I broke off as he swiftly dismounted from the downtrodden animal that had carried him.

"No, I must insist, m'lady."

I backed away, my eyes darting from him to his animal, and I wondered if this was the chance I had been waiting for after all. He was a long, lean man, but even so I doubted I could win in a skirmish. If I could outwit him, there was a chance I could claim the animal as my own. It was clear that it needed a better master, and in any event, it would get me that much closer to returning home.

He stepped closer, his stride confidant as if he could smell my fear. He reached out to seize me, but I ducked, stepping out of his grubby grasp, which only made him laugh. "You know, now that I've had a proper look, your fair complex'ion and your fine clothes make me wonder if you really *could* be a duchess."

"I am," I replied in a voice that wobbled despite my efforts.

"Imagine that. Me, with a duchess." He grinned, seeming well pleased with himself, and I chose that moment to act.

I darted around him as quickly as I could managed and sprinted for the horse. He made a grab for me, but I yanked my skirt away and kept running. I climbed atop the animal as quickly as I could, my heart in my throat the whole while. When I was astride, I kicked my heels, but to my surprise and disappointment the animal did not budge. I looked down in dismay and realized that the man had managed to take hold of the reins, which he clutched like a prize in his grimy claws.

He peered up at me, a mean smile on his face as he sniggered at my misfortune. "Thought you'd steal my horse, did ye? That doesn't seem like somethin' no royalty would do, now does it?" Which a sneer, he jerked the reins and the horse responded by rearing up on its hind legs, bucking me from its back so quickly that I hardly knew what was happening.

A scream lodged in my throat and I had mere moments to process what was happening, during which I became certain that I would break every bone in my body when I hit the ground.

When I hit, I slammed against something solid, and the air whooshed from my lungs. Only as I gasped, struggling for breath did I realize that I was being held by strong arms around my waist.

"Shh, it's alright, sweeting. You're safe now," a voice murmured into my ear. When I realized that it was my abductor, come to fetch me after all, I could have wept. Whether those tears would have been in self-pity or relief, I wasn't certain.

"May I ask what you think you're doing?" he asked, directing his sharp, clipped words at the man who'd caused his horse to throw me.

"Oh, why, I was just trying to help your wife find her way home, sir. She seemed lost, walking out here alone, unescorted and all. A lady of her station, I don't have to tell ye what could have happened. There are some unsavory persons in this part of the world, Yer Grace."

Hearing the man who'd stolen me in the dark of night being referred to by my husband's title was laughable. As if he could hear the giggles trying to burst free, my captor gave me a quelling glance before speaking.

"I believe you speak the truth on the matter, though it looked as though *your* intentions toward my wife were far from honorable."

"Forgive me, Yer Grace, I'm jus' a humble farmer. I certainly didn't intend to frighten the lass."

"The duchess," he corrected coolly. "And in fact, I saw you make your horse unseat her. Had I not been present, she would have been severely injured."

The man looked at the ground, shamefaced and stuttering.

"A lesser man would see you put to death, but as I am the forgiving sort and am sure it was nothing but an unfortunate mishap, I'll take the horse and allow these transgressions to be forgotten."

The man had gone pale, his ruddy complexion becoming whiter than a bed sheet when the possibility of death was mentioned. Had my kidnapper been royalty, indeed, he could have seen to it. "Thank you, sir. I mean, Yer Grace! Thank you. I'm terribly sorry, I am. Thank you for pardoning such a humble—"

"Very well, sir. You may be on your way." As he spoke, his grip on me tightened the slightest bit. "And if we should meet again, I doubt it would go well for you. Understand?"

The humble farmer nodded again and again, giving a clumsy bow that made it clear that his knees were practically knocking together from fear. "I... o'course, Yer Grace. Forgive me, Duchess, I did not mean... well, that is... I'm very sorry. My humblest apologies."

I nodded, which was all I could muster at the moment. My abductor walked forward and collected the reins from the farmer and led the horse away while the man watched. When he reached me, he signaled that I should follow him, which I did, ignoring the farmer who was bowing so low he practically scraped the ground.

"What in all hells were you thinking?" he asked when we'd moved a good distance away.

Straight from one captor to another, I thought wryly. "I was thinking of getting home, nothing more."

"That much is clear." He barked a laugh. "You certainly didn't think of a horse. Did you think of provisions? Did you—"

"No, I didn't," I snapped, eyes blazing as I whirled on him. "The only thought I had was getting away, and if that man hadn't come along—"

"There would have been another man, one that perhaps wasn't as easily fooled. You need to use that pretty little head, princess, before you end up killed yourself."

His words made me shudder. "How do I know that isn't what *you* intend for me, once you've... done whatever you intend?"

He stopped short, facing my glare with his usual unruffled gaze. "As of now, I've done nothing to make you think I mean you ill, princess."

"I've told you!" I practically screeched. "I am *not*—"

"And I'll tell you another thing," he continued as though I hadn't spoken. "Right now, the only thing I intend for you is to understand the seriousness of your actions."

"I was fine," I snapped. "I was handling everything. I would have managed."

"I see. Well, in that case, forgive me for trying to help you."

The reply caught me off guard, as did the fact that he began to walk again, leading the horse alongside him. I glanced over my shoulder and saw that the farmer had finally left, presumably to return home. I gazed longingly at the road. I'd been so close—so close! Would freedom always elude me?

"Go." The one word pierced my thoughts. "I won't stop you, if you're so eager."

My heartbeat quickened at the thought, even as my eyes took in the sun dipping in the sky, shadows being cast by its dimming sunlight. Reluctantly, I tore my eyes away and began to follow him. We walked toward the inn for several moments, neither of us saying a word. My belly tightened at the sight of the building, but I knew that I didn't have a choice. I didn't have anywhere to stay, and for the present I had no other alternative than to make the best of an undesirable situation. I'd get out of it, somehow. I had to.

"I know that you're frightened," he spoke up at last. "Given the circumstances, that's understandable. But what you need to know is that as much as you desire to return to Hohenzollern, there's no longer a home for you there."

I blinked in surprise, trying to make sense of his words. "What do you mean?"

He sighed and ran his fingers through his hair before turning to me with solemn eyes. "I hate for you to find out this way... I hate for you to find out at all, truth be told, but I can see no way around it. Hohenzollern has surely been attacked by now, and all within it will have been given to the Free Cities. That would have included you, had I not taken you with me."

His words sounded distant and distorted. None of what he said made any sense. What did he mean, I did not have a home? Surely everything he said was nonsense, meant to make me accept my fate, meant to keep me from running away from him. "I don't understand," I said, speaking from lips that felt numb. "Attacked by whom?"

"The people of the Free Cities. It seems that the Princess Susanna—"

"No," I protested, shaking my head. "Susanna is a *good* person, she—"

"Please, I know it's very hard to accept, but you have me now, little one, and I intend to make you my wife."

The more he spoke, the more I trembled. Surely nothing but lies tumbled from his full lips. It wasn't possible. Hohenzollern, no more? What would have become of Susanna, of the other ladies I knew? It was unthinkable. He was only trying to unnerve me, but I was a duchess. I was made of sterner stuff than he realized, and I would not bend to the fear that he attempted to drum up in order to get me to fall in line.

"I shall always treat you fairly, with kindness. You have nothing to fear from me."

Become his *wife*? What did he think of me that made him believe that I would consent to such nonsense? "Thank you, sir, I am sure you mean well," I told him with frost in my voice, "but I already *have* a husband."

He let out a long-suffering sigh. "Madam, I'm afraid your husband is most likely dead."

The knots in my belly tightened but I forced myself to keep walking, to keep breathing evenly as if nothing was amiss. The thought of Wallace dead… oh, how my knees wanted to buckle, but I would not let them. Not for the sake of a lie.

"And as I said, you will have nothing to fear from me," he continued. "Nothing, save the thrashing I mentioned earlier."

As I stopped in my tracks once more, a gasp managed to escape my parted lips. When it reached his ears, he turned his head to look over his shoulder at me. It was, in a way, as if I was seeing him for the first time, because only then did I notice how very like my husband's they were: steely gray and as hard and determined as sharp pieces of flint.

CHAPTER THREE

The man that I thought of as my jailer saw to it that the new horse was bedded safely within the stable and gave the lad there instructions to tend it, as he had been doing for my horse, Fortune. Only then did he turn back to me once more. "Come with me."

He didn't force me to walk alongside him, he didn't lay a finger on me, but I at least had the sense to know when I was beaten. I knew that I could not run again—indeed, it seemed that it had been foolish to do so in the first place.

The moment we walked into the establishment, I saw that the innkeeper was by the door, smiling tightly at the pair of us.

"So, you have found her."

"Yes, madam. Thank you for your concern. Now, if you'll excuse us..."

"Oh, of course. I suspect you'll have... matters to attend to."

He gave her a thin smile in acknowledgement of her words, yet I turned my head to stare back at her. What could she have meant? Did she know... surely not! Surely, he couldn't mean to carry through on such an awful threat! And even if he did, certainly he never would have shared such sensitive information with her!

He opened the door and gestured me inside, but as soon as I'd crossed into the room, I turned to him with arms folded across my chest. "Did you tell that woman that you... that you..."

"Intend to spank you?" he prompted as he closed the door behind us.

My eyes narrowed into slits. "You should know that a true gentleman would never—"

"I do not know what manner of 'gentleman' you've encountered, princess, but I think both of us know that a title and lands don't make a man."

For some reason, the way he looked at me made me think he spoke of Wallace, who I suddenly felt fiercely protective of, if for no other reason than this man was too low-born to look down upon him. "If you refer to the Duke of Württemberg, then it is my duty to tell you that you don't know what you're talking about," I informed him airily. "He was the most noble, most caring, bravest man that ever lived."

My captor stared at me for the span of several long heartbeats, his gray eyes piercing me, as if searching me for lies. When he spoke again, his voice was soft. "You must forgive me my impudence, princess."

He was finally giving me the deference that I'd told him in tone and manner that I deserved, and yet, somehow his gentle, unassuming demeanor made me feel ashamed. My mother had always cautioned me not to wield my nobility like a weapon, and I'd been doing it from the moment I'd met him—if *met* was the proper term. It didn't matter that it, coupled with my razor-sharp tongue, was the only weapon I had, it only mattered that I was acting below my station by being so haughty. And to a man that, though he'd kidnaped me, had been nothing but patient and kind with me.

"Please… I'm not a princess." When I spoke, my voice was mollified.

"I know, my lady. It's my private jest, I suppose, and I pray someday you'll see fit to forgive me for it."

I ventured a small, tentative smile, though I kept my eyes on the floor. "If you have only been looking for something to call me, you can use my name. It's Cecily." I didn't know that I'd ever told my given name to a commoner before, but somehow, it felt right. A peace offering of sorts.

"Thank you, my lady. It's a lovely name. It suits you."

When I dared risk a glance at him, I saw to my surprise that he was not mocking me. In fact, he looked quite serious indeed. For the first time, I took a good, long look at the man I'd been thinking of as my captor. I saw that the eyes which I'd initially thought bore such a strong resemblance to my husbands' were in fact remarkably different. They were gray, that much was true, but they seemed to be full of light and framed by dark lashes, making them look truer to silver than the storm clouds Wallace had. He was taller than Wallace, too, and was good two heads taller than my own 5'4" frame. Wallace had an enviable physique from fencing and sword fighting, but this man far outweighed him and it was clearly mostly muscle. His hair was brown with streaks of gold threaded through the strands, but his most noteworthy feature were the twin dimples in his cheeks. I'd only seen them once thus far, but as I looked at him, taking in the full measure of him, I wondered what it would take to see them again.

"You're too kind," I answered at last. I felt that my response had been late in coming, but he dipped his head in acknowledgement anyway.

"You may call me Antony, my lady."

Antony. The name reverberated through me, seeming to suit his quiet strength and dignified bearing. "As you wish."

We said no more for several long moments, each staring uncertainly at the other. I didn't know where things went from here. Taught to be the epitome of a proper lady since before I could fathom any of it, I did not know how to proceed when one had exchanged Christian names with a man of lesser birth, much less what to do when that same man had promised to spank me.

"What are you thinking, Cecily?"

I could see that he liked trying my name out and it sounded sweet as honey on his lips, making me smile faintly. "Only that I don't know how to… I don't know what we should do now."

"I see. Might I suggest we talk for a bit?"

I nodded and he took a seat in the chair by the door. Mirroring him—for it was all I could think to do—I sat gingerly on the bed.

"Firstly, I want you to know that I intend to keep you safe. I know that might be hard for you to believe, considering the manner in which we met, but I speak the truth. I have no desire to harm you, and intend to protect you from those that would."

I had so many questions, so many things to say that rose to the tip of my tongue, but I swallowed each of them back, waiting patiently for him to finish.

"However, in order for me to do those things that I might ensure your safety, I must know that you will obey me. This is all I ask of you, my lady. You must obey, or suffer the consequences of failing to do so."

The word went through me like a shot, making me freeze. *Consequences.* How did it sound so frightening on his lips, and yet… yet, my bosom heaved in a way that I could not understand.

"Sometimes, those consequences could entail you finding yourself in danger, as you were today. To prevent this from happening again, your consequence for disobeying me will be a sound spanking."

My heart pounded hard at the sincere, calm way that he spoke of such things. It was unheard of, threatening a lady and especially one as high-born as myself. Yet, I felt myself thawing, somehow warming toward this man who'd spirited me away from my home. "You cannot," I murmured, my breath quickening as I stared at him. "It would hardly be proper."

"I'm afraid on this we're going to have to disagree, my lady. Tell me, did your husband never chastise you?"

"Wallace?" I blurted out, his name a laugh on my lips. I sobered as soon as I'd spoken, flushing when I realized how improper I was being right this moment. I cleared my throat, abashed. "The duke would never do such a thing."

It was true, in a sense. Wallace had been ready to beat me in a drunken rage on the day I fled from his presence, but I could hardly imagine him spanking me.

Antony's intense eyes studied me for a long moment before he spoke again. "More's the pity. I've always thought that a spanking, particularly when well-deserved, brings a man and woman closer together."

I wanted to laugh again—indeed, the laughter bubbled in my throat, but one look at his no-nonsense face and it died on my lips. As the humor was fading, I felt something strange stirring in my breast, something that made my chest tighten and my pulse race. "I think I'm going to be ill," I murmured, putting my hand to my forehead.

"The prospect of punishment can be frightening." Antony clucked his tongue sympathetically, while I wondered if we were talking about the same thing. "Best to have it over with, and quickly, so that you can get some rest. I'm sure you're still shaken from your ordeal." When he stood, I once again mirrored him, backing away as he began to move toward me.

I kept moving, my feet shuffling in reverse as quickly as I could until I found myself backing into the wall. I swallowed hard, knowing that I had nowhere else to go. My eyes fixed on Antony as he moved closer still, in hot pursuit. I splayed my hands against the wall, pressing them tightly against the wood as though I could give myself room to run from the sheer will of wishing for it.

Regrettably, the wood stayed solid despite my grasping fingers and Antony was soon upon me. He did not grab me, or even make a move to touch me. He stood, large and looming in front of me without moving a muscle. As I waited to see what would happen next, I took in his large palms. I'd never had cause to consider a man's hands before, but as I studied his I found the knots in my belly growing tighter with every passing moment. They were large and looked heavy. I couldn't help but wonder, my breath hitching in my throat, what such a hand would feel like on my bottom.

He pinned me with his eyes and when I saw how kind yet unrelenting his gaze was, I knew that this was not a fight I should win. In all truth, I was tired of fighting, which was why I turned in slow, shuffling movements to face the wall. I didn't know what came next, so I simply stood there, looking at the cool wood and trying to ignore the rapid beat of my pulse in the hallow of my throat.

"Have you ever been spanked before, Cecily?"

The question caused me to start in surprise. In the life I'd come from, such matters simply weren't discussed, and certainly not so openly. Yet, I knew he expected an answer, and despite myself, something about the soft lilt in his voice when he asked it made my pulse quicken until I felt my breath coming in short bursts. "No."

Though she'd wrapped my knuckles once or twice, my lady mother had believed that disappointed silence was punishment enough—and indeed, I'd learned my lessons well.

"In that case, I feel that I must warn you that this *will* hurt. Under different circumstances, I would go light on you, as this is a first offense, but I need you to understand how seriously I take matters such as these." As he spoke, Antony began to hike up my skirts until my pantalets were visible to him.

Just the thought of him seeing my dainty, carefully sewn undergarments was enough to make my body tense as a blush stained my cheeks. The only man who'd seen them had been Wallace and I doubted he'd taken much notice. He was not the type of man to undress a woman and had often left the task to one of my ladies.

"What you did put both of us in danger, whether you realize it or not," he continued as he arranged my clothing to his satisfaction. "Bend over, please."

I hesitated for no more than an instant before I obeyed his directive. No sooner had I complied than he began to drape my skirts over my back.

"What if it had been a band of men on the road instead of just the one? What if I hadn't been able to protect you? What would have become of you then?"

I was struck by the sincere concern in his voice. "Would that truly have meant anything to you?" I ventured to ask. "After all, I am only stolen goods. Easily replaced, I'm sure."

"Is that what you think?" He punctuated the question with a single, stinging slap of his hand to the back of my pantalets that made my legs lash out as I squeaked in protest. "I'm sorry that you think so little of me, my lady, but more's the pity that you value yourself so lowly."

"Oh, don't mistake me," I replied drily. "I know my value all too well. It is you who seems to be forgetting who I am."

I shouldn't have been surprised when my buttocks were struck again, but I mewled in pain just the same.

"I can see that you need this spanking badly, and for more reasons than one. Don't you worry, my dove, I shall see to it that you get what you need."

The endearment surprised me and it robbed me of any reply I might have made.

"Don't be embarrassed if you need to cry out, but I will not accept you fighting me in any way, do you understand?"

Though my ears understood his words, I didn't know if I could do as he asked. It was all too foreign to me. My bottom was tingling painfully where his hand had fallen, and the knowledge that he intended to do it again had my breath coming in quick little gasps and my heart racing anxiously. "Please, I—" I stood and began to turn, but Antony caught my wrists and with gentle hands he turned me to face the wall once more.

"You have been warned, my dove. It is not a warning I will repeat." Without another word, he put a hand on my back, encouraging me to bend over, fixing my clothing once more after I'd complied. Only when my pantalets were uncovered did the spanking resume, his hand vigorously meeting my buttocks again and again, each smack measured and hard. After each startling spank rained down on my upturned cheeks, he left his hand in place for a few seconds, as though encouraging the burn to sear through my clothing and burrow into my skin.

Initially, I tried to distract myself with thoughts of something, anything but the punishment I was receiving at his hands, but all too quickly I discovered that there would be no such reprieve from the horrible, stinging pain. I had to endure it as best I could—it would be impossible to ignore it. No sooner than I had accepted this, his hand began landing more vigorously than ever, his hard, heavy palm visiting each buttock in turn and then going back again. The stinging pain became a burning in my seat and the burning became a fire in my flesh that had my feet dancing as though to a merry tune.

"All I require from you, my lady, is obedience. I know it might seem much to ask, but I will have it all the same." As his hand fell again and again, stoking the heat in my cheeks, I could not think of one reason to ever disobey him. None that seemed worth the price I would pay, in any event. "You will obey me," he continued, his hand striking hard and true, "or end up with a hot, red bottom. I'm afraid I cannot waver in this." The next smack that landed made me arch up onto my tip-toes, and the succeeding one on the next cheek made me fall back to the floor once more. "It is for your own good, I assure you, and in return you will have my unfailing love and loyalty."

Love. I knew quite a bit about loyalty, but no man had ever spoken to me of love.

"Now, my dove, can you give me your word that you will not run again?" His hand stilled on the small of my back, my punishment stopped for the time being.

Something funny was happening in the pit of my stomach, a tightening and simultaneous loosening of knots that left me feeling very odd indeed. *Love*. The word kept reverberating in my head, radiating throughout my being until I felt dizzy with the implication. It was strange: Antony was not royal-born, nor had he been endowed with titles. Yet, he made my body feel hot and my mind swim beyond reason. It wasn't a feeling I liked in the least.

"I shall run," I informed him pertly. "I will run as many times as need be until I find myself home again." The room went still after I'd spoken and I tensed as I waited for a response.

Antony was silent for several long moments, giving me ample time to regret my words, before he spoke, his voice gruff once more. "Your slipper, if you would be so kind, my lady."

"My... my what?"

"Your slipper."

Confused, I slid the leather slipper off my foot and felt him bending behind me to retrieve it. Before I could fathom why he would ask for such a thing, the reason landed sharply on my upturned cheeks. I found myself howling in a most unladylike fashion as it landed once more and then another time still.

"You may run," he said, using each word as an occasion to apply the slipper to my backside, "but I assure you that I am an excellent trapper. I will find you every time. I will bring you back with me, kicking and screaming if I must, with a red backside as your only reward."

"You… have… no right," I choked out, wincing each time the slipper made contact with my pantalets.

"Have you ever heard of spoils of war, my dove? It gives me every right. But moreover, I intend to make you my wife, which means that there will be nothing you can say or do to avoid a sore bottom except to obey."

• • • • • • •

Württemberg Manor

"The Duchess of Württemberg."

I froze just inside the room as I was announced. I spotted my husband in an instant, bent over a table that was strewn with papers which he seemed to be studying with single-minded intensity.

"Yes?" he called impatiently without looking up. "What is it?"

I looked helplessly at the chamberlain, but he did not meet my gaze. I had no one to tell me what I should do. Indeed, I had never been in this position before and did not know how to go about it. "Ah, husband," I said, tentatively stepping closer. "If I might have just a moment…"

"Can't it wait?" he asked in a voice that told me it would, regardless of my desires.

"Oh, of course. Forgive me for having disturbed you," I murmured. I turned to leave and had gone only a few steps when I thought of my mother. She never would have been so easily dismissed and as her daughter, neither should I allow myself to be. I stood taller with my sudden resolve and spun around, walking toward him, emboldened by my determination. "Actually, I require a word now, if you please."

"Damn it, Cecily!" He slammed his balled fist on the table as his head jerked up. "What is it?"

His hardened tone and narrowed eyes almost made me lose my nerve, but I swallowed hard and faced him. "Alone, please."

His jaw tightened and I knew that he was well and truly annoyed with me. He scowled and did not take his eyes from me as he barked the order: "You heard the duchess! Out, every one of you!"

Well?" he demanded impatiently the moment the doors closed behind us.

"I thought you should like to know… well, that is… I've not had my bleeding this month."

"And?" he snapped, rather peevishly.

"My courses have not come. I am carrying your child, husband." I waited tensely for his reaction, but it was slow in coming. I'd hoped he would be happy to have an heir, perhaps even feel some tenderness toward me as a husband should for his wife. When I'd first discovered the news, I'd had the forlorn hope that things might return to what they'd

been before we'd pledged our troth. Perhaps this would make him love me. Judging from the expression on his face, however, his feelings hovered somewhere between annoyance and confusion. "Well," I gave him a faint smile, "I thought you would like to know." I turned to leave and had gone perhaps a step or two when I heard him moving behind me. In the next instant, I felt my waist being seized, felt myself being turned to face him.

His face had been transformed, eager excitement alight in his eyes, his face aglow with the news. "You are certain?"

I was quite caught off-guard by the sudden change in him and didn't know what to make of it. "Ah… I have written to my mother. She is certain, my lord."

He let out a roar that shocked me so I feared I would faint, but then his arms were around me, holding me close, hugging me tight. "How can this be?" he asked, his voice full of delighted awe. "How can this be, a child so soon? Surely, God favors our match, Cecily. Surely, this is a sign."

I laughed, eager to join him in rejoicing. "It is wonderful," I agreed eagerly.

"Oh, yes. My darling wife, my sweet duchess," he cooed, his finger trailing down my cheek as I beamed up at him. "How are you feeling? Surely, you ought to be abed?"

"Husband!" I reproached him with laughter in my voice. "Do not fret, I am doing everything my mother instructs so that our child will be born healthy."

"Yes, well, it's been a long time since your mother bore you. Mayhap I should fetch the physician—"

"Please, Wallace," I murmured, burrowing my face in his chest. "Please, don't fret. Only be happy, here in this moment, with me."

I thought he might protest—indeed, he seemed to have much more he longed to say, but after a moment I felt him relax, the tension draining from his body as he began to cuddle me close. "Of course I'm happy, sweetheart. You've made me so very happy."

This was what I wanted, I thought as I melted into my husband's embrace. This is what I've dreamt of and longed for. Now we'll be as happy as we were before, and have a little baby of our own to share in our joy. I inhaled slowly, relishing the moment, determined to savor the feel of his arms around me as I basked in his love.

CHAPTER FOUR

"I cannot be your wife," I hissed at Antony, who looked back at me unrepentantly. "I am a woman already married!"

"Yes, and as I've already explained, your husband is surely dead."

"Surely?" I mocked. "Surely is not a certainty, and until I can say with certainty that my husband is not in this world, I will never entertain the idea of marrying another! Why, I would have to wait for my mourning period to be over before—"

"These are troubled times, my lady. Things are not as they once were. I'm afraid it would do you much harm to remain unmarried, unescorted, through these parts."

"Then take me back!" I demanded, glaring at him over my shoulder. "I didn't ask to be brought here!"

Antony tilted his head to the side, surveying me before he answered. "I know you are feeling lost, but as I've said, there is no life left for you in Hohenzollern."

I jutted my chin out defiantly. "I don't believe you. But if you will take me back, and let me see for myself, then perhaps—"

"I'm afraid that's simply not possible. I'm sorry, Cecily. Come to me, my poor little dove."

My blue eyes narrowed into slits. Hearing his show of sympathy made me seethe. *He* was the one who had done this to me. Why should he now plague me with his pity? "Thank you, no. I'd rather you finish the chastisement. That, or allow me to take to my bed." I'd thought to anger him, as he'd done me, but I only saw patience and tenderness in his face.

I'd thought that perhaps he would allow me to rest my eyes and sore bottom, however, when the sturdy leather sole of my slipper connected with my pantalets I realized that he was not finished with me yet. The spank was followed by a flurry of equally hard swats. I bit down on my lip, hard, to keep from calling out. As one followed the next, however, I began to sniffle. These were not the slow, carefully counted spanks I'd endured before, but rather a painful, punishing barrage of strokes that had tears rolling down my cheeks long before they'd ceased. I was crying, just as he'd promised, yet, he did not stop there. Antony cracked my slipper against my covered behind again and again until my cries turned to sobs and sobs turned to incoherent begging. By the time he stopped, I felt like I'd sat in the fire and had my pantalets burned to nothing but ash. Surely, if I removed the garment I would see scorch marks on my very skin.

"I have given you your orders," Antony said, still quiet and quite in control. "If you persist in your disobedience, at least you now know what you can expect." When he lowered my skirts and I felt them caress my aching bottom, I winced. "Oh, and Cecily? Next time you'll take your spanking on the bare. Pray remember that before you choose to defy me again."

I turned around with slow, careful steps, and glared at him through a haze of tears. "When my lord husband comes for me—and I assure you that he will—you will pay for every swat. Let us hope it is not with your life."

Antony surprised me yet again by responding to my words with a slight bow. "If that is your wish, then I hope for your sake it is granted."

"Y-you do?" I stammered.

"I think it's best you go to bed. You need to rest before we continue. Might I suggest you lie on your stomach?"

Tossing my black hair saucily, I didn't trouble to reply as I marched to the bed. I would have lain on my back, just to spite him, if the prospect hadn't been so horrid to contemplate. Antony, to his credit, did not gloat.

The smell of cooked meat stirred me in my sleep. When my stomach rumbled loudly, I had no choice but to wake from my slumber, however reluctantly. I sat up in bed, wincing as my arse hit the bed. Despite Antony's warning, I'd rolled onto my back during the night and now my bottom throbbed as a reminder of the thrashing I'd received. I stretched my arms over my head and turned toward the smell. When I caught sight of Antony walking toward me bearing a large platter, I turned my head away, deciding that perhaps I wasn't that hungry after all.

However, my nose couldn't help but keep sniffing the air, which was all it took for my empty stomach to overtake my stubborn will. When I turned toward the smell I saw that he stood by my side, patiently waiting for me to accept what I suspected was his peace offering. Without a word, he slid a plate in front of me. I mumbled my thanks before I attacked the meat ravenously, eating as though I'd been starved for days. My mother would have been horrified. My husband, in fact, would have disowned me from the shame. Antony, however, watched without comment.

As soon as I'd eaten the last morsel, he offered me a bowl of fruit. "Spiced berries," was the only explanation he offered.

It was on the tip of my tongue to thank him, but I remembered just in time that I was still angry with him and reluctant to talk to him at all. I took the bowl he offered and began to eat, realizing at once that they had been spiced to give flavor because they were a few days old. I ate them just the same, and finally, at long last, my hunger was sated. Only when I finished did I realize that I'd never seen Antony eat a bite. *It's no more than he deserves*, I thought meanly. *Let his stomach pain him the way my bottom does me and see how he likes it!*

"Did you sleep well?"

I deliberately turned away from him once more, appreciating the opportunity to snub him. I was feeling very smug and well-pleased with myself—that was, until my stomach lurched and I found myself bent over and heaving my just-eaten breakfast onto the floor. When I was finally able to stop, tears were streaming down my cheeks and I was much too tired for petty games.

"Perhaps you ate too quickly," he suggested, walking toward me and gently pushing me until I was lying back on the bed. "Rest a little longer."

"But—"

"It's alright," he cut off my feeble protest. "We can leave later. It's best that you have your strength back before we set out again."

"It won't make a difference," I told him, cross that he remained unfailingly kind no matter what I said or did. "It's that horrid food! The Duke of Württemberg never would have given me such poor fare." I glared at him, daring him to contradict me.

I should have known that he would not. It was not his way. "Of course not, my lady. Please forgive me. Now, perhaps after you've had a bit of rest when you've improved we can find something that suits you better."

I'd thought it impossible to sleep, but I found that I was tired from the exertion of being sick and found myself drifting off in no time.

・・・・・・・

Württemberg Manor

"Excuse me." I stepped in the path of a servant carrying a basket of clothing. "Do you know where the duke is?"

"No, m'lady," she mumbled, speaking too quickly, avoiding my eyes and too eager to move past me.

It was in bad taste for a woman to have to ask servants where her husband was. I knew that, and yet I could do little else. I felt like I'd not seen Wallace in days, which I began to find troublesome. I'd seen him in the halls, of course, and at mealtimes, but he no longer made an effort to seek me out. To tell the truth, it wasn't as though I missed his company, but I felt it my duty as his wife to make an effort to seek him out.

Yet, I could find him nowhere. I'd been to his rooms, to his war room, the library, and the great hall. I had it on good authority that he was not out hunting, yet no one seemed to know where he was. Or, at the very least, that was what they told me when I asked.

I knew that I was beginning to look the fool and I was about to turn around and return to my rooms when I heard a high-pitched giggle. It was followed quickly by a playful admonishment from a husky male voice. Something about that voice made me still in my tracks and draw my breath in sharply.

It's not him, I told myself, aware even as I thought it that I was lying, just as I knew that I should turn around and pretend that I'd never found my husband. I should remain blind and deaf, lest I allow whoever he was with to break my heart.

But even as I thought it, I still found myself moving closer, pushing open the door that had been left ajar. At first, I wasn't sure exactly what I was seeing. A woman in a dubious state of undress was perched atop the desk in the middle of the room, her head thrown back as she moaned. Yet, she appeared to be alone.

I'd never witnessed such a thing before, and the shock of seeing her clothing askance and the woman herself clearly nearing a state of rapture was enough to make my entire body freeze. How I wished I'd never come in. How I longed to turn and flee, and yet, my slippers seemed fastened to the stone floor.

"Ooh," she moaned, thrusting her naked chest forward like a common whore. The mere sight of how she behaved was enough to sicken me. "Oh, it feels... so lovely..."

I had just decided to announce myself so that she would know she was not alone when she trilled in a quavering wail, reaching forward to grasp something I could not see. She cried out, her body spasming, and I couldn't tear my eyes away, no matter how dearly I longed to.

"Oh, my lord!" she cried. "Your Grace!"

I felt the color begin to drain from my cheeks even before I saw him. The lady moved, ever so slightly, to give me a good view of my husband kneeling on the floor, placed right between her thighs. I was unable to stop the gasp that rose to my throat, and when the lady spun around I saw that she was indeed a whore, the whore called Anne Clover, who was employed by my husband to clean the chamber pots, and yet apparently did so much more.

"Dear Mother of God," I murmured to myself, my hand flying to my breast. I felt faint.

"Y-your ladyship!" Anne squeaked, her hands flying to her breasts in an attempt to disguise her nakedness, as though I hadn't already seen all that there was to see.

"Cecily? What the devil?" Wallace demanded, sounding annoyed as though I'd just spoiled his fun. And it would appear that I had indeed.

"I... forgive me," I murmured, my cheeks flaming with shame. "I... I did not know you were in here." I turned to take my leave and had even taken a step forward when it occurred to me: it was they who should be ashamed, not me. What did I have to apologize for? Wallace was my husband and had just been caught in the act of betraying me, yet he seemed to feel nothing toward me whatsoever. And Anne Clover! The little whore should be blushing to the roots of her hair and running for the chapel to confess her immeasurable sin!

When I turned back around, Wallace arched an eyebrow, clearly impatient to get back to his sport.

"Have you nothing to say to me?"

He seemed surprised—whether by the fact that I'd addressed him at all, or the biting tone I used, I could not say. "What is it you would like me to say? Good-bye?"

"I am carrying your child, in case it's slipped your mind, Your Grace."

"So might she be," he replied, nodding toward Anne and chuckling at his remark.

My lips curled in disgust and I clenched my fists at my sides. "I want her sent from court." Anne Clover turned toward me with a gasp, her eyes wide as her face paled. I did not so much as spare her a glance.

Wallace did not answer right away and instead took his time standing up. I glanced away when I realized that he was not wearing trousers. "Oh, you do, do you? And do you command at Württemberg Castle now, my lady?"

"I am your wife, I—"

"That's right. My wife, not my ruler. It is I who command here, Cecily, and I say that the lady stays."

"Then I shall leave," I declared, turning away and beginning to stride from the room. I'd nearly made it to the door when I felt my arm being seized. With hard, grasping fingers, Wallace turned me to face him, shaking me like a rag doll.

"You take your leave when I command it and not before. Don't ever forget it, Cecily."

"I am not a prisoner here." I glared at him defiantly, jutting out my jaw.

"No, you are not that. You are my dog—you will obey my every order, or be kicked until I can bring you to heel. Shall I offer you a demonstration?" He raised his hand back and I couldn't help cowering at the wild look in his eyes. I knew that he would not hesitate to strike me.

"Please, Wallace…"

Seeing the fear in my face must have pleased him, because he lowered his arm almost at once. "I thought not. You have my permission to withdraw."

· · · · · · ·

When I felt myself being shaken, I awoke with a start.

"Shh, it's alright. Nothing is going to hurt you."

I blinked rapidly, trying to gather my bearings. When I saw Antony staring at me, I relaxed the slightest bit.

"Are you unwell?"

"I…" I sat up slowly, trying to recover from the surprise of being startled awake.

"You were crying out," he said by way of explanation. "You sounded… I was worried, so I woke you."

I couldn't help but be touched by the concern in his expression and I offered a small smile. "No cause to be alarmed. I must have been dreaming." Though, truth be told, it had been more of a remembrance, but I didn't see the need to tell him that.

"Would you like something to eat?" Remembering what had happened the last time I'd eaten was enough to deter me and I shook my head. "You're certain? We'll be readying the horses shortly, and I'm afraid we'll be riding for most of the day."

"I can manage."

For a moment, I thought he might argue, but in the end Antony nodded. "As you wish."

Antony left soon after to take care of the horses and pack provisions and I did my best to freshen up before we left.

I saw straight away that he'd told it true—we were riding hard, and covering a lot of ground. I winced often as my bottom bounced in the saddle, but I did my best to keep my discomfort from him.

We rode hard and traveled with nary a word between us, which was just fine with me. I wasn't angry at him anymore for the spanking, but I couldn't help but feel embarrassed. I couldn't find the courage even to look him in the eye, much less speak to him. It wasn't a feeling that I was accustomed to, and certainly not one that I enjoyed.

When Antony halted his horse, I was quick to do the same. "Would you care for a break, my lady? I wouldn't say no to a rest."

"Certainly," I murmured, still avoiding his gaze.

Antony dismounted in one quick motion and came toward me, offering his hand. After a brief pause, I took it and allowed him to help me from the horse. It wasn't until I was sitting on solid ground that I realized how badly I was in need of a rest from our wearisome travels.

"It isn't much," he said by way of apology as he offered me an apple and a large piece of day-old bread.

I took what he offered and quickly busied myself with the task of eating so that I didn't have to reply. Not that he seemed to mind—Antony had no trouble filling in the silence.

"My Sarah used to bake the finest bread any man's ever tasted," he remarked as he tore a chunk off with his teeth. I gave him a sidelong glance as I ate my portion in small, ladylike bites. "Sarah was my wife," he explained, though I hadn't inquired. "A finer lady has never been made, before or since." After speaking, he bowed his head for a moment, as though in remembrance.

I wondered what he remembered. My own memories, so fresh in my mind, were nothing one would want to remember. "Your wife?" I ventured, intrigued despite myself.

Something in my tone made him laugh. "Yes, my lady. Did you think me a leper without friend or family to speak of?"

"No," I answered softly, because the truth was, I hadn't thought of it at all.

"She was the most Godly, the most giving of women," he told me, his voice turning reverent. "I don't suppose you can bake?"

I couldn't help but smile at the longing in his voice. "No, I'm afraid not."

"It's a useful skill to have, Duchess. Perhaps you could learn. We'll see to it that you get a lesson when we get home."

I couldn't help but flinch as he spoke of "home" knowing that it meant two entirely different things to us, but I didn't offer a word in protest. In fact, I ate in silence for the remainder of the meager meal, and he seemed too lost in his own thoughts to notice.

As soon as we were both finished, we mounted our horses once more and began to ride for a destination that was unknown to me. It occurred to me more than once that now that I had my own horse, perhaps an opportunity to try to escape would arise. Though I'd become more pliant following my recent chastisement, the desire to return home was one that stayed with me, even if I ceased being vocal about it. But horse or no, I realized that I didn't know the landscape well enough to survive. Nor did I know what road would lead me back to Hohenzollern. And then, of course, there was the matter of the retribution I would face once more at his hands if I were caught, which made it all the more imperative that I be certain of escape before I tried to attempt it.

I kept my eyes fixed straight in front of me, my vision filled with a line of trees that made up the endless landscape we rode along. Was it any wonder that I would need assistance finding my way back home? Every snowy hill and frost-covered tree looked the same to me. The more we rode, the more I silently began to question if even Antony knew where we were going. I became bored early on in our journey and my mind began to wander, thoughts of my life at the castle distracting me. I was so lost in thought, in fact, that I began to take no notice of any of the landscape that whirred by as we rode. I didn't even take notice when the sun began to sink in the great, vast sky and still, we rode on. Only when Antony pulled his horse to a stop did I wake from my trance.

"We can sleep here tonight," he remarked as he dismounted. "The ground is soft enough."

"The g-ground?" I echoed as he helped me down, certain I must have misheard him. "But I... I've never..."

"It's nothing to fear, princess," he said with the gently mocking smile I was becoming accustomed to. "It won't open up and swallow you, I swear it. And if it does, then I'll go to the depths of hell to rescue you."

I was used to courtly flattery, and perhaps it was that—this small reminder of what I'd left behind, the remembrance of the kinds of promises Wallace had once made—that made my eyes narrow as I looked at him. "Perhaps it will do me the favor of swallowing you then, so that I might return home."

"Perhaps," he agreed, chuckling despite the daggers I glared at him.

I hoped that Wallace missed me. I hoped he pined for m and repented of every harsh word, every indecent action. Perhaps this would be a blessing in disguise. If my lord husband rued his treatment of me, then it would not be all for nothing. I would forgive him, of course, after a time. And then I would make him order me ten new gowns, for I found I never wanted to be in a dirty dress again.

"I will go scout for firewood, though God knows it will be scarce in this weather. I don't fancy running after little girls who can't behave, so see to it that you stay put."

I whirled on him, prepared to shout that I was a duchess and far from a little girl, when I realized that was just what he wanted. Instead, I clamped my mouth shut while giving him another poisonous stare, but he only wagged a finger at me in warning as though my withering looks meant nothing to him.

"And if anyone should happen this way, don't attract attention to yourself, and don't speak to them. I am certain you still remember what happened last time."

"I didn't attract attention," I snapped peevishly. "I was only walking…" I trailed off, furrowing my brow at the pointed look he gave me. "As you wish, my lord," I grumbled through gritted teeth.

He gave a little mocking bow in return and turned and walked away as though my barb had bounced right off him and he hadn't felt a thing. I "hmphed" loudly, but by that time there was no one around to hear.

I didn't know what it was about this man that vexed me so. One moment, I felt fragile around him, and the next, I was acting the part of a child, despite my royal station and the years of tutelage I'd had in the genteel arts. I'd never deserted my courtly manners no matter what Wallace had done to me, and yet this man was capable of bringing out a side of me that I hadn't known existed.

I'd met some of the finest, wealthiest lords in the kingdom. What did Antony possess that, even common-born, he should make my heart beat so strangely beneath my breast? Each day, it grew worse; ever since the spanking he'd given me, I'd begun to feel my body flush with heat every time he came near. Even now, just thinking of it made my skin tingle anew with warmth that made a fire seem almost unnecessary.

When I heard the hoof-beats of approaching horses, I ducked down quickly and crawled slowly to the nearby brush, hoping to hide myself from their riders. As much as I might not appreciate being given orders, Antony had a point—in my gown, even as stained and sullied by earth as it was—I was an intrigue that most strangers wouldn't pass up. As the hoof-beats came closer, I shrank back, hoping that the green foliage would shield me from their sight. Better yet if they should keep riding.

I concentrated on breathing slowly, in and out, until I heard them stop near my hiding spot. At that point, I tried to stop breathing altogether. My ears strained toward the strangers and as I heard the *plunk* of boots hitting the snow, I realized that they were dismounting one by one. There were three of them, if I should hazard a guess.

Three. My chest was beginning to ache from lack of air, so I let my breath out as slowly as I possibly could before inhaling in the same manner.

"I'm tellin' ye, there's an inn up the road this way."

"You've already led us astray twice, Smith. At this point, I would be a fool to believe you."

"It weren't *my* fault that the fork in the road was missing!"

I leaned closer, peering between the brush as the men argued amongst themselves. Just then, I saw something with familiar colors flutter in the wind. Why, if I didn't know better, I'd swear that horse bore the Hohenzollern flag! Catching my breath, I leaned closer, turning deaf to the men themselves as I tried to get a closer look at the animals they rode. Each bore the same flag, in the Hohenzollern colors of light blue and deep violet.

So consumed was I with righteous anger that I'd stood to my feet and marched over to the riders before I even knew what I was doing. Even when they caught sight of me and stopped speaking, I was shaking too hard to think twice about my actions.

"Ah, well-met, m'lady. Who might—"

"How *dare* you?" I demanded, my tone heavy with accusation as I glared at them. "Who do you think you are? What in all hells gives you the *right*—" I broke off, my chest heaving as the men looked at each other. I could see now that they were all soldiers. Even though they didn't wear the armor like Hohenzollern warriors, they were each outfitted in the same black jerkins and trousers and each had an impressive sword sheathed on his hip. Too late, I realized that I'd been lecturing men that probably had no cause to be friendly toward me.

"I'm sorry if we've somehow given offense, m'lady," one of the men—clearly the leader—said as he stepped toward me.

I took a step backward, silently cursing myself for my foolishness. I'd done it again—acted without thinking, and I'd be lucky if I could get myself out of it now. Oh, *why* didn't I think before I spoke? "You've stolen these animals," I said, my voice much lower and controlled than before.

The leader, who was tall and well-muscled, shared another glance with his companions. "They weren't stolen," he informed me, looking me over carefully. "They were spoils of war."

He continued speaking, but I didn't hear anything that was said. My entire body was going cold, the blood in my veins turning to ice as his words washed over me. Their implication was enough to make me feel faint, but the proof was right in front of me, in the form of the animals that bore the mark of my home. What Antony had been trying to tell me all along, what I refused to believe…

"M'lady? Perhaps you should sit. You look unwell." His hand found my shoulder, but I brushed him off without sparing him a glance.

"Of course I am unwell, you brute. Don't deign to touch me."

"Very well then. Tell me, are you traveling alone?"

My mind spun with the horror of what I'd learned and my breath began coming in short, sharp gasps. I couldn't make any sense of what he was asking me. The only word that made it through to my dazed brain was *alone*. God knew I'd never felt more alone in all my life.

"No, she is with me."

When I heard Antony's quiet yet strong voice, I turned my head at the sound of it. For the first time, I was so happy to see him that I longed to run to him and pitch myself in his arms. I would have done, if my feet hadn't melded to the ground I stood on.

"I see." Though I didn't turn my head, I could feel the other man sizing Antony up. "You ended up with better spoils than we did, friend."

I tensed at the words, even though I saw Antony smile easily.

"Perhaps you would not think so if you knew what a tongue lashing the lady can deliver."

The other men snorted laughter and the leader replied only with, "Perhaps. A good horse is as valuable as a good woman, I always say."

"Well said, friend. Is there any way I can help you?"

"Yes, as a matter of fact, we've gotten turned around somehow. We're on our way to Amshire and were looking for a place to rest our heads for an evening."

"Ah, well, you're headed in the right direction. Only an hour's ride down this road and you'll find a quiet inn. The rooms aren't much to speak of, but the food will keep you warm and full."

"Many thanks to you. M'lady," he said, nodding in my direction.

"Wait." I swallowed hard, already fearing the answer to the question I knew I must ask. "Did you… the Duke of Württemberg. Do you have any news of him?"

"Ah, the Duke of Württemberg, you say? As a matter of fact, I'd heard that he was mortally wounded fleeing the battle. Was he a friend of yours, my lady?"

Fleeing the battle. So, he'd come for me, after all. He must have assumed I'd ridden for Hohenzollern, and instead of me, he'd found a battle and his untimely end. "No," I answered, feeling hollow deep down inside where my heart should be.

"Then perhaps it's nothing to you that he's dead. Thank you again for your assistance."

I didn't trouble to make a reply and instead watched as he climbed in the saddle and snapped the reins. In moments he and his companions were out of sight. I stared after them without truly seeing. My mind was spinning with what I'd learned and all of the emotions that came with it. I simply couldn't believe it.

Nearly as soon as they'd vanished, Antony turned to me, and I could see in a glance that he was not well pleased. If I'd had any doubts, his first words to me would have alleviated them. "What did I tell you specifically *not* to do, Cecily?"

For one moment, I felt like a scolded child. I was ready to give him an abashed apology when I remembered that I was still angry. I was more than that—I was shocked and hurt and grieving and I wouldn't be spoken to in such a manner. "Have a care for the way you address me, sir. I don't think I like your tone."

He regarded me with stern gray eyes that any other time would have brought me to heel. "Indeed? Well, I don't care for the way you disregard my instructions. Which were, if you recall, *not* to speak to strangers who might come riding by."

"And who are *you* to order one such as me?" I demanded, narrowing my eyes and drawing myself to my full height.

"Your protector, in case you haven't been paying attention."

"And that gives you the right—"

"I told you, Cecily. You're to be my wife. That gives me every right."

"Perhaps I don't care to be your wife!" I said with a little toss of my hair. I wanted to hurt him—God help me, he'd been nothing but considerate to me in every instance, but my heart was bleeding and I wanted someone to hurt the way I did, even if it was only to the smallest degree.

"Very well," he answered with the bland aplomb I'd become accustomed to. "Be that as it may, so long as we travel together you need to follow my instructions. We've had this conversation before."

"They were riding on Hohenzollern horses!" I exclaimed, my words running together in an angry hiss. "What was I to do? Ignore their impudence?"

"Yes, my lady. That is exactly what you were to do." Though I had no doubt that he meant what he said, his voice held a measure of regret. "I feel for your situation, Cecily. Please believe me, I do. But you won't do anything but harm if you keep accosting every man that displeases you. And Cecily… I truly am sorry for your loss."

I was still trying to assess my own feelings about what I'd learned and certainly wasn't ready to discuss it. "Did you bring the firewood?" I asked, my voice mulish.

Antony stared at me with a firm gaze that made me drop my eyes and turn away. "As a matter of fact, no. I came back when I heard the horses. I had a feeling that, despite my explicit instructions, you would manage to get yourself into trouble."

"Well, then you worried for nothing. As you can see, I'm fine."

"Yes. But I wonder, do you think that would still be the case if I hadn't come along?"

I folded my arms across my chest, turned my back on him, and refused to answer.

Antony did not speak for a long moment and when he did, his voice was gruff. "I am going to see to that firewood now. Though I know you won't heed me, I feel I must tell you once more to stay out of sight."

I didn't answer, but it didn't seem that he'd expected me to, because the next thing I knew, he was gone. Strangely, once I'd been left all alone, the anger drained out of me until I felt as sad and hollow as a shell. My legs gave way beneath me and I found myself crumpling to the ground. My breath left my body in a long, anguished cry before I began heaving with sobs.

It couldn't be true—it couldn't, and yet, it must be. Antony had tried to tell me, but I'd been too stubborn to hear him, convinced that he would only say those things to hurt me. But now that I'd heard from someone else… seen with my own two eyes the proof, it was indisputable. My home was gone. There would be no escaping from Antony, for even if I could, there was nowhere I might return. The castle I'd grown up in was taken, the life I'd once led was no more.

All the faces of the people I'd once known flashed before my mind's eye in a blur. My ladies-in-waiting. Susanna. What had become of them? Would they have been raped, or even… killed? The thought was too horrible to bear, and soon I was doubled over with heaving sobs that seemed to go on and on until I feared that they would never abate. Finally, I caught my breath, and with it I got control of myself. I couldn't stay here, crying on the cold, wet ground. I had to get up. I had to *do* something. Even if the only thing I could do was find wood for the fire.

That was how Antony found me when he returned, on my knees and brushing snow off icy leaves to scout for twigs. "Cecily! Whatever are you doing?" he demanded as he marched toward me.

"I'm looking for firewood," I explained as I accepted the hand he extended. After he'd helped me up, I began brushing the dirt and leaves from my gown, not even taking notice of the filth. What did it matter now? I would be going to a place where no one cared how fine my gown was, or if my headdress was in the latest fashion—which was good, for I had none.

"Why do you trouble yourself with things I've told you I will worry about?" he asked, sounding more than a little irritable.

But of course he would be. I'd been nothing but trouble for him from the very start. "Forgive me, sir. I didn't mean to anger you." I'd spoken in my humblest voice, and I could see that he'd taken notice. After I'd spoken, he also seemed to be taking notice of my tear-streaked face. Embarrassed, I turned away from him.

He laid a hand on my shoulder and I did not shrink away. "What is it? Are you feeling alright?"

"I…" I took a deep breath and my lip quavered. How did I explain to him that I'd only just realized what he'd known for days—what he himself had tried to tell me? "I'm just thinking of my home, that is all."

"Ah." He gave me a pat on my shoulder and didn't push any further as he dropped his hand and walked away to begin to lay the fire.

Strangely, I found that I wanted nothing less than the fate of being left alone to my thoughts, so I turned around and began to help. I began to fill my arms with the wood he'd found and when I brought it to him, he thanked me sweetly. Only on my way back to the woodpile did I notice a small bundle of twigs that lay separate from the rest. For some reason, seeing them made me still in my tracks.

"What are these?" I asked, striving to keep my voice light though my heart began thudding ominously.

I could feel Antony's eyes on me as he answered. "They're switches. I want you to pick one."

I swallowed hard. "Why?"

"Firstly, because I asked you to, my lady. As to what it will be used for, I think you already know. However, I could show you, if you like."

I'd begun shaking my head long before he'd ceased speaking. "No, thank you," I whispered, unable to take my eyes off them. "It's not necessary."

"I thought not." I watched silently for a few moments as he worked on the fire. Once he had a small blaze, he turned to me once more. "Come, little dove. Warm yourself by the fire."

I thought of saying that I was not his servant to order around, but I had been drained of every emotion, which robbed me of even my oft impertinent tongue. As such, I walked toward him and sat down on a fallen log in front of the small blaze, watching as he tried to coax it higher by adding the dry leaves he found to the flames.

"It's been a hard day for you," he acknowledged, his eyes on the fire.

"It has." My voice was soft and defeated.

"I'm sorry for it, my lady."

I couldn't help it—a laugh broke free from my lips before I knew what was happening. I smothered it quickly, but not before he noticed. "Why ever should you be?" I queried. "I am the one who has lost everything."

"Yes, and that is why I am sorry, Cecily." This time, he looked directly into my eyes as he spoke. "Do you think it gives me any joy to see your pain?"

"What were you doing at the castle that day?" The words came tumbling out before I knew I was going to say them. "Were you there to steal horses too?" The question propelled me to my feet, and I began to pace, struggling not to set free the tears that prickled my eyes. "But that doesn't make any sense! How could you have known what would happen?

"Cecily, come, sit back down." His tone was warm and inviting, but I refused to be swayed.

"I demand to know," I told him, keeping my voice as strong as I could manage.

"Ah, I see. And who commands me? Is it Cecily, Duchess of Hohenzollern, or the frightened widow I saw only moments ago?"

"I suppose… I suppose if what you say is true, those people are one in the same." I did not turn back to look at him and there was a silence that seemed to stretch on forever as Antony let my words hang in the air between us.

"No, my lady," he answered at last, "I was not there to steal the horses. I was sent as a scout for the Holy Roman Empire. I was to report back and tell my findings on whatever I could spot. How many horses, for example, the condition of the armory."

When I turned to him, moving so slowly that I hardly moved at all, all the blood had drained from my face. "You… you are my enemy."

"You have always thought it so," Antony replied levelly. "Why should learning this make you look at me in such a manner?"

Yes, indeed—why? I didn't know the answer to that, and my head was spinning with the new information, so much so that I didn't know what to think. "How dare you?" I managed at last, my voice as soft and fragile as a whisper. "You…"

"I what?"

You made me think—even if it was just for a moment—that you cared for me, I answered silently. I didn't even know when I'd begun to think so. Perhaps I hadn't until right that very moment, but the realization was followed by a swifter one: that no matter what he'd said, what reassurances he'd given, everything he'd said had been a lie. "Never mind. I'm tired. Are we going to ride on or stop for the day?" I could feel his eyes on me, appraising, but I could not bring myself to meet them.

"Cecily—"

My head snapped up and I regarded him with an icy glare. "Do not call me that. Only a friend can call me by my given name, and you, sir, are no friend of mine."

"As you wish, my lady." When he answered, Antony sounded just as forlorn as I felt. For a tiny instant, I longed to comfort him, but I immediately pushed that inclination aside. He didn't deserve it.

CHAPTER FIVE

When I'd awoken the next morning, cold and stiff, I'd found Antony had already risen and was cooking fish over a fire. We hadn't spoken another word to each other since his revelations and I wasn't feeling inclined to change that. Yet, the sight of him sitting alone at the fireside made me ache in a way I couldn't understand. What was *wrong* with me? He'd played a part in my family's destruction... I'd thought of him as my captor, my jailer, but it was more than that. He was Judas—he had betrayed my family, and for what?

Not having known my father very well, I didn't think of him often. Yet watching Antony, I thought of him then. My father had been a warrior too. I had a memory of him coming home from battle, and the weariness on his face had nearly torn out my heart. I'd watched silently as my mother fretted over him, pulling his boots off and wiping his brow, even though they'd had servants that could have tended to such things.

"Are you hurt, my love?" I'd heard her whisper.

"Not anywhere that can be seen by the human eye," he'd replied with a smile that was hardly a smile at all. Even as a child, I'd known he'd only done it for her benefit. "War is such a dirty, terrible thing, Katherine."

I'd been a child and unable to make much sense of his words at the time. But now, looking at Antony, I wondered at what he'd said. Perhaps, in his own way, Antony felt as my father did. Did I owe him the chance to explain himself?

Just then, he turned his head and saw me staring. Not having decided my next course of action, I froze in place.

"Come, you must be cold and hungry. Come sit by me."

For a moment, he sounded just as wearied as my father had that day. I could see no other alternative—I *was* cold, and my stomach was so empty it hurt. So I took a seat beside him and accepted the fish he offered on a tin plate. I ate, and even though it didn't taste very palatable, I continued to eat, as much to fill my belly as to keep from talking. When I'd eaten it down to the bones, there was nothing left to do but wipe my hands on the bark of the trunk and look at Antony. He was poking the fire with a stick and seemed just as content to avoid talking to me as I was to him.

"We should get riding soon," he said, looking toward the sky that was brightening as the sun began to rise.

"Where are we going?" It was a question I had yet to raise, but he didn't seem in the least surprised.

"I had planned to take you home with me."

There was a frank vulnerability in his voice that mere days ago I would have attacked. Feeling so raw from the rush of emotions I'd had the day before, I didn't have it in me to exploit anyone. "What will I do there? What kind of life can I truly make for myself out in the countryside?"

"I suppose that's something you're going to have to find out for yourself, Cecily. Tomorrow we will reach a small town about a day's ride from my house. There, I hope to find a priest."

"A priest?" I echoed, dropping my eyes to my hands in my lap.

"Yes. I had hoped…"

It was not like Antony to be shy, and for some reason my belly began to churn with a nervous energy that I couldn't explain. "Hoped what?"

"I'd thought… well, that is, I'd like… I wanted you to become my wife."

The air whooshed out of me for the second time in as many days, though when I contemplated his words, I realized that I had expected this. Did I want to become his wife, especially after what I had learned?

"I am not going to force you to marry me, if that is what you fear," he was quick to assure me. "If we marry, then you will have to consent. But I feel you should know that if we enter into such a contract, I expect you to respect and obey me always, regardless of the situation."

"You do not seem to require a marriage contract to expect such things." Out of the corner of my eye, I saw Antony smile at my dry remark. I went back to staring at my hands, unsure how to respond. He was the enemy, and he'd stolen me away from my home that was no more. Perhaps if he hadn't, I would have gotten away with my cousin, or my mother, or… but I had not. Still, despite the spanking I had mentioned, he had not mistreated me. He had not forced himself upon me, or struck me even when my tongue warranted it.

"What would you expect?"

"Excuse me?" I queried, startled out of my thoughts.

"If we were to marry, what would your expectations be?"

I had never been asked such a thing before, not by my mother, and certainly not by my husband. I did not have the first idea how to respond, but Antony seemed content to wait. "Do you truly believe my husband is dead?" I asked at last, my voice as soft as the whisper of the morning wind.

"Yes, my lady. I am sorry for your loss, but it is nearly certain, especially since he was in Her Majesty's army."

I nodded, no more moved by these words than by his expectation that we should wed. "Why did you take me that day?" The question escaped my lips before I could reconsider. Once the question was out there, it hung between us, in the delicate balance of what the future would hold.

Antony considered carefully, as though he knew the great importance of his answer. And of course, he must have, because Antony always seemed to know such things. "I couldn't bear to leave you there." When he answered, his voice was gruff with emotion. "Knowing as I did what was coming. It took but one look at you for me to see that…"

"That I'm beautiful," I answered, my voice wooden.

"Oh, you're beautiful, there is no doubt of that. You are as pretty as the princess herself is rumored to be, but that is not what I meant, my lady. No, I took one look at you and I saw your fiery spirit, your tender heart. I knew that you'd undoubtedly fight when the army came, just as I knew that your side would have to lose." He paused here, as if to allow my objection, but I was too focused on what he was saying to make one. "In that one moment, I saw a hundred possibilities of what might become of you, and I couldn't allow it."

"Did it ever occur to you that I might prefer to die where I stood, with my family, than to be taken by a stranger?"

"Of course it occurred to me, Cecily," he answered, his voice as gentled as though he spoke to a babe. "And just as soon as it had, I knew that I could not allow it. I'm afraid you must forgive me for it, if it offends you."

I weighed his words against the level calm with which he watched me, and I knew him to be sincere. When I searched for my own feelings, I found that I was not nearly as angry at him as I would have liked to be. I delved deep to find a scorching remark or quelling glare, but I could summon neither. Instead, I bowed my head and answered, "I will need time to think."

"Of course," he replied, in the same gentle, considerate voice. "As you wish, my lady. If you've finished breaking your fast, we should ready ourselves for the day's journey."

Nothing more needed to be said, and we stood and began preparing to depart. Though Antony did not seem angered by my response—or lack of one—there was a teneness between us, a bevy of things that had been left unsaid. As we rode, my mind was plagued with thoughts that would not be dismissed, no matter how hard I tried. I thought of the life I'd once led, as a duchess. It was all I'd ever been raised to want and I was carrying the duke's child. That should have made me the happiest woman in all the kingdom, but I'd been far from happy. Then, that night I'd seen him with that slender harlot on his lap… the memory still caused bile to rise to my throat. He had dared to humiliate me in front of the entire court, simply because he could.

I could not imagine Antony ever doing such a thing. I'd known him for such a small time, and yet, couldn't I say the same of Wallace? It was how such things were done. Antony did not possess a single drop of royal blood, and yet, he was the only man who'd ever told me I had the right to choose. Where would I go, if I did not become his wife? Somehow, I sensed even without asking that he would find a place for me and honor his word to never force me.

Yet, he was the enemy. How could I feel anything but contempt for someone who had helped destroy the only life I'd ever known? Who had destroyed my family?

Just then, I felt a short, sharp kick in my ribs that made me draw in my breath loudly. I looked down at my rounding belly and slowly, a smile of wonder spread across my face. It was the babe inside me, making its presence known.

"My lady?"

I looked up at the concern in Antony's voice and saw that he'd drawn his horse up next to mine and taken the reins so that my horse would stop.

"Are you unwell?"

"No," I answered, my smile growing as I looked at him. "Not at all."

I could see by his expression that he did not believe me. "Perhaps we should take a brief rest."

"Antony!" I protested with a laugh. "We've only just begun to ride."

"Yes, but…" He trailed off slowly as he looked at me, and then a smile broke across his face as well. "Do you realize that is the first time you've ever said my name?"

"Surely not," I objected with a shake of my head and another laugh.

"It 'tis. And I must confess, Duchess, that the only thing I can think of is how to make you say it again."

I dropped my eyes shyly, looking once more at my growing stomach. The gown hid it well, but I knew that my child was there, biding his time until he would make his appearance in the world. The thought filled me with an unspeakable joy that I could not contain. "You… you asked me what I would expect."

"Yes, my lady. Have you had time to think?"

Had I had time to think? Was I even thinking clearly? Everything felt so wondrous and beautiful in this moment that it was hard to focus on the evil in the world, or the wrong that had been done to me. The heart of the matter was this: if Wallace was truly dead—and how would I ever discover otherwise?—I needed a husband. A woman of any position could not survive without one, and more importantly, I needed a father for the child I carried.

What kind of husband would Antony make? He seemed kind, but then, Wallace had seemed kind in the beginning, too. Despite how tenderly Antony cared for me, he too might turn on me. Yet, I knew that I did not truly have another viable option. Without Wallace, I had no standing. I was not a royal duchess any longer. I had no lands or wealth to pass on to the child I carried. There was nothing for me to do but agree.

"You asked me what I would require in a husband," I said once more, raising my head to look him straight in the eye. "I will promise to obey and respect you, and in return, I ask that you provide for me, protect me, and treat the child I will bear as your own." I spoke as matter-of-factly as I could, though there was no denying that I wished to turn and flee the moment the words were out. I'd never spoken of my baby before—neither, for that matter, had Antony, though I realized that even though I was not beginning to show, he might at least suspect that I was with child. But if I were going to marry again, I had to lay out my concerns now before vows were said between us.

Rather than answering, Antony dismounted his horse and swung me down from mine in one swift movement. Then he shocked me further by dropping down on a knee in front of me and taking my hand in his. "I solemnly give you my word that I will do these things. As my wife, you may not have the comforts you are accustomed to, but you will never go hungry or be without a roof over your head. I will raise your child as though it were mine, be it male or female."

"Thank you," I murmured humbly.

"It is my pleasure, my lady. Only, it surprises me that you do not speak of love."

"Love?" I tried to laugh, but found that I could not manage it. "It has been my experience that love is not often a term of marriage, sir."

"I see. Perhaps, in time, you will come to love me."

"Perhaps." I wished I could offer him more, but just then I could not see how I would ever grow to love him or he me. We were enemies, and nothing would change that, not truly. No matter how well we might live together, or even if I bore his children, I'd always know in the back of my mind what he was. I'd always know that my son or daughter had him to blame for the death of their father, at least in part. Yet, I pushed these thoughts aside and ventured a tiny smile.

When Antony saw it, he bent his head and brought his lips to my hand. "I promise that I shall do my best to ensure that you never have cause to regret it."

"And you accuse *me* of not speaking of love," I said wryly.

"Shall we ride on, my lady?"

There was no denying the renewed spark in his eyes and I couldn't help it—I found myself pulled into his gaze, forgetting, even if it was just for a moment, that he was my enemy.

· · · · · · ·

That night we sought shelter in a barn owned by a kindly farmer along the road. Once upon a time, I would have been quite indignant at even the suggestion, but a night on the hard ground had changed my expectations. I doubted I would ever stop longing for my soft down bed, but I did my best to push thoughts of it aside.

The farmer's wife had even gone so far as to bring us each a serving of fresh eggs and a side of ham, along with cups of sweet milk. My stomach had rumbled embarrassingly at the sight of the food, and while all I'd managed to do was blush, Antony thanked her for her hospitality.

"You see?" he teased as he sat beside me on the barn floor. "Farmers' wives aren't so bad after all."

"Hmph," I grumbled, ignoring the remark as I began to eat. Yet, for all my protest, there was no denying that something had changed between us and I had no idea what to do about it. Perhaps it had happened when I'd accepted his proposal of marriage and had come to realize that I would spend the rest of my life tethered to his. Whatever the reason, I was seeing him in an entirely different light, no matter how many times I tried to remind myself that I should hate him.

Antony said nothing more as I ate, and to my surprise, when I finished he put half his portion on my plate.

"What is this?" I asked, looking at him with wide eyes.

"I find I'm not very hungry. I wouldn't want to be wasteful."

I knew it for a lie the moment the words were out of his mouth, yet I couldn't deny my hunger, which gnawed at me as though I were being eaten away from the inside. So I bent my head over the plate and murmured my thanks before I began to eat once more.

"You know, I do believe that's the first time you've ever thanked me for anything." His voice was light and teasing and I found myself smiling at the sound of it.

"I shall thank you not to snore tonight, then," I commented between bites.

"I do not snore," he protested, bumping me playfully with his elbow.

"You do," I accused. "And if I am to become your lady wife, I demand you stop it at once."

"You *demand*, do you?"

I heard the mock-challenge in his voice and having eaten my fill, decided that I would rise to it. "Yes, and there is one other thing."

"I see. And what would that be?"

"This business of spanking me is much too foolish. Why, it's practically barbaric, and I won't stand for it!" The moment the words were out of my mouth, the air between us seemed to still. I felt my cheeks heat with a mixture of embarrassment and excitement. I didn't know what had caused me to bring it up at all. I should have been grateful that he had not chastised me since the first time, but for some reason, the thought of it now seemed to put an energy into me that I'd never before known existed.

"That's right, I'd nearly forgotten. How could I have been so careless?" Before I could say a word, Antony had taken the plate out of my hands and set it aside before putting me over his lap.

"What do you think you're doing?" I cried out, kicking my legs and trying to push myself up.

"If my memory is correct, I still owe you a thrashing."

My breath hitched and I could feel my nipples become taut against the bodice of my gown. "No, you musn't." Yet, the words came out sounding breathy and weak, and soon Antony was peeling my skirts back one by one, taking his time and chuckling as I squirmed over his lap.

"I musn't?" he echoed, his own voice husky and rich with desire that only fed my own. "Please, Cecily dear, tell me what else I musn't do?"

Before I'd had a chance to reply—with every layer of clothing that he touched, I was finding it harder and harder to concentrate—his hand came crashing down on my pantalets. It certainly wasn't soft, but it wasn't very hard either. He paused before delivering the next blow, which came down with just as much force as the first, causing me to whimper in a way that had nothing to do with pain. I wasn't sure what was happening to me. My cheeks were flushed, my breath was coming in small, shallow gasps, and with each and every firm spank that he landed on my clothing, the knots in my belly contracted and then loosened once more. It was a feeling unlike any I'd ever felt before. Was this what he spoke of when he talked of love? If so, I wasn't entirely sure that I liked it.

"Stop, Antony! Let me up!" I protested, writhing on his lap as I tried to sit up. He had a good hold on me, however, and I was kept right where he wanted me.

"Be a sweet, biddable maid and take your punishment," he returned, the teasing still present in his voice.

But I couldn't simply lie there and let him continue to make me feel things that were surely sinful. Each time his hand came down, smacking me soundly but leaving only a light, tingling pain, a rush of warmth filled my cheeks and ran down the length of my body until I was sure all of me must be aglow. If that wasn't of the devil, I didn't know what was.

"This isn't what it was like before," I murmured, so low that I was certain he wouldn't have heard me.

"What was it like?"

My cheeks warmed at once and I clamped my lips tightly together as he continued to give my bottom firm, slow spanks that stoked the fire growing inside of me.

"I said, what was it like, Cecily?"

"I don't know what you're referring to."

He answered me with a smattering of swift, hard spanks that surprised me with their sting.

"Ow!"

"Do not hold out on me, my dove. If I ask you a question, I expect an answer. I expect—"

"Obedience," I finished petulantly. "I know, I know."

I was quickly rewarded with a dozen of harder spanks that left me crying out and struggling to catch my breath. "That hurt!" I reproached, looking back at him over my shoulder.

"Thank you for telling me. It shall always hurt when you disobey me, my sweet."

"You can't do that," I scowled. "You can't call me your *sweet* one moment and thrash me the next!"

"Why ever not?" he queried, grinning unrepentantly.

"B-because!" I spluttered. "It's simply not done!"

"So far as you know," he countered. "Where I'm from, men rule their households, and their wives are dutiful and respectful, or their bottoms pay the price."

"Nonsense." To my utter surprise, the spanking stopped and I found myself being helped up until I was sitting on Antony's knee.

"It is nothing of the kind," he told me, his voice stern yet tender at the same time. "Men and women have been living this way for generations, even if it isn't something you saw in the castle of Hohenzollern."

"That doesn't mean *I* should have to," I said, but my voice did not sound nearly as strong as I would have liked.

"We have already had this conversation, Cecily. You will not play me false, my dear. If you vow to be my obedient wife, then I will hold you to your word." He softened the words by running his hand over my dark head. "However, it isn't as bad as you may think."

"I know exactly how bad it can be," I said. "I've felt your hand against my backside before."

"So you have. What I meant to say is that at least you will never wonder where you stand with me. I will do everything within my power to keep you happy and safe. As long as you do as you're bid, you needn't worry about anything."

He made it sound so easy, but I knew from experience that men often said one thing and did another. I supposed there wasn't a woman alive who didn't know that.

"And as for me not tending to your spanking yesterday, don't think I've forgotten. I simply thought, considering everything you learned, that you would appreciate a reprieve."

"Thank you."

"You're quite welcome. Unless... unless you'd *like* me to punish you?"

I should have said no. I should have thrown my head back and laughed at the absurdity of him saying such a thing, but even more absurd was the fact that I was thinking about it. If I'd only said, "Thank you, no," perhaps everything would have been different. But instead, I tilted my head back, looked into his light gray eyes and handsome face, and put my mouth very near his as I whispered, "Will it hurt?"

I knew I was getting to him when it took him a moment to answer. Something about that fact delighted me. I'd never thought of myself as being a beautiful woman before, but something about the way Antony studied my face, the way his eyes were drinking me in even now, told me he thought otherwise. And God help me, but enemy or no, I delighted in it.

He cleared his throat, but didn't break eye contact with me. "Yes, Cecily, it will hurt. You disobeyed me. You endangered yourself. If I am going to punish you for it, then you will receive exactly the kind of punishment you deserve. And yes, it will be a long thrashing, and yes, it will most certainly hurt."

Something told me that even then I could have demurred and gone to sleep. I should have, but I did not. "I think… I think that it would not be a good thing to begin our marriage with things left unsettled between us."

"I see."

The scrutiny in his warm eyes made me squirm. I was so uncertain as to whether or not I was doing the right thing. I had better be sure, because once I said I was, it was my bottom that would pay for it. As I looked at him—every strong curve of his handsome face—I realized that more than anything I wanted to trust him. I didn't, not entirely, but I was beginning to believe that it was possible for that to change. Perhaps in order to discover him trustworthy I had to extend a little trust.

"Please punish me, sir," I said at last, holding my breath as soon as the words were out of my mouth.

Antony leaned over and pressed a quick, reassuring kiss to the top of my head before answering, "As you wish. Please go to my saddle bag and retrieve the switches."

"You… you kept them?" I swallowed hard.

"I thought it would be wise."

Without another word I stood up, reluctant to leave the comforting warmth of his lap and equally reluctant to return to it, knowing I would then be over it. I took my time walking to his saddlebag and opened it slowly. A long switch was poking out the moment I pushed back the opening. When I slid my hand inside, I found two more next to the first. I took a deep breath and let it out slowly as I took them in hand, stiffening my spine against the inevitable. How silly I had been to ask for such a thing! Surely, there could even now be a reprieve if I asked for one? Yet, I knew that I wouldn't. I'd meant what I said: if I was going to marry again, I wanted to at least do what

I could to ensure that it might be an amicable one. I was beginning to think that was the best a woman could hope for.

"Pick one," he ordered, not unkindly, when I held them out to him.

"I… I'm not certain…" I looked down at the switches helplessly, not seeing much difference from one to the next. I was sure that they could each light a fire in my backside, so I didn't see much point to choosing between them. Yet, Antony had asked me to do it and I knew it was part of the punishment. After a few moments, I settled on the thinnest one of the three, hoping that since it was smaller it would hurt less.

Antony's face gave nothing away as I showed it to him. "Very good. Now, pray you don't ever give me cause to use it."

"I'm sorry? I don't think I understand."

"I'm not going to switch you this time, Cecily. I'd intended to, that's true, but given what you've been through, I would like to show you kindness. Now mind, that won't sway me if there is a need to punish you a second time."

"Yes, sir," I agreed, eager to be agreeable.

"Go put your choice back in my saddlebag, please. Then I want you to come stand in front of me and pull your pantalets down."

Just the thought made me blush so hotly that I feared my skin might stain permanently from the shame of it. "Sir?" I queried weakly.

"Put it in the saddlebag, Cecily," he ordered once more, clearly not intending to explain his instructions.

I hurried to do his bidding, but I felt my footsteps slowing upon the return. Slow or no, it was inevitable that I would end up standing in front of him, facing his inscrutable expression as he waited patiently for me to carry out the rest of his commands. I dropped my eyes to the straw on the ground, unable to look at him as I slid my hand beneath my gown and petticoats. I pulled my pantalets down as far as I was able and stood, my cheeks flaming as I waited for him to speak.

"Look at me, Cecily." His voice was firm and I felt my eyes being drawn to him despite myself.

"I can't bear it," I murmured. "Are you trying to humiliate me?"

"If it will keep you from disobeying me in the future, then yes."

I gasped at his pronouncement, but he held up a hand to silence me before I could reply.

"I only ask you to do things for your own good, Cecily. It is not my plan to degrade you or treat you as anything but the lady I believe you to be. However, when you chose to disobey me and thus endanger yourself, you will be subject to any punishment I deem fit. Now, tell me, why are you being chastised?"

"I… ah…" I could feel my cheeks blaze with such heat that it began to spread to my neck.

"Because you disobeyed me," he prompted. "You were told to stay put and avoid strangers, yet when men came riding by, you sought them out. You could have been hurt, Cecily. They could have had their way with you had I not been there."

"But you were," I protested weakly.

"And if I hadn't been?" he demanded, his voice suddenly sharp. "Do I need to further explain myself? They could have taken you with them, to God-knows-where. They could have raped you, each taking his turn before they left you lying on the ground. There are endless possibilities, each more horrifying than the last. I thank God I *was* there, but that in no way excuses you from the lashing you so richly deserve."

Before he stopped speaking my eyes were wide with realization. What he said was true. I could have been beaten or violated. I was so accustomed to having my word obeyed that I took careless risks that would have only served to get me hurt.

"Now, come here and take your spanking."

Tears had risen to my eyes while he'd been scolding me, but the pronouncement that my punishment was at hand made a lone tear streak down my cheek. Still, I moved toward him and placed myself as gracefully as I could manage over his lap.

Antony immediately peeled back my petticoats, exposing my naked skin to the cool night air. "You'll remember that I told you last time that if I needed to punish you again, it would be on the bare."

"Yes, sir," I replied, trying unsuccessfully to hide the tremor in my voice. It was matched by the one shaking my body.

"Are you afraid of me, Cecily?" he asked suddenly, sounding so concerned that it took me aback.

"No, sir."

"Truly?"

"Truly—I fear only your hand."

"As it should be, my dove. When you deserve it I will always endeavor to teach you a memorable lesson. I can promise you that."

"Why is every promise you make me in regards to a sore bottom?" I should have minded the mulishness in my tone, because Antony responded by three swift, sharp cracks of his hand to my bottom that had me wincing and mewling in pain.

"Because they are the kind of promises that suit you, my lady. Now, remind me why I am punishing you, Cecily."

"Because... because I disobeyed you," I whispered.

His hand came down hard on my quivering flesh, bouncing from one cheek to the next as he exacted justice for my sins. Each smack of his hand was firmer than the one before it and the desire to kick my legs and try to escape was nearly irrepressible. It was only his strong arm looped around my waist that kept me from trying.

"What else, Cecily?"

It was hard for me to concentrate on the sound of his voice. Right then, it was hard for me to think of anything other than my aching arse and the tears that I was trying to blink back. "Ah…"

Two hard, resounding swats on each of my cheeks had me gasping and arching my back. "Think hard, if you must."

"I… I brought attention to myself."

"It was a dangerous thing to do, was it not, sweeting?"

At that very moment, I began to wonder if I wouldn't have been safer with the looters than with Antony. I very much doubted my bottom would be in such agony! However, I knew better than to say so aloud. "Y-yes," I answered, tears beginning to roll down my cheeks.

"All I endeavor to do is to keep you safe, my lady." With that, the spanking resumed, his hard hand coming down again and again until I thought I could bear it no longer.

"I'll be good!" I cried out, a sob lodging in my throat. "Please, I beg you! It shan't happen again!"

"I intend to see to it that you keep that promise, Your Grace."

I should have told him that no one would ever dare spank a duchess. That I had learned my lesson well, that it hurt too much. I should have told him something, anything to make it stop, but as I cried, words were lost to me, turned instead to piteous moans which only grew in frequency and volume as his hand continued to punish my hot, defenseless cheeks.

And part of me kept my silence because I knew, in truth, that I deserved the punishment I was receiving at his hands. He was right: I could have been raped, or worse. I could be *dead*, and my baby would have suffered the same fate. That in itself was worthy of receiving a sore bottom. The other part of me said nothing because I realized that Antony was the only man in my life who'd ever cared enough about me to correct me. I knew he would not play me false. He meant what he said—he spanked me because he didn't want to see anything bad befall me. How humbling it was to be loved like that, especially when I'd done nothing to merit such kindness.

As his hand continued to work its way up and down my hot, aching flesh, something within me broke. Suddenly, the dam of sobs I'd been storing up inside me burst free and I was crying my heart out as though I would never, ever stop. Everything—my marriage to Wallace and the way he'd begun to shun me, being taken from my home—all the things that I'd refused to cry about came pouring out in long, shuddering sobs and piercing wails. It wasn't until I was spent from crying and was lying limply over Antony's lap that I even realized he'd stopped spanking me.

"Do you feel better, my lady?" he asked as he helped me sit up.

A mewl of pain escaped my parted lip as my inflamed flesh landed on his hard leg. "I… I believe so. I'm… I'm sorry."

"Shh, sweeting. Everything is alright now. You were very brave to take such a hard spanking." He emphasized his words with a kiss pressed to my forehead. "Now, tell me, Cecily—do you still wish to be my wife?"

"What?" I blinked up at him through watery eyes.

"Tell me truly, my dove, for I shall only ask you this once. Do you wish to marry me? If you're only going to say the vows so that you will have a home, let me assure you that I never would leave you out in the cold. I can arrange a place for you. You'll have to learn to work to earn your keep, but marriage isn't something you should enter into because you feel forced to do so."

If it wouldn't have been so unladylike, I would have gaped at him. Antony may not have been of noble blood, but I didn't think I'd ever met a more chivalrous man. It was that, combined with how safe I felt in the shelter of his arms, that allowed me to confess. "I'm afraid of marriage."

"Afraid? Whatever should you have to fear, Cecily?"

"I... I lied to you, before." Knowing that I'd just been punished for that very thing, I swallowed hard before I continued. "My marriage to the duke... it was not what I said. He... he did not much care for me, I think."

"I find that hard to believe," he murmured, his mouth soft against my ear and his words softer still.

"No, I fear it's quite true. I caught him in bed with a maid, and he humiliated me for it. He reveled in my humiliation, in fact."

"Oh, my poor, poor little dove," Antony cooed, his arms going tighter around me. "You have had to endure so much."

"For that reason," I continued, keeping my voice as strong as I could manage despite the tears that threatened, "I can't say I relish the prospect of being a wife once more."

"I see." He began to stroke my hair and, like a cat, I tilted my head back to allow him access. "I can't promise you that you will always enjoy being my wife, my lady. There is the matter of discipline, which I insist upon, as you know. And you will have to work hard, I won't deny it. But I will always strive to make you happy, if I can."

It would have to be enough. I knew that, in every fiber of my being: what Antony offered would have to be enough for me. Besides which, he truly was the kindest man I'd ever met. I honestly believed that other than a hot backside, he would never hurt me. In the end, wasn't a smacked bottom better than a bruised heart?

"Yes, my lord." It was the first time I'd ever said such a thing, and I could feel Antony's smile even if I didn't look up to see it. "I shall be your wife."

CHAPTER SIX

The farmer's wife had sent us off with saddlebags full of bread, apples, a side of meat, and even a small jug of ale. From the moment she looked at me, I was sure that she'd heard my wailing as Antony had spanked me, and I couldn't bear to look her in the eye.

Antony had thanked her and pressed a few coins into her hand as payment before helping me into the saddle. "Are you feeling well?"

I considered the question. My arse throbbed horridly, and I sensed that it would only grow worse after long hours in the saddle. Yet, despite that, my heart felt lighter than it had in days. I'd cried until my eyes were red and my throat was raw, but somehow I found myself smiling shyly at Antony when I woke in the morning. "Yes, thank you."

"Good." He gave my waist a squeeze before he released his hold on me. "We won't be riding too hard today considering your… ah… condition."

I blushed to hear him mention my spanked bottom and was thankful that the farmer's wife had already departed and wasn't there to witness my flushed cheeks. "Thank you."

"I thought we'd stay at an inn tonight. Would you like that?"

The prospect of an actual bed and a fire, perhaps even a bath, was too wonderful for words, though I was sure my beaming smile was sufficient a message of gratitude.

"Then, after we break our fast, we will ride for my farm. We should be there before dinner time."

I watched as Antony mounted his animal. He had such a fluid, easy grace. How had I never noticed it before? He straddled the animal with confidence—the same way he did everything. My eyes took in his long legs and traveled upward, to the hard thighs I'd been bent over to take my punishment the night before. I caught myself wondering what he would look like out of his jerkin and trousers. No sooner than the question crossed my mind, Antony looked back at me and I dropped my eyes, feeling my face flame with heat as though he could read my thoughts.

I shouldn't be thinking of him in such a manner! Yes, soon he would be my husband, but even so, it was indecent! I'd certainly never thought of Wallace in that way, even after we'd bedded many a time. My shame was only heightened when I recalled that the nobility had always talked—behind closed doors, of course—of the peasants' wantonness. Surely that was why they had so many children—more than they could ever hope to feed! Was that what was happening to me? Was spending time with Antony and coming to have feelings for him changing me?

"Are you ready to ride, my lady?"

His husky voice broke me out of my thoughts and I found myself smiling even before I'd begun to nod my assent. If Antony was changing me, I decided, it was only for the better.

• • • • • • •

Though we stopped riding long before we normally did, by the time we reached the inn my backside felt like it had been lit on fire. I was grateful when Antony came to lift me out of the saddle. "Do you think a bath might be possible?" I ventured as we walked inside.

"Tonight, you shall have anything that is within my power to give, sweeting."

His words warmed me and I was smiling by the time we approached the innkeeper. "I require a room for the evening," he told the wizened man. "And perhaps you might tell me where I can find a priest?"

His eyes darted back and forth between the two of us, seeming to read my flushed cheeks and Antony's smile in but a moment. "Ye'll be wanting to speak to Bishop Williams, then." He gave us directions, chuckling as Antony took my hand and guided me from the inn.

"Let's walk," he suggested once we'd gotten outside. "It's close by, and it will give the horses a rest."

I nodded my assent. I couldn't imagine how walking could be any worse than riding. Though Antony seemed content to walk alongside me without a word, I found my nerves mounting with every step we took. A marriage contract was nothing to enter into lightly, but somehow knowing that I had feelings for him made it almost more difficult. It was true that I had few options available to me, but the more my heart warmed toward him, the more I worried. Inevitably, he would tire of me, and what happened when the sweet words and kind smiles were nothing but a distant memory? This time, my heart would truly bleed, for I would have already given it to him.

Yet, I found that I could not say any of these things. When the time came, I did as I'd vowed to and stood beside him, saying "I do" in a voice that was clear and rang through the room like a bell. The smile Antony gave me as he squeezed my hand made my heart flutter with hope.

It was done in minutes, finished with a prayer led by the bishop, and then we were once more on our way back to the inn. It had taken no time at all, certainly not the amount of time that should be required to commit yourself to one person for the rest of your life. Antony was so cheerful he practically strutted, the veil of silence seeming to have lifted now that the deed was done.

"A hot meal will do us both good," he commented as we made our way back to the inn. "I would love a good piece of fish, but it will probably be stew." I could feel his eyes on me but couldn't bring myself to reply. "Come, now." He bumped me playfully with his shoulder. "It's your turn to guess."

"I don't know. Mutton, perhaps."

"I can see you're not in the spirit of the game." His eyes shone at me, filled to the brim with a happy light. "Are you alright?"

"Yes." I made myself smile for his benefit. "I'm fine." Truth be told, I *was* fine—it was only that I was consumed with thoughts that had nothing at all to do with food. In fact, for the first time in a fortnight I felt like I wouldn't be able to eat a bite. The only thing I could think of was the wedding night. I hadn't very much enjoyed performing the duties of a wife, but I knew that it must be done.

Antony and I were greeted by the innkeeper with hearty congratulations and the news that a small cake had been prepared in our honor. The man pinched my cheek and laughed as I blushed. Antony was full of smiles and kind words for every person that stopped us to offer congratulations.

When Wallace and I had married, we'd had a wedding feast, as was the custom. The meal that Antony and I shared together could hardly be called such, and yet, it was a warm, enjoyable affair. All the patrons of the inn gathered around us and filled the evening with lively conversation and innocent jests that, after a time, made me forget my fear. It was not long before the cake was served, which Antony cut into small pieces so that everyone present could sample some.

I watched my new husband with awe. He was among his people now, and it was clear to see that he was a true leader. He could make them laugh, and he listened with rapt attention each time anyone spoke and genuinely seemed to care about each and every one. Long before the meal was over, I found myself feeling a certain sense of pride concerning Antony.

After the cake had been eaten, my cup was filled with wine and I was urged to drink. It went straight to my head, which seemed to be the point as the guests present laughed at my flushed face. I joined in the laughter, happy to be a part of the merriment. One man began to play a fiddle and another had a flute. Before long, the room was full of dancing and Antony was quick to pull me to the center of the room and spin me around until I was dizzy with the dancing and drink.

"Oh ho!" he exclaimed, cradling me in his arms when I swooned. "Not too light on your feet tonight, my dove?"

"It's your fault," I accused, my words slurring slightly. "You only wanted a reason to catch me."

He leaned forward until our lips were nearly touching. "Guilty as charged," he murmured, moments before his mouth met mine. In another life, I would have been horrified to cause such a scandal. Yet, in this moment, with this man, I knew no shame. I kissed him back with all the passion I felt, hardly hearing the hoots of laughter and encouragement that surrounded us.

When we pulled apart, Antony's eyes sparkled brighter than before. "I think it's time we were to bed, wife."

"As you wish, my husband."

Antony thanked the people who had dined with us, waving off their invitation to see us to bed. Then, with an arm protectively around my waist, he led me to our room. "I got you a gown," he surprised me by saying.

"You did? When?"

"You recall I bought a replacement harness for your mare? I picked up a few supplies while I was there."

"How thoughtful," I remarked, pleased that he'd thought of me. When he showed me the gown, nothing more than a plain cotton garment with only a strip of lace for decoration, I thought it the prettiest thing I'd ever seen, simply for the thought he'd put into it. I began to unbutton my dress but quickly found that my fingers were slippery and useless.

"Here, let me," he suggested huskily as he stepped behind me.

"I normally have someone to help me," I admitted.

"Now you have me to help you. There is no shame in asking your husband for help. That is why I am here."

True to his word, Antony unbuttoned me from top to bottom and helped me step out of the gown without complaint. Wallace had much preferred to rip the fabric from my body. Though I tried to push thoughts of my first husband out of my mind, today of all days it was hard not to compare them.

Antony said nothing as he helped me from my chemise and then slid the nightgown over my head. Only when it was in place did he smile and lean forward to kiss my lips. "You look beautiful, my dove. I knew it would suit you."

"Thank you." I dipped my head, humbled by his gesture and the compliment.

"You must be exhausted, sweeting. Let's put you to bed."

It was not until he'd tucked me into the soft bed—which felt remarkably better than the hard ground, particularly where my sore arse was concerned—that I realized that he truly did intend to sleep. I waited for him to say or do anything that would show another intention, but when he slid underneath the blankets alongside me I realized that he was not planning on bedding me. To my surprise, I found myself feeling disappointed. Did he not want me? How could that be possible? Surely he'd only married me so that he could lie with me as a husband would.

"Are you unwell, my dove?" Antony asked as I shifted in bed for the tenth time. "Can you not sleep?"

I wasn't sure that I was going to say anything, but when I opened my mouth to reply, I found the words tumbling out. "I thought you would wish to consummate our union."

"I see. I thought given your... condition, and the long ride today... I assumed you'd rather not."

"Our marriage is not valid before the eyes of God until we lie together as man and wife."

"Is that what worries you, Cecily? I told you that I would honor you and protect you as a husband should. I will keep that vow regardless of whether or not we consummate our union this night."

"You don't want me then," I said flatly.

The bed shifted as he sat up. "Is that what you think, wife? Don't let such falsehoods sully your lips again, or I am afraid I will have to clean them with soap."

The threat made me shiver in a way that I found strangely erotic. "You are the one who is talking of sleep," I pointed out.

"Yes, I wanted to have a care for your condition. Forgive me, next time I shall simply pull your gown up and have my way with you."

"Indeed," I rejoined, catching his teasing tone. "Do you intend to marry me a second time?"

With a sound somewhere between a growl and a primal yell, Antony lunged for me. In mere moments his mouth seized me and I knew at once that this kiss would be quite different from the other. It was a hard, possessive kiss that stole my breath and left my heart fluttering madly. When Antony pulled away, I could see his face in the light of the candle by the bedside and he looked decidedly unrepentant.

"Wait here," he commanded, his voice throaty. "I have something that will teach you to mind your tongue."

I smiled in the darkness, my heart feeling lighter still as he climbed from the bed and padded across the room. I did not know what he was in search of, but it did not matter. The only thing that mattered was the way he looked at me, the way he kissed me—as though he would never get enough of the sight of me, the feel of me. I'd never been loved like that.

"Did you miss me?" he asked upon his return.

"The loneliness was horrid," I said with a breathy little giggle that made him lean down and kiss me once more. When he sat back up, I saw that he held a black strap in his hand. The sight of it made me gasp. "Husband?"

"Don't worry, my dove," he crooned, caressing the side of my face. "You aren't being chastised tonight. Well, only lightly, at any rate."

"What is it for?" I asked, awed at the sight of it in the candlelight. It looked so hard and inflexible, yet somehow pretty as the light shone off the leather.

"You shall see, my lady. Indeed you shall." With that, he slowly began to lift the hem of my gown. He kept moving it higher until every inch of me, even my breasts, was bared.

My breath hitched in my throat as I waited, my eyes wide with expectation. I flinched when I saw him raise the strap, but I needn't have bothered. When it flicked my breast it was as light and gentle as a caress.

"Do you like that?"

I could not find my tongue, even if it wouldn't have been indecent to answer. When he brought it down again, the contact was only the slightest bit harder. To my surprise, the nipple he'd struck became a hardened bud of desire. I writhed in shame to see it, but he only chuckled. The next slap came down on my other breast, and I found myself arching my back and mewling.

With each flick of his wrist he showed my breasts attention—the stinging, teasing kind that somehow led to a moisture developing between my thighs.

"I think you *do* like it, lady wife." His smile was wolfish and so handsome that I squirmed on the bed beneath his eyes, wanting things I didn't even know how to voice.

"Please."

"Please what, sweeting? Do you want me to spank your naughty quim next?"

I gasped to hear him say such a thing, at the way his eyes crinkled with pleasure when he said it, and the deliciously naughty way it made me feel. "Antony…"

"I love it when you say my name, Cecily." He bent down and kissed my lips, gently teasing my bottom lip with his teeth. "Pray say it again."

"Antony." The moment the word was out of my mouth, he flicked his wrist and the strap landed with a soft thud on my sex. The feelings it sent coursing throughout my body, so ripe with need, made me shudder.

"Again, my sweet."

"Antony."

Down came the strap, its touch feather-light, yet with just enough force to make it sting the tiniest bit. The lady I was raised to be was horrified at how much I enjoyed it. She was further shocked when I spread my legs invitingly. "Antony," I repeated, just to feel the leather make my whole body tingle once more.

On and on we played our game until his name was nothing more than a moan on my lips. When he finally set the strap down, I was flushed from my hairline down to the very tips of my toes and his breathing was nearly as ragged as my own. I watched in fascination as his hands went to his trousers. When he pulled them down, my eyes were drawn to his member as it sprang out eagerly, long and hard.

"Are you certain, my lady?" he asked in a throaty murmur.

One look at him, at his handsome face and shining eyes, and I knew I could not deny him anything. "I am certain."

When he entered me, I found that it hurt not at all. I'd been tensing for it, but all I felt was unfettered pleasure at being made one with him. With him inside me, somehow I felt as though I'd been made whole. When he began to move, thrusting slowly in and out, I gave myself to him with abandon, vaguely aware that I had found something I hadn't even known I'd been missing.

I moved beneath him, wanton in my desire, and he responded to my affection with eagerness, increasing the speed of his thrusts. When I cried out, he smiled down on me and moved faster still. I had no name for what I was feeling, as I'd never felt it before. The only thing I knew for certain was that I felt like my body was being torn apart, yet I loved every moment of it. Tears came to my eyes, and for once, I let them flow down my cheeks, the only true sign I could offer of my joy.

"Oh, sweet Cecily," my husband murmured as he loomed over me. "You are the most beautiful of women. I am a lucky man indeed."

"Antony," I answered, my voice rich with emotion. Instead of the slap of a strap, he buried himself deep within me, enough to make me arch my back and mewl my pleasure. I thought that the joy would never, ever end. Even when we'd spent ourselves, he pulled me close beside him and I closed my eyes feeling, perhaps for the first time in my adult life, wholly and completely loved.

• • • • • • •

The feeling did not fade even when we woke the next morning. The innkeeper had left a basket of fresh berries and newly baked bread outside the door and we broke our fast without a stitch of clothing on. As we ate, we sampled each other. I would pop a berry in my mouth and gasp moments later to discover Antony's tongue tasting my shoulder blade. Shyly, I explored his body as well, as much as I dared.

We were both aglow as we dressed for the day, and my heart felt as though I'd never known a moment's worry. Surely this was what it meant to be loved. There was a part of me that wanted to feel pity for Wallace, who'd most assuredly never known such a thing, but I pushed thoughts of him aside. I was enjoying my new husband far too much to worry about the old.

"It won't be long until we reach my farm," Antony told me as he helped me in the saddle. "I... I can't wait for you to see my home. It isn't much, but—"

"I will love it, dearest. As I do you," I assured him warmly.

He grinned up at me to hear me speak so freely of love but said nothing more as he mounted his own horse.

I could not have said if our journey took minutes or hours, for I kept sneaking glances at Antony, and each time I did, my body filled with a rush of delicious excitement. I tried to turn my mind from such unladylike thoughts, but I couldn't help but wonder if he would make love to me that evening—or perhaps even when we'd reached the farm. The occasions when he caught me looking at him were best of all because then I'd get to see the light of his smile which would make me giggle with a giddy rush of delight.

When he drew up his horse, I pulled on the reins to stop beside him. "This is my home," he said, and the note of pride in his voice was unmistakable.

At first, I was too absorbed in watching him to see anything, but when I let my gaze follow his, I was astounded by what I saw. Instead of the run-down farmhouse I'd been expecting—indeed, he'd made mention more than once that he lived on a farm—a large, sprawling house sat tall on a large stretch of land. It was pretty—all green and gold in the sunlight, which was rare for the winter months. Surely it couldn't all be his.

Yet, when I turned to him and saw the twinkle in his gray eyes, I knew that it was. I looked at the land again, seeing field after field of silver wheat waving in the light breeze, a few apple trees, and animals herded into pens. I wondered, not for the first time, what kind of life I could expect as his wife. My very next thought was that it would be bigger and more beautiful than I'd ever expected.

"You... you're a lord." The thought hadn't even been made clear to me until the words were out, yet I knew them to be true. "You never said."

"Forgive me the deception, my lady. It was not my intent. It is not something I boast of."

I turned back to him, my gaze sharp, but one look at him and my gaze softened. He had a point, after all.

"All shall be made plain over dinner, wife," he assured me rather cheerfully as he dismounted his horse. "But suffice it to say that I inherited the title from my father and am a small lord of an even smaller land."

"Yes, *my lord*," I murmured pointedly as I allowed him to help me down from my horse.

"Ah, do not sass me. I fear your bottom has not yet recovered."

I was about to reply when his fingers tilted my chin up and his lips seized my own, robbing me of words. By the time he released me, I couldn't begin to remember what I would have said if given the chance. Just then, out of the corner of my eye, I saw a boy walking toward us. I turned to my new husband, the question ready on my lips when I looked at the lad again. There was no need to ask who he was. The child was no more than eight or nine, his hair long and sandy blond, his eyes a bright, cornflower blue, but there was no mistaking that hard jaw and the dimple in his chin. He was Antony's through and through.

Antony caught my eye and clucked his tongue. "Do not fault me, my lady, for you never asked," he chided me gently.

I bit back any remark I might have made, for he was right, of course. I hadn't asked a single thing about him, and having the fact before me filled me with shame. Antony had been so unendingly kind to me that I feared I might never be able to repay him.

"Do not worry," he whispered in my ear as he looped his arm around my waist. "There will be plenty of time to learn about each other."

I had only just relaxed when the lad stopped in front of us. "Hello, m'lady," he said, offering a clumsy bow that made me want to giggle. His eyes were so serious as he looked at me, though, that I forced myself to squelch my smile. "May I introduce myself? I am John, son of Antony of Briar Farm."

"Well met, John," I said warmly, bobbing him a little curtsey.

The boy's eyes grew as wide as saucers as he looked from me to his father. "Is she the princess?" he asked in an awed whisper.

Antony's burst of laughter made me turn to glower at him. "No, my boy, but she thinks herself as good as."

My hand rose to my chest as I gasped, affronted. "Antony! How could you say such a thing?" It wasn't until I'd asked that I saw how his eyes laughed at me. Annoyed at being the butt of his joke, I turned away from him with a loud "hmph!" Out of the corner of my eye, I saw him reach for me, but I sidestepped his grasp.

When he lunged for me, I wasn't quick enough and found myself caught up in the web of his arms. "Let me go!" I demanded, but the moment his mouth came crashing down upon my protesting one, the little bit of fight that I'd possessed fled.

"Now, is that any way to speak to me in front of my son?" he murmured close to my ear so that only I could hear. "Especially to your lord and master?"

The words sent a shiver of pleasure throughout my body and I blushed to know that his son was watching the exchange between us. "I don't know that I will ever call you that."

"Perhaps not," he allowed with a smile. "But you think it just the same. Ah," he warned, holding up a finger as I opened my mouth to reply. "Before you sully your lips with a lie, think of the consequences, for I know you far better than you realize, Cecily. Far better."

After delivering his warning, he released me and I dipped down in a low, elegant curtsey. "As you say, sire."

Antony laughed out loud, clearly delighted by my jest. Just then, my gaze flitted over to his son, who was watching us with wide eyes. He was a handsome lad, even at such a young age, and strong, from the looks of him. I knew without having to ask that he made Antony proud. "Would you be so kind as to show me the house?" I asked, directing my words at the boy.

"A-ah, yes. Of course, m'lady," he stammered, blushing as red as a beet after he'd done so. I kindly schooled my features to show no reaction. "As you wish. Right this way."

"Thank you, sir," I said, following into line behind him. Antony and I exchanged amused glances over the back of his head before his hand found mine and we walked, hands clasped, to the place that was to be my new home.

It certainly wasn't a castle—and what house could compare with the splendor of the Hohenzollern palace? Yet, it was far more vast than I'd expected, and I found it endearing and sweet. I complimented the cleanliness generously, much to my young host's delight.

"I've been sweeping every day, m'lady," John informed me, shyly ducking his head as he seemed prone to do.

"Why, how very dedicated of you," I replied warmly, resisting the urge to pull him to me for a hug. He was too old for coddling, I supposed—though I couldn't help but hope that he might indulge me once we'd known each other a bit longer. "Your father is blessed to have such a bright lad for a son."

"Oh, that I am," Antony agreed, ruffling the boy's hair.

"Thank you, m'lady," John mumbled, offering another bow before saying that he was going to see to the chores and excusing himself.

"What?" I demanded, taking in Antony's arched brows.

"Nothing, just that John seems quite taken with you is all."

"And why shouldn't he be?" I asked with a saucy toss of my head. "Perhaps if his father had the same sense, we wouldn't find ourselves at opposite ends so often."

"Ah, but the reason we find ourselves at opposite ends, my dove, is your tendency to be disobedient." He walked toward me in quick strides and caught my wrists, holding them firmly between us. "And do recall that his father had the good sense to know a valuable jewel when he found one. I did marry you, after all."

Mollified, I allowed myself to be kissed, and it wasn't long before I was raising my head so that my lips could fully enjoy his attention. Antony pulled away just as my quim began to hum, and long before I was ready.

"We have chores to attend to as well."

"Chores? But we've only just gotten here!"

"Yes, that's the life of a farmer, I'm afraid. And, sadly, as you'll come to know, the life of his wife. Now, I think it is time you learn to make bread."

Instantly, a memory came rushing back to me and I nibbled my bottom lip before I found the courage to ask. "Sarah... your wife. She... she is John's mother?"

"Yes," he answered, hefting a flour sack onto the counter.

"And... you never did tell me... how did she die?"

"She gave birth to a little girl," he said without preamble. "She died of childbed fever, and the child a few days after her."

"Oh," I gasped, the words hitting me like a blow. "I'm so sorry."

"I am too," he admitted frankly, avoiding my gaze. "John has gone almost three years without a mother. I should have told you about him—especially after you were so forthright about your own condition."

"Why didn't you tell me?"

Antony looked up, staring me in the eye at last. "I suppose it's because I'd fallen a little bit in love with you even then, and I feared if I told you… it was a foolish thing to do."

"Mayhap," I agreed, moving toward him. When I reached him, I put my hands on both sides of his face and looked deeply into his gray eyes. "But I assure you, I am happy to have married you. God willing, he will come to love me, in time."

Antony's smile stretched widely over his face. "I cannot see how he could not, my lady."

• • • • • • •

Baking bread did not turn out to be nearly as simple as I'd always assumed. By the time we'd finished, there was only one decent loaf, although we'd made five and I was covered head-to-toe in flour and had an aching back and sore elbows to boast of as well.

John had finished his chores long before we had finished and had come in to sit and watch. He never made one comment, though I sensed his amusement, particularly when I was at my most frustrated.

"Perhaps the boy can learn to bake," I suggested when I was at my breaking point. I'd looked pitifully at Antony, but he had only chuckled.

"You're supposed to knead it," the lad had supplied helpfully from the stool he sat on.

I'd turned to Antony, my hands spread wide as if to say, *you see?*

"Though I'm certain he won't mind helping you when he can, I'm afraid his chores keep him much too busy. This is something you're going to have to learn sooner or later, my wife."

I put every ounce of energy, every bit of stubbornness I possessed, into learning and at the end of it, all I had to show for it was one good loaf of bread. But every time I looked at what I'd made—John and Antony both agreed it looked nearly as good as what they'd seen in the baker's shop in town—I felt such a surge of pride as I'd never known before.

"I think it would be nice if you took half of this over to the neighbor's wife," my husband mentioned casually.

"What?" I asked sharply, nearly glowering at him. "I put all that effort into making it and now you want to give it away? I thought you said that you liked the look of it! Why, if that's all it means to you, feed it to the pigs for all I care!"

Antony's stern gaze pulled me upright and made me still my tongue before I did any more damage. I could tell by the hard set of his jaw that he was not happy with me and felt doubly embarrassed when I realized how rashly I'd spoken in front of John. "I was not asking because I don't like it, Cecily," he answered in the cool, level tone that belied his irritation. "I think it would be a neighborly thing to do, and I thought that since you are newly moved here, you would care to make a friend."

"Yes, well, as you pointed out *I* am the one new here. If anyone should be bringing bread to anyone, shouldn't she come to me?" Though I spoke quieter, without as much rancor, I could see that Antony still was displeased. "I don't have anything to wear," I offered weakly before he could scold me in front of his son.

His eyes looked me up and down again before he nodded. "Very well, I'm sure that I have a gown or two that will suit until we can get you your own things."

I glanced at John and back to Antony, knowing that I was helplessly trapped. "Very well," I said, with as much dignity as I could muster.

"My boy, fetch my saddlebag, won't you?"

"Yes, sir," John said, moments before he scurried to do his father's bidding.

I knew that my husband was not well pleased with me, and the feeling was mutual, but the moment he turned those stern eyes on me, I wilted. "Antony…"

"Come, I'll show you the dresses and you can take your pick."

Knowing I had no other choice, I followed behind as Antony led me into the room that must have been his late wife's.

"Most of her things were donated," he explained. "But we kept a very few of her favorite gowns." He opened the wardrobe doors, then turned in my direction, scrutinizing me. "You're more fair, but as I said, these should serve for now."

"Thank you," I murmured humbly. I knew it couldn't be easy on him, seeing me in his dead wife's gowns, yet he was offering them with a free heart to make me more comfortable.

"Choose what you like and I'll be back in a moment to help you dress."

Antony departed quickly and in his absence I took a look around the room. It was very well-kept, though sparsely furnished. There was a simple wooden chair by the window, a small bed piled high with homemade quilts, and a pretty basin on top of the wardrobe. Once upon a time, such a room would have made me turn my nose up, but knowing that these things had belonged to Antony's wife, to John's mother, made me see them in a different light.

I walked to the open wardrobe and looked inside, seeing three homespun gowns. I reached a hand inside, gently fingering the soft cloth. One was a pale yellow, one a serviceable brown, and lastly a deep burgundy calico that made me pause.

"I thought you'd pick that one."

I spun around, surprised to find Antony behind me, watching. "Oh, I didn't hear you."

"Forgive me, I didn't mean to startle you, my lady."

Yet, I was more startled still when he stepped into the room and I saw that he held the strap he'd bought tightly in his left hand. "Antony, please," I pleaded, my eyes searching his face for a sign that his intentions might be different from what I thought. If anything, the hard set of his jaw and the firm line of his mouth told me that my suspicions were correct. "Please, what if John was to overhear?"

"No need to worry yourself, my dear," he replied drily. "I've sent him out to feed the animals and milk the cow. We'll be long finished by the time he gets finished."

"Antony, I'm sorry. I..."

"Yes?"

"I... I don't know, I suppose I should have thought before getting upset."

"You suppose?"

"I should have," I amended. "And I'm very, very sorry. Please, there really isn't any need to... use that."

"Who decides if there is a need, Cecily?"

His husky voice was authoritative and even though I knew I was in danger of being chastised, I couldn't help but feel weak in the knees at the sound of it. "You do, sir."

"That's right, my dove. And I'm afraid you've earned yourself a spanking."

"Please, Antony—"

"Save the rest of your apologies for when the punishment is over. I'm going to help you remove your gown."

I was biting down on my lower lip as Antony approached me. He stopped right in front of me, crossed his arms against his chest, and waited, his eyes pinning me where I stood.

My heart was beating hard in my chest. I hated knowing that he was angry with me, and hated even more than I deserved his wrath. "Forgive me," I tried again. "I never should have spoken to you so, especially in front of your son."

"No, you shouldn't have," he agreed. When he said nothing further, I knew that he was still waiting for me.

Realizing that no matter what I said or did there would be no respite, I turned around and waited. In moments his hands were at the back of my gown, his fingers nimbly undoing each of the buttons. When the last one had been undone, the gown fell to the floor and was quickly followed by my shift.

Antony offered me a hand to help me step out of the puddle of fabric.

"Bend over the bed, please."

The words sent a shiver of nervousness traveling down my spine, but I knew better than to disobey. With tentative steps, I moved toward the bed, spreading my fingers wide as I placed them on the mattress and bent over. I could feel Antony behind me and I tensed, waiting for the first crack of the leather against my arse, but he seemed happy to make me wait. I could hear his breathing and I longed to look over my shoulder at him, but instead I stayed in position as he'd ordered. The longer he waited, the more anxious I became until I was practically a bundle of nerves.

When the leather strap came whistling down on my bare flesh for the first time, it was almost a relief. That relief lasted for half a second before the searing pain set in.

"It is one thing to disagree with me, Cecily," he said, ignoring my whimper. "It is quite another to voice it in such a disrespectful manner." Down came the strap again, so hard and fast and imparting pain I would not have believed possible considering the pleasure it had brought me the night before. "I will never speak that way to you in front of John, or the child you carry. All I ask is for the same courtesy. Is that understood?"

"Y-yes, sir," I whined, knowing very well what came next.

Antony did not disappoint. His aim was swift and true, the strap smacking down on my quivering cheeks again and again until the tears flowed freely down my cheeks and my feet were hopping in time to the strokes. As soon as he'd finished—I assumed that it had only been a dozen, though I hadn't been able to concentrate on counting—he dropped the strap to the floor and caught me up in his arms, kissing and murmuring reassurances as he wiped my tears away. "Shh, it's over now. There's no need to cry."

"I really a-am so-rry," I said, sniffling through my tears.

"I know, my dove. And I just want to ensure that you will think before you speak next time. I wouldn't ask you to do anything that would harm you, and I think meeting a neighbor might be good for you. You never know, you may take to each other."

I strongly doubted it, but rather than saying so, I offered him a weak smile and let him wipe away my tears. When I'd calmed down, he gave me a quick kiss on the lips before setting me on my feet again.

"Come, let's get you dressed."

In moments I was in a fresh chemise and the burgundy gown I'd admired. Looking at my reflection in the mirror, I noted how it brought out the blue in my eyes and highlighted my fair complexion. I was well pleased with it, but I couldn't begin to think what Antony must think when he looked at me.

"You look lovely," he said as he drank me in. He said it with the warmth and sincerity I'd come to expect from him, and to look at him, you'd never know that he was thinking of another woman as he looked at me.

I quickly decided to leave it at that and thanked him for the compliment. "Wash your face and then come back into the kitchen. I'll slice up the bread for you."

I nodded my assent and did just as he'd asked. When I reached the kitchen, Antony had a tin plate in his hand which he'd covered with a cloth. John was back to sitting in the stool, waiting, it seemed, for my arrival. When he saw me, he smiled bashfully.

"You look very pretty, m'lady."

"Thank you, John," I replied, surprised by his generosity.

"I can take you to the Gerald's farm, if you like."

"Make sure you wash your hands and face first," Antony answered for me.

"You... you're not coming?"

"I'm afraid I have things to tend to here. As big a help as John is, he's only a boy. I need to see how the farm held up in my absence."

"But I..."

"You have to get used to doing things on your own eventually, Cecily," he told me gently. "Today is as good as any other day."

"Well, then perhaps tomorrow—"

"I think not," he interrupted, chuckling. "But I admire your effort, my dove."

Knowing then that I was well and truly defeated, all I could do was wait until John returned, which wasn't long. He was all too happy to go over to the neighbors' and kept up a steady stream of chatter as we made our way there. He told me everything he knew about Mr. Gerald, though he didn't have much to say about his new wife. Either he didn't care to investigate such things, or there hadn't been much time. I rather got the sense that he'd been kept quite busy in his father's absence.

I decided that I liked the boy. He seemed bright, though perhaps a little shy. He looked like a hard worker, which I knew Antony must require in a son. Until that very moment, I hadn't thought what kind of life my child would lead, but I supposed that if I had a son, Antony would raise him to be the same. Strangely, the thought didn't bother me nearly as much as I would have once suspected.

"There it is," John told me, pointing at the white farmhouse that loomed ahead.

"Hmm," I answered noncommittally.

"I'm sure she's nice."

I glanced at him out of the corner of my eye, embarrassed that he knew I was nervous. "How do you know?"

"Mr. Gerald wouldn't have married her if she wasn't, just as father wouldn't have married you."

The frank sincerity in his voice made me smile. He certainly was his father's son. "Alright. If she's mean, can we make an excuse to leave?"

"I promise," John replied, so solemnly that I had to feign a cough to cover my laugh.

As it turned out, I needn't have been so worried. Mrs. Gerald, who introduced herself as Julia, was indeed very nice. She was of an age with me, and short with round curves, thick, curly brown hair, and a smile that was impossible not to return.

She'd taken one look at me and ushered me in, insisting I take a seat before I'd even introduced myself. "This bread smells heavenly," she declared, putting in on the table. "I have some fresh-churned butter that would go nicely with it." She excused herself and then returned not only with the butter in hand but a pitcher of milk as well.

"You know," she said, turning thoughtfully to John, "our goat just had its litter. Would you like to go to the barn and see? I believe Mr. Gerald is feeding them now and I'm sure he'd be delighted to have your help."

John's eyes went wide as saucers and I knew at a glance that he wanted nothing more, but he turned to me first. "Is it alright, lady mother?"

Both surprised and touched to hear him address me so, I couldn't manage anything beyond a nod of assent. It was enough for John, who raced out of the room as though he was being chased.

"He seems like such a helpful lad," Julia commented as she poured a glass of milk and pushed it toward me.

"He is." I took the cup from her and sipped it, just to have an excuse not to speak. At first, I felt a bit uncomfortable now that we were left alone, but Julia had an affable air about her and it was impossible to stay so for long.

"You've only just moved here?" she asked, her brown eyes sparkling. "Why, I've only been here for a few weeks myself!"

Long before the visit was over I found myself relaxed enough that I didn't even realize how long we'd been talking. I hadn't had many women that I trusted enough to confide in back at Hohenzollern, but during that time of my life, I had to be careful who I put my trust in. Here, Julia and I were equals and she had nothing to gain by hurting me. I was surprised by how refreshing it was to share with someone who I knew wouldn't use my thoughts and feelings against me.

When the door opened and John came running in, followed by who I assumed could only be Mr. Gerald, I glanced to the window. To my surprise, the sun was already beginning to set.

Julia seemed to see it at the same time and jumped to her feet, wringing her hands as she looked from the window to her husband. Mr. Gerald was a tall man and well-muscled from, I assumed, long hours in the fields. He cut an imposing figure and made it more so by the fact that he looked at his wife without speaking. "Forgive me, William," she began, before he'd said a word. "Mrs. Jennings came by to introduce herself, and I…"

"Spent the whole afternoon talking and not getting one bit of housework done," he finished, his voice deep and stern. "Nor do I see dinner on the table, wife."

"It won't take me long to—"

"Forgive me, Mr. Gerald," I interrupted, standing to my feet. "The fault is mine. I'm afraid I'm new here and don't know all the rules yet." I gave him my most charming, courtier smile. "And I should have mentioned earlier that my husband and I would like to invite you to dinner this evening."

Mr. Gerald raised an eyebrow. "Indeed? How very kind of you, Mrs. Jennings. I'm afraid we won't be able to this evening, but we would love to share a meal with you and your husband soon. Julia, I believe you made enough last night to make another meal. Why don't you serve the meat with some of that fine bread I smell? That will be enough for me." There was no mistaking the look of relief that crossed Julia's pretty features, and I couldn't help but wonder if she too was spanked by her husband. "In fact, why don't you send some home with Mrs. Jennings? I know how much her husband enjoys a good piece of meat."

I knew then, coupled with the stern look that Mr. Gerald gave me, that he knew I'd been lying about the invitation. That didn't bother me much, as long as it kept my new friend out of trouble. I feared she wouldn't want me to come calling again if she was punished because of my foolishness.

I thanked the pair of them and even gave Julia a brief hug before we accepted a covered plate of meat and went on our way. John had been given the gift of a baby goat, so he'd ignored the exchange entirely and spent the entire walk home chattering on about his goat. I had to reassure him half a dozen times that his father would let him keep it, and even then I wasn't sure he believed me.

Antony gave me a broad smile when I showed him the plate of meat that I had brought home with me and talked enthusiastically with John about the new goat, promising that they could find a baby bottle to use to feed it. "Perhaps we should go into town tomorrow to get a few things," he remarked over dinner. "We could find some fabric for your new dresses, Cecily."

"As you wish," I replied, listlessly poking at my food.

"Is something the matter, sweeting?"

"No, no, of course not."

After the meal was finished, John was dismissed to go to the barn to tend to his goat and I began to clear the dishes from the table. Antony came up behind me and wrapped his arms around my waist. "What is it, Cecily? You hardly said a word and you didn't eat at all. Is something wrong?"

I turned to face him, contemplating how I'd tell him when the words broke free all on their own. "I lied, and I think Mr. Gerald knew it. And now I fear that Julia will be in trouble on my account."

"Shh, calm down, sweeting. You can tell me everything and we'll figure it out."

It had seemed like the right thing to do at the time, but as I explained it to Antony and felt the disapproval in his gaze, I knew that I would have done better to have said nothing.

"I see," he said when I finished.

"And now I fear that he won't want her to speak to me," I said miserably.

"That won't do," he said, clucking his tongue. "She's the closest neighbor we have, and you need another woman to talk to. I doubt much harm has been done, but if you wish, I'll speak with William. In the meantime, I know one wife that will be getting punished tonight."

"Oh, Antony," I gasped, my head snapping up as I looked at him with wide, pleading eyes. "Please, no. I didn't mean any harm."

"I know, darling, but in trying to get Julia out of trouble, you've just put yourself there. Next time, offer to cook dinner with her, or help her clean house. But you're not to lie for her or anyone else. Think what kind of example you're setting for our boy."

Hearing him called *ours* made tears sting my eyes just as much as the reprimand had. "I'm so sorry, Antony."

"I'm sure you are, my dove, but I can't let something like this go by unpunished. I'm going to the barn to fetch John. When I send him in, I want you to kiss him goodnight and then go to your room and wait for me in the corner."

I held my tears back long enough to greet my new son and kiss him goodnight. "Thank you for helping me today," I whispered before pecking his cheek.

John only blushed and ran for his room, but I got the sense that he was pleased.

It was a feeling that I could not share as I went to the bedroom and waited. Left alone with my thoughts, I quickly became antsy and began to pace the room until I heard the sound of footsteps approaching outside the door. When Antony opened the door, I was sitting in the chair staring morosely out the window.

"What am I to do with you, Cecily?" he asked with a long sigh.

"I don't know what you mean, husband."

"Do you not? Well, then let me enlighten you: when I tell you to do something, I mean it. And that includes when I tell you to wait for me in the corner."

My skin flushed with warmth. Somehow it had escaped my mind that he'd told me to stand in the corner.

"It seems that I have more than one point to make tonight."

"Please, Antony—"

"Hush, sweeting. Your mouth has already gotten you in trouble once today. Let's let that be enough, shall we?"

Snapping my lips closed, I walked over to him and turned around so that he could undo my gown, pulling down my pantalets along with the garment. I thought that he would perhaps allow me to dress in my nightgown, but when I went for it, he shook his head. I watched with wary eyes as he walked over to the chair I'd occupied only minutes earlier and sat down.

"Come here, Cecily."

Taking a deep breath and wishing for courage, I walked toward him, stopping just out of his reach. "What if John hears?"

"He's worked hard today and is probably fast asleep by now. Even so, the best I can suggest is for you to try to keep it down."

Knowing that he referred to my wails, I flushed. When he crooked his finger at me, I came forward and laid myself over his lap.

"Good girl," he crooned, but the praise only made me flush harder. "Some wives need constant attention from their husbands," he remarked, gently patting my bared cheeks. "You're going to be one of those, aren't you?"

Without waiting for an answer, Antony went to work, his hand smacking each cheek in quick succession. Remembering that John was asleep, I bit my lip hard to keep from crying out. I'd never been aware of how loud the spanking itself was until that moment, and I found myself wincing each time his palm smacked my flesh.

"I'm sorry," I moaned. "Please."

"I know you're sorry, Cecily. And you don't know how much it means to me that you came to me and told me what you'd done. But it's my job to ensure that you don't let it happen again."

"I won't," I promised, but Antony seemed deaf to my pleas as his hand continued to punish my poor, defenseless arse. As the spanks continued to rain down, I did everything I could to conceal my pain. I muffled my cries into his trousers, and when I began to cry, I did it silently. Antony certainly didn't make it easy—by the time he finished my flesh felt like it was on fire. I suspected that was due in part to the spanking with the strap I'd gotten earlier.

"On the bed," he instructed, his voice husky and authoritative. I scampered over the bed and was sliding beneath the covers when he shook his head. "Lie on your stomach."

I wanted to wail that I'd already been punished, that I'd learned my lesson, but I stayed quiet except for the cries I muffled into the pillow. Antony took his time joining me. I could feel his eyes looking me up and down, drinking in the sight of my bare flesh. I wondered what he saw when he looked at me. Wallace had never seemed too impressed with my voluptuous figure, but somehow Antony made me feel that he only saw the very best in me. It was enough to make a woman still love a husband, even when he'd just set her bottom aflame with the flat of his hand.

When Antony finally joined me on the bed, I turned my head to see him, but he was behind me, looming over me. At first, I feared that he meant to continue the spanking, but then I felt his hand tracing the curve of my buttocks with a feather-light caress. I could feel goose bumps prickle my skin one by one at the gentleness in his touch. Then, when he bent over and kissed my shoulder, I let out a moan that had nothing to do with pain. His lips moved over the nape of my neck, and then to the other shoulder blade. He followed the trail that the goose bumps had left for him, letting his lips taste nearly every inch of my fair skin. With each brush of his lips against my skin, I felt a shiver run through my body until I was nearly humming with the sensation.

On and on his mouth traveled until he reached my hot, punished flesh. I tensed slightly as I waited to see what he would do. I felt the bed shift as he sat up, and to my surprise, one hand gripped my hip, lifting me toward him. The other hand snaked around, and a finger slipped into my quim, testing the wetness.

"What a naughty girl," he scolded, clucking his tongue reproachfully. "It seems that you haven't learned your lesson after all."

"Oh, but I have!" I protested. "Antony, please, I avow it! I truly have!"

"How could you have, when you obviously enjoy your spanking so much?"

I opened my mouth to say that, of course, such a thought was absurd, but before I could speak, I realized that perhaps it wasn't altogether untrue. I didn't like the hot, throbbing feeling in my backside at the moment, that much was certain, but I couldn't deny that the way he was treating me made me feel cherished. If that was what it took, I would endure the spankings.

"Perhaps I should spank you a little more?"

"No, thank you," I whispered.

"Ah, then whatever shall I do with you, my dove?"

I took a deep breath, summoning my courage before I opened my mouth to reply. "Could you... would you make love to me?"

"Is that what you want, sweeting?"

I was too embarrassed by the fact that I'd spoken such desires aloud to retain speech—all I managed was a nod, but it seemed sufficient to Antony. Only moments later, Antony inserted two fingers into my sex and began to flick them in and out in a way that drove me to insanity. I'd never been touched so before and had never thought that it would have felt so wonderful, but as his fingers moved in and out, I found myself moaning and writhing in the most shameful manner, and caring not at all.

"I can't wait any longer," he whispered, moments before he withdrew his hand and turned me to face him. He began by kissing each of my cheeks, then my mouth. When I tilted my head back, eyes closed in pleasure, he kissed my eyelids and the nape of my neck. As he kissed me, I felt his member enter my quim, and I nearly wept then and there for the pure joy of it. Then we were moving together, as one being, as God had intended a husband and wife to be. It was an odd thing, knowing that I'd been married before but had not felt one tenth of that same joy until Antony had found me.

CHAPTER SEVEN

Six months later

I could hear them talking outside the door and I knew that Julia had come. "She's inside," I heard Antony say, and the anxiety in his voice was undeniable. "Please, take care of her for me."

"You needn't worry, Mr. Jennings," she tried to sooth him. "Cecily is going to be just fine. I'll see to it."

Yet, I did not know how she could keep her word. My body felt like it was being ripped in two, and it was all I could do to bite back the screams. When Julia swept into the room, all calm self-possession, I managed to smile.

She went to work at once, kneeling between my knees and checking the baby's position. I knew we must have a long way to go, because she began to talk about the church service I'd missed and fill me in on the scant gossip there was to hear. She didn't encourage me to talk, and she herself went silent when the pains came close together.

"Really, Cecily," she scolded, her fondness for me plain in her voice. "You can scream, if you need to. It won't do to keep all that pain bottled inside."

"Antony," I answered weakly.

"Hmph," she snorted, spreading my legs the slightest bit so that she could get a better look. "I told him to wait outside."

"He... he won't be able to bear it..."

"So you must," she finished with a sigh. "I know, but all the same, I think you should let it out."

"My mother... my mother never... screamed."

"Well, *my* mother nearly yelled her head off, to hear her tell it, and she was no worse a mother for it," she replied, her brown eyes narrowed at me and her hand on her hip.

"Forgive me," I replied with a smile. Julia was forever telling me to stop being so hard on myself. What she didn't realize, even after all this time, was that I was simply doing things in the way that I was raised. For all the callouses on my hands and the simple gowns I wore, a part of me would always be gentry.

"Oh, never mind, I forget that you—Cecily, I see the baby!"

I could have wept in relief, if I'd had the strength for it.

"Push, Cecily, push! That's it! Yes, harder now... oh, Cecily."

I hardly heard her last words, because the cry that pierced the air was so loud and beautiful that it drowned everything else out, even the pain that I felt. "My baby?" I rasped.

"Yes, Cecily, he's beautiful. Absolutely beautiful."

A son. For one short moment, my heart stopped. So it had been a boy, after all. Wallace had his deepest wish. Then I remembered that it was Antony who would raise my boy, Antony who would be his father. John was such a wonderful boy and I knew he too was eager to help rear the child. Thinking of them helped me to relax, and I held my arms out for my baby. From the moment I first saw him, all other thoughts fled completely. He was still screaming pitifully, his face red and his fists clenched, but I thought that for all the jewels I'd once worn, I'd never seen anything more precious.

"He's perfect, Cecily," Antony murmured, stroking the baby's cheek. I smiled up at him and nodded my agreement. "You're certain you're feeling well?"

"Yes, Antony," I assured him as I stared down at my newborn son. It was a question I'd answered already a dozen times, but I would let him ask it as many times as he needed to satisfy himself.

"What will you call him?"

"I was thinking of George," I answered, beaming at my sleeping child. "George Antony."

"Well," my husband replied after a long pause. "If that is your wish."

"It is."

"Hello, George Antony," he whispered, and there was no mistaking the pride in his voice.

Being a mother was harder and yet more rewarding than I ever would have imagined. I found myself enchanted with this tiny human being that had formed inside of me, and baby George cast a spell that seemed to bewitch everyone. Antony doted on him, snatching him from the floor the moment he came in from the fields and bouncing the baby on his knee until his gurgled laughter filled the house. John was very protective of the baby, and very helpful to me as well, always willing to fetch a fresh blanket or entertain him while I caught my breath.

Of course, it was nothing like it would have been if I'd still been a duchess when he was born. He would have had a wet nurse and his own governess. I still would have been expected to live with the court, as I'd done before. There were moments when I longed for the easy existence I'd taken for granted, idle moments when I thought of Susanna, or my mother. But as a farmer's wife, idle moments were hard to come by so there wasn't much time for thinking of the past or what might have been. Besides which, being present when my son laughed for the first time, or to see John play on the floor with him, made all the hard work worth it.

Antony was as patient as he was kind. He showed me how to perform the tasks I needed to learn and remained encouraging no matter how many times I had to ask him to show me the same thing. I'd thrown myself into my new life with abandon, and in time I'd built a name for myself in the small, widespread community that we lived in. It was shocking to me how easy it was to make friends with other wives. They seemed desperate for friendship and all it took was a single kindness to build a relationship. Julia and I visited one another on a weekly basis and while I feared I'd never become accustomed to the easy rapport commoners enjoyed with one another, I had come to value her friendship.

So much so, in fact, that I'd told her my secret. As soon as the words were out of my mouth, I'd gone rigid in my chair, watching closely for her reaction.

"Well, that it explains it," she'd said as she set her cup of milk down. "I'd thought for some time now that there was something a bit different about you. Now I know."

I'd been surprised but relieved at how easily she'd taken the news and subsequent meetings had proven that it really didn't bother her.

"You see?" Antony had said when I'd told him. "I keep telling you that you have to give people a chance."

How right he'd turned out to be. It seemed that the people around me—the more time went by, the more I stopped thinking of them as *commoners* and thought of them as friends—were a constant surprise. I was even surprising myself. I'd never imagined that I could live in such an isolated community, doing hard labor day after day. Why, taking care of children without help from a governess was, in and of itself, a monumental task. Yet, somehow I was surviving. To tell it true, I was even thriving.

"Lady mother!"

I turned at the sound of John's voice, shading my eyes with my hand. "Yes?"

"I've got to get something from the house! I'll be but a moment!"

"Of course! See you shortly, John." I turned back toward the fence, laughing to myself as I watched for Antony to come home for the day. He'd gone into town on business and as I was every time he went away, I was anxious to see him safely returned to me. In these times, John took his father's orders to watch after me and the baby very much to heart and seemed reluctant to take his eyes off us for even a second.

I'd mentioned it to Antony the last time he'd been away, but he'd simply smiled. "You don't see it, do you, my dove? John's grown very fond of you. He's afraid if he gives you the chance, you'll fly away."

It had made me feel good to hear that my stepson felt as bonded to me as I did to him. Yet at the same time, I sincerely hoped that it was a fear that he would outgrow.

Just then, George began whining, a sound which I'd learned in the past three months would quickly turn to wails if I didn't act quickly. He was beginning to cut teeth and had become quite the fussy baby at times.

"Poor George," I crooned down at him sympathetically. "That mean old tooth will break through soon, I avow. It looks like we need to join your brother in the house and get you something to gnaw on." I had just turned away, moving the baby to my hip as I walked, when I heard a noise behind me. Before I had a moment to think on it, I heard my name.

"Cecily."

I knew that voice. I knew that grating, self-important tone all too well. It was one that I'd never expected to hear again, and I was so convinced that I had to be imagining it that I ignored my initial instinct to break into a run—he'd never expect *that*—and turned around instead. The moment my eyes fell on him, every muscle in my body tensed and I would have fainted if not for the need to protect my son.

It was as though I'd seen the dead come back to life, for while I'd never seen the duke's lifeless body, in my heart he had been as good as dead for some time now.

"You've forgotten your manners," he remarked, his tone light but clearly reproving.

"Hello."

"Tsk, tsk. Is that any way to greet your husband?"

"You're not my husband," I said, my voice loud and strong despite the tremor within it.

"Ah, yes, I'd heard you chose to remarry rather than to look for me." He spoke casually, but I knew Wallace well and the look in his eyes told me that he did not appreciate what he considered to be my betrayal. "Does that amuse you?"

I realized then that I was smiling. The thought of Wallace feeling betrayed in spite of everything he'd done to me *was* rather humorous. "What are you doing here, Wallace?"

He seemed taken aback by my directness, but it only lasted a moment. "Why, I've come for you and our son, of course. It *is* a boy, is it not?"

I felt a frisson of fear crawl up my back, making my entire body go cold despite the blazing sun overhead. "I'm needed in the house. Good day." I turned away from him and began to walk as fast as my feet would carry me, but I'd only gone a little ways when he darted in front of me, blocking my path.

"Come, now," he urged, his voice gentle for a change. "Let me see him."

I held the baby to my chest as I shook my head, my face pinched and tight. "I wouldn't dream it. He is not *your* son, Wallace."

"Oh, but he is." Though he still spoke softly, there was an underlying threat in his voice that couldn't be mistaken for anything else. "Why, you have only to look at him. He looks just like me."

This I could not deny. Though every day I tried to see more of myself in him, when George looked at me I saw Wallace looking back. But nothing, not even that would persuade me to hand him over to such a man as my former husband. "My husband will raise him to be a fine man. You needn't be concerned for him."

Wallace's gray eyes narrowed into slits as he loomed over me. "It is not him I fear for, Cecily, but you. Tell me, did you think me dead? How long did you mourn me? Not the proper amount of time, obviously," he sneered.

"In truth, I did not mourn you at all, Wallace." I didn't know where I'd gotten the strength to speak so freely, but once the words were out I felt a tumult of others like them waiting to spill forth. "Perhaps I mourned the life I used to know, but never you. Now, let me pass."

"I don't understand how you could say such things." His words were mournful and meant to inspire pity, but I couldn't find any for him. I knew all his tricks. I tried to sidestep him, but he seemed to anticipate it and moved once more to block my path. "I can't believe you'd forsake your family. What about Hohenzollern?"

I felt a pang of sadness to hear him speak of the place that had once been my home, but I pushed it aside. "Hohenzollern is lost, Wallace. You should know that better than anyone!" My brow furrowed as I contemplated him. "Were you taken as a prisoner of war and released?"

"Don't be ridiculous," he chuckled. "A man of my station? I couldn't risk being captured. Surely even you can see that."

"I don't understand," I said slowly.

"For God's sake, woman!" he snapped. "Are you daft? I didn't join the fight, of course!"

"You ran?" I gasped. "But... but Susanna was counting on you! How could you—"

"Don't be such a simpleton!" He waved my words away. "The best thing we can do now is go back and reclaim Hohenzollern in the name of our son. He might be as near as can be found to Susanna's rightful heir. Most of Susanna's kin were dragged off as brides to bastards and common soldiers, after all. And even if he isn't, we can make a claim good enough to bring allies to our side. I'll raise an army and—"

I shook my head, drowning out his words. "No. No, I have a life here now. I won't have any part in your schemes."

Suddenly, Wallace's hand shot out and clamped down on my arm. I gasped at the grip, but I couldn't shake him free. "I think you misunderstand me, wife. I don't need *you*. Now, while it would be ideal for you to realize the folly of your ways and come with me, all I need is the boy. And don't mistake me—I *will* have him."

With an anguished cry and a fresh burst of strength, I pulled away from him and broke into a run. Surprise must have slowed Wallace down a bit, but it wasn't enough. Soon, he was upon me again, grabbing my braid to yank me back to him. I knew that I would do everything in my power to get away from him. He would not drag me back to a place best left forgotten, stuck as a puppet in his damnable plans.

The poor baby, surely feeling the wildly erratic beat of my heart, began to wail, but Wallace ignored him as he grabbed me, one hand on each of my arms griping so tightly that I winced. "I'm ashamed of you," he spat. "A royal duchess and this is the way you behave? You haven't just been living with them, out here in this muck! You've become one of them, haven't you?"

I glared at him, his mockery causing me to despise him more than I'd ever done before. "You should be ashamed of yourself! You ran like a coward when Hohenzollern needed you and now, you grasp at something that doesn't exist!"

Despite the fury that contorted his features, I still didn't see it coming. When Wallace raised his heavy palm and slapped me across the face, I stumbled. I didn't even have time enough to scream before his hand cracked down again, this time knocking me to the ground. George was wailing so piteously that it tore at my heart, but I'd been blinded by the explosive pain in my face and all I could do was cling to him.

"St-step away from her."

My head swiveled around to see John standing behind us, his face pale and frightened and Antony's dagger held so tightly in his hand that his knuckles were white.

"Ah, who's this?" Wallace's voice and smile were light and derisive.

"Don't… don't touch her," he insisted in the terrified voice a child trying to defend his mother. "Go now. Get out of here."

"Oh, I intend to. And I'll be taking my wife and son with me," Wallace replied in the easy, unconcerned manner of a lion being threatened by a cub. "You look to be a good, strapping lad, but you still have some growing to do. Why don't you put that knife down before someone gets hurt? There's a good lad."

My vision was still blurred and my cheek was numb. My heart was beating so quickly that I feared I might faint, but I knew that was not an option. Now I had both of my sons to protect and the only way I could see to do that was to give Wallace what he wanted. "John, please go to the house."

"But, lady mother, I—"

"Listen to your mother, boy." Wallace's voice held too much contempt for my liking, but I knew there was nothing I could do about it.

"Please, John. I need you to obey me."

John looked at me, his eyes so full of hurt and betrayal that it nearly broke my heart in two. Yet, he did not move, his eyes going to something beyond me.

"She's right, son—you should listen to your mother. And put that knife back where you got it. You won't be needing it."

I spun around so quickly that I nearly toppled over. Yet, the sight of Antony coming to our rescue was enough to quiet me. "You too, Cecily," he issued, his voice firm and controlled. "I believe it's time for George's nap."

My eyes went between the two men. Antony seemed as calm as I'd ever seen him, yet I knew the signs: his tense shoulders and clenched jaw told me he was ready to do battle, if need be. Wallace was surveying him with narrowed eyes and a sneer on his lips, assured as ever that there was no battle he couldn't win. Fear rose in my throat and made me indecisive.

"Cecily," he prompted, his voice growing in authority.

"I'll... I'll be waiting for you," I said, turning away from the two of them and walking to my son. When I reached John, he offered me his hand and I took it, walking with him to the house and resisting the strong urge to look back over my shoulder.

"Do you think father will be alright?" John asked as soon as we'd entered the house.

I closed the door behind us before turning to him. I saw that he was trying to be strong, to be a little man, but there was no mistaking the way his lip trembled. I knelt on the floor and opened my arms to him. "Of course, sweeting," I murmured when he ran to me. "Of course. Your father will return to us, don't doubt that."

John began to quiver in my arms and George still wailed. I very much felt like doing the same myself, but I knew that I had to remain strong for the boys' sake. I held them close to me and patted John's back, unable to take my eyes off the closed door.

• • • • • • •

As soon as George's cries had abated, I'd put both him and John to bed early. I doubted very much that John would be able to sleep, but if I had to keep pretending to be strong, I would surely falter. Although I believed in Antony with all my heart, I needed to come up with a plan in case Wallace should somehow best him. I knew nothing but trickery would allow him to do it, just as I knew that Wallace was not above using any ploy to get anything he wished.

If only we could get to the Geralds' without attracting any attention. Perhaps we could slip out the backside of the house and go quietly down the road. But what if George cried and drew attention to us? What if we heard the sound of swords clashing? I couldn't risk subjecting John to such a thing.

I didn't know how I myself could bear it.

I paced the house helplessly, agonizing at the decision to be made when it felt that there wasn't much of a choice at all. When I heard the first sound of steel against steel, I couldn't help it: I was at the door as quickly as my feet would carry me. Opening it a crack, I peered out just in time to see Wallace slash toward my husband. Antony side-stepped it quickly, bringing his sword up to meet the attack. My heart jumped to my throat and lodged itself there. Truly, I could feel it pulsing there and making it hard for me to breathe. I knew that I should go back inside, that I should be trying to form some sort of escape route, but now that I knew they were fighting, I couldn't look away.

Antony did not try to harm Wallace. I could see his lips moving and knew that even now he was probably trying to reason with him. What Antony did not know was that when he wanted something, when he was in a rage as he seemed to be now, the duke could not be reasoned with.

Wallace moved with the agility of a wild cat, jumping and thrusting his weapon with the expertise of years of training. I had never asked after Antony's own swordsmanship, but he parried and met every of Wallace's attempts to injure him. I could see that the duke was not taking it well. Every time Antony blocked his sword, his face reddened until he looked like a ripened tomato. Wallace was dangerous at the best of times; when he was angry, he was a man to be avoided at all costs.

Almost unaware of what I was doing, I slipped outside the door, closing it softly behind me. I moved forward a few feet before I crouched down low in the grass, trying to obtain a better view while still remaining hidden. With every clash of swords, my pulse quickened until I felt certain that I'd faint and be helpless to my children regardless of the outcome.

Wallace charged forward, swiping at Antony's middle, an attack which my husband staved off. When Wallace immediately pulled back and aimed his sword at Antony's shoulder, he was not quick enough and I heard the sickening sound of flesh being hit.

I would never know if Antony had grunted in pain, for I was on my feet in an instant, a horrified scream tearing past my lips. Antony never turned his head toward me, but Wallace made the mistake of looking my way. I could see the surprise and confusion warring on his face, only for a second, but it was long enough for Antony to step in and disarm him. When I saw his sword fall to the ground, quickly pinned with the tip of Antony's boot, my breath began to come out in jagged gasps.

"Do you yield?" Antony demanded.

Wallace was still looking at me, even as he shook his head. "Never."

My chest expanded, and the air was rushing out of my lungs at even a faster rate. I didn't know what I hoped for—did I wish Antony to kill him, to make me a widow in word and deed, or did I want him to spare Wallace's life? My mind spun with the implications of each until I thought I would be ill.

"I told you to stay in the house, Cecily." Antony never took his eyes off the duke, even as he spoke to me. His words and the firmness they carried gave me the guidance I needed, and without a word, I tore my eyes from the pair of them and turned and went into the house.

Once the door was closed behind me, I sunk to the floor. How I longed to weep, but all I felt was empty. I wanted nothing more than to have Antony's arms around me, his gentle reassurances being whispered in my ear. It felt like hours had passed before I heard the sound of his boots approaching the door.

I leapt to my feet and threw the door open, taking in his wearied expression moments before I threw my arms around him. "You're hurt," I whispered, even as I clung to him.

"Cecily," his voice was heavy with admonishment. "You shouldn't open the door when you don't know what waits for you on the other side."

"Oh, but I knew," I assured him, standing on tiptoe to kiss his cheek. It was lined with both sweat and dust, but I didn't care.

"You couldn't have," he chided.

"Yes, I could. I saw... I knew..."

"You knew?"

"That you would do... what you must."

"Yes." He sighed heavily. "That I did. Wallace won't trouble us again, you needn't worry."

I squeezed him tighter as I began to cry.

"Shh, sweeting. What is it, my precious dove? Do you cry for him?"

"No," I sobbed, burying my face in his chest. "It's only that I was so frightened. Forgive me, I never doubted you, but—"

"I know, darling. I know. But don't cry anymore, please. The children are safe?"

"I put George to bed but I doubt John was able to sleep."

"I suppose not. I'll have to see to the body before morning. And Cecily? I don't want you looking out the door, either. Do you understand?"

"Yes, sir."

He held me at arm's length and eyed me sternly. "I mean it. And as for your little excursion outside later, after I *specifically*—"

"Please, Antony," I whimpered piteously. "Can't you punish me tomorrow?"

He eyed me for a long moment, the fierce expression on his face making my bottom tingle in anticipation. At last, he nodded and his features softened as he leaned down to kiss me on the mouth. "Yes, this once I shall wait. But expect to be a very sore and repentant wife tomorrow."

"Yes, sir."

Antony bent his head and kissed me again, longer this time, on the mouth.

"I look forward to doing that many, many more times tonight."

I nodded my agreement, even as more tears streaked down my cheeks.

"Don't cry, love. All is right now."

"We'll have to see to that wound," I reminded him, sniffling. "But first, you should go to John. You can't imagine how worried he's been."

Antony gave me another squeeze. "Yes, let's go see to our sons."

Though I was still shaking, I was beginning to recover with Antony by my side. It helped, knowing that in time Wallace and the life I left behind would be nothing more than a distant memory. While at one time it had been unthinkable, I could now say with certainty that I was exactly where I was meant to be.

EPILOGUE

"I don't want you to get your hopes up," Antony said, speaking gently.

"Antony, I'll be fine," I said, impatient to get inside the inn we were standing outside.

"Gossip is often unfounded and—"

"Yes, yes," I answered with a dismissive wave of my hand. "I know that already." My husband stilled me with a firm look that got me right down to the core. I swallowed hard before offering an apologetic smile. "I meant, yes, sir."

"Be sure you remember that," he warned before opening the door for me. "Wait right here."

Although I wanted to protest, I knew I was closer to getting in trouble than I would like. Best not compound my problems. So instead I watched Antony as he walked toward the innkeeper. I sucked in my breath and held it, as I would until he turned back to me and sadly shook his head, as he had every time before. After that, the air would spill from me in a disappointed exhale. One would think that after a certain amount of disappointment it would stop hurting so badly, but thus far I had felt it as keenly each and every time.

After Wallace's sudden reappearance, Antony had indeed notified the captain he'd scouted for, after which he'd begun placing delicate inquiries and discovered that there were women from Hohenzollern living in nearby communities. He only brought the news to me after he had found a woman who he'd hoped was my mother. Unfortunately, it had turned out to be a woman I didn't even recognize. But she knew the locations of some of the older women taken from the castle, and thus began the hunt that we'd been on for the last fortnight.

Each and every time we thought we'd found her, it turned out to be only wishful thinking. Yet, now that the seed had been planted, our reunion was the only thing I could think of. Antony, for his part, could have said long ago that it was a lost cause, he could have instructed me to stop hoping to find her, but he didn't. Instead, he accompanied me any time we had a good lead and was there to hold me each time my hopes were dashed.

My foot was bouncing up and down of its own accord, yet I hardly noticed. I only had eyes for my husband. I watched as he spoke with the innkeeper, and I wished I could hear what he was saying. I knew he would be relating key portions of the story and asking to see the baker, who we'd been told bore a good resemblance to the description I'd given of my mother. The man Antony had spoken with had said that the baker came from Hohenzollern, but we wouldn't know the truth of it until we saw her. I was so anxious that I felt like I would burst at any moment. Antony had often scolded me for my impatient nature during this venture, but even his scoldings and the spanking I'd earned for being impertinent could not cure me of this tendency.

I bit down on my lip as I caught sight of Antony walking back toward me, and I tried to read his expression. The innkeeper hadn't refused, had he? No one had thus far, but it was always a fear in the back of my mind. "Antony?"

"Shh, now," he soothed as he stood by my side, reading my expression easily. "She'll be out in just a moment. But, Cecily, if it isn't her, I don't want you to be upset. We'll keep looking, I promise you."

I slipped my hand into his and squeezed hard, unable to convey the extent of my gratitude. I knew that I might never find my mother, but I thought I could make peace with that as long as I had my husband.

Just then I glimpsed a movement out of the corner of my eye that caught my attention. I turned, and then I saw her. She was standing stock still looking back at me, her face the most beautiful thing I'd seen. Her hair had more silver than I remembered and was held tight in a thick bun on top of her head. Her face contained more wrinkles, but was infinitely dear. It was her. At *last*—my mother.

"Cecily?"

"It's her," I answered, my heart so full that it was overflowing. We began to move toward each other at the same moment, and when we reached one another, we were both in tears.

"How can this be?" she murmured as she pulled me to her and wrapped me in her embrace. She held me tightly, as though she would never let go. "God has finally answered my prayers.

"I have been looking for you so long," I told her through my tears. "Even before I began to hope…"

"I can't tell you how happy it makes me to see you safe." She pulled back, beaming at me. "You look well, Cecily. You were taken?" Her brow wrinkled with concern. "When the castle fell?"

"I… it's a long tale, Mother. I would like you meet my husband." I turned to gesture toward him, and seeing me, he came forward. "May I introduce my husband, Antony?"

"It's an honor." He gave her an elegant bow that made her smile.

"The honor is mine," mother replied graciously. "It is obvious you've taken good care of my daughter, and from the bottom of my heart, I thank you."

"That has been my pleasure. Though not always easy," Antony allowed with a smile.

To my surprise, my mother laughed. "Oh, Cecily has always been a bit stubborn. There is no doubting that she has her father's spirit," she said, smiling as she patted my arm.

"How did you come to be here?" I asked, still unable to believe we'd actually found her. "You made it out of the castle safely?"

"Not to parrot you, sweeting, but it's a long story. One saved for another time, perhaps."

The thought of leaving her had never occurred to me. I'd only just found her!

"On that matter, I would like to offer you our hospitality, my lady."

I turned to Antony in surprise. Though we'd never spoken of mother living with us, the thought filled me with unspeakable joy. Truly, I had the most thoughtful husband in all the world.

"We have the room," he remarked, nodding at me. "It isn't a castle, of course, but you're welcome to any comforts we have."

"The greatest comfort will be being near my daughter!" she exclaimed, clutching my arm in excitement.

"And your grandson," I told her, giggling at the wonder that crossed her face.

"Oh, Cecily," she breathed, almost reverently. "You didn't lose the baby then. I was so fearful for you, child. And all alone…"

"I wasn't alone, Mother. I had Antony." I smiled up at my husband. "And George is fine. Why, he seems ready to crawl, and then we'll certainly stay busy!"

"A grandson."

"I have two sons," I told her, unable to stop smiling at the pure joy of the moment.

"John is a lad of nine," Antony explained. "And I must tell you, he'll be happy to have you. I hear you're a baker?"

"Oh, yes. I had to learn a trade, to get by."

"Well, perhaps you could show your daughter a thing or two." Antony winked at me, but even his teasing criticism couldn't temper my happiness.

"I'd be happy to." She released me at last and wiped her hands on the apron she wore around her waist. "Now then, when do we go home?"

• • • • • • •

My lady mother fit seamlessly into our little family as though she'd always been there. John took to her immediately, and I loved to witness their easy bond. She didn't take over the baking, as I'd expected, but instead spent long mornings teaching me. It was odd—I'd never imagined that the two of us would be up to our elbows in flour, yet as strange a picture as it must have made, we both wore smiles on our faces.

We never spoke of Hohenzollern, nor Susanna, nor any of the rest. Yet, there were moments when I'd see her staring wistfully off into the distance, and I knew she was remembering times past.

In such moments, when my heart would grow wild as it ached in my chest, all I had to do was look down to see George clutching at my skirts, or listen to John as he read aloud from one of the books from our meager library, and my heart would go still and calm again.

The best part of my day was when Antony would come find me. I never knew where I'd be or what I'd be doing, but at some point during the day he would seek me out and stop me from whatever I was doing, scoop me up in his arms, and carry me to our bedchamber. Some days, I laughingly protested, and on others I simply snuggled into his embrace, eagerly anticipating the moment when he would lay me down on our bed and begin to ravage me with nothing more than his hungry eyes.

Though at one point I hadn't been able to imagine such a life, now that I was immersed in it, I discovered that it had pleasures to offer that I never would have known I was missing before.

THE END

Stormy Night Publications would like to thank you for your interest in our books.

If you liked this book (or even if you didn't), we would really appreciate you leaving a review on the site where you purchased it. Reviews provide useful feedback for us and for our authors, and this feedback (both positive comments and constructive criticism) allows us to work even harder to make sure we provide the content our customers want to read.

If you would like to check out more books from Stormy Night Publications, if you want to learn more about our company, or if you would like to join our mailing list, please visit our website at:

www.stormynightpublications.com

Printed in Great Britain
by Amazon